# THE MORTAL SLEEP

## BOOK FOUR OF THE HOLLOW FOLK

GREGORY ASHE

H&B

The Mortal Sleep


Published by Hodgkin & Blount
https://www.hodgkinandblount.com/
contact@hodgkinandblount.com

Published 2022
Printed in the United States of America

Version 1.03

Trade Paperback ISBN: 978-1-09170-295-0

much to be straight. At that point, he usually tackled me and gave me a very pointed lesson about how straight he was.

"We don't have to run," he said, his breathing easy in spite of our pace. "I own a car."

I pushed myself a little faster, the running shoes biting the gravel.

"Sara will buy you a car," he called after me. "Then we really wouldn't have to run."

But we ran. I had to run or I'd go crazy, go out of my mind. Chewing the wallpaper, foaming at the mouth, padded room. That kind of crazy. Because they were out there, Urho and the Lady and whatever lunatics had survived the battle at Belshazzar's Feast. And they wanted me.

"Slow down," Austin huffed as he pulled up alongside me. "We're going to be all sweaty."

"You're going to be all sweaty."

"Your shirt is sticking to your back."

"Good. You like that."

Austin grinned. Then he snapped the elastic in my underwear and shot forward, sprinting away from me.

"Son of a bitch," I roared and charged after him.

Around me, life was coming back to this tucked-away corner of Wyoming. Wildflowers bloomed at the edge of the gravel shoulder, popping up in clusters of blue and violet and yellow. Junegrass was already beginning to green, and where the topsoil thinned and hardened, dusty clumps of sage grew together. On my other side, a snow fence buttressed the road, and a few slushy patches still shone where the shadows were thick at its base. In winter, when storms swept across the plains, the snow had piled as high as the fence. Beyond the fence loomed the Bighorn Mountains, Cloud Peak eaten up by its namesake.

I had dreamed about the mountains. About high valleys and a cabin lit against the night. I had dreamed about the clouds gobbling up the stone in huge bites. I had gone to Cloud Peak once, not physically but by projecting myself to the other side, and I had thought I would find Urho and the Lady. I found gray and black stone, steep slopes of scree and talus, and a mountain lake frozen to glass. The dreams kept coming—those were the dreams I could talk about, the ones I could tell Austin about, not the other dreams, not the ones where I had to run—and I tried to get Austin to drive me into the mountains so I could hike up there and check out the space in the real world. It was February. It was a few days after Valentine's. And thank God I'd been a good boy at Valentine's because I've never seen Austin get angrier. When we both cooled down, I realized he was right:

people died hiking to Cloud Peak in the summer. In the dead of winter, with the snow drifting deeper and deeper, I was asking for a death sentence.

My shoes beat the gravel on the side of the highway, and I sucked in deep breaths of the cold, wet spring air. There was the mineral flavor of the rain, pelting my lips hard enough that they felt puffy, and the prairie grass dust and a faint smear of motor oil. Farther up, a patch of asphalt gleamed with a greasy rainbow.

I didn't try to catch up to Austin—not really, anyway. He had settled into a good pace twenty yards ahead, and he ran like a goddamn machine. I liked my view. I liked those shoulders that had gotten bigger over the last few months. They were a brick wall; you could balance a Prius on them. And the trim vee of his waist. And the shelf of his ass. Practically a goddamn cliff.

He glanced back, tugging up his shirt to wipe his face, and wriggled his tush.

"Slut."

"Perv."

But he didn't slow down. And I didn't try to catch up. And the goddamn showboat kept pulling up his shirt, not even pretending anymore that he was wiping his face. That boy had a killer back, and he liked showing off for my benefit.

It's pretty nice, having people that care about you. It's pretty great. Sara kept me fed. She kept me in clothes. Austin was probably right: if I wanted it, I thought she'd buy me a car, or find a way to help me buy one. She talked to me, asked about my day, and she made me trim my hair, and one time she grounded me because I stayed out past curfew with Austin. And I didn't like being grounded, not at all, but I stayed in my room because I figured I'd put her through enough. I liked having Austin drive me to school. I liked him curled up in my bed as we did homework. I liked him kissing me goodnight, a really serious goodnight, every time like he might not see me again.

So everything was good. Everything was great. All the things that had been wrong in my life, all the things that had driven me, one day last year, to perch on the bridge over the Bighorn River, to push off so that the air whipped my legs and the water came up at me, slapped the breath from my chest and swallowed me—all those things were better. And even if there was just this little spot at the back of my head, just this little black dot, just nothing really, just a little smudge on the glass, even if that was there sometimes, everything was great.

Maybe I had trouble sleeping some nights. Maybe, those nights, I dreamed that I was running through a trackless forest. Maybe I dreamed of something that ran behind me. Something with sharp teeth. Maybe, some nights, I didn't run fast enough, and I woke with scratches on my back, on my neck, on my ankles. Maybe that was just imagination.

Maybe I had trouble sleeping some nights, but everybody had trouble sleeping sometimes. Maybe, some nights, I had to get up and walk. Maybe I had to sit in the shower sometimes, the water so hot it left my skin pink and shiny, so I could breathe. Maybe I had to run every day. But those things were normal. Everybody had stuff like that. That was just how everybody felt, some days. And that thing at the back of my head, it wasn't even that big. Most days, it wasn't even that black. More like gray. More like this gray smudge, and nobody noticed a smudge, not a little one like that when everything else was great. And it was. Everything was perfect.

Our steady pace ate up the miles to town. Vehpese straddled the Bighorn River. The old stone bridge crossed the water; I kept my eyes fixed on it as buildings grew up around us until the city swallowed the shore and the water and the bridge. I remembered the rush of cool air in the late summer heat. The taste of blood in my mouth. The current driving me into the rocks. The way the water had been so blue at the bottom that it had been black, and that black had washed away the edges of my vision and left a perfect, blank nothingness behind it. It was all right there, right behind that glass at the back of my head—right behind that smudge. Sometimes when I got up at night, sometimes when I had to walk around the house, sometimes when I was in the shower with the water steaming against my back, I thought about how cold and clean and quiet it had been at the end. Even with all the splashing and gasping and choking, part of my brain had finally been quiet. I would think about that. I would think about how magical that quiet had been.

Ahead, the town came closer. By now, Vehpese didn't feel strange anymore. The move from Oklahoma had been hard for a lot of reasons, but one of the biggest reasons was just how different Vehpese had been. It was small. It wasn't just another suburb curled up around a city. It wasn't street after street of McDonald's and Applebee's and Home Depot and Pottery Barn. Not that a lack of chain stores made it better; that's not even close to what I'm trying to say.

It was old. That's one thing I had noticed when I first came here. Everything recent had been built in the seventies when the mines in the Bighorns were just getting started and a lot of money was coming into town. And the color scheme was old too. A lot of faded pastels. A lot of yellow. A lot of tan. And it was poor; that was the other thing. A lot of that money from the mines had gone into tattoo parlors and carry-out pizza and payday loan joints. Sure, there was more. Sure, there was a nice, updated section of town along the river. But the strip mall we were running past seemed to sum up the real essence of Vehpese: paint chipping off cinderblock, a vape store called *Smoke Em If You Got Em*, two nail salons—*Emperor's Nails* with the closed sign twisted against the door; *Thai Nails* with a neon hand flashing fingers, 1-2-3-4-5—and a personal tax business with a Lady Liberty costume hanging limply in the front window, like somebody had strung her up and left her as a warning.

Garry's (two R's, God and Garry only knew why) Greasy Spoon had only a handful of cars on its cracked asphalt lot. I recognized the yellow Camaro, the mammoth Silverado, and the brown Ford sedan. The other two were F-150s. This was, after all, truck country. The Greasy Spoon's chrome-and-red exterior, like something that had outlived the sock hop and the poodle skirt, had dulled with sun and years. The red was almost pink. The chrome always looked cloudy like someone had just breathed on it.

Austin slowed to a walk and paced a circle. Plucking at the sleeveless tee, he gestured to his pits. "Told you."

"You're hot."

"I'm hot."

"Yes, you are."

"That's not what I meant."

Rain continued to needle me; I shook my head. "I'm not standing out here just to cool down."

"We could have driven."

Looping arms around his neck, I walked him backward toward the Greasy Spoon. Nose to nose, I said, "We could have driven."

"Yeah. And then we wouldn't be stinky when we ate with our friends."

"Uh huh."

"And we'd be dry."

"Uh huh."

"And warm."

His back bumped the glass.

"I thought we already established this: you're hot."

He opened his mouth to say something else, and I kissed him. Firmly.

When I pulled back, his eyes had narrowed.

"Are we in a fight?" I asked, my eyebrows going up.

A smile crooked the corner of his mouth. He slapped my ass like he was beating hell out of an old rug, and then he slipped out of my arms and sprinted into the diner.

Asshole. He was just one big beautiful asshole some days.

Inside, Becca, Kaden, and Jake already had a booth. Becca and Jake took one side; Kaden took the other, and I had to swallow a growl when Austin slid in next to him. Kaden, the little motherfucker, hooked Austin around the neck and pulled him in for a hug. Because he knew. He knew Austin still had his first little gayboy crush on him. He knew, the little fucker, and he did stuff like this, and then his eyes met mine, and he tried to look innocent as a newborn babe, and I was having fuck-all of it.

"You have a car," Jake said. "It's a little pansy thing—"

"Hey," Austin said, squirming out of the hug and darting a single, evaluating glance at me. It was just a hug, I told myself. They're friends, lifelong friends, and it was just a hug. I hoped all of that was perfectly visible on my face. Austin's attention flicked back to his little brother. "It can go faster than that beast you drive around."

"—but it can get you to town."

"Maybe we wanted to run."

"And get wet?" Becca said.

"And get sweaty?" Kaden said, pretending to wave away BO.

"It's nice weather—"

"Aunt Sara would buy him a car," Jake said. "You know she would."

"We just wanted to go for a run."

"Fuck all of you," I said. "Stop picking on him."

And that broke the rest of them up into laughter. Even Kaden, that little shit, who elbowed Austin and grinned that huge, perfect grin and was probably giving Austin a boner the size of King Kong's.

We ordered. We ate. It was a school night, and it got dark early, and the rain licked the windows all night in long black tongues. But nobody wanted to go. Becca pulled out a laptop—a very fancy, very new laptop, which told me her freelance work was going well—and started on her homework. Kaden dug out his AP Psych textbook and a fat green Sharpie and started underlining. Jake slipped out of the booth, squeezed my shoulder, and cuffed Austin lightly on the back of the head before heading out to see Temple Mae.

Austin and I hadn't brought homework, but that didn't make much of a difference; Austin and Kaden were taking the same psych class, and so Austin just crowded closer to Kaden. They talked in low voices as they flipped pages. Their heads bumped once, and Kaden laughed, and Austin shoved him and said he'd done it on purpose. And he had. I chewed through Austin's leftover sausage biscuit and watched. Kaden had done it on purpose. And it had been fucking cute.

And he was such a cocktease I wanted to crack his head against the window.

Watching them, the way my boyfriend crowded up against his first crush, the way his face lit up when Kaden talked, the way he seemed tuned to some radio wave that I couldn't pick up—every signal, every shift, every breath Kaden made—I couldn't help but count the seats. I couldn't help but think that we were four. With Jake, we'd been five. Temple Mae never came; I didn't think she ever would. But there were seats for six. And we could have had six. Six. One last person who should have been there.

I didn't let myself think about Emmett Bradley. I never thought about him, really. I'd trained myself not to. I saw him at school, sure. He held court on the opposite side of the cafeteria. He passed me in the hall, moving like magma. His eyes never touched me. They never came anywhere near me. I'd vanished from Emmett's world. Or, more accurately, I'd been cut out of it. And he'd been the one holding the scissors. So, in turn, I'd cut him out.

And I never thought about him anymore, not ever. I never thought about his short dark hair. I never thought about the rich dark brown of his eyes. I never thought about the way he felt against me, I never thought about how he kissed me, I never thought about how broken he was, or how much he needed me, or how I was the only one who seemed to see past the bullshit he threw up for everyone else. I never thought about it anymore. I didn't let myself think about him.

Six seats. There should have been six of us.

Austin bumped me, and I shot out of my thoughts so hard that my knee clunked against the table.

"Come on, sleepy. Let's go."

"I'm not sleepy."

"You were on another planet then. Let's go."

Becca was packing up her computer; Kaden shoved the psych textbook into his bag.

"You guys don't want to keep working?" I asked. "Just keep working. I'm fine."

"You're practically drooling," Becca said. "You're comatose." She tucked her arm under the laptop bag's straps and patted my cheek. "See you tomorrow."

"Come on," Austin said, butting me gently with his head. "Or am I carrying you?"

"You?"

He grinned and butted me again.

"With those twinkie arms?"

"Twinkie arms, huh?"

"Like a toothpick."

"You think my arms are small. Like a toothpick."

"I'm surprised I didn't have to hold the fork for you."

With speed that took my breath away, Austin slid one arm under my legs, snugged the other around my shoulders, and heaved me out of the seat. He came with me, stumbling once, and then we were free of the booth. He grunted, hefted me like he was testing my weight, and slung me over his shoulder.

"Put me down for God's sake."

Austin chucked a twenty on the table and marched me toward the front door. Becca, lingering at the entrance, rolled her eyes. I glanced around, my face burning. Two old men sat over identical plates of chicken-fried steak. One of them saluted me with his coffee. Our waitress, who had to be as old as the diner, clapped her hands and cooed. Behind the enormous griddle, the short-order cook scrubbed at his hairnet and looked like someone had whacked him on the back of the head.

That was more or less how I felt too.

Austin carried me outside.

"Don't say anything," I told Becca as I sailed past her.

"It's very caveman."

"I said don't say anything."

She just laughed, and the sound was as silver as her eyeshadow.

Outside, night blanketed the city, fuzzed around the edge of the asphalt lot by a perimeter of sodium lamps. In the buzz of orange light, the Camaro didn't look yellow; it was washed out, almost gray. Austin set me down just outside the diner. The wind picked up, and I shivered, and Austin locked his arms around me. He was warm, and his head fit perfectly against mine, and he smelled like sweat and maple syrup and coffee.

"Are we in a fight?" Austin asked, just a whisper in my ear as his fingers tugged at elastic again, his nails dimpling my waist and making me forget all about the night, all about the wind, all about the start-stop prickle of rain.

I kissed him.

"I'm not driving you home if your tongues are down each other's throats." The Camaro beeped, and Kaden started toward it.

"Good night," Becca called again. "You're making me sick, by the way. I'll probably puke on the drive home."

I waved goodnight with my middle finger.

As Becca lifted the latch on the driver door of her little brown Ford, a car shot into the parking lot and came to a screeching halt. The Corolla—a late model that looked hardly used—cut off Austin and

Kaden and me from the row of parked cars. Becca stared at the Corolla, and then her eyes cut across its hood to meet mine.

In the weak light from the closest streetlamp, the Corolla's driver mixed with the shadows. He was bald and big; I could tell that much. Bigger than Austin. Bigger than me, I guessed. Then the passenger door opened, and a guy stepped out. I'd seen him around. He was a transfer student, red-headed, and I'd overheard him talking about playing offensive line next season in football. He certainly had the build for it.

The redhead glanced at Becca. Then he fixed his attention on me, and he gave a half-shrug. His cheeks colored, but his voice was steady and carried across the Corolla's hum when he said, "You want to come with me?"

From the Corolla, exhaust drifted across the asphalt, hot and dry and tickling my bare legs. Kaden giggled. Austin still had one arm around me, and he didn't exactly squeeze me against him in some kind of pre-verbal signal of ownership. But he came pretty damn close.

"That's a lame pickup line," I said.

"Look, they want to talk to you, and I'm supposed to ask if you're ready to come."

"You're not very good at this," I said to the redhead. "Try starting at the beginning: full sentences, proper nouns."

"You don't even know what a proper noun is," Austin muttered.

The driver snapped something, and the redhead's cheeks darkened with blood and he shook his head. Then, to us, he said, "Look, I'm not fucking around with you faggots. Either get in the car or don't."

"You can't talk to him that way." Becca jangled her keys; she had several of them between her fingers, an improvised weapon, and she brandished them at the redhead. "Shut up and go, all right?"

"To go talk to somebody," I said to the redhead.

"Are you getting in?"

"Go," Becca said, taking a step toward the Corolla. "I'm telling you to leave, right now, before things get messy."

The redhead craned his head at her. "Bitch, be quiet."

"All right," I said. I took a step, and then Austin had one of my arms. I tried to take another step—he was a lot stronger than I realized—and Kaden caught my shoulder. "Get off. I'm just going to talk to him."

"Now the faggot wants to talk," the redhead muttered.

"I told you not to call him that." Becca came around the Ford's trunk, her fist cocked at her side, the keys pointing between her fingers. "Now get lost before I—"

The redhead shoved her, and Becca stumbled back and landed on her butt. The keys rang out as they spun across the blacktop.

"Let me go," I said, twisting to pull free of Austin and Kaden. "Let the fuck go."

The redhead smirked at me over the Corolla's roof. Then he leaned into the brown Ford, pumping the trunk so that the car rocked on its suspension, like he was testing it out and might want to take it for a drive. Then, with a laugh, he said, "They want to make you a deal: leave, and we won't bother your friends."

Then he dropped into the passenger seat, and the Corolla buzzed away. The taillights winked at the turn, and red light smeared the wet pavement, and then the car was gone.

Austin let me go, and I shoved Kaden off and ran. Becca was already on her feet by the time I reached her. She waved me off.

"I'm fine," she said. Tears filled her eyes, though, and a tremor shook her. "I'm so clumsy; I can't believe I fell."

"I'm going to kill him."

"Come on," Austin said, tugging on Becca's wrist, turning up her hand to expose road rash on her palm. "Let's get you cleaned up before you go home."

"I'm going to kill that son of a bitch," I said.

"Becca, let's go inside for a minute."

She was shaking pretty bad by then, and Austin curled one arm around her waist and helped her toward Garry's. Over his shoulder, he tossed his head at me. "You too. Both of you."

"I'm going to kill that fucker."

Kaden laid a hand on my shoulder. "Right, man. Totally."

I shook him off, but he trailed me toward Garry's.

When we stepped through the door, though, Kaden grabbed my shoulder again.

"Lay the fuck off, Kaden," I growled, wriggling free of his touch. Trying to wriggle. He had gathered a handful of my running shirt in a death grip. "I'm going to break your fucking nose just for practice if you don't—"

"Something's wrong."

Austin was guiding Becca into the bathroom, and he threw me a look and motioned for me to wait.

"Yeah," I said, "something's wrong. That redheaded piece of shit just shoved Becca."

"Language," the waitress called, and when I glared at her, she just put one hand on her hip and glared back at me.

"No." Kaden twisted the handful of athletic fabric, and his eyes were wide as he glanced back at the lot. "No, fuck. Something's really wrong with the car. With the metal, something's wrong, something's—"

Kaden was a lot of lean, hipster muscle, a kind of grass-fed pretty boy, but he did a pretty good tackle. He crashed into me, bearing me down onto the floor. Something—syrup, God, let it be syrup—stuck to my hair when I rolled my head, and my nose brushed a cigarette butt and sent it rolling.

Then, outside, Becca's car exploded.

# Chapter | 2

I pushed, and Kaden rolled off of me. From across the parking lot, the smell of burnt rubber and electrical wire and steel rolled into the restaurant. I got up, beads of tempered glass rolling underfoot. The diner's double doors were gone, the glass blasted out by the force of the explosion, and the metal frames had been forced inward until they caught on the uneven floor. I stared out at the flaming wreckage.

Because that's what it was: wreckage. It wasn't like someone had started a flame inside the Ford. It wasn't like someone had splashed gasoline or lighter fluid or kerosene on the windows and threw a match. Once, when Gage and I had spent a weekend together, a full weekend with his parents gone, and we'd fucked our brains out, I'd found last year's fireworks stashed in his garage. And I'd taken a Matchbox car from his old toy chest in the basement and jammed it full of Black Cats and tied the fuses together. That explosion had been a huge pop that had rung in my ears for the whole afternoon. It had left nothing but a pretzel of zinc alloy.

Becca's car didn't look much better. Flames licked up through the open roof, tasting the night air. The tops of the tires bubbled. At the back of the car, the trunk had popped open, and the lid bobbed as currents of hot air brushed against it. A pink spaghetti-strap dress hung halfway out of the trunk, dangling over the bumper, its plastic dry cleaning bag shriveling in the heat.

"What the fuck?"

Austin's voice sounded distant; the thunder of the explosion lingered in my ears, and it took me a moment to realize Austin was shouting. He ran across the Greasy Spoon to grab my arm; behind him, Becca froze in the bathroom door.

"What happened?"

"I don't know."

"It exploded," Kaden said. He kept grabbing the shoulders of his cardigan and pulling, as though he were sliding out of the garment.

Someone—maybe Kaden, maybe whoever he was dating this week—had stitched a crude outline of a marijuana leaf on the right breast of the sweater. He yanked at the shoulder again, even though the cardigan wasn't going anywhere.

Austin just shook his head at Kaden's response. He cupped my face, looked me up and down, and asked, "Ok?"

"Ears," I shouted back.

He nodded. His eyes darted to Kaden and then back to me.

Grunting, I shoved him toward his first crush.

Austin repeated the process, checking Kaden for visible injuries and then asking, "Ok?"

Kaden stared past Austin. He reached up absently, yanking the cardigan into place—it still hadn't shifted.

"Hey," Austin said, taking Kaden by the chin—Austin's eyes cut to me for a moment, blue-green mirrors that gave me nothing—and he wagged Kaden's chin side to side. "Kade, buddy. You've got to talk to me."

"My car," Kaden said, fingers searching for the cardigan's shoulder seam again.

A soft hand touched me, and I jumped. Becca planted a hand in my chest and gave me a push. "Go."

"What?"

With her voice muffled by paper towels and by the aftershocks in my hearing, I could barely understand her, but I managed to make out her words: "You've got to go. Now."

Shaking my head, I said, "No way, we're witnesses. I'm going to tell—"

Becca brushed past me and grabbed Austin's shoulder. I couldn't hear her then; the thunder in my ears was too loud. Whatever she said, though, made Austin freeze. He nodded. He wagged Kaden's chin again.

"Kade. You've got to be with me. Right now, buddy."

Kaden blinked. "My car, my fucking car."

The yellow Camaro that was so pretty and so goddamn expensive was parked two spots away from the burning Ford. The paint blistered, and heat shimmered above the metal.

"We're going," Austin shouted, grabbing me with one hand and Kaden with the other and dragging us through the mangled doors.

"But Becca—"

"She'll be fine." Austin patted down Kaden; granola boy was still in a daze, staring at the funeral pyre of Becca's car, and didn't even seem to notice. Christ, I thought as the thick outlines of Austin's fingers worked under the denim of Kaden's pockets. When this was over, they'd both be having wet dreams for a month. Then Austin produced the keys and pushed Kaden into my arms. "Get him in the back seat."

With the kind of grace that only real athletes, natural athletes, have, Austin spun himself out of his shirt, the whole movement fluid and singular and carrying him closer to the Camaro. With the fabric wadded up around his hand, he yanked on the latch, and the driver door opened. "Now, Vie," he shouted.

I moved to the passenger side, and even here, the heat off of Becca's car hit hard, and the greasy smoke made my eyes tear. I packed Kaden into the back and dropped into the front next to Austin. The Camaro roared to life, jolted into reverse, and swept a long arc across the blacktop. Metal shrieked, and then a clattering, cat-with-tin-cans cacophony started up as Austin drove out of the lot. I glanced back; an uneven length of metal that looked like it might originally have been part of the Ford's frame tumbled and clanked behind us. At the next turn, it spun free, glittering once under a vapor lamp and then was swallowed by a storm drain.

The Camaro's engine roared as Austin punched the gas. He bent low over the wheel, his eyes fixed on the white circles the headlights cut out of the night. I flipped on the dome light.

"Shit," I said. "Your back."

"It's fine."

Shirtless, he had stood with his back to the inferno, and in the crisp blue-white LED light, the skin was pink. I pressed a fingertip into his shoulder, and a blanched spot remained behind.

"Ow. Don't do that."

"Oh fuck," Kaden said from behind. He was scrambling on the back seat, moving from door to door, jabbing at the window buttons. Window lock must have been on because the glass stayed in place. Groaning, Kaden squirmed across the leather again, hammering on the windows. "Oh fuck. Guys, we've got to get out. We've got to—oh fuck, oh fuck."

"Vie." Austin jerked his head without his eyes leaving the road. "You handle him."

"I'm driving."

"I'll hold the wheel."

Blindly, Austin grabbed a handful of my shirt and yanked me toward the back seat. "Will you get back there and take care of him?"

My knee cracked against the center console, and I squeezed between the seats. Take care of him. Austin was never physical with me—never physical in a way I didn't want, at least. Take care of him. Grabbing me like that, manhandling me like that. Take care of him.

Who the fuck did Austin think he was? And why the fuck wasn't he worried about taking care of me?

I crushed the last thought out as I came down on the leather next to Kaden. He was dragging on the door handle, trying to open the door, but it was locked. He must have realized his mistake because he gave a little moan and scrabbled at the latch.

"Shit." I grabbed. Too late.

He got the handle again, and this time, the door cracked open. Air pressed against the door, forcing it closed because of the speed of our passage, and Kaden swore. He shifted position, swinging his legs in front of him, planting both feet on the door, and shoved. This time, he got it open, and the cold, wet drizzle sprayed my face. The sensation, on skin still superheated from the burning car, shocked some clarity into me.

Kaden's back was to me, just a few inches away. I wrapped both arms around him and pulled him against me.

You'd think I'd stuck a knife in him. He went crazy. Insane. He screamed—the only words I could make out were, "Let me go," but most of the noises weren't even close to words, they were just high-pitched, animal shrieks. He ripped at my hands. He was begging.

"Jesus Christ, Vie," Austin shouted, his head whipping toward us for a moment before the Camaro swerved and he had to jerk his attention forward again.

"Me?" I shouted back, "why am I—" Then Kaden's head came back and caught me in the mouth.

It was just a glancing blow, but it cut the inside of my mouth against my teeth, and blood pooled under my tongue. For fuck's sake. I twisted backward, dragging Kaden with me. I was bigger than he was. I was stronger than he was. I wasn't a little twinkie granola boy who owned too many goddamn cardigans, and even with him spinning and spitting and kicking and clawing like a Tasmanian devil, it wasn't that hard to get him on his back, my knee in his chest, his wrists locked in my hands.

"For the love of fuck," I said. I swallowed blood, touched the tongue to my teeth, probed for any that were loose.

"Get off me. Just get off, all right? We've got to get out, please, Vie, the car's going to blow, it's going to fucking blow, all right, just let me—"

Metal popped somewhere: the sound of bolts being forced, maybe. Or of the frame twisting. Kaden's eyes were wide and blank; they'd been scraped clean by terror. His ability to manipulate metal was going to be a real bitch once he remembered it. Or, for that matter, if panic made him do something stupid unintentionally. He might rip off one of the Camaro's wheels. He might tear off a door. He might crumple the frame and crush us to death. Or he might do what I figured he'd been wanting to do for a while: accidentally find a way to put a nice long piece of steel through my chest.

Another gust of air swept through the Camaro before the wind knocked the door shut, but the prickle of that cold April rain on the back of my neck made me shiver. It wasn't quite at the level of conscious thought, nothing I could put into words, but it was there anyway: the sudden realization that I had this little cocktease right where I wanted him, and he was so fucking hysterical I could do just about anything.

The slap knocked his head sideways. It sounded a hell of a lot worse than it was; it sounded huge, and as the noise clapped through the small space, I knew I was a piece of shit for doing it. Kaden's shrill pleas cut off. The only noise was the engine revving, the tires buzzing through planes of water, the whistle of air through the door that wasn't all the way closed.

Austin bent farther over the steering wheel. His foot must have dropped because the Camaro launched forward like a rocket.

Beneath me, Kaden made a clicking noise in his throat, and he rocked his head back and forth. The print of my hand was huge and red on his cheek. Christ, my hand had never been that big. I touched the side of his head—not that ballooned print, I wasn't stupid, at least, not that stupid—and he flinched and pulled away.

With a sigh, I eased my weight off of him. He took a shuddering breath and pulled inward, his whole body contracting. His breathing was ragged, but he wasn't hyperventilating, and he wasn't screaming, so I figured it had all worked out. Except my face was still hot, and my hands were still tingling, and I thought throwing myself out of the car might be better than this silence.

"You all right?" I touched his arm this time; he flinched again.

"Yeah."

"You don't look like you're all right. Will you sit up?"

"Leave him alone, Vie."

"I just want him to sit up so I can check him out. He was pretty freaked, and—"

"Leave him the fuck alone."

I eyed the back of Austin's head. The back of his head could be pretty damn angry sometimes. I eyed the door, where air still bled through the imperfect seal in a high, shrill noise like a train that couldn't stop. Yep. Throwing myself out would be a lot better.

"I'm ok." Kaden squirmed away from me, his back against the opposite door. That print on his cheek, it was a joke. It was colossal.

It was clownish, so exaggerated there was no way it could be real. My hand wasn't that big. And I'd never hit him that hard. Never.

But I thought of Dad coming at me with the belt. I thought of Mom looping the vacuum cord around her hand. I thought never was a lot fucking closer than everyone told themselves.

Kaden's hand waved up and down, almost to his cheek, away, back, away, back, away, never quite touching, and his eyes did this amazing circumnavigation of the whole damn Camaro without ever meeting mine. He looked at the back of Austin's head. I wondered if it looked as pissed off to Kaden as it did to me.

"Hey," Kaden said, reaching around the seat to ruffle Austin's short, preppy hair. Then his hand dropped, skating along Austin's chest. Brotherly affection. Just a couple of straight-guy bros who were comfortable with each other. Or just Kaden being a goddamn tease. In a few more months, would he run his hand lower? Would he blink, his eyes huge and innocent, and tell Austin he was flexible, he didn't need labels, this was just something all guys messed around with? "I'm ok, Aus. I am. He didn't hit me that hard." His hand settled right on Austin's shoulder, and he squeezed once. He laughed shakily. "Thanks, Vie. I needed that."

Then his eyes cut to me.

Fucker, I mouthed to him.

He didn't smile. He didn't smirk. His eyes didn't light up like he'd scored a point. He just stared at me, his hand on Austin's shoulder, and I realized Kaden didn't have to do any of that. He didn't have to pull a face or grin or mime a tally in the air. Because both of us knew I'd fucked up. And both of us knew he was winning. I didn't even know the game or the rules or the end of it all, but I knew he was winning.

When we reached Sara's, the house was dark; she was still at Bighorn Burger, still making sure her crew of teenage delinquents—which normally included me—didn't burn the place down. But there was a car in the driveway: a boxy blue Volvo with reddish-orange crusts around the wheel wells. There wasn't any moonlight or starlight, not with the clouds so thick. The rain still came down in brief, furious fusillades. But even with all that darkness, I could see shapes inside the Volvo. Waiting.

The War Chief, I thought. And the Lady. They were here now, waiting for me. The explosion at the Greasy Spoon had been them beating the bushes, trying to scare me out into the open, and I'd come running back here, right into their arms, where they were waiting for me. In a Volvo, a dry voice asked at the back of my head. I ignored it. The terror that they were here, appearing after all these months, was too strong.

Austin hit the brakes, and Kaden and I bounced off the seats. Kaden's eyes had gone cartoon-size. Metal squealed somewhere inside the Camaro, and then from outside the car, there was a snap. A length of Sara's wire fence whipped free from the post, lashing the black sky. A piece of wire that gauge, moving that fast, could take off a limb. Could open an artery. Could break bone. I punched Kaden in the shoulder, hard.

"Get it together."

Shuddering, he licked his lips. "Sorry."

The squeal of metal died. The fencing wire dropped, limp, to the ground.

Ahead of us, the Volvo's passenger door opened. A figure stepped out, and Kaden sucked in a breath, and beneath me, the Camaro gave another squeal.

"Fuck, it's her, it's her—"

I slugged him again.

"Keep him from doing anything stupid," I said.

Austin reached back and grabbed my arm. "I've got my hands full with you. Literally."

"That's Shay. Tyler and Hannah's mom. She lived next door to me."

Nodding slowly, Austin peeled his fingers away. "Why's Kaden so freaked then?"

"Because he's a baby. Dark and stormy night. All that."

Austin grunted.

Unlatching the door, I stepped out into the Wyoming night. The wind roared across the prairie. It was a dark wind. It clapped me between the shoulder blades, propelling me toward Shay. She was barely more than a blur in the next volley of rain, blond and frail, and the wind pinned her against the door like a butterfly wing.

A few months before, I had snuck into this woman's bedroom. I had faced the thing that had taken possession of her, Mr. Big Empty, and I had fought him, and I had won. My heart beat so fast it was like a fire. The cold, the rain, the wind—these were miles off. I was hot with blood. Hot with the desire to throw the first punch. Did she remember? Had she come here to shoot me, to stab me, to complete some final line of subliminal code that Mr. Big Empty had left inside her?

When I reached her, she leaned into the blue Volvo. The rust climbing the panels leached into her khakis, staining them every time another gale buffeted her against the car. Blond strands hung in her eyes. She shoveled them away, and rain left trails on her face. Not just rain, I realized. Tears.

"Shay—"

"They're gone. Please tell me you know where they are. Hannah and Tyler are gone."

# Chapter | 3

In general, I didn't have much use for—or belief in—women collapsing. Women, in my experience, were generally the more resilient sex. God knew they had to put up with a lot more shit. But in this particular case, with the wind howling and another barrage of rain needling my face, with Shay slumped against the Volvo's glass, with the rusted-out wheel well running red streams down her leg, I figured I'd better get her out of the weather and into a chair.

When I rapped on the Volvo's glass, though, Lucy Harwood—Shay's mother—just gave a stiff shake of her head. I nodded toward the house, and then I beckoned for Austin to follow. The headlights flashed once; I beckoned again, and Austin trotted out to join me. Kaden scrambled out of the back and took the spot behind the wheel. The wind and rain licked Austin's preppy-boy hair flat; he had pulled on his shirt, and it darkened with water. Then the Camaro rolled backward, and Kaden was gone.

Inside, I let Shay take the armchair, while Austin and I sat on the sofa. In the sixty-watt light, Shay didn't look much better. The weather—and her tears—had made ragged curtains out of her mascara, and her hair was a bleachy mess. The wounds, however, had healed—the ones I could see, anyway. The bruises were gone from her face. The cuts, with a few exceptions, had vanished. At the corner of her mouth, and low on her jaw, two thin white lines remained. Before the rain, I guessed that some sort of concealer had made even those lingering reminders vanish. Mr. Big Empty had a nasty method for taking possession of someone. A very nasty one. Body and mind and spirit. They were all connected; break one, and you could break all of them. Mr. Big Empty always started his breaking with the body.

"What's going on? What do you mean they're gone?"

A minute ticked by. At my side, Austin poised, ready to jump to his feet. Every muscle was tense, and it made him incredibly solid, like I was leaning against a rock.

"Maybe she needs some tea."

"She doesn't need tea."

"She's probably freezing."

"Fine. Get her some tea."

"I don't want to leave you alone in here."

"Then don't get her the tea. Or get it. Whatever."

"I dream about you." Shay's words didn't sound dreamy, though. They weren't vague or breathy or wispy with some far-off recollection. She hissed the words. They sounded like steel on a whetstone. "Some nights, when things are really bad, I dream about you. In my room." Her eyes shot toward me. "Is that real?"

"Why don't you tell me about Hannah and Tyler?"

"Is it real?"

"I was there. Once."

Someone cut her strings. Boneless, she slumped across the armchair. And then she started to cry in earnest. It was silent. She didn't move, she didn't shake, she didn't cover her eyes or wipe her face. It was one of the most unnatural things I'd ever seen, and I'd never wanted to run farther or faster in my life.

"When Lawayne broke my big toe," she said, "they put a splint on it. When I was sixteen and Ronnie Sandovar was pulling on me, trying to keep me from getting out of his dad's Impala, when he broke my arm, they put a cast on it." Her hand settled on her chest. Her fingers tented as though the full weight were too much. "Nobody can do shit for what's broken inside, though. I'd look at my babies and they weren't mine anymore. They were someone else's. They were something else. They were . . . little shits. They'd whisper about me." Her whole face tightened in a spasm, and she seemed unaware of it. "They'd watch me. Their little eyes crawling all over me. Little shits. I wasn't going to let them . . . wasn't going to let them . . . wasn't . . . get away with it." Another spasm rippled across her face, as though something lay underneath and wanted to get out.

"If those kids are missing," Austin said low in my ear, "we need to call the sheriff. Right now."

"She's messed up."

"And those kids might be dying. She's out of her damn mind, Vie. Listen to her. She sounds like she did something to them."

"If she had, Lucy Harwood wouldn't be sitting out in that Volvo so calmly."

"Who?"

I pushed up from the seat and walked over to Shay. I threw open my inner eye. The thickly textured reality of the other side came into view, and I focused my attention on the woman in front of me. There was no poisonous cloud around her. No sign of the beast of smoke and hate that I had ripped out of her and shredded. But Austin was right: something was wrong.

Since that day at Belshazzar's Feast, my powers had worked more or less at my command. I wasn't yanked around by them anymore. But I also wasn't really sure—most of the time—what I was doing. What I did next, though, I had been doing as long as I could remember. It was like falling off a log. A really high log. Into a really deep pile of shit. I went into her mind.

Inside Shay's mind, instead of the normal silence and black emptiness, I found a storm surge. That was the closest I could come to conceptualizing it: a rush of filthy water choked with flotsam that was rising, threatening to spill over the fragile walls of Shay's sanity. And on top of that water, slicking its surface, was something else. Crude oil. It wasn't oil, of course, but that was what it felt like: greasy and black and stinking. It was something left over from Mr. Big Empty, something like the way smoke deposited carbon on stone and brick. A stain.

I wasn't sure what I could do. For that matter, I didn't even really know what the hell I was doing. Whatever I tried might cause more harm than good—and I didn't want to harm Shay. She'd been through enough. She'd caused her mother and her children enough pain. But I couldn't leave her like this either.

More and more over these last months, I'd found myself digging deep into my own memories. There was something to it that affected people; they responded to my memories like some kind of sympathetic harmonics, like the tines of a tuning fork resonating together. I'd done it with Emmett. I'd done it with Kaden. I did it now with Shay: I chose a happy memory and let it resound inside her. I started with the merry-go-round at the elementary school, the centripetal pull, the heat on my back. And then something answered in her: the merry-go-round, yes, and the sight of a blond, gap-toothed boy grinning as he tried to hold on, the smell of the hot pebbles paving the playground, the smell of dust and iron from gripping the merry-go-round. It was her memory, but it was an echo of something in mine. That was how it worked. That sun-drenched memory rose up inside her and the dark waters stilled.

Then I was free of her, and my third eye snapped shut, and I probably would have fallen if Austin hadn't caught me.

Shay, her arms and legs akimbo, raised her head. Tear tracks still marked her cheeks, but her eyes were clear, and she took a low, slow breath.

I tried to get my feet under me, but my legs were still noodley, and Austin just wrapped his arms around my waist and helped me stay upright. "You all right?" The words were so quiet they barely tickled my ear.

"Yeah."

"What did you do?" Shay pressed the back of her hand to her forehead; on anybody else, it might have looked affected, but on her it was just one more stroke of exhaustion. "My head hasn't—it isn't better, is it?" Her eyes focused on me, and she drew herself upright in the chair. "It's just quieter."

"I don't know how to fix it."

"But it's quieter." She kept her hand where it was. She might have been an oil painting: *Woman in Chair about to Have the Vapors, c. 2018.*

"Ma'am," Austin said, then grunting as he hoisted me to keep me from sliding out of his arms like hot spaghetti. "You want to tell us what's going on?"

"They're gone. Hannah and Tyler are gone."

"That's something for the police. Have you called the police?"

"No," I said. My ankles and knees were finally feeling semi-solid, so I squeezed Austin's arm, and he reluctantly let go. "She's here because she wants me to find them."

"Of course that's why she's here. That's why everybody comes to you. That's how you keep getting yourself right in the middle of the worst things that come through town. But it's not your job."

"I need to know what—"

"No. It's not your job. Lady, you seem like you're really upset, and I'm sure you're a decent person, but it's not his job. You can't come here and ask him to do this. You can call the sheriff. You can go to Highway Patrol. You can get the FBI involved for that matter. Your kids, I'm really sorry they're missing, but he's a kid too. You are, Vie. Don't do that. Don't shake your head at me. You're a kid, we both are, and you don't need to get involved in this. You shouldn't get involved in this."

I looked at Austin, taking in the preppy-boy part, the turquoise eyes, the rugged lines of his face.

His cheeks colored, and he said, "It's not your job, Vie. I know that look. I know you want me to shut up. I know you think I'm an idiot and that I'm embarrassing you and you just want me to disappear right now. But I'm right. And lady, if you've got any kind of conscience, you won't ask a sixteen-year-old kid to stick his head into some kind of trouble."

Neither Shay nor I spoke.

"For the love of—he doesn't even have a driver license."

"No," I said, kissing him on the cheek and squeezing his arm again. "But you do."

"Don't do that. Don't—don't use my fucking emotions against me like that. No. Don't. Whatever you're going to say, you're going to twist this all around, and I honest to God can't stand that. Not after everything you've been through. Not after what I've—" His voice broke, and he had to swallow and look away. "Not after what I've had to watch you go through."

Shay's face had lost its manic edge, but the desperation was still there, and the pain and heartache wisped off her like the smell of rot.

Gently, as gently as I could, I said, "Maybe you should go, then."

Austin actually twisted away from the words as though they'd been a slap. A tremor ran through him, one single tremor from shoulders to toes, and then he jerked his head savagely to the side. "No. I'll stay."

"All right," I said to Shay. "Go ahead."

"He's not wrong. Maybe I should . . ." She crossed her arms, and her nails bit so deep that purple crescents stamped her fair skin. "You're just a kid. And Mother . . ."

"You'd better tell me now before he breaks my nose."

"Don't make fucking jokes like that. You don't get to make jokes like that." The words were so savage that I glanced at Austin, and I was surprised—no, shocked—to see tears. He leveled me with one furious glare and then jerked his head away again.

"You can't go to the sheriff," I said. "Or you already tried. Or you think he can't handle this. Which one is it?"

"All of them. I . . . I did talk to him. Not at the station, but I talked to him. I've been picking up shifts at the Cow Poke. Just lunches mostly; breakfast and dinner are busier, and those girls have been there a long time. I just fill in. But the sheriff eats lunch there some days. Most days. And I guess I knew I couldn't talk to him, not officially, but I was out of my mind, and he was sitting there, chewing his ribeye sandwich, watching me like he does, and I just started talking."

"Go back all the way. When did they disappear?"

"Saturday."

"All right. Where'd you last see them?"

"They went to the park." Her hands found the gimp braid on the cushion; her nails scrabbled at the trim. "I think."

Austin dashed his arm across his eyes—Christ, how could somebody telegraph anger so goddamn vividly with just one move of his arms—and said, "You think?"

"I had a lunch shift. It came up last minute."

"Your mom," I said.

"Mother had already left for the day. She was driving to Cheyenne to see a friend. I didn't know I was going to have a shift; I would have asked her to stay and watch the kids. But it came up, and Saturday lunch is better than what I usually get, and if I said no, Tony would . . ."

"You took a lunch shift so you could get Mrs. Pritzker's fifteen-percent tip on her tuna salad? So you could make a buck twelve? And you left your kids alone, without anyone to watch them, for a buck twelve? After everything they've been through? After what you've been through? After I told you, I fucking told you the first time we met, that you weren't ever going to do that to them again—"

"All right," Austin said, clutching my shoulder. Until he did, I hadn't realized I'd taken a step forward, and Shay shrank back into the chair, her nails ripping up a two-inch section of the gimp. "Easy."

"I'm not going to take it easy. She knew. I told her she wasn't going to do it again, or I'd—"

"Ok. Take a breath. Lady. Shay. What time was all this?"

"I don't know; ten-thirty. Maybe eleven. I left sandwiches in the fridge." Her chin came up; she didn't quite meet my eyes, but she was trying. "I was going to be back for dinner."

"Fuck dinner," I said. Austin's fingers bit into my shoulder as he hauled me back, and it only made me yell louder. "They were gone by dinner!"

This time, Austin grabbed a handful of that fancy athletic t-shirt and shook me so hard that a seam popped. It sounded like a gunshot in the small room, louder even than my lopped-off breaths.

"You can either cool down and figure out what she has to tell you, or you can be a total asshole." Austin shook me again, but more gently. "Which one?"

"I can do both," I growled, rolling my shoulder away from his touch. "All right. You were out of the house by eleven. And?"

"And they knew they weren't supposed to go any farther than the park. St. Raphael's. It's not even a park, really; it's the playground for the Lutheran preschool. But we just called it the park. You can—" She cut off, pressing a hand to her chest. When she spoke again, her voice was reedy. "You can see it from our house."

"From your mother's house," I said, just because I wanted to be a bitch.

Austin shook his head. "When did you get home?"

Shay ran a hand over her eyes.

"What time?" I said.

"It might have been seven. A little after."

"You were gone for eight hours."

"Vie," Austin said.

"Eight hours. You left those kids alone for eight hours with a fucking plate of sandwiches. That's it."

"Vie."

"They can—"

"If you fucking say they can fucking take care of themselves, I will kill you."

"Vie!"

My breathing still had that staggering, lopped-off sound. Outside, the wind battered Sara's small house. Anger prickled across my back, an invisible tattoo of heat and sweat that stung, and I couldn't believe I'd ever been cold in my whole life.

"That's more than a shift," Austin said.

"All right. I'm a terrible mother. I'm the worst mother in the history of the world. Fine." Shay threw up her hands as though waiting for the cuffs. "You don't know. You don't know how hard it is, being a mother. You don't know what it's like."

The worst mother in the history of the world. The candles. The iron. The cigarettes. The vacuum cord.

"Where'd you go?"

"I worked my shift. I took my tips to the bank; we're saving up for our own place. It was closed, but you can do the after-hours deposit. And I had to talk to a friend."

"What was his name?"

"Vie, just drop it."

"No, Austin. I want to know what his name was. And maybe you can tell me how much weed you scored. Or what kind of booze he stocks. Or if he had horse or coke or whatever you wanted. Or maybe you can just give me the measurements of his cock, and maybe that'll explain why you left them. Again."

"The measurements of his cock?" Austin rolled his eyes.

"Rich is a good guy, all right? He's got a job. He sells insurance." Shay squirmed to the edge of the seat; her nails picked at the gimp again, and Sara was going to rip my ass in half when she saw what had happened to the chair. "He treats me nice. You know what he said? He loves kids, and you know what he said? He said we should take a family trip to Disneyland this summer. That's the kind of guy he is."

"And when Rich had finished throwing it to you—"

"You're being really crude," Austin said.

"—you, what? Finally decided to go back home and check in?"

"I went home. They were gone." Tears welled in her eyes, and her nails—at least two-inches long, peacock-blue with iridescent tips, the kind of nails that must have cost a fortune—ripped out another length of the gimp braid. "I looked everywhere. I called the school, but it was Saturday. I called their friends. I called up at St. Raphael's, and all I got was the janitor, and he didn't remember seeing any kids."

"But you didn't call the sheriff," Austin said quietly.

Shay shook her head.

"Why?"

"Cribbs—that's their dad—he's complicated."

"Hold on. His name is Cribbs?"

"His name is Todd Anthony Cribbs, but he went by Cribbs through high school. And yes, he's from here. And yes, we both went to school here. And yes, he was my high school boyfriend. And yes, I dropped out when I had Tyler. So there you go. Is that all of it?"

"Don't get pissy with me because you fucked up your life."

"He's complicated?" Austin said in that quiet voice. It was hard to reconcile him now—composed, compassionate, reserved—with the furious tears I had seen only minutes before. But he'd been going to therapy. He'd been getting all sorts of nifty self-help tricks. I, on the other hand, had my own kind of tricks. The self-fuck kind that I used every day.

"He's bad enough. He hit me. He broke my nose one time. That's before I was dancing, thank God, or Lawayne would have put me on the street. And he's not clean. He drives long distance, and he put his willy in every puss-trap from here to the coast. Brought home all sorts of bugs and didn't mind passing them along. But he loved those kids. He's a shit dad, but he loves them."

"He's out of the picture, isn't he?"

She shifted, her profile now toward us, but her body inclining toward the door. "He was."

"So call the sheriff," Austin said. "God, I feel like I'm talking in circles here. If you think he kidnapped the kids—"

The worst mother in the world, I thought, my fingers like chips of ice. The worst mother in the history of the world, and the candles, and the iron, and the cigarettes—

"You don't have custody." I didn't recognize my own voice.

Austin glanced at me, a reflex, and turned back to Shay. Then he looked at me again. Harder. Like a goddamn sledgehammer. And his hand found the small of my back.

"You need to sit down."

I shook him off. "You don't, do you?"

Shay, still needled toward the door like a damn compass, shook her head once.

"Of course you don't. Why would they give custody of two kids—two nice kids, two kids that deserve a good life, two kids that deserve somebody home, somebody watching out for them, somebody who cares about them—why would they give them to a stripper, to a drug addict, to a goddamn fucking prostitute?"

She flinched at the end like I'd hit her.

The candles, the iron, the cigarettes. The vacuum cleaner cord. Christ, I knew what that flinch was. That flinch was a lot of practice taking blows. I knew because I'd had a lot of practice myself, and all of the hate spilled out of me like a ruptured infection, and my knees sagged again.

I didn't fall, not exactly—no fainting women, not in my life, just one big fainting queer-boy—but I staggered, and Austin steered me onto the sofa. He kept his hand at the small of my back. He rubbed small circles. I wanted to cry; my eyes burned with the need to cry. For myself, mostly, because that's what kind of selfish shit I was.

I was so caught up in the struggle not to start bawling that I didn't realize Shay was talking at first. ". . . heard he was back in town, the first time since they set custody, and he was shacked up with Maggie McKenna, who was probably the only girl from high school that out-slutted me. I saw her once in the C-Mart on 97. I didn't go in. Thank God." She whispered those two words. "If I'd gone in, I would have done something. I know I would have done something. She had Hannah and Tyler with her; I guess Cribbs was back on the road, or maybe sleeping one off, or maybe he just told her to take the kids and get out of the house for a while. I hadn't seen them in six months, I think. Hannah was four. She followed Tyler around the inside of the C-Mart clutching a Whatchamacallit; Tyler had a Laffy Taffy rope. Strawberry."

A four-inch section of the gimp had come loose, and she worked her index finger under it, the nail flashing out like lapis lazuli. "Maggie wasn't even paying attention to them. Not even when they went over to the beer cave and Tyler tried to open the door. They could have gotten stuck in there. They could have suffocated or frozen to death or something, but she was too busy talking to the clerk and trying to get him to look at her tits. I'd been clean for four months. And I knew I could do better for them than Maggie. I could do better than Cribbs. He loves them, but he doesn't know what to do with them, and so he'd shack up with girls like Maggie and hope they could figure out how to handle kids. So I picked them up from school one day." She smiled at me, and I forgot about crying, and I forgot about my own shit, and I figured out, for the first time since I'd known her, why a guy might pay money for Shay to smile at him.

"That's it?" Austin said. "They just let you pick up the kids?"

"That's it. Nobody even looked at me. I was just sitting at the end of the block, and when Tyler and Hannah walked past, I rolled down the window. I had that place out by Slippers by then, and I had a job, and we drove home."

"Cribbs?" I said.

She shrugged.

"He didn't come after you? He didn't send the sheriff?"

"I think he knew it was better. That's what's so funny about it. The fight, the whole custody battle, that was about getting back at me. He loves those kids, sure, but that was really about teaching me a lesson. He didn't want them around; he didn't want to do the hard stuff with them. Once he realized how much work kids are, he must have wished he'd slashed my tires or something instead of fighting me for custody. I honestly think he picked up Maggie because he needed a nanny. He left her a week after I picked up the kids. I saw him a few times after that; he drove for Lawayne sometimes, and he'd stop by the club. Aside from being a general asshole, though, he didn't really want anything to do with me. He liked to see the kids. Take them out for dinner or ice cream and a movie. But he saw them less and less."

Lawayne's name lit a fuse at the back of my head. He was dangerous, and he had a hand in every awful thing in the county, and he had gotten tangled up with Urho and the Lady before. "But?"

Shay spread a wrinkled paper across her knees and passed it to me. I scanned it. It was a page from the Kane Motor Court registry. On the left, three hole punches feathered out where they had ripped from the rings. Two-thirds of the way down the sheet, in a blocky all-caps print, someone had written Cribbs.

"He signs his name that way?"

"It's the Kane Motor Court," Shay said. "It's not the Ritz."

The date was for March 30th, the Friday before. I teased the torn hole punch as I studied the paper. "So he stayed in Kane the night before they disappeared."

"It's thirty miles away," Austin said.

"It's twenty-seven."

"Why didn't he stay at his house here?"

"He doesn't have a house. He drives all the time. When he's around for a few days, he stays with a buddy, or he stays at the Kane Motor Court or the Gypsy or the Hunt Public House. He used to sleep in the cab of his truck; maybe he still does when he's driving. But when he's in town, he likes to—" Her mouth twisted. "Get out."

"He has legal custody." Catching the ragged edge of one of the hole punches, I twisted until it tore free. "If he took the kids, he's got every right to them. And when you talked to the sheriff, just a casual talk over lunch, that's what he told you. He said you shouldn't make it official. He said it wouldn't go anywhere. He said he couldn't do anything."

Shay nodded.

"So get a lawyer," Austin said. Jerking a thumb at me, he added, "This guy's not a lawyer. He can't help you."

"Thanks."

He was still rubbing circles at the small of my back, and he gave me a tight grin, but those eyes were hard as turquoise.

"It's something else," I said. Something was hollowing out Shay's expression from the inside, collapsing her face into a horrified mask. "You don't even really believe Cribbs took them. Or if you do, you don't think he took them just because he decided he wants to play dad again."

My final words made Shay jerk as though I'd pricked her, and her hand came up. With a long, stuttering rip, the gimp braid pulled all the way to the corner of the seat. I sighed. Sara was going to whip me through the streets.

"I keep hearing them. Well, her. Hannah. I can hear her at night. When I'm trying to go to sleep. Not that I'm sleeping much. But I can hear her."

Austin's hand, in the middle of one of those small, comforting circles, froze.

"You can hear Hannah?" I spoke quietly. Calmly. You don't yell at a rabid dog.

"Not words. Not even all the time. But at night. When I'm in my room upstairs." She giggled, the sound terrible and shrill, and clapped both hands over her mouth. "Because I'm upstairs. Like a radio tower. I can hear her screaming sometimes. Screaming and screaming and screaming." She giggled again. Her nails bit into her cheeks; blood enameled little red pommels at the tips.

Austin's fingers at the small of my back had enough tension to pull a trigger. "Jesus," he breathed.

"Mother thinks I'm absolutely insane, coming to you. But the sheriff can't do anything. Won't. Can't." She shook her head. Some of the blood curved around her fingers and slid under her nails, staining the beds purple. "She thinks I should get a lawyer. She thinks she should put me in a home. But I can hear her. I can hear Hannah calling me."

Next to me, Austin just breathed out low and slow. It was worse, somehow, than when he muttered *Jesus*.

With a suddenness that startled me, Shay shot out of her seat. She was coming for me. I brought up one arm. Austin launched off the sofa. But both of us were too slow. Shay clutched my leg, her nails slicing skin, embedding in flesh, her blood mixing with mine.

"Tell me. Tell me you'll find them."

"Get off him, you batshit fuck." Austin slammed into her, and Shay was a tiny thing, maybe ninety pounds when she was sopping, but she didn't budge. "Get the hell off him."

"Promise me you'll find them."

Blood. Her blood and my blood. It laced my knee, branched, fanned along my calf.

"Promise me."

"You're hurting him. Get off him."

"Promise me."

"I'll find them."

"Get the fuck off him."

Shay stumbled backward. Austin, his chest heaving, planted himself between us. She looked at me. She looked at her hand, the fingers crooked into a claw, gore staining the peacock blue of her nails. Then, with a shuddering sob, she plunged out into the wind and the rain and the night.

"What the fuck."

I stood up, my injured leg pulsed, and I shut the door.

"What the fuck."

When I faced him, those eyes were still hard and cold as turquoise.

"What the fuck was that?"

I shook my head.

"You're not serious. You're not serious about what you just said. Tell me that. You need to leave town, Vie. You heard those guys earlier. You need to get out of here, now, tonight."

I rolled my shoulders. The look on his face transformed into that vicious, shutter-click rage I had seen before, the one that preceded tears. But there weren't any tears this time. I could take him in a fight. The calculations ran just under the surface of conscious thought, but the conclusion was startlingly vivid. With him looking at me that way, with rage closing his face like the shutter on a lens, he might swing. And I could take him. He was stronger now. Maybe stronger than I was. But I was bigger. And I was meaner. And I fought dirty. So I could take him because deep down, Austin was a good guy. And I wasn't. And that meant I'd win.

"Just tell me what you said, tell me it was just to get her out of here. Tell me you wanted her gone, so you said what she needed to hear."

If he swung—when he swung—it would probably be a wide right hook. That's what he'd used last time.

"Tell me you're not going to get dragged into some insane custody battle between a prostitute and her drug-dealing trucker boyfriend."

"Austin."

"Oh my God."

"Austin."

"You know what? You were right. I should have left." He looked around, as though he needed to snatch up his jacket or a bag or something so that he could make his dramatic exit.

"Austin, come on. They're kids."

"They're not your kids. They've got a mom and a dad. You're a kid too, all right? This guy, Cribbs, I've heard of him. He's not just a trucker, ok? Kids buy from him. Kaden's bought from him. He's a piece of shit. Even if she's telling the truth and he really does love his kids, he's a piece of shit. And he's—he's a fucking lunatic. And there's no way I'm letting you get involved in this."

"You're not going to let me?"

The temperature in the room dropped. I could feel that rain again, icy and needling my chest.

"No."

"You don't get to say things like that. You don't get to make decisions like that."

"Yeah, I do. I'm your boyfriend—"

"You don't own me."

"I'm your boyfriend, damn it, and I'm telling you that I'm not letting you get involved with this."

"Or what? You'll break up with me?"

Rage shuttered his face again.

"You'll hit me? You'll break my legs so I can't leave the house?"

His hands curled into fists.

That feeling of rain, of icy barbs driving into my chest, was heavier now.

With what looked like a lot of effort, Austin relaxed his hands. Staring at the carpet, he said, "Do you want help with your leg?"

I managed to shake my head. The blood was a network of streams now, a delta of red down my calf and into my sock.

"Do you want help upstairs?"

I worked my jaw, trying to ease the tension. "Yeah." That was the hardest part. And I knew I could do a little more and try to make up for being an asshole. "Yeah, why don't you come with me? We can, you know. A shower. It's a tight fit, but we've made it work before, and—and it'd be fun."

"Yeah. Fun."

I slid my hand along his arm, hooked his fingers, and tugged.

Austin pulled away. "You go on ahead. Unless you need help up the stairs."

"You don't want to . . ."

"I'm just going to stick around until Sara gets back."

"I didn't mean it. Will you let me take it back?"

He dropped my hand. "Forget it. It's fine. Vie, would you tell me if something was wrong? With—I don't know. With you. With us."

"I should shower." The words came out sharper and colder than that fucking miserable day.

And nothing from Austin. Just that sensation of ice prickling my chest, sliding through skin and muscle all the way to the heart.

I limped to the stairs and dragged my sorry ass up, step by step. About three steps up, I stopped and looked back. Austin had stretched out on the sofa, heel propped on toes, hands behind his head as he stared at the ceiling.

Other people say they have regrets. I just had a black hole at the back of my head. It was bigger now. It wasn't just a smudge on the glass. It was a black hole. Everything had been great, everything had been perfect, and that black hole had been there the whole time, eating up light and life and energy, until this. Until I fucked up everything again.

I made it up the stairs. Someone had managed to cram a stall under the eave of the house, so the shower head hit me at the chest. Still, the water was hot, and the pressure was good, and I scrubbed off blood from my thigh and knee and calf. The towel came away pink when I dried my leg, but the scratches looked a lot better. I tossed the towel in the hamper and limped, naked, into my room.

Emmett Bradley, dark-haired and slender and raising every hair on my body like he was a lightning storm, was sitting cross-legged on the bed.

# Chapter | 4

Nothing. No raised eyebrow. No smirk. No heavy-handed attempt to ravish me. Not so much as a leer.

Months. It had been months since I had been this close to Emmett, and my body still reacted to him like somebody flipped a switch and sent electricity into me. His hair was still in short, messy spikes; his tan had faded over the winter, but he looked almost better this way, the contrast between dark hair and dark eyes and the pallor of his skin. He was so beautiful he could have started a war, or ten wars, or a hundred. The scar on his neck, though, that was new. It was still shiny, and it hooked like a J toward his collarbone. He still hadn't said anything.

"It's a bad time, Emmett."

He nodded. His eyes were all over me. My face, my chest, my arms, my crotch. I grabbed at a drawer, yanked out boxers, and stepped into them. They didn't hide anything. Hell, they just made it worse. And those eyes. Worse than touching. If he'd touched me, I could have slugged him, I could have knocked him down the stairs. But those eyes, all over me, and my skin prickling, my breath sizzling. I snagged a pair of clean running shorts, jumped into them, and yelped as they scraped along my scratched leg.

Better, I thought, checking myself. But not by a whole lot.

"It's a bad time. What happened? You disappear for a few months and now you're deaf?"

He slid to the edge of the bed.

"Go." I pointed to the window he had used—the window he had used once before to sneak in and catch me like this. At least that time I had a towel. "Get the hell out. If you want to talk, you can come to the door and knock like everyone else."

He stepped around me, and his hand fell on the doorknob.

"Don't go out there. Austin's here, and he's pissed, and if he knows you were up here like this—"

"Like what?"

The old Emmett would have grinned. He would have smirked. It would have been like running the wheel on a lighter, sparking all over the place.

"Like this, dumbfuck. Like you eye-fucking me and me naked."

"You're not naked. And I'm not . . ." He paused and shook his head. He turned the knob.

"I'm serious. Don't."

"Don't worry; your watchdog won't know I'm here."

With that, he opened the door and stepped out onto the landing.

Downstairs, the sofa springs pinged as Austin shifted. Footsteps padded across the floor. Emmett didn't hurry; he sauntered toward the bathroom, a full-on, goddamn saunter like he was walking down a runway and wanted everyone to get an eyeful. As Emmett passed through the bathroom door, Austin poked his head around the stairs.

"You don't have to babysit me," I called down to him. It just popped out of my mouth, and I wanted it back as soon as it did.

Probably thirty seconds passed and Austin stared up at me. "I'm going downstairs. I'll leave the door open; if you need anything, just shout."

"If you want to work out, you can go work out."

Another thirty seconds. He looked tired. Beat. Worn the hell out. "Just shout."

No sooner had Austin thumped toward the basement than Emmett emerged from the bathroom, still moving in that goddamn saunter like a cat swishing his tail. In his arms, he held an orange tackle box.

"Put that back."

He bumped up against me, forcing me into the bedroom, hooking the door with the toe of his sneaker, his chest against my chest. I could feel him. The lean heat of him. The slight dampness of the cotton. The stiff nubs of his nipples. His breath on my neck.

A few months ago, touch like that would have sent my abilities into overload. I was psychic—I didn't know if that was the right word, but it came close enough to describing my abilities. I could read people: their emotions, their thoughts, their memories. And I could send my own thoughts. I could overload them with guilt or pain or rage. I could soothe them. For most of my life, I couldn't control it, and touch would send it into hyperdrive. Now, thank God, I had some modicum of control, and I didn't get swept into Emmett's mind.

The last time I had been this close to Emmett, he had been in a hospital bed, bandages swathing his neck, and I had been lying next to him, holding him as he wept. I had watched him stab Makayla

Price. And then I put him to sleep. And he hadn't called. In four months, he hadn't picked up the phone. He hadn't visited. He hadn't stopped by Bighorn Burger. He hadn't talked to me at school. He hadn't so much as looked me in the eyes. As far as I knew, Emmett hadn't even known I was still alive. And I knew—I knew—that Emmett knew exactly how much that hurt me.

And now he was here. His goddamn nipples poking through wet cotton. His goddamn nipples poking into my chest as he barreled me toward the bed. Here. He'd come here, right into my room, caught me naked, put on that face like he didn't know me from a guy on the street, watched me like he was taking me apart for his own private porno, talked about Austin, called him my watchdog. Emmett kept coming, the edges of the tacklebox biting into my hip when he bumped me, his face smooth as slate.

I pushed back.

He shoved me toward the bed. Nothing on his face.

I slapped him. And I put my shoulder into it. His head cracked to the side, and his lip split against the heel of my hand, and the first drops of blood were so hot against my palm that they could have been embers.

He staggered a little. The tacklebox fell, and the lid flipped open. Gauze, medical tape, a pair of silver snippers, Hello Kitty Band-Aids, and a foil-wrapped condom that was probably older than I was bounced across the floorboards. Emmett shook his head and straightened up.

I'd gone to a funhouse with Gage once, back in Oklahoma. And one of the rooms at the back was a total blackout. You walked in, and one of the workers slammed it shut, and boom. Dark. And then the floor dropped on a mechanical lift. Not far. Maybe an inch. Maybe two, tops. But for that fraction of a second, there was no light, no space, no up, no down.

Emmett's dark eyes met mine, and that was what it was like: no up. No down. I wasn't even falling, not yet.

From deep below us, metal clanked. Austin. Austin was down there, lifting those damn weights that he'd installed in the basement. I could shout. I could shout loud enough that he'd hear me because he'd promised to come running if I shouted, he'd promised he'd leave the door open so he could hear me.

Emmett ran the back of his index finger under his lip, collecting beads of blood.

If I shouted now, Austin could be here in forty seconds. Maybe thirty.

Emmett wiped the blood on his shirt, right on the Dolce and Gabbana emblem.

"You son of a bitch," I said.

Dropping into a squat, Emmett ripped off a length of gauze and wadded it against his lip. Then he stood again, eye to eye with me. My bare chest prickled.

"You knew. You knew, Emmett. You goddamn fucking knew I was worried about you."

Crimson wicked along the gauze, diffusing as it went, darkening individual threads at the edge of the fabric.

"I wanted to know you were ok. I needed to know. And you—you wouldn't even look at me. And now you're here? You just show up, you're just in my room one night, sitting on my bed, and you goddamn knew I was in the shower. You could hear me. And you're such a fucking little perv that you stayed right there and waited for me. And I needed to know, Emmett. God damn it. I needed that much from you."

Peeling off the gauze, Emmett gave a shadowy little smile. It wasn't the real thing, but it was the closest he'd come to looking human since I found him in my room. "You don't always get what you want, tweaker."

Something about his look, something about my standing shirtless, about the boner that hadn't completely gone away, about that ancient derelict condom near my foot, made the goosebumps worse. My skin was so tight I felt like it might split.

"Are you going to tell him I'm here?"

"That depends."

"On what?"

"On why you're here."

And then Emmett did smirk, and it was scorching. He dropped to his knees, his mouth level with my bulge, and his fingers hooked inside the elastic band of my boxers.

"Are you going to tell him now?"

"Christ, Emmett, what are you—" I grappled with him, prying at his fingers, but all I was doing was helping him inch the elastic lower, exposing pale flesh and, then, an oblong of blond fuzz. "I'm not—we're not fucking doing this, not like this—"

Laughing, he pushed, and I stumbled backward. The bed hit me at the knees, and my legs folded and I sat hard on the mattress.

"Relax, tweaker. I told you before: your virtue is safe with me. I just needed to get a closer look at that leg."

I tried to draw away, but he caught my ankle and planted my foot on the ground. Scooting closer, he swept the tacklebox toward the bed. He picked up the hundred-year-old condom, turned it once like a card shark, and flipped it. The damn thing landed right there, right at the hot spot at the center of my lap. Right goddamn there, like he'd been playing the ring toss. Emmett just grinned and started winding gauze around my leg.

"I can do that."

"Sure."

"Austin can help me."

"Yeah, it sounded like he'd be happy to help."

His head, at the level of my knees, was distracting me, and I kept fighting the urge to run my fingers through his hair. "You, uh. You heard that?"

Frank, brown eyes came up at me.

"Oh."

"There might be a few people who didn't hear it."

"All right."

"Back east."

"I get it."

"Across the Atlantic."

"You're such a prick sometimes. And you shouldn't have been eavesdropping."

He just gave another of those shrugs. With surprising skill, he taped the gauze in place. Then he dropped back. He looked good there, between my knees, that perfect face fixed attentively on me. He looked really good. The heather-gray shirt had slipped down, exposing the smooth flatness of his chest, and his pulse beat in his neck. A very fast pulse, I realized. I thought maybe if I flicked that condom in his lap, it might be a little like ring toss again.

This time, I couldn't stop myself. I touched his hair. Just the side of his head, just the tips of my fingers, just a short line above his ear, and then I managed to pull back. Because I was dating Austin. Because I had a boyfriend. And because Emmett had made it perfectly, painfully, one-hundred-percent clear that I was not dating material—not for him, anyway.

"Are you?" I asked.

"A prick? Yeah. Most of the time."

"No. Are you ok?"

His face shuttered. He retreated to the rocking chair Sara had insisted on putting in my room, and his clasped hands hung between his knees.

"Emmett, I need this. I don't ask you for shit, but I'm asking for this. Give me this."

"No."

The word was a quiet, emotionless slap, and now I knew how Emmett must have felt when I hit him. It practically knocked my head off.

"What do you mean—"

"What do you think I mean, tweaker? I mean no. We're not going to talk about that. About any of it."

"Not going to talk about what?"

"Don't play stupid. You're not stupid. You're big and you like to act like you're all muscles, but you're not stupid."

"No, I want you to tell me. What aren't we going to talk about?"

He wiped at his face. When his hands swung between his knees again, he was blank again. "You know they're coming for you."

"You just said we're not going to talk about—"

"And you know that whatever they want from you, whatever they think you can do for them, that's not going to be the end of it. You know they're all in on this. Life or death. Your life. Your death."

I rolled my shoulders. What he was saying was true. It was scary true. It was the root of the fear that sent me out into the freezing April rain to run. To try to run far enough and fast enough to get away from that fear. And I didn't want it here with me, with Emmett, with Austin, with me. So I pushed it away. I wanted to be here, only here, in this warm room with the rag rug between my toes and the rain spitting on the window.

My wet hair brushed my shoulders, the tips chilly, carrying a whiff of Dove shampoo. That didn't seem fair. I didn't want to smell Dove shampoo and wet hair. I wanted to smell Emmett. I wanted to smell that hot, citrus cologne he wore. If he were next to me again, on the floor between my knees, his hand on my ankle, if I bent forward, I could pull in a deep breath of him. Pure Emmett.

The condom in its foil wrapper jostled and slid right off the front of my shorts.

"Try to focus, tweaker." But he was smiling again. "I'm talking about you getting killed. And I'm not going to allow that."

"You don't get to come in here, play doctor, poke and tickle, whatever the hell you were doing, and then shut me out."

Emmett shook his head slowly. "You still don't understand, tweaker. I get to do whatever I want. Whenever I want. And you'll let me. Now sit on the floor."

"Fuck you."

"Come on. Scoot your ass."

"I'll let you? You think I'm that pathetic? Yeah, Emmett. Yeah. One time, one lousy time I let you see a part of me that cares about you. But that's over." That was a lie; my heartbeat, my thick tongue, those gave it away. And Emmett knew it was a lie. Once, on accident, I had let Emmett see how much I loved him. And he had run. Shoeless. Practically naked. Into a Denver winter. And that, more than anything else, had made it pretty clear how he felt about me. Somehow, I managed to keep talking. "If you think I'm some head-over-heels sap who's going to let you walk all over him, if you think—"

"I think," he said quietly, "that you should keep yelling if you want your watchdog to come up and sniff around."

From the basement came another clank, heavier, of weights hitting concrete, and then the creak of steps.

"Call him that again," I said evenly, levelly, perfectly, sanely, reasonably. Total control. "And I'll do more than bust your lip. I'll break your jaw. I'll break it in so many pieces you'll be slurping soup until graduation."

That shadow-smile darkened Emmett's face.

"Vie," Austin called from the living room, his voice coming nearer. "What's going on?"

"Tell him I'm here," Emmett said. "I want to see his face. I want to know what he thinks, you naked, water dripping down those big pecs, all cozied up with me?"

"Stay the fuck quiet," I hissed at Emmett, moving to the landing and drawing the door closed behind me.

Austin took the stairs two at a time, at a jog, his face flushed and sweaty. All of him, in fact, was flushed and sweaty. And all of him was very, very visible. He'd changed clothes, and now he wore a skimpy pair of workout shorts, and they did nothing to hide one of my favorite parts of Austin. That was all: just those shorts. They were so damn distracting I probably would have been able to focus better if he'd been naked.

Maybe it was Emmett in my room, maybe it was having him so close to me again after all these weeks, maybe it was the painfulness of the arousal I felt for both of them, Austin and Emmett, maybe it was the fight with Austin. It might have been a dozen things. It might have just been that I needed a lay because I was a teenager and my hormones were pumping out sex 24/7. But I saw Austin, really saw him, and how he'd changed over the last few months.

He hadn't just cut his hair. He hadn't just lost baby fat or bulked up his arms a little. He was ripped. He was shredded. He was—he was a fucking Hulk. Not as tall as Emmett, not as tall as I was, but more muscled than either of us. With Emmett and his slender frame, that wasn't much. With me, though—it had been a long time since I'd met a guy more built than I was. His arms. God damn. How had I not noticed how big his arms had gotten?

And Jesus Christ. The veins. Getting his pump. Getting his swell.

When I took my next breath, it sounded like a train whistle.

"What's going on? Why are you yelling?" Another step up. His head swiveled, and one of those huge arms came up as he scratched behind his head. Good Lord. "Are you ok?"

"What?"

"Is something wrong? You sounded upset."

"What? I mean. No. Yeah. I don't know."

Those thick eyebrows shot up. He swiped at some of the sweat on his face. "Are we fighting? Because last time, at least I knew we were fighting. And if we're fighting, I've got to start thinking of a way to make it up."

"We're not fighting."

Another step up. The heat pounding off him threatened to give me a sunburn. "You're sure?"

"We're not fighting."

One of those huge arms wrapped around my waist, tugging me forward. For a moment, I balanced on the lip of the step, and then I teetered forward as Austin hugged me to him. Easily. He lifted me, wrapped me against him, and squeezed until I grunted and whopped him on the back.

"God, you're going to put me in a wheelchair."

He buried his face in my neck, kissing, his teeth nipping lightly. The hard-on, which had started to fade, came back like the goddamn Terminator. I ran my hand through his short, short hair, enjoying the way it bristled just above my fingers.

When he set me down, I wiped at his sweat slicking my chest and arms. "Now I need another shower."

"You had an interesting idea about that earlier."

"Yeah. Well—"

His fingers looped the elastic at the front of my waist; his knuckles dug into that strip of blond fuzz that was just barely visible. "You're not going to be a tease about this, are you? You know how I get when you tease me."

"Emmett's here."

His hand slackened. Blue-green eyes swept to the door. Then he elbowed past me, taking the last three steps together and launching into my room.

I flew after him. "Hold on, Austin. It's not what you think—"

I expected to find Emmett on the ground with most of his teeth sparkling on the floor around him. I expected to see just how hard

Austin could hit after lifting weights for the last four months. Hulk smash. That kind of thing.

Instead, Austin stood in the center of the room, facing Emmett with an intense expression that I couldn't quite read. I opened my inner eye a fraction. Concern wisped off Austin. And a last smoke signal of lust. But mostly he was a tangle of noxious green jealousy and frustration, a fever blister that he couldn't quite scratch. Somehow he managed to keep it from his face, and that worried me more than anything else. I had tried, for most of our relationship, not to read his mind. It didn't seem fair or right. But right then, I was really tempted.

"Look at you," Emmett said. "All oiled up. Those tiny shorts. Abs like a goddamn mountain range. You turned gay six months ago and all the sudden you're a gym bunny?"

Austin's response was to cross his arms over his chest, and a pretty pink blush, almost girlish, ran up his cheekbones. "You're starting tonight?"

"Waiting isn't going to help."

"We talked about the end of school."

"You talked about the end of school. You talked about waiting. You talked about giving him more time." Emmett's grin hooked the corner of his mouth. "Then I heard what happened tonight."

Austin's hand compressed. Knuckles sheared steep ridges across the top of his hand. I waited for it: that fist to hit like an asteroid, the force of impact rippling through Emmett's smooth, soft skin.

But even though the pink in Austin's cheeks intensified, dusky and rosy all the way to his jaw, all he did was nod. He was gritting his teeth like he could chew through the hull of a battleship. But just one simple nod.

Then he turned and kissed me. Hard. His arms went around me, and he pulled me to him. That kiss melted me. It liquefied me. It was the kind of kiss that in a cartoon would have left nothing but a pair of steaming socks.

"All right," Emmett said, and he didn't sound quite so cool and collected anymore.

One of Austin's hands slapped the wall, and he leaned into me, his tongue deep in my mouth, his arm bracing me against him.

"Cut it out."

Austin loosed me just long enough to run his hand down my chest, his nails biting into skin hard—hard enough to sting, hard enough that the kiss took on a painful intensity. He drew my lower lip between his teeth, biting, pulling his head to the right—toward Emmett, I realized, and at the same moment I realized I could hear

Emmett, could hear a hate-filled hiss in his throat and the rocking chair squeaking under his weight.

"Get a fucking room." It didn't even sound like him anymore. It didn't sound like anyone, not anyone human.

Austin gave one last savage tear of his head, and then he released my lip and pecked me on the mouth. With a grin, he said, "We're in a room."

"What the hell was that?" I said, my fingers pressed to my throbbing lip. On my chest, five sharp red lines ran to my navel.

"Just a reminder," Austin said. "That we're not fighting."

Good Christ. I definitely wanted to go on not fighting with Austin. I could not fight with him until my head exploded.

"Get lost, Austin." Emmett's fingers curled around the rocking chair's arms. His nailbeds were white from pressure. Ugly purple mottled his face and throat. "You agreed."

"I agreed to after school was over."

"What are you two talking about?"

"Will you get the fuck out of here? I don't have all night."

"Somebody tell me what's going on."

"Night, bae," Austin said, squeezing my wrist and heading for the door.

"Night?"

"Yeah. He'll stay until Sara comes."

"That's not what I meant. I'm not worried about—"

"But I am. Night."

And then he was out the door, clomping down the stairs, and a moment later, the front door squeaked shut.

My lip was still throbbing. Emmett was glaring at me, and I yanked my fingers down, but it was too late. He shook his head in disgust.

"Don't say anything," I said.

"What? You don't want to talk about your boyfriend pissing all over you to mark his territory? Fine. I won't say anything. I won't say a word. Nothing about how insanely jealous he is. Nothing about how weird that is, how fucking messed up, that he has to mark you like that. Nothing about how he doesn't trust you, doesn't even pretend like he can trust you to be alone with me—"

Easing the door shut, I put my back to it and studied Emmett. The purple still hadn't left his cheeks. He met my gaze for a moment, and then his eyes cut to the rug, and he ran his hand over his mouth once, and then twice, as though Austin had been on his mouth—or as though he wished he'd been on mine.

"Let's get this over with."

"Not until you tell me what's been going on with you."

That, to my total surprise, changed everything. Emmett's shoulders went back, his head came up, and the tension oozed out of him. He looked all of a sudden the way he had when I'd first found him in my room: cold and distant and totally in control.

"I already said this, but I'll say it again: no. I'm not talking about that. Any of that. Not with you. Now, sit down."

He dropped onto the rug, legs crossed.

"I want to know—"

"Tweaker." It was almost gentle. Almost. "No."

"Then fuck you."

"Sure, fuck me. But sit down."

I sat. My fingers teased out strands from the rag rug.

"They're here. They're here for you."

"Jesus Christ. We already talked about this, and I don't want people worrying about me—"

"No, that's pointless."

"—just because. Wait. What?"

"It's pointless. Stupid. A total waste of everyone's time and resources."

"Hold on. I mean, it's not a totally stupid—"

"Yes. It is. We're wasting our time." His dark eyes slashed across my face. "On an ungrateful asshole."

"I'm not ungrateful."

"Sure you are. For some reason, we all just put up with it."

"I'm not ungrateful. I'm really grateful. The things—"

"Tweaker, I'm not here to argue with you."

"You're here to break into my room. You're here to eye-fuck me. You're here to pick a fight with my boyfriend—"

That iron control slipped, and Emmett growled, "He was the one chewing on your lip like it's a goddamn dog toy."

"You're here to mess with my head. But you're not here to tell me what's going on with you. You're not here to tell me if you're ok. So why are you here, Em?"

I didn't mean for it to come out like that. I didn't mean to say his name like that, catching so hard in my throat that I couldn't get it all out. I didn't mean for my whole chest to lock up so I couldn't take the next breath.

He stared at me. For the second time that day, for an instant, the floor dropped out from under me, and everything went dark, and I was in that funhouse suspended in nothing. Those dark eyes. I was floating in those eyes.

He had to clear his throat, and that noise broke the stillness.

"I'm here to make sure when they try next time, you don't make a total jackass of yourself."

# Chapter | 5

I stared at Emmett. He had this annoyingly smug little smile. I was thinking about smacking it off his face. Again.

"What?"

"I'm going to get you ready."

"Yeah. What the hell does that mean?"

"I'm going to train you."

"Oh."

"Genius, right?"

"Yeah, yeah."

"That's all you're going to say?"

"Just taking it all in."

"See, you've got these amazing abilities."

"Right."

"But you're a chickenshit."

"Uh huh."

"And so you haven't done anything with them except when you're absolutely, completely, totally pushed, like, back-to-the-wall pushed."

"Sure."

"So I'm going to fix that."

I nodded. "Let me get this straight. I'm a chickenshit."

"With powers."

"I'm a chickenshit with powers. And you, with no powers—"

"I'm really, really, really hot."

"With no psychic powers—"

"Sometimes I know what you're thinking."

"With no legitimate psychic powers. And I don't trust you. And you've shut me out totally, like blackballed me from your life. And you refuse to tell me anything remotely significant about what's been going on with you after vanishing four months ago. And you're going to train me to use my abilities, which, by the way, are the thing I hate the abso-fucking-lutely most of everything in my life. Is that about right?"

He ticked items off on his fingers. "You do trust me, even if you feel like you have to lie about it. I didn't vanish four months ago—I've been here the whole time. And I did tell you something significant: I told you I'm hot."

"You need to leave."

"Make me."

"Ginny already did this, you know? She opened up my abilities. I don't need any help."

"Sure she did. So make me."

"I don't want to hurt you."

"Tweaker, you have never, ever been able to hurt me. If you want me to leave, you're going to have to make me."

"If I have to." I rocked forward, but he pressed a hand against my chest, and the salt on his skin stung the furrows that Austin had left.

"No. The other way."

It was so easy when he was touching me. I opened my second sight and—

Someone was laughing. Giggling.

The sound was so shocking that my second sight shuttered, and I stared at Emmett.

"You can't, can you?"

"Shut up for a minute."

I opened my second sight again. Nothing. No giggling. No laughing.

Had I imagined it?

Another few seconds passed, and then I turned my attention to Emmett. With his skin against mine, it was so easy. I could do it without touch, but it was so very easy this way. So easy with him, in particular, like trailing my hand through water, like there was nothing separating us. I opened my inner eye and reached.

I had done this before; only a handful of times, to tell the truth, only since I'd managed to unlock the full extent of my power. I could send emotion, trigger physical reactions, search thoughts and memories. Getting Emmett to leave? That was going to be child's play. I'd give him a scare—just a little one. And then, when he bolted, I'd chase him down. Maybe give him a hug. Just to be sure he was ok. Just to be—

The memory hit me so hard that I actually felt it whump in my chest. Me. I was seeing me, like I was looking in a mirror.

No, that wasn't right. Because I'd looked in plenty of mirrors before, and it hadn't been anything like this. And anyway, I didn't look like that anymore. This version of me had dark hollows under his eyes, cheeks stretched tight, face like the period at the end of a nasty sentence. This was me eight months ago. This was me right after I'd arrived in Vehpese.

And then the rest of the memory began to take shape: the part of me viewing the memory was sitting on a brick landing near a flight of stairs. I recognized the spot; it was the courtyard in front of Vehpese High School. My stomach dropped. I knew, then, what I was seeing. I was seeing the first day I had shown up for school. And I was seeing it from Emmett's perspective.

Memory-me stepped down from the bus; Tyler and Hannah scurried past me, tugging at my arm, waving, and then zipping toward the elementary building. Memory-me swung his head in both directions and glanced toward the high school's front door.

Desire prickled down my breastbone: a series of discrete sparks, like someone striking match after match. I wanted this big, hulking blond stud. I wanted—

I jerked out of the memory. Something cold tickled my throat. My eyes focused, unfocused, and focused again.

I was staring up at Emmett, who had pulled my head back by the hair. In his other hand, he held a knife to my throat.

"Boom, tweaker. You're dead."

Shoving his wrist away, I fought to control my surge of disorientation. The lust flickered out slowly, and that was a damn confusing feeling since it was directed at me. Thoughts began to cohere. I was going to kick Emmett's ass. I was going to show him exactly who he was messing with. I was going to give him nightmares that would keep him awake for a week. But through all of that, the only thought that I could really hear, the only one that came through clearly, was: had Emmett really felt that way the first time he saw me?

"Just like that," he said, wagging the knife at me. "Dead."

"That was a trick."

"Of course it was a trick. Do you think they're going to play fair?"

"I wouldn't fall for something like that."

"Try it again."

This time, I wasn't touching him, but it was still like parting water with my hand. With my inner eye open, I reached for him and—

The big, hulking blond stood on the bottom-most step of the bus. It still rocked a little under his weight. He had deep hollows under his eyes, and his cheeks were so tight that it looked like he hadn't had a decent meal in his whole life. He bounced down another step, and two little kids streaked past him. The way they tugged on his arm, the way he looked at them as they ran toward the elementary building, struck a fire in my belly. Not just in my belly. A line of hot points from my breastbone down—

I shoved the memory away again and came back, again, to cold steel.

"Stop fucking doing that." I knocked his arm away, and Emmett danced back with a smile.

"You're dead." His smile flattened. "Again."

I wasn't going to fall for it this time. I flowed. The world vanished between us, dissolving like sand falling into a strong current, and the blackness of his mind swelled around me. As the last of the world disintegrated, I readied myself for the memory. His memory. Of me. And I was so busy getting ready, so busy bracing myself, that I saw his fist an instant too late.

He hit me. He didn't pull the punch, and he didn't just give me a tap. His fist connected at my solar plexus. All the breath rushed out of my lungs—and a lot of spit, too. The world kept dissolving, but it wasn't that psychic fade of the other side. This was just a whirl of black because I couldn't get any oxygen. I slumped forward, gasping, my whole body on fire with the need for air. I could hear the gasping, sucking noises as I struggled for breath.

Emmett gripped my hair and tilted my head back. I was still gasping. Still sucking. Still spitting, a little, and some of that spit scattered along his face like shrapnel. My eyes were tearing up, and I had to blink furiously to keep him in my sight.

Cold steel touched my throat again.

"You're dead, tweaker. They won't wait for you to get your act together. They won't wait while you meditate and hum and center yourself and get all zen with the universe. You close your eyes, you drift away, and they'll crush your windpipe with a baseball bat, or they'll put a bullet between your eyes, or hell, all they need to do is give you a little tap like I just did. Now try it—"

I didn't let him finish. I swept into his mind. The memory surged up, washed over me, and dragged at me like an undertow. For a moment, the sheer sexual lure of it caught me, the need to fuck that blond stud, to fuck him until those hollow eyes filled up with something real and bright and alive. Me; that's what he was thinking about me.

I swatted the memory away. Emmett was coming at me, the knife a hot white line in my vision, and I clamped down around his wrist. I twisted, and with a grunt, he released the blade. It clattered on the boards next to me.

He was smiling, but not with his eyes.

"Don't do it again."

"You learned something, didn't you? They're not just going to sit and wait for you to come at them. They're not going to roll over for you. They've been doing this a hell of a lot longer than you, and they're better than you, and they're nastier than you, and if you keep up your chickenshit and don't try to get as strong as you can, they're going to kill you. And I'm not going to some dumbass tweaker's funeral."

That last part, with the hook of his smile, put me over the edge. I reached for him psychically. He tried to bring up the memory, but this time I was ready for him, and I forced my way past it until I floated in the dark emptiness at the center of his mind.

He wanted to see me be strong? He wanted to see me use my abilities? Fine. Great. Perfect. He was going to get a taste of what I could do.

It wasn't an exact science. It wasn't anything as simple as flipping through a stack of photographs or turning the pages on a calendar. Part of it was like tuning in a radio station, and I focused on grief, pain, anger. And part of it was about focus. Images washed over me: Emmett as a boy standing over a bicycle with a flat tire; Emmett on the cusp of puberty, a giant pimple swelling on his nose, while a group of boys laughed at him; Emmett dishing himself Rocky Road out of a paper carton. They were all from too long ago, and I let them rush past me. More images. And more. I sifted as best as I could and tried to hurry. Time didn't stop when I was in his head, not exactly; it was warped. I didn't know how long I had before he tried to get away from me.

What I wanted was deeper, more visceral. And recent. I tracked it by its scent: total despair, self-hatred, loathing. Then I saw it: the knife coming up in his hand, coming down, the supple resistance of the muscles layering Makayla's stomach and then steel piercing flesh. Blood squirted out, hot, and I brought the knife up again, brought it—

My world whited out. I was distantly aware that a star had collided with my eye. Then, with a slightly clearer sense, I realized I was on my back staring up at the ceiling, and my right eye was the size of a baseball. He had punched me. And he'd done a pretty damn good job of it. I blinked; the ceiling bulged, shrank, and settled. Something was whistling.

Pushing myself up, I froze. Emmett hunched forward in the rocking chair, face buried in his hands, his whole body shaking with laughter. Silent laughter. But the jerking motions of his shoulders were violent, and he still wasn't making any noise, just that horrible shrill of air that I realized was his breath.

I got to my knees. The room bulged again. My eye threatened to drop out of my head. Then I crawled toward him. I grabbed his wrist and pulled his hand away from his face.

"Emmett, stop it."

He twisted away from me, and his hands snapped back into place, covering his features. It didn't matter though. I had seen the wide eyes, the puffy nose, the shine on his cheeks.

"Stop. Hey. Emmett, you've got to stop. I'm serious. Pull yourself together. Whatever you're feeling," I grabbed his wrists, wrestling with him this time, prying his hands away from his face. "Whatever you're feeling, it's just a memory. It's just something I pulled up, I didn't mean to do it like that, I didn't—"

His head cracked to one side. He twisted, staring up at me. Snot and tears glistened on his face. I don't even know if he saw me, not the way he was looking at me. He just shook his head, slowly, a steady 1-2 swing with his eyes on the floor. Then he froze.

I should have been ready for it. I should have guessed. He hit hard, first with his shoulder and all of his weight behind it, and then, as I fell, with his knee connecting just below my diaphragm, duplicating his earlier blow. It was about as effective as shoving the hose from a vacuum cleaner down my throat: it sucked all the air out of my lungs, and I went down with my eyes stinging.

Emmett scrambled over me, and then I knew: the knife.

"No," I croaked, catching his sneaker. I couldn't breathe. I couldn't even get my lungs to pump. But I could see him, I could see the black holes in his eyes. I dragged back, as hard as I could, and he skidded toward me. His fingers squealed against the floorboards. He flipped over, onto his side, and scrabbled, trying to get purchase, trying to drag himself just a few more inches so he could reach the knife. He drove his free foot into my stomach, and my breath whooshed out again, and an army of tiny black ants began nibbling at the corners of my vision.

I hauled him backward again. This time, his ass popped up off the floor, and when he came down, he landed on the rag rug. I kept dragging, and the rug slid easily over the floorboards, and Emmett came face to face with me. He was gone. Those huge eyes, emptied all the way to the bottom, didn't see me. I don't think they were really seeing anything. He slapped me, his nails curling at the end to rake one side of my face. He drove the heel of his other hand into my forehead, and my head struck the floor and caromed back. My grip slackened, and Emmett twisted away, planting one of his big feet right across my stomach, the rubber of the sole gripping painfully against bare skin.

For the first time in what felt like an eternity, breath rushed into my lungs. I twisted, reaching after him, and realized too late that I'd made a mistake. Emmett didn't go for the knife. He leapt, shooting toward the tacklebox like a runner diving for home. The orange plastic box toppled, and the lid popped up, and gauze and medical tape and a flash of silver and a half-flattened tube of Preparation H spilled out.

The snippers.

His hand closed around them. Those long, elegant fingers tightened until the knuckles bulged. He rolled onto his back, his head falling to the side, the long, smooth expanse of his neck bare. A pulse fluttered like a dying hummingbird in his throat. He brought up the scissors as hard as he could, driving them straight toward the artery.

I caught his wrist. I was sucking and blowing air like an old horse, and my spit flecked his face, sparkled on the back of his hand, on the steel of the snippers. He roared at me, past words, past anything except the need for what I wouldn't give him. He clubbed me on the side of the head. Those ants rushed back and forth across my vision, swallowing parts of the room. I was falling sideways, I realized. And when I hit the floor, when I didn't have the leverage to keep the snippers away from his neck, he was going to get exactly what he wanted.

Gravity only pulls down. At least, that's as far as it goes for me, for a guy who doesn't know physics. But throw a baseball. Kick a rock out over a canyon. Shoot a goddamn cannonball. The same thing will happen every time: gravity pulls down, and there's something perfect about the parabola of the fall, the long, graceful arc toward the ground. Mr. Spencer, in English class, had read to us about how the ancients thought that all things were attracted to their home, and so when you dropped a stone, it fell toward the earth, and that explained gravity. An explanation like that didn't do much for science, but it sure as hell made sense to me.

When I reached for him, it was like falling. It was easy when it shouldn't have been easy. All I had to do was fall, and gravity pulled me home.

Inside, a storm blew through Emmett. All the hate and pain and guilt and sorrow that I'd dragged up spun across his psychic landscape. I wasn't even sure what I wanted to do. I just knew that what happened next, happened, again, like gravity pulling me down. I let the memory that he'd been throwing at me wash back over both of us. The blond guy stepping down from the bus, the slight rock of the suspension, the hollowness in his eyes, the kids streaming past and tugging on his arm, the fireworks detonating in sequence 1-2-3-4 from my breastbone down.

The storm stopped. Everything inside Emmett was there, with me, inside that memory. The fireworks kept exploding, points of heat moving deep in my belly, lower, almost painful between my legs.

With a gasp, I came back to the real world. I was lying next to Emmett, still holding his wrist, with the snippers shining in his hand. I rolled on top of him, squeezed his wrist and turned, and he whined. His fingers spasmed, and the snippers clattered against the floor.

Then it was just the two of us, and the wet cotton of his shirt rubbing against my bare chest, my whole body so sensitive that it felt like sandpaper. Emmett was breathing funny—huge, gasping breaths. He rolled his head to the side, his eyes closed, and a flush ran from his chest to his eyebrows.

Shifting my weight, I reached for his face.

"Please." It was a whimper. It was Emmett begging, honest-to-God begging. His head snapped toward me. His eyes shot open. The pupils had almost swallowed the swirl of his irises. "Please, Vie. Please."

"What?"

"Oh fuck me. I don't know. Fuck me. Fuck me." It shifted in tone and intensity. "Fuck me. I want you to fuck me right now. Oh fuck."

Then I felt the hardness in his pants pressed against my knee. He was shaking.

Sucking in a breath, Emmett said, "Oh Christ. Don't move. Just—ah. If you move. If you move, if you touch me, I'm going to—oh don't fucking move. Or—or do it. Just do it, maybe. I don't know, oh Christ. I don't know."

I wanted to. I wanted to shift my weight, apply a little more pressure with my knee, and watch him come apart just from my touch. Nobody else would ever be able to do that for him. Nobody else would ever have him like this, so totally open, so vulnerable, so desperate. It would be easy. He'd probably thank me. And then—

And then what? I'd have tricked him into wanting me, and he'd shoot in his pants and probably have an out-of-body experience. And then tomorrow? What would happen then, when he realized I was still the kid that wasn't good enough for him or his family? What would he do? Shit, what would I do? Would I trick him again, make him beg for my touch again, because now I knew I could? Would I keep him coming back like an addict? Would I do that, as selfish and horrible as it was, because it would give me a chance to have Emmett in my life?

I didn't know. And I hated myself for not being able to say no.

He was still moaning, tossing his head in tiny, helpless gestures.

I eased away from him, careful not to brush against him, and when I was clear, I scrambled to my feet. I gathered the snippers and the knife, and I backed toward the door. The wood bumped my shoulder blades.

Emmett's breathing, deep and raspy, sounded like someone revving an engine, sounded like the best bass line, sounded like sex. He propped himself on his elbows. I wanted to dive into him again, knowing how easy it would be, knowing I could have him tonight, completely, totally, in a way he would never give himself to me otherwise.

"Don't go."

"Oh fuck," I said, and it sounded a hell of a lot like a moan. I jostled the knob with my elbow, managed to get it open.

"Vie, get back here. Peel off those goddamn shorts, get out that cock, and fuck me until I hit the stars."

"You're not thinking straight."

The look in his eyes was obscene; I'd made out with him, had him pressed up against me, and I'd never seen him like this. He palmed himself, his lower lip pulled between his teeth, his irises moonless.

"Damn right I'm not. Not straight at all. Just thinking about that cock."

"This wears off, Em. It's going to wear off. You can stay up here until it does."

"Don't even think about walking away from me. Get that ass back here. If you won't fuck me, take off those goddamn shorts and I'll sure as hell fuck—

I slammed the door. I took the stairs backward, stumbling, not able to take my eyes off the door. Because if he followed me, if he kept talking like that, like gravel spinning under rubber, it didn't matter what I thought was right. I'd give in. I wasn't a good guy. I wasn't even a decent guy. But I was trying really, really hard not to be a shitty guy, and I wasn't even going to manage that if Emmett came after me.

Three steps from the bottom, I missed a stair. I slipped, fell, and hit ass-hard on the floor.

The shock and the pain helped a lot with the arousal. It was hard to chub up when I was mostly wondering if I'd broken my tailbone and cursing myself for being the biggest idiot in a hundred miles. I lay there, contemplating exactly how stupid I was and staring at the sagging ceiling. What the hell had I been thinking? I knew how easily I could damage someone psychically. I knew how easily I could mess up Emmett—I'd done it before, although never that bad. But he pushed my buttons, and the minute I felt threatened, I lashed out. I might not want to be a shitty guy, but I was feeling pretty damn close.

I was still lying there when a shadow flicked across me. Sara, her red face floating in her cloud of frizzy blond hair, stared down at me.

"Vie, honey. Are you all right?"

"Yeah."

"You're lying on the floor. Did you fall?"

"Yeah."

"In your underwear?"

"Um. Yeah."

"With a knife?"

I sighed. "I guess so."

"Can you get up?"

"I'm not sure."

"Is this something I should know about?"

I shook my head, and somehow, that made my ass hurt again.

"Vie, I know you and Austin—" That boy was her nephew, and her face got even redder. "Should we have a talk? About being safe, I mean?"

"Is there a safe-sex talk that covers the really weird sex stuff like falling down stairs with knives?"

"Well, I just meant . . ."

"Austin's not even here."

"It's not—well, I was reading a parenting article about auto-erotic—"

That managed to get me on my feet faster than a lightning bolt. "Look at that. Miraculous recovery." I shot up the stairs, still holding the knife. "Thanks, Sara."

She called after me, "If it's something that Austin's making you do, I want you to tell me."

I groaned. This might actually be the worst day of my life.

When I shouldered open the door, I didn't know what I'd find: Emmett naked on my bed, Emmett ready to pounce and rip my clothes off, Emmett trying to make a noose out of a bed sheet.

Instead, I found nothing. Just an open window, rain, and the night.

# Chapter | 6

Emmett, the little bastard, didn't answer any of my calls, and I didn't even know he was still alive until the next day at school when he passed me in the hall.

It was eight in the morning; the first bell was about to ring, and I was lingering in the hall to avoid Mr. Lynch, my sadistic math teacher. Some of that lingering was also motivated by the fact that I might, maybe, possibly have thought I'd see Emmett if I waited long enough.

And then, while I leaned up against my locker, there he was: Armani tee, jeans hugging his ass, big old combat boots. He had something to prove, I guess. Guys like Emmett always have something to prove. He was coming down the hallway, surrounded by his new group of friends—an assortment of juniors and seniors, the jocks and the weed-heads who kept the jocks supplied with what they wanted.

I had every intention of apologizing. I had a whole speech prepared. Yeah, I'd screwed up last night. I'd screwed up really, really badly. And I was willing to take whatever punishment he named. If he wanted me never to go near him again, fine. It'd kill me, but fine. If he wanted to beat my ass, fine. If he wanted to grab me by the jaw, push me up against a wall, and—well, Jesus. I cut off that line of thinking fast.

All of that went out the window, though, when I heard him say, "That goddamn tweaker did it."

Rachel Emmenthal kept rising up on her toes, pouting, and trying to touch his lip. "You poor baby. You need to tell Mr. Hillenbrand. He attacked you. He's psycho. Amanda Abbott said her dad heard that the cops picked him up for blowing truckers, and Amanda Siegfried said her dad said that he killed a kid at his last school."

I focused on Emmett's lip. It was definitely split. It was puffy as hell. And that brought out my first smile of the day.

He didn't want to look at me. He was trying hard not to look at me. But he would have needed a brace, a big old clunky iron thing around his neck to keep his head from swiveling toward me.

"What the fuck are you grinning about?"

"I like your new look." Over Emmett's shoulder, I saw Austin. He bobbed through the crowd that was beginning to gather. Teenagers could smell a fight like sharks scenting blood. Austin bulldozed between a pair of blondes that looked about as big as his wrists. One of them bounced, literally bounced, off the drinking fountain. "The boots," I added, flicking my gaze back to Emmett. "Really butch."

"You're such a fucking fag," one of the juniors said. I didn't know him; I didn't need to know him. Guys like him are the exact same everywhere in the world. They've been the exact same ever since they evolved those thick necks and empty heads.

"Shut up, Jack." Emmett shook his head. "Quit looking at me."

"It's a free country."

"Quit grinning."

"I'm having a great day."

"You want me to beat his faggot ass?"

"Christ, Jack, if you open your mouth again, I'll knock the shit out of you."

"Go ahead. Tell him to beat my faggot ass."

Jack hopped up and down like he was about to get into a goddamn boxing ring.

Then, with a shake of his head, Emmett stepped around me. He didn't so much as blink when I caught his sleeve.

"Hold on, I'm not done talking to—"

He just shook me off, and his new group of friends clustered around him. One of them, a big, red-headed kid, checked me with his shoulder, laughed, and slapped five with another guy as he caught up to Emmett's little posse. I froze and stared after the departing group.

The redhead was the same guy who'd blown up Becca's car. And he was hanging out with Emmett, part of his gaggle of morons.

And then they were gone.

The sharks that had gathered for a feeding frenzy looked at each other in disappointment. The static buzz in the air began to dissipate. A whiff of cedar and tobacco reached me, and a moment later, Austin pushed through a giggling gaggle of sophomores who were picking me apart with their eyes.

"Which one of them?"

"What?"

"Was it Jack?"

"Nothing happened."

"All right." Austin turned to the girls. "Who called my boyfriend a faggot?"

"Will you drop it?"

The girls had dried up; they quivered, trembling against each other and staring at Austin.

"Who. Was. It."

"Leave them alone. Hey, you girls. Go to class. Boo." I clapped my hands, and they took off like I'd announced a Lululemon giveaway in the next room. One of them screamed.

"It was Jack. I know it was Jack."

"It wasn't anything. It was Emmett being a prick. Putting on a show for his friends."

"Fine. It doesn't matter. I'll find Jack later."

I took handfuls of his shirt and pulled him toward me. He was getting too big for his britches. Literally. The button-up was ready to pop when I tugged on it. It did, however, make him look damn fine.

"First, I've got to decide if we're having a fight."

"What?" Those turquoise eyes blinked sleepily. "We talked about this last night. We're not—"

"That was before I knew that you conspired with Emmett on some insane plan to make me a better psychic."

"The bell's going to ring."

"I'll take the tardy."

"Mr. Lynch is going to write you up."

"Unlike you, I've had detention before. I'll survive."

"But Mr. Lynch might not."

"Start talking."

"Conspired. That's a big word for a guy with all those muscles." He was leering at me now, taking me in, and then he leaned toward me for a kiss.

I planted a hand on his chest. "I'm practicing for the ACT. If you try to change the subject again, we really will be in a fight."

"Come on, Vie. You already know all of it. What do you want me to say?"

The bell chimed.

"I want you to tell the truth."

"Emmett came up to me one day in the weight room. Just showed up out of nowhere. He's never down there, not unless he's—"

"Not unless he's what?"

Austin eyed the rapidly emptying hallway. He looked like he was trying to decide if he could outrun me.

"Not unless he's what, Austin?"

"Not unless he's selling."

"What? Like, he's got a job?"

"Not a legal one."

It took a minute. I loosed the wrinkled bunches of fabric that I'd been gripping. "You're telling me Emmett is selling drugs? What? Weed?"

"He came down to the weight room, like I was saying, and he moved right behind the bench, grabbed the bar, and told me we had to talk."

"Hold on. Back up. You can't just skip over that. Who told you this?"

"A lot of guys."

"So give me a name. Give me a lot of names."

"It doesn't matter, all right?"

"Yeah, it matters. I know Emmett. He's not selling drugs. And whoever's saying that—"

Red stained Austin's cheeks. He jabbed a finger in the direction Emmett had gone. "Him? That piece of shit that just walked past you? You don't know him. Come on, Vie. You're so smart most of the time. And you don't trust anybody. You thought that fireman, the one who was collecting change in the intersection, you thought he was running a scam. And last month, when we went to Billings, I saw you eyeing that nun."

"She was suspicious—"

"She was selling apple pies outside a convent, for Christ's sake. Just listen, ok? You won't turn around when you have your shirt off because you think somehow I'm going to forget what's on your back. You can't sleep half the time I'm in bed with you—"

My face caught fire. "Dude."

"—no, don't try to tell me you're sleeping. I know what you sound like when you're sleeping. Sometimes you're awake, Vie. But sometimes you're dreaming and you scream. You're terrified. And it's not just the sleep, you know? You've got a backup plan every time I promise to do something because you're convinced one day I'm not going to show up. And you won't tell me what's wrong, what's really wrong. With us. Or with me. Or with you."

"This is over." I knocked into Austin with my shoulder.

Digging fingers into my shirt, he spun me back around. He was stronger. God, he was so much stronger than he'd been a few months ago. "You're so smart. You're so careful. You're so fucking suspicious about everyone and everything, even me, but you trust Emmett Bradley. Well, here's the truth. He is a drug dealer. Colton told me. And Kaden told me. And Harry Cash. And Dan Williams. And JJ

Whaley bought a goddamn dime of weed off him while I watched, ok, so I know it's true."

I shrugged him off. I had a whole plan to storm down the hall, but my legs weren't working. My heart was pumping blood somewhere, but it wasn't my legs.

"Right there in the weight room, he sat down, and he told me you needed to start getting ready. And he's right. And we agreed we'd start working on it after school got out. So I was going to tell you. Don't make that face like I lied to you or hid something from you. I knew how you'd react. The first time I said his name, you were going to go flying out to his house and see if he was ok. So I waited. And then Emmett did what he always does: exactly what he wanted. He showed up without telling me. And he fucked with your head, just like he always does. And you know what? When we'd finished talking about you," Austin's finger jabbed toward my chest. "When we'd finished worrying about you." It jabbed toward me again, not touching but coming close. "Because we're always worrying about you." Again. "He tried to sell me steroids right there on the goddamn weight bench." All the fight went out of Austin; his shoulders slumped, and he sighed. "Get a clue, Vie."

# Chapter | 7

School dragged by. A few times, I thought I saw the clock moving backward.

It was Friday, which should have meant I was looking forward to the weekend: work at Bighorn Burger, time with Austin, and a chance to feel semi-normal. Instead, though, all I did was think about that day and the night before. I had fucked up with the two boys I was in love with; I never should have acted that way toward Austin; I never should have done that psychic stuff to Emmett, even if he was being a hurtful piece of shit by refusing to talk to me about how he'd been doing.

My distraction wasn't even, not really, about Emmett's second reaction the night before, the way his pupils blasted open with arousal, that bulge under wet denim, although there were a couple of times in gym class when I got distracted, and once Austin had to punch my arm and tell me school was strictly PG-13 and maybe I'd better go take a shower, a cold one. He didn't smile. He didn't give me a peck on the cheek. He just shook his head again and I felt like I'd shot his dog or something like that. Austin's warning didn't really help, though; later, a kickball whammed me in the back of the head, and when I looked behind me, Colton, with his stupid faux hawk done up, was miming a really impressive jerk-off session. After that, I decided I should stay a little more focused.

No, what really distracted me was the fact that both boys had been right. Austin had been right that I trusted Emmett. I still trusted him, even if I shouldn't. And Emmett had been right too. I certainly wasn't going to tell him that. He wasn't right about everything. But he was right about enough. He was right that I'd been avoiding my abilities, avoiding learning about them and mastering them and controlling them. And he was right that, deep down, I was a selfish chickenshit. Sure, I bitched and moaned and whined about everybody watching out for me. But I still let them do it. And if I'd learned anything from Emmett the night before, it was two things: one, I could be killed very, very easily; and two, I was a danger to the people I cared about the most.

With those kinds of thoughts, it was hard to pay attention to anything, and the school day rushed by in a blur. Austin, who was in most of my classes, noticed, but he was obviously still angry with me, and aside from a lot of watchful glances—angry, watchful glances—he seemed content to wait.

The only new thing that day was in science. After Mr. Warbrath had been murdered, and after his psychotic replacement, Mrs. Troutt, had disappeared in the massive fight at Belshazzar's Feast, we'd had a carousel of substitutes in chemistry. None of them really seemed to know where we were at in the course, what we were supposed to be doing, or, for that matter, anything about chemistry. It was probably no surprise that it was the only class I had an A in.

Today, we had another substitute. She was tiny—short and thin, and she probably wouldn't have come up past my chest. Her dark skin made her a rarity in Vehpese; the only people of color were the Crow on the nearby reservation and immigrants from Latin America, who worked the ranches and some of the wage jobs in town. She announced that she had taken a long-term position with the school, and that made me very, very suspicious. I had a sinking feeling that my science teacher was going to try to kill me. Again.

Her name was Ms. Meehan, and she was wearing a t-shirt that said *God Loves Black Nerds* and on the back *Too Bad They Don't Believe in Him.* If she recognized me, if she were already planning my murder, she didn't give any sign of it. She just read the roll, told us we would get assigned seats the next day, and handed out instructions for a lab that we would be doing tomorrow.

When class ended, she stood at the door, practicing students' names and wishing everyone a good day. As I passed her, I saw that she was older than I had first realized. Maybe even middle-aged, although she was so small and thin that it seemed shocking she could be that old. She nodded at me, smiled, and said, "I recognize you."

Austin clapped me on the shoulder, bumped me toward the door, and said, "Gotta go, Ms. Meehan."

"You were out running yesterday. Both of you."

"It's a small town," Austin said, giving her his best boy-next-door grin as he hustled me into the hall.

"Have a nice day," she called after us.

"What was that all about?" I said, shrugging off Austin as we plunged into the chaos of passing period.

He didn't answer; he cut off to the right and the crowd swallowed me, and I ate lunch alone. On the other side of the room, Emmett was holding court. Rachel Emmenthal was touching his lip and fussing over him. The other girls were staring at her, obviously waiting for her to make a mistake so they could drag her down. The boys were laughing at whatever Emmett was saying. My fingers pinched the white bread in my hands so hard that jelly squirted over my fingers. Fine. They could laugh at his jokes. The girls could bat their eyelashes. He could sit there, thinking he was king of the school. But whose room had he been in last night? Who had he begged, goddamn begged, to—

Rachel darted in and kissed Emmett.

I threw my half-eaten sandwich into the trash and spent the rest of lunch on a toilet seat, my feet holding the stall door shut.

After lunch, I had Mr. Spencer's English class. Things had been weird with Mr. Spencer. Part of it was the fact that he had spooned me. Naked. He did it to keep me from freezing to death, but still, all the important parts had been there, and it had been a very, very difficult memory to set aside. Part of it had to do with the fact that when I'd felt my absolute shittiest, I had kissed him. That, too, was hard to forget. But a lot of it had to do with the fact that, ever since the day at Belshazzar's Feast when I'd seen Jim Spencer turn into the Human Torch and burn down an entire ranch, he'd been trying to pretend he had no idea who I was.

Like today. He was blond. He was beautiful. He dressed like he'd just walked out of a J. Crew catalogue. And today, he smiled at me, nodded at me, and his eyes never left a spot on the wall behind my head. He could have been a goddamn greeter at Walmart.

"I need to talk to you," I said.

"Sure, Vie. I stay after school Tuesdays and Thursdays, and I've got one of your papers that I'd like you to—"

"No. Today. Right now, maybe."

He was still staring at that damn spot behind me. He was looking through me. He wasn't even seeing me, and I knew he never, ever wanted to see me again. "Gotta start class. Give me a few minutes to get everyone working, and then we can look at your—"

I grabbed his arm. Even through the poplin shirt, I could feel the supernatural heat that he radiated. "Now. Not about some goddamn paper. There's a new teacher—"

Heat flashed under my hand, and I yelped and snatched my fingers back. Wisps of smoke curled up from the cotton, and a pair of brown singe marks showed where my fingers had rested. When I looked up, the copper in Jim's blond hair was brighter, and cinders swirled at the back of his eyes.

"Don't ever grab me again, Vie."

He couldn't have sounded more serious with a gun to my head.

Then he went into the classroom, said something, and everybody laughed. It took me a minute. I walked to the end of the hallway and came back. Then I went into the classroom, ignoring Mr. Spencer calling out, "That's a tardy, Vie." I found my seat. I didn't kick the desk. I just bumped it. On accident.

Mr. Spencer started talking about the *Odyssey*. He had all sorts of things he wanted to say about it. He wanted to talk about heroes. He wanted to talk about monsters. I wanted to walk up there, grab him by the throat, and shake him. I wanted to make him talk about the real monsters, the ones we'd faced at Belshazzar's Feast. I wanted to make him talk about everything that had happened to me since moving to this town. I wanted to make him talk about that damn kiss and why I couldn't stop thinking about it.

"Are you sick?" Georgia Dunlap, in the seat next to me, asked. She had hair like a golden retriever; I'd seen her buying the store-brand dye off the discount shelf at the C-Mart.

"I'm fine."

"You sound like you're going to throw up."

"I'm fine."

That last part came out louder than I intended, and the classroom went silent. Mr. Spencer, chalk in hand, paused. Those eyes swept over me and then past me to an innocuous spot behind my head. He smiled like a cardboard cut-out. "Vie, is something wrong?"

"Sorry."

"Then maybe you can tell us your definition of a hero."

"No, thanks."

"I'm going to ask you again in a minute, so think about it. The Greek heroes had two essential traits: they were doers of deeds and speakers of words. Odysseus, as we're about to see, meets both of those requirements easily. But Greek heroes also had to deal with conflicting demands placed on them. On the one hand, they were expected to achieve kleos. Glory. And this meant the glory of great deeds on the battlefield. It also meant a glorious death on the battlefield.

"The opposing pull to kleos is nostos. Does anyone recognize that word? What does it sound like? Nostos. Any words in our language that might come from it?"

Crickets.

Mr. Spencer smiled. "Nostalgia. Nostos means the return home, where your glory could be celebrated, where your wife and children could be proud of what you'd achieved and your glory transferred, at least in part, to them. But if you died to achieve the ultimate kleos, you couldn't have nostos. And if you were too eager for nostos, you might not achieve kleos. Now, Vie, I just bought you a few minutes by rambling, so I hope you've got something ready to share for us. What's a hero?"

I shook my head, face turned down to the desk. Kleos I could understand. Dying for something, I could understand. But nostos? The desire to go home again? Who wanted that?

"Vie?"

I knew what he wanted. I knew why he was pressing me. I had my own questions I wanted to ask. What's a hero? Is it a guy who fucks up every good thing in his life? Is it a guy who's a chickenshit and afraid of himself? Is it a guy who has nightmares, a guy who lets his dad whale on him, a guy who lets his mom burn cigarette tracks up and down his back, a guy who psychically controls Emmett Bradley and runs away from Austin Miller?

"Vie, we're not moving on until you give us an answer."

"A hero is somebody too fucking stupid to stay out of trouble."

There was no dramatic silence. Somebody at the back of the class snickered, and just about everybody shifted in their seats, and the clothing rustled.

"All right," Mr. Spencer said, shaking his head. "Go on down to Mr. Hillenbrand's office."

I gathered my bag and my notebook and I headed out the door.

"What about you, Barbie? What do you think a hero is?"

The door clicked shut behind me.

Turning around, I faced the door, and I stared through the window set into the wood, and I waited. Because he knew I was standing there. He could see me out of the corner of his eye. And he was trying to pretend he couldn't. He was hoping I'd go to the office. He was hoping I'd let it slide.

Five seconds.

He scrubbed at the board with an eraser.

Ten seconds.

He dusted chalk from his hands.

Fifteen seconds.

His head jerked toward the door. It looked involuntary and painful.

I gave him the finger. And then, speaking loudly and clearly, I said, "Fuck you."

He heard me. The whole damn class heard me. Jim Spencer took one step toward the door, and then he reined himself in. He pointed in the direction of Hillenbrand's office. I counted off ten more seconds with my finger up, locking eyes with him. God damn, the copper in his hair was bright. If I stayed long enough, if I pushed the right buttons, maybe he'd light up right here, right in the middle of school, like a Roman candle. And then let him try to pretend I didn't exist.

"What are you doing?"

Becca came down the hall in quick steps, her head swiveling as she checked each classroom she passed. Becca, at least, hadn't changed over the last few months. She still had the same platinum hair. She still wore the same silver eyeshadow. She still looked terrifyingly fierce and lovely, and if I hadn't been gay, I probably would have married her. When she reached me, she grabbed my wrist and jerked my hand down. Her eyes went to Mr. Spencer, who, for the first time in weeks, looked like he was genuinely seeing me. The red in his hair was almost auburn now.

"Are you trying to get suspended?"

"It seemed like a good idea."

Waving at Mr. Spencer, Becca shoved me, and I stumbled down the hallway. "Come on."

"I have to go to Mr. Hillenbrand's office."

She shoved me again, and this time, I had to jog a few paces to keep from falling over.

"Ease up, Becca. I'm not—"

"Vie, come on. I've got to talk to you about something."

She tried to shove me again, but this time, I danced back. I grunted when I hit something solid. Something massive. Something like a goddamn brick wall.

Warm hands caught my arms and steadied me, and the air brought the fragrance of cedar and leather and tobacco. "I knew you'd fall for me," Austin whispered in my ear. Then, even lower, "Are we in a fight?"

His breath on my neck prickled every hair on my arms, and I shook my head because I couldn't get any words out.

"What's going on?" I finally managed to say.

"Becca's organizing the Great Escape." He spun me so I was facing him. "She wanted all of us to talk." He paused, and his eyes wouldn't meet mine. "All of us."

Then it sank in. I shook my head. "No."

"Vie, she wanted all of us to—"

"Becca." I whirled to her. "You didn't—"

"Of course she did, tweaker." Emmett slipped around the corner like he was all silk. "You guys need me."

"Don't look at me like that," Becca snapped. "I can't keep up with when you're fighting with Emmett and when you're best friends, and anyway, he's right, we do need him."

"We don't need—"

"Come on," Becca said, "before he pitches a hissy fit right here in the hall."

Austin, throwing an arm around me, tugged me after Becca. Emmett fell in beside us. Close enough for me to smell the metal-and-citrus of his cologne. Close enough for my hand to brush his if either of us shifted an inch. But he didn't shift. He didn't talk. He didn't so much as look at me.

Becca led us to the girls' bathroom. I balked at the door.

"Will you get in here already? Before someone sees us, for God's sake."

"It's the girls' room."

"Then you should be fine," Emmett said.

"Fuck you. You want to start—"

"All right," Austin said with a sigh, hooking me forward with that arm around my waist. "You can claw each other's eyes out later."

The girls' bathroom was, well, weird. It smelled better. It had more lights. There wasn't toilet paper pasted all over the floor. And there were so many stalls. I was surprised to see Kaden and Jake and Temple Mae already in there. Jake and Temple Mae were holding hands. Kaden was trying hard to look like he didn't care.

"Lock that, will you?" Becca said, and Emmett turned toward the door. Before he could touch the deadbolt, it spun to the locked position all by itself. I glanced at Temple Mae, who jerked her head in a negative, and then at Kaden. He had the good grace to blush and shrug; it looked like he, at least, was becoming more comfortable with his new ability. The red print my hand had left was gone from his cheek, and I couldn't explain why that was such a relief.

Becca moved to the sinks and set a manila envelope on the counter. The clasp was bent at a vee, and something about that envelope, about the way Becca handled it, about the crease along one corner, about that brass vee of the clasp, made my stomach drop.

"What's this about?"

"We've all been doing what we can since—since Belshazzar's Feast." She was the color of the tile now, an ugly shade of cream, and the silver on her eyes and lips sparked like fireworks. "Austin and Temple Mae and Jake and Kaden have been keeping an eye on you."

"Wait, what? They've all been watching me? When? Like, all the time?"

Becca spoke over me. "And Emmett's been—"

Emmett's smirk could have started World War 3. "He knows what I've been doing."

Becca cocked her head, her lips ready to form a question, and then she just said, "And I've been, well, researching."

"Researching what?"

"Everything." She grimaced. "Sometimes that actually feels like the truth. Everything I've had time to research, anyway. Belshazzar's Feast and the Lady and Urho and these abilities and missing kids in Mather County and—well, everything."

She had changed something. She had been planning on saying something else, and her eyes had flicked to Emmett, and then she had lied. Becca had lied. To me. About something to do with Emmett.

"What's going on? You guys didn't think you might want to talk to me about this. You didn't think you should tell me what you've been doing? You didn't think—"

Becca pinched the clasp, peeled open the envelope, and shook it out. Photographs printed on white copy paper tumbled across the counter. Becca shuffled them and then she paused. Her upper teeth had silver on them from biting her lip.

"They're coming, Vie. They're here, actually."

"What? If you're talking about the guy with your car—"

"Like last time. Like they did before Belshazzar's Feast."

I took a step forward to study the photographs. I fingered one. And then I knew what she meant. "You're not just talking about that guy, are you?"

Becca shook her head. "The Lady and Urho are bringing their army to Vehpese."

# Chapter | 8

Their army. Becca probably hadn't meant for it to sound like that. Becca probably hadn't meant to scare the rest of them. But the words had slipped out. Temple Mae had her face buried in Jake's flannel, and he was stroking her hair and glaring at me like he wanted to knock my teeth out for fun. Kaden bounced on his toes; behind him, the latches on every stall door rattled in time with his bounces, and he seemed totally oblivious to what he was doing. Even Austin's arm tightened around me, and I could feel his breath like a gasp, like I'd just sucker punched him in the solar plexus.

Only Emmett seemed unaffected. His dark eyes roved the room and then settled on me. He still wore that mocking grin. His lips moved soundlessly as he mouthed the word *army*.

"Fuck you, Emmett."

His eyebrows shot up, and his grin exploded, a thousand times brighter because, as always, he had gotten exactly what he wanted out of me.

I turned my attention back to the photographs. Five. There were Five of them. Five was a small army. But last time, it had been—three? Four? And we'd barely survived. My hand was shaking, so I clamped down on the first piece of paper to hide the tremors. Austin must have noticed; he was practically holding me up at that point. But he didn't say anything. He still looked like he was trying to get air back in his lungs.

The photographs. I had to focus. Becca had printed them from her computer, but she must have had a good printer—even on white copy paper, the images were vivid and clear. The first one I recognized.

"That's Ms. Meehan," I said, sliding the photograph to the left.

"Lightning."

"What?"

Becca cleared her throat. "She's had four husbands die after being struck by lightning."

"What?" Kaden said.

"She lived in Cleveland before she moved here. I guess after the fourth guy, people started talking. A reporter did a story. He—" Becca pressed her hands over her face and laughed. It sounded like she was choking. "He got electrocuted. In his bathtub. With nothing else in there. No loose wires. No radio that had fallen into the tub. Nothing."

"Four?" Emmett said. "She's not that pretty."

"You're such an asshole sometimes," Austin said. "All right. I'm in chemistry with Vie, so at least he won't be alone. We'll have to watch where she goes during the school day; Mrs. Troutt has tried to get him other places. The locker room. Damn. The showers. The sinks. Any place with water."

"Sorry, Vie," Emmett said. "Guess you won't be able to spray off with the boys."

"Will you shut up?" Jake said, still stroking Temple Mae's hair. "Don't you ever shut up?"

"It's a joke. If you can't take a fucking joke—"

"Enough," I said. "Emmett, shut up for a while." I thumbed the next photograph toward me. "What about this one, Becca?"

The picture showed someone familiar: a red-headed boy, big in the shoulders, big in the thighs, built like he could break through a wall, Kool-Aid Man-style. I recognized him from the hallway. And from the Greasy Spoon's parking lot.

Austin, though, grabbed the paper, and it wrinkled in his grip. "That's the kid who blew up your car."

"I've seen him," Jake said. "He's the one that's always tagging after Emmett."

"He doesn't tag after me." Emmett snatched the paper, glanced at it, and tossed it back at the sink. Becca caught it out of the air and passed it to Jake. "He's been hanging out with JR and Welch. They just bring him along sometimes. His name's Leo. I don't know his last name."

"Leo Lyden," Becca said.

"What can he do?" Jake asked.

Becca frowned. "Blow things up, I guess."

"You're sure it was him?" I said. "It wasn't the driver?"

"There's one article about him. It's not even an article. It was in the police beat, and I had God's own luck finding it. A little newspaper in this flyspeck Kansas town. Barbarossa. Something like that. And it was about his homecoming. He got arrested. And then I couldn't find anything else."

"Explosions, huh." Emmett slouched against the wall, arms folded, leering at me. "Literal? Or metaphorical?"

"What kind of explosion is metaphorical?" Kaden asked, even while I shook my head, trying to forestall the question.

Emmett smirked. "Like some kind of spontaneous, remote orgasm trigger. Maybe Vie should ask him to prom. Get some real action."

"That's enough," Jake said.

"Cool it, cowboy."

"You need to stop talking."

"I can talk whenever I want. If you don't like it—"

"I don't like it. And I'm going to break your face if you keep talking to him like that."

I wasn't exactly used to Jake taking my side; a few months ago, he'd beaten the shit out of Austin for being a fag and then tried to beat the shit out of me. A lot had changed, though. And some of that change, I was starting to realize, had made both the Miller boys fiercely protective.

Emmett's face screwed up with anger, and he opened his mouth. I laid my hand across his chest.

"Not right now."

He blinked. His jaw shut. With a goofy smile, he pushed my hand away, and the sleeve of his tee hitched up, and the inside of his arm came into view, and I saw what I knew I'd see.

Emmett didn't notice. He just said, "All right. Later, then." And he crossed his arms, and his sleeve slipped down, hiding the track marks.

"What did he get arrested for?" Austin said.

"Blowing up a cow."

"What?"

Becca mimed an explosion in the air. "A cow. It was the school mascot. And it exploded during halftime."

"He shot it with something?" Jake said. "A big caliber gun? Something that tore it to pieces?"

"No. It blew up. Thousands of pieces. Millions of pieces. They thought somebody had managed to get an explosive device inside the cow, and then somebody remembered seeing Leo near the holding pen, and that's why they picked him up."

"But there wasn't an explosive device," I said, my eyes searching Becca's face. "There wasn't anything."

"There was a lot of ground beef," Emmett said, and then he glanced at Jake and zipped his lips with two fingers.

"Emmett's right. The police report was just a blurb, but it said pieces of the cow were found in the parking lot. On the cars. All the way from the center of the football field."

"Was anybody hurt?" Temple Mae lifted her head from Jake's chest. Her tilted, feline eyes were red. Her nose was puffy. The hard slash of her mouth was harder than usual. "Besides that poor cow, I mean."

"No." Becca's voice was gentle. "Nobody else. And Vie was right: they dropped the charges after they realized they couldn't prove anything. I mean, I don't even think they really believed there was anything to prove. They never found evidence of an explosive device, and they issued a public apology to Leo."

"It was a cow. At a football game. And one person saw Leo near it." Emmett shook his head. "That's not a really convincing case for the theory that he has magical powers. I mean, what's the explanation? His ability is that he can blow up cows?"

"And Fords," Becca said. "He touched my car last night. Remember? He was pushing on the trunk. And then he got in the car and drove off."

"He did something to it," Kaden said. He glanced at each of us and blushed. "I don't know how to explain it. The metal got . . . excited."

"See?" Emmett said. "He'd be perfect for Vie on prom night."

"It didn't explode when he touched it," Austin said. His voice was calm, but his fingers bit into my side, and his eyes never went anywhere near Emmett's face. "Same thing with the cow. So there's some sort of delay."

Becca paled. "I could have been in the car. I could have been driving when it . . ."

"But you weren't," I said. "Kaden warned us."

"Vie, if he can start a countdown, he might do it to anything. Anywhere. Austin's car, for example. Or a drinking fountain. Or the propane tank behind the school."

I nodded. "So that means Kaden needs to be on the alert."

"If it's metal." Temple Mae's feline eyes looked redder and puffier than just a few moments before.

"What?"

"Kaden will only be able to help if the explosion has metal elements. If it's an animal like that poor cow . . ." She brushed at her eyes, her whole face twisting as she fought not to cry.

"There's nothing we can do except be careful," Jake said. "Next."

I grabbed the third photograph. It was a boy with dark braids and the amber skin of a Native American.

"I don't know his name," Becca said. "But I saw him lurking outside school and snapped a picture. When I ran a reverse image search, he came up on a conspiracy theory blog. They call him Old Man Coyote. That's from a Crow story, by the way. He's a kind of creator figure. And the traditional trickster figure."

"This boy's supposed to be a god?" Austin slid his hand across mine, toying with the edges of the page. "He doesn't look like an old man."

"The blog doesn't talk about him being a god. It talks about—"

Jake spoke over her. His eyes were wide, and his arms dropped away from Temple Mae for the first time since we came into the bathroom. "Conoco. That goddamn Conoco station."

"You read that blog?"

"He was there at that Conoco station when it got robbed. Austin, remember. After the rodeo in Billings, when we were driving back, Dad and I, and we stopped at the Conoco."

I opened my mouth, but Austin squeezed me around the waist, and he said, "Yeah, I remember. You said the guy behind the till was dead. Dad wouldn't let you see, but he told you—" Austin swallowed. "He told you the clerk was shot right through the head. And there was a kid carrying an armload of those cupcakes or—"

"Sno Balls. He had a mountain of them, and he was barefoot and running as fast as he could." Jake wiped his face. "Damn. Do you think he killed that guy? I just thought he was robbing the place. He looked too young—I just thought the killers were already gone and he was taking advantage."

Becca shrugged. "It's . . . a possibility. He's on a handful of security camera stills that people uploaded to that conspiracy site. People say he comes before a robbery. Or after. Like a black cat."

"Crossing a black cat doesn't get you shot in the head," Jake said. "A kid like that? How old is he? Twelve? And he's out there shooting up gas stations and killing people for a bunch of Sno Balls."

"What's his ability supposed to be?" Emmett asked. "Eating disgusting junk food?"

"I've got no clue." Becca shrugged. "But a kid sitting on the edge of campus, watching the school like he's here to stay, that makes me curious. And when the same kid shows up on a conspiracy theory site, as an omen of bad luck, and linked with a series of robberies and murders, that's enough for me to want to keep an eye on him."

"Two more," Austin said. "God, how did you do this, Becca? Did you hack every security camera in town? Cross all the images against a visual database of Vehpese? Run anybody who didn't fit through facial scanning software?"

She glowered at him. "You're starting to sound like him: stupid with lots of muscles."

Austin wrapped both arms around me and pulled me against him. His chin settled on my shoulder. "Good."

"I couldn't hack every security camera in town. Not even if I wanted to, and I don't. There's no point."

"So what'd you do?" I asked.

"I paid off Mrs. McLees."

"The registrar?"

"New student records," Emmett said. "Smart."

"That explains Leo," Jake said. "But what about the rest of them?"

"I got lucky with the Crow boy. If he hadn't been so obvious about watching the school, I probably would have missed him. But you're wrong about Mrs. McLees."

"She's not the registrar?" Emmett said. "Or she wouldn't give you the records?"

"She gave me names, not records. But that's not what I meant. She's the biggest gossip in the entire state. Maybe in the West. She knows everybody. And she knows everything about everybody."

"She doesn't know everything." Emmett's smile thinned into a white line. "Trust me."

"She knows a lot. And I asked her who was new to town."

"And she told you? Come on, Becca. That means she's going to turn around and tell everyone about you and what you wanted. She'll probably tell Ms. Meehan and the rest of them all about it."

"Emmett's right," I said. "Why would she tell you? Even if you did pay her, she must have wondered what you wanted."

"I told her what I wanted." Becca's smile gleamed silver.

"You told her you were keeping watch for psychic thugs coming into town to form an army for a crazy Indian ghost?"

"I told her," Becca said, her smile threatening to break into laughter, "that I was trying to set up a dating website. Kind of like Farmers Only, but exclusive to Wyoming and Montana."

"You told her you were coding a Farmers Only knock-off?"

"She was very interested. She thought it was a great idea."

"Of course she did," Austin said. I couldn't see it, but I could almost feel him rolling his eyes.

"What does that mean?"

"Nothing," I said. "Tell us about the last two."

Becca pointed to the fourth photograph. The man in the picture had rough, thick features; he was bald, but his eyebrows were so fuzzy that they almost made up for the lack of hair on top. He was big, too.

I mean, I'm big. And Austin's getting big. But this guy was built like a tank. Like a goddamn Panzer.

"The driver," Kaden said. "Last night, he was the driver."

"Kyle Stark-Taylor. His mom was divorced and remarried."

"We need his life story?" Emmett said, lounging against the tile again.

"Maybe. This time, maybe. He killed his dad. The biological one. He beat him to death."

"He looks like he could do it," Jake said with a shrug.

"He did it when he was thirteen. There wasn't enough left of the dad for a funeral. They cremated him, or whatever they could scoop off the floor. And they sent Kyle to prison—he was tried as an adult."

"Take a look, Vie: a real prison-sculpted body."

"Why do we put up with this asshole?" Jake said. "Austin, what's his deal?"

Austin, his chin wedged in my shoulder, shook his head.

"It's not a prison-sculpted body," Becca said. "Longhollow Penitentiary fell down."

"Like, the roof fell in?" I asked.

"No. The whole prison fell down. Boom. Clouds of dust. Like an implosion."

"Only it wasn't an implosion, was it?"

"I dug up the structural engineer's report—"

"Kickass," Austin said, his chin burrowing deeper into my shoulder.

Becca flashed him a smile. "The structural engineer discussed what happened in great detail; she was very thorough. The key phrase in the summary was 'systemic structural damage consistent with, but not identical to, seismic activity.'"

"This guy can make a fucking earthquake?" Jake said.

Temple Mae, wiping at her face, pulled back from his chest long enough to say, "Consistent with but not identical to?"

Becca shrugged. "A fancy way of refusing to commit to what looked like it was impossible: an earthquake that no seismograph detected, that didn't affect anything beyond the walls of Longhollow, that didn't so much as buckle the parking lot asphalt."

"How the hell are we supposed to fight an earthquake?" Jake said.

"Maybe he's not here for Urho or Vie," Emmett said. "Maybe he's just looking to buy a summer home."

"According to Mrs. McLees's sources, he's come into town twice to buy supplies. He's staying somewhere up in the Bighorns."

"All right, so maybe he's going to bring down the whole mountain range." Emmett had that goddamn annoying grin stretching his face again. "You've got one more, Becca. How bad's this one going to be?"

The silence that came after prickled the skin across my chest. I shivered, and Austin squeezed his arms around my waist. Becca wouldn't look at Emmett. She wouldn't look at any of us. She lifted the final photograph, turning it in her hands. Her silver eyes flicked on and off like klieg lamps. She was about to cry.

"That bad?" Austin said.

Emmett took two steps and snatched the paper from her. He studied it against the light and then clapped it against my chest hard enough to hurt. When I raised it to my eyes, it showed a blond girl, the dark roots revealing how long it had been since the last dye job. She was cocaine pretty, so thin a good sneeze would break her, and in five years, maybe less, she'd look a lot like the girls I saw going into Slippers, the local strip club.

"What's her story?"

Becca shook her head. She was looking at the grimy tile, and her sneaker traced an arc in front of her.

"Becca, come on. It can't be that bad."

"What's her ability?" Emmett slouched between the hand dryers, arms across his chest, shoulders drawn up to his ears.

"How'd you find her?" Jake asked.

"She's been showing up around town. Mrs. McLees thought she was an out-of-town girlfriend."

"Whose?" Emmett snapped.

I glanced at him. Purple slashed his cheeks. He glared at me and gave me the finger.

"What the hell's gotten into him?" Austin murmured in my ear.

"Whose girlfriend?" Emmett asked again.

Becca shook her head. "I don't know. Mrs. McLees didn't say. Anyway, I don't really—"

"What's her ability? You put her picture there for some goddamn reason. So what's her ability?"

Becca drew herself up. Silver flashed around her eyes and mouth. She took the picture from me and smoothed it on the counter, and then she met my eyes, and I saw what she'd been afraid to show me earlier.

She was sorry for me. I'd seen pity in her eyes before. Becca had seen me in some pretty dark places. But what I was seeing there now, it made me want to tie my laces, head out to the highway, and run. Run until I ran out of highway. Or run until my heart exploded. Either would be better than what I was seeing in her eyes.

"You're freaking him out," Austin said, his arms tightening around me. "Just spit it out, Becca."

"She's been arrested a couple of times, although she's under eighteen, so I think they've been short stays in a juvenile facility."

"Arrested for what?" Temple Mae must have sensed the change in the air too because she had finally turned to face us. Jake's arm was around her, and I knew he'd die to protect her, but I also knew that Temple Mae would do a lot more than die to keep Jake safe. And something in the room, something right then, was making Temple Mae look the way she did when she'd thrown a pickup truck through the air with her goddamn mind.

"Both times, they were drug possession charges. But I called her old high school. She's from Evanston. I talked to her teachers." Becca blushed and smiled. A small smile. Very small. "I told them I was the principal here and that I wanted to know what had happened with her. And they told me. Two of them were really eager to talk about it. Fighting in school. Boys. Lots of problems with impulse control. She did every stupid thing that came into her head. She kicked a teacher's computer to pieces one day because he told her to put away her phone. I asked about drugs. I thought maybe she'd been using. Or dealing."

My gaze flicked to Emmett again; he didn't notice me. The purple stained his cheeks even more darkly now, and he was staring at Becca, biting down on his busted lip, unaware of the blood spreading across his teeth in tiny red fissures.

"And they told me it wasn't dealing. She had a boyfriend. And he was a big deal in Evanston. In terms of drugs, I mean. He had distribution. And he had supply. He was growing weed in an abandoned warehouse on the edge of the city. And when the police picked him up, they picked up Krystal too—that's her name—and they only laid on the possession charges because she was a minor." Becca took a deep breath. "They said there was no water. No lights. The woman who told me all this, she said it like she wanted me to know that Krystal and her boyfriend almost got away with it. Like they were pulling up stakes when the police got there. But I don't think that was it."

"She's a magical drug maker?" Jake said.

"Plants." Temple Mae passed a hand over her eyes like she was suddenly unbearably tired. "She can control plants."

"Something like that," Becca said.

Then her eyes cut to Emmett.

He flinched. If I hadn't been watching him, if my whole body hadn't been tuned to him, I would have missed it. And I would have missed the flicker of fear in his face. And the flicker of something else. Something that made me want to run my fingers through the short hair above his ear and tell him it would be ok.

And then anger burned off everything else in his expression, and he said, "Don't be a bitch about it. Show them."

Becca stared at him. The silver leached everything from her eyes.

"Don't be a fucking bitch. I know you've got it. So show them."

"Don't talk to her like that," I said.

"I can talk to her however I want, you fucking tweaker moron. She's being a fucking bitch, so I'm going to call her a fucking bitch, and a stupid tweaker moron faggot like you, no matter how big your muscles are, can't make me do anything else."

I tried to take a step, but Austin held me. The flat of his hand pressed against my stomach, rubbing a small circle as he whispered in my ear. I rolled my shoulders and pulled at his wrist.

"Don't talk to her like that."

"Vie—" Austin tried.

I knocked his hands away and pulled free from his grip. My first step toward Emmett sent the dark-haired boy backward, and he hit the tile wall.

"Stop it," Becca said.

"Show them. You're so fucking proud of yourself, so show them."

"What the fuck is wrong with you?" I said. "Why can't you be halfway decent for—"

"Vie." Becca's voice was so thick I barely recognized it, and when I looked over my shoulder, I saw why. She was crying: huge tears trailing silver eyeshadow down her face in lines. She was holding something, too—holding it out to me, a folded white rectangle that I guessed she had been hiding in her pocket. And a dark voice pointed out that Emmett was right: she had been holding something back.

My fingertips buzzed as I took the paper. I couldn't feel the edges. I couldn't even feel them when one sliced the pad on my thumb and left a red stripe. But somehow I got the page open.

I knew the bedroom, with its wall of windows. The picture had been taken from outside, from the wild sea of buffalo grass. It had been taken at night. Inside, warm yellow light blossomed around the desk, the TV, the guitar stand, the bed. That same yellow light crowned a figure at the window. And whoever had taken this picture—Becca, the fucking bitch, that dark voice said, you know it was Becca—had used a telephoto lens, and I could see everything like I had my nose pressed to the glass.

The girl named Krystal stood in front, her blouse unbuttoned, a lacy black inch of bra exposed. A familiar hand—long, strong fingers—

slid between the blouse's buttons, crept under that inch of black lace. Behind Krystal stood the owner of that hand. Emmett was bending down, his mouth on her neck, his dark eyes like collapsing stars in the reflected light.

"All right," I said.

Was it weird that I still couldn't feel my fingers? Not anything past the last knuckle. Not even a buzz. I bet I could run a table saw and stick my finger right down on the blade and not feel it. And somehow that idea excited me. It made me feel . . . interested. That image of the huge, turning blade, sharp enough to cut me to pieces. Anything sharp would do. Anything at all.

"All right."

Austin grabbed my collar. "Why don't we take a walk for a minute?"

"Why? I'm fine."

"Because you're not fine. Come with me. Come on. Let's take a walk."

Laughing, I shook him off, waving the picture at him. "This? This isn't anything. You think I'm upset about this?"

"Vie, don't do this. Please. Jake, help me get him—"

"Why in the ever-fucking world would I be upset about this?" I shook the paper at Emmett. "You like her, right? So you're fucking her?"

"It's not any of your business, tweaker."

"No, of course not."

"Vie," Austin said. He settled his hands on my chest and pushed me. "You're going to do something—"

"You're damn right I'm going to do something. Get the fuck off me. Get off, Austin. You're damn right. Did you hear him? It's not any of my business. No. Of course not. Because it wasn't any of my business when he was fucking Makayla—"

"Don't say her name, tweaker."

"It wasn't any of my business when he was fucking Makayla, and so it's not any of my business now when he's fucking this girl. And it's the same thing. He didn't care that Makayla wanted to kill me."

"Say her name one more fucking time, and I'll kill you."

"He doesn't care that this girl wants to kill me. All he cares about is getting his skinny cock wet with whatever cheap piece of trash comes along, just like he did with—"

"Enough." Austin shook me so hard my teeth cracked together.

"You'd better explain yourself," Jake said to Emmett. I hadn't realized until then that Jake was holding one of my arms, that Becca had curled up against the counter with her makeup a silver waterfall across her face, that Temple Mae leaned toward us, her eyes narrowed with concentration, and that the laces on my shoes were drifting upward as though some enormous thermal current were trying to lift me into the air. "Start talking. Who is she? How do you know her?

"Come on, Emmett," Kaden barked. "You're being a dick."

Emmett shook his head. "You're all such fucking tools. You know that? You all play at this stupid cops-and-robbers game. You're all kids, and you think you have an idea about what the real world is like, and you don't know anything. Not jack shit."

"Jesus Christ, Emmett." Austin's voice was broken, but his hands on my chest were rock solid. "You're killing him, all right? Are you happy with that? You're ripping his goddamn heart out." And part of me knew I was the shittiest guy in the world. I heard Austin's soul bleeding out in his sentence. "Just tell us what's going on. Jesus, do it for him if you won't do it for the rest of us."

"Fuck all of you." Emmett looked at each of us in turn. "Fuck you. And you. And you. And fuck you, tweaker. Fuck you, fuck you, fuck—"

I didn't remember charging. All I remembered was a sudden vertigo as something—Temple Mae—flipped me into the air and sent me crashing back against the closest stall. Jake and Austin stumbled after me, pinning me, but they didn't need to. I couldn't have moved a muscle. I couldn't have blinked or winked or breathed. And that didn't have anything to with Temple Mae.

But I could see. I could see very clearly as Emmett shook his head, took all of us in with one final glance, and hit the deadbolt. The lock spun free, and he jerked the door open, and then he was gone.

# Chapter | 9

I needed to go back to class. But first, I let Austin help me over to the boys' bathroom, and Jake and Kaden came after us. Austin wetted some paper towels and ran them along my neck and my forehead. He pressed on the back of my scalp, checking to see if I'd broken my head on the stall—I deserved a broken head, but I was fine—and he asked me the same questions about a dozen times until he was sure I didn't have a concussion. But I didn't. I didn't even have a headache. Temple Mae was strong. But she was also very, very controlled.

That whole time, Jake and Kaden lingered at the door, faces red and turned toward their sneakers, not looking at each other, not looking at Austin, and certainly not looking at me. I got the feeling they were there for Austin's sake. In case the crazy tweaker decided to hurt his boyfriend even more, as if that were even possible.

Because I knew what I'd done. Austin knew I had feelings for Emmett, of course. He wasn't oblivious. But I'd just exposed how much I cared for Emmett. And I'd done it in front of everyone that mattered in my life. And Austin had seen it, and he'd tried to help me, and now he was here, washing my face with a scratchy paper towel, and I realized I had snot under my nose and my eyes felt like they were the size of eight balls.

"Oh fuck. I fucked up so bad."

"It's ok." At some point, my hair had pulled out of its bun, and he ran his fingers through the shoulder-length blond locks. I liked it; he knew I liked it. "He's going to calm down, and you guys can talk—"

"Austin, I fucked up with you. Jesus. Why are you here? Why are you putting up with this shit? And please, please, will you tell them to go away so I don't have to keep making an ass of myself in front of an audience?"

Jake met Austin's gaze and gave a short, sharp shake of his head.

"Maybe you need an audience," Kaden said. "You're pretty good at making an ass of yourself."

"Go on," Austin said.

Jake shook his head again, that single, sharp, vehement no.

Austin sighed and ran the paper towel under my nose. Again. "Let's just get through the day, all right?"

He cupped my cheek. His hand was cool. The calluses from roping and riding and from hitting things hard scratched my hot skin nicely.

"Yeah," I said. And in my mind, the table saw turned faster and faster. It was shining now at the back of my head, the kind of flickering white shine of metal moving faster than the eye can track. "Yeah. I just. I left my bag in the girls' bathroom, I think."

"I got it," Jake said, tossing it to Austin.

Austin caught the backpack and held it out of my reach.

I tried to wipe everything off my face. I just needed my bag. I was going to go to class. I was going to get through the day. I tried to make the thoughts louder. I blasted them to drown out anything else—so that they'd hide anything else.

"All right. We can go to class now."

I shook my head. "I still feel kind of sick. I'm going to take a minute. Like—in the stall, you know."

Those turquoise eyes were so bright. "You guys get going."

"I'm not leaving you—" Jake started.

"Yeah. Get out of here."

Kaden and Jake shuffled in place for a moment, and then Kaden caught Jake's arm and tugged him toward the door.

And then we were alone.

"I'm going to give you the benefit of the doubt. I'm going to assume you said that because they were in here. Now tell me."

Emmett, face turned into that girl's neck. His fingers sliding under the lace of her bra. The flicker of yellow light exploding in a corona behind them.

The table saw whipping faster and faster. The shine was steadier now. Stable. At that speed, the teeth could tear through just about anything.

"I'm going to take a dump, all right? Is that what you want me to say? What? You want to watch or something?"

"Please tell me."

"What?"

"What's wrong? This isn't just about Emmett, Vie. Something's been wrong for months and . . . and I don't think it's me. I don't even think it's us. But something's wrong, and I can feel it."

"Something's wrong with me. That's what you're saying."

"We agreed: no more lying. No more hiding. No more going away where I can't see you."

"Yeah." I reached for the bag, and Austin pivoted, keeping it out of reach. "Yeah, that's what we said. But it wasn't supposed to be fucking literal. It wasn't supposed to be you watching me every time I need to take a shit. That was just talk, all right?"

"You promised. If you're going to do this, you promised you'd be honest with me about it. You promised you weren't going to block me out. I want us to get to a place where you don't have to do this anymore. I want to help you."

Austin holding my arm. Austin, hands on my chest. Austin asking me to go for a walk, to go for a goddamn walk with him, because he knew how bad it was going to be and he wanted to spare me.

The white hum of the table saw. It could tear through anything. Those teeth were sharp enough for metal or wood. Or flesh. It could chew right through me. The thought was hypnotic. On its own, a saw blade might be sharp, might be able to cut. But like this, when it spun thousands of times per minute, so fast that it became steel and shadow and glow, it could go through anything. It could go through me. It could slice through me. I wouldn't even feel it. That's how clean the cut would be. I wouldn't even feel it. And wouldn't it be great, wouldn't it be perfect, to be taken apart, completely taken apart, and not feel a thing? Not feel it ever again?

"I'm not doing anything, all right? I want to take a fucking shit. If you want to watch, fine. I'll keep the door open. I didn't really think raunch was your thing. Guess I was wrong."

He was blushing now; he was still such a straight boy in some ways. He dropped the bag and kicked it under the first stall. "Fine. Jesus Christ, Vie. Why the fuck do I—"

My tongue was so big it was hammering on the back of my teeth. "Go on."

He just shook his head. "I didn't—I shouldn't have said that. But I don't know what to do."

"Easy. Go to class."

"Hey, will you look at me?"

"Just go to class, Austin. It's fine. I'll take my dump. I'll even record it for you. You won't miss anything."

"Look at me for five seconds. Right there. Like that. Look at me like that. And tell me what you'd do if I took that box of razor blades out of your bag."

"I'm taking a dump, Austin. I don't even carry those things around anymore."

"So we're all the way back here. Things go bad with Emmett, and somehow we're all the way back here, with you lying, with you hiding, with you putting up a wall to keep me out."

"I'm sorry I'm not this fucking perfect boyfriend that you imagined—"

"I've got to get out of here. I can't do this with you right now. Not again."

His footsteps echoed through the bathroom, and the door thudded shut behind him. The son of a bitch in the mirror looked like shit. Some of that was the fluorescents buzzing overhead. Some of it, though, was the fact that he was shit. A huge piece of shit. I didn't like how he was looking at me, so I went into the stall and kicked the door shut behind me. It bounced back. I kicked it again. And again. And again. And finally, my breath hot, my chest jerking, I slammed the latch home, and it stayed shut.

The table saw whirled brighter and brighter at the back of my mind. That black hole was there too, this giant, gaping emptiness fueled by the pain and the anger, and it was eating me up. It swallowed up everything so that I couldn't think, couldn't breathe. I was going to feel this way for the rest of my life if I didn't do something. The saw, white and bright as the moon, would be one way. One wonderful, perfect, gleaming way. But the table saw wasn't here.

The razor blades were in the pocket where I always kept them. I dropped my jeans, dropped my boxers, and stood there. The air was cold. I was cold. That was the only explanation I could give for the way I was shaking, for the way my skin pebbled, for the way the hairs on my arms stiffened. I was cold. I was freaking freezing. The air smelled like piss. A wet S of toilet paper snaked under the stall partition. I was cold in a filthy bathroom. I was so cold.

For a moment, the world was in flux. The hypersaturated colors of the other side bulged, pressing against the thin barrier to reality. From outside the stall came a noise, a soft scuff on the tile. A shoe. But not a man's shoe. Not a woman's. A child's.

And then the world was normal again, and I listened, heard nothing. I was alone. I was still so cold.

I drew the blade across the inside of my thigh.

The table saw slowed, stopped, and hung at the back of my head: just as sharp, just as bright, but frozen. Like the moon. Everything was sharp. Everything was bright. Everything was frozen. The black hole had stopped its cosmic spin. I took in a breath, my first breath in what felt like hours. I was in charge again. I was in control.

And when it ended, I was tired, and I had to wad toilet paper against the cut until the bleeding slowed, and I pulled my clothes into place and went out of the stall, and Austin was there.

His face was red. His cheeks were wet. And he looked at me for five seconds. Maybe five. Maybe four. Maybe three. Maybe one, maybe one goddamn second, maybe that was all he could stand to look at me. And he turned. And he left.

I got to the trash can, and I dropped the blade inside, and I gripped the hard plastic rim to steady myself. It wasn't anything new. He'd known. He'd known from the minute I said I needed to be alone. He'd probably known from the minute I asked for my bag. He'd known, and he'd left anyway, and so fuck him. Fuck him for judging me. Fuck him for looking at me for one motherfucking second. Fuck him for leaving.

The trash can came up easily. I swung it. Hard. One, two, three, four, five. Five times. He couldn't even look at me for five seconds, and I swung it five times. And then that mirror was all over the place, and the son of a bitch staring back at me was gone.

And a voice, rasping and ancient and tattered like hundred-year-old buffalo hide, spoke into my mind, the words clear and precise and amused. *Now I see you.*

# Chapter | 10

Mr. Hillenbrand had been looking for me, and he heard the glass shatter, and that pretty much put an end to the school day for me. First we had to talk. Then he had to tell me how much potential I had, and why was I throwing it all away, and was everything all right at home. At least he had the decency to look embarrassed at that last part. He mentioned Saturday like it was a big accomplishment. Like living long enough for someone to shove more candles into a cheap-ass cake was a win.

Then, after we'd talked, he had to get Sara on the phone. Only she wasn't satisfied with a phone call. She had to drive over from Bighorn Burger. And then we had to talk all over again. And then Mr. Hillenbrand left us alone in his office for a moment. To talk.

Sara was a big woman, and her cloud of blond hair made her seem bigger, and the way she held herself, like she was ready to charge in and defend you, that made her seem even bigger. But right then she looked very small and very tired, and the dust storm of blond hair was settling on her forehead, and all she said was, "Let's go."

It was a week out of school. For the mirror and for everything with Mr. Spencer.

She drove like she'd never touched a car before: we hit every stop sign like a brick wall, and then her little car reared up and shot forward. At Bighorn Burger, she undid her buckle and opened the door.

"I can still work my shift."

She froze halfway out of the car. I'd never in my life thought Sara might hit me, but something about the way her back twisted, about the way her hand whitened around the frame, about the sudden stillness in the air reminded me of Dad. And Mom. And my heart started beating so hard I couldn't breathe.

"I can't talk to you right now. Please don't say anything else until I'm ready to talk to you."

She disappeared into Bighorn Burger. After the first minute ticked by, reality started clicking. She was going to call Ginny, my caseworker. And she was going to have Ginny take me away to one of those group homes. If I was lucky, to a group home. Maybe to juvie. Sara couldn't talk to me, couldn't even look at me, and so she was going to get rid of me.

Ok. I blew out a shaky breath and flattened my hands on my knees. I'd had so many ups and downs already that day that this new surge of adrenaline turned my stomach. The cut on my leg started to throb harder. Ok. She was going to get rid of me. I'd be out of Vehpese for sure. I'd be gone. No more Austin. No more Emmett. No more Becca. No more anything.

I could steal the car. It was a tiny Ford Focus. It could have come in a cereal box, that's how big it was, but it would get me out of Vehpese proper and into one of the state or national parks nearby. The boy I'd been when I came here, the boy from the big flat openness of Oklahoma, he would have been a dead man running out there. But I'd spent a lot of time now with Austin and his friends out in the countryside. More importantly, I knew that a lot of people had cabins out there. Cabins that were infrequently used. Cabins with liquid propane for heat. Cabins stocked with canned goods in case of a snow-in. I could make it six months out there easily. In six months, I could have a real plan.

I unbuckled myself and reached for the latch as Sara emerged from Bighorn Burger. She settled into the car, and the Ford sagged under her weight, and she said, "Seatbelt."

Clipping the buckle back into place, I fell back against the seat as she punched the gas. We drove in those herky-jerks all the way back to her house, and we went inside, to a cloud of cinnamon and vanilla potpourri and the sofa where I lay at night when I talked to Austin on the phone and the kitchen where Sara, the first person in my whole life, had asked me how I liked my eggs, to the first house that had ever felt like a home.

My eyes were hot and stinging. I ran my arm over them and trundled toward the stairs. I'd pack my stuff; I could do that much at least. It'd be less embarrassing when Ginny came to haul me away. Or—or maybe I should leave it? Sara had paid for all of it, after all. And God knows I didn't deserve to take it with me.

"I'm not trying to be cruel," Sara said, the words stilted. "My parents wouldn't talk to us as a punishment, and I always thought that was cruel. That's not what I'm doing. I'm just so angry right now that I'm afraid I'll say something I don't mean. I'd like you to go upstairs and stay there for now. I'll come up when I've cooled down."

She tried to smile; it didn't get far, but she tried. "I've always had a temper. Go on upstairs now."

So I did. On my bed, staring up at the cracked plaster ceiling, I lay and I waited. It might have been an hour. It might have been longer. Outside, branches clacked against the glass; the Wyoming wind never died, and today was just as cold and gray and stormy as the day before. The phone jangled, and Sara's heavy steps crossed the room below me, and then the jangle cut off. It jangled again a moment later. And then the house was silent for a long time.

When the knock came at the door, I sat bolt upright. Voices mixed below, and then the steps creaked, and a second knock came at my bedroom door. Austin. My heart skipped up into my throat. Christ, how was I supposed to tell him I was sorry?

"Come in."

It wasn't Austin who came in, though. It was my social worker, Ginny Coyote in Sage, who was so tall her head practically brushed the ceiling and was built wide from shoulders to hips. She wasn't pretty, but her eyes were wide and large and dark, and something about the way she looked at me made me feel like I was a human being.

Except today she wouldn't look at me.

She shuffled into the room, her big feet clanging off the wastebasket and sending it rolling, and perched on the edge of the rocking chair. The wood groaned in distress. Her eyes moved over the rag rug and settled on my stockinged feet.

"It's not like I killed someone."

She smiled, a saccharine grimace, and her eyes moved up to my knees. "I hear you had a rough day at school."

"Can Sara hear us?"

Ginny didn't move, but I felt something shift, and then she shook her head. That was Ginny's ability—one of her abilities. I wasn't really sure how it worked, but she could make other people go to sleep. Kind of. It was a convenient way of holding a private discussion and ensuring that it remained private.

"Why don't you tell me what happened today?"

"No."

She nodded. Her eyes were still fixed on my knees. They were fine knees. They worked pretty well. But they weren't so goddamn fascinating that I could figure out why she was staring at them. "How are you feeling right now?"

"Ginny, I'm not doing this therapist bullshit with you. I fucked up at school. I know that. But I've got to talk to you about something else. Something important. Urho and the Lady are making their move."

Her eyes shot to mine. They were as wide and dark as a Wyoming night, and fear ran through them like the wind.

I shifted to the edge of the bed, leaning toward her. "This is it. You've sat on the sidelines long enough. When Mr. Big Empty was torturing and killing people, you buried your head in the sand. When Urho and the Lady tried to get me the first time, you were gone like fucking smoke. But not this time. This time you're going to do your part."

Color stained her cheeks like wine. "I'm not a—"

"If you tell me you're not a warrior, I'm going to rip your hair out of your head. You're not a warrior? Fine. So who is a warrior? Me? I can fucking read thoughts. Sometimes. I can glimpse memories. Emotions. Kaden can move metal, sure, but he's got PTSD or something like it; he tried to jump out of a moving car last night, he was so freaked. Temple Mae can throw pickup trucks, but she won't look at me, talk to me, acknowledge me unless she has to. Anyway, she's a kid. And what about the rest of them? Austin, Emmett, Becca, Jake. They don't have any abilities, and they're still out there doing more than you. The only one who comes close to being a warrior is Jim Spencer, and he's decided it's too much of a risk to even acknowledge I'm alive."

"I'm not—"

"Say it. Say you're not a warrior, and you're walking out of this house bald as a fucking eggshell."

Her head dropped, her chin tucking against her chest, and she rubbed the heels of her hands against her eyes. "I can't do anything," she said in a whisper. "I'm a guide. I helped you, didn't I? I showed you a way to your abilities. That's all I can do."

"Then help the rest of them. Help Kaden so he doesn't crack up the next time there's a loud noise. Help Temple Mae so she's not always trying to hide. Help Emmett—" My voice cracked. My fingers tightened, gathering folds of the quilt, and I shook my head. "Fuck it. You're just going to run away again."

Her head came up a little. She was back to looking at my socks. "I think we should talk about you for a while."

"Get lost, Ginny."

"This isn't a permanent solution, Vie. Foster situations are always meant to be temporary. The best thing for children is for them to be with their biological parents whenever possible. What do you think about that?"

My fingers gathered more quilt. "You're sending me back to my dad."

"That's not what I'm saying."

Trapped in the quilt's folds, the pulse in my fingertips felt like micro-detonations. "You're sending me back to my mom?"

"No. I just want you to know that your father has made a lot of progress. He's still making a lot of progress. And while I know Ms. Miller has been very responsible—"

"Responsible."

"She's an exemplary—"

"She's—she's—" I couldn't form the words. She's my mom, I wanted to say. She's the closest fucking thing I've ever had to a parent. She's the only person that's ever given a shit about me.

"We really believe it's in the best interest of the child to make every effort to improve the living conditions at home and return—"

"Why? So I can—" I had to bite the inside of my mouth, and I tasted blood. "So I can be buddies with my dad? So we can play catch? So he can take me fishing and buy me an ice cream and have a serious talk with me about girls and then, at the end, give me a rubber to keep in my wallet? Jesus Christ. Have you met that man?"

"He's making a lot of progress, Vie. He knows he's made mistakes. He's getting treatment for his addictions, and he's attending counseling, and I think you'd be really proud—"

"Get out." I stood, and my socks slipped on the wood, and I had to catch myself on the bed. I shot a finger toward the door. "Get the fuck out of my room."

"Your behavior at school is a sign that things aren't working out, no matter how hard Ms. Miller tries—"

"Get out!"

She was tall. Taller than me. And built like a brick wall. But damn if that woman didn't scurry out of the room. I slammed the door shut behind her.

Anger sat on my chest, making my breaths difficult. I paced the length of the room. Every other step, my socks would slide, and I'd have to catch myself, and I'd get angrier. One. Two. Slip. Dad. They were going to send me back to Dad. One. Two. Slide. Dad. They were going to send me back to Dad.

I dropped onto the bed and ripped off the socks. My feet were sweaty. I was sweaty all over, in fact, but my feet were so goddamn sweaty that I couldn't get the socks off, and I just kept ripping at them, pulling as hard as I could, until the seams gave on one and tore with long, stuttering pops.

"Fuck," I screamed. Downstairs, the muffled conversation between Ginny and Sara halted.

And it was so stupid and so ridiculous that it actually made me feel better.

I flopped backward on the bed. My heart was racing, but the practical side of my mind began to take over. Ok. They were planning on getting rid of me. Sending me back to Dad. Well, I wasn't going to live with that piece of shit again. I wasn't going to let him hit me again. I wasn't going to let him blow my cash on crystal again. I wasn't going to be afraid to go home ever again.

A part of me, though, was still a kid. A part of me still had hope. It was a stupid, tiny part of me that I couldn't crush no matter how hard I tried. That part of me remembered the good times—the few good times—with Dad. Like the day he'd taken me to Lake Thunderbird, and it had been late autumn, with giant red maple leaves bobbing on the water like flakes of fire, but it had been warm, too. And I remembered how he had helped me cup my hand around a flat gray stone. And how he had held my arm just right, shown me how to throw, and the whick of the stone in the air, and the wet smack as it kissed the water once, twice, and then flopped down into the depths.

No. I wasn't going back, no matter what.

Opening my inner eye came easier to me now. It overlaid the world with texture, as though I were seeing everything through a microscope, the warp and weft of molecules staining everything like the grain in wood. Color changed too; some colors grew deeper or brighter. The world seemed hyper-saturated; the colors lay over everything in a scrim, visible and not visible at the same time. It was enough to give me a blinding headache.

Over the last few months, as I had explored this ability, I had started to learn some of what it meant. Some of the colors had to do with emotion—excess emotion, strong emotion. My whole bedroom was stained in various shades of red, and the psychic echoes of lust and love made me dizzy. A lot of that was Austin; the damn bed squeaked so loud that we had to wait until Sara was gone, but we'd still found plenty of opportunities. I didn't even want to know what the shower looked like. But some of the red in here, the parts that looked like flame, some of that was Emmett. And there were tinges of blue and black now. Like a bruise. Like thick ice on dark water. Like the heart of winter. Some of that was what he was still carrying around for Makayla, for himself, Christ, for what had been done to him. I'd turned the spigot and let all of that come rushing out, and I'd damn near killed him doing it.

The next part still didn't come easily. I pushed. It was like sitting up, like doing a sit-up or a crunch, but with a different set of muscles. I separated, peeling out of my physical body, projecting myself into the other side. And then, once it was done, it was like—well, a bit like being in a dream. I had a body, and I moved through the world. But at the same time, my real body was lying on the bed, my eyes almost closed, my breathing slow. I could travel more easily like this. I focused on the living room below, and just like that, I was there.

It was empty. The phone, on the table next to the sofa, had the receiver off the cradle, and I circled around. Sara had pulled out the cord and let it fall to the floor. It looked like she wasn't in the mood to take any calls. Ginny's bag sat next to the chair that Shay had peeled the gimp from. From the kitchen came voices. Sara's was rough and low. Ginny's was pure bullshit: an emotionless sympathy that sounded like it had been drilled into her by a corporate training video. I drifted to the kitchen and risked a quick look.

Ginny's ability placed her on both sides—the real world and the other side. And I knew I was taking a risk of being seen. In fact, that was kind of the whole point. I actually thought that might work to my advantage. If Ginny noticed me, I hoped she would assume that it meant I was doing typical teenage things: lying in bed, sulking, and trying to eavesdrop. I needed her to think that was all I was doing.

When I looked into the kitchen, I saw Sara at the sink, running hot water over two sudsy mugs. I guess they had finished coffee or tea or whatever Sara had served. Her back was to me, and her frizz of blond hair glowed in the weak afternoon stormlight. Sara paused as I watched, the sponge stuffed inside one of the mugs, and her shoulders heaved once.

Ginny, at the table, folded and unfolded her hands like a schoolgirl reciting. She sat at an angle, and the kitchen door was in her field of vision. But she didn't even blink when my projected self slipped into the room. She just kept talking to Sara.

"—it's not anything you can really help with, of course, but you understand that we have to take these kinds of things, this kind of behavior, seriously, especially in the case of a boy with a history of deviant—"

The shatter of ceramic made me freeze, and Sara turned around so fast that I thought, for one heart-stopping moment, that she had somehow sensed my presence. Instead, though, Sara took a single step toward Ginny and raised one hand. Suds dripped off it and spattered the floor. Framed by the weak gray light that came through the clouds, her face lost in shadow, she looked ancient and terrible and domestic all at the same time, like some sort of forgotten goddess.

"You won't ever say something like that again about Vie. Not in my house. Do you understand me?"

Ginny made a gasping, fishy-faced struggle for words.

I was too distracted by something else to enjoy the moment fully. Where was Ginny's coyote? When I had met Ginny, I had tried to get a psychic sense of her. Instead, I had run flat into a wall of her own power, and with my inner sight, I had glimpsed a ghostlike coyote that accompanied her. But here I was, a few months later, and the coyote was gone. What did that mean?

Maybe nothing. Maybe something. I wasn't exactly the expert on psychic-ghost-coyotes. Maybe she was just having an off day. Maybe it was something else; a few months ago, she'd had a bad skiing accident, and that might have affected her abilities. Maybe she'd lost her powers somehow. Maybe that was why she wouldn't help me. Of course, if that were true, why wouldn't she just tell me?

I lingered for another moment, waiting for something—for Ginny's eyes to flick in my direction, for her expression to betray annoyance at my presence, for anything that might tell me that she had noticed me. I got nothing. After Sara's rebuke, there was an awkward silence, and then Ginny gulped and started listing reasons they were going to put me with Dad again.

Letting my astral projection fade, I opened my physical eyes and sat up. I swung my feet off the bed, stood, and winced when the boards creaked. For this next part, I needed to be very quiet. My torn sock flapped on one foot. The other sock, thank God, was still whole. I crept toward the door.

One problem, though, was that I was over six feet tall, over two hundred pounds, and physiologically not built for sneaking. The other problem was the house. It was old. Not like, thirty or forty years old. Like, pre-electricity old. Like, they'd cut the timbers up in the Bighorns and hauled them down with teams of oxen. And although they'd built the house well and built it to last, and although Sara had done a good job of keeping it up, it was still old, and nothing could fix old.

So it creaked. Everything. Everywhere. Every step I took, something else seemed to creak. The floor. The door. The stairs. From the kitchen, Sara's voice came clearer and angrier.

"I don't care if you have the Pope on record saying he thinks it's a good idea, I'm telling you I know that boy, and the first thing he's going to do is go to pieces. The minute you tell him—"

"It's not exactly that simple, Ms. Miller. I want you to look at this. This is a sample of what I'll give Mr. Eliot, and he knows that things aren't going to be swept under the rug. Look here, for example, about the regular visits."

Ginny kept talking, and from time to time Sara grumbled. The chairs squeaked on the kitchen floor, and I imagined Sara's body language: arms folded across her chest, chin thrust out, her face redder and redder by the minute. There was something about Sara that always made me think of a wild animal that would charge in to defend its young. For the last few months, I'd deceived myself into believing Sara could hold off anything bad—anything from the ordinary world, at least. I hadn't counted on Ginny being one of those things.

I reached the main floor. My ripped sock flapped away, exposing one sweaty foot. And a sweaty foot, in this case, was a sticky foot. I could hear my skin peel away from the floorboards. Jesus, why hadn't I taken a page out of the Hulk's book and ripped my shirt instead?

Step. Then the soft snick of my sticky, sweaty foot peeling away. Step. Snick. Step. Snick. The voices in the kitchen continued. Ahead of me, less than five yards away, was Ginny's bag. I felt a pang of guilt, but it was like an echo, not the real thing. If anybody asked Sara, she would have sworn herself blue that I wasn't a thief. But here I was, about to prove her wrong. And she was wrong about me in a lot of ways, I decided. She was wrong if she thought I was going to fall to pieces. She was wrong if she thought I needed her. She was wrong if she thought I couldn't take care of myself. Because I could. I could take care of myself without any help from anybody. I'd done it for a long time; I'd just gotten out of the habit for a few lousy months.

The rug swallowed the noise of my steps, and I crossed the rest of the distance in a flash. Squatting next to Ginny's bag, I pulled the mouth wide and peered inside. A travel pack of tissues. A roll of Lifesavers with its paper tail spiraling up. A hang-tag, the kind you'd put in your car, with 7A marked in blue ballpoint. A gun. A row of manila—

Hold on.

It was a revolver with a long barrel and a walnut-plated grip. S & W was stamped on the metal. My hand was halfway into the bag before I caught myself, and it was hard not to wrap my fingers around walnut and steel. I had held a gun before. I knew how this one would feel in my hand: heavy at first, cold but warming under my skin, like the only solid thing in a universe of mist.

Why was Ginny carrying a gun? The thought diverted the sudden wash of gun-lust. Self-protection, I thought. Protection against what, though? Against Sara? That was laughable. Sara might want to hurt Ginny. If things got really bad, and if Sara really thought she was protecting me, she might go so far as to throw a punch. But she wouldn't kill Ginny. She wouldn't ever hurt her, not really.

Against me, though? Well, that was a different matter. Ginny had never really seemed comfortable with me, and time had only strained the relationship. Did she really believe I might attack her? Did she really believe her life was in danger?

My pulse burned like match tips in my fingers. Ignoring the Smith & Wesson, I thumbed through the folders. Several of the family names I recognized, but I stopped when I got to the one I wanted. Vie Eliot ran across the tab in Magic Marker. It was thick. Heavy. And when I shimmied it free of the bag, something slid inside the folder, and I had to catch it: plastic, square, its edges fitting neatly into the crease of my palm. A microcassette in its case.

The swell of voices behind me made sweat pop under my arms. I emptied the folder onto the rug. Then I grabbed a sheaf of pages from another folder and shoved them into mine. A decoy. A temporary diversion. It wouldn't last long, but I hoped it would last long enough to get Ginny out of the house without noticing that she'd been robbed.

I crept back across the room, my foot sticking and snicking with every step, and launched myself up the stairs. It wasn't until I had the papers and the microcassette in my backpack that I dropped onto the bed and let out a breath. Footsteps moved below me, enough motion that I didn't dare look through the material I had stolen. Ginny might be coming back to apologize. Sara might just want to check in. Maybe they'd teamed up and decided to throw me out on my ass together.

Breathe, I told myself. I studied the cracks in the ceiling, following one crumbling line of plaster to another. Just breathe.

But sweat kept popping out under my arms, along my back, and in hot spots that felt the size of quarters on my forehead. What was on all those pages that Ginny had about me? And what the hell did she have on the cassette?

# Chapter | 11

Breathing didn't help. If anything, it seemed to make things worse. Every breath made my heart race. My pulse became this frantic, unstoppable thing in my ears, so fast it was basically one long drumming note. And that sweat. Christ. I'd never been a sweater, not like this, but I was basically swimming in the sheets.

I cupped my hands over my mouth, and when I breathed, the air smelled like my skin and my sweat and the school's industrial hand soap. Once, a few weeks after everything happened at Belshazzar's Feast, Sara had to visit a cousin who was dying in Bend, Oregon. She was only gone for a weekend, and she arranged for me to stay at Austin's house, and she made me swear up one side and Austin swear down the other that we'd behave. But we'd snuck out, of course, and come back to Sara's house alone, together, and it had been surreal, like we were living together, a kind of dream. And Austin had cooked eggs in nothing but an apron, and I'd told him there was nothing sexy about a guy cooking eggs, naked or not, and then he'd sat on my lap and that pretty much proved I was lying about my first point.

But that night, the one night we spent together with no one else in the house, Austin woke up screaming. Only he wasn't awake at first, and the screaming was so shrill and so panicked and terrible that I shot out of bed and stubbed my toe and punched the first thing I saw, and I was lucky it was a stuffed llama that Becca had put on my dresser and not a lamp or the dresser or the wall. And Austin just kept screaming and screaming, and then he kind of woke up, but he was groggy, and he didn't know where he was. I tried holding him, and he didn't want any of that. He just put his hands over his mouth, just like this, and breathed. After a while, he fell asleep again, and I spent the rest of the night ready to punch the first lamp or dresser or wall that moved. When I asked Austin about it in the morning, about all of it, and about the thing with his hands, he blushed and said it was just something his shrink had told him. And I guess it worked.

But all I was getting was a lot of air that tasted like my hands. It wasn't just the fact that Ginny was going to put me back with Dad. That, I could handle. That, that was nothing. But the papers. All those papers. And the cassette. And something about the way Sara had said, *The minute you tell him—* Like she knew the truth, whatever it was, would drag me below the waves, a kind of psychic undertow that I could swim against, struggle against, but that would eventually drown me.

She was wrong. I sucked air that tasted like my skin, like pink hand soap from a pump dispenser, and I told myself Sara was wrong because she didn't really know me. And then the whole nightmare reel would play from the top.

My heart thudded. Thud thud thud. Thud thud thud. Thud thud—

And Christ, it wasn't my heart. I almost laughed. It was the door. The thudding continued downstairs, and then the creak of the joists under Sara's passage, and then the door. The voices were too low for me to hear anything; I popped open my door an inch to listen, but I was too slow, and the front door shut, and the lock clicked.

Steps moved toward the stairs, and Sara's head came into view. She eyed me through the cracked door.

"Can we talk?"

I pulled the door open the rest of the way and retreated to my bed. I wasn't quite sure how this would go. Sweat prickled under my arms. My heart was crammed sideways in my throat. Mom had never talked. Dad had never talked. There had been the vacuum cord. The iron. The cigarettes. There had been fists. The belt. The buckle. I dragged both hands under my arms, patting down the cotton, trying to soak up all the sweat. I could smell myself. I had smelled this before. It was a zoo smell. A cornered animal smell. Christ, how long could it take to come up a flight of stairs?

In the doorway, Sara paused, breathing heavily, her face flushed. She dabbed at her forehead with the back of her hand, and then she dropped into the rocking chair. Wood groaned, and she smiled and fanned herself and said, "I'm off my diet."

"That's ok."

"It's not ok. But I'll just try again. Another time, I guess."

"Sara, I really fu—"

Her penciled-in eyebrows shot toward the ceiling.

"I really screwed up."

Rocking gently, she nodded. This was the worst part; I remembered this with Mom. With Dad, it was always a lightning strike: one minute, things were fine. The next minute, I was on the ground. But with Mom, there was a buildup. Like this. There was lots of quiet. There was this long, long pause. What would it be? The vacuum cord? Sara had a vacuum. She'd asked me, once, to run it, and I'd gotten so sweaty and white that she'd thought I had the flu. So maybe it was the vacuum cord. Because she had seen me get sweaty and white, and I think the next day she knew it hadn't been the flu because she never asked me to vacuum again. She never even ran the vacuum again, not while I was in the house. And she didn't smoke. And the iron would leave a scar. So it would be the vacuum cord. She would say something, she would tell me to take off my shirt and go downstairs, she would say—

"Is that all?"

"What?"

"Is that all you want to say?" The rocker creaked against the floor, steady, like a heart pumping out the last of my blood.

I nodded.

She blew out a breath, ran both hands through her cloud of hair—it split between her hands, turning into cones on either side of her head, the whole effect so bizarre that I couldn't stop staring at them. Like horns. Like she had these huge blond horns now.

"Well, the first thing I want to say is I'm sorry."

"I'm sorry."

"What?"

"I'm sorry. I am sorry. You're right, that's the first thing I should have said. And I am, I am sorry, I—"

She was crying, touching the insides of her wrists to the corners of her eyes. "Vie, honey, just stop for a second. I didn't say that was the first thing you should have said—although, to be fair, it's never a bad way to start. Especially with a woman." She tried to smile. "Or, in your case, with a young man who just spent half an hour hammering on the door in the pouring rain. I'm saying I'm sorry. That's the first thing I want to say to you. I'm sorry for how I treated you earlier. I know I've got a temper, but that's no excuse." She blew out another breath. "But since I don't have the self-control God gave a skunk and I can't even steer clear of your box of sticky buns, keeping my temper seems like a lost cause."

She wiped her eyes again and then just watched me. And it took me maybe a hundred heartbeats to realize she was waiting. For me. She was waiting for me to tell her—

"Sara, it's not—you don't have to—you didn't do anything."

"I shouldn't have spoken to you like that. I'm very sorry."

And then more of that waiting. I was really sweating now. My armpits were goddamn rivers. I might as well have been in a swimming pool.

"It's fine. It's nothing. Just don't cry, all right. It wasn't anything."

"It's not nothing, sweetie." She touched the corners of her eyes again. Her voice was a little steadier when she spoke again. "That's going to be a long lesson for you, I think. Learning how people ought to treat each other. To tell you the truth, that's the only thing I worry about with you. You're plenty smart. If you don't get yourself expelled, I expect you'll go to college and do just fine. You work hard. You're honest—until it comes to boys, I suppose, which is the same for any teenager, so I can't fault you for that. But there's a whole world out there full of people who will eat you for dinner, and they'll do it in a way that makes you think they're doing you a favor, and that's what I worry about. I worry you'll always think cruelty's a kindness. And what am I supposed to do about that?"

I didn't really understand what she was saying. Cruelty was cruelty; I wasn't stupid. But I got the feeling that I wasn't supposed to answer her question, so I stayed still and waited.

"Of course," she said, and her tone dried out a little. "I suppose I also have to worry about your temper, don't I?"

"Umm."

"You know you can't just hit things when you're angry. Especially not things that don't belong to you. I ought to make you pay for that mirror. And for the trash can. It wouldn't even do for a sieve now, not after what you did to it."

"I will. I'll pay for it, with my own money, what I earn at work."

"That's good. That's the responsible thing to do." But her eyes cut left, and her next words went straight toward the door. "It could be a lot worse, sweetie. Someone could have been hurt. If you were an adult, they might have pressed charges. It doesn't matter how big of a barn-ripper fight you've got going on with Austin, you can't act like that. That's got to go into your head right now, understand?"

"Yes. But I wasn't. We weren't. It wasn't a fight, Sara."

The rocking chair creaked forward, and her eyes finally came back to me.

"I mean, it wasn't really a fight. Not completely."

"I see."

"It's just—" The cut on the inside of my thigh stung. "It's just a misunderstanding."

"That is what every stupid boy has said about every stupid thing in every relationship since God put grass between his toes."

"It was my fault."

Sara snorted so hard that one of the cones of blond hair toppled, and she had to shake it out of her face.

"Austin's mad at me. He's right to be mad at me."

"Sweetie, let me tell you something: anger's a fire, and every fire has fuel. If he's angry, it's because something else got that fire started."

"Yeah. Something did. Me. I got it started."

She shook her head. "Anger always comes second. That's what I'm trying to say."

"He was mad, Sara. He was furious. And he's right to be furious."

The rocking chair clunked against the wall as Sara heaved her bulk out of the seat. She brushed at her shirt and plucked a half praline—from the sticky buns—and shook her head.

"I'm telling you, he was angry because he's scared. Or hurt. Or something else. And if he was angry, he's over it."

Chewing my lip, I shook my head.

"Fine." Sara shook the praline half at me like it was a yardstick. "But that boy called up here blubbering so hard I couldn't even understand him."

"That was Austin?"

"Yes, you great galoot. I had to unplug the phone for him to get the message."

"That was him the second time?"

Her eyes slid toward the door again. "Then, when I finally managed to get him to understand that I wasn't letting you take any calls, he drove over here and just about knocked down the door."

"Is he—I mean, did he—"

"No." She waved the pecan menacingly. "And don't even think about going downstairs. I told him you were grounded. And you are grounded, mister. You might be grounded until you're a very old man. You'll go to work, and you'll go to school, and you'll come straight home. Austin can drive you if you need a ride, but he's not going to hang around and kiss you and tell you how pretty your eyes are because you are in trouble. Capital T."

"He doesn't say that. He's never said that. About my eyes, I mean."

"I live in this house, Vie Eliot. And you are too lazy to shut your door sometimes."

Oh God. Sweet, merciful God. My face probably melted off.

"You'd think I told that boy you were being shipped off to Siberia, the way he acted." Sara shook her head. "I told him you're fine, and he looked at me like I was the biggest fool on the green earth. So I want you to tell me right now: is there something I should worry about?"

The cut on my leg throbbed with my heartbeat. I shook my head.

"You're not thinking about hurting yourself? Nothing like that?"

"God, Sara."

"Well, people do things when you don't expect. I'm not smart, but I'm not so stupid that I don't know that much. Would you tell me if you were?"

"I'm not going to do anything."

But for a moment, my entire brain was bright with that table saw again: the whirr of perfect metal, the light on steel, the vibration in the plastic casing. Piece by piece. I could take myself apart piece by piece and I wouldn't even feel it; I knew it like a lullaby. My finger first, sliding toward the blurred teeth. So perfect. My wrist. My elbow. I had to get an artery just to be sure. And then no pain, not anymore. It was in the basement. I could go down there when Sara was asleep. I'd smell the metal of Austin's weights. I'd let the fluorescents flicker. I'd stand there, the cold seeping up through bare feet. And then, when I was ready, I could flip one switch, one simple switch, and it would start.

Sara harrumphed. "He's standing out in the cold, and I think it serves him right for being a fool when I told him to get in that fancy car and go home. But did he listen to me? No. You can have five minutes, but I swear, if you set one foot past the front door I will have you clean the deep fryers every day for a month. Do you understand me?"

I nodded. "Not one foot."

"Not your big toe."

"Not my big toe."

"Not even a hair, Vie Eliot."

"All right, all right."

"Not even if he wants to—"

"Oh my God. Please, just, oh my God. I get it, I promise."

"Then why are you still sitting on your bottom?"

I flew down the steps. My feet actually went out from under me when I hit the hardwood at the bottom, and only a quick grab at the banister saved me. Then, sliding, I crashed into the front door and yanked it open.

His hair was oh-so-short and neatly parted. The collar on his flannel shirt was nice and crisp. He had those boots on that I loved, the ones that were beaten to hell and that he rubbed beeswax into and that looked perfect with the rough denim of his jeans. Everything about him was perfect. Everything except his face. Everything except the fact that he was a wreck, a complete and total wreck, and anybody could see it.

"Are we in a fight?" I asked, and my voice buzzed up and down so that I could barely hear what I was saying.

"No. No. No." He kept shaking his head. "No. We're not. No."

"Will you come inside?" I laughed, but it got all big and wet and bubbly in my mouth. "Sara said she'd kill me if I stepped past the door, so will you come in here?"

"She said she'd kill me if I went inside, but who the fuck cares." He staggered over the threshold, arms clasping me to him, face buried in my neck. "Jesus, Vie. I'm so sorry."

"You can't be sorry. I'm the one who—"

Then he reared back and kissed me, and my knees exploded, and my head exploded, and for all I knew, the whole world had exploded and he was the only thing holding me up.

"That's enough," Sara said, the stairs groaning as she came down. "Austin Miller, I'm going to whip your bottom if I ever hear that language again, and if you don't have the brains to remember that I told you to stay outside my house—"

Austin squeezed me once more and then darted backward.

"That's better." Sara looked at each of us and sniffed. "It would do you both a lot of good to have fifteen minutes apart."

"We're apart all the time," Austin said, his cheeks pink.

"You've got four minutes, mister." And then she dropped onto the sofa. Right there. Less than ten feet away. Watching us. "Three and a half, and I'm not going away, so you can both stop looking at me like that."

"Uh, Sara—"

"You're down to three minutes."

"Look, I fu—" I swallowed it. "I messed up. I messed everything up. But the stuff about Emmett, I shouldn't have—"

"I don't care about that. How bad did you—" He dropped his voice. "Do you need stitches?"

The table saw's whine whited out the inside of my head. I managed to shake a no. "That's really hard for me. To let you watch. To let you be there. I freaked out today, and I know I promised I wouldn't lie, but I freaked the fuck out."

"Language. That's another day on your grounding."

Austin shot her an irritated look. "It's all right. I shouldn't have pushed you like that. Sometimes I just get so worried, and then after . . ." He didn't finish, but his cheeks purpled with blood. The turquoise in his eyes had gone to the hard, dark chop of seawater.

"I'm sorry."

"A minute."

Austin shot her another angry glance.

"Don't glare at me. I'll call your father and tell him the kind of look you've got on your face."

"I'll see you tomorrow. We can talk tomorrow."

Shaking my head, I said, "Sara said I can't. I mean, you can't come over, and I can't go out."

"But tomorrow is—"

Saturday. The pink-and-white swirl of a candle. The flame swelling around a black wick. Wax on the buttercream. Wax on my cheek just below my eye. Wax on my shoulder. Wax on my back. And then—

"You just mind your own business, Austin Miller." Sara was on her feet, bumping me away from the door and swinging it shut.

"Hold on. That's not fair. Tomorrow is—"

Saturday.

"Everybody knows just perfectly well what tomorrow is, Austin. You go home. Right now. I really will call your father, and I think he'll have plenty to say to you about all this."

"At least let me say goodbye," I said.

"You've said goodbye to that boy a million times. Goodbye, goodbye, goodbye. There. All done."

"Call me," Austin shouted.

Then the door clicked shut, and Sara turned the bolt and set her back against the wood like she thought Austin might try to break it down. She looked at me, and the expression was surprisingly frank.

"You don't even think of sneaking out."

I nodded.

"I mean it. Trust goes both ways."

I nodded again.

"No phone, either."

"I know."

"Well, I don't suppose you've got any homework, on account of how your day ended. But Lord knows they'll be sending plenty of it home next week. Why don't you go up to your room for a while?"

"Do I have to stay in my room?"

"Nine days out of ten I can't get you to budge, and the one time I say you should go to your room, you assume it's a punishment."

"Is it?"

"Will you just get out of my hair? I'm no good at this. I'll make dinner, and you can wash up." The collapsed blond hair swung into her face again, and she shook it out of her way. "And you can mop the floor."

I was having a hard time not smiling. "Ok."

"I mean scrub."

"Yes, Sara."

"Don't you laugh at me, Vie. I've got a whole basement that needs work. You'll be sweeping up spiderwebs until you're an old man, so don't you dare laugh."

A whole basement, and the spotlight in my head only showed one beautiful circle, a white circle cut out of all the black, and at the center of the spotlight, the teeth glittering and silent and waiting.

"No, ma'am."

But halfway through Sara's cooking, the phone started ringing again, and even from upstairs I could tell that Sara was upset. Pots banged against each other. Water roared in the sink. Something—the flour canister, I guessed—toppled over like a bass drum. The whole thing sounded like the symphony of a woman looking to beat the hell out of whatever got in her path.

The house creaked and shifted as Sara crossed the room beneath me. I cracked the door, and when her head appeared at the bottom of the stairs, she pointed an enormous, gravy-covered spoon at me.

"I have to go into work."

"That's all right. I can warm up something."

The spoon wavered. Gravy beaded along one side, and the drops quivered, as viscous as Elmer's glue. Sara said she wanted her meals to stick to my ribs; looking at the gravy, trembling as she waved the spoon at me again, I figured it was definitely going to stick to something.

"All you have to do is take the chicken out of the oven."

"Thank you."

"The oven mitts are in the bottom drawer."

"I know."

"And there's a packet of Country Time. It's the raspberry one; that's what you like, isn't it?"

"I like it fine."

"You and Austin drank a whole pitcher last time he was here. I thought you might like that to drink."

"Yeah, sure." I took a step out onto the landing. Sara's spoon trembled again. She fumbled it in a quick rotation to keep the fat gobbets of gravy from falling. Sara threw a series of rapid glances at the front of the house, with a few in my direction. "Is everything all right?"

"You don't go outside, all right?"

"I'm grounded. I get it."

"Not one foot."

"I said I wouldn't."

"I mean it, Vie. If you do, I'll—" She waved the spoon, seemingly unsure how to finish, gravy splattered the stairs. "Oh Lord."

"I'll clean it up."

"I want you to promise."

"What is it? What's going on?"

"And you keep the door locked. Don't let anybody in. Not even Austin."

"Sara, what's got you so upset?"

"Well, Kimmy just about cut off her hand, and Joel and Miguel ruined an entire container of ground beef because they wanted to see if they could make blue-cheese-and-vinegar burgers after I told them to do no such thing and—"

"Well, go."

"Promise me right now, Vie. Promise me you won't sneak out while I'm gone."

"Yeah, I promise. Will you go? Kimmy's freaking out, and you can't leave her with Joel and Miguel. They'll probably try to see how far she can squirt her blood or mix her severed finger into the fries or something like that."

"Lord, Lord, Lord, they will." Sara whipped around, the spoon whistling a trail of gravy behind her, and then she froze. "You promised me, Vie Eliot. I know you. That ought to mean something to you."

"I'm not leaving this house unless it's on fire, Sara. You need to run."

"Not even then. You stay where you are until a fireman carries you out."

And then she sprinted out of sight, and a moment later, I heard the front door crash shut. And then the bolt went home. And then the distant spin of her tires. And then the wind rocked the house, and then nothing.

I cleaned up the gravy. I could see Emmett again, standing at the window in my memory, the golden light ringing him with a corona. I shook it off and went to the kitchen. I retrieved the chicken—breaded and fried and cooked through in the oven. I could see him backlit by the ring of yellow light. I ate more than my share. I ate more than just about anybody's share. I could see him. In that damn photograph, I could still see him with the light picking out the texture of his hair. On the counter, I found the Country Time envelope, and I emptied it into a pitcher. Reddish-brown dust sifted up, staining my fingers, and when I breathed, it was bitter all the way down into my lungs. I could see him with his face in her neck. With his face buried in her fucking neck. I added an extra cup of sugar; Sara didn't need to know about that. It would only hurt her diet. And, as she predicted, I drank most of the pitcher.

I could still see him. I could see his hand sliding under the lace of her bra. I hadn't lied to Sara. That was a poisonous thought, and I tried to push it away. I tore into another drumstick, the skin crackling under my teeth, the hot fat and juices of the meat spritzing the inside of my mouth, and I chewed, and I took another bite. I hadn't lied to her. Not exactly. That was really important. It wasn't a lie. I wasn't lying. I hadn't lied. I wouldn't do that to Sara, not after everything she'd done for me. I wouldn't sneak out of the house. I wouldn't. I absolutely wouldn't. Not while she was gone; that was what I'd promised. I wouldn't sneak out while she was gone. So I wouldn't. I wouldn't do it even though at that exact moment, Emmett Bradley was on the other side of town probably raising a hickey the size of Vermont on some new skank's neck.

It was a bullshit technicality. It was a sophistry. It was a lie; my throat was still bitter no matter how much fried chicken I ate, and the raspberry lemonade was too sweet, and I dumped the rest of the pitcher down the sink. A window looked out above the sink; beyond, Sara's trimmed lawn ran for twenty feet before it ended at the wire fence. The wind was strong tonight. It was huge—that was a better term, because it wasn't just about strength. Not out here. Out here, in Wyoming, wind was more about space, about the thousands and thousands of miles of high plains and buffalo grass and Junegrass and sage. Out in that emptiness, where the wind became bigger than anything I could imagine, the War Chief was hiding, and the Lady was working, and their army was coming together, and—

Something surged out of the darkness. I jumped back; the pitcher, still in my hand, cracked against the sink. Glass shattered. It didn't matter; I kept moving back, bringing up the pitcher's broken handle and the jagged rim of glass still attached. I could take somebody's throat with it. I could get an artery.

And then, sweat needling my back, I stopped and let out a sigh. The tumbleweed was about the size of Sara's Focus, and it slammed into the wire fence again, and the wires bulged in toward the house. But the fence held. And that enormous tumbleweed rolled back and then launched forward again. A tumbleweed. Sweat made my underarms gritty. I dropped the broken pitcher handle in the trash and began scooping glass out of the sink. A goddamn tumbleweed. I focused on that, and by the time I'd finished cleaning, I'd almost convinced myself I wasn't lying to Sara. Not really.

Sara had plugged in the phone again. Kaden answered on the first ring.

"I need to do something tonight."

"Oh, cool. Cool, man. I'm so glad you called me. I was worried about you. And I've really been thinking that we don't hang out enough, just the two of us, we don't—"

"Run out to Walmart. Or wherever. I don't know. And buy one of those recorders. The kind that can play a microcassette. Do you know what I'm talking about?"

"Like a little tape?"

"Yeah. Then park on the state highway at midnight. Turn off your lights before you get close. In fact, you might want to kill the engine and coast the last half mile."

"Uh. Yeah. I want to. That'd be fun. But it's, like, a school night. And I don't know if Austin wants me—"

"Good. I'm glad you brought that up. You absolutely are not going to tell Austin about this."

"Sure, sure. That sounds great. It's just that, well, he was really clear about this. Really, really clear. Like, he ripped an orange in half."

"About what? Wait. What? An orange?"

"About uh. About nothing."

"What did he say?"

"I think I got confused. What were we talking about?"

An orange? "So you're coming over at midnight."

"The thing is, though, it's really dark, and if I coast without my lights on, somebody might run into me, and it's a good plan, Vie, like, a really good plan, and I'm so glad you called me—"

"Kaden."

On the other end of the call, a woman's voice hummed, and Kaden said, "Yeah, yeah, Mom. God, I know. Just let me talk on the phone, all right? Yes. Yes. Oh my God, yes, kids still talk on the phone. God, Mom. It's Vie. He doesn't have a phone, all right. Yes, he has a phone, but I mean, he doesn't have a phone with texting and—God, I said I'd do it already." Then Kaden's breath chuffed across the mike, and he said, "My mom says hi."

"Midnight."

"I can't—"

"Don't tell Austin."

I hung up.

The rest of the night passed slowly. I turned off the lights downstairs and went to my room. I tried to read, but I'd never really been much of a reader, and I didn't want to watch TV. When I heard Sara's car in the drive, I turned off my light. She came into the house slowly. She came up the stairs slowly. I closed my eyes, and when the door creaked open, I smelled the remainder of her perfume under the hot oil smell from Bighorn Burger's fryer.

She was breathing funny. Heavy breaths. Irregular. A heart attack? Had the stairs finally done it? But she was still breathing, and I kept waiting for her to fall, for her to moan, for her to say my name or something like, "Oh God, my heart." Nothing. Just that harsh, irregular breathing. And then she sniffled, and I realized she was crying.

Never in my whole life, not that I can remember anyway, was someone so careful about closing a door quietly. I thought about that after she left, with darkness carpeting my eyes, as the digital minutes on the clock formed and reformed until it was midnight. Then I kicked off the quilt, dragged on my sneakers, and grabbed my backpack with the stolen pages and the microcassette. I left through the window. I climbed down the side of the house on the same trellis that Emmett used. Halfway down, the wind just about knocked me loose. That giant tumbleweed creaked and scratched as it pushed at the fence. The black cup of the sky didn't have a single star.

On the highway, Kaden's yellow Camaro sat a hundred yards down from Sara's house, tucked off onto the shoulder. Even from a distance, I could see the paint blistered from the heat of Becca's burning car. I guess he really was worried about someone crashing into him, even though this particular road didn't get much traffic. I jogged. The air smelled fresh: wet sage and gravel and the fabric softener Sara used on my shirts. I wasn't excited. I wasn't. I had to keep a cool head about this. I had to think clearly. A hundred percent clearly. No emotions, not tonight. I had to be perfectly, completely, totally rational about Emmett-fucking-Bradley sucking on that bitch's neck.

When I popped open the Camaro's door, the dome light sprang on, a vibrant LED white, and I slid onto the seat. Leather. Nice, new, still had the smell. And something else. Cedar. Maybe even something like tobacco—not smoke, but tobacco leaves crushed in the palm of the hand. I glanced at Kaden, and his eyes had white rims and he was trying to shrink into a ratty cardigan that had a bumper sticker pasted on one sleeve: *Free Love; Ask Me How.*

Kaden was already shaking his head when I figured it out.

"Hi, babe," Austin said from the back seat. He was just a shadow with the dome light glaring in my eyes. A big shadow. A huge shadow, with his legs spread wide, his hands on his knees, his jaw ready to take a punch. "Are we in a fight?"

# Chapter | 12

"You are a fucking rat."

Kaden squirmed deeper into his cardigan. He had nice shoulders; tonight, they were so high they buried his ears. "I had to tell him, all right? I—"

"Shut your mouth or I'm going to shove that bumper sticker down your throat. Free fucking love. Hipster son of a bitch." I turned to Austin. "Hi."

He cocked his head. I couldn't see anything, not his eyes, not his mouth, nothing but those hands on his knees, the fingers spread, each digit dimpling the denim. I slapped at the dome light, and it took two tries before I decided to shut the car door, and then the only illumination came from the red flush of the dash.

"This isn't a big deal."

"Good."

"I've got something I need to take care of."

He gestured with an open hand: *Go right ahead.*

"And I asked Kaden to do this one thing without bothering you."

"I wasn't bothering him. I just—this is a big deal, Vie. Oh, and I got that microcassette player you wanted—"

"It's not a big deal." I snagged the player and shoved it in my bag. "And I fucking told you what I'd do if you didn't keep your mouth shut."

Austin's hand closed over mine. "So?"

"What?"

"Are we in a fight?"

"That's up to me?"

"Feels like just about everything's up to you these days."

I swallowed. The red glow of the dash painted everything in the car at an angle, and I had to close my eyes for a moment. Just a moment. Because what he'd said, the way he'd said it, made me dizzy.

Then the table saw whirred to life, bright and white as the moon in the spotlight at the back of my head. And I could breathe again.

"It's nothing," I told Austin.

"Good. This'll be a fun drive then."

But it wasn't. I told them where to go, and Kaden drove too fast. Austin, taking up almost the entire back seat, was too quiet. I was too damn stupid to figure out why I had ever thought I could trust Kaden, and I spent the drive thinking of inventive ways to hurt the hipster. Smashing his fingers in the Camaro's door would be pretty satisfying; I'd like to see him roll a joint when I was finished.

Before long, Vehpese shrank behind us, a grimy, dishwater bubble of light at the base of the Bighorns. Ahead, the world unfurled like a great black canvas. Roadside thistles with heavy purple crowns flickered in the Camaro's lights, and a cat's paw of wind played with the Camaro, hitting hard enough that the car drifted on the asphalt, and the double yellow disappeared under its wheels. When that cat's paw hit us, it was almost the same sound as the thrum of the tires, and the two noises hummed in my head. Like the whine of a drill. Or the thrum of gears. Or the cry of a saw—

The Camaro thumped onto the gravel shoulder, and I touched Kaden's arm, stopping him before he could turn down the drive. Emmett's house stood at the edge of a sea of buffalo grass and sage and dirt bleached to gray by the moonlight. It was huge; the architect had taken the building blocks of a log cabin and blown them up into a McMansion: lots of timber, lots of glass, lots of light cutting amber rectangles in the lawn. His bedroom, on the far side of the house, wasn't visible from the road, but it didn't matter. I could see it in my mind, on the top level of the house, an entire wall of windows looking out onto tumbleweed and sage. I could see him. His head bent. His face turned in. His mouth on her neck.

Kaden drummed his thumbs on the steering wheel. "So we're here. And you know what? I think we should head back. Right, Austin? I think we should head back because this is kind of a bad idea. It's late, and they're probably asleep—"

"The lights are on."

Austin didn't say anything.

Swallowing, Kaden nodded. "Yeah. But. It's really late. And I think, um, Vie, I think you're still maybe a little worked up. About this afternoon, I mean. And nobody would blame you. I don't blame you. It was . . . it was messed up, what happened. So I think you're totally right to be angry."

"I'm not angry." I undid my seat belt. "And I'm not worked up."

Austin still didn't say anything. He didn't even blink.

"Sure. Of course not. I didn't mean you were angry. Not like that. I just meant, well, think about it like this: we go home. You get a good night's sleep. You come at this thing tomorrow, from a fresh perspective." He glanced back. "Right, Austin? I mean, tomorrow, Vie, it's Saturday, it's—"

"It's just another day. One more fucking day. Same as every other day." I popped the door open. The wind caught it, cranked it wide, and weeds streamed and hissed toward me. They'd grown long at the side of the road, and I doubted the Bradleys were happy about that. "Stay here. I'm just going to look around."

"I don't think—I mean, Austin, just, will you tell him, I mean, will you ask him—"

Austin hit the latch on the seat, and it slid forward. He climbed out of the car, stretched, and the cedar smell, the crushed-and-dried tobacco smell spun on the wind and was gone. He put his hands on his hips. Those arms. Those goddamn arms. His eyes, hard as turquoise again, were waiting.

"Fine," I said. "But Kaden stays."

He just shrugged. "Duh."

Together, we jogged the length of the drive. A tall iron fence surrounded the lot, following the division between trim, lush grass and tangles of scrub. The fence, however, was purely ornamental; it was tall, but it didn't have a damn thing at the top, so I boosted Austin—I was still taller, even if he'd decided to pack on muscle—and then jumped, caught high on the fence, and shimmied the rest of the way up.

We landed together on the other side, where dry, brambly creepers tangled around the fence. The Bradleys had been cheaping out on their landscaping; somebody wasn't keeping up with his job. Moonlight caught Austin's face in profile, and it was a hard face. Without the baby-fat that had bled away over the last few months, the strong lines that made him rugged instead of pretty were inked bold and true. It was the kind of face that could stare into the Chinook for fifty years and the wind would blink first. And this guy, this guy with a face like that, with a heart like that, this guy was here with me. Tonight. After all the shit I pulled.

"Austin, I just want to tell you . . ."

"What?" One of those thick, dark eyebrows curved.

"Nothing."

"You hurt your ankle?"

"No, I'm fine."

A beat passed between us. The other eyebrow shot up. "You're thinking about Valentine's Day."

"I'm not fucking thinking about Valentine's Day. Never mind. Forget it." I took off at a trot, cutting away from the drive so that the house lights wouldn't pick me out against the night.

Coming after me, Austin said, "You were all misty-eyed. If you didn't hurt your ankle, then you were probably thinking about Valentine's Day."

"I was thinking about how I can't go anywhere without my jealous boyfriend following me."

"You were probably thinking about those teddy-bear boxers I got you. The most romantic gift of your entire life. You get tears just thinking about them."

"You're out of your damn mind."

When I glanced at him, he was grinning, and then he tweaked the soft skin at the back of my arm hard enough to make me yowl. He jetted ahead of me, his sneakers leaving tracks in the wet grass, curving around the side of the house toward Emmett's room at the back. I followed him. I didn't mind Austin teasing me. I kind of liked it, in fact—most of the time he was so serious, most of the time he was so earnest, and I liked that too, but the teasing was fun. He wasn't like Emmett. Emmett could hardly say two words without one of them making him an asshole. Of course, most of that was Emmett's defense mechanism; he was just about the most vulnerable human being I knew, and he hid it behind the armor of being an unbearable shit.

And the thought flashed through me that maybe Austin's teasing, when he saw me looking at him in the moonlight, was because he felt vulnerable too. He had watched, earlier that day, as I exposed how much I still cared for Emmett. I had lied to Austin today. I had pushed him away. I had tried to go behind his back. But he was still here; no matter how hard I pushed, I couldn't seem to budge him. The teasing tonight, when I looked at him, when I wanted to tell him how I felt about him—was he worried? Was he afraid? I wanted to laugh. Afraid of what? Of what I'd do?

Clear as crystal, I could see it in front of me: Emmett's lips on her neck, his hand between the folds of the blouse, that inch of black lace riding up over his fingers. What would I do? I wasn't sure. Burning down Emmett's house felt like a good place to start.

I tamped down the impulse. Following Austin around the house, I snaked a path through the grass. It was long here, where the house's shadows fell thickest. It was so long that it slipped wetly against my jeans at the knees, the blades rasping against each other. I got my first glimpse of Emmett's bedroom. The lights were on. Like the rest of the house, the windows blazed with a warm glow, and I shivered as the wet, Wyoming wind cut through my jacket. Austin watched the wall of windows, and I joined him, slipping my arm around his waist.

He glanced at me; his surprise was almost comical.

"I, uh, love you."

"What?"

"You heard me."

"Yeah, Vie. I know you love me." He kissed my cheek, nuzzling against me until I laughed and pushed his head away. "I love you too."

"That's why I got all, um, quiet. After we got over the fence."

"You didn't get quiet. You got teary-eyed."

"I didn't get teary-eyed. I'm just saying, that's what I wanted to tell you. When we jumped down. I was just thinking about it."

Those goddamn eyebrows shot up again. "Not about the teddy-bear boxers?"

"No. For fuck's sake—oh. You're joking."

"You're not exactly impossible to read, blondie. Not like you think you are." Something like a blacklight shone across his face. "Not even when I ask what's wrong."

"I'm sorry I'm a total fuckup. I'm sorry I was a total fuckup today in particular."

"You're not a total fuckup." He let out a breath and tilted his gaze toward the windows. "Emmett, on the other hand—"

"Why are the lights on?"

"Vie, when it gets dark, some people still need to do things, and they need to see, so—"

"I'm going to make you sit in the car with Kaden."

He nuzzled against me again, hard, peppering my face with kisses until I laughed again and pushed him away. The grass whispered against me, flexing, teasing wet lengths along denim. For a wonder, the ever-present Wyoming wind seemed to have died, and suddenly something felt wrong, and the skin down my spine itched, and every noise was too loud. My laugh faded quickly as I studied the house. "Seriously. Why the lights? It's past midnight. Even if Emmett is up, even if he's having some friends over, why is every light on in the whole house?"

Austin gave the house a moment's consideration. "Maybe his parents have friends over."

"Who?"

Shrugging, Austin said, "Maybe it's like this on the weekends. Or maybe it's like this every night. Maybe they leave the lights on. Or maybe his mom is a night owl. I mean, it could be a million things." He paused, and tension tightened his body against mine. "What are you looking for?"

"What?"

"I mean, what do you think you're going to see? And if you see it, what good is it going to do you?"

"I want to see who Urho and the Lady brought into town."

Words tumbled out of him now. "If you see them up there, pressed against the glass like they were in the picture, if that's what you came to see, what are you going to do? Go inside and shoot him? Or shoot her? Beat him up? Yell at him? Drag her out by the hair? Try to get answers out of her?"

"I just want to see her. That's the smart thing to do. Get an eye on the enemy. Protect myself."

Austin shook his head as though what I'd said was too stupid for words. Then he ran his hand up the nape of my neck, through the thick blond hair, and I thought of the day before, when he'd marked me with his nails, scratching five long lines down my chest. "Baby, you've never, ever known how to protect yourself. Coming here like this is about as far from protecting yourself as you can get."

The wind whistled across the plains, clawing through the buffalo grass and leaving gouges that disappeared into the darkness. I pushed aside Austin's words and focused on the house, the lights, the empty glare of the windows. It wasn't a party. My heart thumped a little faster. It wasn't a late night. The lights were on, and his mom wasn't a night owl, and his dad wasn't having scotch with a friend, and the lights were on, past midnight, every light, the whole house blazing like a lamp at the end of the world, and it wasn't any of the things Austin had said. Every light. Every goddamn light. And the wind shrieked in my ears, carrying pellets of rain that exploded against my nose and my cheek and my jaw. Every single goddamn light.

I started back, and Austin ran easily at my side. I felt bad for him then, for the way the tension slackened in his shoulders, for the relief that softened his face. I felt bad because he thought we were leaving and I wanted to give him what he wanted, I wanted it so bad, but I couldn't. Not with the wind in my ears. Not with those lights swimming in the windows. I felt bad because I couldn't even tell him, because my throat was so tight and my heart was hammering on it, trying to get out.

As we passed the door that led into the kitchen, I stopped and checked the handle. It turned.

"Jesus Christ. You're kidding."

I couldn't look at him; I couldn't stand to see how much this was hurting him, so I shouldered through the door and kept going. The kitchen was huge, with stainless steel and granite and hanging racks of pots. It wasn't big enough to feed an army, but it could have fed a couple of battalions pretty easily. The lights were on. They ovaled along stainless steel like the edge of a galactic disc. They puddled deep in the granite.

Beyond the kitchen, a hallway ran the length of the house. Every light was burning. I knew they were electric. I goddamn knew it. But in my blurred vision, they burned and bent like flames. Every light. Every light in the whole house. And even inside, the wind was shrieking in my ears, and I realized it wasn't the wind, it was something inside me, a noise that couldn't quite get out. Every light. And the house was silent. How could it be so bright and so quiet?

"Vie, this is a bad idea." Austin hooked my sleeve. "A really bad idea, even for you."

I kept going, towing Austin behind me.

The house hung on the axis of a central staircase, a massive wooden affair overlooking an enormous foyer on one side and, on the other, a tastefully appointed living space. I took the steps. My soles squeaked once, at the bottom; I looked back, but I couldn't stand what I saw in Austin's face, so my eyes skimmed over the wet prints of my shoes and then I kept going. He let go of my sleeve, then. That was better. And, at the same time, so much worse.

Emmett's bedroom was on the third floor, but I stopped on the second because the door to his dad's study was open. Someone moved inside the room—I couldn't see them, but steps rasped across the rug, and then there was the soft clang of metal: a filing cabinet, I thought. Or a desk drawer.

When I met Austin's eyes, he shook his head once. His eyes were an absolutely hopeless shade of blue, like the bottom dropping out from the ocean.

He was right. We should leave, right then. I should turn around. I should get the hell out. But he didn't understand; every internal alarm I had was ringing out, and they all had to do with Emmett, and I could just as easily leave as I could cut off my own arm. And then, looking at those blue eyes darkening at the rim of the iris, thinking of a shelf of ocean floor crumbling, of the waters seizing up with blackness, I thought maybe he did understand. He was here. He had followed me.

I crept to the edge of the study door and peered around the frame. A man sat behind the desk, but he wasn't Emmett's dad. This man wore a flannel shirt open at the top, exposing a thatch of dark hair and muscled chest. He was a big guy—muscled, with the extra weight of an athlete just starting to go to seed. He had a nice face; he looked like your neighbor, like the kind of guy you'd trust to help you move a piece of furniture or jump your car. He was Lawayne Karkkanew, and he controlled the drug trade—and pimping and prostitution and every other vice I could imagine—throughout Mather County and beyond. He was a killer. And he had conspired with a dirty deputy to kidnap me and offer me up to the War Chief and the Lady.

If I'd had the Glock, I would have put a bullet between his eyes. I'd stolen the gun from his office the year before; it was valuable insurance, but it hadn't kept Lawayne from turning on me. Since his betrayal, I'd waited and tried to decide what to do about my ace in the hole. Pulling the trigger—figuratively—would remove Lawayne from my life, but for the moment, I thought it was better to know who my enemies were. If I got rid of Lawayne, someone would replace him, and I might not be able to identify his successor.

Right then, though, seeing him in that chair, rifling the desk, I wasn't thinking that far ahead. I just wanted to blow out the back of his head.

It was the change in Austin's breathing that made me tense, and I glanced back and froze. Above us, on the next flight of stairs, Emmett shirtless and barefoot, leaned coolly against the wall. He pointed a compact, black pistol at me. Something flickered on Emmett's face. A footstep sounded farther up the staircase, and Emmett glanced up, over at me, and then toward the open study door. "Lawayne. We've got company."

"Put that down," I said. "You're not going to hurt me."

A smile tore at one side of Emmett's mouth, pulling on his split lip. In a mocking echo of the words he'd spoken in my bedroom, he said, "You still don't understand, tweaker. I get to do whatever I want. Whenever I want."

"You wouldn't shoot me."

He just shook his head. That smile opened the side of his mouth like a gash, and the gun twitched toward Austin before settling on me again. "Maybe I would. Maybe I'd shoot your boyfriend instead."

"What the fuck is wrong with—"

The shot came so abruptly that I never had a chance to prepare myself. The clap of the gunshot rocked me. On the step below me, splinters jagged up.

"No more talking," Emmett shouted over the ringing in my ears. "Or I'll shoot Austin. And you know I won't lose any sleep over that."

His eyes were that funhouse darkness I remembered. I was in shock: the sense of vertigo, of weightlessness, of falling while I was standing still. He had shot at me. He had actually taken a shot. The little fucker had actually . . .

"What the fuck is going on?" Lawayne barked from the doorway.

"These two were sneaking around. Krystal caught them when they got on the grass; she told me."

And then I remembered the grass that was too long, that was wet, that whispered and rasped and flicked against my legs even when the wind had stopped, and I knew what some intuitive part of my brain had already figured out: the grass shouldn't have been moving when the wind stopped. That had been Krystal.

Lawayne grunted; then, still speaking loudly over the aftereffects of the gunshot, he said, "You always go breaking into people's houses?"

"I didn't break in. The door was unlocked."

"That's a nice technicality. I wonder how well it would hold up in court."

"The next time you're in court, it'll be when they're putting you away."

Lawayne's face eased into a smile, and he clapped me on the shoulder. "Jesus, I always forget what a tough little prick you are. Come on in. Let's talk. Emmett, get Krystal and come down here. If they try to run, have Krystal stop them." Lawayne cocked his head. "And then shoot them."

Without another word, he disappeared into the study.

Emmett, with a kind of bro-ish swagger that made me want to clip the grin off his face, shoved the pistol in the front of his gym shorts. "Better go in there. You heard the man."

"Vie," Austin said.

I shook my head and stretched out a hand behind me. After a moment, Austin took it, and I tugged him toward the study. As I passed through the door, I shot a look back at Emmett and gave him the finger; for an instant, that sharp grin disappeared, and I saw calculation in his eyes.

Lawayne sat behind the desk again, yanked out the bottom-most drawer, and gestured to the chairs. Austin and I stayed in the doorway. As Lawayne pulled out file folders and strewed them across the floor, he said, "I bet you want to do something really nasty to me. Am I right?"

"What are you doing with Emmett?"

"He works for me." Lawayne paused, fingered open a folder, and then scowled and threw it down. Meeting my eyes, he said, "I offered you a job. A couple of times, if I recall correctly. You weren't smart enough to take me up on it. Your buddy was."

"What are you doing with Emmett?"

Lawayne smiled. He dropped the folders back into the drawer, slung his heels up onto the desk, and leaned back. Hands laced behind his head, he studied me. "Jesus, kid. You beat them once. They came after you hard, with everything they had, and you handed them their asses. But you know what your mistake was?"

"Not handing over that Glock to the sheriff."

"Your mistake was not working with me. If you'd told me everything, if you'd started at the beginning, everything that happened with Tony and with that kid Luke, if you'd told me what was going on—" He broke off with a laugh that sounded genuine. "Jesus fuck, kid, the kind of stuff that's been going on: mind control and ghosts and psychics. If you'd even told me some of it, I would have made you the richest kid this side of the Mississippi, and I would have had your back against those crazies. But you didn't want anything to do with me, and a guy's got to make a living."

Austin grabbed my arm. "We're leaving. And if you try—"

Emmett appeared in the door, the pistol dragging down the waistband of his gym shorts, and his arm curling around a skank-skinny girl with dark roots. I recognized Krystal Giblin from the photographs; I recognized the bad dye job, the way the cocaine made her ribs show through her shirt, the way she fit under Emmett's fucking arm. Now, from a closer distance, I could see a mountain range of hickeys running along Emmett's collarbone and up his neck. There were a lot of things pissing me off right then, but the biggest one was that Emmett was just such a fucking slut.

"You want to know what Emmett's helping me with?" Lawayne stood, and the office chair skittered back on casters, the noise shrill and jolting me in my seat. "Well, you know what? This kid is pretty smart. And he's been looking into a few things for me." Another of those buddy-next-door laughs spilled out. "He's been my little research assistant. And it's time to see if his research has paid off."

I shook my head. I turned to leave, only now Emmett had the gun trained on me again.

Lawayne pulled a folding knife from his pocket. Opening the blade, he circled behind the chairs. I wanted to move, but Emmett had the pistol nuzzled under my ribs before I could take a step. I froze and watched as Lawayne moved to stand behind Austin. His fingers threaded through Austin's preppy cut, jerked his head back, and laid the blade against his throat.

"Now," Lawayne said. "Emmett told me you're getting better with your magic powers. I bet you could get inside my head and scramble me pretty good. But here's the thing: I bet you'll have a hard time messing with my head if Emmett puts a bullet in you. He's still a kid; he's tough, but I'm not sure if he's hard. Not yet. So maybe he wouldn't put you down. But he'll put a bullet in your leg. And something like that, something that hurts like a real bitch, I bet that pulls you right out of my head. And then I'll cut your boyfriend's throat. So you should think really carefully about what you do next."

The electric lights blurred and bent as I blinked, trying to control my breathing. Emmett would shoot me. He would; I could see it in his face, I could see it in that nightmare, funhouse drop in his eyes, that darkness, the void where for the last year I had found my footing. Emmett might not kill me, but he would shoot me. That was the truth. And that would definitely be enough of a distraction for Lawayne to slice open an artery, and Austin would bleed to death. My heart wasn't even beating anymore; it thumped, hard and heavy, like a stone rolling downhill.

"Be smart," Lawayne said. "Walk over there and take off your jacket and shirt. Tell your boyfriend to sit like a good boy."

My hands froze at my sides. My fingers burned like I was holding ice. Like frostbite had taken them to the first knuckle.

"Leave him alone." That was Austin, his voice so thick the words barely came out.

"Walk over there, face the wall, and lean up against it, or I'm going to take off your boyfriend's ear. Whichever one I like."

"Fuck him, Vie, fuck—" Austin cried out, and I jerked in response; my vision went to him long enough to see the cut at the top of his ear where Lawayne had set the blade.

"I'm going. Don't hurt him, all right?" My first step, I bumped into the chair, and it scraped along the floor and fell over. The wood clattering was the only sound in the whole universe. Another staggering step, and then another, and I worked my way to the spot against the wall that Lawayne had indicated. As I went, I wormed out of the jacket, and then I stripped off my shirt and let it fall. I leaned against the wall, my forehead and the inside of my arms the only thing touching the paneling. It was real wood. It had a slight waxiness to it, and lemon rubbed off from the polish.

Face to the wall, I could only trust my hearing to tell me what was going on. Austin's erratic breathing meant he was still just as freaked out as I was, and I could hear steps as Lawayne marched him to one of the chairs. Krystal hummed the jingle from an orange soft drink ad. Emmett—not a sound. He might as well have been dead. He was dead, as far as I was concerned. Dead to me. And he'd be literally, physically fucking dead as soon as I got a chance with him alone.

"Krystal," Lawayne said. "Take over for me."

Lawayne's first step toward me scuffed on the rug. His second step caught a warped board that creaked. I tried to slow my breathing. I forced air in and out. From inside the command center of my brain,

I struggled to relax my muscles. When he hit me, I wanted to be limp; I wanted to flow with the punch, to absorb as much of the force with my own movement and try to minimize the damage. I concentrated all my focus on those things: the tension in my core, in my legs, in my fingertips. Flow with the punch. But what if it wasn't a punch? What if it was a vacuum cleaner cord? What if it was the winking red eye of a cigarette? What if it was a knife?

His touch was hot and cold at the same time, and I jerked away from him and made the most goddamn embarrassing noise of my entire life. It was a whimper. Worse than a whimper. Because he had touched one of the scars. The first one. The very first. And all I could hear was the tune to "Happy Birthday."

"Get your fucking hand off—ah."

"It's fine, Aus. It's fine. Just—" The next shudder broke up my words, and I had to clench my jaw to keep from biting my tongue. "Just be quiet, all right?"

Lawayne's hand moved. There was a pause. No, that wasn't right. Not a pause. At the level of an animal, at the level of instinct, I recognized what it was: hesitation. He wasn't certain. And then he exhaled and settled his finger on the second scar, the watery triangle left by the tip of a hot iron, and my heart became a white hiss in my ears beating so fast I couldn't tell the pulses apart.

He knew some of it. He was guessing the rest. How? I'd only ever told Austin. How could Lawayne know so much?

His finger landed with more certainty on the third injury: the first time she used a cigarette. And on. And on. Sometimes he hesitated. A few he got wrong. Toward the end, they were so frequent and so close together that he might have been getting them right and I didn't know it; I'd lost track. Whatever hellscape my mom had laid out on my back, I'd gotten lost a long time before she'd finished. But Lawayne wasn't lost. He kept touching. And touching. And touching. And his touch was so hot that it might have been cold. Or so cold it was hot. I didn't know. I was shivering, and the seam in the wood panels dug into my forehead.

"Get the fuck off him, get the fuck off him, get the fuck off him right now, I'm going to fucking kill—"

Emmett spoke for the first time since I'd taken off my shirt, and I knew from the sound that he'd left the doorway. His voice came from the same direction as Austin's, and that meant Emmett had walked across the room, had stepped up to my boyfriend, and—what? Nuzzled the gun against his chest? I didn't know, but I could guess. And I could hear his words. "Shut the fuck up, cocksucker."

"This gets you off?" I said, trying to draw all their attention, trying to draw out Lawayne. The words sounded as shivery as I felt. "Touching a boy, that's what gets your rocks off? Fuck, if I'd known that, I would have let you blow me when I lived with my dad."

"Kid, you don't even want to know what gets me off." Lawayne's hands moved to my hips, his touch clinical, the nails fishing under the line of elastic. "Keep talking and you might find out."

"Not down there." Emmett's voice was hard and flat. "I told you, didn't I?"

"You did. But sometimes people miss things."

"This fucking faggot is so desperate for me to bone him that he's always getting naked around me. If he had anything down there—" A sneer came into Emmett's voice. "—anything I was interested in, I mean, I would have noticed. And I would have told you."

For the second time that night, Lawayne's hesitation filled the room. He shimmied the elastic down another inch, bunching the denim and exposing the top of my ass. His thumbs settled into the cleft like he wanted to keep going. Or like he wanted to rip me in half with his bare hands.

"Fuck, kid. Lots of guys would kill for an ass like that. Your boy Emmett sure would." Then he laughed, slapped me like he was telling me good game, and let the elastic slither back into place. From the way his voice changed, I could tell that he had turned away from me, facing Emmett as he said, "You were telling the truth."

"Why wouldn't I?"

"About all of it?"

"Of course."

"All right." Lawayne's excitement glimmered underneath his best efforts to keep his voice expressionless. "We have a deal."

"About time."

"What deal?" I asked. "What the hell did you do, Emmett?"

"I'm going to kill you," Austin said. His voice had taken on an eerie calm. "You know what this kind of shit does to him, Emmett. You know what you do to him. And you put this together. You did this to him, even though you knew. And I'm going to kill you for that."

"Not if I kill you first."

"What deal?" I said again. "Whatever the fuck you think Emmett's going to get you, you're wrong. He's a goddamn cheat and a liar." The air was too thin; my lungs burned and heaved no matter how much I sucked in. "If he'll do it with you, he'll do it to you."

Lawayne laughed. The sound was so startled and so honest that it had to be real, and that made it worse somehow. I wanted to sink into the wall; the grit scrubbed my forehead, my cheeks, my wrists, the soft flesh on the inside of my arms. Lemon stuffed up my nose. Then Lawayne's hand tangled in my long hair and jerked my head back.

"He'll do it to me, is that right? Damn, kid. You've got a perfectly nice guy right here, ready to get his ear cut off for you, and you've got your panties in a twist about Emmett fucking Bradley? I thought you had more brains than that."

"What's the deal? What's he offering you?" My mind flashed back to Sara's living room, to the white-out desperation in Shay's face, and I said, "Did you get involved with Cribbs and those kids—"

The movement was fast and hard, and I never had a chance to prepare myself. Lawayne yanked on my hair, drew my head back, and then drove my face into the wall. My nose bent. Blood sprayed across the paneled wood. I flailed, and Lawayne hammered me against the wall again, dropping his elbow across my neck and bracing me. His coffee breath tickled my ear.

"Now why'd you have to go and say something stupid like that."

I spat blood, and the crimson loogie slid down the wood paneling. "That's it? You're going to break my nose? That's all you've got?"

"Kid." His fingers tightened, and even though I was tall, I had to rise onto my toes as Lawayne hauled on my hair. "I really tried to like you. I've given you all sorts of chances. But you just don't make it easy, do you? Where are they?"

The shock of the question took me by surprise. Lawayne thought I knew. He thought I had something to do with it.

Casually, he smacked my head into the wall again. "So this is it: this is the last one, the last chance, the last time I make an exception, because I want to like you, kid, I really do. Where?"

"They're not with their dad, are they? They're not with Cribbs." I had to swallow; my mouth was all sparky and coppery, and someone was playing the radio loud, really loud, and it was a high-pitched noise like an emergency broadcast. "You were supposed to have them, but you lost them."

Lawayne drove me into the wall with another of those indifferent blows, just a guy doing a job he didn't find very interesting. Then, shaking out his grip on my hair, he let me go, and I slid down the wall faster than my own bloody loogie.

With his sneaker, Lawayne pushed me onto my side—nudged, really, the way another guy might have nudged his dog out of the way. And then his shoe came down on the back of my neck. A lot of the world had disappeared into the shrill whine of that radio. And part of me knew there wasn't a radio, and nobody was broadcasting an emergency. I couldn't worry about that, though, because I had to swallow again. The inside of my mouth was too slick; it was like a waterslide.

"—fucking knocked his brains out." That was Emmett.

"He's fine." That was Lawayne.

Long, slender fingers turned my face. The lights were still bending and flickering no matter how hard I squinted, and that radio was still shrieking in my ears.

"He's no good to us if he's in a coma."

"He's no good to us at all. Not like this. No. Shut the fuck up, Emmett. I'm handling this." Then someone began to dial back that godawful radio, and more of the world came into focus, and I recognized the change in Lawayne's voice as he spoke into his phone. "Bob, shut the fuck up and listen. I called you, all right, so shut up. I'm doing the talking."

Bob.

For a moment, the radio warbled back to full volume, and that emergency siren canceled out all thought. Bob. There were a lot of guys named Bob, but Lawayne wasn't calling a lot of guys. He was calling one guy. One Bob. One Bob in particular. Bob Eliot. My dad.

"Your baby boy's over here at the Bradley place. Uh huh. Uh huh. I'm not trying to jam you up, Bob, so shut it. I'm telling you your boy is over here and he knows something. And you know what? Uh huh. Uh huh. Yeah, he's got fucking rocks for brains. So I think it's time Daddy gets his house in order. Get over here, now, and take care of this. No. No. No, I don't want to hear your excuses. Well, why the hell did you drive all the way out there in the first place? Bob, the only reason I haven't shot off both your kneecaps is because you promised me you could make him heel. Well, he's barking like hell and I'm telling you to make him heel, and what are you giving me back? Just a bunch of bullshit, that's what."

The worst of that shrill whine faded from my ears. My vision cleared a little, and I found myself staring up into Emmett's dark, funhouse eyes. But right then, with the hard lines of his face softened in my fuzzy vision, they didn't make me think of that funhouse drop. Right then, with his long fingers curling along my jaw, he looked worried. And furious. And helpless. And he blinked once, and long lashes came up heavy and glistening.

From Lawayne's phone came the soft buzz of my dad's voice, and then Lawayne grunted. "Well, that's something. That's really something. They were sending him back to you anyway? Good old U. S. of A. Fine. That'll be fine. But I'm telling you, Bob, I want him on a leash. In a fucking kennel, if you have to. I mean that literally. Fine. Fine. Tomorrow, then."

With an abruptness that surprised me, Lawayne dropped the phone from his ear and disconnected the call. Tension tightened Emmett's fingers, and then he let my head drop and stood. As he rose, that trapdoor in his eyes opened again, and all I could see was the black space of a funhouse drop.

"They haven't decided what they want from him." It was the first thing Krystal had said, and her voice was deeper than I expected, almost husky.

Lawayne rolled his shoulders. "I know what they want."

"I'm going to take him—"

Lawayne spun on her, and Krystal recoiled, her hip bumping the desk. She didn't look afraid; she was too tough to be scared. But she was unsettled. Uncertain. Wary. The blade in her hand trembled centimeters from Austin's throat. My head was still thrumming from the blows, but I tried to focus on what I was seeing, on what it all meant. They were allies. But they didn't trust each other.

"You know." Lawayne punched a finger down onto the desk. "You know that's not how we're playing this."

"We've got him right here." Krystal hugged her skinny chest. "It's stupid to go on playing some game when we've got him right here."

"Get the fuck out of here. Emmett, you too. If you have to drag their sorry asses to the gate, do it, but get them out of here and then get the fuck lost for the night."

Krystal shook her head, exposing a network of dark roots, but she didn't argue. She stomped to the stairs, and her passage down echoed through the house. Emmett followed her to the landing and then stopped.

Stiffly, as though he had aged years over the last few minutes, Austin levered himself up out of the chair. One of his hands floated up toward the cut on his ear, but he stopped himself, and he shuffled over to me. By the time he reached me, I was on one knee, so Austin helped me dress and dragged my arm over his shoulder.

"Sorry," I croaked.

Austin just squeezed me around the waist and dragged me toward the landing.

Emmett watched us, fingering the gun at his waist, sneering. He jerked his thumb at the stairs, and so we went first. By the time we got to the ground floor, the worst of the fogginess in my head had burned off, and I was walking better. I tried to slide my arm free of Austin's shoulder, but he caught my wrist and tugged.

"Play it up," he whispered.

So I did. I let him support me all the way to the front door, underneath the massive chandelier, and I slumped against him while he juggled my weight and wrestled the heavy door open. Krystal paced at the other end of the foyer, chewing a nail, watching us. On the black wave of night came the crispness of freshly watered grass and, muted, the not-far-off dustiness of the high plains. Security lights on the front of the house arced across the grass, washing everything milky-white. The wind howled, plucking at the grass, stirring it, drawing it out and spinning it into threads.

As we walked, the night air cleared my head, and I noticed again how badly overgrown the yard had become. Weeds choked the split asphalt. Had Emmett's dad gone broke? The whole thing seemed like a joke. Why were they letting this place go to hell? I glanced back at Emmett, who stood ten yards back, hand curled around the pistol in his waistband.

At the gate, we stopped. I glanced back at Emmett, who said, "You can go out the same way you came in."

"He's hurt." Austin shifted my weight. "Jesus, Emmett, just open the gate."

"He's faking."

"Your boss," Austin laid pure disgust on the word, "just about smashed his face in."

"He's fine. You're not fooling me, tweaker."

"Open the goddamn gate."

Tugging on Austin's shirt, I shook my head. "Leave it. He's going to be a dick about this, so let's just go."

"I don't want you climbing—"

I tugged on his shirt again. Hard. "Leave it. Please?"

Austin's mouth snapped shut. Lacing his fingers together, he held out his hands, and I settled my foot into the stirrup. The weeds were blowing again, snaking against my leg, the thorny creepers catching in the denim and tugging. With a grunt, Austin propelled me up and braced my foot with his arm fully extended. I caught the top of the gate, the metal cold under my bare hands, my head just clearing the top bar.

Ahead of me, at the end of the drive, Kaden sat inside the Camaro, its halogen lights cutting out a strange shape on the shoulder. Inside, Kaden was nothing more than a silhouette.

Then Austin grabbed my leg and pulled. I slipped, banged my chin, and tasted fresh blood. "What the hell—"

I looked down and choked. It wasn't Austin pulling on me. It was those damn creepers. They wound around my leg, thorns nicking the fabric of my jeans, looping tighter and tighter. I kicked. As if by reflex, the creeper closed around my ankle like a noose, and its thorns drilled through denim and into my flesh. Then, with a ferocious jerk, the creeper hauled me back toward the ground.

I barely caught myself on the top of the gate. Pain ripped up through my leg—in part from the force of the pull, and in part from the thorns digging deeper. I let out a grunt. Panic swam up at me, and I forced it away. I had to think. Christ, I had to think and not freak the fuck out because a plant was trying to rip off my leg.

On Emmett's porch, illuminated by the glow from inside the house, stood Krystal: shoulders hunched, arms around her cadaverous ribcage, dollar-store blond hair spilling over her face. Ten yards behind me, Emmett held the pistol in his hand now, and he was spinning in a circle, trying to figure out what was going on.

Choking noises made me look down. Creepers and brambles bound Austin to the fence. His raised arm kept the creepers from tightening around his neck and cutting off his air, but blood coated his hands, running freely from his wrists where a knot of thorns held him fast. His face was red as he twisted against the fibrous noose pulling tight. Looking up at me, he rasped, "Vie, I can't breathe."

"Let him go," I shouted. "Let him go, you fucking cunt, or I'll kill you. I swear to God, I'll—"

A thick vine lashed out of the darkness, wrapping around my wrist binding me to the gate. A second vine came almost as quickly, wrapping around my forehead, and the iron bars clanged as my head crashed between two bars. I was able to turn my head slightly toward the porch. The taste of rust filled my mouth, mixed with something else, something like the rot of old mulch, of grass clippings heated by the sun.

"I'll kill you, you fucking cunt, I'll kill—"

Below me, Austin arched his back. His head rang the bars like some horrible bell, and his toes—those boots, the worn, scuffed, beeswax-polished boots—dug into the turf. He twisted his face toward his armpit, trying to relieve the pressure on his throat and draw some air into his lungs. His features were puffed with trapped blood and the strain of his panicked struggles. He didn't even look like Austin, not really, and at the same time he did, and he had kissed me, and he had tweaked the skin on the back of my arm, and he had laughed and said, *I know you love me, I love you too.*

"I'm not letting you walk away," Krystal called. "They'd be furious. They'd . . . they'd punish me."

My eyes cut toward Krystal. I could barely see her; she was just a mop of cheap blond hair framed by house lights. It didn't matter, though. She could have been in China. She could have been on the moon, and I would have reached out the same way I did right then, and I would have touched her just as easily. If Emmett wanted to shoot me to stop me, he could goddamn well shoot me. My third eye flashed open, and I stepped into her mind.

A faint resistance met me, and then I was past it, inside the waiting darkness. And I knew, this time, what I wanted to do. I found the right memory: dusty carpet, the scratch of wool on my cheeks, the thin line of light under the door, footsteps, her shadow, pee blotching the cotton between my legs with the warmth of an infection. The helplessness. The terror. I couldn't force the memory on her, but I could call up its simulacrum, and I felt it splash as it broke the surface of that perfect darkness inside her mind. I caught glimpses of it. Robbie—whoever the hell Robbie was—holding her arms, and Cage shouting, "Do it, just do it, oh my God," and dissolving into laughter, and then the brush of furry legs on my face, and it was going to eat me, it was going to eat me . . .

Sensory detail from my body crashed over me: the pain in my arms and in the ring of puncture wounds on my ankle, Austin's wheezing, Emmett shouting something—whatever it was, I couldn't understand—and then screams. Horrified screams. Helpless screams.

From the porch, Krystal plunged out into the night, running and twisting and tearing at her face. I'd never heard anyone scream like that, not in my entire life, and something inside me shriveled at the sound. I'd done that to her. I'd given her back her worst terror, and Christ, what kind of monster did that?

The vines flexed, and something popped in my elbow, and the thorns ripped furrows along my flesh. Austin's wheezing grew even more labored; his eyes bulged, and his body shook like he was having some kind of seizure. The noose around his neck and arm pulled him up, and his heels left the ground. Tighter. Jesus fucking Christ, it was getting tighter.

In her panic, she was going to kill us. Just like she would have anyway. I'd tried, and I'd failed, and we were going to die. Fuck, who cared about we? Austin was going to die. Austin. The toes of his boots, still burnished with beeswax, kicking feebly in the air. This boy had transformed from the biggest asshole in town into someone I couldn't get out of my head, let alone out of my heart. And he was going to die because I couldn't keep him safe.

Weeds grew out of the driveway at hyper speed, like an old movie sped up for special effect. They snapped out at Emmett, and he stumbled, shouting. He came around in a full circle, and he leveled the pistol and squeezed off a shot. The clap of gunfire muted the hissing of the vines and creepers for a moment. On the road, tires squealed. Kaden bailing. Kaden jetting out of here like a coward. Over my left shoulder, in those milky-white panels of light on the grass, I saw Krystal had dropped to her knees. Her nails ripped bloody furrows down her face. Reflected light cast a sheen over her; the blood wasn't red. It was silver. And the sheen made it hard to see details, but I was pretty sure she'd clawed out one of her eyes.

Another squeal of rubber on asphalt, and this time, the sound was closer. Maybe Kaden hadn't left. Maybe he was turning around, maybe he was coming closer, coming to help. I squirmed against the plants chaining me to the gate, breathing short, shallow breaths against the rush of pain as they pressed my forehead tighter against the crossbar. I looked up through the bars toward the highway.

The Camaro, its yellow paint shining in the reflected glow of the headlights, was still parallel to the house, sitting at the edge of the road. But now it was the shoulder closest to the house. And then I spotted Kaden: in the middle of the goddamn highway, his chin on his chest, his palms out like the Da Vinci sketch I'd seen in my history textbook.

The Camaro rattled.

Austin spasmed again; the bar rang out as his head struck again, and the sounds he had been making stopped mid-whimper.

On the Camaro, metal shrieked, and glass cracked and pebbled the shoulder.

Austin's boots no longer drummed on the fence. Now there was only an ominous silence below me.

Kaden grunted, and even from the road it reached me clearly. It was a familiar sound. Austin made it all the time. That sound came up to me from the basement with the clang of weights falling, with the smell of rust, with his sweat. It was the sound of somebody lifting something really, really heavy.

Then the Camaro flew. It wasn't this long, graceful blur like somebody pitching pro. This wasn't Temple Mae's level of work; this was amateur. Not even bush league. Close to four thousand pounds of metal and leather and glass wobbled, spun, turned end over end, and looked like a five-year-old's first toss. Maybe a drunken five-year-old. Maybe a drunken five-year-old who needed glasses.

But it was moving. And hell, it was moving fast. And it got faster. And it was so surreal that I didn't even think about shouting a warning. All I could do was stare at the tumbling hunk of American autobody and think that Kaden had the ability to control metal, and instead of the fence, instead of the guns, instead of anything else he might have chosen, he'd picked up his own car and used it like a rock in a catapult. My boyfriend's best friend, the boy he was still head-over-heels crushing on, was an absolute, tremendous, fucking idiot.

The Camaro sheared through the fence to my left. The noise of torn metal and shattering glass swallowed everything else. After clearing the fence line, the Camaro thunked once into the lawn, tearing up a stretch of grass at least thirty yards long, and then it flopped over, slid another ten yards on its roof, and came to a stop. One wheel was still spinning. Kaden let out a whoop, and I had to admit it was all very impressive.

Except for the fact that he'd missed Krystal.

The Camaro lay a good five paces from the girl, and she hadn't even shifted when all that steel and metal tumbled across the ground like hell's worst tumbleweed. The shock and noise, though, must have penetrated the fears terrorizing Krystal because her head came up. Her face was ruined. There was nothing poetic about that description; her face was no longer a face. It was skeins of raw flesh, and a limp balloon of one eye, and the gleam of teeth where she had clawed open the cavity of her mouth.

But she was still alive. She was still moving. And when her gaze snapped past the tangled metal of the fence and toward the road, I realized she was still dangerous. Kaden let out a surprised shout. Glancing back, I saw him falling in a tangle of rangegrass.

The stretch of fence where I was pinned drooped slowly toward the ground, its structural supports demolished by the Camaro's passage. With the loss of tension, the section under us separated from the rest and sagged inward under our combined weight, the base still anchored in the ground. My feet caught the pavement and I stepped backward awkwardly, supporting the length of fence across my chest. The creepers loosened enough for me to duck my head out from under their hold. With my feet on the ground and my head free, I had more leverage. Krystal's attention was still fixed on Kaden, and I took advantage of the distraction to rip free of the bramble shackling my ankle. I braced myself against the fence and shoved, pulled, and tore myself free of the remaining vines.

Austin lay in front of me, senseless; he had slipped to the ground when the fence fell. I scrambled toward him; he was trapped under the fence, the creepers holding fast around his neck and arm, and he was lying so still. As big as my wrists, the thick vines were impossible to shift or pull free. I was running out of time before Krystal turned her focus back on us.

I spotted Emmett lying on the driveway, barely twenty feet away. Weeds wrapped him in a straitjacket, the pistol a dull polymer block just a few feet from his hand. I ignored it. I had to ignore it because it wouldn't do shit to the vines. Instead, I rushed over to Emmett and gathered handfuls of the weeds and yanked on them. They came away in fat clumps—maybe Krystal had gone easier on him because of their relationship—but they were thick, and it was taking so damn long. I ripped, I ripped, and I ripped, and the smell of chlorophyll and rot and dirt made me choke. Then I saw a swatch of gray fabric. I dropped onto my knees, plunged my hand into the pocket of Emmett's gym shorts, and prayed. He was such a cocky bastard. He was just so damn cocky. And he'd been right when he came into my room, he'd been right that I was a chickenshit. Please, God, I thought. Please let Emmett be as cocky as I think he is. Please let him be the kind to carry around a trophy when he's really proud of himself. Please. Please, God, please let him be just as cocky as he always had been.

My fingers closed over the folded compact knife. The same knife Emmett had brought to my house. To teach me a lesson.

On the way back to Austin, my knee buckled, and I fell onto the edge of the fence, bounced, and scrambled to keep my footing. I tried to move faster; Krystal was coming back. I just knew it.

The vine snaked around his neck and arm, thick and rubbery near his face. The knife skated along the surface at first, peeling away a thin layer that oozed clear, wet sap. I gathered a loop farther from his head. This time, I sawed with the blade, forcing the edge deep into the vine as I used all my strength to keep tension on the loop. When the cut ran deep enough, I yanked, hard, to snap the vine. I peeled off the next coil, and then the next. As I peeled and cut, they fell thrashing and mindless and furious, still alive. Already the first one that I had cut was curling around the iron bars, moving up toward Austin again. I had to get him out of here.

Then the last loop around Austin's neck gave way, and I dragged him free. I caught him up against me, where he slumped, boneless. He was so still. And in the reflected glow of the security lights, he was so pale. So washed out. He was limp. He wasn't dead, though. Austin couldn't be dead.

Austin couldn't be dead.

A tendril of vine slid around my wrist, and I jerked backward, away from it. Someone was screaming. Not me. My screams were stitched to the inside of my throat. My screams couldn't get out. And not Austin, because Austin was—I crushed the thought. And not Emmett. I'd recognize his screams. So who?

Metal warped and bent and thrummed like someone running a mallet down a xylophone.

Kaden.

Kaden was screaming like he was being ripped limb from limb. That was a possibility. A very real one. The vines curling around ankles and wrists, tugging, tugging, fueled by Krystal's ability. I just needed to get a little farther. I just needed to get to the asphalt, and then I could run to the garage, get—I had to bite back a hysterical laugh—pruning shears, get gasoline and a match, get a goddamn weed whacker.

In my arms, Austin weighed more than I'd ever remembered. I'd held him in bed. I'd hugged him. Once, in the shower, I'd gotten him up against the wall, his feet clearing the floor, and his head had bonked the low, sloping ceiling. None of those times had he ever weighed this much. Especially not in the shower. That night, he hadn't weighed anything. Not for me. When his head bonked the ceiling, we'd laughed, and the water streamed off his face and ran onto mine, touched the corner of my mouth, tasted like him, and he'd squeezed my biceps and said maybe I should think about the circus. Be a strong man. And I'd bitten him on the collarbone to teach him about teasing.

Only I didn't feel strong tonight. When it mattered, I hadn't been strong enough, when it mattered—

Something caught my ankle.

I stumbled. My knee hit the asphalt hard, the pain running through me in a shock wave, and Austin slipped to the ground in front of me. I grabbed for him, tried to steady him, and then something latched on and hauled me backward. Another of those damn vines had caught me, and it tightened around my ankle until bone grated and popped. I let out a howl. Twisting around, I hacked at the vine around my ankle. Maybe it was anger. Maybe it was luck. This time, it parted in two blows, and I scrambled back. The rough abrasion of asphalt burned my palms. I had to get Austin out of here. Through the back maybe. In the pool. I wanted to laugh. Plants couldn't swim, could they? No. No, they damn well couldn't swim. But they didn't need to swim. I was willing to bet they could reach me from the shore. So the pool was out; I had to get out somehow, though. The garage, maybe. If one of the cars were still there. Maybe. Maybe. I flipped over onto hands and knees.

Then I saw Emmett and froze. Somehow he had wrestled free of the weeds, and now he knelt facing me with Austin sprawled on his back. As I watched in disbelief, Emmett rolled him roughly onto his side, struck him between the shoulder blades, and rolled him onto his back again. He bent low, his face over Austin's. What the hell was he doing?

"Get the fuck off him." I crawled across the broken asphalt, caught Emmett's shoulder, and tried to push him away from Austin. "Leave him the fuck alone."

Emmett's right hook was huge and sweeping and was so fucking telegraphed somebody probably could have read it all the way in England, but all I was thinking about was Austin, and by the time I realized what was happening, it was too late. His fist connected with my eye. The world went dusty white. My momentum pitched me forward, and the only thing that saved my chin from cracking on the driveway was the fact that I landed face first in Emmett's lap.

Emmett's fingers wove through my hair and shook my head once, gently. Then he shoved me away and scrambled back to Austin. Chips of broken driveway had tracked a line of road rash down the side of Emmett's face, and the blood and torn flesh made black and white motley. His mouth slashed a hard line across his face. His eyes were dark and furious and, I thought, afraid. But controlled. Sweat curled hair at his temple, and he was beautiful, really beautiful, and I was the only one—I knew this the way I knew my own heartbeat—who had ever seen this part of Emmett. He pressed two fingers gently against Austin's throat, paused there, and then leaned down to place his ear against Austin's mouth.

"Quit looking at me like you're having a fucking stroke and do something."

"What? Should I . . ." I made a helpless gesture at Austin's mouth. "Do you want me to—"

"I don't fucking need you to fucking kiss him. He's not fucking Sleeping Beauty."

"No, I wasn't—"

"Shut up, tweaker, and do something about Krystal."

From the street, Kaden gave a shriek that cut off abruptly. That wasn't good. That meant that our distraction might be over. It meant Kaden might be dead. It meant, in the next moment, Krystal might stop Emmett, and then Austin would be—

This time, something pulled on my leg so hard that I left the ground. I didn't fly far, maybe a yard, but when I came down, I hit so hard that the air left my lungs. Groaning—a breathless, empty noise—I flopped onto my side. Vines wrapped my ankles together, and they ran in a straight line back to Krystal.

She was on her feet now. Her left eye sagged and hung down over the eyelid, like a water balloon with a slow leak. Behind the mask of scratches, Krystal looked beyond pain, beyond fury, beyond sanity. There was nothing left that I recognized in her face except murder, and when I glimpsed her through my third eye, she wasn't even a whole person anymore: she was like two thunderheads clashing together, a kind of cloudlike, substanceless collision of madness. And then the vines dragged me toward her.

I had lost the knife at some point while carrying Austin, and I grabbed at the ground, trying to catch hold of anything to slow myself. Vines shot out of the darkness, twisting my arms behind my back, turning me onto my stomach so that my chin dug into the grass. Unable to move, I found myself staring back at the driveway, where Emmett still knelt over Austin. Then a coil of brambles snared Emmett around the neck and dragged him into blackness.

I was still watching. Waiting. Praying—not to any god in particular, but to whatever would listen. I didn't want the world. I didn't even want my own life. I just wanted to see him move. I just wanted a breath, a single breath. Kaden was gone; I had heard his death-cry. Emmett was gone; I had watched the brambles spool him back into the darkness. But not Austin. I couldn't lose Austin. No god would be that cruel—or, if one of them was, all of them couldn't be.

But Austin just lay there.

I came apart.

My inner eye flashed open. I stepped into the other side. Those things had happened before; I had done them before. But this—this was a different order of magnitude. It was like I'd been striking matches in a dark room, so impressed with the light I could create, and then the sun had come out. It was like I had walked around with my eyes closed for my whole life. It was like, for the first time, I had really woken up.

And it did feel like waking, the way I slid out of my body as though everything—Lawayne's hands on my back, the way he had counted out every horrible thing in my life; Emmett watching me with a smirk; Austin, his back arching, as light slowly left his eyes—had been a nightmare, and now I was awake.

Of course, that wasn't the truth. It had all happened. All of it. But standing on the other side, it all seemed to matter . . . less, somehow. Distant. Like it had happened years and years ago. Or like it had happened to someone else. And it was easy, so very easy, to brush aside the hurt of it all. It was easy to feel good, in a way I'd never felt good, not really, in my whole life.

It was easy, too, to turn back and look at Krystal. Her savaged face was still twisted in hatred. She studied my physical body as the vines dragged it across the lawn. She was thinking of all the ways she would take me apart: thorns and brambles and incredible force and saplings growing out of my eyes. I didn't have to step inside her head to see it; the thoughts were there on the surface, as easy to read as a picture book.

It was easy to see the threads that made up this side of reality. It was like turning over a piece of embroidery and spotting all the stitches. It was clearer than it ever had been for me. And it was easy, so easy, to see how Krystal was threaded together. It was easy to see the loose threads and the dropped stitches. I thought of what Mr. Big Empty had told me: a true psychic can touch both sides. He can pull things across.

And it was easy to pull.

At first, she didn't seem to notice. Maybe it was the fact that she was in so much pain already. Maybe it was her broken mind that hid the truth from her. Maybe she knew, but the horror of it didn't reach her face. But as I ripped the soul from her body, it came free in a series of stuttering pops, like seams giving in a pair of old jeans, and then, all at once, I dragged her across to the other side. The glowing, hypersaturated version of her—her spirit, her soul, whatever you wanted to call it—hovered for a moment, overlapping her physical body, doubling it like a mirage. It flaked away like ash in a high wind. And then it was gone.

Her body dropped. The vines flexed, quivered, and went still. Everything in the whole night went still.

And then, ahead of me, figures slipped from the shadows. Leo Lyden, the red-headed boy who had been buddying up with Emmett at school, came first. He was the one who had made a cow explode. After him came a rough-featured man, massively built, who had to be Kyle Stark-Taylor. He had knocked a prison down with an impossible earthquake. And then came the boy, his skin like copper in a forge, dark braids spilling over his shoulders, his eyes ringed with smoke. The Crow boy. He looked at me. He saw me. He pointed.

That was fine. Let him see. I smiled; it was so easy to smile. Why hadn't I smiled more before this? Why had it always seemed so hard? I thought about how easy it had been to rip out every stitch in Krystal's existence, how easy to pull her across to the other side. My smile spread until it hurt, and even that felt good. When you could do something like that, when you could unravel somebody like an old sweater, why wouldn't you smile? And when you could do it again and again and again—

The Crow boy said something. Leo and Kyle paused. Then, sharing a glance, they backed away.

The Crow boy took a step toward me. Something flickered at the edge of my vision, and I glanced to my right.

The Crow boy was there too.

And to my left.

Three of them.

By the time I looked back at the first one, he had crossed half the distance between us, and he carried a buck knife as long as his forearm. My grin tore the corners of my mouth. This was going to be so much fun. I settled in, ready to pull him apart—all three of him—as soon as he was close enough. I was going to enjoy him. I'd go slower this time. I'd coil each thread around my fingers, feeling the pulse of his heart wild and erratic, and I'd let myself have a taste, just a taste, of his terror. It would be sweet, it would be sweeter than anything in my whole life, but I'd only let myself taste. And a part of me, deep down, was screaming, but it didn't matter. I would twine the fiber of his existence around my hand and drink deep of his terror, drink until it filled me, drink until—

I was standing on the other side. That was the only explanation for how I survived, for how I managed to keep my sight. In this projection of my psyche, I watched as a lightning bolt struck from a clear night sky.

# Chapter | 13

Even without physical eyes to damage, I still lost sight for a moment. The flare from the lightning whited out everything. It didn't lift the hairs on my arms; at least, not on the other side. But behind the lightning, energy thrummed. Real energy, something more powerful than the lightning. A version of the same energy that had carried me here, into the other side. A version, but not the same. And that seemed important. It was like tasting two vanilla ice creams. They could be very, very similar. But they weren't the same. And that was important, that was—

Exhaustion hit me so hard and so suddenly that I never even had a chance at keeping myself on the other side. My physical body dragged me back, and the hypersaturated, hypertextured vision of the other side vanished.

Croaking, I gasped for air. My next breath was nitrogen and ozone, all the oxygen fried out of the world. I gasped again, and again, and then air, real air, rushed into my lungs, and I propped myself on my hands and threw up. My arms trembled. My fingers slipped along the cool grass. I had to fight to keep my head up. I had to fight to drag my knees up under me. And that was it, that was as far as I could go. I didn't have any more fight left.

Not until I remembered Austin. And then I managed to crawl. My eye throbbed from the punch Emmett had landed earlier, and it was already starting to swell. Squinting through the puffy folds of flesh, I tried to orient myself.

The lightning had ripped open a hole in the ground. Krystal was gone. No smoking, severed leg. No burnt-sole sneaker. Nothing. And I thought of how her spirit had flaked into ash and blown away. How much of her had been left for the lightning?

There was no sign, either, of the Crow boy. No sign of Kyle or Leo. My ears were ringing, I realized, but the sound was so high and so persistent that it had passed until now for background static. Dirt stained my knuckles, and small lumps of clay clung to the dusting of blond hair on my arms. When I crawled forward another pace, dust rolled between my shoulder blades and curved along my spine. So much fucking dirt. The lightning had blown a metric ton of it into the sky.

But the lightning hadn't knocked out the lights, and they still spilled their milky enamel along the lawn. I found the edge of the driveway and crawled. Grass tickled between my fingers. I couldn't think about that. I'd never look at grass the same way again. Not grass, not weeds, not creepers, not brambles.

When I got to the length of vine, dead and limp, I couldn't go any farther. Not for ten seconds. Maybe twenty. And then I made myself think of the time I had fallen off a horse and Austin had caught me, and the way his arms had felt around me, and the smell of his shirt and the way a patch of skin on his chest, visible at the collar, pebbled when he held me. I hadn't known, back then, what I knew now. And that was enough for me to force myself to slide one knee gingerly over the vine, to wait for it to lash around my wrist or ankle or throat. Nothing. It was dead. Krystal was dead. I had shredded her spirit, the same way I had shredded Mr. Big Empty. I had dragged her from one side to the other and left less than nothing of her spirit.

I gagged, but there was nothing left to bring up. I kept going.

Austin lay there, exactly as before. He looked so small and helpless. Maybe people looked somehow bigger because when they were alive, there was something filling them up: air, water, light, life. I touched his chin, tilted his head, and withdrew my hand. His head lolled back. Heavy. Dead weight.

"What the fuck are you doing?" Emmett stumbled out of the darkness. Weeds had scratched red tallies along his wrists, up his arms, in the hollow of his throat. The death of a thousand cuts. Fuck, it looked like it hurt. But his face still held the same luminous intensity that had transfixed me earlier. No matter what everyone else saw—the kids who laughed with him at lunch, the girls who fainted when he walked past, the boys who trailed in his steps trying to be like him—this was the real Emmett: hurt to the point of breaking, frightened to the edge of rational thought, and yet holding everything together through sheer force of will. And mine. Here, tonight, alone, only the two of us, he was mine. The way he was meant to be.

I crushed out that last string of thoughts as Emmett came closer. He dropped next to me, yelped as his twisted foot shifted, and elbowed me out of the way.

"He was breathing before, tweaker. Start the CPR checklist."

Shaking my head, I put up my hands. “I don’t know CPR. I never even had a class, I never even—”

“You’re so fucking useless. All those fucking muscles and you can’t do anything. Move.”

I scooted back, and Emmett took my place. Kneeling over Austin, he performed the same routine he had done before, setting two fingers to Austin’s neck and his ear against Austin’s mouth. I watched in a daze. All I could do was watch. In the background, ringing the edge of my mind, the pain was waiting. The physical pain, sure. The cuts and bruises from Krystal’s vines and weeds. The puffy eye Emmett had given me. Even the concussive aftereffects of the lightning bolt—it was all waiting, and in a minute, it would rush in and take me. But for that minute, all I could do was watch, my lips moving silently.

Or I thought they were moving silently until Emmett told me to shut up.

“Quit watching,” Emmett said. He didn’t look at me. “Skeev.”

But his split lip tugged at the corner.

I was about to say something back. I was about to ask what was going on—how he could hold a gun on me, how he could watch while Lawayne touched my back, how he could kneel here, now, and tend to Austin like all he’d ever wanted to do was help. But before I could pull the words together, movement caught my eye, and I looked up the length of the driveway.

Two figures were coming toward us, and it was easy to make out who they were because one of them was on fire. Mr. Spencer wore oxblood loafers, chinos cuffed to show bare ankles, and a paisley shirt with the sleeves rolled up. He probably could have passed for a guy walking off an ad shoot—Gucci, Armani, J. Crew—except for the fact that fire plumed and curtained out around him. His hair trailed embers, and the blond had vanished into a red like copper in a furnace.

At his side, in a t-shirt that said, *Conan, what is best in life?* and a pair of Chuck Taylors, came Ms. Meehan. She looked tinier than ever next to the enormous, flaming whirlwind that surrounded Mr. Spencer, but she didn’t seem troubled by the heat. As I watched, a line of blue static charge worked its way to the end of her short hair and arced out into the night. Nothing on her face changed; I wasn’t even sure she noticed.

Then Austin groaned faintly, and my eyes snapped back to him.

“Austin.” I didn’t remember shouldering past Emmett. One minute I was flat on my ass, watching everything fall to shit, and the next minute I was pressed up against Austin, drawing him into one arm, my other hand touching his face, his chin, his jaw, his ears, his eyebrows. I had to scrub my arm over my eyes. He just had such fucking beautiful eyebrows. And then I had to scrub my eyes all over again.

"Vie?" he croaked.

"Yeah. Hey. Oh fuck, I'm here, Aus. I'm right here. Don't try to talk all right." I couldn't stop touching him. His lips. The hollow of his temples. The line of his neck. The vee of chest that showed above his collar. "You're fine, you're going to be fine, right? Just don't try to say anything. Just—just keep breathing, all right? We're going to get you to the hospital, and we're going to make sure you're fine, and all you have to do is keep breathing, all right?"

His head lolled, and he snuggled into the crook of my elbow, and then he paused. In that same horrible, broken voice, he whispered, "Why are you touching my eyebrows?"

"I don't know. Fuck me, I don't have any fucking idea." But I didn't stop, either.

I wasn't sure what made me look up, but I did, and my eyes went to Emmett. Some of the control had gone out of his face. Some of the fear. And there was something else there, something like a shadow swallowing all of him except those dark eyes. And they weren't funhouse eyes. They weren't darkness. They weren't that empty void where I didn't know up from down. They weren't empty at all, in fact. They held one thing reflected in the firelight that Mr. Spencer threw off. One thing that filled them up completely. Me.

And that scared me so bad that I looked down at Austin again, and I was sure, a moment later, that it had been my imagination, or a trick of the light, or anything but what, for a moment, I thought it had been.

"Where'd they go?" Mr. Spencer's voice reached me at the same time as the heat he was throwing off. Red and orange light streamed across the asphalt, brighter and brighter, until he stood a few feet away, and I had to put my free arm over my eyes. Even then, the heat was so intense that my skin prickled like the start of a sunburn. "Kaden called us from the car. Where are they?"

"I don't know." I jerked a thumb where I'd last seen them. "Everything went white for a while. When I could see again, they were gone." I swallowed. "Krystal's dead. The Crow boy, too. That kid, I mean. He was standing—"

"That one isn't dead." Ms. Meehan's voice was crisp, dry, and disappointed.

"I'll check." Mr. Spencer jogged toward the edge of Emmett's property. I could see, now, where a chunk of fencing had been ripped away. In the light cast by Mr. Spencer's fire, the cement at the base of each post was visible. Someone—Kyle, I guessed—had ripped out an entire section of the fence. Alone. And he'd pulled it out of the ground like me pinching out a staple, all the way down to the cement foundation. I shivered.

Mr. Spencer followed the property line. His feet burned black tracks into the ground, and fire dripped off him, sizzling and leaving pinprick holes in the grass. It was like watching someone who had been doused with jellied gasoline and set on fire decide to jog a mile. Then he disappeared around the side of Emmett's house, and all I could track was the bubble of orange light bobbing on the other side of the windows.

Sharrika Meehan walked a tight square around the three of us. When Emmett tried to stand, she settled one hand on his shoulder. He sank down again, and she paced the square again, and nobody said anything. I glanced at the gaping hole in Emmett's lawn. Nothing was left of Krystal. No shoes with smoke wisping off the soles. No fried corpse. Not even the lingering aroma of singed hair. The only smells were the woodsmoke heat of Mr. Spencer's fire and the lingering whiff of burnt electronics. Ozone, courtesy of my new science teacher.

"I need to leave." Emmett didn't look up. I studied him, waiting for a glance, a flick of his eyes, anything, but he didn't look at me. For the first time that night, he didn't look at me. He'd looked at me down the barrel of a gun. He'd looked at me while Lawayne pawed me, counting every scar out loud. He'd looked at me after he'd brought Austin back to me, and at the thought, my arms tightened reflexively around my boyfriend. He grunted, the sound cracked and warbling, but he nuzzled deeper into my arm. His breathing still sounded good, and that was because of Emmett. I had Austin here, now, in my arms, because of Emmett.

"I need to go," Emmett said again, his gaze shifting now to Ms. Meehan. "I can't be here. I've probably already fucked up everything."

"You're not going anywhere."

Ms. Meehan boxed us in again, and this time, her attention was on me. I met her eyes—dark, very large in her small, delicate face. No more electricity climbed her short, stiff hair, but she still carried herself like a woman with a rifle up against her shoulder. Only she didn't need a rifle. She was the rifle. She was a goddamn ballistic missile.

"What?" I finally said.

"I really need to get out of here," Emmett said.

Neither of us so much as glanced at Emmett. "You're cute," she said to me. "Your grades are shit, but you're cute, and I bet you've ridden that a long way. Grades are more important, though."

"What the fuck is this? An after-school special? Who the fuck cares about my grades?"

Austin's hand found my wrist and squeezed once. A warning.

"You're going to want good grades when you apply to college. You can't fix the semesters that are already closed, but you can still do well going forward. I pulled some of your testing. You're smart."

Smoothing Austin's hair, I bent over him and tried to ignore her.

"You're not a genius. You're not going to be valedictorian."

"If I go, right now, I'll still have time. But I've got to go."

"But you're smart. You're not going to get into Harvard. But you're smart enough to get in somewhere."

"I don't want to go to Harvard. Will you shut up? I'm trying to listen to his breathing."

"You're definitely not going to get into Harvard if you tell your teachers to shut up. You're not going to get into Wyoming State if you tell your teachers to shut up. You're going to be lucky if you get into community college if you tell your teachers to shut up."

"Lady," I said, my eyes finding hers. There was no emotion in them. Only a detached interest, like I was a beetle she'd trapped under a glass. "If you don't shut up right fucking now, you're going to find out exactly how I feel about my teachers."

A static charge hummed in the air, and the hair on my arms lifted. Austin twitched and tried to stiffen. When he ran his hand up my arm, his touch sparked along my shirt.

"If you want to scare me," I said, surprised at how calm my voice was, surprised at how easily my arms curled around Austin, surprised at how ready I was—eager, even—to come apart the way I had earlier, to be fully on the other side, and to rip out every stitch of this woman's soul. "You're going to have to do better."

Sharrika Meehan stared at me. I stared back.

"I can get my car," Emmett said, and then his voice died, and he shrank into himself. So much, a distant part of my mind thought, for that beautiful, furious, defiant Emmett I had seen just a few minutes before. What had changed? But the voice was too small, and I was too angry, and the thought vanished in a heartbeat.

The squeak of sneakers of asphalt broke the tension. Mr. Spencer trotted to a stop next to Ms. Meehan.

"Everything ok?"

I bent over Austin again, my fingers teasing down his hair.

"What happened?"

Ms. Meehan didn't say anything, but her clothing rustled as she shifted her weight.

"I really need to go," Emmett said. "Mr. Spencer, you've got to let me go. I've got to get out of here before—"

"Before I remember," I said, my head coming up, "that you're a fucking traitor, that you drew a bead on me, that you would have shot me, that you—"

That you let him do that. That you let him touch me. That you let him count every scar, and you watched, and you knew what it would do to me. Austin was right about that. He was right about you, and damn you for making him right. You knew what he'd do to me, and you let it happen.

I shook off the thought, but it had come on too strongly and too clearly, and I'd lost the train of my words. In the back of my head, the bleak gleam of the table saw began to spin again. Emmett had arranged this. He had wanted it to happen. He had known what it would do to me. And he had watched. The blade spun faster. And faster. It burned white. It shone like water off a high cliff. It was the moon.

Then Austin's fingers found the cuff on my sleeve, and he slid his hand under the cloth, his grip soft and solid on my arm.

"I want somebody to walk me through what's going on," Mr. Spencer said. "Emmett, let's get inside—"

"No," Emmett and I said at the same time.

"Lawayne's still in there," I said.

"I've got to go. Right now. Mr. Spencer, can I just talk to you? Alone? One minute, that's all I'm asking."

"No. We're all going. Mr. Spencer, we're going to have to take Emmett with us, but we can't trust him. You'll have to watch him; Austin's pretty bad, and I need to get him to the hospital now."

"One minute. One minute, Mr. Spencer."

"No fucking way. Jim, get him on his fucking feet, and get him somewhere you can keep him. I'm taking Austin to the hospital right now. Kaden's got his car—shit." I shook my head, hearing Kaden's final scream again, watching the car tumble through the air like a sloppy pitch. "I'll have to borrow your car. When I know Austin's stable, I'll come back, and we can take Emmett somewhere else. Somewhere we can talk."

I leveled a look at Emmett, waiting for him to shrink, for those funhouse eyes to flit away, for the color to leach out of his cheeks. Instead, though, he squared his shoulders. His eyes came up as far as my chin; not my eyes, but close. And he was looking dangerously resolute again. And dangerously beautiful. And his eyes, if he looked up another inch, just another inch, would swallow me again.

"All right," Mr. Spencer said.

Ms. Meehan's head whipped toward him. "Jimmy, there's no way we're letting a kid—"

"He's not a kid. Not anymore. And I trust his judgment." Fishing his keys out of his pocket, he added, "Car's up at the road. Kaden's in the back. He's probably still moaning, but he'll be fine. They just need to clean him up."

"Kaden's alive?"

"He's alive. He's in pain." Mr. Spencer's voice went dry. "He'll tell you how horribly he's hurt, I'm sure, but I burned off the vines before they could do more than give him some bad abrasions."

He tossed the keys, and I caught them with a jangle. Getting my shoulder under Austin, I helped him sit up, and then to his feet. He rocked against me. He'd packed on all that muscle, and it made him really easy on the eyes, but it also made him a goddamn elephant. "Watch Emmett," I said. "Somewhere else. He's right; Lawayne's still here, and as soon as he thinks he's got a shot, he'll take it. Maybe literally."

"Sharrika's car is here too; I'll let you know where we take him. Yes, Sharrika, we're doing it this way. Tonight, at least, you've got to go with it."

"He's a kid."

Mr. Spencer just shook his head at her. "Go on. I'll make sure Emmett—"

"No."

Austin's word was so cracked that I barely understood it; with his head rocking on my shoulder, he spoke into my chest, mouthing against the flannel of my shirt.

"Aus, babe, you're hurt bad. Really bad. You need a hospital right now, and—"

Somehow, he brought up his head and met my eyes. Blood fissured the whites of his eyes; he looked like he'd just smoked the worst pot of his life. His face was still puffy from the trapped blood that was slowly draining away, and he trembled against me, his whole body vibrating like he was plugged in and set to low.

"No."

"No? That's crazy. You're going to the hospital. That's not even a question."

He hooked my collar with one finger. His hand shook with the effort, and the movement was sloppy, uncontrolled. His nail scraped a furrow down the hollow of my throat, the lacerated skin stinging at the touch of night air. This had happened before. This was the night in my room all over again. I thought I knew what was happening, and then the sting of Austin's nails on my chest, and he was going to say something now, something that flipped it all on its head. It made me so angry that I forgot, for a second, that Austin had pretty much died that night. It made me so angry that I wanted to push him away, let him fall, and walk. Just walk and be done with this. Done with him, his secrets, all of it. Done with feeling so absolutely shitty every time I turned around.

"No. Let Emmett go."

"What? Why? What are you talking about? You were in there, Aus. You saw him with that gun. You saw him . . ."

But Austin was shaking his head. He was shaking all over, trembling like a leaf in a gale, but he was shaking his head harder, denying me, refusing to give me what I was asking. He beckoned for Mr. Spencer, and when Mr. Spencer came over, he pressed his mouth to Mr. Spencer and whispered something.

Secrets.

My boyfriend was keeping secrets from me. Secrets about Emmett. And that sent thoughts cascading through me. The way Austin looked when I couldn't sleep, when he knew I couldn't sleep, when he wanted me to sleep with his arm over my chest and I couldn't, no matter how hard I tried, and I opened my eyes and he was still awake, waiting for me to sleep, his eyes telling me how tired he was of all my bullshit. And Gage, all the running around behind my back with that boy, that piece of theater trash that Gage had hooked up with. And the way Austin's toes had dug into the dirt, how his back arched, as I watched him die and couldn't help him.

The blade at the back of my head spun faster. A table saw blade was a blade that could cut through anything. Just press down, lightly, and a thousand micro-serrations would meet wood or flesh or bone. It would be spinning so fast that the cuts would be perfect and clean. For an instant, at the very moment of laceration, the cuts would even be dry, and my heart started beating faster, and my mouth went cottony. Dry at first, the flesh ripped away, the bone ground to dust, and then the blood would come. It would well up, the first drops coming slowly, redly, glistening and spreading and capping the stump. I worked my tongue in my mouth, trying to keep my anger, trying to keep my rage, trying to keep my pain. Anger and rage and pain broke under my fingertips like branches on a dead tree. Anger and rage and pain couldn't help me. They couldn't fill that black hole in my heart.

The blade was sharper and cleaner and so, so much easier. Because the blade, with its shining steel, was control. I could cut away everything I didn't like. I couldn't cut away a black hole; that was laughable. Impossible. But I could cut away everything around it. I could cut away everything until I got to the place where nothing hurt anymore. Ever again.

The other side.

The thought came with such clarity and force that for a moment, I didn't notice that Mr. Spencer was pulling Austin's arm across his shoulder, shifting his weight away from me.

"Hold on."

But Mr. Spencer turned his body into my path, blocking me, and he helped Austin take a step away from me.

The saw, white water, the moon so bright I couldn't see anything else.

"Hey, hold the fuck on."

"We're just going to talk." Mr. Spencer spoke like they were deciding which fly to tie on their lines, like they were trying to pick a spot up the river. Guy talk. Nothing but ordinary guy talk. But copper sparked and swirled in his hair. "Go wait with Kaden. Emmett and Austin and I are going to talk."

I knew what they were going to say. I could write the script for their little meeting myself. Inside me, the saw was spinning faster. They were going to talk about how I'd wrecked everything. They were going to talk about how I couldn't keep anyone safe. The moon was rising inside me now, so bright, so sharp, turning so fast. They were going to talk about how I was nothing but a worthless piece of shit, no good for anything if I couldn't keep them safe. They were going to laugh about it. Laugh about me, about all the times they put up with me, about all the times they'd seen me cry, about the scars on my back. They'd probably count them up. Austin could help them. They'd count them, and they'd laugh, and the moon was so bright inside my head, so huge that my skull was going to crack open and spill everything out. I knew none of it was true; I knew they'd never say any of that about me. But at the same time, in some weird way, I didn't know it, and the words were real, right on the edge of hearing, and the moon in my head was rotating so fast that it was music, it was the last sound, the sound when everything else would end—

"You're going to talk to that fucking traitor." I took a step forward. Then another. "You're going to listen to him."

"Austin—"

"Austin just about died. He needs to be in an ER. Right now. Whatever he thinks he knows, he's out of his damn head."

Some of the embers in Mr. Spencer's hair cooled. His forehead creased, and he darted a quick, questioning look at Austin.

"Get Emmett somewhere else. Hold him. I'll take care of Austin, and then I'll meet up with you, and I'll take care of Emmett too."

Mr. Spencer threw another look at Austin. Austin gave a weary shake of his head.

"Just wait with Kaden, Vie. You need a few minutes to calm down."

Shadows hid the corners of his mouth. Were they twitching? Was he laughing at me? In his voice, the tone, those words. He might as well have said, *You're a fucking lunatic.* He might as well have said, *You're one hysterical son of a bitch.*

"Calm down."

"Oh boy."

"You think I should calm down."

"Yeah. I think that's exactly what you need right now."

I spun on my heel. My ankles, bruised and swollen from being lassoed by Krystal's vines, throbbed in time with my pace. Asphalt and dry, dead weeds crunched underfoot. The sky looked very huge and very black, even with the clouds gone and the stars blinking back. Ozone still soured the air. When I climbed over the fallen fence, the bars chimed softly under my sneakers, and when I hit the asphalt on the other side, my heart moved up to my throat. But I kept walking.

Where the asphalt plateaued and met the highway, I stopped and looked back. The scene below me, moonlit, was surreal: an enormous hole blasted in the lawn, vines and weeds growing along every surface as though the place had been abandoned for decades, and a length of fencing ripped straight out of the ground. In contrast to all of that was the glass and wood and light of the house itself, pristine and untouched, every window yellow and opaque like candlelight.

At the garage, Emmett, Austin, Mr. Spencer, and Ms. Meehan clustered together. I stood and tried to ignore my heart hammering in my throat. Maybe the wind would carry their voices to me. Maybe I'd hear what I knew they were saying. I tried to slip into the other side, to project myself down there, but I was exhausted, and my inner eye wouldn't open.

Movement in the house, a shadow swooping past a window, caught my attention. Lawayne, I decided. He was the only other one in the house, and he was still there. Watching. Waiting. And his phone call came back to me.

You promised me you could make him heel.

I want him on a leash.

Tomorrow.

I shivered. The spring chill raised goosebumps on my arms; with my adrenaline dying, with exhaustion rolling in, I wanted a heavier jacket. Or a blanket. And a bed. Instead, I had to stand here like a kid with his nose in the corner and watch while my boyfriend kept secrets from me. While they all kept secrets from me.

They were still talking when I started toward Mr. Spencer's car. Out here, burnt rubber still laced the air, and skid marks tracked along the highway where Kaden had pushed the Camaro. The buffalo grass was long. Longer than it had been an hour ago when we arrived. The last, wavering tips were higher than my head, and they swallowed the horizon so that the sky was just a flat, empty pane above me. The buffalo grass hissed, and it made me think of Krystal, and I forced myself not to walk any faster. I didn't need to walk any faster because Krystal would never hurt anyone again.

Mr. Spencer's blue Chevy Impala was parked on the shoulder, a ring of burned weeds marking the perimeter. The ash stirred when I stepped through it, licking the sides of my sneakers, curling up against my jeans. Inside the car, the dome light caught Kaden in a golden bubble. When he saw me, he flinched, and the Impala vibrated like a strummed chord. Then he must have recognized me because he grinned, that 100% sunshine, bullshit grin that he always wore, and the Impala went quiet. A long abrasion marked one side of his face, and the grin tugged at it, but Kaden otherwise looked all right. He practically tumbled out of the car to get to me. On the passenger seat was my backpack.

"Oh my God. Oh my God. Vie. Are you all right?"

I nodded.

"Where's Austin?"

"Back there. With Emmett."

And why in the fuck had I said it like that?

Kaden's eyes grew huge. "Did you see that, man? Did you see that girl? With the plants?"

"Did I see her?"

"I almost shit myself. Honest to God, I almost did. And then I thought about you guys down there, and I got mad, Vie. I did. I threw a car. I threw my car." The last words got higher and higher, helium-pitched, with his lingering shock. "It exploded."

"Yeah. That was awesome. Hey, Kaden, Mr. Spencer needs you down at the house."

"The Camaro, oh Christ. I threw a motherf-ing Camaro. My car, man. My parents are going to kill me."

"Only if they know you did it. If that's the case, I think your parents are going to be more worried that you can psychically move metal, Kaden. The car's probably going to be second. They need you down at the house." An idea flashed. "Austin wants you to help with something."

"Shit, yeah. He's all right, yeah? I mean, it was bad. The fence. Those creepy snake vines. He wants me to go down there? Yeah, I'll go." But he stayed. And I noticed that half of one of the cardigan's sleeves was gone, along with half of the bumper sticker, which now read only *Free Love*. And it made me think about how Austin looked at him, how Austin would look at that fucking sticker, and that made me think about how the cartilage in Kaden's nose would crumple under my knuckles. I pictured it in slow motion. "Hey," Kaden said. "What about you?"

I shook off the very pretty picture. "What?"

"Austin was hurt pretty bad. Why are you up here?"

Another flash. Like lightning. And this one burned like lightning, too. It hit so hard, so true, that it burned me out of my fucking socks. "He was worried about me. Lawayne's still in the house, and Austin wanted me away from that son of a bitch."

It must have only been an instant, but it felt like Kaden looked at me for a lot longer, like he could hear the lie, could hear the truth underneath it, and like he felt sorry for me.

"Yeah, man. Right. I'll get down there. If that piece of shit has a gun, he's going to wish he had plastic bullets."

"Don't give him any ideas."

With a jaunty thumbs-up, Kaden jogged up the highway. I waited until I heard his steps turn onto the asphalt drive, and then I started Mr. Spencer's car and drove away.

# Chapter | 14

Driving through the emptiness of Wyoming, at night, with the stars muted to the color of dead cinders, wasn't the exact same as driving through a black hole. Not exactly. But black holes were on my mind. There was one of them inside me, gobbling up every spark of happiness that came my way. And when you were fucked up like that, seriously fucked up like that, everything looked different. A guy with a hammer sees a hell of a lot of nails. I saw a lot of black holes, and I was in one right then, space and matter and time compressed around me into the white dot of headlights that traced a path ahead. Once, a tumbleweed spun through the light, its skeletal branches throwing a huge shadow across my face. And then it was gone. Just me. The hum of the tires. Darkness compacting around me, crushing me, until my chest threatened to cave in.

They were safer without me. That was a fact. Their lives were easier without me. That was a fact. They were happier without me. My eyes stung so badly that I couldn't even see the ghost-patch of road ahead of me. I hammered on the wheel with the heel of my hand.

"Fuck, fuck, fuck, fuck, fuck!"

I drove the rest of the way in silence, trying to hold the wheel steady.

On 97, the state highway that ran north through Vehpese, an ocean of broken asphalt reflected the blink-blink-blink of fluorescents spelling out a single word: Slippers. The strip club occupied one end of the lot, a sprawling concrete structure with blacked-out glass doors at the front. At the other end stood a row of apartments. Between, rusted out Fords and Chevys and a few foreign models—shunted off to one side, their drivers obviously ashamed to be driving them—filled the lot. A pair of guys in Wranglers and puffy down jackets stood near the turn-in, while a third man peed into a drainage ditch. I turned hard, cutting close to the men. The two in Wranglers swore at me; the third guy toppled face-first into the ditch.

At the end of the apartments, I swung Mr. Spencer's car into a space and killed the engine. The headlights picked out the plate on the car ahead of me. Magnified by the bumper, the light was suddenly too bright, and I closed my eyes and fumbled on the side of the steering column until they were off.

I kept my eyes closed. This was it: a black hole. Not the center of it, not yet, but I was already in the funnel. I couldn't believe I was back here. I couldn't believe that I'd gotten away—I'd escaped by some miracle, by Sara's intervention, by the grace of God. And now I was back. I had one thing to take care of, one final thing, and then I'd leave. I'd take Mr. Spencer's car until I had to abandon it; he'd get it back after a few days. I'd hitch. I'd go anywhere.

Shouldering open the door, I stepped out into the April night. It was colder here than it had been near Emmett's house; I didn't know if that was too much imagination or if it was just the reality of micro-weather patterns. Above the asphalt the night air stirred eddies of mist, tumbling the clouds into the oversized tires on the F-150s around me, and then the mist would dissolve until another drift of air carried more across the lot. The air smelled wet: the smell of water meeting dust, of water splashing into oil, of water tracking through rust.

When I turned toward the apartments, the wind snapped tight a line of distant barbed wire. I had stood there, at the beginning of autumn, and leaned against the wire until my weight drove the barbs into the tender flesh of my belly. I had stood there and run the wheel on a lighter and held the flame against my arm. My finger found that spot now, blindly stroking the shiny length of scar. Why had I stayed? Why had I cut myself, burned myself, walked myself all the way to the bridge over the Bighorn River and jumped? Why hadn't I just left?

I started walking. My sneakers squeaked on the wet asphalt, and when I splashed through a puddle, the smell of motor oil came up stronger than ever. Rainbows rippled across the pooled water in the fluorescent glow. Why hadn't I left? Because there was something fundamentally, unfixably fucked up inside me: the fact that I couldn't be happy, hadn't managed to be happy, even when everything was going right for me. Call it psychosis. Call it borderline personality disorder. Call it a black hole at the back of my head.

Stepping up onto the cement walk that ran in front of the apartments, I paused. I had met two little kids here. I thought they'd just needed someone to look out for them. Now, I wasn't so sure. Maybe they'd just wanted to look out for me. And they were gone. Shay had asked me to find them; Shay had believed I could find them.

But Austin was right: I was just a kid. I couldn't even keep the boy I loved safe. How was I supposed to rescue two kids who had vanished?

When I reached for the doorknob on the last apartment, I froze. Lawayne's words butterflied inside my head. On a leash. In a kennel. Tomorrow. A couple of days ago, my worst fears for tomorrow had been blowing out candles on a cake. Now, tomorrow was a cliff, and I was running right for it. Tomorrow. He wanted my dad to take care of me tomorrow.

Under my fingers, the brass was cold. I tightened my grip. On the phone, Dad had told Lawayne that he was out of town. And Lawayne had believed him probably because very few people lied to Lawayne. But Lawayne didn't know Bob Eliot the way I knew him. Lawayne hadn't heard that same pleading, whining, pathetic inflection behind a lifetime of excuses: where had he been for days; what had he been doing; where was all the money; why was he leaving? Lawayne hadn't heard the lies that came every time. But I had.

And I knew Bob Eliot wasn't out of town. I knew from the sound of his voice: he was stoned out of his mind. He was home.

For a fraction of a heartbeat, the brass resisted. Locked, part of my brain said. You can just go. You can leave the way you were planning on leaving and not have to do this. But then the knob twisted, and the latch pulled free, and the door lurched a quarter-inch away from the frame. I could leave. I could get in Mr. Spencer's car and drive. But I'd be running away, and I'd learned a few months ago that once you started running, you never stopped. I pushed open the door; the smell of wet carpet, Kraft Mac & Cheese, and burning plastic puffed out into the night air. I was going to end things with my dad. Tonight. And then I'd leave, but at least I wouldn't be running away.

My first step inside, though, made my stomach shrivel. I bumped the switch with my elbow, but the lights didn't click on. The darkness was deep; it swallowed the red flicker from the parking lot and gave nothing back. Now, mixed with the meth-pipe smell that was all too familiar, I noticed something else: shit. I bumped the light switch again, flipping it with my elbow. Still nothing.

A picture was unfolding in my mind: he had gotten high out of his mind. He had knocked over the lamp, broken the bulb, and now he was lying here in the dark. He had shat himself. That was all. It was a simple story. It was an easy story because it had been the same story for so many years.

But I tried the switches again, and still nothing, and a voice in the back of my head warned me that the ambient light from the parking lot was outlining me, and I either needed to close the door or run. That same voice told me to run hard, fast, now.

I shuffled another pace inside the apartment, caught the door, and shut it behind me. The red glow from the Slippers sign outlined the blinds, but otherwise, I stood in darkness. I took a step forward, bringing up one hand, groping the air. The layout of the place I knew just fine: the kitchenette with peeling linoleum on my right, the living room with the vinyl sofa on my left, Dad's room and the bathroom straight ahead. But I kept my hand up anyway. I was waiting for something to rush at me out of that darkness, and I wanted to grab it when it did.

Another step. The sound of the footfall was different this time, softer. I rocked on my heels, testing my footing, listening again for the subtle change. When I peeled back my toes, the sneaker came away from the carpet with a sticky, ripping sound, like a kid's sucker that's been allowed to dry on the carpet. I let my foot back down and tried again. It made the same stiff, tearing noise. A chill ran from my tailbone to my shoulder blades. Behind me, the blinds crinkled metallically, and I spun. I flailed once at the air, a wild, invisible punch, before I got myself under control.

Nothing. And then the blinds crinkled again, the thin metal chiming as it flexed, and something buzzed against the glow filtering between the slats. A fly. My next breath was ragged and wet. Just a damn fly.

I kept moving deeper into the apartment. My right foot made that long, ripping noise every time I pulled away from the carpet, and my mind kept filling in possibilities. Beer, maybe, that had mostly dried and I'd stepped right into it. Or sometimes when he was high, Dad got those Icees, the cherry ones that were bright red. Maybe he'd walked down to the C-Store, bought an Icee, and carried it back. And then he'd stumbled and dropped it. Or he'd balanced it on the back of the sofa and it had fallen. Or he'd just plain forgotten about it, knocked it over when he was stumbling around. My breath was coming faster and faster. I could picture the deep red liquid spreading, shifting, staining. Cherry red. Sure. That's all, just cherry red Icee.

Rip. My shoe came up again, and I didn't believe it was anything close to an Icee that I'd stepped in.

My fingers scraped something, and I froze. I moved my hand again. The noise was shrill. Nails on a chalkboard, and I had to bite the inside of my cheek. Under my touch, the door to Dad's room wasn't smooth; it was rough, textured. Thin strands of something that had dried. A few sticky spots. I thought of carving pumpkins with Gage, the one time I'd ever done it, and how we'd scraped the guts out onto newspaper, and the fibers had dried in thin strands just like what

I was feeling right then. Only it was April, not October. And nobody here had been carving a pumpkin and spreading its guts—oh Christ.

Stomach heaving, I jinked toward the bathroom. My shoulder forced the door open. The corner of the sink caught my hip. I staggered. My knee clipped the toilet, and the blow jostled some of the aches from where Krystal's vines had clutched at me; my whole leg turned to fire. I hit the towel rack, my fingers knotted in the worn cotton pile, and I grunted. I had to make some kind of noise, and a grunt was better than screaming my damn head off.

The pain helped, though, and took the crest off the nausea. As the throbbing in my leg dwindled, I took a step, and then another, and I found the light switch in the dark. Up. Down. Up. Down. Nothing. And that was bad. My nice little story about Dad shitting himself and breaking a lamp didn't hold up, not now. Because there wasn't a lamp in the bathroom. The bathroom had a tiny ceiling fixture with thick, frosted glass, and Dad couldn't have broken it without climbing on the tank and hammering on the damn thing for half an hour.

Up. Down. One last try. Still just darkness. An even deeper darkness if that was possible. Back here, without even the razor-slices of red fluorescents through the blinds, the darkness was total. The temptation to slip out of my body and into the other side was strong. Really strong. I would have done it just to escape the darkness, but I was still so tired that I couldn't even open my inner eye.

I took a step back toward Dad's room. My shoe gummed against the linoleum, and the ripping sound, and the cherry Icee that wasn't an Icee, and the dried pumpkin guts that weren't from a pumpkin—I froze. I needed to get out of here. One last showdown with my dad, that wasn't going to make any difference. One last effort to convince myself I wasn't a pussy by—what? Punching it out with my old man? Come on. That kind of shit, that didn't even fly in the movies anymore. So I'd just go. I'd make my way to the front door. I'd walk all the way around the sofa just so I didn't step in that spilled Icee again, and I'd walk out into the lot, the smell of water and dust and rust and engine oil, and I'd just drive. I could get to Salt Lake tonight, I thought. I wouldn't even be running, not really. I'd just be keeping people safe.

But I didn't circle around the sofa. And I didn't step out into the red wash of the Slippers sign. My fingers rasped along painted wood and found those same thin, dried strands on the door. The latch rattled, and for a moment I thought it was broken, and then I just realized I was shaking so badly that I wasn't even turning the damn knob. So I yanked on it, and the door sagged inward, and I kicked it the rest of the way. The burnt plastic smell was thicker here, stinging my nose. And the smell of unwashed clothes. And stale air. I raked my arm along the wall, and I caught the switch, and light supernovaed inside the room.

I had to blink and drop my head until my eyes adjusted, but I watched for shadows, movement, anything that would tell me someone was taking advantage of my momentary blindness. There was nothing. After a minute, I glanced up, bracing myself for the worst: blood and gore staining everything, a mutilated body, the signs of torture.

Nothing. The room looked a little emptier than usual—Dad had stripped the sheets, and the mattress showed the stains from bodies where the thin bedding had been oversaturated. The flat cube of pillow was yellow with oil from his hair. No blood. No gore. No severed limbs. My knees sagged, and I caught myself on the jamb.

But no clothes either; Dad usually had clothes strewn across the floor. His boots were gone. The last time I'd been here, he'd hung a Stetson on the window casing, and that had disappeared too. No dirty socks balled up under the bed. Some of the usual stuff was still there—green and black cans of Monster, Nutrigrain wrappers, the lid from a Western Family cottage cheese container. But that was just trash.

I checked the door. The sticky spots were red and small and had dots with little tails, like they'd struck the wood with force. But there were only a few of those. They could have come from a spilled Icee. They could have. I didn't know who I was trying to convince, but I was trying hard. And the dried strings I'd touched were just paint drips that had hardened in fine lines—invisible all those times I looked at the door, but revealing themselves when I ran my hand over the wood.

I went back to the front room. With the light behind me, my shadow loomed large on the wall, but I could see what I needed to see. The sofa. The dark red stain on the carpet, and the drying half-prints I had tracked away from it. That didn't look like spilled Icee no matter how much I tried to tell myself. It wasn't a very big spot, maybe the size of a silver dollar. You could bleed that much and be just fine. You might bleed that much and not even notice it. But I thought of those red dots with little tails on the door and I thought he'd noticed it, he'd sure as hell noticed it, someone had made sure he was noticing everything.

Taking a deep breath, I moved into the kitchen. The cabinets were open and empty. The table had its usual film of grease and crumbs, but the refrigerator was bare. So. He'd skipped town. Or he'd skipped out on the apartment. He couldn't make rent. Or his dealer had found him here and knocked him around, and Dad had decided it was smarter to get lost than to get whaled on. So he'd left. He'd forgotten to replace a few lights on the way out, or he'd taken some of the bulbs with him like a real cheapskate, and he'd left. And I'd freaked out because of the dark, just like a little kid. I blew out a breath. I felt jittery and jello-y all at the same time like I might shake myself into a puddle. I took a step toward the door. Good riddance.

But there, tucked to one side of the sofa where I hadn't been able to see it before, was a duffel. It lay on its side; the loose sole of Dad's New Balance flopped out. I squatted, pulled the bag open, and saw the shirts, the balled-up socks, a brown plastic bottle that had held my antibiotic prescription with two refills left. Dad had left. He had left. His dealer had shown up, knocked him around, and he'd left.

So why hadn't he taken the duffel?

A timeline unfolded inside my head: Lawayne called. Dad lied. Then he started packing. He hadn't been planning on running, otherwise he would have been prepared, and everything about this place looked like the packing had been done in haste. Maybe in a rush of terror. And then what?

That silver dollar of blood. Those red comets on the door. He hadn't been fast enough. In my mind, I replayed the fight with Krystal. Lawayne had stayed inside. He had, undoubtedly, called for backup because Kyle and Leo and the Crow boy had shown up. But so had Mr. Spencer and Ms. Meehan. And when Ms. Meehan blew the fuck out of Krystal, Kyle and Leo and the Crow boy pulled back. They weren't expecting resistance, not that level of it.

And they came here. They found Dad as he was trying to clear out.

Did I have proof? No. I couldn't even open my inner eye to scan for traces of violence. But I knew. In my gut, I knew that was what had happened. Because they wanted Dad to put the hurt on me. They wanted him right where they could get him because they knew a kid like me, a kid who's had a black hole blown open in the back of his head, that kind of kid just keeps letting Daddy hit him over and over again.

My hands were shaking again, so I hefted the bag. Paper rustled. And Bob Eliot wasn't a novelist, he wasn't a poet, he wasn't a playwright. He wasn't civic-minded enough to read the newspaper, and he wasn't literary-minded enough to pick up a book. I'd once heard him telling a neighbor about ripping pages from *War and Peace* when he'd been squatting in a place on the edge of Cheyenne, no toilet paper, and how bad he'd clogged the toilet. So why did he have paper in the bag?

I carried everything into the bedroom and dumped it on the bed: the floppy-tongued New Balance shoes, the balled-up socks, a baggie of weed—I slipped that into my pocket—a jerk-off mag called *Teacher Tits* from June 1997, dirty shirts, all of it. And at the bottom, their shape compressed by all the shit that had been piled on top so that they looked like a massive paper airplane, was a stack of documents. I smoothed them out, best I could, on the mattress.

It was my entire life. Copies of official stuff like my birth certificate, school records, vaccinations (a frosted donette had smushed into the stack at this point, smearing chocolate and yellow cake crumbs over the date for my MMR shot), and more serious things, more recent things, like the forms transferring my custody to Dad, the initial Child Protective Services report that Sara's phone call had instigated, the paperwork putting me in Sara's care, and the follow-up reports conducted by Ginny, my caseworker, as she continued to visit my dad. The last page was dated the day before, and I wiggled it free from the stack.

Before I could give it my full attention, though, I saw the newspaper. The dramatic part of me wanted to call it yellow, as though it was a hundred years old and crumbling at the edges. It wasn't. It wasn't yellow. It wasn't crumbling. But it had a picture of Mom, and the sight of her, even flattened into black-and-white print, made my heart stop.

I cleared everything off the newspaper. My thumbnail cut a half-moon in the edge of Mom's picture. She was beautiful. I looked like Dad; Mom always made a point of telling me that. It was just another thing like the vacuum cord. But looking at her from a distance, when she was younger—she couldn't have been more than twenty in the picture—made me realize I looked like her too. My cheekbones. My eyes. Maybe that was all, but it was so strange that my thumbnail punched right through the old paper.

And it was old. Older than I had first thought. Not yellow with age. Not a hundred years old. But old. I tore my eyes from that picture of Mom—twenty, and beautiful, and hurrying down marble steps with a scarf over her head, very much like an old Hollywood starlet might have run from the press—and found the date. 22 February 1951. Yeah, right. 1951. When Mom was, oh, negative thirty. She hadn't been born until 1981.

Maybe it was one of those novelty papers. Maybe it was one of those gags people give each other for their birthdays—here's what happened the day you were born, but a weird variation. Only it wasn't. The feel of the paper was a dead giveaway. It was authentic. So maybe it was just somebody that looked like Mom. Maybe Dad had stumbled across this paper when he was squatting—on the edge of Cheyenne, maybe, no toilet paper, clogged the damn toilet—and I shook my head and told myself to shut up. Because even if my brain didn't want to accept it, my heart knew. My gut knew. It was a sick, twisting cramp, but it was confirmation. Whatever I was seeing, it was real. And I had no idea what it meant.

The paper was called the New York *Volant*, and Dad only had a half sheet of it, torn raggedly along the vertical crease: two pages, one on each side. The front included the masthead, the date, a snappy column about etiquette, a squib lampooning a local politician's love of cigars, a three-day weather forecast, with each day occupying its own cartoon cell, and three main articles, each about a murder. The back had an ad for Viceroys cigarettes, with a caption by a dentist recommending Viceroys for whiter teeth.

I went back to the murder articles and made myself read slowly.

MURDERESS ESCAPES

WIDOW SLEEPS ON THE STREETS

Miss Lillian Bellis left the courthouse like Aeneas sailing from Troy: she might have escaped, but she left the whole world burning behind her. Miss Bellis didn't seem to have any concern for what she left behind. When asked about the case, Miss Bellis refused to comment. Miss Bellis came to the attention of good citizens everywhere after the brutal stabbing of Mr. Arturo Fabiniani in one of the nightclubs he owned. While today's case may have decided Miss Bellis's fate as it regards criminal law, her ill-gotten wealth, bequeathed to her in a will supposedly altered by Mr. Fabiniani hours before his death, remains in hazard. Mrs. Fabiniani has pledged to fight in the courts for her money, but in the meanwhile, she has taken to sleeping on a bench outside the courthouse. Experts agree that—Continued on A3.

Below, the second article.

INSIDE FABINIANI'S DUNGEON

The plebeian mob has raised hue and cry about Miss Lillian Bellis, who has since become an object of great interest. Equally of interest is Mr. Arturo Fabiniani, a nightclub owner and, according to some, a gangster. Interest in Miss Bellis is justified; this reporter has been hard-pressed to uncover anything beyond her arrival in the city two years previous, when she made print in the society pages by appearing on the arm of Bertie Rowan—much to the dismay of eligible young ladies along the Hudson. What is known about Miss Bellis is known everywhere: that she is an accomplished pianist; that she is an exceedingly great beauty; and that her animus toward the press, including any inquiries into her past, has no equal. Beyond those simple facts, the Book of Life is closed with regard to Miss Bellis, even after a flurry of attention following the charge of murder.

Regarding Mr. Fabiniani, however, a great deal has come to light, not the least of which is word of an infamous chamber kept hidden below Mr. Fabiniani's brownstone, a kind of Amontillado catacomb, rumored to be filled with the victims of Mr. Fabiniani's legendary temper—and equally legendary cruelty. Having recently managed an exclusive visit to Mr. Fabiniani's home, this reporter is eager to share his first-hand observations about the dungeon, and that word is not used lightly. Ladies and children should forego the following—Continued A3.

And the third article.

WITCHCRAFT IN THE MODERN WORLD

Following the sensationalist trial of Miss Lillian Bellis, in which a parade of chorus girls and waiters and the armed thugs of Mr. Arturo Fabiniani described pagan rituals, many of them so obscene that they cannot be printed, much to the dismay of the prurient among us, a kind of infection has spread through the city. At least a dozen people have approached the staff of the Volant asking to publicize their eyewitness accounts of lewdness, debauchery, and violence committed behind Mr. Fabiniani's walls. More surprising still are the tales these same people—by any other measure, hard-working, honest, industrious Christians—carry about demonic possession, incantatory powers, and secret workings. While such superstitions have often plagued the weak-minded, this latest surge of the supernatural seems directly tied to the Fabiniani scandal and the outrages that have been described from the witness stand. One might hope that ridiculous stories about women levitating above the Empire State Building, or men calling up spirits of fire to serve them, or strange faces interrupting a dream at night had vanished when Edison's invention burned away those Popish shadows—Continued A4.

The half-moon under my thumbnail had widened into a jagged gash, and I dragged my hand away from the paper, half-expecting the page to crumble or blow away. It didn't. A column of ink smudged the side of my hand: f a k l e s r m, an acrostic that didn't make any sense. Where the ink had come off the page, the letters had washed away almost to nothing.

In 1951, my mother hadn't been born. My mother had been born in 1981. And her name was Lily. Not Lillian. Lily Osprey, not Lillian Bellis. Lily Osprey Eliot.

I turned over the page, found the dentist grinning at me about his Viceroys—a pack was tucked into the pocket on the front of his smock, I noticed—and so I turned the page face-up again. I wanted to read the rest of the story. I needed to read the rest of it. I needed to know about Lillian Bellis and Arturo Fabiniani. I needed to know about dark rooms and dungeons and . . . and—a force ran through me, stronger than a shudder, and the paper rustled in my grip—and about vacuum cords and cigarettes and candles with pink frosting clumping at the base. I needed to know about women who could fly over the Empire State Building, about madness, about witchcraft in New York City in the winter of '51.

How had my dad gotten this? How much had he known? How much had he suspected? Mertrice Stroup-Ogle was a nasty woman and a viciously self-interested reporter, but she had told me a lot of useful things. And one of those things came back to me now: she had told me that my dad had come to her, asking about Belshazzar's Feast.

Now, more than ever, I needed to know why. So much had changed for me over the last year. I had learned about the dark forces behind what had happened in Vehpese over the last two hundred years: the disappearing children, the murders, the trafficking of drugs and people, more. But it wasn't just knowing the truth about the crimes in Mather County that had changed me. Everything at Belshazzar's Feast—everything involved in the Dust Feast, what the Lady and Urho called the game they were playing—had opened a new chapter in my life. Being psychic was one thing; knowing that there was an immortal old woman trying to bring back her dead husband, knowing that she'd been waiting for centuries to find the right psychic to help her do the job, that was another.

I studied the picture in the newspaper again. Mom, barely twenty. And she would have lived almost another fifty years before she had me. So that left two possibilities: this woman wasn't Mom, or she was. If she wasn't Mom, then she was doing one hell of a good impression. Maybe a grandmother? A great aunt? I snorted and wanted to flick my own ear for being stupid.

Ok. So. This was my mom. Almost seventy years ago, someone had snapped a picture of her in New York City.

What did that mean? I wasn't sure I wanted to know, but I knew it meant something bad; that twisting, cramping sensation in my gut, like I needed to go drop onto the toilet fast, made me grit my teeth.

It didn't matter. The thought floated up, so beautiful and so clear that I almost laughed. It was weird. It was really fucking weird, but it didn't matter. Mom was in my rearview mirror. I had so many other problems to worry about, so many real problems, right-now problems, that I didn't have the time or energy to worry about Mom. So maybe she had an ability. That wasn't starting to sound so weird.

I'd been running into people with abilities my whole life; I had an ability. My dad didn't, so my power must have come from my mom. She lived a long time. All right. Mystery solved. She lived a long time, and she was a royal bitch back then, just like she was today, mystery solved, case closed, show over.

I folded the broadsheet twice, and I moved to replace it in the stack, and then I folded it once more and stuffed it into my back pocket. I grabbed the other papers, skimmed off the birth certificate and the vaccination record with the donut crumbs and glaze pasted to it, and I shoved them in my back pocket too. I had everything I needed. Glancing the length of the apartment, at the silver-dollar spot of red on the carpet, at the door with its little red comets dragging their tails across the paint, I let out a breath. If Lawayne or the Lady or Urho wanted Dad, they could have him. I wasn't going to fight any battles for him. I took a step for the front door.

There was that one page, though. That one page at the bottom of the stack, that official-looking document from CPS with Ginny's name on it. The one dated yesterday.

My mind went back to the afternoon. Two phone calls. One from Austin. I thought about Ginny in my room, telling me she was sending me back to Dad. I thought of Sara saying, *The minute you tell him—*.

Leave it alone. Leave it alone, please. I was begging myself like I was a total stranger. Just walk out into the night, into the red glare from the sign, into the way this whole state smells after the rain moves through, and get in the car and drive until you hit Salt Lake or until you hit the end of the gas or until you hit a bridge embankment. But just leave, just go, right now.

The pile of pages toppled as I worked out the bottom-most sheet.

It was a letter. A form letter, with phrasing that sounded like legalese and a few specifics tailored to the circumstances. I read line by line, but only phrases popped out at me.

. . . interviews including foster parent(s), friends, and other significant individuals . . .

. . . careful observation of biological father . . .

. . . inadequate living conditions . . .

. . . substantial improvement in behavior . . .

. . . departmental belief that every effort should be made to keep children with their family . . .

. . . happy to inform you of this provisional return of custody . . .

And at the bottom, in uneven blue ink from a cheap ballpoint: Genevieve Coyote in Sage.

They were giving me back to Dad.

Interviews including foster parents. Interviews including friends. Interviews including other significant individuals.

Who did that mean?

They were giving me back to Dad.

Foster parents. That was Sara.

They were giving me back to him. Back to a guy whose only goal in life was to get stoned and get laid, and the second one was optional.

Friends. Kaden? Becca? Kimmy? Joel?

They were giving me back to the guy who hit me, who stole money from me, who spent all his cash on meth so that we never had food in the fridge.

Other significant individuals. Austin? Emmett?

I didn't remember letting go of the paper, but it brushed against my jeans as it fell, rasping down my leg. The walls were shrinking down around me, not enough space for air or light or me.

I found my backpack. I found the tape player, the sheaf of stolen documents, and the microcassette. I let the papers fall; they drifted like eiderdown, their edges curled like feathers. I jammed the microcassette into the tape player that Kaden had found for me. *Interviews including foster parent(s), friends, and other significant individuals.* The outline of the Play icon bumped under my thumb.

Just go. Just go now and you never have to know.

My thumb pressed down. The player clicked. The tape rolled forward. A woman's voice came out of the tiny speaker.

"I never want you to apologize for saying how you feel. You need to say how you feel. Your feelings are valid, even when they're painful for you. Maybe especially when they're painful for you."

The words were followed by silence. Then a hiccupping sob. Then more silence. "I shouldn't have said that."

"In this place, you can say whatever you want—"

My thumb hit the Stop button so hard that the plastic creaked.

Austin. The woman was talking to Austin. And a string of lights went on in my head, one after another. Your feelings are valid. Austin was crying. You can say whatever you want. I'd heard that kind of talk before. That was shrink talk. This was a recording of one of his therapy sessions.

Who had recorded it? The therapist? Or Austin? Or someone else?

That last part buzzed in my head, an ugly little conspiracy thought, and I shooed it away. That left two options: the therapist or Austin. *Interviews including foster parent(s), friends, and other significant individuals.* That line from the letter settled in my gut. Austin had recorded this, I decided. Austin had kept it. Some bullshit effort at self-improvement. And when Ginny had asked him about me, he'd handed it over.

Why?

Just go, I told myself. Just go. Just walk out the door, take a cold breath, clear your head. This is like eavesdropping. A really nasty, really dirty kind of eavesdropping. This is Austin's private conversation with his therapist, and you've never asked him about therapy, you've never pried, you've always told yourself you respect people's privacy. You wouldn't read his mind, would you? So put down the tape player and walk outside and maybe go for a walk, maybe just walk forever, but don't listen to this.

I ran the tape back. I pressed play.

"—not even really his fault." Austin's voice was steady, with a frustrated twinge at the end. "I know that. None of it is his fault. He can't control what other people do. I get that."

Then the slight hiss and scratch of a cheap microcassette in a cheap player. Say something, I thought. He was paying this woman, this therapist, to get his brain straight, so why didn't she say something, why didn't she open her fat mouth and say one thing, one simple, fucking thing that could make this better for Austin, why didn't she just say—

"It's just, sometimes I think it'd be so much easier if he weren't here."

Through the speaker, his sob sounded like it came from inside a tin can. He gasped for breath. He choked. He sniffled. The background noise, steady and shrill, sounded like an emergency warning on broadcast TV.

"I know I'm—"

I punched the Stop button. I let the player drop into my bag. I staggered out into the living room, and the papers that I had let fall slid under my sneaker, and I collapsed onto the sofa, and the vinyl squeaked. I lay there for a moment, not really standing, all of my weight held by the sofa's wooden frame. Then I punched the cushion. And I punched it again. And again and again and again. My breaths were soft little grunts. I quit when my arms gave out and I was just too tired, and then I lay with my stomach across the sofa's back because I couldn't get up.

Eventually, though, my legs worked again. I patted my cheeks. Dry. No sweat. Nothing. Dry, with a hectic heat that I could feel turning my skin red in patches. I staggered for the door. I plunged out into the night like it was ice-water and I was a burning man. Rainbow light ribboned across the asphalt, and I hit one of those shiny patches and my foot went out, and my knee—the same one as last time—

smacked the pavement. I scrambled up. Adrenaline put my heart in my ears, and it was so loud I heard everything else like it came underwater: a semi whooshing past on the state highway; the thud of music from within Slippers; a caw of laughter.

They were sending me back to Dad. And they'd talked to Sara and Austin and Emmett and Kaden and Becca and—and everyone, and they'd let it happen. And the rational part of my brain knew it didn't matter. The rational part, which was small and hard and compact like a diamond at the bottom of a mine, totally out of my reach, the rational part told me I was running away, and I shouldn't get so worked up because nobody could make me stay with Dad.

But it did matter. It mattered because I had trusted Sara. I had trusted Austin. I had trusted Emmett. I had trusted Kaden, Becca, Kimmy, Jake, Temple Mae, all of them. And they had let this happen.

Austin had let this happen. Austin had wanted this.

*Sometimes I think it'd be so much easier.*

The betrayal of it went through me with claws and teeth, shredding and biting and tearing up my insides. I staggered again, and I cracked hard against a bumper, my elbow clanging against the trunk and denting the sheet metal. Someone cawed laughter again, and then the laughter choked off.

"Hey, man. What the fuck? What're you doing to my car?"

The rest of them, Sara and Emmett and Becca, the rest, they had let this happen. They had sat there, and they had looked Ginny in the eyes, and they had let it happen. Or—

Horror prickled up my spine. Maybe they hadn't just let it happen. Maybe they'd wanted it to happen too. Sara had gotten tired of grounding me, of feeding me, of talking to me. Becca wanted a new career and a new life without all the drama. Emmett just wanted to fuck me over because he still hated me for everything that had happened with Makayla.

"Fuck-face, I asked you a question. What are you doing to my car?"

The guy was basically a bulldozer with legs: blunt face, thick from his neck to his knees, a lot of muscle packed under yards of flannel.

I looked from him to the car, a little Ford Fiesta that had probably rolled off the line in the late '70s, its original color obliterated by a chop-shop job of lime spray paint.

"Your car?"

"That's my car, fuck-face. Get the fuck off it."

They had wanted this. Of course they had. The thought was like a bad fluorescent light flickering on and off in my head. They had wanted me gone. They had wanted me back where I'd come from.

*Sometimes I think it'd be so much easier.*

I took a breath, but it didn't help. That flicker, that on-and-off in my head, disrupted any kind of real thinking. I was out of control. I was out of myself. And there was only one way to fix that, only one really good way, only one way that put me back at the center, put my hands on the wheel, put me back in charge.

"Your car?" I dropped my elbow again, and this time the sheet metal buckled, and the dent looked like something a really good piece of hail might have left. "This one? Is this the car you're talking about?" Clang. This time, the dent was something a baseball might have left, like a kid had knocked one out into the parking lot.

"What the fuck's wrong with you? I'm telling you that's my car."

"Oh. This. This is your car." I sidestepped, brought up my foot, and drove my heel through a taillight.

"You're dead."

He rushed. Guys like him always rush. Guys like me, we rush too, and so I barreled into him. His first punch clipped the back of my head, and it was like someone had shaken up a hive and sent the bees swarming into my brain. I rocked to the side but kept moving. His second punch came around low, clobbering me just above the kidney, but I was still moving, and he had a bad angle, so it glanced off. Just a blip, just a hot little blip.

Then I caught him under the jaw. It was a classic uppercut. It was so damn classic you could have found a picture of it in a textbook, and if the guy had been sober or smart or halfway decent in a brawl, he would have recognized it and ducked his chin or pulled back or tried to knock the blow off course. He wasn't any of those things, though, and my fist connected like I'd been following a dotted line.

The force of the blow ran through his face like shockwaves. He didn't come off the ground, not exactly, but his toes peeled back. His eyes were wet and reflective, just like the asphalt after rain, and there was something funny about the way he fell, like he was trying to sit down and forgot how. It was really, really funny. A little like the Three Stooges, like Moe getting bopped between the eyes and going down in slow motion. I'd tried to get Gage to watch the Stooges, and he'd told me they were too old; they were dumb. I hadn't tried with Austin. Then I didn't feel like laughing anymore.

A couple guys still huddled together near the drainage ditch. Their cigarettes winked, and one said something to the other, but they didn't make any other moves. Maybe they didn't care that I'd knocked out flannel-guy. Maybe they didn't want to get in the same kind of mess. The orange tips of their cigarettes described a wavering point in the distance.

At the back of my head, that swarm of bees was still buzzing. The guy might have gotten me better than I realized. I dropped to my knees next to him; he wasn't moving, and I wasn't moving, and my head was fucking killing me all of the sudden. His flannel-covered chest rose and fell; his breathing bubbled at the end of each exhale.

*Sometimes I think it'd be so much easier.*

A couple of lousy punches weren't going to knock that kind of thought out of my head. Picking a fight with a drunk, picking a fight with a fat, dumb drunk, wasn't going to knock that kind of thought out of my head. At the back of my head, where that black hole was quietly, invisibly pulling me apart, metal gleamed and whirred and spun.

I didn't want to cut tonight. I wanted something else. I stumbled to the Impala, jammed the key in the lock, and got the door open. The glove box held a map of Wyoming, an LED flashlight with the batteries dead, the Impala's owner's manual, and a flattened sleeve of Ritz crackers. The sandy crumbs sounded like a rainmaker when I bumped them. Fifty-seven cents in loose change in the ashtray. I thumbed the plastic covering, a hope sparked. But no. The electric lighter was gone. Three pale, soggy McDonald's fries hid under the seat, with leaves and gravel and salt tracked in over autumn and a long winter.

I had my blades, but this called for more than blades. This called for something bigger. The saw, a small part of me thought, and I pushed that thought away. But I couldn't find anything. Not a damn thing. Maybe the guys with the cigarettes. Just about every guy that went into Slippers had a lighter or a matchbook or—

Just about every guy.

Behind me, the Impala's door wobbled shut with a soft click; I didn't care if it was really latched or if it had just caught halfway. My skin was starting to itch. Sweat dampened my shirt, and it clung in a wet diamond between my pecs. Flannel-guy was still where I'd left him, blowing his bubbly breaths. Maybe his jaw was broken. That was an interesting thought. Maybe his teeth had cut something inside his mouth. Maybe that was the sound of blood trickling down his throat. Those were interesting thoughts too. But not interesting enough, not when another thought, a blinking-red-traffic-light thought, went on and on in my head: they were sending me back to Dad.

My hands shook as I patted flannel-guy down. Keys. Wallet—eighty-eight bucks, which meant the guy either hadn't even gotten inside Slippers or he'd left early for some reason, before he'd had a chance to blow it all. The cash went into my pocket. A cinnamon disc in crinkly plastic. A condom. I pocketed this too. Then, a piece of hard plastic. I shoved it toward the top of the pocket, and the steel wheel emerged first. My fingers were shaking so badly I could barely work it all the way free, and then I had it: three fingers around the tube, with its stored cloud of butane, and my index and thumb bracketing the wheel and the head.

I almost went back to the Impala; the dome light was still on, a sure sign that I hadn't actually closed the door, and that spooked me. I didn't want light. I wanted to be off on my own. I wanted that black hole in my head to swallow me up—to finish eating me, instead of this piece-by-piece bullshit. I wanted total dark. Privacy. But I heard Austin saying, *You promised.* My empty hand clutched at my jeans, the palm sweaty and the denim rough and slippery all at the same time. I could get in the car, I could drive to the hospital. He'd be there. He'd talk me through this. He'd make sure it didn't go too far—just far enough, just so I could pull myself back together again.

And then the words from the interview flashed red and hot, stoplight red, in my head: *Sometimes I think it'd be so much easier if he weren't here.*

Fuck that promise. And fuck Austin.

I walked, all diagonals like some kind of crazy drunk, back into the apartment. The bedroom light was still on, this huge, God-like eye stabbing at the back of my brain. I shut the front door, flipped the lock, and tripped over one of Dad's New Balance sneakers, the one with the sole lolling like a dog's tongue. One hand on the couch to keep me walking a straight line, I plunged into that God's-eye light. My hip caught the jamb. Just like in the kitchen. Just like when he'd had me cornered against the counter, my hip checking up against the laminate. And the light washed out everything else. Just like his fist in my eye, that explosion of neutron white. I slapped at the wall until the switch caught, and then everything was dark.

At the window, my nose on the cool glass, I rolled the wheel. Sparks jumped. No flame. I undid the button on my jeans. I shimmied out of the denim, and it pooled around my ankles. My boxers next. The cold off the glass was like ice-water from the waist down. I struck the lighter again, and sparks flew up. The glass caught them, reflected them. I saw the cut from earlier that day—or had it been the day before?—weeping red through the bandage. I saw my own face. It looked a lot like that kid in Emmett's memory, the one stepping off the bus, with his face hollowed out. That was just the shadows, though. I rolled the wheel a third time, and the flame caught.

And then I held that flame against the inside of my thigh. The red on-off in my head went off, one final time, hard and dark and absolute. The bee-buzz went quiet. The itch on my skin went flat. I howled because it hurt, and I dropped the lighter. Sagging against the glass, the cold sharper against my wet cheeks, I had to hold that leg up because it was trembling so bad, because it wouldn't take any weight.

But after a while, the shaking stopped, and everything was quiet, and all the pieces were back where they were supposed to be. I tried to pull up my boxers, but it hurt too much, so I shuffled to the bed and lay with my legs spread, a blob of heat pulsing on the inside of my thigh.

In the back of my head, the whirr and gleam of metal had solidified and steadied into a white, rising disc. The moon. That was soothing. That pale light that I got from cutting and burning, that glimmer of illumination, was so much better than the black hole that usually chewed up the back of my head. I took my first real breath all night and enjoyed how steady I felt, enjoyed how my head was glowing and calm and serene.

And as I dipped toward sleep, I heard the rustle and snap of canvas, a rattle of tentpoles, and then, for a moment, I was in that vast and ancient forest again, and behind me came the beast, always running faster than I was. A voice came. A voice that I recognized from my nightmares. The voice of Urho Rattling Tent, War Chief of the Tribe That Walks Apart.

*You're making this much too easy.*

# Chapter | 15

It was a dream and not a dream; I recognized that much from the beginning. The forest was gone. The beast was gone. The clouds came first, and then the mountain walls and the low, swooping bowl of the valley, and then the Junegrass green under dew so white that, at first, I took it for frost. Then the lake. The water reflected the tumble of clouds without the faintest ripple. On the other side of the lake, set on a stone shelf that overlooked the valley, was a log cabin. Not one of the ultra-modern glass-and-timber constructions like Emmett's house, but not a dinky one-room that somebody's grandfather had thrown up. I looked straight at the cabin. I had an audience, and I wanted them to get their money's worth.

I had been brought to places like this before. Luke—Mr. Big Empty—had done it, scooping me out of dreams and dragging me into nightmare fantasies that he constructed. Always I had been able to tell that the place I was in was not a dream: everything had a flattened quality, as though I were moving through a set on a soundstage. This place had the same feel, but the difference was one of quality. These background pieces were painted by a finer hand, with little touches to add realism. Seed-heavy, a stalk of Junegrass bobbed and brushed droplets of dew across my sneakers. That, for example. That had been a very nice touch.

"All right," I said. "You made your point."

"You're making this so easy for him."

River made his way through the tall grass toward me. Where he passed, he left a trail of bent stalks, their tops dark and matte with the dew wiped clean. The trail led back maybe thirty yards until it vanished in the center of a long swath of grass. River was dead; I supposed it was easy for him to appear and reappear. This place, not quite a dream, brushed the other side. Or maybe this wasn't River's spirit at all; maybe it was just another special effect. He looked the way he had looked in life: my shoulders, my height, but his hair was curly and tucked behind his ears. It made sense that we shared so much. We were half-brothers.

"I thought you were dead."

"I am dead."

"No, I mean really dead. Gone." Months before, I had done something to River; I had hurt him somehow. The same way I had shredded Mr. Big Empty's spirit. The same way I had popped the seams holding Krystal's soul together. With River, it had been unintentional, but I had still frayed whatever psychic connection held him to this plane of existence.

"I'm here."

"You're still working for Urho."

He shrugged; his spirit wore the same denim jacket he had carried in life. "I don't really have a choice. Unlike you, little brother."

"What's that mean?"

River's features twisted in pain, and he shook his head savagely from side to side. "Every time—ah, fuck. Fuck that hurts." He shrugged, and his face relaxed as he said, "Urho told you himself: you're making this easy for him."

"Every time I what? Every time I go to sleep? Every time I close my eyes? Every time I go to the other side?"

Worry flickered in River's eyes, and he turned toward the lake and, beyond the lake, the cabin. "I've got a message for you."

"From Urho."

River swiped at a long, bushy tail of Junegrass, and it slid through his hand with a wet smack.

"What?" I said. "You're going to tell me I'm making it easy for him. Fine. I'll make it as easy as he wants, right up until I rip him apart like I did to Luke. Message received, River. Go on back to whatever you've been doing."

"I've got a message for you."

"Maybe I don't want whatever message you've got. Maybe I don't need you haunting the afterlife, hanging around like you're the goddamn psychic mailman. Maybe you should just disappear, go wherever you're supposed to go and leave me the fuck alone."

"I've got a message for you, little brother."

"Then give me the message already."

"Urho Rattling Tent, War Chief of the Tribe That Walks Apart, says this: 'Defy me again, and I will take everything from you. The children you cared for. The boys that you love. The woman who shelters you. Your teachers, your friends, anyone your shadow falls upon. These things I will take from you. And when you have nothing left, I will leave you with your pain, and I will raise up new tools.'"

I waited until the silence thickened and I was sure that River didn't have anything else to say. Then I walked through the grass, the blades heavy and wet and soaking my clothes until I reached the edge of the water. I threw a double bird at the cabin.

Urho's anger went through the dream like an earthquake with its point of origin at the cabin. Concentric waves of force rippled out. The stretch of rock and earth sloping down from the cabin sheared away, and the landslide rushed toward the water. The lake drew back from the shore near my feet for half an instant, and then it splashed toward me, the water cresting at my knees and flooding across the valley floor. Where the lake hadn't swallowed the Junegrass, deep fissures ripped open the ground, swallowing clumps of sage and purple-headed thistles, and below, where everything fell away, there was nothing.

I staggered against the water battering my legs. Invisible beneath the flood, the ground split and shifted. I stumbled, scrambling to keep my footing. The heel of my sneaker slid along wet, crumbling earth, and then there was nothing underneath. The spray soaked my shirt as I regained my balance and struggled away from the disintegrating ground.

But it didn't matter how far I went. The lake spilled out of its bed, unrelenting, the volume of water seemingly—impossibly—limitless. But possibility didn't matter here; it was a dream, and there was as much water as Urho dreamed there was. If that water knocked me on my back, if the slate-gray flood closed over my face, if the ground washed away, I'd fall into that black dream-void. Whatever might happen after that, I didn't want to find out.

I tried to open my inner eye, but nothing changed. I was asleep, but that didn't change the fact that I was exhausted, physically and emotionally. In fact, the emotional exhaustion—for a moment, I could feel again the red throb on the inside of my thigh—seemed to matter more than anything else. And without second sight, I couldn't find my way out of this place—I couldn't stretch and reach and shatter Urho's hold on me here.

Another chunk of earth dissolved beneath me. I splashed backward, paddling in water that soaked me to the middle of my chest. When my feet left the ground, the current caught me and spun me hard, driving me toward the valley's edge. I flailed, rowing against the rushing water with my arms, digging my toes into mud that was too thin to hold me.

A hand caught my arm, jerking me tight against the current, and I swung around to face River. His face twisted in pain. One eye swelled grotesquely, and a runnel of blood curved along the bridge of his nose and dripped off his upper lip.

"You're making it too easy for him. It's like you're lighting these signal fires on the darkest night of the year, and he can see you from miles away. He can reach out and touch you, then. Vie, you've got to remember that she's hungry. You've got to remember she's—"

River's voice cut off as he gagged with pain, and his fingers shot out straight. Without his grip holding me against the current, the water launched me toward the edge of the valley. For a moment longer, I could see River, blood running down his face in rills, and then he started screaming. Rust-colored water bubbled up around him, like some hidden well geysering to the surface, and then he was gone.

I spun myself into the current, thrashing with arms and legs. I strained to open my inner eye. It was like heaving my weight against a boulder. I hit it again and again. But I was just so tired. So tired of the broken pieces tumbling around inside me. So tired of the black hole at the back of my head. So tired of being open, of being hurt every time I opened myself up.

But I didn't want to die either, and the water was colder and blacker as it sped me toward the edge of the valley, where the dream dissolved into shimmering spangles and, beneath the shimmer, blackness.

Fueled by desperation and fear, I forced my inner eye open. The hypertexture of the dream rose to the surface, and I braced myself and pushed against it. It was like trying to punch through thick cloth, like canvas folded over on itself again and again. There wasn't resistance, not in the same way as striking stone, but the dream didn't break. It bent and folded and warped. But it didn't give.

Cold, now. Frigid. The water sucked the heat from me as it swept me toward the abyss. The cold ate its way into me, gnawing at nerves and joints and ligaments so that each movement was clumsier, slower, uncontrolled. My paddling became ineffectual slaps that skipped along the black chop of the water. My kicks lost direction and strength. I felt myself moving faster.

An arm hooked me around the neck. I flailed at my attacker, trying to catch whoever had come up behind me, and then River's quiet words reached my ear. "When I've got his attention, that's your chance."

Before I could look behind me, before I could say yes or nod or give any sign that I understood, River was swimming again, dragging me cross current, moving with an ease that had nothing to do with physical strength and everything to do with the strange rules of the other side. Urho's shriek rang throughout this tiny, private dimension. I watched as the force of his anger descended on River: River shook his head, and then his back bowed, his fingers fumbling their hold on me.

I could feel it then: the sudden thinning of the barrier between worlds. I flexed again. I was exhausted. I was half frozen. I had barely survived a nasty battle with killer plants. But I sure as hell wasn't going to stick around while a dead man tried to kill me. I brought as much of my power as I could against the grayscale fabric of the dream, and this time it ripped like wet, rotting cotton.

Shuddering, I launched upright in bed. I was wet. Not with sweat; there was too much of it. I sniffed. Not pee, either, thank God. Water, real water, and when I opened my mouth and pulled in a breath, the drops on my lips ran down onto my tongue, and I tasted clay and calcium and magnesium. Hard water. Mountain-lake water.

The cold hit me a moment later: I shivered so badly that I bit my tongue. The heat was off in the apartment—of course it was off; Dad must have used the money for another dime—and my skin prickled with goosebumps. Far off through the window, tacked against the dark velvet of the Wyoming night, a blue-white security light glittered. It was barely enough illumination for me to recognize where I was.

Still shivering, I dragged myself upright. My shirt and coat were soaked through; I shed them and stood naked in the darkness, but naked was better than the heavy, wet cold of flannel. I found my pants where I had left them by the window, but I couldn't drag on the boxers and jeans; they were dry, sure, but they were too tight. The burn on the inside of my thigh flared. I had to bite the inside of my mouth to keep from crying out. Asphalt crumbs, the spines of dead leaves, something wet and cold and sticky—blood, my brain supplied, that silver dollar of blood—clung to my bare feet as I crossed the front room in darkness. I rummaged through Dad's bag. My shoulders kept heaving. My hands wouldn't do what I wanted. I thought of the last time I had been in Austin's arms, the sweat pasting my back to his chest, and how stupid I'd been because all I had been able to think about was opening a window.

In the bag, I found joggers that I dragged on. Even the soft, broken-in cotton felt like I was rubbing sandpaper across the burn, but I could handle that. Then I found a sweater, real wool, scratchy against my chest and under my arms and tight around my throat. But it was warm. I curled up on the couch, the vinyl sticking to my wet cheek, and tucked my feet between the cushion and the couch's arm. Then I was shaking so badly I couldn't do anything else. I kept seeing the lake, and sometimes it was that valley lake rising around me, swallowing me. And sometimes it was Lake Thunderbird, and the only noise was the hiccup of water as the stone skimmed the surface. And at some point, I stopped shaking and went to sleep.

# Chapter | 16

You're making it too easy for him.

I groaned, and the vinyl farted as I rolled onto my side, trying to burrow deeper into the sofa. My feet were cold. All of me was cold, but my feet in particular, and I dug my toes under the cushion. I wasn't going to open my eyes. Not yet. It was still too early; I could feel how early it was in the cold damp. Even with the cold, even with the throb behind my eyes, even with the burn on the inside of my leg, I was going back to sleep. I could sleep for as long as I wanted. I could sleep forever if I wanted. The black hole at the back of my head yawned at the idea. Forever. Just quiet, black forever.

You're making it too—

I scrubbed away the thought. I wasn't going to worry about the War Chief and the Lady. I wasn't going to worry about Sara and Emmett and Austin. I wasn't going to worry about my dad. I was just going to sleep.

Except for the cold needling my toes.

Except for the rash of heat on the inside of my leg.

Except for the very, very real fact that I needed to pee.

So I got up, and I stubbed my toe, but I made it to the toilet and peed like a race horse. In the dark. Because the fluorescents still weren't working, and only a gray scum of third-hand light—filtered first by the blinds and then by distance—reached the bathroom. And while I peed, I laid out my plans. I was going. I was leaving. I was out of here.

In the dark, I couldn't see all the scrapes and bruises that Krystal's vines had left on me, but I sure felt them. I should have felt guilty for what I had done to her. I did feel guilty, I guess, but it was an intellectualized guilt—it was only in my head, not in my heart. In my heart, nothing. I'd felt absolutely nothing when I was on the other side and ripped Krystal apart. And that should have made me feel guiltier.

That reflected light in the bathroom made me just a pair of blue eyes floating in the mirror. And then those blue eyes weren't mine anymore. They looked a lot like someone else's. A lot like they belonged to a boy who had told me I looked like Thor. Or maybe like they fit the face of a girl who had seen too many bad things in her short life. I splashed water on the glass, arcing a big handful of it across the reflection, and then there wasn't really anything to see anymore, and that was better.

I went back to the bedroom, gathered up my clothes—shirt and coat still soggy—and tried to get my boxers on again. They were too tight. Austin liked them tight. He liked to work his fingers up the back of my thigh and let the red fabric snap back into place. He liked to tug on the elastic until he was halfway to giving me a wedgie, until I was on my tiptoes and grunting, and then he'd laugh and let both of us fall back onto the bed. The boxers were so tight that they rubbed like hell on the burn I'd given myself, and I wasn't ever going to see Austin again, so I hooked my thumbs in the waistband to take the damn things off. But after a moment, I left them on. And I dragged on the jeans after them.

You're making this too easy—

I crushed that thought underfoot and ground it out.

Picking through Dad's clothes, I found a pair of long-sleeved tees, and I dragged one on and then pulled on the sweater again. Until my coat dried, I needed layers. With a shiver, I worked my wet socks into place; the cotton bunched and pulled, and then one of them ripped and my big toe shot out the front. I sighed and laced up my sneakers. It was just going to be one of those days.

I packed the paperwork, including that strange newspaper, into Dad's bag. Then, after filling Dad's bag with the rest of his stuff—maybe I'd sell it, maybe I'd use it, maybe I'd toss it out the window when I was going ninety miles an hour—I grabbed my backpack and stepped out onto the cement pad that ran in front of the apartments. The day was cold. The sky was a fuzzy blue-gray, the texture of pilled wool, without a sun. Maybe somewhere it was going to be a good day, but in Vehpese, it was going to be another slog. The only good thing I could tell myself was that I was leaving.

He said I looked like Thor.

Flannel-guy, who I'd tangled with the night before, was gone. In the bleak, muted light, Slippers' empty parking lot looked worse than ever: slabs of asphalt buckled and split, weeds—damn, I'd never look at a weed the same again—a streamer of wet toilet paper running for almost twenty yards like someone had tried to throw a ticker-tape parade last night. I'd been in this town almost a year, and the parking lot hadn't changed. Nothing had changed.

I hadn't changed. I marched across the parking lot to Mr. Spencer's car, worked the key in the trunk until it creaked open, and dropped Dad's bag inside. I was still me, the beaten-down, fucked-up, cut-and-burn version of me that had come here. Even after things had gotten good, even after things were good, really good, even after things had gotten great with Austin, with Sara, with life, even after life had been better than I ever thought it could be, even after all that, I couldn't be happy. I was the kid with the hole in his brain, that black hole swallowing everything else. And if I couldn't be happy here, if I couldn't be happy with Austin, if I couldn't be happy with Sara, if I couldn't be happy now, then that was on me. That was just how fucked-up I was. So I couldn't blame Austin for wanting me gone. I couldn't blame the rest of them. They were being smart. They were cutting me out before I ruined their lives too. They still had a chance.

I turned out onto the state highway, heading south. In a couple of hours, I'd hit I-80, and then I'd have a straight shot wherever I wanted to go. Salt Lake. Sure, why not? It was spring here, even if it didn't look like spring. And spring was the time to be hopeful. It was spring, so I was going to be hopeful. It was spring even if the sky was just a rumbling mass of black and gray. It was spring even if I was so cold my teeth were chattering while the car warmed up. It was spring even if the only things growing on this stretch of road were flattened styrofoam cups and skid marks and the brown glass of broken beer bottles. It was spring, and I was starting the newest, next, best part of my life.

He said I looked like Thor.

The apartments slipped away, and the Slippers sign blinked once in my rear window, and then a swell of the low, rolling ground swallowed it all up, and there was only miles and miles of buffalo grass and sage and tumbleweed and fencing and snow, still goddamn snow, shrinking along the fence posts. I'd come running this way. My very first day in Wyoming, I'd come out this way running. And I realized, with a sense of déjà vu, that I'd been thinking the exact same thing then that I was thinking now: this is a fresh start, this is a new place, this is when life is going to be good and I am going to be happy.

He said I looked like Thor.

I jammed on the radio, and Metallica crashed over the speakers. I rolled down the window, and the cold air whipped my hair behind me and stung my eyes. Cowshit came in on the wind. I spat, and all there was was more cowshit.

Because I'd been wrong. I punched the radio, and Metallica whined off into silence. I'd been wrong about the most important part. Yes, coming here had been a fresh start. Yes, coming here had given me a chance at happiness. Life had gotten better. It had gotten better than I'd ever hoped it could get. And it still hadn't been enough. Whatever was in the back of my head, eating away at my brain, that was the reason. That was always going to be there. And no matter where I went, no matter how good things got, that was going to be there: swallowing light and hope and energy until there wasn't anything left of me. I wanted to close my eyes. In contrast to that emptiness, in contrast to the darkness, I could see the round, white glow of the table saw. I could hear the metal purring.

There was one place I could go where that black hole couldn't follow me. There was one door I'd never gone through. Not all the way. There was one place I could be . . . well, not happy. But nothing. And it sounded pretty damn good to be nothing.

He said I looked like Thor.

I jerked the wheel so hard that the Impala skipped along the shoulder, throwing up a cloud of gravel and dust. I grabbed two handfuls of hair so hard that my eyes filled with tears, and then I coughed and choked on the dust, and I let go of my hair and let my forehead rest on the steering wheel. Molded plastic bumps bit into the thin skin.

River's voice came back to me, speaking Urho's words. His threats. *Defy me again, and I will take everything from you. The children you cared for. The boys that you love. The woman who shelters you. Your teachers, your friends, anyone your shadow falls upon. These things I will take from you. And when you have nothing left, I will leave you with your pain, and I will raise up new tools.*

For one moment, with my eyes closed, the world seemed to spin too fast. That black hole irised open at the back of my head. The glow of the saw, the perfect hum of steel, were so close. All I would have to do was drive to Sara's house and—

. . . *The children you cared for* . . .

The words hit me with such clarity and force that my head came up off the steering wheel and I stared out the windshield. A mule deer was picking its way along the highway's shoulder, and when my head shot up, the deer froze. Then its black tail twitched. And then it bolted, its legs carrying it in long, graceful leaps, the buffalo grass swishing beneath it, and I didn't move, didn't breathe, didn't blink.

. . . *The children you cared for* . . .

I had been so busy bitching and whining and moaning that I hadn't even thought about the dream. I'd been busy letting my heart bleed out because one boy, one stupid boy—ok, maybe two—didn't want me. Jesus Christ. I was such an idiot.

I checked the Impala; I was well onto the shoulder and clear of the highway, so I killed the engine. The car shuddered, the vents gasped, and everything went silent. Then the tick of cooling metal worked its way up the frame. I barely heard it.

He said I looked like Thor. I could still remember it. I could still remember the repressed excitement in his voice, the trill at the end of it, and the uncertainty too. It was the first thing he had ever said to me. I had walked past them; I hadn't wanted anything to do with them. Not because I was cruel but because they were kids and I was sixteen. But then he had said those four words, and there had been something so open and vulnerable about his innocence, his wonder and excitement, that I had stopped. They had become Tyler and Hannah to me. And after that, nothing had been the same.

My skin pebbled, and my next breath was unsteady. Nothing had been the same. I'd watched over those kids. I'd fed those kids. I'd stayed up nights so that they could sleep. I'd let Tyler take a bullet instead of me, and seeing him hurt had almost killed me. Nothing had been the same in my life after those four words, and if I could lie to myself and hide from myself and pretend everything else had stayed the same, I couldn't lie about what Tyler and Hannah meant to me. What they had done to me. And for me.

And they were missing.

*. . . I will take everything from you. The children you cared for . . .* Those were Urho's words as River reported them to me. And I parsed them as carefully as I could. Mr. Spencer might not think I paid much attention in class, but I wasn't totally oblivious. Something was strange about the words. Something that I should have noticed earlier.

Cared for. Past tense. Not care for, present. What did that mean? Did Urho believe I didn't care for them anymore because they were living with their mother and grandmother? Did he believe I didn't care for them anymore because they weren't my neighbors, because I didn't see them every day, because I wasn't feeding them dinner and making up a bed for them on the sofa?

That seemed sophistical. So what were the other options? That the kids were dead?

A semi roared past, the blast of air from its passage rocking the Impala. I jumped and banged my head against the headrest. Then I wiped my face and shouted a fuck you into the truck's wake. I wiped my face again. The kids weren't dead. They weren't. That was a nonstarter. I wasn't even going to consider it. I wasn't even going to let it be possibly true.

So what did it mean, the children you cared for? I ran through the rest of River's message. The boys that you love. The woman who shelters you. Something about my shadow. It was all present tense. Just the part about Tyler and Hannah was in the past.

*. . . I will take everything from you . . .*

Their dad had taken them. That's what Shay wanted me to believe. But Shay had also told me that she had heard Hannah calling her name. And I had heard something too, hadn't I? Not my name. Laughter. The hairs on the back of my neck bristled. If Shay were right, and if Cribbs had taken them, then why was she hearing Hannah's cries? Why had Cribbs kidnapped his children? Why take Hannah and Tyler when someone higher up than just the local police might notice their disappearance because Mather County—

Because Mather County had too high a rate of missing people. Missing kids, in particular. And even if the government didn't know and the sheriff didn't know and nobody else knew, I knew why those kids were disappearing. And that meant I knew why Hannah and Tyler were gone. For the same reason all the other kids had vanished, and only some had returned: for the Lady to wake them from the mortal sleep, in hopes of producing a psychic.

*. . . I will raise up new tools . . .*

Shay had shown me the guest book from that shitty motel, the Kane Motor Court. Kane was thirty miles away, give or take, and I'd never seen the motor court, but it wasn't hard to imagine. It would be like a thousand other roadside flops: run-down, ill-used, an easy place to stay cheap and to stay discreetly.

I tried to remember the rest of what Shay had told me. March 30th. That was the day Cribbs had signed the Kane Motor Court's guest-book. And March 31st, the next day, Hannah and Tyler had disappeared while their mom finished her shift at the restaurant and was off trading blowjobs for coke or for cash or maybe just for companionship.

I will take everything from you.

No, I thought, cranking the key and hitting the gas so hard that the Impala sputtered and choked before lurching forward. I spun the wheel hard, cutting a U across the highway and heading the opposite direction. No, you won't.

# Chapter | 17

The drive through rural Wyoming gave me time to think. On either side of the car, the buffalo grass rolled toward the horizon. With the exception of the Bighorn Mountains, where Cloud Peak hid among its namesakes, the land rolled and swelled and dipped but kept more or less on the same plane. Some of the sage was already greening up. When I crossed the Bighorn River, the water was clear, and huge slabs of turquoise-colored stones showed at the bottom, where trout darted between patches of shadow. It was hard to believe that this place was coming alive. Hard to believe I hadn't seen it an hour before. Hadn't seen it ten minutes before.

Thinking felt good. Thinking felt like breaking the surface of quicksand and gasping in air, a sudden, reflexive easiness that I hadn't even imagined was possible a short time ago. Part of my brain registered all this; part of my brain warned me that this, too, wasn't normal, that I needed to consider this more carefully, that maybe I should talk to someone. But I didn't want to talk to anyone. More importantly, I didn't have time to talk.

I thought about Urho and the Lady. They had taken children before. They had taken lots of children. Mather County had a shockingly high number of missing children relative to national averages. In the reports Becca had unearthed, government officials offered mealy-mouthed suggestions about the unforgiving nature of the environment, the local culture of independence, and the town's lack of road services. In other words, the same old excuses: it's your fault they wandered off, and either that desolate wilderness killed them or a stranger did.

Those weren't answers, not really, and my experiences at Belshazzar's Feast, where I had met the Lady and glimpsed, at the edge of my mind, Urho, had convinced me that most of those missing children, maybe all of them, had been taken by the Lady—or, more precisely, had been taken at her orders. She had been taking children for decades, maybe centuries, using her abilities to awaken powers in the children, at least, in those who survived the experience. Luke had gotten his powers that way. So had Mr. Spencer. And Kaden. And Temple Mae. And Makayla, and Mrs. Troutt, and Hailey. And I was willing to guess that this new crop—Krystal and Leo and Kyle and the Crow boy, even Ms. Meehan—all had connections to this part of the world. They had come through here on a family vacation. They had stayed the night on a road trip. They had lived here, or worked here, or visited family here. And then they had disappeared, only to return a few days or weeks later. Alive. But different.

And, with the few exceptions like Mr. Spencer and Kaden and Temple Mae, they had come back as raging psychopaths.

Luke had claimed that the Lady was trying to create a psychic. That she needed a psychic, a real psychic, someone who could cross back and forth to the other side. At the time, when I faced Luke on the other side, I thought I had understood what that meant. She wanted to bring Urho back from the dead. More specifically, she wanted me to bring Urho back from the dead.

Ever since my experience at Emmett's house though, when I had felt myself come apart, I had started to wonder about my conclusions. That experience had been singular; always before, I had crossed over to the other side as a projection, aware of my body behind me, dragging on me like an anchor. But at Emmett's, when I had come apart, I hadn't felt anything. And that smooth, perfect numbness, had been . . . invigorating. Empowering. It had been so easy to unravel the threads holding together Krystal's soul and drag her across to the other side.

Ahead, a flock of quail burst out of the grass, their wings a flurry of shadow against the sky. I followed them with my eyes until they narrowed to dots on the sky, soft little graphite points like the tips of a pencil, and then I studied the road again. I could go back. I could try, anyway. Try to pull myself apart and see if it felt as good as it had the first time. I shivered, and I punched at the heat and then I punched it off again and I wiped one hand on my sweater like my fingers were dirty. They felt dirty; I felt dirty. Because it had felt so good to come apart like that. Because I felt guilty—that's how good it had felt—and embarrassed. I couldn't put into words why, not really, but it was there. And so was the urge to jerk the wheel right, thump off the shoulder, let the car roll down into the buffalo grass where no one would see it, not immediately, and try. Just try. Maybe nothing would happen. Maybe I'd just sit there, and after fifteen minutes or thirty I'd guide the Impala back up onto the highway and keep driving. But maybe it would work. Maybe I could get there, to the other side, all the way. My face was flushed. My armpits were sticky. I wiped my hands on my chest again.

For another minute I struggled to keep the wheel straight, to keep from turning onto a weed-choked gravel cutoff. Then I rolled down the window and pulled up the sweaty knot of hair at the back of my head and let the air cool my neck.

Fuck. Nothing that felt that nice could be good for you.

Well. Ok. One exception. With Austin. But nothing else.

Dragging my scattered thoughts back together, I tried to focus on Tyler and Hannah. The Lady had been gathering children for decades, longer even. She had wanted a psychic. Instead, except for her halfway success with Luke, she had managed to produce only—what had Luke called them? Kinetics? And that raised two questions: first, now that she knew about me, why would the Lady take Hannah and Tyler? And, second, where had my powers come from?

The image of that faded newspaper came to mind, and I batted it away. I focused on the first question. The simplest answer was to accept Urho's message at face value. Urho and the Lady had taken Tyler and Hannah for the same reason that they had taken my dad: to control me, to threaten me, to frighten me. That had been a stupid idea, of course. They would do whatever they wanted to Dad; I didn't give a rat-shit about him. And taking Tyler and Hannah hadn't made me frightened. It had made me angry. Anger was an old friend. Anger made me strong. I'd had seventeen years, seventeen years today, to get to know my anger, to learn how to use it, to make it serve me. And Urho and the Lady were going to find out just how angry they'd made me.

The outskirts of Kane cut out a silhouette ahead of me. It was a small town, even smaller than Vehpese, and it showed all the wear of long, hard years on the high plains: brick houses hunkered in the constant wind, their roofs peeling, their glazing thin but double-paned against the harsh winters. I passed a Kum-n-Go, an Arby's, and a Mexican restaurant called Guadalupe's with an inflatable cactus sagging against its doors. I passed a post office, and a strip mall abandoned by everyone except a single occupant—to judge by the giant wooden tooth hanging out front, its white paint gone dove-gray, a dentist. Two dogs, long-haired mutts, sniffed their way down the length of the strip mall. One was limping; the other had a bullseye of mud on its flank. They were the only living things Kane had to offer me.

Built on the west side of Kane, where the state highway left town and headed deep into nowhere, the Kane Motor Court was a single U of detached buildings: an office with a dead neon sign that, at one point, had probably flashed a vibrant blue Vacancy, bracketed on both sides by three cabins. Probably as a concession to the dead neon sign, someone had pasted cardstock letters in the window spelling a single word: ROOM.

I parked the Impala. I went back down to the state highway and looked in both directions. No semis. No big trucks. Nothing parked along the shoulder, and nothing in the motor court's lot except for the Impala.

But I wasn't stupid enough to leave it there. I went to the closest cabin. I listened at the door. At the window, I squinted against the glare and the watery reflection of my face—I looked like shit, which made sense because I felt like shit—and tried to pick out anything inside. I saw a trim of what looked like a very roughly used polyester quilt, a half-circle of a particle board table, and an empty black ashtray that could have come off the set of *Mad Men*. Around back, I shimmied halfway up the log wall and slapped my hand against the furnace exhaust pipe. Cold. Then I froze. A small window with frosted glass was set into the wall. The bathroom window; I was sure of it. The screen had been sliced and flopped out of the frame.

Somebody sneaking out to avoid paying for another night? Or something else?

I checked the other cabins in the same way. I wasn't really sure what I was looking for. The kids had vanished a week ago today. The only information I had—and it was questionable at best, considering my source was Shay—told me that Cribbs had stayed here more than a week ago. It was too much to ask that I'd find him holed up here, playing house with Tyler and Hannah. But I had to check. And something in my gut told me that if Tyler and Hannah had been taken, Cribbs had been involved. I didn't know how to start looking for Tyler and Hannah any other way, so even if I was wrong, it was kind of a moot point.

I didn't find any sign that Cribbs—or anyone else—was staying at the Kane Motor Court. I didn't find any sign that anyone would ever want to stay at the motor court. I didn't find any sign that this place would still be standing in three months, let alone in a year. But places like this had a kind of grim tenacity. It would probably stay here long after someone had tamped down six feet of earth above me.

The office door jingled when I put my shoulder into it. The cramped box of the lobby smelled like artificial vanilla, some kind of air freshener that I guessed was called Sugar Cookie or Grandmother's Fresh Chocolate Chip or whatever the hell marketing people came up with. There was a nickel gumball machine full of gumballs that had to be at least as old as I was; the colors had faded to pastels. Someone had wadded up a chewed piece of Big Red in the nickel slot. Behind a warped sheet of plexiglass, a big, bald guy was reading *Car and Driver*. Between the white straps of his A-shirt, coarse, dark hair matted his shoulders. His eyes flicked up at me and then back to the glossy pages.

"No kids."

I leaned against the counter. "I just need a favor."

"Get a friend with an ID. Over eighteen. He can pass you the key if he wants, but I don't rent to kids."

"I'm not looking for a room."

"Great. Get lost, then."

"I've got a question."

Rolling the magazine, the guy looked me full on and seemed to take me in for the first time. "You from around here?"

"I want to ask you about someone who stayed here."

The guy tapped on the plexiglass with the rolled-up magazine like he wanted to swat my nose with it. "Kid, just get lost, all right?"

"Cribbs. He's a trucker."

The magazine hovered a quarter-inch off the plexiglass. "What about him?"

"Everything. Whatever you can remember."

"Kid, come on. What is this?"

"I told you: whatever you can remember."

He seemed to consider this for a moment, and then he wagged the rolled-up magazine side-to-side and unfurled it. "Get lost, kid."

As he sank back into his reading, I reared back, studying the plexiglass. I couldn't break through it. And I was willing to bet part of the wall—the parts around the window—were reinforced so I couldn't break through those either. Places like this had to deal with worse people than me. The door to the back part of the office was steel and set in a steel frame. I wanted to get back there and break his nose, but today really just wasn't my day.

For a moment, my third eye opened, and I reached out across the distance between us. Inside the darkness of his mind, I rifled, searching for memories of Cribbs and Hannah and Tyler. It wasn't easy; I knew how to work through people's emotions, finding their fears and hopes, even finding the parts of their brain where exhaustion and sleep and dreams and relaxation were processed. But specific memories, memories that were just data, those were hard. Needle-in-a-haystack hard. And after a few extended moments, I returned to my body.

All right. I was going to have to do this the hard way.

I hammered on the plexiglass, which flexed under the blows. "Hey, I'll pay you."

"Yeah?"

"You've got nobody in those rooms."

"I already told you: I don't rent to kids."

"I'll pay you what you would have made off a night."

"You got sixty bucks?"

"The sign out front says thirty. I'll pay you thirty."

"It's been really slow, kid. Sixty."

"Forty."

"Cribbs stayed two nights. You want to know anything else, you pay two nights." He paused, as though struck by how very intelligent this arrangement seemed. "Yeah. Two nights."

Pulling out the wad of cash I'd taken from flannel-guy the night before, I peeled off the bills and slid them under the plexiglass. "Sixty bucks. Now quit jerking off and talk."

The guy wagged the magazine side-to-side again. "Kid, you got a mouth on you. You want me to come out there and take care of that mouth for you?"

"Sure. Come out. Take care of my mouth. And I'll take care of your knees. You'll be walking with two canes for the rest of your life. Come on out here."

"I've got your sixty bucks. I don't have to do anything."

"You have to come out sometime to pee. And I'm really good at waiting. So either start talking, or let's see how long you can stay in there."

"I can call the cops."

"Yeah, I'd like that. You're running a place like this, and you call the cops. I'd really like that. Call them."

The magazine dipped again, and the guy's eyes went to the phone and then to me. His hairy shoulders dropped. "Look, he was here two nights. That's it."

"Keep going."

"I don't know what you want me to tell you. He parked his rig up the road. He went out for dinner; I saw him walk back with carry-out from the diner. I—" He hemmed. "I don't know, kid. There's nothing to tell you."

"Why two nights?"

"What?"

"Why did he stay two nights?"

"I don't know. He was tired. He wanted to be off the road for another day. It's not like he told me."

I shook my head. Another place, another time, maybe that would be true. If he was somewhere he liked, somewhere it made sense to stay an extra day—a little fun, a little relaxation. Maybe if there was a girl in the picture. But not in Kane. Not the same weekend that Cribbs's kids went missing. I didn't believe in coincidences.

"Did he have anybody with him?"

"Shit, kid. I tell them they can't bring those girls in here, but it's not like I do room-checks."

"So he did have someone."

"I don't do checks, I told you."

"That's a bullshit answer. You saw him with someone. You saw him with the carry-out bag. You would have seen somebody else, too. Who?"

"Look, it was dark, all right. It was . . . it could have been anybody."

"Who?"

"A woman. I mean, she had a dress on. But she didn't look like those girls that work some of the lots and rest stops. The dress, it was like, a dress. I mean, long. And I couldn't see her face because it was dark, but she was, I don't know . . ."

"Old." The word leaped from my mouth before I realized I was going to speak.

"Yeah. Like, maybe his mom. Something like that, right?"

"Two nights. Which night was that?"

The guy tapped the plexiglass with the magazine as he thought. "Saturday. The second night."

The Lady had come here Saturday night. Why? To talk to Cribbs? My heart pounded in my chest. When I ran my hands along the laminate strip of counter, sweat made them slick.

"Anybody else?"

"What are you—"

"Kids. Did he have little kids with him?"

The bald guy reared back, dropping the magazine. "Now, look. Just look. I try not to get involved. If this is a custody thing, I don't want anything to do with—"

"Did he have kids with him? His kids. His son and daughter. They'd be, I don't know, eight and six. Something like that." I couldn't even remember how old they were. How messed up was that? I was supposed to care about them. I was supposed to protect them, and I couldn't even remember how old they were. "Did you see them?"

"Look, they were his, right? His little boy. His little girl. Normally I don't let kids stay, but they were his, weren't they? I said one night, they could stay one night."

I left. The door jangled shut behind me, and the chilly spring air came to me over the high plains, carrying dust and wet pollen and blowing away the last whiff of Sugar Cookie air freshener. I clasped both hands at the back of my neck, but sweat made them greasy, and I couldn't stand touching myself.

I made it to the Impala and slid into the driver's seat. Ok, so he had brought the kids back here on Saturday. He had stayed two nights, and the second night he had seen the Lady, after he had grabbed the kids. Why? Because already, over a week ago, she had been putting her plan in motion. And part of that plan had to do with taking Tyler and Hannah. Just like Urho had said: he was going to take everything from me.

I paused. Something didn't feel right. They wanted me to leave, didn't they? What did they want?

Right then, staring out the windshield at the motor court cabin, I felt helpless. I wasn't going to just roll over and let Urho and the Lady take the people I loved one by one. But I didn't know what to do. Cribbs had swooped in and taken his kids while Shay was distracted. I didn't have any idea where he'd taken them. My one lead, the only shot I'd had, had been here at the Kane Motor Court, and it had been a dead end.

I thumped the heel of my hand on the steering wheel hard enough that the horn bleated. Damn it. I'd come up against bad spots like this before. I'd come up against riddles and mysteries, things that felt like dead ends. But I'd always gotten around them.

Jangling the keys in my palm, I reconsidered that last part. I had gotten around them. That part was true. But I hadn't done it alone. I'd had Austin and Emmett and Becca. And they'd done a lot of thinking and digging and working to help me. Becca in particular. She was just so damn smart.

But I couldn't ask her for help. I couldn't even put my reasoning into words, not really, but some of it was the pain of learning that Ginny had talked to Sara and my friends without telling me, part of it was the shame that they all knew how messed up my life was, part of it was the decision I'd made to leave. And no matter how much I told myself that I was leaving to protect them, that I was leaving so they wouldn't have to deal with the train wreck of my life, I knew that was only part of the truth. I was leaving because of how bad it all hurt. And going back to Becca, asking for her help, would be to walk straight into the worst of that hurt. I knew it was stupid to think like that, but it didn't matter. I couldn't change it.

As I bounced the keys on my palm, a realization hit me so hard that I fumbled. Scrambling to recover the keys, I tried to work through the thought again. I didn't have Becca here. And I was too messed up to go ask for her help. But maybe I didn't need to have Becca. Maybe I just needed to think like her.

What would Becca do if she were searching for Cribbs? She'd do some sort of profile of him. She'd trawl social media for information. She'd look up property tax records. She'd search white page listings and news databases. I couldn't do any of those things because I was shit with computers and, even if I hadn't been, I didn't have access to one. But I still had a profile of Cribbs. An imperfect one, yes, but still a profile. Shay had given it to me.

I ran my thumb along the edge of the Impala's key, trailing my nail along the ridges. What had she told me? That he was abusive. That he was petty and vindictive. That he was self-centered. That he used people and disposed of them when he no longer needed them. How had Shay put it? He'd been dating that girl just so he had a babysitter for Tyler and Hannah, and then he'd kicked her to the curb. Something like that. Shay had told me that he didn't have a house and that instead when he passed through the area, he liked to stay at the Kane Motor Court—

My nail skipped along the key's ridges. He liked to stay at the Kane Motor Court. Or the Gypsy or the Hunt Public House.

Maybe three nights in one place had been too much of a risk. Maybe showing up with kids at the Kane Motor Court after two nights alone would have drawn too much attention. Maybe he'd just gone to one of his other favorite places. Maybe.

The drive was a blur of the pilled-wool sky and the sage and the first greening of the Junegrass. As I headed toward Vehpese, I thought. I was going to have to make a decision where I would search next. The Gypsy was a roadhouse, south on Route 127 from Vehpese. That might have been where Cribbs had gone; it wasn't far from town, and it wasn't so rough that anybody would wonder about kids—well, they wouldn't wonder too much. The Hunt Public House was another story, and a pair of kids would definitely stand out. But the Hunt Public House was also east of Vehpese. Closer to the mountains—closer to the Bighorns, and closer to Hunt Mountain in particular. And I had dreamed of mountains.

I turned east. I drove through Vehpese, following the state highway through the center of town. In the pallid spring light, with stormwater jeweling the windows and following the draw of aging caulk in heavy runnels, Vehpese looked better. Not newer, exactly. Cleaner, definitely, where the rain had floated away the clamshell takeout containers from Bighorn Burger. But—scenic. Picturesque. Those weren't the right words, but I couldn't come up with what I wanted to say. The enormous sky cottony with clouds, the bright glitter of the remaining raindrops, the cement and asphalt dark and wet—it wasn't beautiful, but it was dramatic. And damn if I wasn't feeling dramatic as hell that day.

I passed Bighorn Burger where I was missing my shift—it didn't matter because I was going to be dead or gone in the next day, but I still felt guilty about leaving Kimmy and Joel and Miguel shorthanded—and I passed The Big Swirl and Lumber Jack's and the redone stripe of town along the river with its lines of young, springy lodgepoles and its metal and its borrowed Portlandia look. I passed the coffee shop where I had talked to Austin, really talked, for the first time. Not a date, but it had been the day our lives crossed. As I drove a thread unspooled from my heart to that back corner of the coffee shop with the dead plant, and the farther I drove, the harder that string tugged. I crossed the bridge over the Bighorn River, and my stomach dropped and kept dropping, and I remembered what it had been like: the cold water needling my face, plugging my nose, scraping my throat raw as I swallowed and tried to get air. The sand and pebbles scraping my cheek. Emmett's face set in concern, his wet hair flat across his forehead. The sound of his guitar. The dark and the wind and the sea of buffalo grass. The realization that he was alone.

After that, I drove faster because I had to find these kids and get the hell out of this place before I made the same mistakes all over again.

Hunt Public House sat in a cluster of businesses, an island of commerce in the ocean of juniper and scrub and cottonwood that grew thirstily along the Bighorn River. The public house itself was a squat two-story building with a sheet metal roof and a pan-formed plastic sign: a black-tail doe in mid-jump, a red iron sight on her flank. They were taking the name Hunt rather literally I realized, and I sighed as I pulled into the parking lot. It was going to be one of those places.

The asphalt made an E, with the public house at the center leg. The upper leg terminated at the Suds 'n Shop; judging by the wall of industrial washers and an endcap display of dollar-store Easter decorations (an enormous plush bunny, legs sprawled indecently, took the upper shelf), I decided it was some sort of combo laundromat/general store. The lower leg of the E met a single-story brick structure with plate windows. On the windows, someone had made a weak attempt to scrape off white lettering that read *Hunt Personal Computing Experts You're Best Shot* (nobody had worried about the grammar, and I figured Mr. Spencer would be proud of me for noticing if he weren't so pissed I'd stolen his car) and below that line of half-erased script, bright yellow letters said *We Buy Gold*, but the windows were dark, and a thick chain wrapped the door.

So much for the brief commercial boom in Hunt, WY.

I drove behind the Hunt Public House, where an ancient F-150 was pulled up against the back wall. There was a Cutlass with duct tape holding one door in place, and there was a Firebird sloughing its cherry-red paint. A few yards back, where the asphalt broke off and dirt and weeds sloped down toward the cottonwoods, a soapy blue semi-tractor was parked with leaves across its windshield. It was just the tractor—the front part of the whole assembly, with the cab and the engine so that it could be driven independently but without the long hauling trailers that it normally towed. Cribbs's tractor, I guessed. No. I hoped.

The Impala ticked as it cooled behind me, and I trotted toward the tractor. I made a circuit of it. The leaves on the windshield were a good clue, but I checked the crumbling asphalt under the tractor — lighter in color than the wet patches exposed to the weather—and the mud flaps—dry on the inside, the mud stiff and crumbling to my touch.

The semi-tractor had been here for a day. Maybe two. Through the rain, which had been on and off for almost two full days. Never long enough for the roads to dry out completely. And never long enough that someone could drive it without picking up wet mud and splashing a lot of water on the vehicle's undercarriage. Take the Impala, for example: as it ticked and cooled, I could see spatters of fresh mud in the wheel wells.

Why was Cribbs here? Why not—well, I paused as I took a step back and studied the public house again. I didn't know what Cribbs wanted. Something, obviously. He must have been involved with some of the illegal shipping—human trafficking, drugs, black market merchandise—that Belshazzar's Feast had coordinated through this part of the world. There wasn't any explanation of why or how he would know the Lady otherwise.

Asphalt crumbled, tiny black crumbs shifting under my sneakers as I worried the edge of the pad with my shoe. Suspecting that Cribbs had somehow been involved with the Lady and her operation out of Belshazzar's Feast didn't explain the rest of it, though. What did he get out of turning his kids over to the Lady? The only way that made sense is if Shay were wrong and Cribbs didn't care about Tyler and Hannah. And even if Shay were wrong, even if Cribbs didn't love his kids, why go to this kind of trouble? Why risk a kidnapping charge, even if it got dropped after the truth came out about the divorce and custody settlement?

I followed the asphalt around to the front of the public house. Aspen leaves, brown from last autumn, clung to my sneakers. Money. People did all sorts of things for money. That seemed too obvious. Too simple. It might have been money, sure, but I didn't have anything to base my guess on. A thud, thud, thud had started, and it sounded like it was in my chest, more rhythmic than my heartbeat, buried deeper in my flesh. Money. What kind of piece of shit sold his kids out for money? Thud, thud, thud. Thud, thud, thud.

A part of me was still in the asphalt lot, pausing at one of the misaligned parking stops to scrape an aspen leaf from the toe of my sneakers. But a part of me was back in Emmett's house, in his dad's study, my shirt off and Lawayne pawing my back like every scar was just part of his personal tally instead of another fucking seam where my life had broken. That inside part of me, the part that didn't care shit for the aspen leaf on my shoe or the fact that nobody had ever straightened the parking stops or that the thud, thud, thud was coming from inside the public house, the bass line to shitty pop music, that inside part of me was hearing Lawayne talk to my dad, telling him to put me on a leash, to put me in a kennel, to beat my ass. And my dad's voice like a bumblebee trapped in an aluminum case, buzzing yes, yes, yes. What kind of piece of shit. That leaf wouldn't come off my sneaker no matter how I twisted my foot, no matter how hard I scraped along the parking stop's snub end. What kind of piece of shit. I ran my foot the length of the parking stop. That damn leaf bent in half, its wet tip trailing along the stop, but it didn't pull free. What kind of piece of shit. I brought my foot down hard, so hard that the shock ran up to my knee, and I knew I was being stupid, I just goddamn knew it, but I didn't care because that leaf wouldn't get off my fucking shoe, and what kind of piece of shit did that kind of thing to their kid?

With one final, savage kick, I ripped the leaf free, and it spun, its tip shredded from the parking stop's cement, and lay flat on the asphalt. I shook myself out. Who cared about a leaf? And who cared about the kinds of pieces of shit that got to be parents? That was just biology. Stick your dick in the right spot, and if you were lucky/unlucky, a kid popped out. You didn't have to be smart or decent or talented. And anyway it was just a leaf, just a leaf, they were all over the soles of my sneakers, so what did it matter if there was one more.

And sure enough, I picked up another leaf, an identical one, on my next step.

Fuck my life.

Inside, the Hunt Public House did have a decent bass line going—the thud, thud, thud I had heard outside. It wasn't pop music, though, as I'd guessed; at least, nothing I had heard before. Older stuff, maybe. Or just something obscure. Hipsters popped up everywhere; maybe one of them owned the Hunt Public House. With the weak bulbs behind thick yellow glass, the inside of the building was mostly shadow with the occasional burl of light knobbing the darkness. There was a bar, a row of taps, and a chalkboard menu with pizza listed as the special of the day for February 22nd. It had been a long time since February.

Behind the bar, a pair of guys did prep work: one sliced limes; the other washed bar mats and metal trays. They looked like Wyoming boys, brothers: rangy, mud-haired, and each of them in red flannel.

"No kids," the one with the limes shouted over the music.

"I've been hearing that a lot today."

"What?" He shook his head. "Axton, tell him no kids."

The one scrubbing bar mats—Axton, God love him for a name like that—looked at me over his shoulder. "No kids."

"Yeah." When I got to the bar, I glanced around. Bathrooms were on my left. On my right, an archway opened onto another room with a pool table and more seating. A curtain covered an opening further down the wall, and I guessed that was my destination. "I'm looking for somebody."

"You can't be in here," the one with the limes said. "No minors. It's against the law."

"I'm not trying to buy anything."

"Still can't be in here."

"Are you sure about that?"

"Axton, get rid of this kid, will you?"

"No kids."

"Jesus Christ. I'm just looking for somebody and then I'll go."

"Didn't you hear him—" the one with the limes started.

Axton waved him to silence. "Who?"

"A guy named Cribbs."

The one with the limes froze, the knife halfway through a green wedge.

"Kid, you should just go, all right?" Axton was trying hard to meet my gaze, but he was looking over his shoulder, and I was better than most people at being cold as ice. After a moment, he shrugged, turning his attention back to the bar mats. But as he turned, his eyes slid toward the curtained opening. "Just get lost."

"Yeah. I'll get lost." I pushed off from the bar and started toward the curtain.

"Hey, kid. You can't go back there. Kid! Axton, for Christ's sake, Cribbs doesn't want anybody—"

"Will you shut up, shit-for-brains?"

Behind me came the sound of the rubber mats splashing into the sink, then footsteps. The brothers behind the bar, if they really were brothers, hadn't looked tough. They were both smaller than me. But they also worked in a pub, and they'd probably had to get rough with customers before, and they might not feel bad about tossing a kid out on his ass. They might not feel bad, for that matter, about doing a lot worse.

The industrial vinyl underfoot bristled with the spillage from sticky drinks, a fur of dust that had settled since whenever this place had last been mopped—a few decades ago, I guessed—and a snack mix of pretzels, peanuts, and those little bagel wafers. They probably put out bowls of the stuff from time to time. Every step I took sounded like velcro ripping, and behind me, Axton was coming faster.

As I grabbed the curtain—thin cotton that had gotten thinner with age, a layer of oil and nicotine filming the surface yellow—a hand grabbed my arm and hauled me back. Tried to haul me.

"Kid," Axton's voice was low, almost sad, and then something pricked me low on my back. Steel. Sharp steel. "You should have just gotten out of here."

# Chapter | 18

The steel dug into me again, the point passing easily through my sweater and dimpling the flesh low on my back. Warm blood trickled into my waistband. Just a trickle. The edges of my world went red—not from the pain, it was just a pinprick, but from the sudden rush of fear and anger.

"You want to see Cribbs. Why don't you tell me why?"

He hauled on me again, and the top of my body went with him, while the lower half tried to remain fixed in place, bent against the narrow point of steel embedded in my skin. Axton hauled on me once more.

I was big. I was heavy. I was mad. I didn't haul.

He was touching my arm. It would have been easier if I had turned to look him in the eyes, but I didn't want to give him even an instant of satisfaction. He was touching my arm, and that would be enough. My inner sight opened. The hypertexture of the other side overlaid the public house: the tobacco-smoke haze on the curtain suddenly gained depth and complexity; the lines of my veins, blue like river water under winter-pale skin, became sapphire threading through snow. I heard a soft voice at the edge of consciousness, but I ignored it and reached across, into Axton's mind, and found the darkness waiting for me.

It was quiet in here. I hung in that void. And disappointment rasped inside me like a match on a strike strip. I didn't feel any better. That black hole in the back of my head, the thoughts about my dad, about Austin, about Emmett—they didn't quiet down, they didn't go away. They were still there, eating me up in pieces.

Why? When I had come apart, when I had entered the other side fully and ripped Krystal's soul across planes, I had felt great. Beyond great. It hadn't just been peace; it had been bliss. Here, now, in the darkness of this Wyoming bartender's head, I still felt like shit.

I had to go deeper into the other side. I had to go farther. Away from me, away from myself, away from my body. The thought glowed; it was like that security light I had seen from Dad's window the night before, just a speck of white tacking the void into place.

Time was passing, I realized. Slower here, but still passing. I needed to deal with Axton, and then I needed to get upstairs.

Dipping into the dark stillness of Axton's mind, I looked for the source inside me: a memory from my own childhood. Nothing terrible. Nothing that might cascade through Axton the way I had set off that landslide inside Emmett's head. This was simple, small, safe. It was the memory of lying on a quilt spread on the grass, the sky dark and open, and a daddy long-legs crawling onto my arm. My first reaction, my only reaction that persisted in the memory, was stark, brainless terror. Then I was free of Axton's head, and my inner eye snapped shut, and the hypersaturated colors of the other side faded.

Axton squealed. It was the only word that fit the noise: a high, desperate glottal sound. Then metal chimed, and the knife dropped down to bump against my sneaker as Axton jumped back.

I spun around. Axton's mouth was wide. That squeal, deep in his throat, was still choking him. He took a rickety step back; he caught up against a chair, and it tumbled, and the clatter seemed to snap whatever was holding Axton. The squeal turned into a full-on, "Fuck," and he ran. He crashed into the pub's front door at speed, slipped, and his legs went out from under him. The next instant he was scrambling out between the doors on hands and knees. I met the other brother's eyes and pointed the way Axton had gone.

Other-brother ran too.

A knife. I glanced down at the long deadly blade. Not a paring knife for slicing limes. Not a box cutter for breaking down cardboard. You could skin a deer with a knife like this. Or you could bury it in a kid's back. If you hit low, the kidney maybe, you might not even give him a chance to scream. I didn't have definite proof. I didn't know, not for sure. But I had a pretty good sense that Axton had planned on killing me before he let me get to Cribbs's room.

Suddenly, the pub's emptiness made my skin crawl. Water still ran in the sink where Axton had been scrubbing the mats. The brother had left a lime slice only half-cut. The thud, thud, thud of the music continued, and I stooped and grabbed the hunting knife, and then I twitched aside the curtain long enough for a look.

A flight of stairs.

I hesitated a moment and then moved back behind the bar. I found the radio and shut off the music, and I hit the tap with my elbow; the water sputtered once and dried up. Everything smelled like limes back here. Keys. Where would they keep the keys to the rooms they rented? They would have to be close, right? I pictured the public house in the small hours. The music would still be hammering. The crowd would have shrunk to the loyal, the desperate, and the wasted. The loyal would probably have a place of their own; the desperate and the wasted, probably not. They might stay in their cars. They might try to drive into the vast expanse of the high plains and find a flophouse like the Kane Motor Court. But why risk a DUI? Why go out in the cold, in the rain, onto roads where the Highway Patrol wouldn't mind having a friendly chat with you and then another, longer chat in the county lock-up? Why do something stupid like that when the Hunt Public House had rooms for rent? And cheap, too. The desperate and the drunk would come up to the bar. They'd settle the tab. They'd pick up a key.

At least, that was what made sense to me, so I scanned the cramped space behind the bar. There, above a shelf with pickled jalapenos and pearl onions and an open box with plastic-wrapped tampons spilling out, keys hung on hooks. Two keys with identical tags that read 1. Two keys on the next hook—2. Only one key each for hooks 3, 4, and 5.

Five rooms. Three of them occupied. I grabbed the keys tagged 3, 4, and 5. Then I took the stairs.

The rooms ran shotgun toward the end of the building; a window punctured the far wall, exposing a rectangle of that dirty-wool sky. All five numbered rooms were on my left. On my right, one door was unmarked, but the addition of a serious-looking deadbolt told me it was probably the office. A little farther down on the right was a second door. No deadbolt. It was opposite Room 3, and judging by the screw holes on the wood, I figured at one point it had borne a plaque of some kind.

I jiggled the handle on the door with the missing plaque. The sound was loud, and my heart beat a little louder in my ears. The handle turned, and I opened the door. Mops in stagnant water, a dolly with chipped red paint, metal shelves with a few sad rolls of paper towels. A utility sink filled with bloody bedding. Fear swam in my gut. Was I too late?

Shutting the door, I studied the hallway again. Ok, so the janitorial closet was opposite room 3. And rooms 3 through 5 were the backmost rooms, with five against the exterior wall. So if they've only got one guest, maybe they put him in 3 right away because it's the easiest room to clean. And 4 goes to the next guy. But 5—5 didn't make sense. The third guy should have gone in 2, right next to three.

Minimize effort and work. Don't schlep the cleaning supplies all the way down to 5 if you don't have to.

I paused. I wanted to club myself on the side of the head. I was a psychic, right? I didn't need to go through all this process-of-elimination shit. I could just project myself into the other side and walk right through the walls, check each room, and go from there. I opened my second sight, and as the ultra-fine weave of the other side appeared, I hesitated. To project myself onto the other side, even partially, would leave my body here. Helpless. And if Axton worked up the courage to come back—or his brother, which was more likely—then I'd be easy prey for them. I'd likely die before I even knew they were there.

The swim and surf of blood was louder in my ears. For the time being, until I had someone to watch my back, I wasn't willing to take the risk. I worked key 5 in my hand. I'd have to do this the hard way.

Up here, a nickel's worth of carpet covered the floor. The damn stuff didn't muffle anything; every step I took sounded magnified by the cheap flooring and the bare walls. If I were Cribbs, if I had taken my kids off the street and hauled them out to this dump, if I were locked up and hiding with them—God only knew why—what would I do? I'd be worried. Not scared, not yet, but on edge. That much was obvious by how Axton and the other brother had acted downstairs. They hadn't just wanted me to go away; Axton, at least, had been willing to hurt me, maybe kill me, to keep me away from Cribbs.

So if I were Cribbs, holed-up in the Hunt Public House, and if I were worried enough to bribe the two sons of bitches who worked here so that they'd keep anybody from getting into my room, and if I were stupid enough—the rush of blood, mixed with shock at the stupidity, made me pant, a doggy grin on my face—if I were so goddamn stupid that I still parked my semi-tractor out back where anybody who took an extra two minutes could find it, and if I'd been here for days, the worry and fear ramping up, getting stronger, putting me on the edge of my seat because I was here with the kids, nowhere to go, nothing to do but wait, what would I do?

I'd go out of my damn mind. I paused as my sneaker passed room 4. After a few days of that, hiding out, stupid as shit, I'd be getting paranoid. I'd start wondering if the Lady was going to deliver on whatever she'd promised. I'd start wondering if the cops were already looking for the kids. I'd start wondering if Axton and his dumbass brother might not be willing to sell me out to anybody who had an extra twenty.

The hiss of blood in my ears made me brace myself against the wall. If I were feeling like that, I'd be ready for somebody to show up at any minute. And I'd be ready to do something stupid. Maybe really stupid.

I backtracked to the supply closet. I snatched the mop, wrung out as much of the stagnant water as I could, and scuffed my way up the nickel's worth of carpet until I was just past the door to room 4. I didn't want to get much closer. Any closer and I might get caught up in the wrong kind of stupid.

Flipping the mop around, I grabbed the wet nylon strands, grimacing as the water ran down my wrist and soaked the sweater. Then, the long wooden end of the mop wobbling, I swung and rapped it against the door to 5. Once. It was a sharp, clicking sound. I brought the mop back again, ready to crack it against the door again. It wasn't a perfect replica of a knock, but to a guy who's been holed up for days, worrying out of his mind, it might sound like—

The shotgun's boom crashed through the hallway. Pellets chewed through the door, gnawed away a good chunk of the mop handle, and dug deep into the drywall on the other side of the hall. I staggered back, my ears ringing. A second shotgun blast followed, the sound even louder this time, as a grinning chunk of the door peeled away and fell into the hallway.

"I'm gonna kill you, motherfucker," came a shout from inside the room.

Cribbs, I guessed. What an introduction.

On my next breath, I tasted gunpowder and the dry gypsum of wallboard. Dust swirled in the air. My ears were still ringing from the two successive gunshots, and when another flap of wood fell from the door, I heard nothing as it hit the ground. I edged a step closer to the door. I needed to see him; I needed that much, or I doubted I'd be able to make the connection that I needed to reach his mind and disable him.

"Mr. Cribbs." Christ, that sounded stupid. I opened my second sight, and the ultra-textured reality of the other side washed over me. "Mr. Cribbs, my name's Vie. Vie Eliot. I'm a friend of your kids—"

"Vie?" Hannah's voice was small, barely audible over the lingering thunder that the gunshot had left in my ears. It hammered right into my heart like a silver spike. "Vie, he's got a gun. He's not my dad—"

He's not my dad. I didn't know what that meant, but I could sense Hannah's fear like a poison cloud. I didn't care about Axton or his brother coming back. I didn't care about my body lying helpless on the floor. I pushed, the feeling like I was trying to sit up, and projected myself into the other side. Whoever was in there, I was going to walk right through that wall and rip his mind into so many pieces they could use it for confetti.

Before I could do more than project myself into the other side, though, I felt a surge. It was like what I had felt in the power Ms. Meehan had used at Emmett's house, like my own power, but another variation on it. The door to room 5 buckled. The hinges bent and squealed. One of the screws ripped free from the jamb, and then another, and all I could do was stare as an invisible force yanked the door out of its frame. Wood and metal shrieked, and the door flew inward, as though a giant had pitched it. Stranger still was the way the other side reacted: the threads making up this part of reality stretched, the weave drawing tight, snapping in places, subjected to forces that went beyond the physical. It grabbed me, my psychic projection, and slammed me against the wall. Whatever was happening, it was ripping the whole universe.

And then it stopped. I fled back to my body, dragged myself to my feet, and stumbled toward the door. Sure, whoever was in there had a shotgun, but I was willing to bet that guy didn't matter anymore. Something bigger and nastier had gotten him. Something had come for these kids, and I wasn't going to let him—or it—have them.

When I got to the broken door frame, I stopped and peeked around the jamb. Like a million other shitty roadside motels, the Hunt Public House had two queen beds with cheap polyester coverlets, a utilitarian chest of drawers, and a bulky CRT television on top. All of that, my mind took in without registering it. My attention was drawn to the man who was dying in front of me.

He was shorter than I had expected, with a compact muscularity that had gone to seed. He had a pot belly, likely from too many hours on the road and too few hours on his feet. A jagged end of the wood had punched through his torso and protruded from his chest, surrounded by gore. Pieces the ruined door lay around him, shrouding him like some bizarre postmodern burial custom. Suburban Death: A Visiting Installation. Like something Gage would have dragged me to see at the OKCMOA, and part of my mind flicked on at the thought, warning me how bad this must really be, how bad this was fucking me up because it had to be bad if my brain was skipping all the way back to Gage.

It wasn't the fact that this guy was dead that had my brain scratching and skipping like a shit record. I'd seen death before. What froze me was the kids.

Tyler crouched under a three-legged card table behind the dead man, his face set in a vicious snarl, his throat working noiselessly.

Blood made a thin line under his nose. Tyler had done this, I realized. He was in a straight line behind the man, and somehow he had ripped the door out of its frame and pulled it toward himself—spearing the dead man in the process. He'd managed to drag my psychic form toward himself too; he'd managed to twist the threads that made up the other side. An extraordinary combination of powers.

"Hey, it's me. Tyler. It's me, Vie. Ty, come on. Ty. Can you hear me? Where's Hannah?"

At the sound of his sister's name, Tyler jerked his head viciously, and his snarl became audible.

My second sight unfolded. The saturated colors of the other side bloomed: the coverlets suddenly looked ultramarine, the carpet textured brown and gray and black, even the cheap nightstands glowed like the best walnut. Except Tyler. Only Tyler looked the same as he had with only my physical sight, and that didn't make any sense. I didn't have time to think about it, though. Everything slowed down. The vicious jerks of Tyler's head became comically exaggerated pantomimes. I stretched across that distance and touched the mind of the boy I had tried to keep safe. Tried and failed.

Instead of stepping into darkness, I met a barrier of sharp edges. Like broken glass. I forced my way past it, ignoring the pain, and stepped into a hellscape of fire and pain. A sickly orange fire. The glow of a candle inside a plastic Halloween pumpkin. I had seen this color before. I had felt the hectic, fever heat of it. This was the Lady's touch, warm like infected flesh.

Inside myself, I found a soothing memory: dusk on the bank of the Bighorn River, late autumn, the rangegrass spiked with catkins at the water's edge, the cottonwoods spinning flame-colored leaves out against the sky. A purple sky. A quiet sky: no sun, no stars.

In the flickering sickness of Tyler's mind, a memory answered. That was how it worked: an echo to whatever I could find in myself. For Tyler, though, the memory wasn't of the river. It wasn't the cottonwood leaves tipped with fire against the void of the Wyoming sky. It wasn't the sound of the river, the smell of mud turned up by my sneakers, the brush of a catkin tickling my neck.

For Tyler, the memory was one that I recognized: the vinyl sofa sticking to his cheek, the scratch of an unfamiliar blanket, the leftover taste of chicken strips in his mouth, chicken strips that Vie—me, I thought, me—had brought home from work, and the smell of Hannah's hair kind of like his mom's hair as they shared the sofa. His eyes fluttered, a kind of watchfulness as he scrambled to keep from falling into sleep, and he saw me, my hair tied up in a bun, as I slouched against the wall, my chemistry book in my lap, a pencil between my teeth.

The memory poured over the fire like glacial water; Tyler's mind went dark and still. I shook myself free and found myself back in my body, staring out at the warp and weft of the other side. I didn't remember that night. I mean, sure, I remembered having them over, night after night, as they slept on the sofa until Shay got home from work. But I didn't remember any one night in particular, anything special, any night that might have left that kind of impact on Tyler. I was shaking. Part of it was from exhaustion, and part of it was—I wasn't sure. I wasn't even sure I wanted to know.

Fatigue dragged at me, and I felt my third eye sliding shut. Then I saw something else. Something I hadn't noticed before.

I saw Hannah.

Tyler's sister perched on the edge of the bed, wearing a short yellow dress that might have been perfect on a warm spring day, a day spent at the playground, but that was far too light for the recent bouts of Wyoming cold. She was kicking her legs. And what made me freeze, what made me struggle to keep my inner sight open, was that she appeared to me in the hypersaturated colors of the other side. And then, next to her, I saw her body. Her physical body. Stretched out along the coverlet.

"Hi, Vie," she said, her face drawn with fear, her kicks a little faster now. "Do you know why I can't wake up?"

# Chapter | 19

Somehow, I kept my third eye open long enough to drag myself to the bed. Tyler had curled up under the card table, his breathing even, his eyes half-shut and liquid beneath his lashes. I could deal with him in a moment.

"I keep trying to wake up. I keep opening my eyes, but nothing happens. I even pinched myself. That's what Grandma said you should do when you have a nightmare: pinch yourself. But I can't wake up."

"I don't know." I had to clear my throat as I dropped onto my knees next to the bed. Next to the tiny body. Was she in first grade? Christ, how shitty was that? I didn't even know. I raised my hand to take her pulse, and I froze again. I couldn't do it. I couldn't.

"Vie?"

I had to clear my throat again, and my voice still sounded like I'd swallowed an egg beater. "Just a second, Hannah."

"My dad can't wake up either. He's in the other room."

Too late, I thought. I was always too late. Too late to keep River alive. Too late to keep Emmett from having to kill Makayla. Too late to keep Austin from almost dying at Krystal's hands. Too late. Over and over again, too late. Too late for these kids, who hadn't done anything to anyone. If I'd gone looking for them right away, right when Shay asked, I might have been able to do something. Instead I had dicked around, moping about Emmett and trying to convince myself that he still cared about me, that in spite of all signs to the contrary, I meant something to him. If I'd just done what Shay asked and come looking—

"Do you think I'll wake up soon, Vie?"

I still couldn't move my goddamn hand.

"I'm not scared," Hannah said.

My eyes flicked toward her, the spirit version of her. Her eyes were wide and earnest. Her legs kicked easily. Here she was trapped on the other side of reality, just happy as a jaybird, and I couldn't so much as move my hand.

"Why?"

"Why what?"

"Why aren't you scared?"

Hannah thought about this for a moment. Her waifish face twisted in indecision. "I don't know. That old lady came and did something, and it hurt, Vie. It really hurt." Her hand caressed a spot below her ribs. "And then I was like this. I couldn't go back. Dad didn't like it. He didn't like what the old lady did, and when she went outside, he made Tyler climb out the bathroom window, and then he carried me out, and we came here. I was scared for a few days. At the beginning. And then it just seemed silly to be scared for days and days, and I thought about how Tyler would have loved something like this, and I was worried about him because—because then the other man came, and he hurt Dad, and the other man wasn't nice to Tyler at all, and then I—I just got unscared." Pausing, she seemed to consider it. "I guess I was a little scared. Right now. Because of the door. But I don't feel the same way I used to feel. Things are different when I'm like this, aren't they, Vie?"

I didn't know, but I remembered how I had felt when I was fully on the other side. I didn't answer. I flexed my fingers. One knuckle popped, and it startled me so bad I pulled my hand back like I'd touched the stove. And then I reached for her inanimate form, settling my fingers on her neck, holding my breath. For one agonizing moment, I remembered seeing Hannah for the very first time: small and hungry and helpless. Like a kid on the back of a milk carton, if they even still put missing kids on milk cartons.

Her pulse bumped against my touch. Maybe just my imagination. Maybe just a dream. And then it bumped again, a tiny knot of pressure passing under my fingers.

I blinked. I dragged the sleeve of Dad's nasty, scratchy sweater across my eyes. I smelled the burnt plastic stink—the crystal meth stink—that had been baked into the wool. I smelled mop water. My chest hiccupped, and I had to scrub again with that wool, scrub hard enough to start a fire in my eyes.

"Are you all right?"

"Stay here for a minute."

I went back to the hallway and checked the door marked 4. Nothing.

I checked the door marked 3. A dead man lay in the bathtub, wrapped in a shower curtain. His face, although bloated with death and age, reminded me of Tyler. Cribbs, I guessed. He had tried to save his kids, and someone had hunted him down. And they were holding on to the kids as a power play. Or, I guess I should say, they had been holding on to the kids.

I went back to room 5.

"We need to get you to a hospital," I told Hannah. "Both of you."

"You don't look very good."

"I'm fine."

"Tyler looked like you once. Mom said he had cottage-cheese face. Then he threw up his whole bowl of Fruit Loops, and he got his throw up right into my bowl of Fruit Loops. And Mom made us both go to our room." The last sentence carried a note of injustice, and Hannah looked at me expectantly.

"I'm sorry."

She nodded, and then she slid off the bed and skipped over to Tyler. "Tyler's got loopy-lips, Tyler's got loopy-lips."

The fact that Tyler was dozing and, even if he'd been awake, couldn't hear her didn't slow Hannah in the slightest.

Gathering Hannah's limp body, I carried her out to the Impala. I came back to her teasing—

—loopy-lips, Tyler's got loopy-lips—

—and carried Tyler to the car too. He grumbled a bit, twisting in my arms, trying to get comfortable. He managed to elbow me in the mouth, dig his knee into my solar plexus, and squirm halfway out of my grip before I caught him. He might have been dreaming about wrestling a tiger or kayaking through white waters or shooting lasers in outer space. Whatever he was dreaming about, he had a second round of it when we got to the car, and that time he got me good enough to bust the corner of my mouth, and I grunted in spite of myself.

His eyes flitted open, blue and clear and empty, and he blinked, not seeming to see me. Then he huffed a breath, squirreled deeper into my arms, and mumbled something.

"What?"

"He says you've got cottage-cheese face," Hannah said helpfully. She sat in the front seat, looping her hand around the seatbelt and then giggling as her fingers passed through it.

After getting Tyler settled on the Impala's rear bench, I belted Tyler and Hannah into place. There was something so odd about fastening the buckle around Hannah's slim body while her spirit made faces—with no visible result—in the rearview mirror. But I figured that was just the tip of the iceberg with how weird things had gotten lately. I climbed into the driver's seat and started the car. Behind me, two dumpsters overflowed with the Hunt Public House's garbage. I eyed them in the mirror as I shifted into reverse, adjusting the turn so I wouldn't clip them.

"When Mom has cottage-cheese face, she usually needs to eat something. Or sometimes she definitely shouldn't eat something. Sometimes she needs something to drink. Like medicine." Hannah crossed her eyes at me and stuck out her tongue. "One time she needed her medicine, and instead Tyler cooked eggs, and the eggs burned, and Mom said he was trying to kill her, and he's not allowed to make eggs anymore. But I never tried to make eggs." Her eyes uncrossed. Her tongue shot back out at me.

"I don't need a drink," I said, still gauging my turn in the mirror, but the truth was that a drink actually sounded really good. Really, really good.

"But your cottage-cheese face—"

"I don't have cottage-cheese face."

Hannah's whole face screwed up in concentration. I knew that face. Even glimpsing it out of the corner of one eye, with my attention fixed on making this turn, I knew that face. It was the face I made every single time Mr. Lynch put a new proof in front of us.

"Why do Austin and Emmett want to kiss you on the mouth?"

I hit the gas too hard. The Impala shot backward. The rear bumper clanged against the dumpster, and the dumpster answered with an enormous, hollow boom. I rocked forward, my head narrowly missing the steering wheel. Then I fumbled the car into neutral.

Hannah was giggling, her hands pressed over her mouth.

"What are you—I don't—I wasn't—They never—"

"I saw you. I went to your house sometimes. When I was bored because Tyler couldn't hear me and Dad didn't want to hear me. And sometimes when I went, Austin kept kissing you on the mouth. And you kept trying to find something in his pockets. But one time, it was Emmett, only he didn't kiss you on the mouth, but he looked like he wanted to, and then he got on his knees—"

"Ok. Hold on. You were watching me?" Then it came to me: that giggle. That damn giggle that I had heard.

Hannah nodded. "And Tyler told me. He said that Jerry Casevich told him, and he said Jerry's friend Rodney told him, and Rodney's a fifth-grader, and Rodney's sister is a sixth-grader."

"What?"

"Tyler said he's seen Austin kiss you on the mouth. Sometimes a lot."

The Impala rumbled under me. The heat from the vents tasted faintly like exhaust. Out above the rangegrass, a falcon gyred.

"Tyler said that Rodney's sister told Rodney, and Rodney told Jerry, and Jerry told him, that Emmett Bradley wants to kiss you on the mouth, but you don't let him."

The falcon's spiral slowed.

"And Tyler said that Jerry called you the f-word and he had to punch Jerry in the face. And that's why he got three days in the office. And then he asked Mom why you wanted boys to kiss you on the mouth, and Mom said, 'What boys?' and Grandma said, 'It doesn't matter which boys, Shay, just leave it alone.' And Mom said, 'I'm just asking him which boys, I think it does matter, especially if it's that one we always see him with.' And Grandma said, 'It's nobody's business.' And Mom said, 'I know it's nobody's business, but sometimes I just want to know,' and that's when Tyler said he'd seen Austin kissing you on the mouth a lot at school, but I've never seen it at school because I have a different recess than Tyler, so I don't always see the high school kids. I only ever saw you in your room. When you have your shirt off."

The falcon straightened out its flight, dropping down slowly against the tumbled-up gray of the clouds.

"And then—" Hannah said.

I groaned.

"—Grandma said, 'It's a shame it's not the Bradley boy.' And Mom made a face, and Grandma said, 'Well, I've still got eyes, don't I, and those two together would make anybody have dirty thoughts.' And then Tyler said that part about Jerry calling you the f-word, and I wanted to know why he called you a fart, and Tyler laughed and said I was too young to understand, and I said I wasn't too young, and Tyler just kept laughing until Mom said, 'That's enough, Tyler.' And then Grandma said, 'Well if it's both of them, I ought to smack his hand. He can have a cookie, but he can't have the whole cookie jar.' And Mom said, 'All right, Mom, we get it.' Because Grandma is her mom, so she calls her mom. And Grandma said, 'He'd look better with that Bradley boy on his arm.' And Mom said that was enough and told Tyler and me we could eat dinner in front of the TV, so we did, but Tyler said she was just doing that to get us out of the room, and I knew that already, so we put the TV low, and Mom said, 'Do you really think he's with both of them?' And Mom said she'd pick Austin if she had her choice, and Grandma said Mom never had good taste."

I groaned.

"Do you like it when they kiss you on the mouth?"

The falcon shot toward the earth, scooping up something—it was too far to see what—and carrying it into the sky. A vole. A mouse. A rat. A rabbit. Something that was dying a vicious, brutal, sudden death. Maybe, I thought, it wouldn't be so bad to be a rabbit. Or a rat. Or a mouse. Or a vole. Any other goddamn thing in the universe wouldn't be so bad right now.

"I think we should have quiet time," I said.

"Vie?"

I shushed her.

Hannah fidgeted with her hair. "I just have one question, Vie."

"I really think we should just have quiet time—"

"I just wanted to know which one walks funny."

"Huh?"

"Those boys. The ones who kiss you on the mouth. Which one walks funny? Because Grandma said the only way to know which one you like was to watch and see who walks funny on Saturday morning, and I thought maybe Austin hurt his foot, because one day Tyler said he saw—"

"Ok." The word was a squeak. I fumbled with the gear shift. "Ok, um. I think we have to stop talking. Right now." Forever, I thought. We have to stop talking forever. "Because we don't want to wake up Tyler. So let's be quiet the rest of the way."

Somehow I got the car into drive, and the Impala lurched away from the dumpster, and somewhere out among the rangegrass and the buffalo grass and the Junegrass, a vole was being ripped to shreds and having a much, much better time than I was.

"Vie." Hannah was hunched toward me, hand to the side of her mouth, her voice a child's attempt at a whisper. The hypersaturated colors of the other side pulsed with her curiosity. "Vie!"

"Dear God," I muttered.

"I only asked you that about those boys kissing you on the mouth because I don't think they're going to want to kiss your cottage-cheese face."

# Chapter | 20

I expected the kind of frenetic emergency response to my arrival at the hospital that I had seen on television hospital dramas. I carried Tyler in first, and while everybody seemed really curious about how I had gotten hold of a child, there was no dramatic rush of action. An orderly came out to the Impala with me, helped me get Hannah's body situated on a gurney, and then took her back inside. I parked the car; by the time I grabbed my backpack and got back into the ER, they had Hannah and Tyler in a curtained-off exam room.

"Are you family?" The nurse who asked me was a large Hispanic woman. She had kind eyes and a dusting of a mustache.

"Yes."

"Do you have ID?"

"No."

"You'll have to wait out there."

Out there meant a row of plastic chairs at the registration desk. The nurse followed me to the desk, watched me until I sat down, and then disappeared back into the examination area. Hannah's spirit, which had drifted along behind me, said, "I'm going to go watch Tyler."

I nodded, and as she left, I let my inner eye shut. As soon as I did, my head began to throb. It wasn't an ache or a pulse or a thrum. It was a goddamn hammer-to-the-skull pounding. I'd never had my inner eye open that long before, and I felt like I'd managed to split my skull in two.

Letting my head drop onto my arms, I tried to enjoy the cool of the laminate countertop, and I took slow breaths to keep the pain from taking up too much space inside me.

Shay and her mother arrived. Something about the sound of their steps—a frantic, hurried clicking—made me lift my head, and there they were: Shay glancing around the waiting room, and Lucy trailing after her. Spotting me, Shay hurried over.

"Are they here? God, where are they? Why aren't you with them?" She raised up on tiptoes. "Someone called and said—"

"Mrs. Cribbs?"

"Me. It's Harwood again, but that's me. Mom, come on." Shay scurried after the nurse and disappeared into the closed-off examination area.

Lucy Harwood lingered, though. She hadn't changed in the months I'd known her: trim, coiffed, her back ramrod straight. Her platinum hair didn't have any roots showing; I figured she paid enough to make sure they never did. The corners of her mouth made daggers.

"They're fine. Or they will be."

Lucy brought up one hand; a hundred years ago, she would have been trailing lace, a handkerchief between her fingers. Today she wore a Michael Kors watch with a rose-colored strap, and she dabbed at her eyes with wadded tissue. "How bad was it?"

I shrugged and laid my head down again.

For a moment, Lucy drifted toward the exam area. Then she stopped, and her heels clicked as she came over to me and ran one thin hand through my hair. "I won't tell her. And I don't want you to. But one of us needs to know."

"Bad."

Her fingers froze at my nape, tightening around the locks of thick blond hair, enough to hurt. I spoke out of that pain.

"Cribbs is dead."

Her exhalation whistled, and a tremor ran through her. I saw it shake her little pink pumps, and I felt it in her fingers, trembling in my hair. Then she shook her hand free and smoothed the back of my head.

"I'm sorry. She shouldn't have asked you."

"It would have been worse if it had been someone else." That was true; at least, I more or less believed it was true. Someone else might have gotten a knife in the back courtesy of Axton or his brother. Someone else might have taken a spray of shotgun pellets. Someone else might have gotten caught in Tyler's miniature hurricane and gotten a door jamb through one lung. And nobody but me would have been able to talk to Hannah.

"I didn't want her to ask you." Her thin hand—it was so thin, the weight almost nothing, as though the bones were birdlike and hollow, and I wondered what it would have felt like to have a grandmother to brush my hair—rested on my head again. "You picked them up on the side of the road."

"What?" I raised my head, or I tried to raise it, but she gently forced me to stillness. Her fingers ran through the locks again, her nails gently scratching my scalp, and it felt so good that some of the ache went away.

"You picked them up on the side of the road. Do you understand?"

"On the way to Hunt."

"On the way to Hunt," she said. "I'll make sure Tyler and Hannah remember exactly where you picked them up. On the side of the road. On the way to Hunt." Then her voice changed. "I thought Sara Miller was keeping your socks darned and your stomach full."

I shrugged. Her nails continued their rhythmic massage of my scalp.

"Why do you look beat to hell, then? Your daddy catch up with you?"

There was a frankness to the question, an absolute lack of judgment, that robbed me of the anger I would normally have felt. "No. Something else."

"Does Sara know you're here?"

"She doesn't need to know."

Lucy's hand stopped again. With my head buried in my arms, I couldn't see her face, but her voice thickened when she spoke again. "Boys are all the same, no matter what age they are. You think you're half diamond and half dynamite, like nothing can touch you, and you're all so stupid nobody can tell you different. I ought to call Sara right now and tell her to get down here. I spanked her bottom once in Sunday School for kissing Gene Peterson behind the pulpit. I ought to haul down her drawers and purple her ass again. It's gotten plenty big."

I lifted my head, then, shaking off Lucy's touch, and I met her eyes. "But you won't."

She sighed, and she dabbed at her eyes again, and she twisted her watch around and around like she thought she could shake back time. Finally she shook her head. "No, I won't because I might be old, but I'm as stupid as ever for a pretty face." She rummaged through her purse and drew out something that she pressed into my hand. "There's more of that. Come by the house. Or call; I can always wire it."

I pressed the crinkling bills toward her, and Lucy shrugged her purse back up her shoulder so furiously that I actually wilted. She watched me for a moment, waiting to see if I'd do something stupid again, and then she sniffed and turned and walked toward the exam rooms. She might have been sixty, or thereabouts, but she had those pink pumps and she had a sway in her hip, and an old man with a straw hat just about fell out of his chair watching her go.

Two hundred dollars. Christ. I could get a lot farther now. As soon as I took care of things here, I could get as far away as I needed to. California, maybe. Not on two hundred dollars, not all the way, but I could get a lot farther now.

I just had to scrub Urho out of existence.

Laying my head down again, I tried to plan. Before I could make certain decisions, though, I needed answers. Sleep came unexpectedly, washing over me as I sat there, my head on my arms. It was patchy, broken by the noises of the waiting room, and when I woke—an hour later, to judge by the clock on the wall—my neck was cricked, and my tongue had dried up.

I walked the length of the waiting room, checking out the connecting hallways, and I followed one and then another. Then, near a pair of recessed bathroom doors, I saw them: a bank of payphones and, more importantly, a drinking fountain. I took a long drink. Then I went to the phones.

With the plastic receiver smooth in one hand, running my thumbnail along the seam, I held down the hook. The phone was dead in my ear. All I had to do was lift my finger, let the line open, and dial.

Down the hall, a middle-aged man with a mop of curly brown hair moved from trash can to trash can, removing the filled trash bags and stowing them in his cart before replacing them. A Bluetooth earpiece blinked on and off, and he mumbled into it as he walked, stopping as he shook open each fresh liner to laugh and deliver another short burst of response in a language I didn't recognize. A pair of girls, sisters, I guessed by their similar hair and clothes, skipped down the hall, singing, "One-two-three, skipadee-doo, skipadee-dee." The bathroom door behind me rattled open, and a cloud of air freshener—something pleasantly artificial to reassure you that the hospital was sanitary—filled the air. A red-faced woman shuffled past me, her skirt on backward, a tail of toilet paper wagging from the heel of her black sneakers. She had a phone pressed to her ear, and she was saying, "I don't care if she thinks the paisley is a better match, Richard, it's your father's funeral and I'm not paying all that money for you to look like a Frenchman."

Nobody. I couldn't call anybody. Trash-can guy could talk to his buddy or his girlfriend or his wife or his brother while he worked. The sisters could hold hands and skip and laugh with each other. The lady with the toilet-paper tail might sound like a holy terror, but she still had Richard on the phone, and it didn't sound like Richard was ever going to get a break.

A little shiver ran through me. My thumb slid off the hook, and it popped back up with a tinny ding, and the dial tone rang in my ear. I punched in a number. I'd had good reasons for memorizing this number. I might need it in an emergency. I might need it exactly at a time like this. I might need it if I was backed into a corner. Sure, I thought as I pressed the digits. Sure, you cowardly little shit, I told myself, keep thinking that's why you memorized it, keep telling yourself all those good reasons, and tell yourself it didn't have anything to do with the feel of him naked against you, the heat of him, the taste of his mouth like smoke and cinders stinging your lips.

Jim Spencer picked up on the second ring. "Hello?"

"I need to talk to you."

The screech of sliding metal came across the line, then heartbeats of silence, and then Jim's voice low. Low, but furious. "Where are you? Vie, what got into you? You know everybody is going out of their minds? Did you know that? Did you even think about that? Austin keeps trying to pull out the IV and go looking for you, and it's about all I can do to keep Sara from falling to pieces. What the fuck were you thinking?"

The harshness of the vulgarity, when he was normally so controlled, normally so precise, normally such a goddamn English teacher, actually lifted my toes from the vinyl flooring. "Is he ok?"

"Where are you?"

I curled the metallic cord around my finger. My breathing sounded funny. It was just because of the phone, I told myself. Just because I had that plastic so near my mouth, it was making everything sound funny.

"He's all right. Will you tell me where you are? I'd come pick you up, but I don't have my car."

"I'm sorry."

"Don't apologize to me. Where are you?"

"I'm at the hospital." I forced some strength into my voice. "I need you to look at someone, two kids, and I need you to tell me what happened to them, and I need to know if I can help them."

It wasn't until I finished speaking that I realized Jim was talking to someone else, his words low and indistinct like he'd pulled the phone away from his mouth. Then, in a clear voice, he said, "What floor are you on?"

"What? No. I want to meet you outside first, and then I can—"

"What floor, Vie? You're making this a lot harder than it needs to be."

"Ground floor. Near the emergency room. I'll head out front, and when you get here—"

"Just stay where you are. I'll be right there."

The phone clicked. I held the receiver against my ear for another moment, and then I hung it on the hook. Something stuck with me about the way he'd said it. Why did it matter what floor I was on? It didn't matter, not unless he was planning on coming inside to meet me. Or—

Or he was already here.

A perverse anger twisted inside me, and I stalked away from the bank of phones. I didn't know why I was angry. I didn't even know who I was angry with. Myself, mostly. Because I hadn't even thought about the fact that Austin would be here, with an IV in his arm, recovering from almost dying. And angry at the universe. And at Mr. Spencer. And at Austin and Emmett. Especially Emmett.

They were here. Austin was here.

I didn't even know where I was going, and then I was lost, and then I had to scramble from station to station, getting directions, until I took four flights of stairs to the top floor and stood halfway down a hallway outside his room and listened.

Kaden was laughing. "Good joke, man. All right. You really had me going. Come on." The forced amusement in his voice, already brittle, snapped. "Come on. Quit messing around."

Silence. Then the faint chime of metal. Kaden was nervous. Like, about-to-get-fried-out-of-his-socks nervous, and all that energy was manifesting itself. The hinges squeaked in response to that energy; the door swung a quarter-inch.

"You're serious?" The weed-and-good-vibes ease of Kaden's voice screwed tighter. "Austin, come on. You can't drop something like this on me. Don't—don't look at me like that." A rubber sole squeaked on the vinyl. Kaden's ugly Chucks, I guessed, as he tried to beat a retreat.

My palm rested on the door. The wood veneer was clammy under my skin. When it swung open, his nose would be right there, right at the perfect level for me to drive the bone right up into his brain.

But the Chucks squeaked again, and his voice had wound even tighter, like a guitar string ready to snap. "You can't just drop something like this, all right? You can't just tell me this and expect me to act normal. I've been cool about everything, right? I mean, everything. I've been cool about you being gay. I mean, it's not your fault. I think I kind of knew, anyway. I've been cool about you hooking up with that freak show."

The toe of my sneaker bumped up against the door. It wobbled another quarter-inch. My thoughts were as high and hard as the Wyoming wind, and it was hard to stay focused, but I was pretty sure—pretty goddamn sure—I could pitch Kaden through the window. The glass would be reinforced, but I was still pretty sure. I was going to try, at least, and see what happened.

"I get it: there's not a lot of guys here, ok? I mean, guys like you. But he's crazy. You know that, right? I've tried really hard to be cool about this. I've tried really hard to ignore the fact that you're making a—making a joke of yourself. I mean, the guys can't even look at you half the time because you're getting so weird. You're always with him. Always. You won't hang out. You just about bit my head off when I asked if you wanted to come over last weekend—"

"You asked if I had cash to get pot and coke and whatever other shit you wanted." It was the first time Austin had spoken in my hearing. His voice was raspy, an after-effect of being strangled by Krystal's vines. "You didn't want me to hang out. You wanted to get high. You just needed me to do it."

"Fuck you, man. He's not a bad guy, ok? I get it. But he's a freak show. Look at how fucked up our lives have gotten since he came here."

"You sold him out. Last year, when things got bad for you, you sold Vie out."

"I was saving my own skin, Austin. I wasn't trying to hurt him. I was—"

"You could have gotten him killed. And he helped you. He saved you. He saved all of us."

"From a fucking nightmare we wouldn't have been in if he hadn't come here. You know what? You know how messed up he is? When we were down in that . . . in that fucking prison or whatever you call it, you know what he did? He kissed me. He straight up fucking kissed me. Ask him if you don't believe me. That's the kind of guy you're going to throw everything away for? Jesus, Austin, you almost got killed yesterday. Just . . . just let it go, ok? Call it off. What you said, about me, about you and me, I never really thought about guys like that before, but if it makes you get this freak show out of your life, yeah, I'll think about it, ok? I'm not promising, but I mean, I'll think about—"

The heel of my hand butted the door, and it swung open. They were a nice little picture. They were a perfect fucking tableau. Austin lay in bed, his preppy hair not quite so preppy, his cheeks flushed, his lips parted, the hospital johnny askew and revealing the friction burn around his neck. Kaden stood with his hands on the bed's chrome rail, leaning toward Austin, his granola smile directed at the other boy. And all of the sudden, I remembered my first kiss with Austin, which had been in a hospital bed. It was like I was looking down a tunnel.

Or falling down a mineshaft. There was this tiny square of light I could still see, and it framed Austin and Kaden perfectly—only somehow, at the same time, it was Austin and me. And everything else was that rushing blackness.

"Hey man," Kaden said, turning to face me and then sliding along the chrome rail away from me. "Hey, it's so good to see you, we didn't know—"

"Vie. Oh my God, Vie." Austin slid toward the edge of the bed. Something—an IV line, a lead attached to his chest, something—caught, and he swore and jerked. "Are you ok? Jesus, I was so worried." He fumbled with more leads and wires and lines that they had him hooked up to. "Fuck," he roared, yanking at them. "Kaden, get this shit off me. Oh, fuck it." He surged toward the edge of the bed again, as though he intended to drag everything—the bed, the machinery, the wall if he had to—with him.

Kaden caught the hospital johnny in a fist and hauled Austin back onto the bed. Then he planted a hand on Austin and shoved him down.

I hadn't even stepped into the room. I hadn't even breathed, I didn't think. I felt like if I breathed, that square of light at the end of the tunnel would flicker and go out. So I just watched them in that tiny frame.

"Vie. Jesus, Kaden, what the hell is wrong with you? Get off me. Get the fuck off me. Vie, will you come over here? Are you ok? What—where did you go? What—Kaden, get the fuck off, I told you. Kaden!"

Kaden was smiling. Not his usual granola-and-sunshine smile. Just a hard sickle cutting his mouth. He knew I'd heard. Or he guessed that I had.

I nodded. It felt like my head might roll off my shoulders, and that little square of vision at the end of all that rushing blackness tilted and threatened to slide off into nothing. Then everything steadied, and I left.

"Vie! Kaden, I'm going to fucking kill you. Vie! Wait up!"

That black wind was eating up more and more of the world, and the spot of linoleum and chrome and tan at the end grew smaller and smaller. I wasn't breathing, but that was ok. I didn't need to breathe. There was so much air flowing past me, sucked into the darkness by that black hole at the back of my head. I didn't need to breathe. Fireworks detonated, huge and brilliantly white, in the collapsing tunnel of my vision. My shoulder caught someone—a nurse, a patient care tech, maybe the Surgeon General for all I knew—and I half-spun, regained my footing, and plunged through the next door.

I had the vague impression of shelves, a dingy yellow bulb, and cracked ceiling tiles. My foot clipped a stepstool, and it clanged against the shelves. Perfect. This was perfect.

I dropped onto the stool and swung my backpack between my knees. Someone was panting—it was a silly sound, and it made me want to laugh because it sounded so silly. I didn't need to breathe. I hadn't breathed in minutes. Those fireworks went off like neutron bombs at the back of my eyes, but I didn't need to breathe. Maybe nobody needed to breathe. Maybe it was just a big conspiracy. And that did make me laugh, but then I was dizzy, and I was lying against the shelves, and I couldn't sit up.

I grappled with the steel racking, and with one hand, I groped for the bag between my legs. I knew how I could feel better. The world was disintegrating, splitting at the atomic level, ripped apart by that black hole inside my head. But I knew how to bring it all together again. I knew how I could take all those things that pulled away from me, all those things that spun away in a cyclone, and have control over them: for a little while, anyway.

The zipper stuttered in my fingers, caught, and held. I swore and tore at it. It stuttered another quarter-inch and caught again. Fast, this time.

That dog-panting was getting louder. I wanted to laugh again. Geez. Geez, somebody was getting desperate. My fingers ripped at the narrow opening in the zipper, trying to force it wider, then just trying to worm inside. My nails caught the cardboard box of razor blades and tipped it into a half-turn. I snagged it and wriggled it free through the broken zipper.

As I fumbled open the box, that dog-pant got louder, and my hand jerked, spilling half the blades across the floor.

"Damn it."

But that wasn't my voice.

I leaned forward, kneeling in the dust bunnies, scraping my hands over the floor to find one of the blades. It was just so damn dark. Even with those fireworks going off, it was pitch black in here.

A hand closed over my arm. "Vie, you need to calm down. Take a breath. Take a real breath for me, ok?" Becca. That was Becca.

That was just so stupid. It was so fucking dumb I couldn't believe it. How could she not understand that I didn't need to breathe—that nobody needed to breathe? I remembered Austin telling me about all his breathing techniques. I remembered him telling me about controlling his breathing to avoid a panic attack. And I wanted to laugh. Why hadn't anybody ever told him that the problem isn't controlling your breathing—it's just plain old breathing? Panic is a fire, and fires need oxygen, and if you cut off the oxygen, poof, no more fire.

“Get out of here, Becca.”

“Vie, Vie, hey, look at me.”

Silver eyeshadow swam into the narrowing tunnel of my vision. The last two stars in the whole universe.

“You don’t have to do this. We can talk about this. I’ve been reading, doing a lot of reading, and I think I’ve got some good strategies. There are ways to cope. You don’t have to do this, all right? Can you just take a breath for me, though? It all starts with taking a breath.”

My fingers closed over a blade. The knot of tension between my shoulders slackened. Reading. Coping. Strategies. Breathing. What a fucking bitch. What a fucking stupid bitch. Breathing didn’t mean anything with a black hole at the back of your head. Nothing meant anything except—

Except that huge, beautiful spin of the saw, the blade shining like water, like starlight, like the moon. I felt a sudden, visceral tug. I didn’t have to settle for this. I didn’t have to cut with a cheap blade in a shitty storeroom. I could trot on down to the Impala, drive back to Sara’s, and start up the saw. I could really get things under control then. I could put everything in order. I could take myself apart, piece by piece, and then put things back where they were supposed to be.

“Give me that. You’re not going to . . . You’re not going to do that, not while I can help. Vie, lots of abused children do this, lots of abused kids end up harming themselves, hey, no, I—”

I turned my back on her. “Get out.”

“Please, I just want to—”

“What the fuck don’t you understand? Just get out. Get the fuck out.”

“Vie—”

“Go!”

I rolled my shoulders, letting my coat fall, and hiked up the sweater. I’d been using my legs lately. That was better; fewer people saw my legs. But this dumb bitch was going to get in my way again if I didn’t hurry, so I just shoved my jeans down a few inches and found the cleft that ran below my abdominals and toward my crotch. It was well defined, a furrow that marked tight musculature and the absence of body fat. Austin had run his tongue down that cleft. It took the blade like water, and red followed. Red like Austin’s tongue.

Everything contracted. The rushing darkness slowed. I started gasping for air, shaking, and the blade rattled out of my hand. Sagging, I steadied myself against the shelves. A prickling awareness returned in my fingers and toes as I felt myself coming back together, back in control, back whole, the way I was supposed to feel. The black hole at the back of my head had quieted. It was like throwing open a window or a door onto a perfect evening, fresh air blowing through an old room, and everything took on the clarity of moonlight. I wondered why I'd felt so fucked up a few moments before.

Soles scraped the linoleum, and I looked up. Becca was slinking out the door, her head down as she left.

I shifted, rising, and my sneaker caught the spray of blades, and they slid across the floor to strike the cabinets, and they chimed. I staggered. It wasn't just exhaustion, though. It was something inside my head. It wasn't the black hole chewing me up again, though. This was different. This was a kind of pressure building steadily behind my eyes. A stroke. I was having a stroke.

The voice in my head had that same singsong elocution I had heard before. It was the voice of the War Chief. And it wasn't even speaking to me, not really. It was like he stood behind me, speaking to someone else, and I just lucked into overhearing.

*They are at the hospital. Go quickly.*

And then, like someone spinning the tuner on a radio, Hannah's voice warbled in and out of static: *Vie*—and then the long, powerful rush of my blood blotting out everything—*can you please, please come get me? I'm scared!*

# Chapter | 21

Hannah's plea hung in my ears. I threw open my inner sight, and the thickly textured reality of the other side wove itself across my field of vision. I listened. I waited. One heartbeat. Come on, Hannah. Two heartbeats. Come on, God damn it. Three heartbeats. Nothing. I plunged out into the hallway.

And I crashed into Austin. He was holding the hospital johnny shut behind him with one hand, and he was patting Becca's shoulder with the other. She was sobbing. A pair of older nurses—one with hair set in huge curls that had probably been set in 1977, the other with hair shorter than Austin's—were moving toward us with the grim resolve of executioners. I knew I was first up on the chopping block.

"Vie, what the hell is wrong with you?" Austin said in that raspy voice. A stranger's voice. He squeezed Becca's shoulder and then took a step toward me. "What did you say to her?"

I skirted him, and he grabbed my coat and hauled me back a step. As he did, my coat and sweater rode up, exposing the lowered waistband of my jeans and the top of the bloody furrow running toward my crotch.

Austin swore, blocking me into a corner with his body. The hospital gown looked pretty damn good on him. You couldn't hide those shoulders under a johnny. You couldn't hide the trim taper of his waist. You couldn't hide—

He blushed a little when he chucked my chin. "Up here. Hey. What's going on?"

"Move."

"I'm not going to move. I'm going to talk to you because we need to talk. I've been worried sick about you. You ran off, Vie. Jesus, do you know what that did to me? Hey. And now you're cutting?"

Over his shoulder, I watched the 1977-curls nurse lead Becca away, but Becca kept casting glances at us.

"You won't even look at me? Is that where we're at? What happened? Did I do something?"

My eyes shot to his, and he stopped. He swallowed. The color got a little higher in his cheeks.

"Move. I'm not going to ask you again."

"You heard that. What I was talking about with Kaden, you heard that."

"Fine, you won't move, I'll move you."

I didn't want to hurt him. Whatever else had changed in the last few minutes, I still loved him. That was the bitch about love. The real stuff, it grew like a fucking weed. You couldn't just rip it out. It was in there, roots all the way down in my soul, and Austin was going to run off and fuck Kaden silly, and they'd be in love for a million years and have a million babies, and I'd still love Austin, and that's the kind of fucking weed love is, that's how deep it ran. In me, anyway. So I didn't want to hurt him. But I did want him out of my way.

I scanned the hallway: two framed sketches of stargazer lilies; a nurses' station with a phone the size of a concrete block, its cord hanging to the floor; an abandoned gurney stripped of its sheets; a row of doors; the nurse with hair shorter than Austin watching us; and one of those curved mirrors at the far end of the hall, showing a splash of movement. Guys in blue uniforms. Security.

Emmett flashed into my head, the night he had tried to teach me something about my abilities. He had used my best emotions against me. And he'd warned me that Urho and the Lady would try to do the same.

I blinked and let tears flood my eyes. It was dangerously easy. Then, hiking up my sweater and the layered tees underneath, I splayed my fingers along the cut. "Aus, I don't know what's going on with me. I think I cut too deep. Something—it won't stop—"

"Hey," Austin shouted. "Hey, we need somebody over here right now, we need—" He glanced over his shoulder, looking for a nurse.

And I sucker punched him. Right in the solar plexus. I heard the air come out like a bad whoopee cushion, and he folded. I caught him, walked him backward until we reached the nurse's station, and ripped the floor-length cord out of the big, blocky phone. Then I tied his arms to the chair.

"You fucking piece of shit," he said, and his face was shiny now, tears lacquering the high red. "Vie, what the fuck is going on? Baby, I want to help you, I'm trying to—"

"You're going to get yourself out of that pretty fast. When you do, you need to run. Get the hell out of here. Get everyone out of here. Pull the fire alarm if you have to."

"Young man," the nurse with the short hair grabbed my arm. "You sit down. Right now. You're going to have a lot of explaining to do—"

I half-spun, let her follow me, and then charged into her when she was off balance. She went backward. Her feet came up, surprisingly little feet in blue Nikes, and she landed hard with a breathy, "Oh!" I charged past her.

The security guys were already at the stairs. They weren't much to look at: no guns, just blue uniforms and walkie-talkies. They weren't even big. One of them, a lanky guy with elephant ears, I'd seen before at the basketball games cheering on his brother. But Timmy Stepp was a shit small forward because he flinched every time another guy came at him. And I was going to guess his big brother flinched too.

I wasn't willing to risk using my abilities on them. For one, I was going to need all the juice I had if it came to a real showdown. For two, if Urho had sent Kyle and Leo, I didn't want people incapacitated with terror or guilt while the building came down around them. Or exploded. Or whatever the hell those guys might do. So I settled for getting these two out of my way just long enough. And that meant doing it physically. And I was looking forward to that because I was feeling the powerful urge to hit something. Preferably, if I could track him down, Kaden.

"Stop right there," the guard, the one I didn't know, shouted.

"Get on the ground," Timmy Stepp's brother yelled.

I kept walking.

"Visual confirmation," the one I didn't know was saying into his walkie.

"Get on the ground right now," Timmy Stepp's brother yelled. His voice had skipped an octave. I let out a smile; he was definitely a flincher.

When I reached the abandoned gurney, I thrust my hands into my pockets.

"Show us your hands," the one I didn't know was screaming. "Show us your goddamn hands."

"He's got a gun," Timmy Stepp's brother called.

Someone down the hall screamed.

Jesus. Just Jesus Christ with these guys.

I whipped out my hands. Both guys flinched.

That's when I spun the gurney out from the wall and into the hall. I charged, pushing the gurney lengthwise across the hall, gathering as much speed as I could. I only had to go about ten yards, and Timmy Stepp's brother and the other guard were still recovering from those big, yellow flinches. I rammed into them at something close to fifteen miles an hour. Timmy Stepp's brother went down, and the gurney bucked over him. The other one took the brunt of the impact, and he flew. He hit the wall, grabbed at a chrome wall plate, and then drizzled down to the floor.

I shoved the gurney aside. Snatching one of the walkies, I bolted down the stairs. Aches and twinges from my fight the day before with Krystal clamored for my attention, but a cocktail of fear and adrenaline made it easy to ignore them. Urho and the Lady were coming. Or they were sending their guys. And I knew what they were looking for: they were looking for Tyler and Hannah.

I took the steps three at a time, risking a twisted ankle or worse and not caring. I caromed off the landing and kept going. My thoughts raced out ahead of me. Cribbs had been hiding them. That thought was clearest, bold and black-lettered. Cribbs had taken his children. He had let the Lady wake them from the mortal sleep. And then he had—what? Changed his mind? Realized he had made a mistake?

I hit the ground floor, and the shock zinged up through my ankles. I sprinted toward the ER. Cribbs had been a good dad; Shay had told me that several times. He'd been a shit husband. He'd done some bad stuff working for Lawayne. But he'd been a good dad. How had it gone down? Had Lawayne lied and told Cribbs that they just needed the kids as bait? Had he not even told him that much? At what point had Cribbs realized that something had gone wrong?

My sneakers squeaked as I slid into a turn at the next corner, and a realization rumbled through me, hitting hardest in my knees, vibrations that made me slip and catch myself on the wall. At the Kane Motor Court. After the Lady had come. After the children had been woken. That's when Cribbs had realized he had made a mistake, and then, at the first opportunity, he had run. The ripped screen on the bathroom window. The shouts. The fighting.

That vibration hit me again, shaking me so hard that I crashed into a kidney disease poster and ripped it clean from the wall. I spun, kept my footing, and ran. But those big shakes weren't coming from realizations. I bit the inside of my cheek to keep from laughing, and I tasted blood. Those tremors running through me, those weren't because I was some kind of genius. Those were a real, genuine, goddamn earthquake. Kyle Stark-Taylor was here, and he was going to bring down the whole hospital on my head.

At the next intersection, I skidded to a halt. Which way? Were the kids even in the ER still, or had they been transferred somewhere else? Another tremor shook the building; one of the drop-ceiling tiles shook loose and fluttered down, spilling foam chips on the floor.

Christ, if I took too much time, it might not matter. All they had to do was get the kids; as soon as the kids were clear of the hospital, Stark-Taylor could bring down the building and kill anybody left inside. All they had to do was get the kids out the front door.

Betting on institutional bureaucracy, I charged toward the ER. The decision saved my life. Something whipped through the air behind me, something I glimpsed out of the corner of my eye. And then it exploded. A globe of fire filled the intersection where I had stood a moment before. The blast clapped against my ears; the force of it lifted me onto my toes, and I jinked right, hard, to keep from falling. I hit the wall and slid along it, keeping my footing out of sheer luck.

When I threw a glance behind me, the intersection looked like a firestorm had spun through it: soot blackened the paint and stained the chrome wall guard, and flames danced along the padded cushion of a wheelchair—which, thank God, wasn't currently in use. The smell of melting rubber chased after me.

"Vie," a familiar voice called. I recognized it from the hallways at school and, more recently, from the parking lot outside Garry's Greasy Spoon. I kept running and threw another glance back. Leo came around the corner, moving over the blistered vinyl without seeming to notice it. He was tossing a balloon between his hands; liquid sloshed inside the plastic, and I was willing to guess Leo hadn't filled the balloon with water. "Hey," he said, flipping the balloon into the air and palming it with another slosh. "Catch."

I put on speed. I just had to make it around the next corner. Twenty feet. Maybe thirty. I could do it. I shot looks back at Leo. He had a grin under that ugly red hair. He was laughing, watching, letting me try to get away. The hallway ahead was clear. Footsteps were moving along it—first responders, maybe, coming to check on the explosion. "Stay back," I shouted. "Just stay the fuck back."

Twenty feet now. It couldn't be more than twenty. Behind me, Leo's ugly red-headed grin got bigger. He pulled back his arm, drew up his leg, a whole show like he was pitching in the Major Leagues, and then his body uncoiled and that balloon shot toward me. He was shit at throwing, I realized as I watched the balloon wobble. Then the balloon vaporized into flame, still spinning toward me with that hitching, awkward lurch like Leo hadn't ever played a decent game of catch. And the flames grew, a cloud of fire rushing to swallow me. Twenty feet to the intersection, but the fire was going to get me before I made it another yard.

I drew in a breath of superheated air, and honest to God, I felt my lungs crackle, felt the dizziness of a breath with all the oxygen burned out of it, and I ducked my head and kept running because I wasn't going to let a fucking ginger roast me standing still. The flames licked my back. Along my neck, there was a hot, stinging flash like a sunburn, and then nothing.

I hit someone. I was running full speed with my head down, and I hit hard, and I went down. We went down, both of us, tangled arms and legs, my head bouncing once on the linoleum that seemed softer than it should have been. Maybe that was just my head. Maybe you can only hit your head so many times before it starts going soft.

I needed to get up, but I was still thinking about my head, wondering if it had a big bruised spot like an apple, and I was breathing in these huge, wonderful breaths of air, and I was tasting campfire smoke, the kind of fire you roast hot dogs and toast marshmallows and huddle up against with a mug of hot chocolate. Nothing like that burnt rubber smell that had been following me. Then I blinked, and Jim Spencer's face drifted into view above me. His hair was copper and gold and a deep red like the heart of a volcano, and heat poured off him.

"Stay down," he said.

That sounded pretty stupid, so as he moved away, I rolled onto my side. Then I stopped. And I stared.

The flames that had licked the back of my neck hung in the air. They weren't frozen; they still snapped and licked and curled, and the foam ceiling tiles smoldered and gave off acrid smoke. But the flames had stopped. I could see where they had stopped, a perfect line drawn in bubbling vinyl and blackened ceiling tile. Jim Spencer had stopped them.

Jim wore what he always wore: a button-down and slacks that made him look like runway material instead of a high school teacher. He stood between me and the curtain of fire. Embers spun and whirled around him, and for a moment, I thought they'd fallen from the tiles overhead, but then I realized Jim was standing too far away. And then the only explanation that made sense—even if it didn't make any sense at all—was that the embers were coming from him. Huge, fat cinders spun in the air around him. Black patches worked their way along his shirt, and when he raised his arms, the cloth flaked away to expose lean, pale muscle. With my inner eye open, I could see him as he was, golden fire haloing his mortal body. He was fucking beautiful.

Then he pushed, and the fire raced toward Leo. Leo yelped. And then Leo screamed. I got to my feet and grabbed Jim's shoulder—his bare shoulder, his well-muscled, very nice, very rippling shoulder—and then I yowled and yanked my hand back.

"I told you to stay down," Jim said. The fire rolled down the hallway like a river, and the cinders drifted like snowfall around him. His face was pale and drawn and dry like a fever was burning inside him.

My inner eye was still open, and when power spiked in the direction Leo had gone, I felt it.

"We've got to go," I said. "He might not be able to control fire, but he can make things explode, and he just—"

The explosion threw me onto my ass, and it threw Jim down next to me. Ahead of us, the hallway collapsed. The walls folded inward. The ceiling bowed. Metal shrieked and sheared away, and then everything came down. Dust and ash swirled out, peppering my face, lining my tongue with the taste of styrofoam.

Another tremor shook the hospital. On the wall, an emergency defibrillator case rattled itself open, and the padded case flopped out onto the floor. A gurney with an unconscious woman shivered in time with the hospital, its rails chiming musically as it inched along the floor. Overhead, a fluorescent tube worked its way free. It fell, battering open the plastic screen and shattering when it struck the ground.

"Where are they?" I said as I scrambled to my feet.

Jim was just as fast; more of his charred shirt flaked away, and the heat pouring off him seemed even more intense. Embers whirled at the back of his eyes. "Who?"

"The kids. The ones I brought in."

He shook his head.

"Fuck. I've got to find them. I need you to—"

Before I could finish, Jim elbowed past me. Even through my coat and sweater, his touch was like a hot iron on bare skin. Fire lanced from his extended hand, blistering the paint down the next hallway. Then, just as suddenly, the fire cut off.

I stared at him. "What was that?"

In answer, the overhead sprinklers spun to life, a deluge that soaked my coat and sweater. The woman on the gurney moaned and thrashed, but her eyes didn't open.

"He's down there," Jim said, staring past me, his arm extended like he meant to shoot another blast of fire. The heavy spray of the sprinklers washed away the ashy remains of his shirt, leaving a lot for me to look at. And I was looking, even though I knew there were more important things to focus on. But the guy had an eight pack. And he was—he was dry. The water steamed off him. And his fucking pants were about to burn away, and then—

Business, I told myself.

"The one that was coming after you," Jim said, jerking his head in the direction he had shot the blast of fire. "He's skulking down there. He just poked his head around."

"I've got to find Tyler and Hannah."

"Go ahead. I'll take care of him."

I nodded; it was as close to a thank you as I could get right then. But when I turned to go, I saw the woman in the gurney. Her eyes were open. They were wide, uncomprehending, a milky blue that made her look older than she really was—maybe thirty, forty at the outside, but those eyes belonged to someone much older. She moaned again. Water slicked her hair and filled her gaping mouth.

"Where's the staff?"

Jim shook off my question and launched another barrage of fire down the hall. Something detonated, and a chunk of metal the size of my fist spun past me. With a grunt, Jim gave a quarter-spin and clapped his hand over his stomach. Blood boiled off him in greasy black smoke.

"Come on," I said, "you can't stay here."

"I said I'd take care of him. Go get those kids."

"Where's the staff? This lady, she can't just stay here. There's got to be—"

"Just go," Jim shouted, and then a column of fire as big as the Impala roared down the hallway. It lasted maybe twenty seconds, and then Jim sagged. Water ran down him in silvery lines. Blood slicked his fingers.

It wasn't boiling off.

That was a red alert. I kicked his ankle and, when he shot me a look, jerked my head in the opposite direction. Then I grabbed the gurney and started pushing. The woman thrashed once, and her bare foot rang out against the gurney's frame, and she shook her head as more water plastered the hospital johnny to her wasted frame.

The floor was slick, and the gurney moved easily. Too easily. I knew I was going too fast, but we were running out of time. The smell of smoke, that pleasant campfire smell, was gone. I smelled blood, though. Jim's blood. And I tasted my own sweat and the oils in my hair as water ran into my mouth. The hypertextured reality of the other side overlay my vision: grief and pain etched into this place like acid stains, with the occasional touchstone glimmer of joy. A new baby—the memory caromed off me, a vision that opened and shut in an instant of a mother and child. In my mind, I pictured Hannah's tiny, weary face.

*Hannah,* I called.

The rush of static filled the distance between us again.

*River,* I tried.

More of the white hiss.

I swore, and at the next corner, I slid into a turn, forcing the gurney against its own momentum. The static—that was Urho's doing. His abilities had to do with the other side. I had learned that before. He was the reason the dead hadn't been able to tell me what was going on. He could control them to an extent—or bind them. Something. The way he had used River to deliver that message, for example. And now he was getting in my way again.

Hannah!

But still nothing except a fuzzed noise that made me want to scratch the inside of my ears.

"Vie." Jim was panting. His hair had returned to strawberry blond. The embers at the back of his eyes had settled. With one hand, he hid the wound low in his gut, but gore stained his trousers, and pink runnels of blood slid along bare skin. "I can't."

"Just a little farther."

Shaking his head, he set himself against the wall. Then he pointed. "Go."

"You can make it. You can. Just a little farther, Jim."

He gave me an exhausted smile. "Mr. Spencer."

"Fuck that, Jim. I'll call you that when we're in school. Right now, you have to keep moving."

Power spiked again behind us. Closer now. Much closer. Leo was closing in. Then another tremor shook the hospital. The floor bucked hard enough that I actually went into the air. The gurney too—it came down hard, and the woman in it screamed, and metal rattled with the force of the landing. A fissure ran up the closest wall, and plaster spilled out. The spray from the sprinklers muddied the dust and spun it into the growing current. When I was done with all of this, I wasn't going to shower for a week. I spat out more water. A month. A fucking month.

"You need to go, Vie. I'll keep him from following. I can do that much."

"But—"

"These kids, they're important?"

"Fuck that. That's not what we're talking about."

"They're important. So go make sure they're ok."

"Fuck you."

That same exhausted smile. And then embers glowed at the back of his eyes, and his hair brightened to copper and sunlight and the sizzle of an old heating element.

"Go," he said, pushing me. The skin on my chest puckered and stung, and I knew I'd have a red patch of sunburn in the shape of his hand.

I stumbled, catching myself on the gurney, and then I froze. Down the hall, coming toward us, was the kid, the Indian boy, the one we called the Crow boy. His twin braids hissed along his back, sweeping back and forth with every step. His dark eyes were locked on mine. Sno Balls. That was all I could think about. Those nasty prepackaged snack cakes with coconut. This kid loved Sno Balls. He loved them so much he'd shot a C-Store clerk in the head and walked out with an armful of them.

Behind me, fire roared, swallowing oxygen and drawing air along the hall. The breeze pricked my cheeks like nettles. It rubbed my raw lips. It pulled at the wet strands plastered to my face, and I could smell something new, something that the wind drew off the Crow boy. Weed. I took in the kid again, the way his braids rasped across his shoulder blades, the way his eyes never left mine. Glassy eyes. Red eyes. And then I let out a laugh. This middle-schooler was coming to a fight stoned.

He'd probably be best friends with Kaden.

The rush of fire died abruptly. "Why are you still here?" Jim shouted. "I can't keep both of them off you."

"I'm not going anywhere," I said, turning to look back at Jim. "Not with the Crow boy—"

But the words crumbled in my mouth. Jim looked like shit, even worse than he had moments before, but that wasn't what stopped me. At the far end of the hall, Leo bounced a basketball. Where he'd gotten it, I had no idea, but with my inner eye open, I could feel the power building in him. In a moment, he'd loose that power, and then he'd throw the basketball, and then it would explode and take off my head. But it wasn't Leo that stopped me either.

It was the Crow boy. He walked past Leo with the same slow stride that I'd just seen a moment before, at the other end of the hall. His dark braids rasped against his shoulder blades. He flicked open a knife and held it low and casual.

"That's impossible. He was just—"

And there he was. At the other end of the hallway, coming toward me, where I'd seen him.

"There are two of him," I said.

"That's impossible," Jim said. He raised one hand, launching a gout of fire. The flames passed through the Crow boy with no effect. It was like he wasn't even there. "That's impossible," Jim said again, his voice lower, and he looked down the hall and shot fire at the second Crow boy. Same thing: the fire went straight through him, and he just kept coming.

"They're not real," Jim said.

"He's got a knife. They've both got knives."

"They're not real!"

But what I couldn't explain, not in the heat of the moment, was that I had my inner sight open. And I could see the Crow boy. I could really see him. And he was there when I looked at him, really there, his spirit and soul and essence mapped out across his physical body. Jim's fire went right through him, and that didn't make sense, but he was really there. In both places. At the same time.

I reached out with my mind, and I found nothing.

I could see him. I could see the thick texture of the other side, the threaded reality of the boy we called the Crow boy, but I couldn't touch him with my mind. And Jim couldn't touch him with his fire.

Leo must have gotten bored because his power spiked again, and he reared back to toss the basketball.

Jim was faster.

The blast of fire was narrow, no wider than a pencil, but it punched through the basketball. And the force of that fire was enough to rock the ball backward. It teetered on Leo's fingertips, and Leo's expression was comical as he fumbled the ball. For a moment, it looked like his desperate flailing might permit him to regain his hold. Then the basketball fell, and it bounced once down the hallway, away from Jim and me.

Swearing, Leo threw himself down.

The basketball exploded.

Jim turned back the rolling wall of fire, but chunks of sizzling rubber flew through the air, and one of them ricocheted off my jeans and left a greasy black patch on the cloth. The wall of fire lasted a moment longer, pushing against Jim's invisible control, and someone was screaming. Screaming bloody murder. Screaming like he was being cooked alive. Leo.

Then the fire collapsed, vanishing as quickly as it had come. Jim gasped. A fresh spurt of blood spilled over his fingers. The flakes of fire tumbling around him in the air hissed and vanished under the heavy spray of the sprinklers. He fell hard against the wall, catching himself with his shoulder, and slid into the ankle-deep water. His eyes were closed.

Smoke shifted, and I saw the Crow boy. I threw another glance over my shoulder, and he was there too. They were about the same distance from me, so I picked the one coming at me from Jim's side. I reached out again over the infinite distance between minds, and again I found nothing. It was like dragging my fingers through air. There was a hint of resistance, of substance, but nothing I could grab. I breathed in the smell of smoking basketball and tried again. Nothing.

He was five yards off. I glanced back. The other one was about five yards too. I'd have to charge. Going up against a knife was stupid, about as stupid as you could get, but letting the Crow boy walk up and plug me with it would be even stupider.

I set my feet and hoped the deepening water wouldn't mess up my blitz. Then, closing my eyes, I tried one last time.

A fist crashed against my nose, and I rocked back. That was impossible. He wasn't close enough to hit me. But those thoughts flashed like lightning and went dark. I made them go dark.

Emmett. That name flashed like lightning too. It burned me. Bad. And then I made it go dark too. But the lesson I'd learned was there, at the surface, where I needed it.

Emmett had hit me like this too. Right when I'd been about to use my ability on him, he'd clocked me. And it had messed up my flow, and he'd gotten a knife against my throat. He'd made a good point, and I hadn't forgotten it.

Instead of reacting to the punch, I slipped out of my physical body and let it fall. From my projection to the other side, I took in everything through my inner sight: the two Crow boys that had worked their way from each end of the hall, and a third one who now stood in front of me, still dropping his hand from the punch he'd landed. Three of them. How in the world were there three of them now?

I watched as my body dropped into the water. With my luck, I'd manage to drown myself. But I could deal with that later. For the moment, I had to deal with the Crow boy. With three Crow boys. Jesus.

And he could see me. The one I had in my sights, the one in front of me, he brought up his head and looked straight at my projection.

"Hi, motherfucker," I said.

What I had done to Krystal, ripping every stitch of her soul across to the other side, that had been instinct. I tried now to do it consciously. I reached for the Crow boy, but instead of trying to slip inside his mind, I grabbed at the shimmering threadwork of his soul.

I caught nothing.

The Crow boy just stared at me, sloe-eyed, neither curious nor afraid nor angry. He slapped at me and caught air, but I still danced back. Thank God. That was the only thought I had. Thank God he couldn't touch me here.

But he could still get to my physical body. And the same thought must have occurred to the Crow boy because he swatted at the air again, his dark little mouth twitching with frustration. Then he turned his back on me. I glanced left and right. The other Crow boys were still there, standing, waiting.

The one in front of me, the one closest to me, squatted. The water surged up, darkening the denim to his knees.

"Oh no you don't," I said.

He grabbed my shoulder. My physical shoulder.

"Not a chance, you little fucker."

With a grunt, he rolled me onto my stomach, and my face went into the water.

It was my body there. My body, face-down in the water, motionless like I was already dead. Only I wasn't dead. I was here, on the other side. And my body was still trying to breathe, and I saw bubbles, and then my physical body jerked. A spasm arched my back. And I watched it. I might as well have had popcorn and a soda because I was just watching, the whole thing happening in front of me, and I couldn't do a damn thing about it.

I could go back to my body.

I might manage to surprise the Crow boy. I might. I could take advantage, maybe get my elbow in his throat, maybe knock him on his ass, take away the knife—

Catching myself before I returned to my body, I hesitated. The knife. Why hadn't he used the knife? Watching my physical body drown, watching the thrashing, the spume that rose on the filthy water, the way my hair trailed in the weak current, it was one of the freakiest, scariest things of my life. But part of my brain was still cranking, and that part was wondering: if he wanted me dead, why didn't he just push that knife into my back?

Because he was a sadist. Because he wanted me to suffer. Because he was enjoying the thrill of knowing that I was watching him kill me. Because he was a twelve-year-old psycho getting off on this.

Maybe.

Or maybe because he was trying to get me to do exactly what he wanted. Trying to get me back in my body. He could knock me out. Hell, he could drown me until I lost consciousness and then pump air into my lungs. He could do just about anything to me once I got back inside my body, and unless I had the best luck in the universe, I'd never have a chance to get away again.

And I knew one thing: I'd never been that lucky.

So I stayed on the other side. I watched my legs kicking weakly. I watched the curve of my spine. I thought about tetanus shots and how

Joey Hayden had told me in fifth grade that if you got tetanus, you just kept arching your back, arching your back, arching until you snapped your own spine. He told me he'd seen it happen to a dog. And now I was watching it happen, watching my body try to flex its way out of the water, watching the brainless struggle of instinct as it sought air. Would this happen to someone else? The thought flashed through me, morbidly clinical. Or was my body different because it was only my soul that had stepped out, making this somehow different from a coma or another type of unconsciousness.

I knew what Emmett would say. Emmett would tell me it didn't matter because I was about to become a human sponge.

I flailed, reaching psychically again for the Crow boy, and again I caught nothing. It was so strange. Even when my powers hadn't been under my control, even when everything had happened by instinct or in those cumbersome, intermediary steps—the bridge and the door, I remembered—it had never been like this. There had never been someone standing in front of me, right in front of me, with as much psychic substance as a TV character.

Trying again, I grappled with the emptiness of the other side. The thickly tapestried overlay of the other side glowed, taking on the crimson of my anger, the sickly yellow-green of my frustration and my fear. The Crow boy's soul was there, visible, a thread-work of blue and silver and coal-dust. He was right there. I could see him. And if I could just reach him—

But again, I caught nothing.

I wanted to come apart. I wanted to be here, fully on the other side, the way I had been with Krystal. I wanted that total numbness, the dissolution of everything that had mattered until the world refracted and took on crystal clarity. I wanted to be outside myself, completely free, without anger or pain or fear. But no matter how hard I pushed, no matter how I tried, I was tied to my body. And my body wasn't going to be alive much longer.

The next part was just pure, toddler rage. It was the psychic equivalent of throwing a fit. An extrasensory temper tantrum. I reached out with my mind, grabbing mental handfuls of the other side, and ripped. I tore at that weave of reality. Pieces began to rip. The colors blurred in long lines, and it made me think that I had seen this before, seen something very similar in the Hunt Public House. But I was furious. I was terrified, and that only made me angrier. I gathered psychic folds of the other side and tore them to shreds.

And then, all of a sudden, I caught something other than the other side. I caught the Crow boy. Only not the Crow boy in front of me; that one, no matter how I tried, passed through my grip like smoke. I grasped the one behind me. I grasped one that I couldn't even see. It had been chance or accident, a kind of mental groping in the dark. And I felt his flicker of surprise. And his fear. And then I tore.

It was like grabbing spaghetti. I caught at him, handfuls of him, and then he would slip away. I couldn't hold on to him long enough to pop the seams of his soul. I couldn't hold on to him long enough to shred him and let the tatters smoke away.

But whatever I was doing must have still hurt like a bitch because the Crow boy screeched. It wasn't a human sound. It wasn't even really an animal sound. I think Krystal might have tried to make something like that noise, only I was too fast, and she was dead before she really knew what was happening. But the Crow boy screeched like I was ripping the noise out of him with fishhooks, and his dark eyes got huge, and he whipped his head from side to side, his braids rattling like rain on a steel roof.

Then two of the Crow boys were gone, and when I looked behind me, the third one was staggering away, feet slipping in the rising water, suddenly looking only twelve years old, small and vulnerable. Good. Small and vulnerable was great. Small and vulnerable was perfect, especially if I could get the middle schooler to hold still long enough for me to put his own fucking knife in his back.

I returned to my body, gasping and choking as I dragged myself out of the water, hacking up what felt like half a lung. I wiped my face, wiped my eyes, and hacked up some more lung. And then I managed to get to my feet.

The sprinklers hissed. I still tasted flaming basketball with every breath, but now there was blood too, my blood. My nose throbbed. I breathed through my mouth, but every breath made that throb between my eyes turn star-white. I was pretty sure I was going to pass out.

Behind me, the woman on the gurney was moaning again. "Be quiet," I told her. "You didn't exactly help."

Splashing across the hall, I scanned both ways. No sign of the Crow boy. Leo was gone.

"Wake up," I said, dropping into a squat next to Jim. His hand had slipped; the wound in his gut looked bad. All that lean muscle, the pale, smooth skin, his nipples. It was just too much of a shame to let a hot guy like that die. I grabbed his hair and shook his head. "Up. Right now, Jim."

"Vie." He licked his lips. "Go."

I rolled him into a sitting position, and he screamed. Then he went limp, and his blood floated red-black clouds into the puddled water. I rocked him, got him over my shoulder, and launched up. The worst part was getting to my feet. The whole world went white, and the center of the white was that glittering spot of pain between my eyes. I slapped a hand against the wall, held myself, and after a few breaths I was pretty sure I wasn't going to fall. Or puke. I got him to the gurney.

"Move over."

But the woman didn't move. She just moaned. So I dropped Jim next to her, and the two of them were ass to ankles squeezed onto the gurney. I blinked and wobbled and waited for the huge white crisscross at the center of my face to let me breathe again.

"Wasting time," Jim mumbled. His hand got my wrist, and his grip was lukewarm. Strong, but not that sizzling heat I had come to expect from him.

"You teach drama," I said, putting my shoulder into the gurney and getting it rolling. Water splashed under the wheels. "Shakespeare. That kind of boring old shit."

His head flopped when we took the turn. I wasn't sure if he could hear me.

"And you're a big old homo. Hey." I whapped his leg. "Wake the fuck up. I'm talking to you."

"Vie."

"You're a homo. Did you hear me?"

"Vie, you—"

That was when I knew Emmett had really gotten into my head. It wasn't just the punch I'd taken from the Crow boy. It wasn't just the memory of Emmett trying to help me. It was his snark. It had infected me, lain dormant, and now it was awake, and I was running my mouth just like him. And I was grinning. And I hated how my heart ka-thumped and I hated Emmett, and I hated that grin, but I couldn't stop running my mouth.

"You know what that makes you?"

"Vie, you've got to run."

"That makes you a drama queen."

The gurney squeaked and rattled as I ran. My breath whistled. My nose was about the same temperature as the sun, and it was getting hotter.

Ahead, double doors opened onto the emergency wing of the hospital. I hit the doors at full speed, praying nobody was on the other side. I got lucky. I didn't knock anybody flying, although I did clip a nurse who shouted something after me in Spanish. From what I'd heard Miguel and Joel say, I didn't think she was very happy.

"Hey, Jim. Did you hear me?"

He groaned, rocking with the force of the gurney's speed, his arms over the belly wound.

"Jim."

"I fucking hate high school."

I whapped him again on the leg just so he knew he wasn't alone.

They were evacuating the hospital. Nurses directed orderlies, and orderlies wheeled gurneys toward the nearest exit. I didn't make it more than ten feet before I got mired in the traffic; a big, balding orderly with a fringe of cotton candy hair shouted at me and rammed his gurney into mine.

"You can have both of them," I said, slipping through the jam. I caught a nurse's arm and pointed back at Jim. "He's got a gut wound. Lots of blood. Something exploded back there."

"Wait," she said, catching at my sleeve. "What—"

But I was gone. I had to keep moving. I had sloppy drunk steps as I danced through the chaos, and I needed to stop, drop, and sleep for a year. But I couldn't stop yet. I couldn't drop yet. And I couldn't sleep, not yet, because Tyler and Hannah were still here. I could still hear the white-out static of Urho's ability blocking Hannah's scream, and I took that as a good sign. That meant she was still trying to talk to me. That meant they were still here.

I cut against the flow of traffic, moving deeper into the hospital. A man in a doctor's coat shouted something at me. Another tremor rattled the building. Ahead, the emergency exit sign hanging at the next set of fire doors pulled loose and swung on a frayed wire, snapping sparks into a cascade. I recognized those doors; I cut left.

And then, between one moment and the next, I was free. The crowd evaporated. Behind me, the hub of voices dwindled, and as I continued forward, the only steady sound was the hiss of the sprinklers. Cold water pelted my face. No more showers. Never again. Maybe I'd take a bath once a year. Maybe. But other than that, I was finished with water. I could see the open space of the emergency waiting area ahead. I was close; I just had to get back to the exam rooms now.

The hospital lurched; the floor heaved. A crack shot between my feet and zagged up the wall, exposing a shifting support beam. The smell of hot electrical wire filtered through the wet air. All of the sudden I thought of oxygen tanks. Compressed gases of all sorts. Would they explode? Christ. Even if Kyle didn't bring down the building, he might still manage to kill a lot of people just with all the incidental destruction.

As though in answer to my thoughts, a stronger tremor plowed through the building. It knocked me off my feet and carried me into the wall; my head punched through a pastoral painting of a cottage and some sheep. The damn thing fell and hung around my neck, and all I could do was slip and slide and try not to fall on my ass.

Then the tremor stopped. Ducking my head, I worked free of the ruined painting. Then I froze.

Someone was shouting.

"—you damn kids!"

I took a step. Puddled water splashed underfoot. Another step. The water rilled, sloshed, slopped. I froze, waiting for a sign that someone had heard me.

Power surged nearby, a psychic signal fire, and a piece of equipment the size of a Prius whipped through the air. The air displaced by its passage rushed down the side hallway where I stood. That air was cold. It was like someone dusting me down with snow. All of a sudden, that white spot of pain between my eyes vanished. A crash came from deeper in the waiting area.

Now or never. Now or never. I worked my chilled fingertips. I took a step. The splash sounded like King Kong doing a cannonball.

At the edge of the waiting room, I stopped.

The man I recognized as Kyle Stark-Taylor lay under the massive piece of machinery. When it had struck him, it had carried him back into the wall, and now both Kyle and the machine were buried in the rubble. But Kyle's big, bald head was visible; his fuzzy eyebrows were visible; the rough, thick features were visible. Something red was spraying across his face, and for a moment, I thought it was blood. Then I realized it was too thin, too glossy, and decided it was coming from the machine. Kyle sputtered and spat and tried to turn his head. On one screen, the machine flashed, ERROR D-187, and I had another of those goddamn Emmett Bradley moments because I wanted to giggle and I wanted to ask who had programmed the error code for being thrown like a goddamn shot put.

With a roar, Kyle squirmed, thrust out his chest, bobbed his head, rocked side to side.

Another tremor hit the hospital. It was like the big bad wolf had gotten a fresh lungful. And God damn it if that huge piece of machinery didn't start to shift. It skidded an inch. And then another. And then a few more.

And then I saw Kyle's hand gripping the frame, and I realized that monster truck of a human being was pushing it. He was shouting like he was performing for the WWE and he was about to knock the hospital down with some kind of psycho-seismic event, and meanwhile, he was just fucking strong enough to push a Prius off his chest. Oh. Yeah. And getting thrown through a wall had barely slowed him down.

I ran.

A screwdriver drilled toward me, and I yelped and dodged. It skinned the side of my head and stabbed through an overturned chair.

"Kaden, you little fuck!"

He popped up from behind the registration desk, rubbing plaster from his face with one sleeve. "Oh. Yeah. Sorry."

Like fuck, I thought. Like fuck he's sorry.

Temple Mae popped up next to Kaden. Her face was drawn. Her cat eyes were hard and flat. Furious, I guessed. With me, with Kaden, with Kyle Stark-Taylor, maybe even with Jake—with everyone who had brought her to this point where she had to use her abilities, acknowledge who she really was. A bloody scratch ran from the tilted corner of one eye down to her jaw.

I traced a mirror of the cut on my face as I ran. "Did he get you too?"

Temple Mae just shook her head and pointed past me.

Behind me, metal screeched, and then a quake rocked the building. The floor canted under me, and for a moment I was falling toward the registration desk. The quake rocked itself out after another moment, and I belly-flopped onto the desk and rolled across it.

"Mr. Spencer called us," Temple Mae said as I slid to a stop next to her.

"How bad?" I asked as I dropped into a crouch next to them, with the registration desk our only barrier—and a flimsy one—between us and the juggernaut.

"Bad," Kaden panted, wiping at his face again with that damn sleeve. "He just keeps coming. Vie, we're done for. We've got to run. We get out of here as fast as we can, and we don't look back."

I turned my attention on Temple Mae.

Shrugging, she said, "He's right. It's bad."

I risked a glance over the desk. With a crash like a thundercloud hitting the Vehpese High School band's brass section, the machine toppled onto its side. ERROR D-187 pulsed one last dim warning, and then the image shuddered into darkness. Kyle shoved a fallen section of wall, and framed drywall spun across the waiting area, clearing chairs and magazine stands like a cyclone. The earth seized; the floor buckled, and vinyl sheeting ripped along glued edges. Kyle dragged himself out of the rubble.

"Jesus Christ."

"I got a scarf around his neck and dragged him all the way to the parking lot." Temple Mae gripped the desk; a flush mottled her fair skin. "He didn't like that, but he just ripped off the scarf.

"I pegged him in the dick," Kaden said, squirming up next to Temple Mae. "Right in the dick.

"Have you tried electricity?" I said. "A live wire? That stopped Hailey for a while."

"With a stapler. I got him in the dick with a stapler."

Temple Mae shook her head. "I didn't even think about that."

"Well, it doesn't matter, right?" Kaden was shooting glances across the desk and then back at Temple Mae. He wouldn't quite look at me. "We're going to go. Right now, right? We're going to get the hell out of here."

"Hannah and Tyler," I said. "He's here for them."

"Then we grab those kids, we get out of here, and we run."

"This building is full of people," I said.

"They're evacuating." Kaden's eyes ping-ponged between Temple Mae and Kyle, who was kicking a path through the chairs in the waiting area. "This is an emergency. They train for this kind of thing. They're probably clear of this place already."

"This is a shit hospital in the middle of nowhere," I said. "The hallways are clogged with people trying to get out. If we leave, Kyle might pull this place down on top of them."

"He could do it anyway," Temple Mae said. More of the color had fled her face; she wasn't looking at me either now, and her gaze was fixed on Kyle.

"Temple Mae."

"He could. He could bury all of us, and he'd just dig himself out and go."

"But not while the kids are here. They're not going to risk hurting them. They can't take that risk." And not while I'm in here either, I thought. The Crow boy didn't want to kill me. He wanted to capture me. I guessed Kyle's orders were the same—that's why he hadn't kicked the hospital over like an anthill already.

"I just wanted to see Austin," Kaden said. "It's not fair. I wasn't supposed to even be here."

"You little fuck," I said. "You're upstairs trying to steal my fucking boyfriend—"

"You guys," Temple Mae said. Her eyes were narrowed in concentration; out of the corner of my eye, I glimpsed chairs whirling through the air and a covey of magazines in flight and what looked like the seat of a toilet and a plastic brochure display that had ripped free from the wall and was trailing a cloud of pamphlets about urinary tract infections. The big machine creaked and wobbled, but it didn't move, and Kyle swatted aside the UTI display rack like it was a gnat.

I barely noticed. I was too focused on Kaden, who still wouldn't meet my eyes. "And then, when I bust you, you come down here and try to steal Jake's fucking girlfriend—"

"You guys." The registration desk groaned. Fissures ran through the particle board.

Beneath me, the floor convulsed, and I braced myself against the straining, trembling desk. "And you're such a cowardly little shit that you can't even pretend to care that Austin's still in the building somewhere, that—"

"You guys!" The last word escalated into a shriek as Temple Mae reared back. The registration desk ripped free from the floor, spun, and launched toward Kyle like an Ikea-style battering ram. It hit him, and even over the whirlwind rush of the winged magazines and the UTI pamphlets and the molded plastic chairs, I heard the thud. And I watched as the desk disintegrated, driving into Kyle with so much force that the particle board came apart, splintering and shooting off to either side.

Not a scratch on Kyle Stark-Taylor. Not so much as one fuzzy eyebrow hair out of place.

Grabbing Temple Mae by the arm, I scrambled back. "Kaden, do something!"

His face twisted in concentration, and he crabbed after me. Temple Mae stared past me, past Kyle, her gaze fixed on something in the distance. I kept backpedaling, half supporting her, half dragging. Metal shrieked, and when I glanced back, I saw the drop ceiling twisting apart. Foam tiles drifted down. A light sparked and then popped. Kyle may not have heard the sound; he was still deflecting the chairs and other airborne debris that Temple Mae was spinning around him. From time to time, he batted something—a pair of broken-backed magazines, an orthopedic shoe, an unfurling roll of bandages—out of his way, but for the most part, he just kept walking. He never looked back. I got the feeling ever since he'd gotten his powers, Kyle Stark-Taylor had never once looked back.

Temple Mae gave a jerk in my arms, and a tiny starburst of blood exploded in her left eye, and then crackling and live and trailing a line of electric discharge, a wire whipped down from the ceiling. It struck Kyle at the base of the neck, and his whole frame went rigid, his body trembling like he was vibrating in a high wind.

"Come on," I shouted, grabbing at Kaden's cardigan, gathering only wool, and still hauling him toward me. His face was still fixed in frozen concentration, but his ass hit the vinyl, and he slid easily enough. "Come on," I shouted, even though the two of them were dead weight. Shouting made it easier somehow. "Come on, God damn it."

Dragging both of them—a fistful of Kaden's sweater in one hand, Temple Mae drooping over my other arm—I stumbled back, watching as a hundred and twenty volts ran down Kyle's spinal column.

And then the juggernaut reached back and ripped the wire out of the ceiling. It fell, dead and dark, at his feet.

"I hate kids. I fucking hate kids." Kyle lifted his foot like he intended to stomp Kaden into jelly; for all I knew, he was perfectly capable of doing that. "I don't got time for this—"

Whatever Kyle Stark-Taylor didn't have time for, I didn't wait to find out. I wrenched open my second sight. My head began to pound, and nausea swept a flood of acid through my stomach. As I reached for Kyle's mind, I shook Kaden by the cardigan. Whatever he was trying to do, he needed to do it now.

The psychic connection only lasted an instant. As soon as I touched Kyle's mind, a wave of memory crashed over me: a knife sliding into flesh, and Austin's eyes huge and wide, and then the way his whole body rippled around the steel, and he coughed and blood darkened the corner of his mouth, and—

The force of the memory, its pure, raw, vividness, caught me. If I hadn't been half-expecting something like this, if Emmett hadn't been smart enough to think this far in advance, it would have ended right there.

Even with Emmett's preparation, though, I barely managed to retreat into my body. I rolled sloppily, slowly, and still fighting to keep the horror of that memory—fake, I told myself, it was a fake, he was psyching you out—from paralyzing me. Kyle's foot came down, and a square yard of the hospital floor collapsed under the blow. Cement dust devils whirled around Kyle's boot.

So much for my theory about wanting to keep me alive.

"Now, Kaden," I shouted, scrambling back. "Whatever you're doing, now!"

Kaden let out a grunt, and the far wall of the waiting room exploded. A lot of the wall had been given up to the sliding glass doors at the entrance to the emergency room, and doubtless that had something to do with how easily the whole thing collapsed.

But a lot of it had to do with the three tons of American steel that launched toward us. I had about half a second to process the vision of a GMC Sierra spinning through the air like a goddamn discus, and then it hit Kyle, and it was like tossing a rag doll in front of an oncoming bus. The Sierra hit Kyle without slowing. The force of its movement carried Kyle with it, and they crashed through the next wall, and the next, and I lost sight of them in the cloud of splinters and broken plaster.

I sucked in a breath. I tasted my own flop sweat, and the fresh-cut wood smell of the splinters, and something that I associated with ozone, something that burned the hairs inside my nose. Kaden was on his back, his eyes rolled up, his chest rising and falling in shallow breaths. I shook him, and he didn't move. Temple Mae's eyes were wide open, and that was worse. She was breathing, but that starburst of blood in her left eye—that looked bad.

Then metal screeched, and I froze. My head spun toward the hole that the Sierra had punched through the wall.

The sound came again.

A long, twisting shriek came next.

The goddamn Sierra. He was pulling the damn thing apart just so he could get out from under it. He was still alive. Fuck me. For all I knew, that hadn't hurt him any more than it would hurt me to do a somersault.

I got to my feet. Every inch of me throbbed. That white star-point between my eyes burned out my vision for a second, but I staggered in the direction the truck had gone: through the emergency room wall. Toward the exam rooms.

Hannah. Tyler.

I kicked my way past a door that had fallen out of its frame. I climbed over a toppled cabinet, its files spilling out like a hundred paper tongues lapping at the floor. I got around the corner, and I saw it: the Sierra, banged to hell, leaking a black shimmer of motor oil. But no Kyle.

Voices. Shouts.

I ran.

As I reached the door to the exam room, I heard a familiar voice.

"You can't take them. I don't care who you are, I'm not letting you—" It was a woman's voice. A familiar voice, although I couldn't name her. "I won't let you."

A terrified voice.

When I stepped into the room, I recognized her: the Park Avenue poise; the elegant silver hair; the drooping eye. Diana Fossey, the doctor who had known, somehow, that I was involved in the madness running through Vehpese. The woman who had offered to help. Behind her, Tyler was curled into a ball, his arms wrapped around his head. On the exam table, on a crisp sheet of paper, Hannah could have been taking a nap.

Kyle took a step forward. Dr. Fossey looked like an aspen leaf, trembling in his path, a medical chart in one hand and a scalpel in the other. She sliced once, caught Kyle's hand as he reached for her, and the blade bounced along the skin like it was steel. He laughed.

Her eyes shot to me.

Kyle flicked her head like a kid shooting marbles. It split from her neck. It hit the wall like a bad grape.

I shouted something. I ran straight at him, and he backhanded me, and the next thing I knew, I was spinning on my stomach across the vinyl. I hit a cabinet. Came to a stop. And I watched as Kyle kicked a hole in the wall. Sunlight came in. And the smell of the high prairie. It had stopped raining, a dazed voice in my head noted. I felt a breath of cold, dead spring.

Kyle grabbed Tyler in one hand. Hannah in the other. He stepped out of the hospital.

And that was when the quake hit.

The tremors came one after another, a series of seismic thunderclaps that seemed to have no end. I'd never been in an earthquake; I had nothing to compare this to except the earlier shakes and rattles that had run through the hospital. This wasn't anywhere close to the same league. This was a distant cousin. This was at the complete other end of the family tree.

Rolling through at that speed, the individual tremors were hard to tell apart. I fell almost immediately; my battered nose whited everything out except the grit of the vinyl under me, and I knew I was still falling. I hit something—a wall, a filing cabinet, God, please, something that wouldn't topple over and crush me—and bounced. Blinking, gulping air, I shook the snow-spin from my vision.

The building bounced like a funhouse. Where Kyle had kicked his way through the outer wall, the weakened structure began to give. A window on an upper floor must have shattered because glass mixed with the dust and wood and plaster and steel that shot out of the wall. I scrambled toward the opening. It was a damning, furtive movement—a rat scuttling for its hole. In that one instant, animal instinct dominated everything else, and I didn't care about Austin or Kaden or Temple Mae. All I wanted was to be outside, under the spring sky, and safe.

I stopped myself and changed directions. Tremors continued to rip through the building, but their frequency was slowing, and I lurched from one spot to the next between them. I didn't know much about earthquakes. Scratch that. I knew nothing about earthquakes. I jagged right as the building trembled again, and a row of cabinets sagged on the opposite wall, doors swinging open to spill medical supplies across the floor. I stumbled on a brick of shrink-wrapped scrubs, slid, and caught myself on a wheeled rack. The rack and I rolled a few more yards, and then another wave hit the building, and I caught myself on the wall. Cracks webbed the plaster; when I shook my head, dust sifted down from my hair. Deep in the building, in its bones, I could hear supports squealing. I didn't know a goddamn thing about earthquakes, but I was willing to bet that when this building came down, it was going to come down hard and fast and all at once. I just had to get Kaden and Temple Mae first.

I skidded a few more yards and came to the opening that the Sierra had plowed through the building, and then I hopped through the ruined series of walls. Temple Mae was sitting up, her hair and face white with dust except where a fresh cut to her cheek bled in a long, fanged curtain down to her jaw. Kaden was still out. I tried to ignore the part of me that recommended leaving him here.

"Gotta hurry." I snagged double fistfuls of Kaden's cardigan; the fabric stretched and ripped as I pulled him into a sitting position. The squeal of the metal supports. "Can you help me? Hey. Temple Mae, I need some—"

The squeal became a scream. It was happening. It was happening right now, the whole place was coming down, it was . . .

But it wasn't. Temple Mae stared at the ceiling, and blood leaked from the corner of her eye in a muddy tear track, and behind me, the exam rooms vanished as the building collapsed. But not here. Not for this heartbeat. And another.

And fuck, I was wasting time.

I got Kaden over my shoulder, and then I caught Temple Mae under the arms and dragged her. If she knew what I was doing, there wasn't any sign of it. Her eyes were locked on the ceiling, and that bloody tear track was a goddamn river, and all around the oval that Temple Mae was supporting, a waterfall of steel and glass crashed down.

We were halfway to the hole in the front of the hospital, that big saw-toothed opening that the Sierra had blasted through the front doors when Temple Mae seized. Her whole body convulsed. A miniature earthquake ripped her brain apart, and then she went still.

I kept going, Kaden on my back, dragging Temple Mae. Gravity was going to pull this whole ruin down on me now that Temple Mae was out, but I wasn't going to stop. My back ached. My head spun. That spot between my eyes was like the North Star, so bright it was blinding me, so hot it was cold. But I wasn't going to stop. I didn't want to die like a rat, didn't want to die without telling Austin I was sorry, didn't want to die without seeing Emmett one last time. I coughed a laugh and tasted copper and that burnt electric taste. The rubble overhead shifted. A dangling light fixture worked its way free of the debris and fell, shattering ten yards to my left. Gravity. What a bitch. The whole place was going to come down, the whole place.

I guessed I had twenty yards left.

I guessed I had made it maybe five since Temple Mae seized.

I guessed I was going to get a million tons of construction-grade steel piled on me.

Something pinged against my cheek, sharp enough to slice the skin and draw blood. It ran down to my chin, warm and then cool all of a sudden. Something else pinged. Something exploded in glass and steel just a few yards to the side. Something hit with a massive thunk. Something winged my shoulder, and I staggered. Something groaned above me, and then that little drizzle of debris became a rainstorm, and I tried to go faster.

Something hit me on the head, and my knees turned like little clockwork pieces, and I was on the ground.

This was it. The end.

Only it wasn't.

The hail of steel and glass and stone ended. Abruptly. Instantly. My pulse pounded in my ears, and in the sudden silence, it roared. It was like a crowd cheering in a stadium. It was like fifty thousand voices shouting that I was alive. For a minute longer. For less.

Someone grunted.

Someone that wasn't me. Someone that wasn't Kaden. Someone that wasn't Temple Mae.

Then another grunt.

And I knew that grunt. I knew that voice.

It had been, how long? A day? Less?

It couldn't be him.

I slithered out from underneath Kaden's weight, letting him sag onto the floor, and then I flopped over onto my belly. I was too tired to stand. I was too tired to think. I was too tired to do anything except stare and try to process what I was seeing.

Emmett was on one knee, one fist pressed to the floor, head down. He looked like something sculpted, something Greek, all the perfect lines and broad shoulders and beauty. The rubble shifted and skittered overhead, and I glanced up, glimpsed a flicker of pearlescent sheen. A dome. Some kind of barrier. Emmett grunted again.

"Em?" I said, and it sounded so dumb, so utterly fucking stupid, that I wanted to take it back as soon as it left my mouth.

He shivered like I'd run my finger down his spine. And then he seemed to brace himself. Not against the weight of the building, but against something else. Against me. Against looking at me.

But he turned his head, and I bit my lip so hard that blood ran down and pattered the vinyl.

They weren't scars, not yet.

I had seen him a day before. He had been so perfect. The kind of beauty that stopped my heart when I turned too fast, when I forgot to brace myself, like catching a lightning bolt with my eyes open and wanting to do it again and again for the rest of my life. And he was beautiful, still.

They weren't scars, not yet, but the wounds were deep and vicious and twisted along half his face. A perfect, exact half. His right. It was as though someone had drawn a line down the center: forehead, nose, lips, chin. And everything on his right had been shredded with claws. My heart gave a kind of hiccuppy skip. Claws. Or scissors. Or a steak knife. Or a screwdriver. And they were mostly healed, which was impossible.

If the wounds hurt him, he gave no sign. His mouth curled in a familiar smirk. "I like you on your hands and knees, tweaker. And I appreciate the offer. Really, I do. But don't you think we should get out of here first?"

# Chapter | 22

When we were clear, when Emmett released the barrier holding up the debris, the rest of the building sagged and collapsed, tumbling down to fill the hollow space where Emmett had saved my life. Our lives. Dust sneezed out, a cloud that licked the wet pavement and stained my sneakers, and then it was over.

The only tally I could keep, the only tally that made sense, was the tally of the people I knew who had survived: Austin, Becca, Jake, Jim, Kaden, and Temple Mae. Jim was strapped to a gurney and unconscious; Kaden and Temple Mae were both out for the count, and to judge by the way Jake grabbed Temple Mae's face and shouted for help, she wasn't in a good way. Kaden didn't look much better.

Austin and Becca stood on the edge of the parking lot. Austin's face looked like steel in a blast furnace: a degree of white that was going to give me a screaming headache if I looked at it too long. Becca was holding him up, and when he saw us, he ran, and nothing ever felt better, ever, than when he hit me at twenty miles an hour and carried me a few yards, like some sort of romantic adaptation of one of his football moves. I wasn't going to complain; aside from the battering my nose took, I liked it.

"Are we in a fight?" he managed to say, his whole body shaking, the words buried in my shoulder.

I shook my head and gripped him tighter. "No. No fight."

Everything from the last day—the recording of him talking to Ginny, the conversation I had overheard with Kaden—popped like a soap bubble. He was here. He was warm. He was mine. He squeezed me until my spine cracked, and then he shook me, and he still hadn't said anything.

*Sometimes I think it'd be so much easier if he weren't here.*

The words slithered at the edge of my subconscious. Ok. Maybe everything from the last two days wasn't gone completely.

When the kissing started transitioning into the shaking and the squeezing and the yelling about taking stupid risks, I grabbed his hand, and Becca, Austin, Emmett, and I moved away from the crowd, huddled against shock and the spring chill. The April sky was the color of a razor. The sun had disappeared behind steel clouds again.

The bigger tally—the tally that went beyond me and what I could hold in my head—was the number of the dead. My limited exposure with the Bible and religion had not impressed me, but the phrase wailing and gnashing of teeth came to mind, and it fit in the worst way. There was a lot of wailing. A lot of screaming and crying and moaning and weeping. There were firetrucks and ambulances. There were dazed men and women, some staff, some patients, some visitors, some passersby. I remember a man, he looked ancient, with his hospital johnny fluttering in the icy April air, his bare ass chapped and red in the cold, one slipper scuffing along the pavement, the other foot bare as he dragged an IV pole. No bag. No IV. Just the pole. He got all the way to the highway, and he crossed the green, and then he was gone down the hill on the other side. I couldn't have gone after him if I wanted to.

Emmett moved in next to me and tried to get an arm around me.

Austin shoved him out of the way. His fingers gathered clumps of sweater like I might try to sneak off. Or like he wanted to make it very, very clear who I belonged to.

"Missed me," Emmett said, rubbing his chest.

"Don't touch him. Don't fucking come near him."

"You're not very grateful. I just pulled his white-trash ass out of that anthill."

"Emmett," Becca said, shivering against another slap of April air. "What happened?"

That sneer again. "I took a trip."

The wounds on his face looked worse in the daylight. They made me dizzy, and not just because I could only imagine how painful they had been. There was a pattern to them. A nightmarish symmetry that wasn't really symmetry at all. Only—my eye would follow the deep cut that ran from the corner of his mouth, and a part of my brain would latch onto the ragged fissures that ran along his temple. Or I'd find my vision looping a long, spiraling cut at the center of his cheek, and I'd have to swallow and look away because otherwise I'd throw up. If you'd tried to do it mathematically, with parallel lines and mirrored images, you'd say there wasn't any coordination. There wasn't a pattern to all of it. Only there was a pattern. You'd say there wasn't a reason behind the madness. Only there was. The madness was the reason.

I wasn't the only one looking; Austin studied him for a long moment before turning his attention back to me. Becca would glance and then her gaze would slide away.

"Take a fucking picture."

I looked away again, my cheeks heating, and Austin tightened his arm around me. "I've got to go after them." I pried at Austin's hand, but he just clutched me tighter, pressing me to him, and that rich, cedar smell with a hint of tobacco filled my lungs, and a tremor ran through me. "I've got to go before he—"

"You're not going anywhere." Austin pulled me against himself, both arms around me. "Vie, you're not taking a damn step."

*Sometimes I think it'd be so much easier if he weren't here.* It rode a dark carousel at the back of my head, swinging into view and then just as suddenly vanishing again. And when it came around, it didn't come alone. I could hear Kaden's voice: *but if it makes you get this freak show out of your life.* And then the carousel would spin, and I could focus on Austin, really see him without any of the last two days clouding my sight.

I wanted to sink into him. I wanted to bury my face in his shoulder, breathe that cedar-smoke smell, breathe his skin and his sweat and the heat of his body, and let him stroke my hair the way he was now, let him kiss my ear the way he was now, let him take away some of what hurt the most.

*Sometimes I think it'd be so much easier if he weren't here.*

I owed Hannah and Tyler more. I groaned and tried to pull away. Austin, shushing me, ran his hand along the back of my neck.

*But if it makes you get this freak show out of your life.*

That touch, and the way his breath tickled my ear, and the feel of him around me, against me, it was weakening me. It was softening the hard edges. My eyes sparked, and I squeezed the lids shut. If I started bawling, I was afraid I'd never stop. The carousel spun again at the back of my head.

*. . . Sometimes . . .*

No.

*. . . but if it makes you . . .*

No. No. No.

Maybe it wasn't a carousel. Maybe it was the cylinder in a revolver. Maybe this was a double-down version of Russian roulette. I forced those worries aside. I thought of Hannah and Tyler dragged off to God knew where at the mercy of Urho and the Lady. I shuddered. "Aus, let go. I've got to—

Austin's arms tightened around me. "You're not going anywhere. You're beat six ways to hell, baby. You need medical help. You need to rest. We can talk about . . ." He was still speaking, but the words blurred into sounds I couldn't understand. A thought came through, as sharp as the razor-blade sky: he wouldn't let me go. Not willingly.

And just as sharp and clear as the first thought, I knew what I had to do.

I broke his grip more by surprise than strength, and when he followed my backstep, I planted a hand on his chest.

"What the fuck are you doing?" I said.

"What are you doing?" he said back, in that calm, even, oh-so-Austin voice.

Just a little, I told myself. Just a little. Just enough that he backs off. And then you can make it up to him. Just the very littlest bit so he backs off.

"I said what the fuck are you doing?"

"Vie, baby—"

"Baby," Emmett snickered.

Austin was coming at me again, and I fended him off, taking another step back. "Jesus Christ. Did you think I'd forget?"

He froze then. It was a kind of lurching half-motion that ended with a huge look of surprise and pain. It was the way somebody might stop if you shoved a spear through him and pinned him right to the spot.

What happened next was worse, though. He didn't raise his arm; I think he was still too shocked, still in those few stunned moments before the pain really hit him. So he didn't raise his arm. He didn't reach for me. But his hand turned, this tiny cupping gesture like a kid might make, like he was begging and he didn't even know what he was begging for.

"Are we—" He had to stop. "Babe, are we in a fight?"

"Damn right we're in a fight. You're up in that fucking hospital room, with fucking Kaden, fucking talking about how you fucking want to date him, and now you want to hold me and hug me and call me baby?"

The whiteness in his face was the color before steel melts. I had to squint against it. I had to blink.

Just a little, please, just let it be a little, just enough that he'll get angry and let me go and I can still come back and make things right.

Austin wobbled, but he didn't move. People had died like this; impaled. That was the word. Like I'd impaled him on my words. People had died screaming. It had taken days. I had to keep blinking; I didn't know what was fucking wrong with my eyes.

"That's not what happened. What's going on with you? What's wrong? Why are you acting like this?"

The firmness of his voice, the certainty behind it, the absolute fucking lie of it hit me like a wrecking ball. It smashed through my pain. It smashed through my fear of hurting him. It smashed through every goddamn barrier in my head until it was just me and that black hole and Kaden's voice saying, *I never really thought about guys like that before, but if it makes you get this freak show out of your life, yeah, I'll think about it.* And then I wasn't just thinking about hurting him a little bit. I went full speed. I went for all of it like a goddamn fucking moron.

"I heard you. Both of you. He's going to think about it. He wants you to break up with me. He's so fucking desperate to get rid of me, he's willing to fag it up with you. And you're so fucking desperate to get rid of me, you don't even care that he's not really gay. All you care about is getting his cock—"

"Shut up." Austin wavered again. The Wyoming wind had picked up. At least, I thought it was the wind. Something was shrieking in my ears, making it hard for me to hear. And Austin was wavering like he was about to fall. So it had to be the wind. What else could make a noise like that?

"What did you say to me?"

"All right, guys." Becca danced between us, her hands flapping at each of us like she could bat us into separate corners until we could cool down. "Let's all take a breath—"

"Take a breath, sure, that's what Austin's always telling me to do." I shouldered past Becca, ignoring her squawk until I was chest to chest with Austin. "I don't want to take a fucking breath. I want you to look me in the eyes and tell me. When did you finally decide? When did you figure out it was worth taking a risk? Were you guys stoned, and he was doing some of his typical cocktease bullshit, and you finally broke down? Were you wrestling and you popped a boner? Were you hosing each other down in the locker room—"

"I said shut the fuck up. Shut your fucking mouth, you fucking faggot."

That wind. That goddamn wind. It was so loud, it was like the background hiss on a cheap stereo. It was the sound of an ocean of blood, the surf pounding in my ears. The words went through me like a yard of rebar. Right through my gut.

"That's enough," Emmett said. Beneath those horrible wounds, his face was twisted into an expression I didn't recognize. He grabbed at my arm. I hit him hard enough that he fell on his ass.

"What did you say?"

Austin was crying now, and he gave a tiny little jerk of his head, and his eyes wouldn't meet mine.

"What did you say to me?"

"We're done. You and I are done."

"Fine. That's just fine with me. You can go fuck Kaden now like you've been dreaming about—"

"Just stop it, all right?" Becca screamed. She was crying too, ugly, silver tears that spilled down her face.

I reached for my bag. I wanted to shove that cassette down his throat. I wanted to make him choke on plastic and magnetic tape and his own fucking words. But I didn't have my bag. I didn't have anything. Jesus Christ, my eyes, what the fuck was wrong with my eyes, I didn't have anything. I didn't have anything. I didn't have anything.

"You know what? You're right." I tried to shrug, but all my muscles were locked with some kind of jittery electrical signal, and all I could do was jerk and jump like I was Frankenstein on a hot wire. "It'd be so much easier if I weren't here. You're right. You're absolutely right."

Austin sagged. He hunched a little, his upper body caving forward as though he were trying to protect himself.

Emmett had picked himself up, and he grabbed a handful of my shirt and shoved. I stumbled, skidded on loose gravel, and caught my balance.

"What the fuck is wrong with you? Get the fuck out of here, tweaker. Just get fucking lost, all right?"

I stared at him. Behind those deep cuts that twisted half of his perfect face, Emmett stared back at me like he'd just kicked over a shithouse and watched everything spill out.

I gave him the finger.

"Fuck you too. Jesus Christ, tweaker. Austin, hey. Come on. Let's get you out of here."

I was still staring as Emmett hooked an arm around Austin and guided him away. Becca, wiping at her cheeks so that silver smeared the heels of her hands, just kept shaking her head. She looked at the sky. She looked at her black flats. She looked at the heels of her hands and made a bubbly, disgusted noise in her throat. And then she looked at me. It lasted maybe ten seconds, and then she started crying again and shook her head and left.

Just a little bit. The words echoed emptily in my head. What the fuck had happened to just a little bit?

# Chapter | 23

I found the Impala. I slid into the seat, started the car, and was surprised that it still started. Under the gray blade-light of the April day, the world had passed into some kind of apocalyptic wasteland. The fact that the Impala still started, the fact that anything still worked the way it was supposed to, made no sense at all. The world had ended. Didn't everybody else get the message?

Emmett looping his arm around Austin. *Come on. Let's get you out of here.*

I drove. I don't remember driving, but I drove. At one point, I ended twenty miles up the Bighorn River, the car nose-out toward the edge of the bluff. With the engine in neutral, I let my foot down, and the motor roared. All I'd have to do is bump the gear shift. I'd done it before, dived into the river before when I'd gotten to that spot at the center of the black hole. Only this time, Emmett wouldn't drive along by chance. Emmett wouldn't swim in and pull me out.

Emmett looping his arm around Austin. *Come on. Let's—*

The engine roared so loud that the Impala was about to shake to pieces. Just one bump. Just one little bump of my wrist on the gear shift.

A numb, asinine part of my brain was still problem solving. I had lost Kyle's trail at the hospital, but I could still try to find him. Becca had mentioned something about Kyle staying outside of town, buying supplies. There would be a trail. Everyone left a trail. I left a trail. Bloody footsteps from walking on a line of broken hearts. Fuck, that was maudlin or melodramatic or whatever the right word was. But it felt right.

I got my hand over the gear shift. The pebbled plastic was cool against my skin. How much pressure before it slid into drive? And then all that power would pour into the wheels, and the car would take off like I was trying to win a soapbox derby, and Christ, with my luck, I'd probably crack my nose on the wheel.

That dry little asshole voice at the back of my head was still trying to problem solve. He wanted to think about Austin. He wanted to think about Emmett.

Emmett looping his arm—

Emmett tending to Austin, tenderly setting two fingers to Austin's neck and his ear against his mouth—

But I wouldn't. I couldn't. Instead, I let the little asshole try to work on the situation with Hannah and Tyler. I could try to find Kyle's trail. I could ask around. I could check the stores. I might even be able to get the sheriff to help me—ever since Belshazzar's Feast, we'd avoided each other, but I think he'd listen if I told him what had happened to the kids.

My mouth still tasted like plaster, as though when the hospital had collapsed, the cloud of dust had rolled straight down my throat. I tried to work up some saliva. I popped open the Impala's door, hung out my head, and spat. Nothing. The air smelled like mud and the exhaust from the Impala. The river was louder. Still nothing. My mouth was still open. Nothing. Dry as a bone.

I pulled myself back into the car, and I slammed the door, and the river went silent, and I stared out at the little white arrows of chop on the water, like they were marking out a landing strip for me, and my wrist bounced on the gear shift, and that little voice was still going. Time. The problem was time. Urho had the kids—or he would have them in the next few hours, whenever Kyle finally reached him. Did the kids need more time for their abilities to develop? Would they help Urho when he asked, or would they fight him? Would dragging Urho's soul into the physical realm require hours or days, or would it be instantaneous?

I didn't know the answer to any of that. But I'd felt the Lady's touch. I knew the poisonous, fever-sick heat that it left. And I knew that nobody—not Kaden, not Jim, not Temple Mae—would tell me what had happened when they gained their abilities. When they were woken from the mortal sleep. I thought of the way Tyler had looked in that motel room, curled up to shield himself, broken. And Hannah, severed from her body, cut off from everyone she loved. How much worse could it get? I didn't want to know the answer to that question. My gut said that it could still get a lot, lot worse.

Time. It would take time to find Kyle. It would take time for all of it: to convince the sheriff, to track him down, to face off with him. Time. And at the end of it, would things end up any different than they had today? Christ, Kaden had smashed him with a truck, and it hadn't done anything. It had barely slowed him down.

Time.

My wrist bumped the gear shift. The Impala lurched into motion. The white flechettes pointed out a runway for me—an escape, a way out of this mess.

But instead, the gear shift settled on R, and the Impala shot backward. The tire spun, flicking out mud and weeds and the occasional chunk of gravel, and the sedan slewed hard to the right. Then the rear tire caught the highway's shoulder, and the Impala skidded a few more feet back onto the pavement. I shifted again. East, the storm butted up against Cloud Peak. I put the clouds in my rearview mirror and headed for Sara's.

At the back of my head, that black hole yawned. Time. I didn't have time to track down Kyle. I didn't have any guarantee that I'd be able to stop him if I did find him.

But I knew one way to get Urho's attention that worked every time, and the saw blade spun silver moonlight through the darkness on my brain.

I put the pedal down and drove.

# Chapter | 24

At night, with the lights out, Sara's house no longer resembled the storybook cottage I had first mistaken it for. Part of that was that I was older. Only a few months older, sure, but sometimes age had more to do with road rash from the miles than from the actual miles themselves. Storybooks were full of stories, and stories were full of shit. A dark smile stole across my face. I might have been a fairy, but I wasn't a fairytale hero. Today had proved that. If anything, I was more like one of those wilting, drooping, listlessly exhausted maidens waiting for a prince to come.

And that hurt. I fumbled with the lights, flashing the brights once before I managed to get them off, because the hurt ran from my chest down my arm. That's what heart attacks felt like, and that made some kind of shitty sense because my heart was in a million pieces. The truth was, a prince had come along. Austin was a prince. Austin was just about perfect. But the thing nobody tells you about storybooks, the thing nobody tells you about the lies inside, is that nobody can save you. You can't even save yourself.

Dead leaves from last autumn scurried in the window; my sneakers trapped a few and chomped them, and they didn't have that crisp autumn snap anymore. They were wet and soggy and half-rotten. They turned into a black paste on the steps. The porch swing creaked at me, and I thought of Austin curled up next to me on it, and the way he looked with nothing but the light from inside the house painting his face—the rest of the world gone to black, just that warm, yellow light sculpting the hollows of his eyes and cheek and jaw.

Inside, more darkness. The smell of lavender and vanilla spiderwebbed the air, sticking to my skin as I walked deeper into the silence. When the old floors creaked, I froze, and silence settled in again. Just me. Alone. I had waited for Sara to go to work, and now she wouldn't be back until after close. Just me here. Just me. Alone.

I could have turned on the lights. No one lived close enough to see the lights. No one was going to drive by and wonder why the house was glowing. But the darkness felt better. Every nerve was raw, and the darkness smothered the worst of the flare-ups. I navigated the maze of furniture.

The kitchen smelled like fish and citrus; Sara was back at her diet again. Good for her. I thought briefly of what might happen. She might find me, and the thought opened a trapdoor in my gut. I felt sick. I felt dizzy. And then all those feelings tumbled through the trapdoor, and I didn't feel anything anymore. It made me think of the other side, of that night—the night before? Christ, was it really only the night before?—when I had come apart, when I had entered the other side fully, completely, and when I had felt nothing. No aches, no bruises, no pains. No black hole gnawing at the back of my head. I hadn't felt anything for the first time I could remember, and it had been wonderful.

Tonight. Tonight, I'd make it across again. Tonight, I'd light a signal fire so bright that Urho couldn't ignore it. He'd come because he was curious. He'd come the way he always came—to taunt me, to bait me, to chase me in my dreams, but most importantly, to satisfy his curiosity. And when he came, I'd come apart and step into the other side fully, and I'd destroy him.

Through the kitchen window, I had a glimpse of the rangegrass rolling out to the horizon, studded with silver where sage broke through the tumbleweeds. It was all dark, of course—just an impression of the long stalks dipping in the wind, glimmers like fallen stars where traces of ambient light glowed along the sage. Something hurtled out of the darkness, slamming into the fence and snapping the wires tight, just as it had the evening before. This time, though, I stared out at the darkness, unmoved. Nothing could startle me tonight. Nothing could frighten me. Nothing could reach me.

Up the basement stairs floated the smells of rust and sweat and the poured cement floor. I waded down into the smells. The rust and the sweat, those were Austin. Whatever I felt, whatever I should have felt, dropped right through that trapdoor in my gut. At the bottom of the steps, I found the ancient switch and flicked it; the two Edison bulbs sprang to light. For the rest of my plan, I wanted light.

Nothing had changed in the basement: the plastic tubs lining one wall, the rolled-up rugs slumped in the corner, the grit that scraped underfoot, the cool, humid air whispering against my skin. Austin's weight bench took up a lot of space, and again I felt that rush of emotion that dropped through that pit in my gut. And there, between a stack of broken-down cardboard boxes and a rolling tool chest, stood the table saw.

Light winked off the blade at me, and I took a staggering step toward it. And then another. A shrill voice at the back of my head demanded why, why, why, and it sounded a little bit like Austin and a little like Becca and a little like Sara and even a little like Ginny, but it didn't sound like me, and that freaked me out in a way that wouldn't fit down the trapdoor, in a way that got jammed sideways, and then the freak-out filled me up like a clogged sink.

Air. That freak-out filled me up, and I couldn't get any air, and the freak-out just got higher and higher like water in my lungs. Air. Breathe. That's what Austin said. Just breathe. But breathing only made it worse. Breathe. That's what his shrink told him. Breathe. I took another step; the movement was lumbering, as though I were walking at the bottom of the ocean. Breathe. I tented my hands over my mouth the way I'd seen Austin a dozen times. Breathe. That's what his shrink told him.

Only, what if breathing didn't make it better? What if the freak-out was like fire, and everybody knew fires needed oxygen? What if breathing just fanned the freak-out, blew it out bigger? Fire. What if you could feel like you were drowning and your brain was on fire all at the same time?

I got to the saw. It was old; the plastic casing had warped, and through a chink at the bottom, rust spilled out. The cord that ran to the outlet was old and thick and braided. But the blade still looked sharp. The teeth grinned back at me. It was the same silver as the trace glow of sage on the high plains.

But I didn't like that it was grinning. I didn't like the smug little sparkle. Those were crazy thoughts, absolutely bonkers thoughts, but they went through my brain like rounds from a .45. My hand found the switch on the warped casing. My thumb traced the angle of red plastic. Why?

Why was I doing this? Because it would bring Urho? Because I thought if I was hurt bad enough, the way I'd been hurt at Emmett's house—if I were about to die, the way I'd been at Emmett's—I could come apart and step into the other side?

It was more than that. This was like every time I lost control. This was like every time I dug out the box of razor blades or fumbled the striker on a Bic. The way my hands were shaking. The way that black hole chewed through my thoughts. Whatever else I told myself, this was just cutting again—on a new level, sure, but still just cutting. And why the fuck was I always cutting?

That's why I heard Austin's voice. That's why it sounded like Becca, like Sara, like Ginny, like everyone but me. They wanted an answer. I could have told them a lot of things. I could have told them I was doing this because a shitty, silken whisper rippled the surface of my subconscious and told me I deserved it. I could have told them I was doing this because of the candles on a birthday cake, because of the vacuum cord, because of the iron, because of the cigarettes with crumbling red tips. I could have told them I was doing this because it put me in control of me. Because it was my body, and I could do something to it that nobody could undo.

My thumb found the top edge of the power switch. I didn't press, not yet, but I let my nail rest along the crack in the casing. I could have told them all of those things, and it probably would have sounded good with my heels up on a tufted couch, with Austin's nice shrink scribbling on a pad—or whatever a shrink did when they were supposed to be listening. I could have gone on and on about all the reasons that I cut—the reasons I liked, and the reasons I didn't. But it would have been a lie. Because the real reason I cut, the reason that drove me into a bathroom stall when Austin wouldn't look at me anymore, that reason I didn't know. It breathed hot breaths on the back of my neck, sure. But I didn't know its face. I couldn't name it. I couldn't even draw its silhouette. And that scared me because you can't stop a thing you can't name. You can't kill a thing you can't see.

Nobody can save you. You can't even save yourself.

The switch clicked. The saw groaned to life, and then its groan became a whistle, and then its whistle became a high droning, like I'd stuck my head next to a hornet's nest. Yes. Exactly like that. Exactly like a hornets' nest because all of the sudden my body was stinging and tingling and prickling all over, and my breath corkscrewed in and out of my throat, and I locked both hands on the saw base to keep from running away. The blade was as pure and bright and white as I had seen it in my head. It would go through me like I was mist. If I wanted to—if I could hold on long enough—I could take myself apart piece by piece. And Sara will find you, that shitty little whisper said. All she's done for you, and you'll let her be the one who finds you, and you know what that'll do to her.

Nobody can save you.

It wasn't going to be a cut. I'd known that driving here. It wasn't going to be like one of those nice, long, shallow lacerations I gave myself. I'd known that, I'd known it right under the point of my ribcage like a bruise. It wasn't going to be like those shiny little scars the Bic left. This was more than that. The black hole yawned wider. The edges of my thoughts were fuzzy. This was it. This was the door that only swung one way. This was the door that I could open when every other door shut. This was the door out. And Austin, that shitty little voice said, and Austin, what about Austin? He came out for you. He loves you. One little fight, but you know better because you know he loves you, and you know what'll happen to him if you do this.

I shook off that swarm of hornets.

Nobody can save you.

And then that shitty little voice was quiet, and I knew what I was doing, and the universe knew what I was doing, and I could face the truth with a kind of sleepy awareness that had eluded me up until this moment. I knew. I knew. And I could do it because I didn't have anything. Not anymore. I had crossed a bridge, and it had burned behind me, and it wasn't determination or resolution or courage or anything else that carried me toward the end. Everything just flowed forward from this point. It was—I smiled, and my eyes were stinging, sending the saw out of focus into an ugly gray blur—it was like a river, and now everything had come full circle. Yes. It was like a river, and all I had to do was let it carry me.

And just like that, I lay my right arm across the saw's tabletop. The brachial artery. I knew it would hurt, but I'd been hurting for a long time. I leaned forward and let my weight carry my arm toward the spinning blade.

I hit a wall.

A millimeter—less than a millimeter-from the whirring blade, my arm stopped. An invisible barrier held me back from the grinning teeth. I grunted, shoving my arm forward again. Again, the barrier held. It was like ramming my arm against a brick wall. I tried again, and this time, I hit my funny bone, and the tingle ran up into my eyes, and they watered so bad that the saw doubled and tripled.

And that flow, that sense of the river carrying me forward, dissolved. The clarity, the sense of purpose, the decision—they washed away like sand in a strong rain. My stomach flopped. My stomach gurgled. I swore and rammed my arm again and again, against that fucking barrier.

My body, like a traitor, began to react to brushing up against death. Adrenaline swamped me, prickling in my throat, stinging under my arms, making my thoughts sharp and fast and flurried. And then I knew. I knew, and I was so angry that my anger actually steadied me, and I managed not to throw up or pass out or just drop from exhaustion. Carried by that anger, I spun toward the stairs.

"Get out here. Right now. Right fucking now."

Emmett came down the last three stairs with the same easy grace as always, and nothing visible betrayed his nervousness: no hunched shoulders, no arms folded across his chest, no fiddling with his hands. From ten yards away, anybody else could have blinked and mistaken him for a guy coming down a runway. Anybody else but me.

"Didn't anyone teach you it's rude to stare?"

I was staring, but it wasn't because I was horrified by the scars. The wounds that covered half his face were strangely normal, in fact. As though they'd always been there, but I'd only noticed them now. And there was something true about that: Emmett had always been two people. He had been the smoking hot icon of perfection, too hot to touch, too hot for anything but a passing glance or you might burn out your retinas. But that had been on the surface. Underneath, the whole time I'd known him, had been a boy with scars. The boy who was so cut up and broken and hurting inside that he was an ass to everyone, that he hurt himself more because he didn't know how to stop hurting. Now both boys were visible, superimposed. When I'd been a kid, my mom had kept around a red plastic View-Master, and she'd had a bunch of the cardboard reels showing mostly tourist destinations: the sights of Rome, Paris, London. Looking through the View-Master had always made me dizzy; my eyes had struggled to coordinate the stereoscopic images. Looking at the two halves of Emmett's face twisted my gut in the same way.

I pushed the feeling aside and said, "Get that thing out of my way."

"So you can saw off your arm?"

"What the fuck do you care? Get it out of my way now, Emmett."

"As soon as you started bleeding, you'd know you'd made a mistake. And you'd freak out. And you'd get blood everywhere. And they'd probably spend like fifteen hours trying to reattach your arm, and you'd be lucky if you ever got enough strength back to finger your little boyfriend."

I let a beat pass; the hum of the old-fashioned bulbs sang along with my pulse. "Say one more thing about Austin—say anything even close—and I'll beat the living shit out of you."

Emmett's eyebrows shot up, and his mouth opened into a shocked O. He even pretended to fan himself with one hand.

"If you don't get that thing out of my way, I'm going to make you get it out of my way."

The unmarked side of his mouth twitched.

Just to be sure, I reached back, grabbing at the saw blade, but my knuckles crunched against the same invisible blockade. I spun toward Emmett. His mouth twitched again. Then that twitch spread into a full-on grin.

"You don't have any fucking idea what I'm trying to do. This is serious, Emmett. I'm trying to save those kids."

"By cutting your arm off?"

"If you want to help, get rid of that stupid barrier. They're in danger, Emmett."

He nodded slowly. "You're going to cut your arm off to help those kids. Makes perfect sense."

I sucked air through my teeth. "Fine. If you don't want to help, I'll have to make you leave me alone."

"Yeah, you keep threatening to do that." His coffee-dark eyes were glitzy in the light from the Edison bulbs. "Go ahead, tweaker. Do me like you did last time. You're not ashamed of that, are you? You go right ahead. Crawl inside my brain and make me want to kill myself. You want to know how bad it was after Makayla? Dig in and find out."

"I will. If you make me, I will."

Color flooded his cheeks. "Or maybe that's not enough entertainment for you. Maybe you want to tie a string around my dick and use me like your little fuck-puppet. That's what you did, isn't it? You liked hearing me beg. You liked hearing me moan when you touched me. Why? I would have fucked you any day of the week. Are your little feelings still hurt because I only want to fuck you? Because you are definitely not boyfriend material, Vie. You proved that today. What you did to Austin—"

"I told you not to say anything about Austin." I took a step forward, my shoulders going back, my fist cocked.

I hit the barrier in front of me so hard that my nose flattened against it. That white point of pain exploded into fresh intensity, and I staggered back, my ears ringing with the pain, fresh blood drizzling my lips. I shouted because shouting kept me from blacking out—just a long string of obscenities. Every nasty thing I wanted to do to Emmett right then. Every way I could think of hurting him. A lot of them involved shoving one of the Edison bulbs up his ass and then giving him a kick. Let the little fucker shit out bloody glass for a month.

When I blinked away the tears, Emmett had dragged the red footlocker to the center of the basement. He perched on the edge, his ass barely touching the brass studs that outlined the trunk, and he leaned forward with his chin in his hands. His eyes were still so glitzy they looked like something out of a magazine ad. An ad for something cheap. Something like knock-off Hollywood. Glitzy like that. But the scars—the scars were just so fucking messed up that they balanced out all that glitz. And somehow he was even more perfect than he'd been before.

This time, I was smarter. I hammered the air, and my fist connected with the invisible barrier in front of me.

"One last chance," I said.

He waggled his eyebrows. His chin was still in his hand like a guy in front-row seats to the best show of his life. Those glitzy eyes looked like they'd gone through a hundred rounds of Photoshop just for the sparkle.

"Fine. Have it your way, but remember: you made me do this."

I took a breath to steady myself. The taste of damp cement mixed with the hot metal of the still-spinning saw. Rust, too—and sweat. Austin. I shut my eyes to keep him out; the last thing in the world I could afford, the last thing I could ever afford, ever again, was Austin. I breathed in, and my jangled nerves evened out like wire snapped straight.

My second sight opened, and I looked out on the rich tapestry of the other side. Emmett was there. The scars on his face shifted, their contours wet and trailing—like ink dropped into water, or like smoke in a rainstorm. The sharp divide that ran along his face, the line that the scars marked out in his flesh from the center of his forehead to the center of his chin, carried over into this place too. Only the divide was . . . deeper. Longer. It went all the way through him, body and soul, like someone had cleaved him from head to crotch. One side was the vibrantly threaded texture of his soul. The other half—swirling ink and smoke.

He had abilities. He had gone away and come back in less than twenty-four hours, but somehow more time than that had passed. I had a million questions, and buried deep inside me, rotting under all the dirt I had thrown over it, was the truth. I'd have to face that truth eventually. The dirt would wash away, given enough time, and I wouldn't be able to hide from it then. But for now—for now, I could pretend I didn't know. I could pretend I didn't care.

I reached out across that space between us. It was always so easy. Like dipping my hands in water. No, that no longer felt quite right. Looking at him, at the twisting coils of light and dark that made up the two halves, I realized it was something else now. Like trailing my fingers through smoke. It was always so easy between us, like—

My psychic self crashed into a brick wall.

The shock of it rattled me so badly that I felt my physical teeth click together. My projection began to fade, and I had to scramble to keep myself planted on the other side. I stared at Emmett; I stared at the empty space between us. What had just happened was totally, completely, utterly impossible.

I focused on the space next to Emmett, imagining myself there, waiting for the sudden shift in location that made traveling through the other side so easy.

Nothing.

I stayed right where I was.

In my projected consciousness, I reached out again and clapped against the barrier again.

Emmett's head came up, and those coffee-dark eyes pinpointed me. Not my body. Me. My projection. The beautiful side of his mouth quirked again, and he said, "You said something about making me leave you alone?"

"That's not—" I managed to bite off the last word because I knew how stupid it was going to sound. It wasn't possible. Except, of course, for the fact that it certainly seemed to be possible. It seemed to be very possible. It seemed to be reality. But I didn't want to give him the satisfaction.

Emmett stood and kicked back the footlocker. He cocked his head, studying me, and then began rolling up his sleeves. As he folded back the chambray, he spoke. "I've wanted to talk to you for a while. I think now's a good time."

"Fuck you. And fuck what you think is a good time. Get this fucking barrier out of my way before I fucking kill you."

He cocked his head again; that grin plucked at the corner of his mouth, and he shook his head. "Everything's always on your terms, Vie. Do you ever think about that?"

It took me a moment to realize he was serious, and the shock that he believed what he was saying—honestly believed it—was so great that I actually lost control of my projection. I slid away from the other side and found myself back in my body, gaping at him. "What?"

"Your terms. You make the decisions. You. It's always you."

"You're out of your damn mind. Take this fucking barrier down, Emmett. Right now."

"You're the one who decides if we're friends or not. You're the one who decides if we're talking to each other. You're the one who decides if something's dangerous. You're the one who decides if we're going after a bad guy. You're the one who decides the next step, and the next step, and the next step."

"This is bullshit."

"You decided what was going to happen with Austin. You decided if you were going to date him. You decided if you were going to break up with him."

"Everybody gets to decide if they're going to date. He got to decide. And everybody has the right to decide if they're going to put themselves in danger. And—" I tried to dam up the next words; I tried to stop them before they got loose. I failed. "—Austin broke up with me, in case you missed it."

The look Emmett shot me held so much scorn it could have withered half of Montana. Shaking his head, he said, "You knew exactly which buttons to push. It was like watching somebody punch in the self-destruct sequence. Jesus, Vie, you basically wound him up and let him go and watched it happen. Bringing up Kaden, throwing that in his face, you knew. You. You always get to make the decisions."

With the chambray cuffing his upper arm, he paused. Then he extended both arms and turned, displaying them to me. Track marks climbed up and down his veins, clustered most densely inside his elbows. One arm had been butchered with the same scars that marked his face. "Not with me, tweaker. Tonight, you just get to listen. And watch. You want to say anything before we get started?"

"You're out of your mind. You're out of your damn mind. I didn't do anything to make Austin break up with me. And I sure as hell don't get to decide everything. You think I wanted this? You think I wanted to be here? You think I wanted my life to turn out like this?" Something about the way he looked at me, at that stellar conviction in his eyes like he knew what he was talking about better than I did, dragged more out of me. More than I would have said to almost anyone else in the world. Maybe even more than I would have said to Austin, if he'd still been talking to me. "You think I wanted my mom to burn the shit out of me? You think I wanted my dad to beat me so bad I couldn't go to school? You think I wanted to have my brain cracked open so I can't ever have a moment's peace? You think—"

"All right," Emmett said. And suddenly the barrier was all around me, cocooning me, so tight that I couldn't move. My jaw wouldn't open. My chest struggled to rise and fall. I wanted to throw a punch. I wanted to kick. Hell, I would have settled for a scream. All I could get out, though, was a yowl in my throat like an alley-cat. "That's enough talking for you. It's time to listen."

He studied the insides of his arms again, the scars on one, the track marks, still holding them out to me, and he bit his lips. "It was bad after Makayla. After I—after what I did to her. I knew I was doing the right thing even when I was doing it. I still know it was the right thing. I've never wondered about that. She would have killed everyone. She would have killed you, Vie, and whatever else you think about me, you need to know—" His eyes had lost some of their glitz. They were liquid now. Ready to spill. They were dark as the bottom of oceans. "Jesus. Things are so fucked up I don't even know how to say it. When I look at you. When I hear you bitching. When you swagger around like you're Godzilla planning on knocking down a city. You're so goddamn clueless most of the time, and that's fine. I like when you're walking around thinking you can knock down a city. I don't mind because I'm enjoying the show. But then, out of the blue, you'll turn around, and you see me like nobody's ever seen me before, not this—" He brushed his knuckles along the unmarked side of his face, and then his hand dropped. His eyes were the bottom of the Pacific. His eyes were miles deep, and I felt that same old flop in my stomach like I was falling—like I'd been falling for a while, maybe, and it had only just caught up to me. He shrugged, and even his shrug was like an A-lister's. "Makayla meant to kill you, and I wasn't going to let that happen. I couldn't let that happen. So I've never regretted it; I'd do it again right now."

This was what I'd wanted. I'd wanted him to talk to me. I'd wanted him to tell me how he was feeling. I'd wanted to know—I'd needed to know—that he was ok after what had happened with Makayla. I'd needed it desperately because I'd known that he wasn't ok, that when he had killed Makayla he had killed some part of himself, and I needed to know that the rest of him, the part of him I loved, was going to come back.

But not like this. Not with me paralyzed, unable to touch his cheek, unable to catch a tear with my thumb, unable to turn his chin so that the breath between his parted lips caught my cheek, so that my mouth could find his, so that I could tell him in the only way that meant anything that I loved him, loved him, loved him like the sun coming up over the Bighorns. I groaned. I thrashed against the bonds locking me in place.

With one hand, Emmett traced the track marks to his elbow, and his fingers rested lightly in the crease, as though he could hide the past. "But even with no regrets, I . . . I couldn't sleep. I couldn't eat. I'd see her when I came around corners, or when I blinked, or when I tried to close my eyes. I'd feel the knife in my hand, and the way it cut into her like she was a tough piece of meat." Another tear slid down his cheek, and he jerked his head once to dislodge it. "I'd feel her blood. It was hot. And slippery. And it was everywhere. One day I couldn't get out of the shower, and . . . and I just couldn't stop crying. And then Austin and Becca showed up. And we talked." He smiled, but the tears were running freely now, drip-drip-dripping from his jaw, darkening his shirt and jeans and the cement. "We talked about you."

The next yowl threatened to tear my throat. I flailed inside Emmett's prison, trying to break free, but I couldn't move: physically, psychically, I was trapped. This wasn't fair. This wasn't right. Telling me like this, telling me when I couldn't touch him, talk to him, hold him, kiss him—it wasn't fair. It was cruel. It was beyond cruel, and he knew it, and the fact that he knew only made it worse.

"Becca talked the most. She's very smart. Too smart, maybe, for her to keep getting involved in stuff like this. She pointed out that Urho and the Lady weren't done with you. She pointed out that you were too stubborn to let the rest of us help you. She pointed out that, whether you liked it or not, you needed us. When they came at you again, you were going to need all the help you could get. And she pointed out that this time, we had to be the ones who made the first move."

Let me out. The words came from a wound deep inside me. If I'd been able to move even an inch, I would have rattled that invisible barrier like the bars on a cage. Let me out, let me out, let me out. His eyes met mine and skated away. Let me out, please let me out, please don't do this to me.

"And Becca pointed out that I could do what none of the rest of them could." A smirk teased the corner of his mouth, and he wiped his wrist through the tear tracks. "Your boyfriend didn't like that. He didn't like that at all. But he manned up. For you, Austin manned up. And he asked me to do it. And I said yes, tweaker. Because I can't imagine a world where you're not bitching and stomping around and raising hell."

Behind me, the whine of the saw was the only noise in the basement.

Emmett returned to the stairs, and canvas scraped on the wooden steps, and he swung something into view. My backpack. I thought I'd lost it at the hospital. Had Austin grabbed it? Or Becca? The questions vanished when Emmett dropped the bag; it landed with a thump, and he kicked it across the floor. It slid to a stop against the invisible barrier at my feet. I thought I heard metal shift against metal beneath the canvas. The saw buzzed; a yowl was building in my throat again.

Squatting, Emmett unzipped the front pocket on the backpack.

No, I thought.

He tossed aside a handful of change, a pair of mechanical pencils, and a rubber band that had gotten knotted around two paperclips. Then he brought out the small cardboard box and lifted the lid.

No.

Folding the cardboard back, he eyed the row of blades as though he were trying to spot the best one. He plucked out one and let the box fall. He turned the blade, and the weak, yellow glare of the Edison bulbs flashed along the edge.

No, no, no.

"Austin said you're still doing this. Becca said she couldn't get you to stop. Me," he paused, flashing me that mocking smirk that twisted the ruined half of his mouth. "I figure nobody's going to make you stop. It doesn't work like that, does it, tweaker? The shit we do to ourselves, nobody can take it away. Not unless we let them." He hesitated, casting a glance at the inside of his arm, at the track marks up and down scarred flesh he wore. The glance was so fast and so furtive that I wasn't even sure he knew he'd done it. Then those bottomless black eyes were on me again, and he spun the blade in his fingers, and his voice came out low and soft. "Nobody can take our shit away, can they, tweaker? Nobody, not unless we let them. And you're not going to let anybody take your shit away from you. That's the whole point, isn't it? No matter what else people do to you, nobody can take away the fact that you get to cut, you get to burn, you get to do whatever you want to yourself. That's power, isn't it, tweaker? For a long time, I bet that's the only power you ever had."

I wanted to kill him. If the barrier had been gone, if I'd been able to move, I would have killed him. The fear inside me—that shriveling, stomach-clenching fear—was so strong that it drove out rational thought.

"Austin probably wanted to love you out of it. Am I right?" He cocked his head, pulling his mutilated lip between his teeth, those dark eyes swimming again. "And Becca, well, Becca probably wanted to talk you out of it. She really believes in all that. But you know what? I know I can't get you to stop. I'm not even going to try. I just think you ought to know what it feels like, watching someone you love do a thing like this."

That word, love, smoked at the back of my brain like fire ready to catch, but I didn't have time to consider it. Pulling in a jagged breath, Emmett set the blade against the inside of his arm. His face looked like cold ashes. He drew the razor from wrist to elbow, and blood spilled and branched across pale skin.

Someone was making the worst fucking noise in the whole universe. It was a scream, a strangled scream, like the sound couldn't get out. It was like a cat going through a meat grinder. It was me, part of my brain knew, but it was so strange, so shockingly loud, that it seemed impossible that I was the one making that noise.

The color had washed out of Emmett's face, and he wavered and then drew himself up straight and planted himself like he was walking into a storm. He transferred the blade to his other hand, dragging the blade across the whorl of scar tissue on his other arm from wrist to elbow. Blood spattered the cement. It sounded like rain. It sounded like the nights I had spent in Emmett's room when rain pelted the glass, or the night Emmett had snuck into Sara's house and the rain hammered the windows, or the nights I had driven in Emmett's car and the rain had drummed on the roof. I was still screaming that horrible, mangled-cat noise the entire time as he drew the blade up the second time.

He sucked in huge breaths. The hand holding the razor was trembling. He shook his hand twice, as though he couldn't quite get his fingers to let go, and then the blade clanged against the cement, and the saw was still buzzing, and I was still screaming, and the blood forked and twined along the lengths of Emmett's arms until it reached his fingers and dripped in steady drops, huge red-black dots marking an exclamation point on the ground between us.

He didn't say anything; his breathing was still ragged, and his face was green. He sagged, and then he dropped to sit on Austin's weight bench. The barrier vanished, and I staggered, caught myself, and froze.

"Go ahead," he said, head down, his shoulders starting to shake. "Cut off your fucking arm so you can find those kids. Or pick up another blade and add another pretty scar to all the ones you've got. But now you've got an idea what you're doing to—" He dragged his head up; it looked like it cost him just about everything he had left. I saw the old wariness hardening his eyes again, the shine of steel armor, the way he always protected himself from me, from himself, from the world. I could hear the words before he spoke them. *What you're doing to Austin. What you're doing to Becca. What you're doing to Sara.* Maybe, if he was really feeling daring, he might say, *What you're doing to the people who care about you.* That would be as close as he came to saying it outright. Whatever window had opened between us, it had slammed shut again, and I was face to face with the old Emmett again.

And then some seismic emotion rippled through him, twisting his face, and he shuddered and dropped his gaze. "What you're doing to me, tweaker. At least you know what you're doing to me."

I felt weightless. I felt like my bones had been hollowed out and the next drift of air would spin me, shatter me. I dropped onto my knees and stared up at him. His blood pattered the ground next to me.

Something in my mind was unwinding, some terrible knot that I'd kept tied for all these years. Something to do with the black hole at the back of my head. Something to do with the nights I slipped out of Austin's arms and wandered the house, trying to breathe. Something to do with the white buzz of the saw that, even after everything that I'd just witnessed, still sounded like the sweetest thing in the world.

I didn't even realize I was crying until Emmett cupped my cheek, and my tears swirled with the blood on his fingers.

"Em, something's wrong with me." I was crying harder. I choked on the words. The only thing in the world holding me up was Emmett's bloody hand on my cheek. "Something's really fucking wrong with me."

He bent over me, his voice weary and thrilling and full of a tenderness I'd never heard before. "Yeah." He cleared his throat. His blood ran down my jaw, my neck, my chest. It was hot and then it was cold. I could smell it like iron. I was shaking, almost falling, and his muscles might as well have been bronze because he didn't even waver. "Yeah, sweetheart, you're really fucked up." His fingers tightened, slick and slipping over my skin, and he cupped the back of my head and cradled me against his knees, bending low, as though shielding me. He spoke softly into my ear. "We both are."

# Chapter | 25

It was the soft rain of his blood that finally made me move. I staggered upstairs, leaving a trail of bloody prints—half a hand here, a smudged finger there, the toe of my sneaker on the living room rug—on my way to get the first-aid kit and bring it back. When I got to the basement, Emmett had slung his arms over the barbell on the weight bench, and blood wreathed his hands.

As I knelt next to him, I opened the kit and began taking out supplies—antiseptic wipes, gauze, medical tape. That ancient condom was still in there, its foil dull and wrinkled. The snippers were still in there, glittering, like a sterile escape key that I could pick up and use whenever I wanted. Nobody had turned off the saw, and in the background, it still whined; when I glanced toward it, Emmett caught my chin and pulled my head back.

"Eyes on me, tweaker."

He looked awful. Underneath, he was a sickly shade of green. Thick shadows blanketed the wounded side of his face, and I wondered again how much the wounds still hurt him. Ripping open one of the wipes, I studied the cuts on his arms and hesitated.

"Em, these are bad. Worse than—worse than I usually do."

"That's because you act tough, but you're really a big pussy."

"You need stitches. You need a hospital."

He shook his head.

"You're bleeding. A lot. And you look terrible—"

"No hospital. No doctor. No stitches, not unless you want to do them. Clean them as best you can and then wrap them up. They'll stop bleeding eventually."

I caught his wrist in one hand and began to clean; Emmett hissed, but he didn't jerk away. "You're not in good shape," I said. "It looks like you've lost a lot of blood."

"Two cuts on my arms, tweaker. I made sure I didn't get any veins or arteries."

"You're really pale; you look like you might be sick."

"Jesus. I forgot that you don't know how to take a clue." He chewed his savaged lip again, and then he gave an odd little laugh, and his hand caressed my chin again. "I don't like knives, tweaker. Blades. Things that can cut. I really don't . . . I really don't like them near me." He bit his lip, tucking the ruined corner of his mouth beneath his teeth, and then he gave a little shake as though trying to throw off a memory. "A million things can change, and you're still dense as a bag of rocks."

"What happened?"

"I kept you from cutting off your arm. That's what happened."

"You know what I mean."

Emmett didn't answer, and I kept working. The gauze was feathery in my touch as I began to wind it around his arm. His skin was warm; the blood, slick in some places and tacky-dry in others, was cool. The thin cotton soaked up the blood instantly, and red wicked along the threads. I set to work on Emmett's other arm, cleaning and bandaging it in the same way, and then I sat back on my heels and stared at the red-stained cotton, at the drip-trails on the cement, at the red on Emmett's shirt and jeans and sneakers. So much blood. His blood, blood that he'd given for me. My stomach flopped, and sweat flashed out along my forehead. Inside, I was still trying to process everything from the last two days: the fight with Emmett at his house, the way he had treated me in front of Lawayne, how much I had hated Emmett in the hours after and how much I had hated myself for not being able to stop loving him too. I rubbed the back of my hand across my mouth, and the skin there was slick with sweat too. Just the aftershocks of the adrenaline, I told myself. Just the shakes. That was all.

"Are you ok?" He turned me by the chin again. His eyes were deep, and that glittering, brittle shine was gone. "Jesus, you look like you're going to puke."

"I'll be fine."

"Tweaker."

"Really. It's just hot down here."

"It's hot? In a basement? In April?"

"And I haven't eaten—" Since the day before? Twenty-four hours? The thought shocked me; for the last day, I'd been running on a kind of nervous energy, wired together with snatches of sleep and adrenaline and caffeine. And all of a sudden, there was a short somewhere down the line, and the power went out. It was like somebody had flipped off all the lights, and all I could do was sag against Emmett, my body finally overloaded from the past two days.

The thought of food darted through my mind again, and my stomach rolled. Christ, had it been since Sara's fried chicken? The thought of the fried food, the breading popping with oil when I bit into it, sent me over the edge. I had just enough time to turn, knee-walk two steps, and I lost the contents of my stomach, what little I had in there. It still managed to catch me by surprise, somehow, and it went straight down the front of my clothes.

Thank God Sara hadn't finished the basement, I thought. The sick was mostly just the thin, mucusy slime of stomach acid and bile; no real food to speak of. Thank God. Thank God.

And then I groaned because I'd just puked myself right in front of the hottest boy I'd ever known.

His hand was cool on my neck. "Are you going to do that again?"

"God, please, no."

He laughed, and for a moment, he sounded like the old Emmett. "I'm not God, tweaker, although I can probably make you see him." His fingers gathered the long hair hanging over my neck and pulled it across my shoulder, and he raked his nails along the sensitive skin below my hairline, the touch somewhere between a scratch and a caress.

To my surprise, it did soothe the worst of the jangling inside me. It took me a moment to realize what I was hearing over the whine of the saw, but then it clicked: Emmett was humming. And I recognized the song. He'd played it for me once on his guitar, while I'd watched the wind comb the buffalo grass from his bedroom window.

"This is a lot for you," he said, his fingers still fretting the back of my neck. "You're exhausted, right?"

I wiped my mouth; the acidic stink of puke made my eyes sting, but I was so tired I just wanted to stay here, unmoving, and let Emmett touch me. I'd wanted him to touch me for so long. I made some sort of noise and shook my head.

He laughed again, kneeling to get an arm around my waist, and said, "Well, you haven't told me to fuck off yet, so I'd say that's a pretty good sign you're exhausted. Come on, tweaker. Let's get you upstairs."

He helped me upstairs, and he got me water and crackers in the kitchen. After a few minutes, I felt steady enough to try something more solid, but Emmett limited me to white bread. Toasted.

After I'd eaten, we went to the second floor. Instead of leading me into the bedroom, Emmett paused on the landing and nudged the bathroom door open with his hip. He grabbed the hem of my sweater and pulled it over my head. Cold air prickled my skin; even exhausted, I felt my nipples stiffen, felt the dusting of golden hair on my chest needle out. I stared at Emmett; the scars that masked half his face hadn't taken away any of his beauty. If anything, they'd given him an edge, a kind of intoxicating bitterness that only made the rest of his perfection sweeter. I grabbed his shirt and pulled him toward me.

"Not tonight, tweaker." His hands found my wrists, but he didn't pull my hands away. Or, he didn't try very hard. "You're exhausted, you're totally worn out, you're not thinking—"

I kissed him. Puke-mouth and all, I kissed him. I was beyond any of that. His hands tightened around my wrists like he was holding on for dear life, and then he kissed me back. It was like my brain imploded. All the charges had been planted and primed last fall. Those first few stolen kisses, the teasing, the months of growing to know the broken boy that I held in front of me—those had been leading up to this. And tonight, that kiss in the bathroom doorway, that turned the rest of my world to rubble. It was the first perfect kiss of my whole life. Even with puke-mouth. Even with a broken nose throbbing between my eyes.

When I broke for air, he tried to pull away again; I didn't let go.

"Vie, don't—we can't. Austin—"

I kissed him again.

He was blushing when I pulled away, his cheeks vibrant and dusky pink. "You've got a boyfriend—"

I kissed him again, harder, meaner, taking his mouth because I wanted it. I'd let him get away because I'd told myself I had self-respect—I wasn't going to fuck around with a guy who didn't think I was worth dating. I'd let him get away because I loved Austin. I'd let him get away because he was broken, but I was even more broken, and I didn't want to hurt him more than he'd already been hurt. None of that mattered anymore. He was here. He was mine. Tonight, at least, he was mine.

When Emmett twisted away, panting, I moved my grip up to his collar. "Austin broke up with me. Tonight. You heard him."

"He was mad. He was scared. He was hurting, Vie, and you can't—"

I kissed him, and his knees went out, and I had to catch him. I carried him, pinned him against the wall, grinding against him and feeling the hardness under denim. He mewled in my ear when I broke the kiss; he breathed like he'd been underwater for seventeen years. I worked at the buttons on his shirt; one of them snagged, and I just yanked on the fabric hard enough that the button popped free. I pushed aside enough of the shirt to see the left half of Emmett's chest. He was clutching at the other half of the shirt, pinning it in place, but it didn't matter; I could get what I wanted from here.

"He didn't mean it, Vie. You've got to—you've got to—oh Christ, oh Christ, you've got to—"

Bathing one nipple with my tongue, I took little nips, and Emmett's back arched until his head cracked against the wall. His nails dug into my shoulders. He screamed, an honest-to-God scream, and the electricity off his skin, the crackle of my touch, made it feel like we were both virgins, like seventeen years of pent-up drive were finally manifesting in a thunderstorm that could have started forest fires throughout the whole of the western United States.

I tugged at his shirt. I wanted it off him. I never wanted him in a shirt again, if I had anything to say about it.

He wiggled out of my grip, backed away until he hit the vanity, and stopped. The mirror showed the mussed hair at the back of his head, the red marks of my hand on the back of his neck, the popped collar that had come undone as I ripped at his shirt. The mirror showed me, my hair wild and fanned across broad shoulders, my eyes blown open with desire, my chest rising and falling like a berserker charging into battle, every muscle taut and defined in my chest and abdomen.

Then I stopped looking at the mirror, and I looked at Emmett, and I saw that he was crying and buttoning his shirt again, his hands like hummingbirds.

When I took a step, he angled his body away from me, and his hands shot away from the buttons to ward me off. "No." The word had a million frayed edges.

I stopped.

"Please, no."

"Em."

"Please, Vie. Please just let me walk out of here, ok? I—" He was crying harder; the ruined side of his face, with its insane symmetry of scars, contorted with the force of his emotion. "Please don't do this to me."

"Em."

He looked at the tiled floor. He looked at my feet. He looked at the rug. His hands played with the collar, trying to fold it back into place. He was crying so hard I didn't think he could see three inches past his nose.

When he took a wobbly step toward the door, I moved into his path. He cut left, and I hooked him with one arm.

"No, tweaker. Get the fuck off me." He rained blows on my shoulder, on my back, hammering down with his fists as I pulled him into my arms. "What the fuck don't you understand about no? Get off me. Get the fuck off me!"

Wrapping him against me, I settled my chin on his shoulder and held him while he continued to whale on my back. The blows slowed to a steady, softer rhythm. Then they stopped. And then he started crying for real, slumping into me. If I hadn't been holding him, he would have fallen. His tears were hot; they stung my shoulder, traced a blistering line around my scapula.

I felt sorry for him; I did. But I also felt a white-hot surge of triumph. He could have left. He could have used his ability to lock me in place. He could have gotten past me if he'd really wanted to.

Mine. The thought rang out like a million Christmas bells. Mine. Mine. Mine. Mine.

He was mine.

I didn't realize I was saying it out loud until his wet nose ran along my neck and he mumbled, "Yes. Yes, I'm yours. Yes. I'm yours, Vie. I'm yours."

Then, planting one trembling hand on my chest, he pushed himself back and met my eyes. "Please don't do this," he said. "Please, Vie. What she did to me." He shuddered, and I locked my arms around his waist to keep him from backpedaling. "It's not just my face, Vie. Please don't—I don't want you to see me like this. You deserve better than this. I wanted you to have me, the real me, not—" He made a furious gesture that took him in from head to toe. "Not some fucking monster."

I took hold of his shirt's placket, my fingers stiff, my grip numb, almost arthritic. It would be an easy thing to pull—once, hard, finally. And the buttons would fly off. And the shirt would open. And whatever he was hiding from me, more scars—burns, I thought, and my mind flicked like slides in an ancient projector: the birthday candles, the iron, the cigarettes—would be visible.

Just like Lawayne had done to me at Emmett's house.

My hands froze.

Emmett was still crying. Little spasms contracted parts of his face—his eyes, his mouth, a tic drawing back his cheek—and the rest of his body trembled like he'd never heard of solid ground. But he wasn't running. He wasn't shunting me aside with his power. He wasn't fighting, not anymore. And with a surge of heat in my belly, I realized that I had won. Emmett was going to let me do whatever I wanted. The heat spread down into my crotch, up into my lungs. I was in charge. Me. In that moment, for an instant, I had all the power.

Under my fingers, the soft-brushed flannel of his shirt felt like sandpaper. I focused on the sensation, running my thumbs up the rumble of the stitching on the placket, the chill of the tortoiseshell plastic buttons, the friction of the wool heating to a soft burn. I could do to him what he had done to me. I could rip off his shirt. I could stare at every wound. I could make him feel what I had felt, naked, vulnerable, humiliated. I could make up for every night of heartache. Fuck heartache. I could make up for every night he'd left me blue-balled because he was a tease who didn't think a tweaker was good enough for a boyfriend. I could do all of that, and I could still fuck him, could still get every inch of his body, could have him to a degree I'd never had Austin because Austin wasn't broken like this.

That heat in my stomach, in my lungs, in my crotch, it made me think of the night Kaden had jimmied the lock on his dad's liquor cabinet and had played mixologist. He'd lined up shots. And he'd lined up more shots. And the third row of shots, when he was just drunk enough to really think he was a mixologist, he'd poured something that he called afterburners, and it had gone through me like this. Like fire. And I felt drunk now, too, with cinders swimming through my belly. The room canted; I couldn't have fallen because I was holding on to Emmett's shirt so tightly, but I felt like I might slide across the tile like it was the deck of a sinking ship. A burning ship.

I could do all those things to him—strip him, hurt him, humiliate him, fuck him, and feel good about myself for fifteen seconds—and if I did, I'd hate myself for the rest of my life. Even with the vertigo, even with an intoxicating warmth between my legs, that part was clear. Maybe not today. Maybe not next week. But I would eventually. Because I knew abuse spun like a goddamn merry-go-round, and I didn't want to be the kid who kept spinning.

"It's my birthday."

The shock of the words steadied him. He blew out a snot bubble and ran his arm under his nose. "What?"

"It's my birthday, and I want a present."

He pulled the savaged, ruined lip between his teeth. He was trying so hard to smile for me. Not a smirk. A smile. "Vie—"

"I want to unwrap my present." I pried at the placket. Force. Just enough force that if I twisted, just a little, the button would slip through its hole. But only if I twisted.

"Vie—"

"It's my birthday, Em. And I want to unwrap my present." I gave him the kind of smile he was always giving me: that kind of boiling-over sex that could melt steel. It wasn't my natural expression like it was for Emmett, but tonight, with that fire in my gut, I came pretty damn close. "I've waited a long time for this."

He was crying again, but softer now. No racking sobs. No heavy breathing. Just streams of tears, and he mopped at them with the heels of his hands, and they just came harder, two clear rills breaking on the sharp lines of his cheekbones.

"Austin—"

"—broke up with me. Today. You heard him. It's over."

"It's not over. Don't be stupid; not right now. Not when it matters. You know it's not over. He loves you. You love him. And as soon as he's done being mad at you, you two will be back together."

I was shaking my head. I still hadn't twisted. I still hadn't taken that last step, forcing the button through its hole. "It's over between us."

"Christ, you're just so dumb sometimes." He pressed the heels of his hands to his eyes again; a long, buzzing moment passed. Then he lowered them and said, "I'm dumb too, I guess, because I don't care. I know you'll go back to him, but I don't care. Not tonight. I'll—I'll do this, all right?" He closed his eyes and shuddered. He was like a leaf in my hands. Like a leaf driven before the Wyoming wind. "But you've got to say it first. Then it'll hurt less."

I stepped forward. He stepped back. His butt caught on the lip of the vanity, my legs straddled his, and there was barely enough room between us for my hands to clench his shirt. He shuddered again when my breath touched his cheek, and he bucked into me, his hips flexing against the vanity to add leverage as he ground his crotch against me. The kid was going to pop one off before I ever got him out of his shirt, I thought, and then I realized maybe that was the plan.

"Say what?"

Another shudder, and he twisted his face away as though my breath had burned him, displaying the unmarked side. Panting, his chest dropping after every breath like he had an anvil on it, he said, "Say you know it. Say you know he still loves you."

I brought his face back toward me. He was still rocking against the vanity, slamming his hard dick against me, breathing like he was in a one-man sprint. His eyes fluttered beneath closed lids, the way kids look when they're dreaming their biggest dreams. Everything about him was breaking my heart.

"Say it," Emmett whispered, eyes still closed, and he moaned and thrust against me. "Say it, Vie, just fucking say it. If I—" Another huge, animal pant, his chest dropping a mile, and he managed to say, "If I weren't such a fucking coward, I'd ask you to tell me you loved him too, but . . ."

My thumb found his lip. The scar tissue was thicker, rougher than I expected, but his lip was still as warm and wet as I remembered, and when his tongue flicked out against my thumb, lightning ran to the end of my dick, and I whimpered.

His eyes flicked open. “Say it.”

“Maybe. Maybe he still loves me.”

Dry, dry, Sahara eyes.

“But he’s better off without me. You said it yourself, Em: we’re both fucked up.” I leaned into him, in the hardness of his dick, my whole body sizzling like a spark down a short fuse. “You’re mine, Em. You said it.”

He blinked away the tears that were coming again, and I ran my thumb along his lower lip. That whiskey-fire burned in my gut again.

“I want you to tell me again.”

“I’m yours.”

“Louder.”

“I’m yours.”

“Like you mean it.”

“I’m yours, Vie. I’m yours. A hundred percent. Everything. All of me. Oh Christ, Vie, please—” His hand found my wrist, clutching at me like a man hanging off a cliff.

“Em.”

“Please don’t.”

“Em, it’s my birthday.” My fingers rolled the button back and forth, working the tortoiseshell edge toward the slit in the placket. “And I want to unwrap my present.”

His chin dropped to his chest; his lids shuttered. For a moment, he wasn’t even breathing, and I thought this was as far as I could take him with words. After this, I’d have to take him by force. And although the thought bothered me, it didn’t bother me as much as it had a few minutes before. I was too hard. The spark was shrieking its way down that short fuse.

Then he nodded.

With a simple twist of my wrist, the button came loose. And the next. And the next. I took my time; no buttons popping free, not this go-around. The fire in my belly whooshed and winked out, and all of the sudden I was the one who was shaking, and the shakes grew harder, stronger, as I worked my way down the line of buttons, until I was surprised when Emmett’s hand carded my hair, drawing the long, loose blond locks together, and I realized he was shushing me. Calming me.

Then I reached the last button. I palmed the bulge in his jeans. Hot. Sahara hot, and that word felt right with the dryness in his eyes back again, with the grit and burn of the denim against my palm. He rocked into my touch, but the noises he made were still soothing, and his gestures were calming, and I was still shaking.

I took the flannel in each hand and looked up. Emmett blinked; bone-dry eyes, but he still blinked. He was working on a smirk again, and it touched the corners of his mouth, and he gave my head a little push, and I dropped.

"I always knew I'd have you on your knees when we started."

My fingers curled under the flannel; the scant dark hairs under his belly button tickled the back of my hand. I was still looking into those dark, dry eyes.

He nodded.

When I peeled the shirt back, Emmett rolled out of it with his usual leonine grace. I ground my teeth to keep from letting out a sharp breath. The disfigurement on his torso followed the same even line, covering one half of his torso in the same rigid strips and whorls of keloid tissue. It followed his arm to the wrist; my fingers traced his hip and found more of the wounds on his back. Someone had done this to him. Someone had hurt him, again and again, and hurt him and hurt him and hurt him, and the rage whited out my mind like snowglare. Emmett was still watching me, waiting, his whole body taut, and so I leaned forward and kissed his stomach. The scars first. Then, on the other side, the smooth ridges of muscle.

He let out a breath; tear tracks glistened fresh on his face again. "It's worse, twea—It's worse, Vie. Down there. She did it. I don't want you to—"

But now the protests were mechanical; we had already gone past the real barriers. Another twist of my fingers undid the button on his jeans, and they slid easily over his flat belly, exposing inches of golden skin, and then thick, dark bush. His hand caught me then.

I kissed just below his navel.

He let go, and I slid his pants to his ankles.

I had to still myself again. I had to be very, very much inside myself, in the icy snowglare of fury that someone had done this to Emmett, so that I didn't let my pain and anger show on my face.

"If you change your mind," he said, trying to make his voice dry and light, "just shuffle on out and I won't—"

I kissed him again, an inch below my last kiss.

His breathing hoarsened. "I won't even hold it against—"

I kissed again. Lower.

"I won't hold it against—"

Lower.

No words this time. Just his rough breathing, and his fingers coiling in my hair.

Lower.

He cried out.

And after that, neither of us needed to say anything.

# Chapter | 26

Afterglow was the wrong word; even after we were both spent, sweating, tangled in each other on my bed, I was on fire. My skin flushed pink, and when Emmett noticed, he laughed and trailed his fingers across my chest. He laughed again when I flinched because every inch of me was raw, so sensitive to his touch that pleasure bordered on pain.

Even when I flinched—damn that boy; my nips could only take so much tweaking—I kept one hand splayed across Emmett's belly. Under half of my touch, rough keloid tissue rasped my palm. Under the other half, my fingers found smooth, knitted muscle. I kept my hand there because Emmett kept laughing, because his eyes kept roving, because his whole body was coiled, and I had the sense that if I eased up, if I removed even the slightest pressure from my touch, he'd spring up and run away. And, of course, I kept my hand there because I liked touching him. Because I liked the velvet softness of his muscles. And I liked the way the scars made him even more beautiful.

I slid my hand to rest between his pecs; I kept the weight of my hand heavy. Not enough to bother him, but enough that he'd take me seriously. He was mine. He was going to have to start learning what that meant. When my hand rested on the chiseled curves of his chest, his heart hammered up, as though pounding against my touch. He wasn't laughing anymore. His eyes flicked: the door, the window, the door.

It was hard not to compare everything to Austin. Austin and I had long since gotten past the awkward fumbles: Austin knew what I liked, and I knew what he liked. With Emmett, however, everything was new. Everything had a kind of breathy hesitation, as though afraid he might hurt me. Or afraid I might hurt him.

Some of that had gotten better, though, once I'd taken charge. In every other situation, this boy with the bottomless eyes wanted to be in charge. Here, though, with me, he liked to be told what to do. He needed it, I think. When he came, he looked like he was breaking and the only thing holding him together was my voice coaxing him, coaching him, controlling him. He needed me; he needed me when he was being bossy, and he needed me even more when he finally gave himself up to me. The truth of it was so simple and so suddenly, shockingly clear. Not just to fuck. Emmett needed me in ways Austin never had. Fucking just made his need a lot more fun.

His eyes flicked: door-window-door.

"You're not going anywhere."

He tried for his usual steaming-hot-sex pose: he spread his legs, sprawled across the quilt, ran his hair into a shaggier mess with his hands, and smirked, every inch of him a loose, cool line of unconcern. Everything except for the floor that had dropped out of his eyes, and the feeling I had in my stomach when I looked there of falling, disorientation, the thrill of knowing that no matter how much I liked telling myself I was in control, there was something about this boy that stole the ground out from under me.

"I can keep you here all day if I want. All week. All year."

He plucked at my thumb, pretending to wrestle it off his chest, and I let him enjoy the fantasy. But when he let go, my thumb snapped back down. Hard. So he wouldn't start getting ideas.

"My mom and dad might wonder if you kept me here all year."

"Not before then?"

I was trying to joke, but his chin came up, and he stared at a spot over my head.

"Sorry. That was a shitty joke."

"My dad's in too deep with Lawayne."

I raised my head to look into his eyes. "That's why your parents were gone."

His eyes were still studying that spot above my head.

"Why were you still here?"

He was trying his hardest. A nervous tremor was running through him, his foot running restlessly over the quilt, his fingers curling in. He wanted to draw himself into a ball. But he wanted to protect himself more, so he was trying his hardest to remain loose and sprawled and give-no-fucks casual. And—as always—watching this damaged boy try to armor up just made me want him even more. Maybe that's why we fit together so well. He was determined not to let anybody see the weakness; I was determined to sneak past every defense, to break through that armor until I got to the boy inside. With Austin, it had been love. Just love. Graham-cracker, vanilla love. With Emmett, I wasn't sure that love was even the right word. It was like glass. Or coke. Or blow. Em was the way my brain was wired. Love—and everything else—was just a shadow.

"Ok," I said, letting my mind work through events. Things Emmett had said to me filtered into my consciousness. I rolled his arm over, pressing down on scar tissue and track marks inside his elbow with my thumb. The skin whitened with pressure; the lean muscle tensed. His breathing was strong, but they weren't even, they weren't steady, they weren't sure. "Becca and Austin asked you to help protect me. That's bullshit, by the way. I can take care of myself, and three people without any abilities shouldn't be getting into the middle of a firefight."

He looped my hair around his hand and tugged hard enough that my eyes stung. "You're trying to say thank you, tweaker. But you're getting it all wrong and sounding like an asshole." He tugged harder. "Try again."

"You said you could do something nobody else could. No, that's not right. You said Becca pointed out that you could do something nobody else could." The skin darkened around my thumb, the track marks on Emmett's flesh white like snakebites. I knew I was hurting him, but he hadn't made a sound. I relaxed my grip, watching blood rush into the spot my thumb had left, and the words just kept coming. "I knew your dad was involved with Lawayne. I've known it for a long time; I've seen Lawayne in your house before. And Austin told me you're dealing. He said you tried to sell to him. And you told me—" My lips had a kind of mentholated, peppermint numbness, tingling and hot and cold. "You told me you weren't sleeping, and the inside of your arms look like you've been carrying baby porcupines. And you didn't tell me, Emmett. You didn't tell me you couldn't even get out of the shower some days. And I asked you if you were ok. I begged you to tell me.

"And now you're shooting up with, what? Heroin? That's what you're doing? You're some kind of fucking junkie, just like—"

My dad. I had to hold my breath to keep the words from getting out.

Emmett traced my face with his index finger; his touch felt cool against the lingering sex fever, and when he pulled his finger away to rub it against his thumb, it glistened wetly. "Vie, it's not always about you."

"You don't get to make those kinds of decisions. Where you're involved, when it comes to you, it is about me. It's completely about me."

"You still don't understand," he said from behind those fallaway eyes, and the brief illusion of control I'd had—the visceral knowledge from fucking that a part of him needed me, needed me more than he needed anything else in the world—shattered against this other part of him. The cold, calculating part of him that had known, from the very beginning, that I was too much of a risk for a boyfriend. That part doing another version of the same icy calculus as he watched me right then. "I get to do whatever I want, tweaker. And you'll let me. If I want to shoot up, you can shout and rant and slap me around and stick your dick in me. But when you're done, I'll go out and find a needle." Those fallaway eyes shut and opened again. "Nobody can take our shit away, Vie. You know that as well as I do."

I was panting such wild, savage breaths, that a part of my brain waited for an animal to show itself, to explain those noises. Then I hit him, and his face rolled against the comforter, and then it rolled back and he looked up at me from dark, dry eyes.

"Don't make me do that again," I said.

He pulled the ruined corner of his mouth between his teeth again. He looked like a kid trying not to laugh. Or cry. "Nobody, tweaker. Nobody can take our shit away."

I slid off the bed and padded barefoot to the window; I would have hit him again if I hadn't moved. It was late. It was dark. The high prairies had vanished into the dark, and the only thing that still existed was the wind rattling the pane in the frame. Cold pimpled my belly, my chest, my arms. The last of the sex flush died into an ash heap.

"I was already using," Emmett said from the bed. I couldn't help looking at him, and he had one hand to his cheek where the red print lingered. He didn't even seem to know he was doing it. "If that makes any difference to you, I didn't start shooting up because of you. I didn't start so I could spy on Lawayne. I was already buying from him. I was already using. I just . . . sometimes I just needed a few minutes when Makayla wasn't there in my head. And sometimes I needed to sleep. It . . . got away from me." His laugh sounded like it was torn from inside him. "Fast."

"But Becca knew. And Austin knew. And they used it. They wanted you on the inside. Your dad had connections; you were already a customer. The perfect one to figure out what Lawayne was up to and how deep he was in with Urho and the Lady."

"Who else could have done it?"

"It doesn't matter who else could have done it."

"Tell me one other person. Kaden? That kid is a moron. In case you hadn't noticed, he's a flake. And he's got some real shit of his own he's still dealing with. Sure, he buys from one of Lawayne's boys—

nothing too hard, and not too much at any one time. You think he would have been a better choice?"

"Nobody should have done it. It was a fucking stupid idea."

"Don't do that. Don't pretend you don't know that it mattered. If you want to be mad at me, be mad at me. If you want to knock me around, fuck, sweetheart, make me your punching bag. But don't shit on me by pretending it wasn't important."

"Taking a risk like that—"

"They were going to kill you. Do you understand that? They weren't going to play grab-around and tease you, ok? Kyle and Leo were supposed to kill you that night in the parking lot of Garry's. They didn't because of me." Emmett's voice cracked, and he hammered his chest. "I convinced Lawayne that you could still be useful. I convinced Lawayne to push back on the Lady, to tell her not to throw away a valuable tool. I convinced Lawayne that you could be made to see reason. If we could get you out of town, you could be useful to him. He's smart enough not to trust Urho and the Lady."

"You told him to blackmail me?" I took a step, stopped myself, and tried to shake out my fists. "You told him to threaten me? To scare the people I love?"

"They were going to kill you. The end, Vie. Over and out. If Leo and Kyle failed, they had Krystal, they had that creepy kid, they had guys who could just line up a shot and blow your head off before you ever saw them. You couldn't fight against that. You wouldn't have had a chance once they made up their minds, so I saved your life. Try saying thank you. Just try it for once." He chewed on his ruined lip. "Urho and the Lady had already decided to move ahead with the kids, and Lawayne figured he could get what he needed from your corpse. They weren't screwing around, Vie. It was a kill order. You might be psychic. And you might be tough. But when someone wants you dead, really wants you dead, they'll get what they want. Eventually, everybody slips up. And I wasn't going to let that happen."

The fierceness in his voice sent a frisson down my back, and I threw a chill. "Hold on." It took me a minute to work up the words and ask, "What do you mean about the kids? And about Lawayne and my . . . corpse?"

Emmett's hand, which had been massaging that spot on his cheek, stilled.

"What did you mean with all that?"

"I meant what I said: they wanted you dead."

"And I'm asking you what you meant about Tyler and Hannah. And about me. About my dead body. You know, the one you said Lawayne wanted." Another shiver shook me, so I stepped away from the window and wrapped my arms around myself. "That's got something to do with what happened at your house, doesn't it? That's got something to do with Lawayne feeling me up while you watched."

"I was making sure you didn't do anything stupid."

I kept my eyes on him, and after a moment, his gaze fell.

"I'm sorry about that," he muttered in the direction of the quilt. "I wouldn't have—well, you put me in a pretty bad position, showing up at the house like that. I had to convince Lawayne I was helping him. I guess I was helping him, at least on some level, until Krystal attacked you and I blew my cover by helping you. He saw all of that, by the way. I knew I wasn't going to get anything else out of Lawayne, so I decided to take a different approach. That's when I left town."

"You're trying to change the subject, Emmett. What did they want with my body? What did you know about Tyler and Hannah?"

The rag rug slipped under me when I took a step, but I caught myself and kept moving. My shins bumped up against the bed frame. The whole bed rattled, and not in the fun way it had done a little while earlier. Emmett kept right where he was, staring at me from behind those fallaway eyes. And I was falling. It was that same funhouse fall that I felt every time I was around him now: just the shock of the drop, the sense of directionless space, as though I were falling up and down and sideways all at the same time.

"What aren't you telling me? What are you so scared to tell me?"

"It's nothing that matters. We need to keep our focus, tweaker. We need to find Urho and the Lady, and we need to come down on them so hard that there's nothing left to hit back. We need to burn them out. This is medieval shit, tweaker. Fire and iron to get rid of the monsters. If we wait, Urho will get what he wants, and the Lady will keep building their army, and we'll be the ones who get crushed."

"You are scared." I almost didn't believe it.

"Of course I'm scared. I'd be out of my damn mind if I weren't. Jesus, tweaker, we're talking about war here. A real, super-psychic throwdown. And to be honest, I don't think we can win."

"You're so scared you're shaking again." I ran my hand down the inside of his thigh, the light peppering of hair teasing my palm. Tiny shakes, barely even visible, but still there. I could feel them.

He slapped my hand away. "Stop it."

"Tell me."

"I'll tell you when I goddamn feel like it. Maybe that'll be never."

"It has to do with the scars on your face. It has to do with where you went. What happened to you? How could it have happened—you were gone a day, Em, how could it have happened?" I brushed the back of my hand along the inside of his thigh. I wanted him like this always: naked in my bed, my own personal drug that could take me away from everything. But Emmett was right about one thing: I needed to focus. "What did you learn that's so terrible that you can't tell me?"

He slapped my hand away again. He jerked away when I tried to touch him, the scarred half of his face turned toward me like a shield.

"Where did you go?" I asked.

He slashed the ridge of his hand under each eye.

"Where? What did you do?"

"Jesus, tweaker." Red-rimmed eyes. Dry eyes, even though he kept slashing his hands beneath them. Fever, fallaway eyes. "Use your fucking brain for once in your life. I went to see your mother."

# Chapter | 27

Emmett drew his knees against his chest, and he continued to glare at me. The scars went all the way down. A dazed part of my mind tracked them. I had noticed during—well, I had noticed a lot about him over the last few hours. Parts I'd never gotten to see before. I had realized that the scars came down his leg, wrapped around his ankle, and ended. It was such a neat, precise thing. As though the wounds had been meant as ornamentation instead of disfigurement. And that same unnerving, corner-of-the-eye symmetry persisted. That was when everything started to slip and slide, and I had to catch onto the dresser to keep from falling.

"Vie?"

I flipped him off, and moved to sit at the edge of the bed, hugging his chest and staring at me.

"I'm going to throw up," I said.

Neither of us moved.

"I'm going to throw up."

"Well—go. Or do you need me to—"

I was still holding up my middle finger like a traffic sign.

Neither of us moved.

"Are you gonna . . ."

I rolled my shoulders.

"Are you really gonna puke?"

"Christ, Emmett, just shut up." The floor wasn't sliding out from under me anymore, but my heart had moved up about three inches and was trying to punch a hole through my throat. Sweat broke out in a thousand pinpricks, and my legs had dissolved. "I am. I'm going to throw up all over the place."

"Do you want me to hold your hair?"

Neither of us moved.

And then I started crying. Not big tears. Not the kind of sobs that could shake me apart. This wasn't even a snotty cry. It was just slow, steady leakage from the eyes. Like I was melting from the inside out. And that kind of made sense because my brain was gone. I couldn't think. I couldn't move. I just had to stand there, holding myself up on the chest of drawers, while my brains dripped out.

"Vie, I'm—"

"Don't say it. No. Stay right there. If you—" My chest was so heavy. I had good lungs. I ran every day. I didn't smoke—well, not really. But my chest was lead, and I could barely pull in any air. Just little puffs that exploded behind my eyes in white. "If you get off the bed." Puff. "If you." Puff. "If you come over here." Puff, puff. "If you." Puff. "If you." Puff. "If you." Puff, puff, puff like the Fourth of July right at the base of my optic nerves. "I'll kill you."

Neither of us moved.

I knew it wasn't a threat. I guess he did too.

I slid down to sit at the base of the dresser; the knobs on the drawers dug into my back and scraped lines of heat up my skin. When they bumped over the raised battleground of scars, my heart thumped double. My butt felt every speck of dust and grit on the floor; my feet rubbed across the rag rug's concentric rings. I should put on clothes, I thought. Not naked; I can't do this naked. I needed clothes. My boxers. My jeans. Socks, hell, I'd settle for socks. I was vaguely aware the words were leaking out of me just like the tears. Even socks would be better than this. Even one sock just to drag up over my dick so I wasn't facing this—this piece of shit, this traitorous piece of shit, this fuckboy—naked.

"You want me to find your boxers?"

Neither of us moved.

"I should go."

Neither of us moved.

"Vie, please. Can you look at me? Can you talk to me? Yell at me. Hit me. Rip my hair out. Throw me around. Tell me I'm a piece of shit. I know I'm a piece of shit. I'm the biggest piece of shit in your life right now. I'm the biggest piece of shit in the whole world. But I—" He drew in a breath. His eyes weren't fallaway eyes anymore. They were bright and alive. A bright darkness. Electricity arcing in a blacked-out room. He was building up the courage to say what he wanted to say.

Every inch of my skin tingled with what he was about to say. It rushed through me like adrenaline, and my brain cleared, and the weight fell away from my chest.

"Don't." The normalcy of my voice, the evenness, the softness, went off like a gunshot between us. "If you say that, I really will kill you."

Bit by bit those electric lamps in his eyes went out. He tried to pull the corner of his mouth into a smirk; a tic thrummed in his cheek, and then he gave it up and just stared at me.

"Get your fucking clothes on."

"Vie, I want to—"

"Get dressed. And get out of here."

My boxers peeked out from under the bed, where they must have fallen when I kicked them off. I snagged them and hooked my feet through them.

"No," Emmett said. He rolled off the bed, landing on hands and knees next to me, and grabbed the elastic band of the boxers as they reached my hips. "Vie, just hold on."

"Get dressed and get out, Emmett." I yanked up on the boxers.

"No." He yanked down.

"Get your fucking hands off me." I yanked up.

"No. Not until you give me a chance to explain."

"I don't want an explanation. I don't want to talk to you. I don't want to hear about any of it. And even if I did, I don't need to be naked to hear your explanation." I yanked on the elastic again.

"Yes, you do." And then Emmett ripped at my hands, and then, somehow, we were wrestling. "Get out of those damn shorts. Get them the fuck off."

I tried to throw him, but he was crazy, clutching at me, clinging to me, tearing at my hands. Elastic stuttered, ripped, and the boxers came free. We rolled across the rag rug, and then we crashed up against the bed, with me on top, and I slammed him down once, hard enough that his head clicked off the floor, and then I slammed him down again.

"What the fuck does underwear have to do with it, Emmett? There's nothing you can say, nothing, that's going to make this better. It won't matter if my cock's hanging out when you try."

He stared up at me; that dark electricity was back, and he shouted, with spittle on his lips, "It does matter. You're running away, you fucking coward."

"I'm running away—"

"Yeah, you're running away. Even if you don't get off your ass, even if you don't leave the room, you're putting on those fucking boxers because you're running away, and I—" The electricity in his eyes was so bright that I could almost see how deep those bottomless eyes went. "I need you."

Ok, then. That was a different story. I let out a ragged breath. That was safer than what Emmett might have said. If he had said *love*—I stopped the thought, and said, "You need me."

"I need you so fucking much I can't breathe when you're not with me."

"Really? You need me?"

"I need you. Every minute, every day, I need you. Heroin? You think that's the fucking dope that I'm hooked on? Fuck that. That's kiddie shit. You, on the other hand. Eating, sleeping, fucking. You're there, inside my head, no matter what I'm doing. You're the only thing I can think about. And I need you without those damn boxers on." He bucked up at the last, as his words rose into a shout, and caught me by surprise.

I tumbled off, rolled into a sitting position and stared at him. He was breathing like he'd run twenty miles. The flush in his cheeks stained his skin like wine. His tongue ran inside his lower lip; his eyes, bottomless and electric, were enough for me to fall into.

And then I heard what he'd said at the end and started to laugh. I laughed so hard that my stomach hurt, the muscles contracting in spasms, my face wet with the laughter. I laughed so hard I doubled over, the rag rug bristling against my face, the smell of dust and old cloth in my nose. I laughed until I choked on my own spit, and somehow that was just so goddamn funny that it made me laugh even harder after I'd cleared my airway, and I fell onto my side and laughed. And laughed. And laughed. And laughed.

His bare toes dug into my side, pushing hard enough to flip me onto my back. "You're an asshole."

"You need me without my underwear on?"

"You're a real asshole."

But when I scrubbed my eyes clear, he was smiling.

"What about socks?" I got onto my side again, head propped on my arm. My hair fell across my shoulders; it tickled my back like cool grass. It sent a shiver through me. "Do you need me without my socks?"

"God, you're the worst."

"I wasn't running away, Em." I couldn't quite meet those fallaway eyes; the tips of my hair felt like frost-fuzz on my bare skin as I turned my head away. "Ok. Maybe I was."

"You know I like you with your cock hanging out," Emmett said, his tone amused and still heavy. "But you know that's not what this is about. You're brave about a million things. You've lived through shit that would break most people, and I'm not talking about the supernatural stuff. But sometimes, you run. You're right here, right where I can touch you—and I want to touch you, I want you here—but you're gone. You talk to me, you look at me. I bet you could even fuck me, throw me a real hell of a fuck, and you'd be gone the whole time."

He chewed his ruined lip again. "Sometimes you go where I can't follow."

I twisted upright, my hair fanning like ice water along my shoulders. I thought I'd gotten away from the cold; I wasn't near the window, and Sara had the furnace blowing. But my skin pebbled from my collarbone to my ankles. How had Austin said it? Not the same words as Emmett, not the same tone, not the same let's-fuck-around-anyway smile. But the same. The very exact same. Sometimes you go where I can't reach you. Was that how Austin had said it?

"The boxers–"

"The boxers are a fucking metaphor."

"They're not a metaphor. A metaphor is when you compare things."

"Fine, tweaker. They're a symbol. Shut your mouth; I don't care if they aren't really a symbol or if that's not the right definition or whatever. I'm trying to tell you it's not about the boxers. It's about you. I need you to listen to me. I need you to be here with me. I need you, not just the part of you that sticks around when you disappear."

"With my wiener hanging out. Come on, don't make that face. I'm just kidding this time. Can we put on some clothes? It's freezing."

Emmett's brows lifted. "Sure. Just as long as you put on a nice show for me."

I ignored him as best I could. I found a fresh, unripped pair of boxers, and I dragged on joggers and a sweatshirt. I still needed that shower; I smelled a little bit like vomit, a lot like sex, and with the tang of blood–Emmett's blood–ringing in my mouth. But the clothes, the clothes might as well have just come out of the laundry. Gain. Sara's favorite laundry detergent. It flooded my nose as I shimmied into the clothes. I winced as my battered nose popped past the collar.

Emmett, naked, sprawled on the bed.

"Move over," I said, but he didn't budge, and so I stretched out on about four inches of mattress that he left me. "You could get under the sheet, you know."

"But then you wouldn't get to look at me." He shivered then and rolled into me, almost knocking me off the bed. "You'll do a good job of keeping me warm."

Four inches. Four goddamn inches of mattress. That was all he left me. But I curled an arm and tucked him against me, and I ruffled his hair with my free hand. I trailed my fingers through the short, stiff bristles above his ears. I traced his ear, his jaw, his neck, his collarbone. Months. I had waited months and months for this.

"I had a theory." Emmett's chin rested on my ribs, and he spoke into my chest, the words muffled by the thick cotton of the sweatshirt. "It came to me after everything that happened at Belshazzar's Feast. After you told me about that video, the one with the politician that they had kidnapped."

"They hadn't just kidnapped him. They were torturing him. They were breaking him down so Mr. Big Empty could get inside him and wear him like a puppet."

"Right. That's what got me thinking: why?"

"Because they wanted power. They could have used him to do all sorts of nasty stuff. They could have gotten access to law enforcement officers at the top of the chain. They could have used him to subvert laws, or to propose new laws, or just to take bribes and funnel the cash back. They could have—"

"I'm not talking about that. That's the wrong way to look at it, the totally wrong way. You're thinking about why."

"That's what you said."

"You're thinking about why like it's a purpose. The end result. I'm asking why that method. Why did they have to break him down? Why did they have to torture him, hurt him? With that girl, the one working for the Biondi, the torture had been so bad that it left a kind of psychic stickiness, and you could still feel it. When Mr. Big Empty was wearing that girl's body, he had to hide all the damage—he couldn't let anybody see that her body had been brutalized."

He lifted his head then, those fallaway, bottomless eyes finding mine, inviting me to drop—forever, really, to just drop forever into those eyes. Like heroin. Love? What the fuck was love when you could fall forever? If you fell forever, really forever, then it wasn't any different than flying. And love wasn't shit compared to flying.

"Hey." A finger jabbed my ribs. "Focus."

"I'm thinking."

The memory was right there, clear and red like an Exit sign. Sneaking into Jigger Boss, Vehpese's only nightclub, and finding my way to the back room. A secret room. A torture room. And the residue—the stickiness—of the psychic horror that had occurred there. The pain. The screams. The duskfall realization that no one would hear her, no one would come for her, no one would save her. My breaths stitched together in short succession, one-two-three, and Emmett rubbed a circle above my heart.

"Ok," I said. "But that question isn't really a question. There's no why. Mr. Big Empty told me that much; that's just how his power worked. He had to break them to get inside their heads. That's why they kidnapped those people. That's why they tortured them."

"Tweaker," his hand continued its smooth, slow caress. "You're still not thinking. Why?"

I bit my lip to keep an answer from shooting out. I let my hand feather his hair again. I stared up at the ceiling with its web of cracked plaster. Why? Why did he have to break their bodies and their minds to take control of them? Why did it even matter?

"I don't know," I finally said. "You think it's not just some . . . I don't know. It's not some arbitrary psychic rule. You're saying it's not like that?"

The circle of skin under Emmett's caress was a warm, red disc of pleasure. His voice went into my sweatshirt, muffled again. "That's what I started thinking. I started thinking about the people that disappeared. I started thinking about why they wouldn't talk about where they'd been or what had happened to them. Have you ever talked to Temple Mae about the time she spent with them?"

"She's never even told us that's what happened."

"Don't play dumb. You're too big and blond; it's too easy to believe."

"Ok, so I guess she must have been taken to Belshazzar's Feast. But she doesn't want to talk about it. She doesn't even want to admit that she's got an ability most of the time. It's . . . it's like she's angry when she has to admit that she's different. I think the only reason she helps us is because of Jake."

"What about Mr. Spencer?"

"Jim—" I caught myself.

"Jim?" Emmett's head came up off my chest. "You guys are buddies, huh?"

"He won't tell me anything. He won't talk to me about it. He's like Temple Mae: as much as he can, he wants to pretend that part of his life doesn't exist."

"Jim treats you like you're invisible," Emmett said, "unless you're in class, and then he treats you like a normal student. I know. I've been watching."

"That's so creepy."

"What about Ginny? Or Kaden? Or Makayla or Hailey or the rest of them?"

"Leave Ginny aside for a minute. What happened with Kaden at Belshazzar's Feast?"

"They took him away. They did something to him."

"And?"

I swallowed. "He started screaming."

"Have you seen him naked?"

I thought of the kiss between the bars, that detonation of a kiss with a boy who was supposedly straight. "God, no. Why would I?"

"I have."

This time, my head came off the pillow. "What? When did you—what were you—I mean." I dropped back and tried to moderate my voice. "Oh. And?"

"Oh God, now you're going to have wet dreams for a year. I didn't sleep with him. If anybody's going to pop his little cherry, it'll be Austin, judging by the way those two like to play grab-ass. But one night we were partying, only I let Kaden party a little harder, and I held back, and eventually he was so stoned he passed out on the couch. I stripped him down and took a look."

"What did he say when he woke up naked?"

"Nothing." Emmett smirked. "I loaded his phone up with gay porn and left it in his hand. He's probably spent the last three weeks desperately trying to convince himself he really is straight. For all I know, he actually is. But that's not the important part. The important part is that I found two wounds. Mostly healed, but still visible. And they're going to scar, tweaker." Emmett rolled away from me and sat up. He touched his bare chest, a few inches below his heart. Then his hand drifted lower, to his navel, and skidded right another inch. "And don't try to tell me he got hurt during the fight. Austin carried him out of there while the whole place was coming down. Kaden got two specific wounds. Two."

"Just tell me what you're trying to tell me. I'm tired. We still haven't even gotten to the part where you went to see my mom, and that's going to be a real bitch of a fight, so I'm saving up. I don't want to waste time going in circles like this."

Emmett got on his knees and shuffled over to me. His arms came around me, as though he were going to embrace me, and then his finger lighted on my back. On the scar. The first one. From the birthday candles.

"Here," he said. Whispered, really. A low, throaty noise that was barely a word, more just the hot gust of his breath on my neck. His finger found another scar, his touch unerring even with the sweatshirt covering my back. "And here. Here. Here. Here."

The cold was back, drawing the skin tight at the center of my chest. I shivered. Then, as delicately as I could, I laid a hand on Emmett's chest and forced him away from me.

"How did you do that? At your house, when you were showing me off to Lawayne—"

"When I was saving your life."

"—you knew. You knew the order she—you knew the order they happened. And now, without even looking, you know where they are."

"Chakras."

"What?"

"Chakras are like these points of spiritual energy that map onto the body—"

"I know what chakras are." I glared at him. I squirmed until I was sitting against the headboard—I wanted something at my back—and then I said. "Ok. I mean, I've heard of chakras."

His lopsided smile looked so much like the old Emmett that it yanked on my heartstrings. "Well, tweaker, I'll give you the benefit of my research." He began touching himself, marking a line from his crown to his crotch. "The big chakras, the ones that get the most attention, especially the way people in the U.S. have picked up on the idea, are the seven." He marked them out again for me, slower, his hand lingering at his crotch and his eyebrows arching into giant fuck-mes. Then, with a laugh, he said, "They're a big deal if you're into that stuff. Meditation. Holistic healing. Tantric sex." His smirk sizzled again; he was half hard, and those dark, bottomless eyes told me he was thinking of ways to distract me.

"Save it. You want to show me a million ways you can make me come, that sounds like a great way to spend a weekend."

*A weekend*, Emmett mouthed, his eyebrows still shot into those fuck-me peaks.

"But for now, stay focused. None of my scars line up with those chakras." I tried to visualize my back; it was disorienting, thinking of my body from the outside. "They're not even close."

All of the smoldering-coal energy went out of Emmett, and he drew himself together, arms hooking his knees. For a moment, he struggled with something, the effort showing in his face, and then he said, "Mine do."

With visible effort, he opened his legs and leaned back on his arms. The movement was so stilted, so clinically asexual, that even though I had seen him sprawled, erect, moaning as I buried myself in him, this was completely different. It prickled on the back of my neck, the sheer vulnerability of the movement, and the fear on his face.

And then I saw the symmetry. Or the insane version of symmetry that my conscious brain could only partially process. He was telling the truth: the scars on his face swirled out of the chakra at the center of his forehead like tongues of flame. The same on his chest, like half-finished spokes of wheels radiating out from the chakra down to his crotch, where his mutilated penis lay.

Emmett's hand dipped, cupping himself like a fig leaf, and he had a schoolboy blush that looked miles from fitting on his face. "Ok, tweaker. You've seen. Now don't look at me like that." He paused. "Please."

I nodded and glanced away; my face was hot, and my chest was hot, and my belly. My eyes came to rest on a knot in the floorboards, and I directed all my attention to that swirl in the grain so I could control my runaway thoughts, because if I didn't . . . I was going to lose it.

"We fucked, Em; it's not like I didn't notice—" I was rambling trying to find a way to put him at ease.

"Please don't do that."

That black knot in the wood drew my eyes again, my breath catching in my throat, and I nodded without looking up. "Maybe you should put on some clothes."

The rustle of the quilt, then the slow rasp of his jeans, and the swish of cotton falling over lean muscle. When the bed rocked under his weight again, his smell poured over me: his sweat, his sex, the lingering bergamot of his cologne. His breathing was even, but it wasn't natural. When he spoke, his voice wasn't natural either.

"Obviously this, what happened to me, that happened a lot later. The first clue was the way Mr. Big Empty was taking control of people. The more I started thinking about it, the more I realized there had to be a why. Some reason that wasn't arbitrary—that's what you said, right? And it hit me one day. It wasn't arbitrary at all. For millions of years—well, ok, thousands of years—people have believed that the body and the soul are connected. Purity of the flesh, purity of the spirit. Respect the flesh, respect the spirit. Acupuncture, chiromancy, sexual magic. The chakras. And that's when I started thinking I was on to something."

"So Mr. Big Empty wasn't just hurting people. I mean," I paused. My eyes went anywhere but Emmett. They went over and over again to that knot in the wood. "I mean he was hurting them, but the torture was purposeful. Directed. He was damaging specific chakras. Breaking them." I visualized my third eye, and my hand came to rest against my forehead, mimicking Emmett's earlier gesture. Maybe it was my imagination. Maybe. But I thought I could feel the pulse of my power there like a silver heartbeat. "But my—"

"There aren't just seven chakras. There are seven major chakras, but depending on which traditions you follow, there might be twelve, or there might be hundreds. Or thousands. Or tens of thousands. One line of belief posits eighty-eight thousand."

My eyes skipped away from the floor long enough to slide across Emmett's face: those fallaway eyes with the electric sheen, like a skein of light unraveled over bottomless dark. And then I was back, safe, to the floor. My thoughts kept moving though; more and more of what Emmett was suggesting started to come together.

"Ok. Ok, but my—"

"Do you remember when I first saw your back?"

The whorl of darkness in the wood was staring back at me now; the quilt's seams bumped up under my fingers. I remembered trying to sleep in the hotel recliner. I remembered the nightmares. I remembered the catch in Emmett's throat.

"Do you?"

I nodded.

"They found Samantha's body that day. In my garage. And my whole world was coming apart. I thought for sure they were going to arrest me. I thought it was all happening again. It was like one of those nightmares where you can't run, or you can't run fast enough, and whatever's chasing you just comes faster and faster.

"Only it wasn't the same. You were there. And somehow you got me into that hotel room, and you got me into bed, and you looked so goddamn ridiculous squeezed into that chair and trying to sleep. I don't even know if that's when it happened, but now, when I look back, that's when I think it started. I never had a chance, tweaker. Not after that night. And when I saw the scars—"

I shook my head.

"When I saw them, I think that was it. No chance. No fucking chance after that no matter how hard I threw the dice. And it wasn't because I have a thing for fucked-up pretty boys. It was because I knew you'd been through hell, and somehow you'd come out like this: stomping around and raising hell and making those ugly tough faces you think you know how to make and trying to sleep in a recliner because you were worried about me. Somehow after everything that had happened to you, you were worried about me. I should have just stopped fighting it then." He touched the fading red print of my hand on his cheek. "I never forgot that. The way your back looked. And I went and started studying. Do you know what I found?"

He waited. He was waiting for me. *I never had a chance.* The words pinballed inside my head, and I stared at that knot in the floor until it blurred, and those words just pinballed faster and faster. *I never had a chance. I never had a chance.* Heroin. I shivered. He was so much worse than heroin. I could try my entire life to get him out of my system, and he'd come back like this again and again. He thought he never had a chance? What about me?

He was still waiting, and those fallaway eyes were waiting, and I had to clear my throat.

"Do you know what I found?"

I shook my head.

"Nothing. I mean, there's a million websites about chakras. And most of them sound like they were written by crazy people. And there's a lot of books written about chakras, and most of those sound like they were written by hippies or by pseudo-hippies trying to make a buck. But I couldn't find anything that would explain what I had seen. I couldn't find anything that would explain how damaging the chakras—specific chakras, in specific patterns—would produce the kinds of freaky X-Men powers I'd seen. So I went back to the beginning and tried to think it all out."

"Why didn't you talk to me about this? Why didn't we work on it together?"

"Tweaker." And he said it with so much affection and a light veneer of scorn like I was too stupid to see what was right in front of me. Then he shook his head. "I went through the facts. What did I know? I knew that the Lady had been alive for a long time. I knew that she'd been changing people, giving them abilities. But only sometimes. Sometimes people didn't come back. And there didn't seem to be any pattern to the abilities."

"Kinetics." I looked up at Emmett, surprising even myself. "That's what Luke—that's what Mr. Big Empty called them. She kept making different kinds of kinetics. Jim—I mean, Mr. Spencer—"

Emmett's mouth quirked, but those bottomless eyes were deadly dangerous at the mention of Jim's name.

"—and Mrs. Troutt and Hailey and Temple Mae and Kaden and, well, all of them. They can affect the physical world. But that's not what she wanted. She wanted a psychic."

"You figured that out?"

"Luke said she needed a real psychic, a full psychic, so she could bring back Urho. But she . . . what's wrong with your face?"

"You knew? He just told you? Just like that?" Emmett groaned. "Why didn't you say anything?"

"I'm sorry. I wasn't invited to the secret clubhouse for the meetings."

"Jesus. Just Jesus, Vie. Didn't you think that the rest of us might want to know that? What else did he say?"

"He said—" My brow furrowed. "Something about other awakeners. Mr. Big Empty thought there used to be others, and that kind of makes sense, I guess, because the Lady made a big stinking deal about how she was given the Montana Territory. That's what this part of the country used to be called, back before statehood. But he said they were all gone now, and . . . come on, Emmett. You look like you've got to take a dump."

"You could have saved me—" His jaw clamped shut. He gave a single, vicious jerk of his head. His nostrils flared with each breath. "Vie, why didn't you tell us?"

"What are you so upset about?"

"Everybody we know, everybody that's got a power, how'd they get it?"

"Does this have something to do with Lawayne? Does this have something to do with the creepy way he handled me, with him talking to you like you promised him something?"

Emmett snorted. "Lawayne is desperate for an ability, but he's not stupid enough to hand himself over to the Lady. I explained my theory about chakras. I told him about you, mapped out what I knew about the scars and what I'd wheedled out of Austin, and that night, he was convinced I was right. That's why he wanted you—dead or alive. He's got some batshit idea that he can create powers himself, just by making the right cuts. He's an idiot, but he was smart enough to play along with Urho and the Lady long enough to avoid getting crushed." Emmett's eyes narrowed. "You're avoiding my question, though, tweaker. How did everyone we know get their ability?"

"They disappeared. Captured by the Lady. She woke them from the mortal sleep—that's what Luke called it. I don't get it; what are you freaking out about?"

"Use your fucking head, Vie. For once, use it. Everybody we know?"

I stared at him. At the ruined half of his face. Emmett had come back with power, I had been wondering at the back of my head where he had gone. But my self-pity, my fear for Hannah and Tyler, the way everything had spiraled out of control, and then I couldn't breathe, couldn't think, couldn't do anything but come here—the way I couldn't do anything sometimes but find my own place and shake the blades out of their box like a deck of cards. All those distractions had allowed me to push the question to the back of my mind. How had Emmett gotten his abilities? Who had done these horrible things to him? Not the Lady; she wouldn't have released him, and none of her victims wore visible wounds like Emmett. How had he returned, after nothing more than a day, looking like months had passed, his wounds healing into lines of fresh pink scar tissue?

"Why does it matter?"

He just shook his head. The electric slick on his eyes had gone out; they were total fallaways now, and I felt myself dropping, my gut rising, nausea spilling into my throat.

"You—"

"I'm not talking about me. Everybody we know, tweaker? Everybody that's got a power in Vehpese? Every single one of them was kidnapped at some point by the Lady?"

My heart stuttered to a stop. I shook my head. "No." It sounded so dumb. It sounded like a kid. Like a baby. But I couldn't make anything else come out. "No."

"Why did I go see your mom, Vie?"

I shook my head.

"Why? Why did I go see her?"

"You're crazy. There's no way." But maybe it wasn't crazy, maybe it all made some kind of awful sense, because I could see that old newspaper in my mind, could practically feel the brittle page under my fingers.

"I went to see her, Vie, because she's the one who awakened you."

# Chapter | 28

I sat there, framing my next question. I thought I should have been in shock, but the roller coaster of emotions over the last two days had finally carried me past the point where I could react. Instead of provoking a response, this last surprise wiped my nerves clean.

"Are you going to bolt on me again? Are you going to freak out or fall down or something?"

I shook my head.

"Are you going to hit me?"

I smiled. "Are you scared of me?"

"Fuck you, tweaker. You don't look good."

"I'm fine."

Emmett's hand ran the length of his bandaged arm; the dark pools of his eyes swallowed me and gave nothing back. "Are you going to make me show you what it feels like again?"

My grin stayed plastered on my face, and I gave a little shake with my head.

"Well?"

"What?"

"You look like you're going to pass out. Come on, just take a swing so you'll feel better."

"I feel fine." That grin still drew on the corners of my mouth. I was biting my lip, trying to force the expression off my face, but it was super-glued there. "So. You saw her."

Emmett nodded. His eyes had become hooded. He watched me the way a beaten dog watches: alert to every movement, alert in a way that turned my stomach. But my smile. I couldn't shake that smile.

"Did you see the apartment?"

"I—"

"The one I lived in with her."

"I don't know if it's the same one."

Patiently—I felt like I could be patient with him forever, patient, patient, patient—I said, "1117 Oakland Terrace."

"Yeah."

"So you saw where the iron fell and burned the carpet."

"Vie—"

"And you saw the holes I punched under the stairs—she didn't get those fixed, I bet, did she? No, of course she didn't. And you saw—" My lips were dry, and my tongue flicked out, and it was dry too so it didn't make any difference.

"Vie—"

"You saw the ashtrays, I guess. You can't really miss them; they're in every room. And you saw my room, didn't you? You saw the bed. No sheets, right? And you saw the closet doors that fell off when I threw a chair at them. And you saw that greasy spot on the carpet where she rubbed the cake in." My tongue laved my lips again. Dry. Bone dry. "It's still greasy, isn't it? And brown, right? You can't get chocolate out of anything, and she told me not to take it upstairs, and she was right. I dropped it. And if you want to know why I don't like birthday cake, it's because I can still taste those fucking carpet fibers when she made me lick it—"

When Emmett's hand cupped my chin, I stopped. I was blinking rapidly. I was trying to find that knot in the floorboards again, trying to find anything I could fixate on, but Emmett was slowly turning my head, and I knew I'd have to see him eventually. I knew what Austin would say if he were here. That he loved me. That he was sorry. That I was brave or amazing or strong or whatever stupid adjective he'd settled on for today. And I knew that when Emmett said one of those things, it'd be over between us. Those words would burn him out of my system like penicillin chasing a bad infection. I just kept blinking and let him turn my head.

Dark eyes. Fallaway eyes. No electric shimmer. Just the drop.

"Are you doing this to hurt me? Or are you doing it to hurt you?" He waggled my head. "Or do you even know why you're doing it?"

Heroin. Crank. Crystal. Glass. They were nothing, nothing, compared to this. I turned into his touch, and his skin was hectic and hot against mine.

After a moment, he let go. "It's the same shithole, Vie."

I nodded. I scrubbed my cheeks. It didn't make any difference; I could feel the flush and the hot, hectic patches.

"She looked fine. I mean, she's not sick or anything."

"Yeah."

"She asked about you. Do you want me to tell you all of it? Or just the parts your boyfriend thinks you can handle?"

"I don't have a boyfriend."

"Say it like you mean it, tweaker." His breath punched out. "I just wanted to talk to her. I wanted to know if I was right. It seemed unreal: an awakener, a monster like the Lady, only living some shitty suburban life. I wanted to know why she had—" He stopped. "That was stupid, in hindsight. I should have realized she would be . . ."

"Dangerous?"

His fine, long-fingered hands spread across the quilt, chasing wrinkles. "I asked her about you. As soon as she opened the door. And she let me in. She was smoking. She's . . . younger than I expected."

And I knew, without looking at his face, that he meant she was attractive, that he hadn't expected to feel attracted to her.

"And she wasn't nice, not exactly, but she let me sit down, and she got me a glass of water. She asked how you were doing. I lied. I just gave her a little bullshit and then went back to asking questions. She wasn't even surprised when I started talking about powers. She didn't even blink. She just dragged on her cigarette and blew the smoke to the side and waited like I had something more interesting to talk about. She asked if you had talked to Gage." His hands kneaded the quilt; from the corner of my eye, I caught the question in the way he turned his head, and I ignored it.

"All of the sudden, she started talking. Just shooting out facts like she was reading off a grocery list. Yes, she made you exactly what you are. Yes, she did it on purpose. Yes, she could have done it a dozen other ways, but she chose the one she enjoyed. Yes, she knew about the Lady in the Montana Territory, and she laughed about that like it was some kind of joke. And then she said—this part I can remember exactly—something like, 'That old bitch lost her touch, though, didn't she?' and then she laughed again."

She could have done it a dozen other ways. God, the grin on my face was starting to hurt.

"I asked her why. Why she made you the way you are. Why she let you go. Why she lived in a shithole apartment when she had abilities most people couldn't dream of."

"And?"

"I think there are all kinds of monsters, Vie. I think we see the big ones easily. Hitler, Stalin, Pol Pot. Serial killers like Ted Bundy or John Wayne Gacy. But there are so many we don't see. So many monsters that hide in plain sight. They don't care about armies. They don't care about world domination. They're . . . domestic. All they want to do is rule their little kingdoms. They're the nightmares that live next door."

For the first time since Emmett had started his story, I shook my head. "I don't care what you think. I want to know what she said."

His voice warbled; it was such a childish sound, so incredibly innocent, that I wanted to grab his hand, touch his cheek, run my fingers through the short hair above his ears. But I didn't move, and he kept speaking. "She came over and sat next to me on the sofa, and she took the cigarette from between her lips."

A moan was building behind my lips. I hated it; I couldn't get rid of it.

"And she grabbed a handful of my hair. And I freaked out. I grabbed her wrist. I tried to squirm off the sofa. She didn't really fight me or hold me. She just said, 'How bad do you want to know?' And I thought about it. Honestly. I mean, my brain was scrambled, but I tried to think. And I said, 'Just not my eyes.' And she laughed and said of course not." His hands spread on the quilt, the fingers stretched to their utmost as though responding to that remembered pain, and then they gathered waves of quilting and clumped it in his fists. "I didn't scream. I wasn't even thinking at that point, I just felt the pain and this weird pride that I hadn't screamed." He was trying to extend his fingers again, but his fists remained tight around the cloth. "And she said, 'How bad do you want to know?' And it took me longer this time, but I told her, 'Just not my eyes.'" A shudder ran through him. "It went on like that for a while. And finally I couldn't. I couldn't. I was crying. I'd been crying for a while. And screaming. I mean, I had been so fucking proud of myself that I could do this, that I could do it for you, but I'd started screaming pretty fast. She sat there for a while, a fresh cigarette between her teeth, just smoking while I cried." A smile twisted his lips. "She even offered me one. When I finally looked at her, she just asked me again, 'How bad do you want to know?' and I told her to fuck off. And she laughed." He suddenly seemed aware of his tightly clenched fists, so he shook them out and stared at them. "You know what makes me the most angry? It took me that long. It took me all that time, and I still didn't figure it out before she broke me."

"I'll kill her." I got off the bed and took a helpless step toward the door. "I need your credit card for a plane ticket, and then I'll kill her."

"She talked more after that. I don't remember all of it; I was hurting pretty bad, and my mind was in pieces. She said I could leave if I wanted to, but I'd be back. She said people always came back. She said they came back no matter what she did to them because they wanted what only she could give to them. She said once she broke a woman's spine, and the woman still came back. In her wheelchair. And she made that woman get out of her chair and drag herself across the threshold. And the woman did it. Dragged herself back to the woman who had crippled her." Emmett's voice took on a strange note. "She said the woman didn't complain when she got to fly."

And I remembered, then, the article in the old newspaper that I had found in Dad's apartment: the woman named Lillian Bellis in New York City who had looked so much like Mom; and Arturo Fabiniani and his dungeons; and the woman who had levitated over the Empire State Building.

"She was right." Emmett's voice cracked again, and the sound made him look five years younger—it stripped the years and the sex off him until he looked prepubescent, vulnerable, aching for comfort. "I knew she was right. I knew I could drive to the airport. Maybe I'd even get on the plane. Maybe, if I had a miracle of willpower, I'd make it the whole flight and land in Billings. But I'd turn right back around. I'd go right back to that shitty townhouse on Oakland Terrace. I'd run back. If I had to, I'd crawl back. A thousand miles. Two thousand, on bloody hands and knees. And I knew if I left, she'd make me pay even more. So I stayed. And I asked for what I wanted. And I let her take her price."

"What did you want?"

He lied to me. The sudden flick away of his dark eyes told me it was a lie. "I didn't want to sit on the sidelines anymore. I didn't want to repeat Belshazzar's Feast. I wanted to be able to take care of myself."

That made sense. It was plausible. It was even, if I hadn't known him better, credible. "And the price?"

He didn't answer. He didn't have to; it had been a stupid question. He pulled the ruined lip between his teeth again; that was a new habit. The thought pulsed, a low, lava red at the back of my brain, that maybe he had learned that habit to keep himself from screaming.

"I think that's how she felt about kids. I think that's why she had—"

"Me."

"No. I don't know."

"What?"

"She likes having people come back even after she hurt them. She liked the . . . the craziness of it. That's what I think. It's one thing to hurt someone. It's another thing to hurt someone, but they keep coming back. That's power. That's maybe the ultimate power. You turn somebody inside out. They're divided. Split. One part of them knows what you're going to do. The other part, though, the louder part, says maybe it'll be different. Maybe you'll get what you want. What you need. She did it with awakening; she did it with that lady whose spine she broke. But . . . shit, Vie. People like her, people who abuse kids, that's a big part of it. The kids don't know any better. They just know it's their mom or their dad. They just know they want to be loved. And sometimes they get that love. And sometimes they get—"

"Shut the fuck up."

Silence.

"You've just got to shut the fuck up."

The house creaked. The wind rapped at the glass, shrieked between the panes.

"Just stop it with that stuff, ok?"

"Ok."

Another blast of wind howled and curled around the house; something downstairs, the refrigerator maybe, clicked-clicked-clicked. I forced my mouth open. Forced out words. "What about the time?"

"Time?"

"You were gone less than twenty-four hours. The wounds look like they're almost healed. Or as healed as they ever will be."

He shrugged. "You said Ginny can do funny things with time. You said time on the other side is strange. It's—it's a blur, a lot of it. Most of it. I remember bits and pieces vivid like pictures, and then long stretches where I just have impressions. The knife. I remember that really clearly. The scratch of the sofa fabric on my cheek. The old potpourri smell in a sachet. Other things. Sharp things. The Lady did weird things with time, too, right? People disappearing and then being found a few days later, but they thought they'd been gone for weeks. And you. People would have noticed a lot earlier if you were always showing up with fresh injuries. She must have done it to you too, to keep her secret as long as she could."

I shunted that thought off to the side. "If you did this for me, we're done. If you did this for me, for some sick reason like you thought you needed to take care of me, we're done. Is that what this is? Is that why you did it?"

"That's some fucking ego."

"Did you? Did you do this for me, I mean?"

"I told you why I did it." And this time, his voice was cold, his gaze locked onto me. No flick-away tell. "I did it because I'm never going to be powerless again. Not everything is about you, tweaker."

"You went to my mom—"

"I went to her for information. And I got more than I wanted."

"You went to her because you—"

"Do you want to find those kids?"

"Of course."

"Then quit bitching about stuff you don't understand and let's start planning."

I threw myself onto the bed. Emmett rode the aftershocks with a small smile, and he reached out long enough to tuck my hair behind my ears. "Still mad at me?"

I pulled away from his touch. "My plan."

"You're going to need one."

"You interrupted my plan." I explained the series of events of the last few days, and my growing awareness that those moments of pain and release, those moments when my psyche caught fire and burned off the self-hate and doubt and pain, made me visible to Urho. I explained how they drew him to me.

When I finished, Emmett said, "So you took the next logical step."

I nodded.

"You did what any perfectly sane, rational person would do. Because you're you, tweaker. And you always do what's sane and rational."

This time, my nod was more hesitant.

Emmett's eyes made Bambi eyes at me. "You decided to cut off your arm."

"I—" I blew out a breath. "It's not—well, not exactly. I mean, I was going to start with a finger and . . ."

Those Bambi eyes were waiting. "A finger."

"Um. Yeah. To start with."

His eyebrows shot up. "To start with. Oh. Ok. That makes it so much better."

"I have to draw him out, Emmett. I don't know where he is. I don't know how to find him. Kyle disappeared with Hannah and Tyler, and even if I can track down Kyle, I can't stop him, so the next best thing is to try to get Urho to face me. At least I have a chance of hurting Urho, maybe even destroying him, if I face him on the other side. But—"

Waving both hands, Emmett shook his head. "It's a shit plan, ok? No. No arguing. It's stupid. It's godawful stupid. And even if you really believe what you're telling me, don't try to pretend there wasn't more to it. You weren't thinking about Urho when you started that saw. You were thinking about—" He pulled back, and a flicker of what might have been compassion crossed his face. "I don't know, I guess. That's your shit. Not mine. But I know you weren't thinking about those kids, not really. You were looking for a reason to fuck yourself up. To really fuck yourself up. And you found it. I don't want to sit here arguing about how you would have bled out and died even if

Urho showed up. I don't. I'm not going to do it. So can we just agree that's a shit plan and we're not going to use it?"

"If it was just one finger—"

"Jesus Christ. I'm up to here with you, tweaker. Up to here. Ok? No saw. No cutting. Not as part of the plan, anyway."

I set my jaw.

"Ok?"

"Ok," I said through gritted teeth.

"You admit it was stupid?"

"Stop pushing it. I said ok."

A slack grin covered Emmett's face. "Let's take it from another angle. Try to use your brain, ok? I know you're out of practice lately—"

"Fuck you."

"—but try. What do we know about the Lady awakening people?"

"We went over this."

"Say it again."

"She kidnaps people. She's been kidnapping them for years. Centuries, I guess. She tortures them—I guess she's mutilating chakras—and then, when they're not psychic, she lets them go."

"That part's strange, isn't it? Kind of like your mom. Why let them go?" Emmett shook his head.

I was thinking about the answer Mom had given: *How bad do you want to know?* And then the cigarette. It wasn't an answer; it was a question. But that could be an answer in its own way. That was her answer. And maybe it was the same answer that the Lady would have given. When I'd been eight, Francis Valentino, who was ten and smelled like his older brother's deodorant and who told us his dad, Ricky Valentino, was in with the mob, had tied an M80 to a stray dog's tail and lit the fuse. And it had blown off a chunk of the tail. The dog had left a trail of blood down the row of apartments, and some of that blood had gotten on Ricky Valentino's white Camaro. When Ricky saw it, he backhanded Francis so hard that Francis did a totally spontaneous and uncoordinated cartwheel and landed ass-up in the rock garden outside the apartment building. Francis was bleeding from scraped knees and elbows and crying, and Ricky kept shouting, "Why'd you do that, dumbfuck?" and cuffing Francis, and Francis kept bleeding and crying. The only answer anybody could get out of Francis, then or ever, was, "It was a stray." And I thought the Lady—and Mom—would have understood Francis's reasoning perfectly.

"Anyway," Emmett said, his voice puncturing my thoughts. "That's not the important part. Keep going."

"What else is there?"

"She keeps getting kinetics instead of psychics. But she needs a psychic."

"She doesn't know what she's doing."

"Or something's wrong with her power." Emmett's voice gained speed. "I've been thinking about this for a while. Your abilities were fucked up, right? But they started coming together. They started working for you, and they worked better as you got through some of your own shit."

"You think the Lady needs a therapist?"

"I think she needed help. Her own chakras might have been fucked up. Or maybe you're right: maybe she never really knew what she was doing, and everything was an accident. If that's the case, she needed a guide. But she couldn't go to another awakener. Like you said—like your mom said—they're territorial."

That word, guide, buzzed through my brain, but I was focused on something else. "You said her chakras, but Em, I've seen inside her. I used my second sight. I . . . I saw this thing. Shriveled. Shrunken. It looked starved and furious, and it was hiding inside her body. I don't think she's human. Or if she was, she isn't anymore." I thought again of that newspaper article from almost seventy years before, Lillian Bellis in New York City. Mom. "I don't know if my mom's human either. I mean—" I shook my head. "Fuck, this sounds like comic book shit."

"Stay with me for a minute longer. You told me you got help. You told me someone helped you. With your abilities, I mean. Someone helped you unlock them. Figure them out."

A guide. "What are you talking about?"

"Think about it, Vie. All this stuff goes down at the same time: all of a sudden, the foster care game is over, and you're supposed to be back with your dad—who's in deep with Lawayne and, by extension, with the Lady." Emmett ticked this off on a finger. "The Lady gets those kids and does something to them that makes her want them bad. She wants those kids in a way she hasn't wanted any of the other kids in two hundred years." He ticked off another finger. "And she brings back her army to make sure nobody interrupts." He ticked this off too. "Vie, everything changed for you—and for the Lady—in a matter of months. And the reason everything changed is somebody started helping her. Somebody showed her what she needed to do. Or somebody fixed her chakras. Or something. But all of a sudden, after two hundred years, the Lady has a—"

Guide, I wanted to say.

"—way to bring her psycho husband back from the dead. Do the math, Vie. There's only one person that we know who can help people with abilities like yours. There's only one person who could have ramrodded you back into your dad's arms. The same person."

"Ginny."

My guide.

# Chapter | 29

The sound of the front door opening stole the rest of our conversation. I stared at Emmett. He stared back at me.

"You've got to decide now, tweaker. Do you believe me? Do you believe your gut?"

Ginny. She had helped me unlock my powers. She had given me a chance at a normal life—she had gotten me away from Dad, helped me land at Sara's house. She hadn't ever fought at my side, but she'd been there, counseling me, warning me, doing her best to make sure I came out ok.

And then I thought of how she'd missed a scheduled check-in a few months back. I thought of the way she'd limped afterward, how she'd laughed about a bad fall on a ski trip. I thought of the missing coyote. And I thought of how she'd told me that she wasn't a warrior, and I'd called her a coward, and she hadn't denied it. Because it was the truth. She was a coward. She had sold me out to save herself. I thought of the paperwork at Dad's house, the letter insisting that my friends and family thought I should be back with Dad. I thought about that microcassette with Austin's voice. Had that been a frame? Had it been a forgery?

How long had she been working for Urho and the Lady? For as long as I'd known her? Or since that missed check-in, and the limp, and the lame story about falling on the bunny slopes? My heart beat faster and faster. I wanted the window open again, and that black Wyoming wind to steal the heat from my body.

"Now, tweaker. Decide now."

I nodded.

"You trust me?"

I nodded. No hesitation, and as much as Emmett tried to hide it, I saw that electric sheen dapple his eyes again. He let out a soft breath and tucked my hair behind my ears again. "Play along. And try to be convincing. Unlike that time you told me that Austin is the best kisser you've ever known."

"That wasn't a lie, I was—"

"Bullshit me later."

And then Emmett sprinted to the door and threw it open.

"Miss Miller. Miss Miller!"

Sara's heavy steps trundled below. Then her voice filtered up the stairs. "Emmett? My God, your face—what happened? What's going on? What are you—"

"Vie's here. He's right here, in his room." He tumbled down the steps, his voice growing softer. "He's freaking out, Miss Miller. He's—I think he wants to hurt himself."

The first step groaned under Sara's weight, but then the sound of movement stopped. Emmett had grabbed her arm. Or put himself in her way. Or given her one of those smiles that could have stopped a runaway diesel. Or his face. Maybe his face had stopped her with its crazy corkscrew scars.

"Can you call someone? Like someone at the hospital? Someone that can talk to him? He won't listen to me, and he says he can't—" I had to admit; Emmett was good. The little hitch in his voice, all that emotion driving a wedge into the words. "He can't let you see him. He's talking about doing something really bad, Miss Miller."

It was all an act, but there was an undercurrent to it, deep waters rolling with real emotion. Emmett cared. People cared. Factually, there was nothing surprising about it. I had always known Austin and Sara cared. I had guessed that Emmett cared, although he was such a little shit sometimes that I figured even he didn't really know what was going on in his own head. Hearing them talking about me, though, and hearing that spike of emotion driven through Emmett's words, and hearing the way Sara's breathing got soft and labored the way it always did when she cried—hearing it was something else entirely.

"Your face, Emmett. God. Was there an accident? How long have you—" Her breathing changed. "If he's going to do something stupid, I need to see him. Get out of my way, please."

"He's going to be mad, Sara. He's going to—can you just call someone first? Just in case? And then if you go up there and he gets mad, maybe someone else can talk him down? Or—or call the police. Can't they arrest him? Like, for his own good?"

Doubt trickled through my gut, a cold sluice that made me rock forward. Had Emmett tricked me? Was this really his plan: to get me into a hospital, hell, to get me into a jail cell, to do whatever it took to get me locked up and—in his mind, at least—safe? I didn't think so;

that was something Austin might have tried, but not Emmett. Still, that cold wash of doubt made me hesitate.

"Please, Miss Miller. It's not good."

"Not the police. He—I don't want to go into it, Emmett, but if he gets into any more trouble, I'm afraid he'll have to go away."

"Miss Miller, there's got to be someone."

Sara's steps were so quick and sudden that for a moment, I took the explosion of creaks and groans for the house falling down. She must have crossed the living room at a sprint. I heard the phone topple, the brass chiming as it hit the floor, and then Sara swearing as she collected it. Sara swearing. Now that was unusual. When she spoke, her voice was too low for me to hear except at the end, when she said, "Thank you," over and over again.

The stairs groaned again. Then she was in my doorway, her cheeks red, her blond hair frizzing like a thundercloud, and the smell of french-fry oil filling the room like smoke. "Oh God, Vie. What happened to you? Where have you—are you all right?" She took a tiny, ballerina-dancer step into the room. "Emmett said you're thinking about doing something stupid." She was still crying; she chuffed little breaths, and after a moment of my silence, she touched the corners of her eyes. "I'm not mad." That only made her cry harder. "I just want you to know I'm not mad."

"I—" A lie was forming on my tongue. And then it evaporated, left my mouth dry and soapy, and I was suddenly telling the truth. "I was. Thinking about doing something stupid, I mean. But Emmett talked me out of it. I'm sorry. And I'm sorry I . . . I'm sorry I broke my promise. And I'm sorry I left." Ran away. That's what I wanted to say, but I couldn't quite bring myself to form the words. It hurt me too much, and I thought it might hurt Sara even more. "I thought I knew what I was doing."

She took another of those tiny steps, just the tips of her toes moving all her mass, and then another. It would have been funny except for the ache that had opened her face and left it raw. And then another ballerina step. And then another. And then she was standing right in front of me, and the smell of french-fry oil puffed off her polyester Bighorn Burger shirt. I leaned into her, my head resting against her warmth, and one of her hands fell onto my back, and she rubbed up and down, up and down, and I remembered how she wiped the stainless steel counters at the end of each shift.

She spoke in rhythm with the long strokes of her hand. "When's the last time you ate, sweetheart?"

I rocked my head in a *no.*

"When's the last time you slept?"

Another *no.*

Her free hand combed my hair, teasing knots out of the long blond strands. "Do you want some ice for that nose?"

I laughed, only it didn't sound like a laugh at all, and then I butted against her gently, and she kept rubbing my back and furrowing my hair.

"Let's get you something to eat," she finally said. "I've still got some of that fried chicken. And then you have to see a doctor."

"I'm not going to do that. What Emmett said. I'm ok."

Her Bighorn Burger shirt muffled the speech, but she must have understood because she laughed and said, "About your nose, sweetheart. The rest of it—we'll talk about it, ok?"

I didn't answer, but I didn't want to answer. Here, at long last, was calm, peace, quiet, rest. Home. I had been fighting for so long. I had fought with Austin, with Krystal, with those human blowjobs at the public house, with Leo and Kyle and Urho. I'd even been fighting with Emmett, and the only difference was that the typical highs-and-lows of fighting with Emmett had, for once, been accompanied by fucking. This was the first time in what felt like ages that I wasn't fighting. And I thought back to the last time I had felt like this, and I thought of Austin, and packing into Bear Rocks, the horse's warmth under me, the sun riding my shoulders, and Austin looking back, framed by the sky and the blue eye of the lake, his face strong and serious and intent, as though I had uttered a cry for help and he was ready to rush into a burning building—the way he always looked at me, I thought now.

And a minute later, that horse had dumped me on my ass, and there hadn't been anything really magical about that trip. Except that moment. That snapshot.

"Food," Sara said, and she gave my back a firm pat. "Before you turn sideways and disappear."

We had barely reached the top of the stairs when a knock came at the door.

"Just a minute," Sara called.

But the door creaked, and footsteps clicked on the floorboards.

"Hold on," Sara shouted, taking the stairs faster. "I said just a—"

The shot was big enough to lift the house off its limestone foundation. That's how it felt anyway. Sara jerked, the way she might have jerked if a bee swerved near her nose. Only it hadn't been a bee. Bright red petals curled on her shoulder, and she lifted her hand toward the blood.

"Get down," I said, dragging her toward me. Another shot rang out, the bullet ripping a chunk of plaster from the stairwell, and the trapped sound raced between the walls. Some of the plaster sifted onto my tongue, and its taste mingled with the iron of blood in the air.

Sara's weight compressed me for a moment. She was moaning, and she began to mumble about being shot. I didn't bother to listen. With another, "Stay down," I wriggled out from under her. Then I hesitated.

Where was Emmett?

"Come out, Vie." It was Ginny's voice. It wasn't firm, but it wasn't shaky either. It was like wet sand. Too much pressure, and the whole thing would crumble, but for the moment it was holding. She had a gun; she'd already shot Sara. Her resolve, even if it wasn't any stronger than wet sand, didn't need to last much longer. A gun would be fast. A gun would be final.

Where was Emmett?

A footstep rapped out on the floor. Just one. But that brought her one step closer to the stairs. She was a big woman—tall, and built like a chimney stack—and how many steps would it take to bring her to where she could see me?

Had he been shot? Had she caught him by surprise, shot him in the back? The thought zinged through me and left my mouth in a reflexive, pained O.

"If you come out now, I'll call an ambulance for Sara."

"Ginny?" Sara's voice was weak. She was raising bloodstained fingertips to the light as if for inspection. "Why did you shoot me, Ginny?"

"She's in shock, but it's going to wear off." Ginny's voice had that nasty, wet-sand grit. "It'll be better for her if we're gone before she does something stupid."

I slipped out of my body and into the other side. I centered myself, reaching out into the emptiness of this half of reality, and brushed Emmett's mind. He wasn't far, but there was something between us. One of Emmett's barriers, maybe. Or maybe he was unconscious. Or dying. I sent my message anyway, like pressing my mouth to glass and speaking into its surface. *She's here. She's inside and she shot Sara.* But I didn't know if he heard me; I didn't even know if he could do anything, even if he had heard me.

Shot right in the back. One of those hollow point rounds that mushroomed out, and he'd have just a tiny hole in his back but a huge, gaping fist ripped out of the front, and his brain might still be flickering little electrical signals, but he was dead. Gone.

The next part, I figured, was hopeless, but I didn't really know what else to do. I was vaguely aware of Sara trying to rise on the steps, but I had abandoned my physical body for the moment so I couldn't do anything to stop her. Instead, I flowed through the other side toward Ginny.

As she had the last time, Ginny lacked the spirit coyote that, for as long as I had known her, had slunk along her aura. I had noticed its absence when she had come to tell me that I'd be moving back in with Dad, but I hadn't really thought about what it meant. Now, in the light of everything Emmett had told me, it made more sense. Something was different about Ginny. She had changed. Whether the loss of her spirit animal was one of the tortures inflicted by the Lady and Urho or simply a side-effect, I didn't know, but I recognized what it meant: she had changed. Emmett had been right—if the gun and the shots at Sara weren't proof enough.

When I had first met Ginny, I had tried to read her with my ability. That time, she had stopped me with her own powers. She might not have been a warrior, as she claimed—although the gun said differently—but she certainly had a good deal of psychic juice. I had grown stronger since then. I hoped strong enough to make a difference.

I reached for her mind, crossing that infinite distance of blackness between us, and crashed into the golden barrier that I remembered from the time before. It was like hitting a bridge abutment at sixty; the psychic shock left me dizzy, disoriented.

Too late, I realized Sara was rising, trying to get to her feet, fumbling with her purse. Maybe she wanted to call for help. Maybe she wanted tissues to press against the bloody wound. Maybe she was so deep in shock that she was just going to freshen up her lipstick. Whatever she was doing, she was going to get herself shot.

I flashed back into my body. Pain broke over me like a wave: my busted nose, the thousand aches and bruises I'd accumulated, and exhaustion. The exhaustion was the worst, the most dangerous, and after I had used my power, it threatened to drag me into unconsciousness.

"Sara, stay down."

But she was on her feet—wavering, and her arm buried up to the elbow in that mammoth bag she called a purse, but on her feet. She was going to get shot. She was going to die because of me.

My unconscious body had slid down the stairs while I was on the other side, and now I was too far away from Sara to tackle her. By the time I reached her, Ginny would have gotten off a shot. Maybe two. I needed something, some way of distracting Ginny long enough for me to get Sara behind cover again. And then I saw it.

I slid on my butt down the stairs and caught my heels on the thin black strip of the telephone cable. The phone. That massive plastic beast of a phone. The one with an ivory-colored casing as big as my head. It lay right there on the stairs next to a gouge in the boards where Sara had dropped it. Call the police. Call Austin. Call Jim.

Those thoughts weren't even really thoughts. They were like the ghosts of thoughts. They never had time to materialize because I didn't have time to think. I only had time to see the phone, for my mind to whirr once, and for me to crouch and grab its bulk. It jangled. Maybe the chime had broken when it fell. Maybe someone was calling. I had the sudden urge to laugh.

Instead, I launched up out of my crouch, the heavy phone held in both hands against my chest. Ginny was looking toward Sara. The pistol in her hand was swinging up at my foster mother. But Ginny must have caught a glimpse of me popping up like some kind of insane jack-in-the-box because the smooth glide of the pistol turned into a kind of stuck-zipper jerk, up and down, a wobble toward me and then a wobble back.

I shoved out with both hands. I wasn't a shot-putter by any measure, but I hadn't been neglecting pecs and triceps and delts on weight days, and that telephone flew like a cannonball. It hit like a cannonball too. My aim was a little off, and the behemoth case of the phone made it arc like a falling star, and the little broken chime chirped madly as it flew through the air, but I still managed to wing Ginny. The phone clipped her arm, knocking her to the side and throwing off her shot. A clump of plaster exploded from the ceiling as her gunshot blasted through the room.

Then there was another shot, and my brain went into overdrive trying to figure out where the bullet had gone. Only I couldn't find it—wall, ceiling, stairs, Sara. Sara. Sara had a gun.

With her blond hair fuzzing out like she'd stuck her tongue to a plasma lamp, Sara straddled two stairs, her body set wide and low in a classic shooter's stance. The gun must have taken up most of the purse because it looked big enough to blast a mule deer in half. My eyes flashed across the room.

Ginny sat on the coffee table, blood welling from her side, her dark eyes swimming somewhere even darker, like the bottom of the ocean. She brought up the gun so fast that I didn't have time to blink. I was staring right at her, right at the gun, right into that dark eye. The darkest. Darker even than hers at the bottom of their black ocean. I was staring into the pistol's negative eye when she squeezed the trigger, and the muzzle flared like she had thrown fire or lightning at me.

I dropped, but even as my brain caught up with me, I realized I'd been too late. I'd seen the gun go off, and no matter how fast I moved, I wasn't faster than a bullet. My hands flew across my chest, my torso, groping, seeking.

Nothing. Just skin and cloth. My breath whistled in my throat, and my nose blared between my eyes. I could taste bile in my mouth; had I puked again?

Two more shots rang out. My ears rang from the concussive blasts.

"All right."

That was Emmett's voice.

"All right, you're ok. You can come out."

Sara yelped and squeezed off another shot. Something shattered, and I rolled onto my knees and looked over the stair railing. Sara had blown her pink-and-blue china potpourri dish into a million pieces. Dried rose petals and bark shavings and whatever else that crazy woman put in her potpourri confettied the air.

Emmett stood in the kitchen doorway, blood seeping from a long, narrow slash to his neck, staining his shirt with a rust-colored fringe. He was focusing on an invisible point at the center of the living room, but his eyes flicked once to me, questing, desperate, and I managed to nod. His breath of relief was barely visible. But it was visible. To me, anyway.

In the air between Ginny and me, three bullets hung suspended in a loose triangle. Ginny slumped on the coffee table, the gun on the floor, its slide locked back; she had emptied the magazine trying to kill us. Now, with one hand pressed over her bloody side, Ginny looked shrunken and old and tired. I'd never seen her that way before. Before, she had always been tall and strong and solid. I didn't know if I was just seeing the effects of the gunshot or if this was the real Ginny: afraid, desperate, beaten.

"I shot her." Sara's voice broke, and the big woman leaned forward. The avenging angel of static electricity slumped against the stair rail, her hair haloed out around her head, whole body quivering, and then she slid to her knees. The movement sent a draft of air my way, and the mixture of frying oil and smokeless propellant made my stomach lurch. "Oh my God. Vie—I've got to call the police. We've got to call the police. My phone. My phone is in my purse. It's in my purse, Vie. I'll just get it out. I'll just get it out now and call—and call the police."

But she wasn't reaching for the purse. And her breathing was strained. Labored. The color had leached out of her face except for two hectic strips that ran under her eyes, and then, in a move that was so classic that it hit me like something off a bad sitcom, she clutched at her chest.

"Oh," she said. "Oh, oh, oh."

"Vie," Emmett said.

"I know."

"Oh," Sara moaned again. "My God. Vie, I think—"

I reached her, wrested the gun from her stiff fingers, and helped her lie back. "I know. Just try to breathe. Just hold on."

Dumping her purse out on the steps, I scanned the spillage of gum wrappers and those small, bewildering cosmetic cases that women always seem to have and a hand-mirror the size of a dinner plate and three packages of tissues and an Alpine Springs water bottle and the knotted mess of her earbuds and, yes, there, her phone. Just an old flip model, thank God, no passcode or security. I dialed 911.

"I need an ambulance," somebody shouted. That couldn't have been my voice. My voice sounded cool, collected, like the ice-water of my thoughts.

"What is the nature of your—"

"She's having a heart attack you dumb fuck. Get an ambulance out here right now."

"Sir, I need you to—"

I rattled off Sara's address and dropped the phone to my chest. My eyes found Emmett's. Fallaway eyes. The electric sheen silverfished across those eyes.

"I'll take care of her."

"I just need to make sure she's ok."

"I said I'd take care of her, tweaker."

"Your neck—"

He ran the tips of his fingers at the edge of the wound like he was smoothing out a chord. "That little Crow boy was back. He kept me busy in the yard. When I heard the gunshots, I tried to get back as fast as I could. He's got some tricks I didn't expect."

"You should see a doctor."

"Take care of Sara. I'll take care of everything else."

I nodded. He turned his attention to Ginny, who barely seemed to recognize where she was; her head nodded, and she dipped as though she might topple off the coffee table at any moment.

"Em?"

A long sigh. A frustrated sigh. "What, tweaker?"

"Thank you."

The silence lasted a full heartbeat. Against my chest, the 911 operator's voice buzzed, but that seemed like somebody rattling greenhouse glass—the only sound in a perfect moment.

He smirked at me over his shoulder. "I'll find a way for you to pay me back. Now let me get this bitch out of here."

While I tried to make Sara more comfortable and handled the operator's battery of questions, Emmett did something with his ability. I watched the invisible barrier sweep across the carpet, pushing a slight ripple of fabric ahead of it, and then it caught up Ginny so that she floated in the air like a doll pressed into plastic packaging. Her blood fanned out against the barrier, like you might see in those displays of plasticized bodies, and then she drifted out of the house ahead of Emmett. He smirked at me one last time, the fringe of blood on his neck and chest only making it hotter, and blew me a kiss. Then he was gone.

In the distance, sirens.

# Chapter | 30

I'd never ridden in an ambulance with someone before. I mean, not this way. I bounced a lot, and every time my ass came down hard, I wondered at the state of Vehpese's roads. I tried not to breathe the clinical, disinfectant-laced air, especially because I kept gulping down the French fry oil whiffs that came off Sara's Bighorn Burger shirt. I recognized the paramedic who rode with me in the back, a hot guy with a faux hawk who patted me on the back a few times but mostly paid attention to Sara.

I tried holding Sara's hand, and I was shit at it. Every time we went over a bump, her hand would slip, and I'd clutch at it harder. Then I'd realize how hard I was holding on, and I'd try to relax, and then we'd hit another pothole or speed bump or whatever the hell was happening to these roads—huge, shelling craters was what I imagined, like a World War II battlefield—and my teeth would click together and her hand would slip and I'd be clutching at her like she was drifting off to where I couldn't catch her again.

Faux hawk patted me on the back again. "Just try not to break her fingers."

He smiled. I didn't bother smiling back.

If I held on to her, she wouldn't die. That was it. Simple as that. And if Sara didn't die, then—what? I could stay? That sounded plausible, like something I might pencil—very lightly pencil—at the end of a really shitty math problem. But it wasn't definite. I wouldn't use ink. Just a real light tracing of the words. I could stay? With Sara? Now that Ginny was exposed, now that I knew Austin—

Now that I knew what?

The ambulance hit another of those World War II-size potholes, and my teeth sheared the inside of my cheek, and I tasted blood. What did I know? I knew Ginny was a traitor. I knew that she'd been working with Urho. First, to get me back in my dad's life, where they'd be able to get to me more easily. Probably with dad's help, if I were honest about it. I knew that she'd tried to kill Sara and me tonight. I knew that she'd almost succeeded.

But the rest of it? I thought of the letter. Of those words stamped in my mind. *Interviews including foster parent(s), friends, and other significant individuals.*

In the snowy tinge of the ambulance lights, with a dozen of my own shadows falling around me, I had to face the problem: I knew she was a traitor, but I didn't know that she was a liar. Maybe Sara really had wanted me gone. Maybe my friends had thought it'd be best if I were back with Dad. And that microcassette. My foot pumped, raising the weight of my backpack. I had collected it from the basement before leaving with the paramedics, and now it rested on my sneakers as we drove. That microcassette was just inches away, clicked into the player, ready to go. I wanted it in my hand. I wanted to unspool the silky magnetic tape and weave a noose with it. It would be cool against my throat. That recording wasn't faked. It might have been clipped. It might have been pilfered. But it wasn't faked. Austin had said those words.

*It's just, sometimes I think it'd be so much easier if he weren't here.*

Sara's hand was slipping again, and I clutched at her, but I wasn't even sure what I was holding on to anymore.

"She'll be all right," faux hawk said with another of those smiles. He must have gotten a twelve-pack of them cheap. He patted me on the back, and I visualized what his wrist would look like with the hand torn off. And then I smiled back.

"There you go," he said.

He goddamn near tousled my hair.

Later parts of that night were a blur: jogging alongside the gurney as the paramedics wheeled Sara into the hospital, and finding myself diverted by a barricade of nurses and orderlies, who shunted me off into a waiting room full of artificial succulents and an abandoned cosmetics mirror, the kind with an oval light ringing the glass, the kind that magnified your face so that the pores were the size of Vehpese potholes.

It took me a few minutes. The walls were lemon curd, with a raspberry border that was probably meant to be cheery. Instead, it looked a little too much like blood; bad taste, I thought, for a hospital to decorate with blood. And then other thoughts started filtering in. Hospital. What hospital? The county hospital had collapsed. Kyle Stark-Taylor had knocked it down like a kid kicking over a sandcastle.

So where the hell was I?

From the waiting room's door, I scanned the hallway. After the big bustle when Sara and I had arrived, everything had calmed down, and now the hall was empty aside from a middle-aged blond tech with dander on his scrubs pushing an old Native American man in a wheelchair.

The reservation? I thought of those potholes, and the blackness of the Wyoming wind and the high prairie rushing past the ambulance. No. Not the reservation. That was on the other side of the mountains, and it would have been faster and easier to go west, forty minutes to Lovell. A minute later, my eyes found it stamped on a list of waiting room rules, below gems like *CMT and MTV stations must be played QUIETLY!!!* And *Snakes and Camels Spit—-LADIES and GENTLEMEN Do NOT!*, there it was, the name: Western Bighorn Hospital.

I went back to one of the vinyl seats and turned on the mirror's halo light. My nose looked like shit. Blue-black and crusted with blood, it filled the mirror. When I shifted, seeing my face in magnified patches, I realized the nose was the worst, but everything else looked pretty bad too. I'd fucked Emmett Bradley like this, looking about as bad as I'd ever looked in my life. All that build-up. All the fantasies I'd squashed about what that first time should have been like: I'd show up in a tux, with flowers—or chocolates, maybe he would have liked chocolates—and I'd be driving a Lambo, something that would have knocked his socks off, or no, maybe I'd hire a limo to take us around. And we'd go somewhere fancy. Maybe I'd rent out a whole restaurant like Clarity, the new place on the riverwalk. Kaden had bragged about dropping two hundred dollars on dinner at Clarity. I'd clear out the whole place, just the two of us, sitting across from each other in a copper shell of candlelight.

I winced as I probed my broken nose, and then I snorted, and that hurt like doubled-up hell. Tux, limo, Clarity. Bullshit. That was a nice kind of fantasy, the kind I had to grind under my heel and squeegee away when I was dating Austin. But Austin and I were done; he had said so. And when it had finally happened with Emmett—my whole face was screwing up tight, my nose screaming, my eyes stinging—it hadn't been a tux and a limo and Clarity. It hadn't been a soap-bubble glow of candlelight holding us together when Em would finally look up and see me, the real me, and realize I was somebody worth dating.

Instead it had been blood. And blades. And scars. And hot, desperate fucking. At least, I told the magnified, watery eye in the mirror, it had been hot.

"They said you looked like shit."

In the doorway, a dark-haired woman with Crow features studied me. She wore a white doctor's coat over a pearl snap shirt and blue jeans. Her boots looked like they'd seen a lot of hard places, but her eyes made me relax. Those eyes looked like she laughed a lot—at all the right things, and at all the right times.

"I feel like shit."

"Come with me, and we'll see what we can do about that."

I snapped off the mirror's light, and my nose looked even worse.

"Are you feral? You don't come when you're called?"

"I'm not a dog."

"You look like something the dog dragged in. Come on. Your mom is going to be fine, and I think she'd be happier seeing you cleaned up than looking like you fell down a mineshaft ass-first."

"She's not—"

She's not my mom. That's what I'd been about to say.

"What?"

"She's not going to die?"

"Not tonight. Why don't you come with me? You look like shit, and you smell like shit. What have you been doing?"

Without waiting for an answer, she took my arm and led me to an exam room, where the paper crinkled under my butt as I squirmed on the table, and I caught a whiff of myself—blood and sex and sweat and exhaustion—in contrast to the chrome-polish air of the hospital. She was right. I did smell like shit.

She set my nose. She wiped my face. She cleaned, with a strong but surprisingly gentle touch, the worst of the scrapes and the cuts.

"I think you're all done. You want to see your mom?"

"Yeah."

"She's resting. You don't need to tire her out."

"I won't."

"You ought to shower before you see her, but you'd just go out and roll in a puddle I think. All right. Let's go."

Sara was resting. She was obviously sedated, but not quite asleep. Her lids fell to crescents of deep blue iris. Deeper blue than her eyes normally were. Maybe the hospital lights. Maybe the dilated pupils. Maybe the shadow of those half-closed lids.

Her hand was puffy and cool when I took it, and she shifted under the thin hospital sheets. She had a million things pasted to her chest and arms—leads and wires leading back to machines that beeped and whined. Her fingers fluttered against mine like she was playing an instrument.

"My chest doesn't hurt so much," she said, and her voice was breathy like she was speaking out of a deep cloud.

"That's good."

More fluttering of her fingers. "I thought you couldn't stand me anymore. I've done everything wrong by you, haven't I?" And then her face shifted—slow, macro, glacial shifts. She was trying to cry, and she was buried too deep in that cloud to do it. "I always told myself I'd be a good mother. My friends told me that too. I'm sorry I did wrong. I'm sorry I made you run away. I shouldn't have yelled."

I stared at her. My jaw was hanging, and it felt cartoonish. Maybe there were birdies chirping around my head too. "You didn't even yell at me." And my brain was telling me that I should say something else, say something about how she'd been the best adult I'd ever met, the only one who hadn't wanted anything from me, who had only ever wanted good things for me, how she had given me a job and then a home and then a life, and how when I got up at night, when Austin's skin was too sticky against mine and I couldn't breathe and I had to walk, had to count steps, had to breathe against the glass and watch my breath evaporate and peel away, how all those nights I hadn't left, hadn't walked out the door, hadn't run, because I knew she was there, and no matter how many bad things got inside me, I knew she was there.

My mouth refused to say any of that, though. I just kept saying, "You didn't even yell. You didn't, Sara. You didn't even raise your voice. You just—you just talked."

And that wasn't right. That wasn't what I should have said.

"I wanted a boy. With Scotty. He would have been big. Scotty was big. Big shoulders." That glacial crawl passed through her face again, tears trying to work their way free of the dope.

"You would have been a great mom." And inside, I was screaming at myself because that wasn't right either. How hard was it to say, you're a great mom, you're my mom, the only real mom I've had, how hard?

Too hard because I just kept babbling, and nothing that mattered, nothing that was really true, the deep-down true, came out.

And then the door snicked, and a wedge of light grew across my knees, and I looked up at Don Miller—Sara's brother, Austin's dad. He nodded at me. His salt-and-pepper hair was still in its meticulous part, and he wore golf shoes and a polo like he might hit the links later, but his whole face shone with worry.

I nodded at him, slid out of the seat, and tried to slip past him. We bumped shoulders, and his eyes swept toward me with something very close to anger, the way you can feel a static charge about to snap. But then he continued, and I continued, and the rush of cool, antiseptic air in the hall cooled my hot cheeks, my swollen eyes.

Austin reached me before I had fully processed seeing him. One moment he was there, filling my field of vision, and then his arms were around me, and he was dragging me against him, and the smell of cedar and crushed tobacco and his hair rushed in on my next breath. For a moment, I let my chin settle onto his shoulder, my mouth rest against his neck, the warmth of him like summer. Then I stepped back, wrenching free of his grip a little too fast, a little too hard, my flush a little too hot, my eyes a little too puffy.

"Are you all right?" His voice was still raspy, but better.

My fingers touched my swollen nose, but I said, "Sara's doing ok."

"They said it was a heart attack."

I nodded.

"Thank God you were there."

"Yeah."

"Vie, she could have died. If you hadn't been there—"

I closed my eyes. The chemically clean air of the hospital was still cooling the back of my neck, and I visualized it streaming in front of me, a blowing storm of a million white particles. Snow. Or sand. I tried to keep myself there in that storm, inside that calming drift of white, because otherwise I was going to do something stupid.

"Seriously, Vie, thank you. You saved her life."

"She almost got killed because of me."

"She—what?"

"Ginny came to the house." How to fill in all the gaps? The saw? The blood like tree roots on Emmett's arms? Sex on the cold bathroom tile, my skin so hot that the cold didn't matter? The truth about where Emmett had gone, what had been done to him? "We figured out she's been helping Urho. Only she came with a gun, and she shot Sara, and Sara—I'm the whole reason Sara had a heart attack, so don't thank me."

The turquoise of Austin's eyes had gone stormy. "We?"

"I've got to get out of here. I've got to get back to Vehpese."

"Becca was with me; I don't know where she went. She was still freaking out about everything that had happened at the hospital. We both were. I was so freaked out I didn't know what I was saying or doing or thinking." There really was a storm in those blue-green eyes. Yes. A storm of anger and tears and helplessness about to rain down. But. I met his gaze. Looked into that storm. And I didn't shrink. Because there wasn't any truth in them. A storm, yes, but no truth. Because the truth was that he had known exactly what he was doing, what he was saying, what he was thinking. *We're done. You and I are done.*

He wanted to take it back. He wanted to pretend it hadn't happened. And I could let him. I could pretend. Even though I was shit at pretending, I could at least try.

"It'd be so much easier."

He blinked. The storm clouds drifted. "What? Oh. You mean—it'd be easier if it were true? It is true, Vie. I was really scared. And I was upset. What I said, it just came out. That's the truth."

I shook my head.

He opened his mouth. He might have tried again. Instead, he set his chin and waited.

It was like a magnet, the tape player. I reached into my bag blindly; I didn't know if I'd ever be able to do this again if looked away right now. The player slapped into my palm like it had been drawn there. The cool plastic. The bump of the buttons. The raised triangle for Play. When I pressed down, I felt a click as the spindles engaged, and then Austin's voice rolled up out of the canvas backpack.

"—not even really his fault. I know that. None of it is his fault. He can't control what other people do. I get that." Then the slight hiss and scratch of a cheap microcassette in a cheap player. "It's just, sometimes I think it'd be so much easier if he weren't here."

Austin wasn't pretty. He wasn't beautiful. He was hot, yes, but his face was too rugged, too masculine, too strong in its features to be beautiful. Only for a moment, pain cracked his face open, and that pain was so enormous that it was transcendent, that it made his face shine, and a loose thread at the back of my brain suddenly tied off, and I knew why people painted saints and martyrs with halos. And then the moment passed, and those cracks sealed over, and the only thing left of that super real moment was in the brightness of his ocean eyes.

"How'd you get that?"

"You're not going to lie about it, then? You're not going to pretend that's not you or that you were talking about someone else, or that this is taken out of context?"

"It is taken out of context. How did you get that?"

I couldn't hold on to the tape player anymore; it weighed a few tons, so I let it fall back into the backpack. The backpack weighed a few tons too. My whole body weighed a few tons. My knees wanted to crack like wishbones and drop me onto the vinyl flooring.

"Did you break into her office?"

I reached for the zipper. It slipped between numb fingers.

"Did you . . . did you hurt her?"

"You're worried about Ginny?"

"Ginny? Who the fuck—I'm worried about Dr. Kilpatrick. How did you get that tape, Vie? Don't lie to me."

"Lie? You want to talk about lying—"

"Don't do that." He didn't raise his voice. He didn't even move, not really, just a tilt of his body, but the threat was so big that I took a step back, ready for a slap, a cuff, a punch, the vacuum cord, the cigarette tip. "You always twist things around. Don't do it. Not right now. How did you get that tape? That's private. That's just Dr. Kilpatrick and me. Nobody else gets to hear that, Vie. I don't care if we are dating—"

"Were. We were dating. You broke up with me."

He shook his head like he couldn't believe what he was hearing. "You stole that. And you listened to it. Jesus, Vie, don't you get how wrong that is? That's like eavesdropping. No. It's worse. It's . . . Christ, I don't know. I can't even think right now."

A violation, my brain said. That's what it was. A violation. Of his privacy. Of his trust. I had wanted so badly not to read his mind, not to take away what everybody had a right to. And I'd done it. Not intentionally. Not knowingly. And I had to bite my lip because I was lying again, to myself this time. I had known that the tape was private. I had listened anyway.

I had to start with *I'm sorry.* I had to start with that and hope that somehow I could rig up the steps and scaffolds and bridges that would get me close enough to him that I could tell him, for real, how very sorry I was. That I could tell him it would never happen again. That I could tell him—

Like a Polaroid, the image of Kaden at Austin's hospital bed flashed back at me. Kaden's voice growing rough like fur stroked the wrong way, saying, *I never really thought about guys like that before, but if it makes you get this freak show out of your life, yeah, I'll think about it, ok?*

I'm sorry. That's all I had to say.

*I'll think about it, ok?*

I'm sorry. Just open your mouth, I told myself. Two words. Just to start, but two words.

*I never really thought about guys like that.*

Two simple words. Those ocean-green eyes were waiting, but they wouldn't wait forever.

*But if it makes you get this freak show out of your life.*

"Private?" I said. And part of me knew, right then, that I had lost him. "Eavesdropping? Kind of like that conversation I overheard between you and Kaden. Is that right?"

He started to turn.

I grabbed his arm and yanked him back toward me. "Were you even going to tell me? Were you going to break up with me? Or was I just going to have to find out—" Like I did with Gage, I almost said, when he started cheating with that trashy piece of theater ass. "—from someone else?" I hefted the bag, letting the tape player rattle against the rest of the junk inside. "Were you going to have Dr. Kilpatrick break the bad news to me?"

"I can't believe I was so wrong about you."

"Yeah, I must have been a big disappointment. So you went to Kaden. You told him all your dirty little fantasies. You told him how you liked to watch him change in the locker room. You told him how you'd eye his pecker through those thin white Calvin Klein's, thinking about how you could get your mouth on it, and—"

Austin had his fist pulled back before I realized it, but he didn't throw the punch. He held himself like a man pulled in two different directions, and when his fist didn't land, I kept talking.

"You can hit me. Why not? It'll make you feel better. Everybody else does it, so go ahead. Hit me. And then, once Kaden's finished thinking about it, you can go tell Dr. Kilpatrick how happy you are, and you can tell her how I threatened you, how absolutely fucking nuts I am, how scared you are that I'm going to hurt you and your new boyfriend, and she can send that tape over to Ginny, and Ginny'll make sure I get locked up where I can't mess up your life anymore. Go ahead. Hit me."

He was still wavering.

I shook him hard enough that I heard his teeth click. "Hit me, you pussy faggot."

He shook out his hand, broke my hold, and stepped back. He ran his hand under his collar, and he cleared his throat twice. "I never wanted Ginny to have that tape. I never told Dr. Kilpatrick to send it to her. I was talking to my therapist, Vie. I was talking through some shit that was hard for me. And yeah, you know what? Sometimes you are hard. But that's life. Everybody's hard sometimes. That doesn't mean I don't love you. If you'd listened to the rest of that damn tape—" He shook his head. "And Kaden? I told him I needed to hang out with him less. I told him how I felt about him because I was tired of lying, and I told him so that he'd understand why I couldn't hang out with him. He came back at me with what you heard. That was him, Vie. Not me. You can believe me or not." He shook out his hands again, as though he'd been holding something burning and had just registered the pain. "I've got to get out of here."

I watched him go a few yards. His words were a bumblebee swarm. If you'd listened to the rest of that damn tape. That was him,

Vie. Not me. It was like I'd swallowed nettles, the prickling rash that ran in a line down my chest and buried itself in my gut.

"You're a fucking terrible liar," I shouted after him. "You're fucking nothing, do you understand? I don't need you. I'm better off without you."

He just kept walking, those big shoulders held even, that preppy hair shining under the fluorescents until he turned the corner.

And then I did what I'd been holding back for what felt like a lifetime.

I ran.

# Chapter | 31

Someone called my name in the parking lot. As I ran across the asphalt, the April chill settling into my lungs, I scanned for the cobalt blue of the Charger. The last thing I could handle, the very last thing, was for Austin to be nice to me. If he somehow forgave me. If he somehow tried to be kind. If he even looked at me with those blue-green eyes, I thought I'd die. Nobody could hurt this much for long without dying.

The clouds were growing thicker overhead, and mist rolled over the high plains, beading the buffalo grass so that each stalk shone with hundreds of translucent jewels when headlights swept across the prairie. My long strides carried me onto the shoulder of the road, where the heavy heads of grass licked my arms and left broad, wet streaks on my jacket. I was exhausted. I was bruised. I was broken. And every stride was shorter than the last because my body needed to shut down. But I kept running.

The roar of the Ducati dragged me out of my fog, and I raised my eyes from the broken asphalt in time to see Emmett skid to a stop on the bike a few yards ahead. He lifted the visor on his helmet and stared at me. The clouds had swallowed the night; the only light was a strip from his headlight shining iridescent waves on the blacktop. Some of that light reflected back and gave a hint of Emmett's features, and of course I would have known that bike anywhere, but I couldn't read his face. Did he know? I wasn't even sure what the question meant; did he know what?

"Planning on running back to town?"

I shrugged.

"And you were going to go back to Sara's house and just hope that guy who can tear down a building didn't show up again. Right?"

"Emmett, will you give me a ride?"

The slight reflex widening of his eyes was the only clue to his surprise, but he only said, "Hop on."

I climbed behind him. I wrapped my arms around his chest. I could still smell our sex on him, and leather now, and the rain.

For one moment, he ran a gloved hand up my arm, gripping at different spots as though testing that I were real. Or solid. Or there.

"It's stupid driving a bike on a night like this," he said, his hand resting on the visor, ready to snap it down. "But Lawayne has the cars lojacked. I'm going to have to go slow, but I'll get you there."

Where, I wanted to ask. But I was too tired. I just rocked into him, and his shoulder cradled my head. My eyes narrowed to slits against the pellets of rain as we slipped into the night.

It seems impossible, but I must have slept. Or maybe my brain just shut down everything but the essentials. The bike hummed between my legs, and the rough warmth of Emmett's leather jacket rustled against my chest, and water ran cold fingers down my cheeks. But I don't remember the drive. Just the end, when the bike coughed and slewed a few inches to the left, and Emmett swore. I jerked awake and saw that he had barely caught us from falling, and now he eased down the kickstand and killed the engine.

He had brought us to a strip of grungy motel rooms bracketed on one end by a flashing red vacancy sign and on the other end by a larger neon display: ROOMS - ROOMS - ROOMS - HOUR - DAY - WEEK.

"Em, I need a ride back to town. I don't have time to stop at a motel that needs a few gallons of gasoline and a match."

"I know, tweaker."

He swung himself off the bike, and I caught his arm. "Please? Please take me back to town."

"What's gotten into you? First you ask me for a ride. Now you say please. It's like you're one of those pod people."

Something broke loose inside me, something the size of a continent. I kept seeing Austin. I kept hearing him. *If you'd listened to the rest of that damn tape.*

Emmett's cool, rain-slick hand pressed against a fevered triangle of my cheek, and I smelled the engine grease on his fingers. "Hey. Hey, tweaker, hey. What is it? What's wrong? Is Sara ok? I figured if you were leaving the hospital, she was ok, but did something happen?"

"Yeah. I mean no. She's fine." In the bloody flutter of the neon lights, the ruined half of Emmett's face seemed more real than the rest of him. I fixed on that part of him, on the looping, twisting symmetry of the mutilated chakras, and it helped. A little.

"You ran into him, didn't you?"

"Who?"

"Who? I'm not stupid, tweaker. I saw him drive up with his dad. I thought you guys were over."

"We are over."

"So what's going on?"

I slid off the bike and took a step toward the road. I didn't know what was going on—not with me, not with Emmett, not with anybody except Austin, who had made it perfectly clear that there was nothing going on, at least, not between the two of us. But I couldn't stand here and talk to Emmett about it.

He hooked a belt loop on my jeans and tugged. I staggered against him, and those lean, muscled arms went around my waist, drawing me closer. The rain had soaked through my coat and sweater, and when he nuzzled into my chest, the sudden bloom of heat followed a trail of gunpowder inside me.

"You're such a fucking mutt."

"What?"

"I swear to God, you're a mutt. And all I can think about is that you need a bath and you need someone to comb your hair, and you need clean clothes, and you need a bed and someone to watch you sleep. It's never that easy, though, is it? Half the time you're trying to bite my hand off. Half the time I'm . . ." He didn't finish, but he didn't need to.

"I'm a mutt?"

"Hush, tweaker."

"I'm a dog?"

"You know what I mean, and I know you know what I mean, so don't pick a fight." He pushed me away and looked up at me. "Are you going to storm off to God knows where if I let go of you?"

"If I stay, am I going to get syphilis just from walking inside that damn place?"

"That's a little more like it. Do you want to bitch some more? Do you want to hit something? Maybe you want to swing your shoulders and stomp around in circles for a while?"

"You're such a fucktoy."

He grinned. "I'm your fucktoy. Come on."

He led me to a room near the vacancy sign, rattled the handle, and called out his name. When the door opened, I blinked. Becca stood inside, and for a moment, all I could think about was Emmett's earlier reference to pod people. She wore a long, transparent plastic poncho, and her peroxide hair was pinned back so that all I really saw was the silver of her eyeshadow and then the glossy translucence of the poncho. It was like something straight out of a bad 50s sci-fi show. She didn't smile or nod or say anything when she saw us; her eyes slid across Emmett's ruined face, and she flinched as though she had forgotten. Then she moved aside, holding the door open, and shut it behind us when we entered.

I stopped just inside the door, and Emmett crashed into my shoulder. It was your standard motel room, two queen beds and some particle board furniture. On the second bed, the one farther from the door, sat Jake. His massive belt buckle was shining almost as brightly as Becca's eyeshadow, but the knife laid out across his knees—a knife as long as my forearm—caught none of the light. His knuckles were white around the hilt. Then they flooded with red. Then white again.

"What's happening?" I said.

Becca nodded at Emmett, and Emmett squeezed my arm to move and stand in front of me. The three of them—Becca and Emmett and Jake—formed a loose triangle. A little, I thought, like the point of a spear driving toward me. I swallowed the urge to repeat my question; better to wait and let them tell me.

"Things have moved beyond a certain point, Vie." Emmett folded his arms. White bandages peeked out of his sleeves, marking the most recent wounds Emmett had suffered for me. The scars on his face, on the wedge of chest that was visible, the scars that covered the rest of his body—those were marks of the same suffering. I felt a dark thrill at that: what he had suffered for me. It turned my stomach. It made me want him even more. "And we've reached a moment," he said, "of making hard decisions."

"We should be finished already," Jake said, his eyes still on the floor, his knuckles blanching and flooding with red in a frantic pulse. "We've wasted too much fucking time already."

"Finished with what?" I said.

"We talked about this," Becca said to Jake. "We agreed that we'd let Vie be part of the decision."

"What decisions? What are you talking about?"

"Ginny is a traitor," Emmett said, spreading his hands, those bandages like signal beacons in the motel room's shaded yellow light. "And she's on the side of an enemy who is vicious. She would have killed you, Vie, and she would have done it without a second thought. Now we have her, and it's time we took advantage of that fact. We need information—"

The knife. The frenzied, cramped whitening of Jake's knuckles. The plastic poncho. The way Becca looked anywhere but at me.

"No. You're—Jesus Christ, Emmett. You want to torture her?"

"I want to get information out of her. She was taken by Urho and the Lady. She knows where they are. She knows their weaknesses. She knows a lot, Vie."

"No."

"And the fact is, we need whatever she knows."

"No."

"You're being stupid!" Emmett's chest rose and fell in the silence that followed his shout. "You're being so fucking thick-headed about this. Listen to me: you don't have a chance. None. If you go up against Urho and the Lady like this, you're going to die. And if that doesn't mean anything to you, then consider the fact that the rest of us will die too. They'll hunt us down. They'll exterminate us."

"No, Emmett. That's the last time I'm going to say it."

"You don't understand, Vie. I—" His whole face curdled, and he tucked his hands under his arms. "I faced one of those things. Your—" His mouth shaped the word *mother*, but he didn't speak it, and he finally said, "You know what I'm talking about. I faced it, and I know. You don't know. You don't have any idea what they're capable of, not really, because she took her time with you. She had to be careful. But the real thing, when she finally lets loose. The power. The hunger—" His chest snapped out like somebody had hooked him and reeled him in hard, and he sucked for air. "Jesus, you don't have any idea—"

"I don't have any idea? I don't? I'm the one that's faced Urho on the other side. He chased Becca and me through a dream, once. Remember that Becca? And he tore open the back of my neck, here, in the physical world. I'm the one that faced the Lady. I'm the one who looked at her with my second sight and saw the real thing: that shriveled abomination hiding inside her body. You haven't seen those things. You haven't faced them. I'm the only one who knows how bad this is, and I'm saying no."

"Fuck you." Emmett looked ready to cry, and the green-white of his pallor made the scars more livid. "You fucking idiot, I'm doing this to help you."

"No, Emmett. You're doing it because you're scared."

If I'd drawn a .45, leveled it at his chest, and squeezed the trigger, it couldn't have been much worse. He didn't take a step back, but he did rock onto his heels, and his mouth drew back into a thin line that tightened all those scars and made his expression savage and horrible. He launched himself at me, and for a moment I thought he was attacking me. Instead, he checked me with his shoulder, knocking me out of his path, and plunged into the drizzle and the gray emptiness of the Wyoming night.

The humid air snaked around my ankles, and I shivered as I shut the door and blocked out Emmett and the rain and the night. When I looked at Becca, she still wouldn't meet my eyes. When I looked at

Jake, his head came up as though on a string and he jabbed the knife in my direction.

"You're wrong."

"Fine."

"He's right. You're a fucking idiot."

"Fine."

"Temple Mae was unconscious for four hours. She's stronger than you, a lot stronger than you, and she almost died fighting that guy."

"I didn't want her—"

"Fuck what you want. I don't care what you say. I'm going to get answers out of that bitch one way or another." He rose off the bed, and for a moment I glimpsed the athlete, the rodeo star, the liquid grace that I had seen—in a less refined way—in Austin. As he surged toward the bathroom though, Becca raised one hand, and Jake flowed to a stop. The huge knife flowed too, as liquid as every muscle in Jake's body, coming up at Becca's body. The tip dimpled the poncho. Where the plastic folded under the point of the knife, light gathered in a starburst. "Get out of my way."

"Let me talk to him."

"I'm getting answers. I'm not going to let anybody hurt Temple Mae."

"Let me talk to him for a few minutes, Jake. Ginny's not going anywhere. Go check on Emmett."

"Fuck him."

"Then go call your dad and see how Sara's doing."

"You're going to let her go. You agree with him, and you're going to let her go."

Becca's eyes were luminous, almost as bright as the plastic poncho puckered around the knife. "I'm telling you we're just going to talk. Ginny's not going anywhere."

For a moment, the knife could have slid into her, parting plastic and flesh, driven by the same muscles that gave Jake his lean, long build. Then Jake swore and stormed toward the door. I angled away from him, and the door clapped shut behind him, and then it was Becca and me.

"He's right," she said with a shuddering breath, one hand hovering above the crease in the plastic where the knife had rested. "It's not going to be hard to talk me out of this." Her eyes came up, meeting mine for the first time. "I didn't like the idea when Emmett came to me about it. I didn't like how eager Jake seemed to be when Emmett called him."

"But you're here. With a poncho."

"I'm here."

From outside the room came low voices—angry voices, Jake's and Emmett's voices—and then a rattling thump that put my heart into panic mode for half a second. Then I recognized the sound: the exterior ice machine churning out new cubes. I caught a mirrored look of fright on Becca's face, and we both smiled.

Her smile faded. "Vie, I don't like this idea. But I don't know what other options we have. Right now, Urho and the Lady hold all the cards. They have Kyle and Leo—both of them a lot more dangerous than any of us, even if Temple Mae weren't out of commission. They have Lawayne and however many guns and guys he can supply. They have—"

"They have Tyler and Hannah. That's the only thing that matters."

"Those are the kids? The ones from the hospital?"

I nodded.

"Why are they so important?"

"They're kids, Becca. They don't deserve to be caught up in this, and Urho and the Lady have already done some horrible shit to them. I shouldn't have to explain this to you, of all people."

"No, I mean, why are the kids so important to Urho and the Lady? They've been kidnapping kids for decades. For centuries, probably. And they've always either killed them or let them go. This time, though, they want the kids. Need the kids. Why?"

I ran through what Emmett and I had unraveled between us: the need for a psychic, a real psychic, who could bring Urho back to this side of reality; Ginny's capture and betrayal; her ability to guide unlocking—or enhancing—the Lady's ability to awaken; and my newfound status of being totally disposable.

"So the kids are psychics?"

I thought back to what I'd seen in the Hunt Public House and shook my head. "Not psychic."

"Then why does she need these kids?"

"I think they might be able to do what she wants anyway. Their abilities, whatever they are, are linked by the fact that they're siblings. Let me show you." I lifted the end of the thin quilt on the bed and pointed to one side. "Tyler is here, on this side. But he's totally here. Not like a normal person. His spirit wasn't even visible on the other side, and that's never happened to me before. He's completely here on this side so he's . . . he's like a nail that's been pounded into this side of reality." I indicated a spot on the other side of the quilt. "Hannah's over here. She's been split out of her body, and her spirit is sitting on this side, completely separated from her body."

"She's nailed to the other side?."

"I don't know, Becca, I'm trying to figure this out too."

"I'm not making fun of you." She frowned, tilting her head. "They're connected. That's what you think? Because they're blood?"

I nodded.

"Why else?"

"What do you mean?"

"Think about it, Vie. Why these kids? She could have picked up a brother-sister pair anywhere. It didn't have to be Tyler and Hannah. Why them?"

"Cribbs was working for Lawayne—"

"That doesn't mean anything. Lawayne probably has siblings in one of those fucking brothels that he could have given her. He definitely could have picked up some stranger's kids. They're using Tyler and Hannah because they know it hurts you. Because they hope it'll make you stupid. They're using them because if you won't leave town, they're going to kill you, and the kids are an easy way for you to mess up."

I blew out a breath.

"So you see, right? Whatever you're planning, they were counting on you coming after Tyler and Hannah. If you wouldn't leave town, they were counting on this."

"Ok, Becca."

She cocked her head at me. "Are you connected to anyone?"

"What?"

"You're a psychic. You said you've gone to the other side. Are you connected to anyone by blood?"

I blinked. "I was."

"River."

Another nod.

"That's why you could sense his ability. That's why you could tell, sometimes, where he'd been, or where he was going."

"Yeah. I kind of assumed . . . I don't know what I assumed."

"Anyone else?"

My heart tumbled against the hollow space in my chest. My mom. My dad. Did I have the same connection to them? If I did, what did it look like? How had it manifested? Or had all the hate and hurt burned away those threads?

"I don't know."

"It might be important."

"I don't know, Becca."

"Ok, ok." She squinted at the places I'd indicated on either side of the quilt. "If what you're saying is right, then Urho coming back to this side is just a matter of time. They've got the kids. Their connection is like some kind of bridge or tunnel that Urho is going to use to cross back to—to where?"

"This side of reality. The real world. The physical world."

"No, to what body? His own? If he died two hundred years ago, that body isn't going to be much use to him." She shook her head. "This is such a weird conversation. Where's he going?"

"He's going—Christ, I don't know. That's the least of our problems. Whoever it is, they're going to have to hurt him bad. In order for a body to be open like that, it's got to have its chakra torn apart. At least, that's how Mr. Big Empty did it."

"Luke."

"That's what I said."

"No, Vie. His name is Luke. That other name, that stupid kiddo name, that's what he wanted people to think of him as. But he was just Luke. Calling him that other name, that's giving him power."

"He's dead, Becca. He's gone."

"You still shouldn't play into his games. No matter what kind of power these people have, they're still people. Dead people. Crazy people. People who have lived a long time. But they're just people." Her mouth twisted. "Do you think he's going to take Tyler's body?"

I envisioned that blank spot on the other side where Tyler should have been. I shook my head. "I don't know. I don't think so. He wasn't . . . he hadn't been hurt in the right ways. But maybe."

"Where, then, Vie? Hannah's? You said her spirit is totally out of her body."

"Maybe."

"We need to do better than a maybe."

"Well, we can't. We don't have enough information."

"That means we're back where we started." Becca shivered, and the poncho crinkled. "We need to do it now, Vie. Before I lose my nerve."

"No."

"Vie, you're condemning two innocent kids to suffer, and you're letting a nightmare come back into the real world. Urho has been terrorizing this part of the world for centuries, and he's been dead. Imagine how bad it's going to be if he's alive. Lawayne, the Biondi—he's going to make them look like bullies on a playground."

"No. That's my final answer."

She shook her head sadly. "You don't get to decide this. I insisted that we at least talk to you about it. I made the others agree to that much. But we're all in danger, Vie, and we all get a vote. And the rest of us have voted yes."

I loomed over Becca, and she shrank back, the poncho creaking and whispering as it crumpled under her, the bed springs squeaking, my shadow slapping like a long dark hand across her face.

"I said no, Becca. We're not doing this. We're better than they are."

"They're torturing children. They're kidnapping and murdering children. Comparing us to them isn't fair."

"They're people. That's what you just said. They're not monsters. They're not soulless goblins created by an entity of pure evil. They're human beings, and yes, they've got powers, and they've used those powers to do horrible things, but they're still people. And we're people too. No, don't interrupt me. I want to finish this, and then you can talk. You know my dad hits me."

Her face turned to chalk. "I didn't—I mean, Vie, if I'd—"

I swallowed. I knew the path I was on. I knew where it led, to that dark sun at the back of my head, to its corona of shadows. I knew what it would do to me. But I had to. I had to walk that path for a moment. I had to tell Becca. So that she would know. So that maybe she would understand.

"It's not an accusation, Becca. I'm just establishing the facts. It's more than that, really. He beats the shit out of me. And my mom, you know about that too, right?"

Becca didn't answer. She was grayish white. She looked like she'd calcified in the last thirty seconds.

"Ok," I said. "My whole life. Or as long as I can remember, anyway. They . . . they could do it, you know? At first I was too little. And then, when I was bigger, something wasn't right." I shook my head. "Something isn't right, still isn't right, inside me, and I couldn't stop them. They always were the ones with power. They were bigger. And they were adults. And they were my parents. They always had the upper hand. And do you know what I did when I started getting control of my abilities? Do you know what I did the next time my dad took a swing at me? Do you know what I did when I was suddenly the one with the power?"

She was shaking her head furiously, drawing one hand under her eyes. "This isn't fair. This isn't—"

"I used them on him. On my dad, I mean. He was coming at me, and I just . . . bam. Right inside his head. And I did every awful thing I could think of. I dragged up all the worst thoughts of his life and set them spinning. And do you know what I did then?

"It's not the same, Vie."

"I left him to drown in those thoughts. I walked away. For all I knew, for all I cared, he was going to drag himself into the next room and slit his wrists or put a gun in his mouth or OD on his stash." For a moment, I was back there in that shitty apartment where the carpet stuck to my feet and the cold frosted the inside of the windows. That was the thing about black holes, I thought. Even black holes that are just at the back of your head. They do funny things to time, and I was back there in the apartment with him, watching him flop like a fish, watching the glassy emptiness of his eyes. "That's what I did."

"He abused you." Her voice was shaking. A delta of silver lines covered her face now. "What he did to you—"

"Was exactly what I did to him. As soon as I was the one with the power, as soon as I was the one who was bigger and stronger, I did it to him."

"You're a kid—"

"I did it to him, Becca. And you know what? Part of me would do it again. Part of me would do it to my mom if I could. Part of me would go after everybody that's hurt me and do it to them. I spent so many years being the one who got hurt. Now I want to be the one who's on top. I want to be the one who does the hurting."

"Stop it." She scrubbed at her cheeks. Her fingers came away radiant with smeared silver. "He was attacking you. You were defending yourself. And now, with Ginny, it's a matter of life or death. It's about—"

"I told myself it was life or death with Krystal. Do you know what I did to her?"

Becca glared at me and looked away.

"I ripped her soul apart. Ripped it to shreds, Becca. And I don't even feel bad about it. I mean, I do. But there's this way it felt good, too. And you know what? I don't know if she would have killed us. Maybe she was just trying to stop us. I really don't know."

"Austin was hurt. He was hurt bad."

"There's always a reason, Becca." I was speaking from somewhere far away now. I had fallen into that dark place at the back of my mind, into the black hole, but my voice came out smooth and steady and gentle. Gentler than that gravitational blackout swallowing me. "I was high. I was drunk. I was mad. I had a bad day at work. I got a speeding ticket. I was scared. I love you, but you made me do it to you." The pressure was worse, like a vise tightening around my head, but it made me feel lighter too. The world tilted, lost some of its color, and my toes were barely touching the ground. I could float away like this. Drift into that darkness and be crushed. "But at the bottom, it comes down to power. What do we do when we're the ones with the power? What are we willing to do to other people? And what aren't we willing to do? The rest of it, those are just excuses. I know,

Becca. I was there that night with my dad. I had every excuse in the world. But I know how I felt, too. And I know it felt good. I was powerful and strong and in control." I was surprised, from where I had fallen into that dark hole, that my arms weren't drifting up, weightless in the sudden vacuum surrounding me, swallowing me. "I won't do that ever again."

She had smeared the silver rivers down her cheeks. The delta was just a muddy silver smudge now. And she wouldn't look at me.

"I'll wait until morning," was all she said. "If we can figure out something else before then—" But she stopped, and her shoulders shook, and she turned away from me.

My feet didn't touch the ground, but it wasn't happiness, it wasn't that kind of lightness. It was that yawning emptiness in my head. It was back again. And I thought about the blades in my backpack. I thought about how easy it would be to shrug out of my clothes, to take a fresh edge and draw it in a clean line down from my nipple, the oblique angle where it would meet the furrow I had dug on the inside of my thigh. Power. Control. This was my power. This was my control. When I had nothing else, I still had this.

I turned and left the room.

Emmett stood in the parking lot, breathing into his hands, huge clouds steaming up in the chill, wet air. Would it snow? In April? It was Wyoming; that was more than a mere possibility. The air tasted like it, that frosty taste on mornings when every guy with a car is scraping his windshield.

With a jerk of his head, Emmett sent Jake back into the motel room. He stood on the asphalt, blowing those frosted breaths into cupped fingers, eyes falling away to nothing.

"I'm supposed to tell Austin," I said, not recognizing my voice.

"Yeah, well, he broke up with your dumb ass. What do you need to tell him?"

I scrubbed at my arms and looked everywhere but those eyes.

"Tweaker? Why do you look more fucked up than usual?"

"I just—I'm supposed to tell him. Before I—" My eyes cut toward him, catching him at the chest, where the rumpled vee of his collar framed the hollow of his throat, half scarified and half smooth and golden.

"So? I'm not your boyfriend. And I'm certainly not Austin. And I already told you I'm not going to try to take that shit away from you."

"Yeah."

"We've got stuff to do. The rest of us are making hard decisions while you're playing Boy Scout. If you want to go cut, go cut."

"Yeah."

His breath blew out in a thin line like moondust or starlight. "For fuck's sake, you're going to fucking drive me crazy. You know that, right? I'm going to be crazier than you."

Grabbing my arm, Emmett marched me toward the strip of motel rooms, but when I tried to slide out of his grip, he just joggled me once and kept going. Instead of returning to the room with Jake and Becca and Ginny, he jammed a key into the next door, forcing open the room and half-throwing me through the open door. It smelled closed-up, musty, and the air still had enough second-hand nicotine to get my head buzzing by the second breath. Emmett slammed the door. Hard. Hard enough that the whole line of motel rooms shook and threatened to fall over like a house of cards. It was just the two of us in the darkness and the old cigarette stink, and then he hit something, and something clattered, and a bright yellow cone made me blink. Then I could see him, and the lamp, and the halo under the light shade ringing his hand.

Wordlessly, he ripped the backpack from my shoulder and emptied it on the bed. Everything came out. Everything. And he knocked aside a half-finished roll of Life Savers—Becca had picked out all the cherry ones—and the ticket stubs from when Austin and I had seen a special screening of *A Christmas Story* at the Wynnham 8, and then the back of his hand flipped over the box and two blades slid out.

He flicked one and sent it spinning toward me over the rust-colored quilt. The other, he snagged between two fingers as he wriggled out of his jacket.

"What are you doing?"

With his head inside his shirt, his voice was muffled. "Don't be stupid, tweaker. Let's just get this over with." Then his shirt came off, and he was bare-chested, his hair flying to the left, the hand without the blade crossing his stomach as though he could keep me, somehow, from seeing him.

"I don't—" I swallowed. "I need to do this. Me. This is my shit, Emmett. You're right about that. It's not your shit. I just—Austin made me promise, and I just need you to know, ok? I don't want you to—I don't want you to do it again."

"Wish in one hand," he shrugged, "and your limp dick in another."

"You made your point, ok? I know this isn't a good thing to do. I get it. But I just need it for a little longer. Until I'm through this."

"Fine. Where are we cutting today?"

"No. Not you. Me. Just me. This is my shit, Emmett."

He rolled those dark eyes, and his laugh was angry and jolting. "The fuck don't you understand about this, tweaker? You're my shit. Get it? Now where are we cutting?"

You're my shit. The words were like antifreeze, sweet and slick and poisonous. I was his shit. And I realized that he was mine. The way he looked. The way his scars only made him better to me. The heat tumbling low in my belly.

"Take off your fucking shirt and let's get this over with." He grabbed my coat and wrestled it off me. Then he wrenched at my sweater until it was on the bed. One hand, his finger pads like ice, pressed on my chest like he was steering me. The other held the blade against the low swell and ripple of his abdomen. "Pick up the fucking blade and let's get this over with, tweaker."

You're my shit.

The black hole at the back of my head, dragging on me, disintegrating me so that I streamed into it like a cloud of particles.

You're my shit. Those dark eyes alive with electricity. My shit.

Nobody can take our shit away from us.

I kissed him.

"You stink." His arm folded, letting me closer, and he wrinkled his nose. "You reek."

I kissed him again, my mouth on his, the rough texture of the scars rocking me like speedbumps.

His arm folded more. The fingers on my chest tensed, flexed, gave way. I hooked one hand in the waistband of his jeans. I twisted, drawing the denim tight, hugging him against me. I could feel how hard he was. I could feel him thrumming like the last note in some enormous bell.

"You haven't been very good," he murmured, his throat bobbing with the effort of controlling his voice. "Maybe I should send you to bed without a treat."

"Who says you get to decide?" I kissed him again. He was rubbing against me now. His other hand, still cramped around the blade, dropped an inch.

For a moment, the dark eyes were flat and deadly serious, and he growled, "Because I get to do whatever I want to you. Whenever I want. And you'll let me, tweaker. Not the other way around."

I nuzzled into his neck. I nipped at his collarbone, on the scarred side of his body, and his back actually snapped tight and he grunted.

That was when I grabbed his hand. I didn't bother trying to get the blade away from him; that would have dragged out the whole thing, and I wanted it over with. I wanted to move on to the next part, to the better part. I just turned his hand, ignoring the flash of pain as

I twisted, and dragged the blade low and horizontal across my belly. Just under my navel. I got the length of my hand before he wrenched away, but I kept twisting, and the blade dropped from his numb fingers.

He stood there, chest heaving, his back still bowing like I'd bitten a nerve, his nipples stiff, his erection visible through the stonewashed denim.

"You stupid fucking cheat."

I crossed the distance. He retreated. I kept moving. He backed into the alcove with the sink and the plastic-wrapped cups and the tiny bar of soap that said French Milled, whatever the hell that meant. I spread my arms and legs, clutching at the alcove's frame, every muscle lean and taut and on display. He could keep moving. He could backpedal into the tiny bathroom with the shower. Or he could try to get past me.

Clarity was coming back to me. A sense of wholeness was coming back to me. Breathing was coming back to me. That hot line under my navel pulled everything together, and I no longer felt like I was dissolving, like parts of me were being siphoned off into nonexistence. I studied him. I really saw him for the first time since coming into the room.

The pulse in his throat. The hollows under his eyes. The way his hands crawled across his chest as though they might successfully cover him if he just moved them constantly.

Blood chilled the top of my jeans. I dropped my arms, rested my thumbs inside the waistband, the wet denim clinging to my fingers. The thin laceration burned against the heels of my hands.

I took a step forward.

"Stop."

I took another step.

He flinched. "Not like this, tweaker. It's one thing if we're—"

"Do you know how perfect you are?"

That brought up Emmett's chin, and gray plastered itself across his face. "Don't do that." His voice was low and serious and full of a kind of wounded dignity.

"I'm serious. Do you have any idea?"

"Don't. Vie, don't. Please. If we're all riled up, if we're just going at it hard, that's fine, but like this, with you—"

I ran one hand down that invisible dividing line at the center of his chest, the scars on one side, the smooth, golden muscle on the other. My index finger brushed a faint, bloody trail.

"You were hot before. You were . . . pretty." My newfound sense of clarity sharpened everything. It was like I'd been sleepwalking inside my pain, and now the world had come back crisper and clearer. The smell of the old tobacco, yes, but the smell of his skin, the metallic tang of my blood, the heat of his body under one finger, the slight hiccup to his breathing that wasn't visible, that could only be felt. "But this. You're incredible. You're perfect."

His head swung down and to the right.

I popped open the top of his jeans, massaged the bulge under the denim until he thrust into my touch, and then I curled my fingers along his jaw, printing bloody ownership all over him, turning him to face me.

"You. You're perfect."

"I'm not good for you." That sensation of falling suspended me again when I met his eyes, and they were surprisingly clear and free from self-pity. "We're not good for each other."

I drew in a deep breath. I smirked, and I felt his breath catch in his throat. Felt it in the tips of my fingers. Felt it in the slight bob of his Adam's apple.

"You said something about how I needed a shower?"

"You smell like a shithouse."

"No wonder all the boys like you." I slid my jeans over my hips and stepped out of them, then past Emmett and into the cramped bathroom. Over my shoulder, I said, "Be sure to grab the soap."

Under the lukewarm spray, Emmett was thorough with the soap. Very thorough.

## Chapter | 32

Afterwards, Emmett went to his bag and took out his kit: the needle and the spoon and the little baggie. Then he disappeared into the bathroom. When he came back, he rolled up everything and hid it away again in his bag.

We lay under the papery quilt, and I ran my thumb over the pinprick on the inside of his arm and smeared a tail of blood to the crease in his elbow. His pupils were hard and constricted, but his voice had turned to cotton candy when he said, "This is my shit, tweaker. Everybody's got their own shit. Just like you do."

I could only nod.

"You're my shit too," he said, his hand trapping mine against his arm, like he was afraid I'd let go.

I nodded again.

Everything still smelled like nicotine, but now it was overlaid by the cheap perfume of the soap and the taste of Emmett in my mouth. His skin warmed when he slid his legs between mine and tucked his head against my arm. He was dozing, or something like it. I drifted; I had reached some kind of state beyond exhaustion, where sleep couldn't claim me.

In that half-waking state, it was surprisingly easy to drift free from my body, and I found myself on the other side. The thick texture of the other side, the warp and weft and vibrancy of color, marked the recent flare of passion inside the room. If another psychic stayed here sometime in the next six months, the emotional echoes would probably act like some kind of empathic Viagra and keep him hard the whole night. Maybe, after this was all over, Emmett and I could come back here. I wouldn't mind tapping into some empathic Viagra myself. I could do to Emmett what I'd done a few nights before: I could flood his mind with desire, open every gate inside him until I could scrape a nail down the center of his chest and watch him come apart just from that, just from that grazing touch. Only I'd ask him first, get his permission, and I'd make him feel things he'd never felt before. Both of us would be hopped up on psychic juice. And then we'd really see what we could do to each other.

That would have to wait, however. I had more pressing things to do. Like find a way to keep Becca and Jake and Emmett from doing something that they'd regret for the rest of their lives.

The most important thing right now was to find Hannah and Tyler. If what I guessed about their abilities was correct—based on what I had seen in the Hunt Public House—they were the key to stopping Urho and the Lady. I had to get them back before they could bring Urho over to this side of reality.

More importantly, if I could find the kids on my own, I might be able to stop Becca and the others from moving forward with their plan. I might even be able to convince Ginny to help me. That felt like a longshot, but it was the only idea I had.

A nudge at the back of my brain reminded me that this wasn't a final solution to my problems with Urho. If Emmett and I were right and the Lady's abilities had improved, she might be able to do this all over again. I might rescue Hannah and Tyler, but what would stop her from catching another pair of siblings—or twins, a part of me distantly recognized that twins would be even better—and repeat the whole performance. I might save Hannah and Tyler, but it would only postpone Urho's return. I would have to face him eventually. Or I would have to run—and if I ran, everybody I loved would have to run too. And I didn't think all of us could run forever.

Drawing in a breath, I focused on the motel room, with its ultra-saturated scarlet that marked the throb of strong emotion. Defeating Urho was a problem for another day. I just needed to find the kids. And I had to find them fast.

I reached out into the darkness around me, beyond the motel, across the high plains with the rangegrass doubling in the wind, the tender stalks of spring growth bending under the same force that sent tumbleweeds rolling and snapped out the dusty silver leaves of sage into streamers. Hannah had contacted me. She had been watching me. She was fixed on the other side, fixed in a way I hadn't ever encountered before. Like a ghost. Urho had managed to silence her—his ability over the other side was incredibly strong—but I wasn't a lightweight either. If I could find her, if I could brush up against her mind even for an instant, I might get a glimpse of where she was. Or the name of a road. Or a landmark. I'd done this before; I'd glimpsed the Widow's Pyre, a rocky outcropping on the Bighorn Range, and it had been enough for Austin to lead me to the cabin where Mr. Big

Empty—Luke, I told myself—where Luke had murdered Samantha Oates. All I needed was a clue. Just one. Just the barest hint of one.

It was like drawing a net through black water. I caught nothing.

I tried again, harder. Around me, the other side faded until I floated in darkness. I tried again, reaching farther. Nothing. A part of me was aware of my body's labored breathing. A part of me was aware of the burn of fatigue as my body tried to fuel the demands of my ability. Again and again my psychic grip trailed through dark waters and caught nothing. I tried again, farther. I tried again, harder. I tried again.

I had never stretched myself this way. Exhaustion bled through the thin barrier between body and soul; I was aware that part of me still lay on the bed, tangled with Emmett, trembling as though I was running the last stretch of an Ironman. But I could also feel . . . something. That image of the net trailing through black water came to me again. Yes. That was close to what it was. I had cast a psychic net over—what? The county? Three counties? My mind felt stretched and raw and burning. Half the state? At the edges of consciousness, where the net was thinnest, the faintest ripples came back to me like minnows slipping between the webbing. I tried again. Harder. Farther.

That burning stretch grew hotter, the feel of friction, of skin on the point of tearing. Those ripples splashed across the surface of my mind: Jim Spencer like a pillar of golden fire, his face bruised and scabbed over as he stared at himself in a dingy mirror, the faintest hint of grunge and porcelain under his fingers. Not his bathroom. It looked like a public restroom. At a convenience mart? A truck stop? A rest area? He looked worse than he had in the hospital. The fire inside him columned in a great whirlwind, and I glimpsed the ancient stainless steel cross-handles droop like hot wax, watched the faucet bend and snake like a falling candle, and then Jim's flicker of surprise, his eyes widening in the reflection, the cinders stirring at the back of his gaze like fireworks, and a single word: *Vie*?

Then he slipped from my net, and my mind continued to grab at the ripples. The next one was a dark place. A few low lights flashed out numbers and charts. A machine beeped. The air smelled like sickness and liniment and a sponge air-drying. *Get out!* It was Temple Mae's voice, furious and raised to a shriek that I'd never heard her use before. *Get out, get out, get out!* And then something hit me with tremendous force, and I caromed out of her mind and into the darkness again.

Another flutter of movement, I seized it, felt the edges of the psychic lacework I had cast out across the night draw tight. I was in another room much like the last one, with the steady drone of a machine, with that identical smell of wet sponge, with cinnamon burning my tongue and Drake pounding away at my inner ear. One hand held a phone, and the screen displayed a series of messages. One-sided messages. Messages sent by the phone in my hand. At the top of the screen was Austin's name, and then a series of blue bubbles: *I'm sorry.* No reply. *I really messed up, Aus. Will you please talk to me?* No reply. *Look, I just need to tell you something in person, ok?* No reply. *Will you just tell me you're ok?* No reply. *I know you're mad. You're totally right to be mad. But will you tell me when we can talk about this?* On and on, those blue bubbles marking Kaden's texts to my ex, his unanswered pleas getting more and more desperate.

That lit a fire inside me. It wasn't some match-and-kindling kiddie stuff. It was bigger and brighter and hotter than that. Like something chemical. Something burning hot enough to make what I'd seen in Jim Spencer's mind, with stainless steel dripping to fall in beads on the cold porcelain, look like the Antarctic.

Then, seeing through Kaden's eyes, I watched a single drop of blood spatter on the phone's screen, and then I heard him thinking, *My head, Jesus Christ, my head, my head, oh Christ—*

And I fled.

What caught me next wasn't a ripple or a tug or a flick of movement at the edge of consciousness. What caught me next was a riptide dragging me across the high plains like I was riding the wind, the buffalo grass rustling under me, the clouds scudding above me, the moon peeping out to cast cold gray radiance across the Bighorns like klieg lights turned up from backstage. And then the darkness dragged me down.

I sat up in a bedroom that wasn't mine, but I recognized it. I'd spent a lot of time there: a room that always had old plates and cups stacked on the dressers, a grease-spotted napkin tenting the remains of a grilled cheese, a trail of socks and underwear and t-shirts meandering to the bed. Where the sheets had fallen back, powerfully muscled legs rode up to the powder blue jock I had given him because it looked like his eyes, their brightest blue when he was happy, and his pale skin glowed almost as bright as the white elastic straps. So sexy.

Austin's breath stuttered in and out, but inside, his mind wasn't afraid.

*Vie? Are you ok? Where are you? I'm sorry, I'm really sorry I didn't just—*

I ripped myself out of his thoughts. Something gave inside me, like a stitch pulling loose, and it hurt. It hurt bad. And I fled, limping, back to my own mind, back to my body, back to the bed and Emmett's legs warm between mine like velvet brushed against the grain.

I was shaking. Sweat stippled my chest, with a ruby glow where the clock radio's light curved along the drops. I wiped my face, and my face was wet; just sweat. I worked the pillow out from under my head and laid it over my face. I held it down tight, breathing the smell of other people's hair and industrial laundering until my hands weren't shaking as bad.

Calm. Austin had been so calm. Why couldn't I ever feel like that? Even with Emmett, it was always fire and ice, always the shuddering draw of the chain pulling me higher and higher until the roller coaster dropped and my head felt like it was coming off. But never calm.

The drugged-out jerk of his voice: *You're my shit.*

And then the clarity in his eyes: *I'm not good for you. We're not good for each other.*

I peeled back the pillow, and I was right. There was no Austin waiting for me. Just the darkness, and the rough ridges of the scars on Emmett's chest as he shifted against me.

At some level, I knew what had happened. I had reached too far. I had tried too hard. I had exerted myself to the point of losing control, and as I had lost control, I had lost focus. Instead of Hannah, I had started picking up the emotional signals I was most attuned to: Jim Spencer, Temple Mae, Kaden, Austin. They were broadcasting at a frequency that I felt day in and day out.

For somebody else, it probably would have been family. You hear stories about it—somebody having a vision when something bad happens to a spouse or a parent or a child, even if they're hundreds of miles away. Or just a gut feeling that something was wrong, and then you learn hours or days or weeks later that there had been a car crash or a fall or an illness.

Not me, though. I didn't have those kinds of family ties. I had my friends. Even Kaden, asshole that he was. I had the people who had fought by me.

I rolled onto my side, away from the scarred ridges of Emmett's torso, needing just a moment of cool linens and space to myself so that I didn't go out of my mind. No matter how bad it had gotten for me, I'd never picked up on even the most remote psychic connection with my dad, much less with my mom—The thought hit me so hard that I had my feet on the floor, the filthy carpet clammy under my soles, before I had fully processed it. I hadn't ever reached out to my mom because she was the one I was trying to get away from.

For me, psychic distress drew me toward the people here, the people in my life, the people I cared about. It was so strong, in fact, that in one case, it had dragged me down like a whirlpool, pulling me straight to Austin.

But I wasn't like most people.

I was so stupid. I wanted to crack a fist against my head. I wanted to shout. But I just sat in the darkness, the bed creaking with every minor shift of my weight, my toes curling in shag carpeting shiny from traffic and bad shampoo jobs. Shay had told me. Shay, Hannah's mom, had told me when she came to ask for my help. She had told me why she was so worried. She had told me why it had to be me instead of the police—the real reason it had to be me, and not the weak excuses she had given her mom.

She had told me that she heard Hannah screaming.

# Chapter | 33

Through the yellowing scrim of the curtain, light from the parking lot gave the motel room a snuffed-out glow. I stared at the window sheers, which looked thirty years old and like they'd spent the entire time absorbing steady blasts of smoke off Pall Malls and Pall Mall Reds and Marlboros—just the Marlboro Blacks—and Pyramids. Those were the brands that populated the images in my head; they were the ones Mom smoked. In the hem of one of the sheers, someone had burned out a series of crescents.

I wasn't really seeing the curtains, and I wasn't really thinking about the nicotine stains or the brands or who might have lain in this bed, sheets kicked down, chain-smoking until the room floated in its own clouds. All of that was happening on the surface of my brain. But deep down, I was trying to remember everything about that night with Shay.

Kneading the quilt, I tried to put the pieces together. She had been waiting for me. She had wanted to talk. I remembered the rain, and the look on Austin's face like he was watching me step into oncoming traffic, and the way her hands had ripped at the gimp that trimmed the upholstery on Sara's chair.

I dropped the quilt, and it fell, scratchy against the backs of my calves. If only I hadn't been so angry. If only I hadn't been angry at Shay for neglecting Tyler and Hannah, if only I hadn't been angry at Austin for interfering, if only I'd listened, really listened, and heard what Shay had been trying to tell me. She had heard Hannah screaming. After the kids had disappeared, when she had assumed they were still with their dad, she had heard Hannah screaming. At the time, I had barely registered the claim. I already knew that Shay suffered from what was, as far as I knew, a unique form of mental distress: something incredibly evil had taken control of her by shattering her chakras and moving into her fractured, broken soul, and then I had killed that creature while it was still inside her head.

The invasion, the battle, the death—they had damaged her brain in a way no psychologist or psychiatrist would be able to remedy.

So I had dismissed her words as either some sort of psychic residue, a kind of echo left by the shrapnel of Luke's mind imploding, or as a fluke. Even after I'd sensed someone watching me, even after I'd found Hannah's spirit in the Hunt Public House, I'd never put two and two together.

And I'd managed to endanger just about everyone I cared about by being such an idiot.

Emmett spooned up close to me, his body a loose question mark on the stained sheets, the stiff ridges of collagen that marked half his body throwing a labyrinth of shadows across the rest of his smooth, golden skin. It was another of those moments where the asshole who normally rode on the surface was buried—or maybe evaporated—and he looked like the boy that I knew was inside: broken, hurting, desperate for love, but also kind and funny and caring. Maybe that was what was so intoxicating about him. Maybe that was why I kept coming back. He just cared so damn much. And it hurt him—that was obvious—it hurt him to care that much. But he kept doing it. And how could I not love someone who put his hand in the fire again and again, not to try to pull me out like Austin, but just to hold on for a minute or an hour or however long I was burning?

I stretched out next to him; springs creaked, and Emmett moved with them. His eyes flicked open, and the asshole was back.

"You weigh like a fucking ton."

"Go back to sleep."

"Are you ok?"

I closed my eyes.

His fingers, callused from the guitar, touched my ear lobe, my jaw, the corner of my eye.

"I'm trying to sleep."

His breath was warm and soft as he exhaled heavily. "Goodnight, tweaker."

"Night."

"If you get up again, remember the bed isn't a trampoline."

"Goodnight."

"You can just lie down. Slowly. Quietly. Softly. You're not trying to bounce to the moon."

"Goodnight, Emmett."

He laughed softly, and those callused pads traced the shape of my mouth, and his breathing softened into sleep.

I stepped out of my body again, but not into the other side. If I had kept my relationship with Tyler and Hannah strong, if I had visited them, spent time with them, involved myself in their lives, I could have found them on my own. The distance between us, though, was too great now. Instead, I stepped into the darkness, the place where I had cast my mind onto black waters. And I cast my mind out again. Exhaustion made the action sloppy, graceless, and I knew I had to hurry before I passed out.

I had been in Shay's mind recently. More than once, in fact. And finding her was easy—not as easy as finding Austin or Emmett or Becca, but easy. I touched her mind, and then I was inside it, and the storm surge of filth rolled up around my ankles—all the oil and tar that marked the remainder of Luke's mind and power. It wasn't the crashing storm that I had encountered the last time, but there was a definite chop to the water, a harsh, pounding force that I visualized as waves on an eroding cliffside.

The next part wasn't something I had done before, not exactly, but I had an idea. For me, triggering emotional responses in people was like a call-and-response, a sympathetic mirroring in which I found the emotion in myself first, and then their mind responded with memories and passions. What I needed to find in myself was love.

That wasn't hard. Here, in this dark place, without feeling like I was center stage, I didn't have any trouble admitting it. I loved Austin. I loved Emmett. I wasn't going to grab a mic and sing my heart out for either of them, but I loved them both. And since I didn't have kids and I didn't have any really good memories of my parents—throwing stones on Lake Thunderbird flickered at the back of my head—that kind of love was as close as I was going to get.

Austin came first to mind. He came quickest. And he came with that sharp, jabbing pain under my ribs that made it hard to breathe. He came in a gliding carousel of images: afternoon picnics as he ran his fingers through my hair, the sun hot on my back; the sticky possessiveness of his arms when we slept together, his sweat pasting him against me; the way he held a gun when he thought I was in danger; that kiss, our first one, in the hospital. It made me angry that he came to mind first. It made me angry that he still sprang forward like that, like he hadn't wanted me the fuck out of his life. Like I was supposed to pretend he hadn't been willing to cut things off when I made one simple mistake. I visualized him in the parking lot, *We're done. You and I are done.* And then I visualized the set of his shoulders as he walked away from me in Western Bighorn Hospital, after throwing those words in my face—*if you'd listened to the rest of that damn tape*—and then I focused on Emmett.

With Emmett, it was even harder. I tried to focus on the day he'd pulled me from the river, but then I was caught up in memories of his house, of the feel of his mouth against me as I wore his too-small clothes, of the chain reaction of explosions his touch set off inside me, and then the way he had told me that we could fuck around but we couldn't date. I tried to think about when he had learned I loved him, and the thought intruded of him running out into the snow, barefoot, so freaked out that he couldn't be in the same room with me. I tried to think about him cutting himself, how he had wanted to show me how much it hurt other people to see me hurt myself, and another memory wormed through my mind, his words from just a few hours before: *We're not good for each other.*

Around me, in the black well of Shay's mind, the filthy storm surge waters rocked and slapped and spat. No image of Tyler or Hannah. No answering echo of love.

What did that mean? Was I broken? Fuck, that was a dumb question; of course I was. But was Shay broken too? Would this not work?

Or maybe—

I was miles past exhausted. I could feel my hold slipping, my power waning, my spirit ready to snap back into my body like a rubber band stretched too far. I just wanted to rest. It felt like it had been years since I'd been able to rest, since I'd been able to sleep without dreams and nightmares and psychic invaders. But it hadn't been years. It had been—two days? Three? How long since I'd last crawled into bed at Sara's house, knowing that she was downstairs, knowing—even though she'd never said a word, never even talked a circle around it—that she'd do anything to keep me safe, and that knowledge had been warmer than any quilt or down comforter, it had been stabilizing, it had been—

The storm inside Shay's mind parted. It was like the sun coming out in the eye of a hurricane, and her memories reeled by in short, vivid images: Shay rocking Tyler, a lullaby building in her throat, one that she remembered from childhood although the words had gone; Shay catching Tyler as he toppled off a stool in the bathroom, the electric surge of fear still cascading down her nervous system, and then the honeyed wave of relief that he was ok, that her universe hadn't ended, the sense of relief so strong it was completely disproportionate to the danger, and the realization that her immoderate reaction, her unmeasured, excessive relief, was like a physical manifestation of love. Then she was holding another baby, and this time Tyler sat on the hospital's window bench, scribbling in a coloring book, and the words *it's a girl, it's a girl* ran like ticker tape through Shay's mind, and sometimes the words were fuzzy and pink and the size of parade balloons, and sometimes they were cramped black warnings, and then—

I seized on that memory of Hannah, and I felt the vibrating line of connection, and I followed it. It was like riding a lightning bolt. It sizzled with energy, beyond my own abilities, beyond Urho's, beyond anything I could imagine. This was elemental. Yet it felt ephemeral too—out of Shay's control, and certainly out of mine. So raw and blisteringly powerful, it threatened to buck me out into the blackness of the universe. But I held on. This was my chance. My one chance at finding Hannah and Tyler, and even though I was exhausted, even though I wanted to slide away from this emotional current and drift into unconsciousness, I held on. They were kids. They were just kids. And they didn't deserve any of this, and so I held on for them. For another heartbeat. And another. And then again, into a place where heartbeats didn't matter.

And then I was there. It was the inside of a cabin, although that wasn't really the right word. It was too spacious, too expensively decorated, too modern to be called a cabin. In those ways, it reminded me of Emmett's house, but I knew this wasn't the same place. It had cedar-log siding, chandeliers made out of antlers, and a ceiling that rose to a steep peak. On all sides, the windows looked out onto snow-capped mountains and valleys, where the spring melt funneled into streams. In the distance, starlight spangled a high-altitude lake, making it seem like a mirror of poured silver.

I recognized this place; I had met River here in my dreams. That time, I had seen it from the outside, standing knee deep in the frigid lake. But that didn't tell me where it was located. I knew they were hiding in the mountains, but the Bighorn range ran hundreds of miles north to south. They could be tucked into a valley I'd never find, one that wasn't marked on any map, and I'd never be able to rescue Hannah and Tyler.

I spun, taking in the large open rooms, and then I froze. Through a squared-off archway, I saw a bulky leather sofa—and lying on the sofa, Hannah's pale, still body. Here, on the other side, I didn't have to walk or creep. I just thought, and I found myself next to her, kneeling, my fingers ghosting through her cheek when I tried to touch her. This was her body, her physical body. So where was her spirit?

On the far side of the room, Tyler sat like a statue. It was the only way to describe it, like seeing him in the Hunt Public House all over again, only worse: the lack of life, vitality, and essence. He registered on this side of reality the same way the sofas did, or the mantel above the fireplace, as if he had no spirit on the other side. Real candles spattered the floor with wax like bird shit. How long had they used this as a secret retreat? How long had they had this hideout, this backup in case anything went wrong at Belshazzar's Feast? Decades, I guessed.

And Tyler still hadn't moved. A yellowing bruise showed along his jawline, but otherwise he looked fine. He wasn't fine, of course; whatever the Lady had done to him, smashing open his chakra like the lock on a tween's diary, had broken him. It had left him fixed on one side of reality. Had it taken his mind? Had it taken his soul? I didn't even really know what a soul was, but studying Tyler, with his dead gaze and the dull, leaden cast to his face, I made a guess. A soul was what made you more than a piece of furniture, and Tyler's soul had been taken from him.

His head snapped up. The movement was predatory, terrifying; the way a fox might scent a chicken. And then something grabbed me, closing around me like a fist, a tremendous pressure that dragged me toward the straw-haired boy. His eyes were fixed past me, but that force still tugged me forward, and no matter how I twisted, I couldn't rip myself free.

"Hannah." I tried digging in my heels. I tried visualizing myself somewhere else—anywhere else. It didn't work. I skidded another foot toward Tyler. The metachromatic weave of the other side skewed sharply, stretching toward Tyler like threads being stressed in loose weaving. "Hannah!"

Hannah's image strobed in-out-in-out near the fireplace like a guttering candle. She was trying to talk to me. She was trying to shout to me. Urho, I realized. Urho was keeping her from talking to me.

I struggled against Tyler, but he was strong. So much stronger than I was. Stronger, I guessed, even than Urho—because Tyler would have to be stronger, he would have to be strong enough to rip Urho across planes of existence. I wasn't going to win a fight with Tyler. His soul was gone or locked away, and whatever part of him I might have been able to reason with, whatever fragment of him I might have been able to use my power on, had been snipped out as clearly as if someone had gotten busy with pinking shears. I couldn't win against that kind of power; he had been built this way, stronger than any psychic because he only had to do one thing and he had to do it well. I'd never be able to beat him.

But I might be able to beat Urho. Just for a second. And a second, I hoped, would be long enough.

I reached out, feeling for Urho, and there he was: deadly, silent, an invisible smoke suffocating the room. I pressed against him. My heels skidded another inch as Tyler pulled, dragging me toward himself. I didn't know what would happen when he got me, but I didn't think I wanted to know. The boy I had fed cold chicken strips, the boy I had covered with a thin blanket while he slept on the couch, that boy wasn't here anymore. There was just this thing that the Lady had made, and if this thing got me, I thought it would rip me into pieces.

Hannah appeared, fractionally longer this time, and she opened her mouth, calling something to me. Then she vanished, and Urho's presence slammed between us. I wrestled with him. I was exhausted; I was injured; I was still new to all of this psychic stuff. Urho was ancient, and he was powerful, and he knew exactly what he was doing. I could feel his shape begin to coalesce, still invisible, and I remembered the dreams, all those dreams going back to when I had first encountered Urho: nothing more than an impression of wild, gnashing teeth that had torn the back of my neck, the dreams when he chased me through trackless woods. That same ferocious hunger was here, now, taking form as Urho concentrated and manifested.

Another tug from Tyler sent me stumbling, and I barely caught myself. His little face was set in a horrible grimace: his lips peeled back to bare baby teeth with the front teeth missing. Milk teeth. That was one way of calling them. An old way. It just popped into my head, milk teeth. Seeing those teeth meant for an adorable, gap-toothed grin, instead framed by that hateful face with peeled-back lips, was terrible in its dissonance. I set myself against the force of his tugging and turned my attention back to Urho.

My eyes flicked up, hoping to see Hannah, but to my surprise the Lady stood in the doorway. I hadn't seen her like this, with my second sight, since that day at Belshazzar's Feast when she had locked me in the basement. I had stared at her then, looked on her with my second sight, and I had seen something that carried me to the cliffs of madness.

Her physical form was nothing to be frightened of: she was prim, old-fashioned, her narrow face and her mountain of pinned hair like something out of a Victorian sketchbook. She even wore clothes to match—a long, full skirt and a frilly blouse. Only her eyes gave her away, eyes that glowed like brick dust. Or like the orange of a plastic pumpkin at Halloween.

Outside, she looked old-fashioned and dowdy and severe. Inside, though, was the nightmare. Inside her was a shriveled thing, a naked, desiccated abomination, as though someone had unwrapped a mummy that had lain under sand and hot desert winds for centuries. It huddled inside her physical body, withered and shrunken, the blackened nipples on its sagging breasts falling over curled knees. It hissed at me, and its eyes flashed the same Halloween orange, and I knew I was seeing the real Babria, Lady Buckhardt, the one who had lived all those centuries.

She was hungry. The thought hit me like a sledgehammer, and it raised a question that flickered in my mind like a coin spinning on its edge, there and gone and there again.

But I didn't have time for questions. I had to do this now.

Urho manifested beside her, a distortion in the air that was most visible at the edges, like light warped through glass. He might have been a hound, but he was the size of a goddamn pony, and I could feel the roil of heat and hate and madness.

Now, I told myself. Now. While he was distracted. While all his focus was on manifesting so that he could rip me to shreds himself.

I threw the last of my strength at the smokescreen Urho had raised, and it wavered and blew apart. Then Hannah was there, staring at me, her mouth open as though I'd caught her in mid-scream.

Tyler grunted, a little boy grunt, and my feet flew out from under me. I felt myself hauled through the air, dragged toward him.

"Tyler, no," Hannah screamed, and I felt her push—a push as strong as Tyler's pull, a push that hit me at an angle. She wasn't trying to play tug of war with Tyler; she just punted me as hard as she could, and I felt myself shear through the line of force Tyler was exerting, and then I was tumbling into darkness as the other side dissolved around me.

I had one last glimpse of Hannah tiny and frightened and alone before night swept the other side out of my vision: her little face fixed with resolve, her little mouth working, and the noise coming to me like the worst cell call in the history of the world.

One word. And so much static I wasn't sure what I was hearing.

Chapee.

And then darkness caught up the last granules of the other side, and I was back in that wild spread of forest, my feet pounding the packed earth as I ran. The beast wasn't there, not yet, but he was coming. So I ran. Then the dream dissolved, and the last thing I heard was hot breath at my heels, and then everything was gone, and I slept.

# Chapter | 34

Birds woke me. I was snug in bed at home, in my attic room in Sara's house, and the birds were singing. Every inch of me ached, so I stayed where I was, my eyes closed, and listened. Birds. That was good. The storm had moved on, finally. No snow. And the birds were coming back. Maybe it really was spring—in Wyoming, even in April, it was hard to tell.

If it had only been the birds, I might have gone back to sleep. But the birds didn't sound particularly happy. It wasn't singing, I realized. Not really. More like squawking. I shifted under the covers, and my body howled at me. It was worse than any post-workout I could ever remember. And the sheets felt rough. Itchy. And my head was pounding. And the inside of my mouth was shit. And—

And bacon.

My eyelids wanted to stick together, and it took some real determination to get them open, but there was bacon on the line. Even with my head pounding, even with those damn birds squawking like a fox was wringing their necks, even with my whole body, head to toe, feeling like somebody had played me like a xylophone, there was bacon. Sara cooked the best damn bacon in the world. So I got my eyes open. I would have cut off my lids if I had to.

No attic ceiling. No Sara.

Emmett sat cross-legged, facing me, and his dark eyes met mine. Then, very deliberately, he tapped his phone. It let off the loudest squawking bird noise I'd ever heard.

"I thought you'd like a soothing wake-up."

"What is wrong with you?"

He jabbed at his phone again. This time, it sounded like a chicken being murdered. "Nothing like the sounds of nature to ease that transition back to wakefulness."

"Back to wakefulness? You sound like a bad infomercial." I rolled onto my back and rubbed at my eyes. Everything hurt. My fingertips hurt. I groaned.

A bird being savagely ripped to pieces shrieked at me.

"Stop it, or you lose the phone."

The next one was a hawk. Some kind of hawk. Some kind of hawk ready to swoop down and catch up a mouse or a vole or a rabbit.

"Fine." I was up, on my knees, before he could do more than squirm a few inches on his ass, and I grabbed his wrist and, pop, the phone fell into my other hand. "And if you've got one of those motherfucking bird call whistles or if you know how to gobble like a turkey or you think it'd be cute to try to imitate a sparrow, give it one shot, one, and I'll hit you in the throat so hard you'll be on a trach for the next year."

Tucking the phone under my arm, I flopped back onto the bed.

But that bacon.

I crossed an arm over my stomach. I could feel it—the traitorous little shit—getting ready to make some noise. I hadn't eaten in days. Had I?

The bed rocked as Emmett got off it, and then, from the other side of the room, waxed paper crinkled. The bacon smell was suddenly about ten times stronger.

I crossed my other arm over my stomach. Don't do it. Don't fucking do it. Because you'll just be giving him what he wants.

"Vie?" More crinkling. And then, the bastard talked through a mouthful of—what? Biscuits and gravy? A bacon-egg-and-cheese sandwich? "Thought you might be hungry."

"I'm trying to sleep." But really, I was squeezing my stomach so hard that I felt my ribcage ratchet up a few inches. As usual, Emmett was being annoying. He'd been annoying about the bird calls. He'd been annoying about waking me up. He'd been annoying about how much I slept. And I was not—I absolutely was not—going to give him the satisfaction of—

More crinkling. Another loud, wet bite. A moan. The little fuck was probably patting his stomach.

My own stomach gurgled.

I lay perfectly still.

Emmett swallowed. It was an intentionally, annoying, assholeishly loud swallow that they probably heard in the Middle East. Then, his words clear of food, "I heard that."

I sat up and pitched the phone at his head.

Laughing, he caught it and resumed his seat on the dresser. Next to him were two sandwiches still in their yellow paper. He tapped one meaningfully. And then he gestured to a brown sack.

"I mean, only if you're—"

"Quit being such an asshat," I grumbled. I felt like I teleported across the room—all those aches and pains vanished as I scrambled to the dresser—and when I peeled back the paper, I saw a burger. A big, fat, quadruple-stacker burger. With bacon.

Emmett was grinning, and it went through his dark eyes like lightning.

"A burger?" I tore off a mouthful and, through my chewing, said, "They didn't have any breakfast food?"

He nodded at the paper sack again. "They did. At six o'clock. And they still did at ten-thirty. But they stop serving breakfast at eleven, so I had to get burgers at two. And at five."

"Five?"

He tilted his phone at me, and the clock flashed across the face: 5:27. So I'd slept—what? Sixteen hours? And he'd gone to pick up food for me four times. Would Austin have gone four times? Or would he have gone once and then just waited for me to wake up, which was the sane and rational decision? I chewed faster and shoved that question out of my head. What did it matter what Austin did—or what he would have done?

My arm was elbow-deep in the paper bag before I realized Emmett was laughing.

"They're cold."

I fumbled around. "Not all of them."

"You already ate two burgers."

"I need to keep up my strength."

"Two big burgers."

"You didn't get any fries?"

"Actually, I did."

"Where are they?"

He cuffed me lightly on the side of the head.

"Ouch. Thank you. For all of this. But where are the fries?"

"You're like a garbage disposal, you know that?"

"Uh huh. Yeah. Sure. Fries?"

"I gave them to everybody else. Along with another sack of hamburgers. And the apple pies."

"Apple pies?"

He laughed again, cuffed me again—so light it was really more of a caress, and I'd never realized how bright his eyes could be when they were so dark. And the scars—he'd probably never believe me, probably never understand it himself, but they made him perfect. They gave this balance to how unbearably pretty he was. They were the dark to all the light. Then I thought of the Lady, and her eyes like brick dust, and I wiped the back of my mouth because the hamburger grease tasted rancid now.

"Hungry," I said.

He laughed again. His fingers kept finding my hair and running away like they'd been burned, and a part of me wanted to ask why, after we'd fucked—we'd fucked really, really well—now he was acting like it was a first date. But my mind snapped to those burnt-orange eyes. And the hunger.

"No," I said, wiping my mouth again. "She's hungry."

He nodded slowly. "You dreamed about them?"

"I found them."

"Where?"

"Some place called Chapee. I don't know; something like that. I heard the word. I'm not sure how it's spelled."

Emmett was already on his phone, tapping out a text, nodding and only half-listening to me.

"She's hungry, Em."

"Yeah, I got you the burgers."

I ripped off another chunk of quadruple-patty and grabbed Emmett's arm, shook him. "Em, I'm talking about the Lady. That's part of what's driving her. That's part of what this is about. I've seen her, the real her, and she's starving. She's withering away. No matter how much she eats, she gets older and thinner and shrunken. That's part of this. That's a big part of this."

He jerked free and rubbed his arm. "What are you talking about? Hungry? She's shriveled? She's two hundred years old. No wonder she's shriveled."

"That's my point. That." I grabbed his arm again, and when he tried to twist free, I tightened my grip. "My mom."

"I told you about that already, and it fucked you up. I don't want to go through it again. And I don't want you yanking on my arm like you want to rip it off."

Crumbling the waxed paper into a ball, I popped it back onto the table, and the paper bag rustled as I dug around inside it. With my other hand, though, I gave Emmett another shake. "My mom. She's like a hundred years old. Maybe older."

"She looks pretty good for a hundred." But his eyes didn't match the snark in his words; his eyes had darkened to that fallaway black that left me without any sense of up or down.

"Somehow, they're staying alive. My mom. The Lady. The ones who can awaken other people's abilities. Maybe that's part of their power. Or maybe it's something they figured out—something to do with the chakras, something they're just taking advantage of. But it's not perfect. It's not . . ." I groped for the right word.

"It's not free," Emmett said in a low voice.

"Yeah. Fucking yeah. It's not free. The dust feast. That's what Luke called all this—all this awakening shit. They're eating us. That's how they're staying alive. They're eating parts of us when they awaken us. That's why some of the kids don't come back, Em. That's why some of them just disappear. Maybe she does it on purpose. Maybe she gets carried away. But she eats them."

His eyes dark and distant, Emmett pried my fingers from his arm and massaged the white-and-purple prints I had left. *How bad do you want to know?* The words my mom had spoken, the only answer she had given when he asked why she did what she did, froze the air in the room. "Vie, this is pretty fucked up, and we don't have any real proof—"

"I know. I know that's what's happening."

"—and it doesn't change anything, does it? So she's hungry. So she's a vicious fucking cunt, pardon my language, in a way we hadn't realized before. But it doesn't change anything. We still have to deal with her."

But it did. I wasn't sure why, but it did change something. It mattered. And I knew I couldn't force it; I just had to wait and let the pieces fall into place.

And then I heard the rest of what he'd said. *We still have to deal with her*. We. We have to deal with her.

We.

Then I saw the Ducati's key on the table.

"Fuck." I dropped another ball of wax paper and massaged my temples.

"Your head?" His fingers found my neck, worked deep into the tissue. "I'm surprised it's not your gut after you plowed through four thousand calories."

"Jesus, it's really hurting. Could you—could you run down the motel office? See if they have some aspirin or something?"

His fingers worked a moment longer. His voice, when he spoke, was all sawdust and smoke and uneven edges. "I like this. I like that you trust me enough to tell me when you're hurting. I like that you trust me enough to ask for help."

That put a hot speck of guilt in my belly, but I forced a smile and squeezed his wrist.

"Stay put," he said, shrugging on the leather jacket. "Actually, lie down with a cold cloth on your head, and I'll be right back."

I smiled. I tried to look like I had a migraine cracking open the inside of my head. And as soon as the door shut behind him, I snatched the key and counted to twenty. I didn't even have to get away with the deception; I didn't care if Emmett saw me running away on his bike. All I cared about was that he was far enough off that I could get away before he could stop me. I counted another twenty. I yanked open the door.

And I froze. Face to face with Emmett, who leaned in the doorway, arms across his chest, shaking his head.

"Very disappointing, tweaker."

"Get out of my way."

"You could have asked."

"Get out of my way. Now."

"I would have said no, but you could have asked."

"I'm not playing with you, Emmett. I'm leaving, right now. Alone."

"Tweaker." He shook his head again, and then he stretched, filling the doorway, his arms braced on the jambs. "You still don't get it. You don't call the shots. You never did."

"Get out of my way, right fucking now, before I—"

"I'm going to do two things that will really, really piss you off, tweaker." A wry smile pulled at his mouth. "Actually, I've already done one of them. The other one is going to have to wait until after this is all taken care of. The sooner you accept that I get to do whatever I want, and you're always going to let me, the happier you're going to be. Understand?"

"Emmett—"

"Understand, tweaker?" The smile was bigger now. The scarred half of his mouth trembled with suppressed amusement.

"What did you do?"

He jerked a thumb over his shoulder, at the parking lot. "I used my natural powers of charisma."

"For fuck's sake."

"There's this book. *How to Make Friends and Influence People*. You should read it sometime. There's something about saying thank you—"

"What did you do, Em?"

"Keys."

I slapped them against his chest.

With an exaggerated wince, Emmett pocketed the keys, and then he tilted his head toward the room where Becca and Jake had watched over Ginny for the night. "Come on, tweaker."

When I stepped out into the parking lot, I knew. Jake's truck was still there. But so was Austin's Charger. And so was the Impala—Jim's Impala. And Sharrika Meehan's Bug. And a boxy silver Lexus crossover that I recognized as belonging to Kaden's mom. And Temple Mae's beat-up Chevy.

They were here. They were all here. I thought about running because how could I face them, how could I face the people who had given up so much for me when I'd brought them nothing but trouble? But I didn't run. I couldn't run; I didn't have a car or a bike or anything but my own two feet. And my mouth pulled into a dry, aching smirk because Emmett wouldn't let me run even if I tried to get away on foot. I'd run smack into one of those invisible barriers.

The little motel room was hot with the damp, unpleasant warmth of too many bodies, but the crisp April air that swept in behind me smelled like snow and cut the worst of the temperature. They sat in a shitty attempt at a circle: Becca to my left, her face scrubbed free of the silver eyeshadow and lip gloss she normally wore, looking older—not old, but mature, like a woman instead of a girl, and so, so beautiful; then Kaden, hangdog, giving me a look like all he wanted was to make up and be best buddies again; then Jake, his flannel rumpled from a bad night's sleep, his fingertips white where he gripped the dinner plate belt buckle at his waist, his eyes not meeting mine; then Temple Mae, who looked at me and only at me, and her eyes were both marked with starburst hemorrhages, and I'd never seen a girl who looked readier to kill; then Jim in a blue button-down and khakis, his hair like autumn, his smile and his eyes frank and warm; and then Sharrika who glanced at me twice before her eyes darted away, and her hands tugged at the Star Trek t-shirt she wore, smoothing it over her hips; and behind me, Emmett, who shut the door with a click, and then it really was too hot, his fingertips tenting between my shoulder blades, not even pushing, just a silent signal until I stepped forward.

And Austin. Austin was on my right. And he had dark circles under his eyes, and his preppy hair was mussed, and while he hadn't lost any muscle, his face looked thin, his jawline so sharp it cut the air. The friction burn on his neck looked worse today, and I could tell he wasn't eating. He wasn't sleeping. Again. He wasn't sleeping again because of me. Because of what I'd drawn him into.

"Hi," he whispered in that raspy voice.

I couldn't even say it, but my lips moved, and a little smile quirked on his face. Or maybe he was about to cry. I couldn't tell. Fuck me if I could tell anything anymore.

*I'm going to do two things that will really, really piss you off.* Those were Emmett's words. But he was wrong. I wasn't pissed off. I'd seen a documentary in history class. Something about the space race or the Cold War or Christ, maybe it had been about Ron Howard. I had no idea what it had been about. But right then, with all those faces turned toward me, I remembered that Apollo 13 had needed to reach a speed of seven miles per second to break free of Earth's gravity. And I thought about how gravity was all about things pulling on each other. I thought about how my heart could never fly fast enough to break free of this.

"I was doing some more thinking," Emmett said, his voice brushing up the hairs on the back of my neck, and he was speaking to me, just to me, even though I'm sure everyone else heard him. "About this ability of yours." And his mouth was close behind me now; his breath hot on my neck, cold on my ears, tickling sensitive skin. "About you, and about all those times it seemed like your ability was strongest, clearest, closest to you." And then his words really were a whisper, so quiet they really were just for me. "About the lake. About the first time I felt you touch me, really touch me."

Then he squeezed between Becca and me, and his eyes swept around the circle, and on everyone's face there was something I thought I should have recognized. It was brightest in Emmett's, in Becca's, in Austin's—and, surprisingly, in Jake's and Jim's. It was a glitter in Temple Mae's furious eyes. It was a gleam like light off an old shoe in Sharrika's expression. It was even there in Kaden's face.

"Please don't do this," I said. My eyes stung, but I didn't dare move, didn't dare bring my shoulder up so I could scrub my face into my shirt, didn't dare blink because it was happening, this was happening, and it was maybe the one thing in the world I couldn't bear. "Please."

I thought I saw pity in Emmett's eyes. But then they were that pitch black again, swallowing me up, leaving me without sense of flying or falling, and he said, "Your ability is strongest when you feel loved. When you're connected to people you love. And people who love you."

The tears were running freely down my face now. I jerked as though someone had driven a pin into me, like some voodoo doll was being stabbed out in the universe, but no one had touched me. Becca was crying too, pressing her fingers under her eyes, her shoulders shaking.

"That's why we're here, Vie." Emmett looked at all of them again. "We love you."

I jerked again, so hard this time I almost tumbled over. It was like a sword going up at an angle, shearing through my gut, slicing off the bottoms of my lungs. I wanted to say please. I wanted to say no. But gravity—gravity speared me in place.

Austin's hand slid into mine. His touch was dry, calluses ridging his palms and fingers, and tentative, like he'd been taming horses his whole life and knew I was ready to spook. "You can't go up against Urho alone. We're going with you."

I shook my head.

"Crack open that thick head, tweaker." The back of Emmett's hand brushed mine. "We're all here. We all care about you. Tap into all that emotion. For once in your life, you don't have to do it alone."

"You don't know what you're talking about. You don't have any idea what you're talking about, and you don't know how dangerous this is, you don't know—"

He bent, and I smelled the leather jacket and the soap from our shower the night before, and his next words tickled my ear. "I remember what happened at the lake. Just try."

And then he took my hand, and he took Becca's hand in the other, and Becca took Kaden's and Kaden took Jake's and Jake took Temple Mae's, and on down the line until Sharrika's dark fingers curled around Austin's, and Austin squeezed my hand once, his blue-green eyes swimming up at me. He raised an eyebrow, and his lips contracted as though he might say something, and then he didn't. His face relaxed. His hand squeezed mine once more. And it was that look I'd come to dread, that expression of absolute trust in me. And didn't he know how fucking stupid that was by now?

But no matter how much I wanted to deny it, that expression worked on me. It was genuine; that was the problem. Whatever else had happened, however badly I'd screwed up everything with Austin, he still trusted me. No. That was skirting the truth. He still loved me. It was blue-white in those ocean eyes, like a blowtorch burning underwater, so hot that water couldn't put it out. How was I supposed to walk away from that? Gravity. So much goddamn gravity.

I could feel what Emmett was describing: a braided cord of power running through the circle—no beginning, no end, because they loved me, but I also loved them. Austin, like a bell struck at dawn. Emmett, like booze on a bad night. Becca and Jim and Jake and Temple Mae. Even Sharrika, who had watched me with calm eyes in the shadows of Emmett's house. Even Kaden, who had tried to steal my boyfriend, but who had gone into the house of death with me and lived. It thrummed—a bit like a live wire, yes, but more like the tingle of excitement that ran down my chest when Emmett touched me, and like the latent heat in my skin when I lay under the sun, picnicking with Austin; it was more than that, too. That corded power wasn't one thing. It was a hundred things, some of them I'd never be able to name. And it was so much more than what I deserved.

On the threshold of opening myself to that surge of energy, I thought about gravity one last time. The way things pulled on each other. The way it kept me in orbit. Trapped me. Held me down. It was now that I had to decide. Not about Emmett. Not even about Austin and the coals, still burning, of what I felt for him. I had to decide right now if I would accept this. If I would let their love be a part of me instead of just being a weight dragging me down. Even if I didn't deserve it.

It was something I saw on Austin's face when I glanced at him. He wasn't looking at me. He was looking past me, at Emmett, and maybe it was because we were touching, and maybe it was because it had always been so easy for me to slip into Austin's thoughts, and maybe it was just because my brain was running on the same tracks, but I knew what he was thinking. I knew in a way that had very little to do with being psychic and a hell of a lot to do with still being in love, no matter how much I wanted not to be. He was looking at Emmett, and he was seeing the day-old clothes, he was seeing the glow in Emmett's scarred and ruined face, he was seeing the bandages on the inside of Emmett's arm and the way Emmett's hand curled possessively around mine, and even if Austin didn't know a hundred percent, even if he didn't know the facts and the dates and times and the places, he knew enough. I watched the realization gut him and lay him open. I watched his face grow transparent with pain, and under the pain, fear and self-doubt and worry.

Maybe it's all of us, I thought in a flash. Maybe we all believe, deep down, that we don't deserve love. Or—maybe not all of us, maybe not some lucky assholes—but most of us. Maybe most of us are just as uncertain, just as frightened, just as desperately hoping that we're worth loving and that the person we love loves us back. Maybe only a fortunate few of us ever believe we deserve the love that comes our way.

And even if I didn't deserve that love, I wanted it. I wanted it like sunlight and oxygen and blood pumping in my veins. Austin's eyes flicked to mine. I could dive into them over and over again. You can't stop being in love, I thought with a shock like a heart attack. You can't stop no matter how bad it hurts sometimes.

I opened up and let the twining current rush into me.

It was power like I'd never dreamed of. I was in their minds, and I was in my body, and I was on the other side all at the same time. Their thoughts were a river rushing past me. Their heartbeats pulsed behind my eyes. Their worries, their fears, their aches. Sharrika Meehan's sore tooth. The slow heat of Jim's attraction to me like a rug burn—and the way his eyes jinked up and left when I glanced at him was confirmation. And Emmett, something that Emmett was struggling to hide from me, like a rug pulled over a trap door and if I wanted, if I even considered it, I could rip back the rug and see what he was hiding.

All their secrets laid bare, all their dirtiest deeds, all their shame, all their hope, all their desires.

Last year, when I had first begun exploring my abilities—with Emmett's help, even back then—I had visualized a narrow passageway in my mind, and a door blocked by a jumble of rubbish. That had helped me to understand how I was connected to people. Now, I visualized something different: a bank vault. And I stowed these thoughts and dreams and secret selves inside the vault and spun the lock and sealed them away. Because I was an asshole, but I wasn't so much of an asshole that I would strip the people who loved me of their privacy.

"Well," Emmett said, his hand popping free of mine, those fallaway eyes wrinkling at the corners. "That was a terrible idea."

"Did it work?" Austin said. Then he breathed out, pressing both hands over his mouth, and his eyes spun in a wild circle. "Of course it did," he said between his fingers. "Jesus."

"You felt that?" I said.

Jim still wouldn't meet my eyes, but he helped Sharrika to her feet and said, "You went through my head like a subway car. I need an aspirin." Under his breath, he muttered, "And a drink."

"A subway car." Becca shook her head; she was still clinging to Emmett. "It felt like somebody shoved the Empire State Building through the back of my skull."

I grunted. "I haven't exactly done that before."

"No joke," Kaden said, screwing himself into his seat, his eyes ping-ponging off Austin.

"It's not like I've had practice."

"Trust me," Jake said, chafing Temple Mae's hand as though she might be suffering frostbite. "We know."

"Well, I'm still figuring out—"

"Tweaker," Emmett said, massaging one side of his head with his free hand. "Have you ever heard a brass band go through a wood chipper?"

"Huh?"

"Because I keep hearing you inside my head. And outside my head. And it's like somebody just shoved the trombones down the chute. So do us all a favor and shut up, all right?"

"Oh." I glanced at Austin. He nodded. I glanced at Becca. She nodded. Hard. I glanced at Jim, but he still wouldn't look at me, and Sharrika was whispering something in his ear. "Yeah."

"Like, right now, tweaker? Shut up right now."

I opened my mouth. Then I nodded.

"Jesus Christ. Can you think a little quieter?"

I visualized that bank vault. I expanded it. I rolled up those connections and shoved them through the door—leaving it open the tiniest crack.

Emmett sighed and nodded. Then, to my surprise, he ran his hands under his eyes, and his fingers came away wet. When he caught me staring, he said, "You're like an icepick digging into a migraine. You might want to work on that."

"Don't listen to him," Austin said. "It wasn't that bad. And it's better now. You're just like a . . . like a dot right here." He tapped the side of his head.

"If we're going to do this, we need to do it fast," Becca said, her phone in her lap as she scrolled through screens. "I've been looking at old land surveys—"

"Chapee."

She looked at me, her expression so ferociously intense that I wanted to take a step back. Then she started tapping at her phone. With a cry, she stretched out her phone like a trophy.

"You found it?"

"I think I found it."

"I just—I mean, Becca, I barely told you—"

"Yeah, well, I've been reading county records for the last four months, Vie, trying to figure out where they were hiding, and I've been thinking about them when I wasn't reading them. It sounded familiar, and I think—" Her fingers paused, and the screen scrolled to a stop. She pinched, zooming in, and breathed out hard. "Here. It's from the turn of the century, and it showed up in the city library when Donovan Metals and Minerals shuttered in the 1950s." Her eyes flicked to me. "That was the mining operation before Shetland Multinational, the ones who are here now. I kept this one on my phone because it was strange, and I remembered the name when I heard it."

"And?"

"And they were prospecting various sections of the Bighorns, trying to find good places to expand their operation. According to this, the surveyor thought it would have been an excellent place to open another mine. But at the bottom—" She turned the phone so we could see it, and she pinched the screen again. It showed a scanned document, the paper yellow with age and hatched with rows listing various technical specifications for an area marked Chapee. Climbing the page at a diagonal in a looping script were three words: *Unsuitable - locals hostile.* And then, cutting across those words in a second hand—a tight, angular hand—two more words: *Superstitious nonsense.*

"It'll take me a little while to figure out where it is. They didn't have the same forest service roads, and they didn't use GPS coordinates, but I think we can narrow it down."

"Austin can help you."

Austin blinked at my words, but he nodded.

"I want to thank you," I said, "all of you, for what you did for me. Not just today. But something needs to be clear: I'm going up there alone. You've given me a chance to succeed; I won't let you risk more than that."

"Then you'll die." Sharrika's voice was clear and dry, and her dark eyes flitted across my face, calculating.

"Maybe. But nobody can stop Kyle, and Leo's almost as dangerous, and that Crow kid was able to get through even Emmett's barriers, so he could reach any of you, and—"

"Vie," Jim said, "we've got a plan."

"What?"

"We're not idiots. We haven't just been sitting around waiting for our fearless leader to tell us what to do."

"That's not what I—"

"Sharrika has been working on Kyle ever since he showed up in town—well, technically, ever since Becca dug up his history. That's why she wasn't at the hospital when he attacked; she was out running a field test. She and I are going to handle him."

"Handle him?" I said. "Fire can't touch him. Dropping a prison on top of him didn't slow him. He can—"

"Vie. We've got a plan. But we need Kaden."

"Me?" Kaden looked ready to swallow his tongue.

Jim nodded, and after a moment, Kaden nodded back.

"And Temple Mae and I are going to handle Leo." Jake's voice was steady, but his fingers were white around his belt buckle again. "Anything he tosses at us, she can toss it back harder."

Temple Mae nodded. I could feel her hatred seething along the bond between us, but it was only partially for me. It was only because I'd brought this back into her life, opened this door, made her face it.

I opened my mouth, but before I could speak, Emmett said, "And I've been thinking about the Crow kid. The one you've been calling the Old Man. I was staring right at him, and he was safely on the other side of the barrier. He was still right there when he almost put a knife through me—there were two of them."

"That's what I saw," I said. "At the hospital. I couldn't even touch him, not until he was so close he almost got me. It was like I was grabbing air."

"I think I can handle him, but I'll need Becca." Emmett's voice didn't change, but his eyes suddenly found something on the wall behind me. "And Austin."

Austin had to clear his throat. I didn't have to see his face to know that, in his mind at least, he was seeing Emmett's rumpled clothes, was smelling the motel soap, was imagining everything that had happened with me. I didn't even recognize his voice when he nodded and said, "Yeah."

"That leaves the Lady and Urho for you," Jim said. "That's the best we can do, so tell me you've got a plan of your own. Tell me you've figured out how to handle them."

"I know how to handle them."

That was bullshit, but I was working on it. I had one last shot at figuring out how I might be able to get to them, so I looked past Jim and Sharrika at the bathroom door and said, "First, I need to talk to Ginny."

# Chapter | 35

Ginny sat in the bathtub. She was too big for it; her shoulders spilled out over the top. When she had come to my house, I had been too busy avoiding a bullet to notice what she was wearing, but it was hard not to notice now. The pantsuit jacket mountained up behind her neck, exposing part of a label stitched with the word *Uptown*, and her black blouse had been snipped away so that someone—Becca, I was guessing—could bandage the wound on Ginny's side. She held a watery icepack on the bandage. Her eyes were red and puffy. Her mouth drew into a sneer when she saw me.

"Hi, Ginny."

"I'm not telling you anything."

I nodded and perched on the edge of the toilet. With the power of my circle of friends running through me, I didn't even have to flick open my second sight; it was open constantly, like a pair of glasses I just had to slide down. And when I looked at her, at the psychic chaos that trailed behind Ginny, I still couldn't find what I was looking for: any sign of her coyote.

"He's going to kill you. You don't have any idea what you're going up against. He's hundreds of years old. Hundreds." She shifted and winced and the icepack sloshed inside its plastic bag. "He's killed more people than you've met. He knows the other side as well as he knows the buffalo grass. Kattie Shakespeare and Elli of New York and the boy Runs Ahead faced Urho Rattling Tent, War Chief of the Tribe That Walks Apart. They defeated him and cut his body into twelve pieces, and he didn't die. He lived on. He's stronger than anyone. And he has Babria, Lady Buckhardt, at his side."

I wanted to ask about what she meant—and how she knew it—but instead I said, "I know where Urho and the Lady are. I know about Chapee. I know how they're planning on using Hannah and Tyler, and I know that you helped the Lady—"

Ginny moaned and shook her head.

"I know all of it, Ginny. They're not going to win. Urho's not coming back, and we're going to put the rest of them in the ground to make sure. Do you understand me?"

She laughed; the shrill sound sheared away at the end. "You don't get it. He can do things nobody else can do. Whatever you're planning, he's already figured it out, he's already prepared for it, and you're going to walk into a trap that you can't get out of."

"This is your chance to help. Help, and you can walk away. You can't stay here; there's no place for you here, not after what you've done. But you can live. You can go somewhere else and live."

She shook her head again, hunching now, looking smaller as she fumbled with the icepack.

"Ginny, he took your coyote—"

"He killed it!" The scream ripped from her throat, and she threw her head back, meeting my eyes for the first time. That was when I remembered Ginny wasn't a small woman, no matter how much she hunched or shrank or shook her head. She was about the size of a bulldozer, and for a moment, she looked like she was coming at me.

The door opened, and Austin tumbled into the tiny bathroom, looking at me and then at Ginny, a revolver in his hand.

I shook my head and waved at the door.

After a moment's hesitation, Austin looked at me one last time and slipped out of the room.

I leaned back, and the porcelain lid wobbled on the tank, and water gurgled somewhere in the pipes.

"He killed it." Ginny's head dropped, her long, dark hair falling the way rain had been falling for the last three days. "I was walking a dream, and then Urho was there, and he killed it. He ripped my coyote into pieces, right there in the dream. It was part of me, and he killed it—" She shuddered, and the next words slipped out in stuttered horror. "He killed it with his teeth." Then her voice picked up speed. "That's not possible. It's not. But he did it, and I ran, I ran from the dream, but they were already there. Men. Men inside my house, inside the bedroom, with ropes and guns and—" She shook her head, and her hair whispered like the rain. "And I'm not a warrior. I told you that. From the very beginning. And they took me. And they made me help them."

"Your last chance, Ginny: help me. Tell me how I can stop Urho. Tell me how I can come face to face with him. Do that much, and I'll do the rest."

"You're not strong enough."

"You don't know everything."

"That little trick? Those threads you've tied back to your friends? I'm not blind, little boy. I haven't lost my abilities. I can see it—you've tangled yourselves together, and you think that makes you stronger."

"I am stronger."

"You've put all your chips in a pile, that's what you've done. All that power runs on love. And love isn't a weapon, little boy. Love isn't a knife you can bury in Urho's throat. You need darker emotions. You need what you felt when you tore Mr. Big Empty to shreds."

That night. I remembered that night, what I had felt that night. My fury at what Luke had done to other people. Fury at what he had done to me. The need to destroy him so that he never hurt anyone else again. And then, more recently, the incandescent anger that I had felt when I thought Krystal had killed Austin. It had burned through me like wildfire and left nothing but open vistas of ash inside me. In that numb clarity, I had left my body and popped every stitch running through her soul and dragged her between worlds. That had been anger, a kind of solar-flare anger that had left me free of remorse or compassion—or love.

Doubt slipped through my gut.

"The minute you try to attack," Ginny said, "the minute you let anger and hate and fear sharpen your mind, become your weapons, that precious lacework is going to burn away, and it'll be you facing Urho alone. No friends. No love. No power."

"That's it, then?" I stood and swiped at my jeans. "You won't help me?"

"Nobody can help you."

"Goodbye, Ginny."

As I stepped out of the bathroom, her voice followed me.

"You can't hurt them or stop them or break them. You can only break yourself trying."

I shut the door.

The motel room had emptied except for Becca, and she studied me now with an unlit cigarette between her lips.

"That didn't sound good."

I shook my head.

"We can't leave her here, Vie."

Taking Becca's arm, I hustled her toward the door.

"Someone's going to find her."

"Fine."

"She might call the cops."

"We're going, Becca."

"She might warn Urho."

And then we emerged into the April evening. The clouds had thickened to a gray roil, and snowflakes dusted the air and smoked away on the ground. To the east, like the edge of the world, the Bighorns spiked up into the clouds.

"Did you find a way to get to Chapee?"

She nodded, biting the cigarette so hard that it bent and drooped between her teeth.

"Then let's go."

"Vie—"

"He knows we're coming. Let's not keep him waiting."

# Chapter | 36

I rode with Emmett on the Ducati, and nobody liked this, least of all Austin. The last I saw, as Emmett pulled out onto the highway, was Austin denting the Charger's side panel with one hell of a punch, and I hoped he hadn't broken his hand.

That was the last thought I could spare for him though. We drove fast into the dark and the snow, and the dry, powdery smell mixed with the leather of Emmett's jacket. Then there were the neon palisades of Vehpese—the glare of the signs hemming either side of the state highway—and a whiff of the late-night donuts at the Big Swirl, and then the mud and water of the river, and snow beaded and glinted like silver on the bridge's stone railings where I had sat one afternoon before I jumped. And then the mountains, and the lodgepole pines, the smell of their pitch and sap filling my nose, and aspens weaving a net of gold and silver as their leaves quivered in our passage. Behind us came the Impala, the Charger, and Jake's big, old truck. We were carpooling to save the environment, and I had to bite the inside of my cheek to keep from laughing.

When we finally left the state highway, the forestry service road was gravel, and so slick that Emmett had to slow down. That probably saved our lives; the rear wheel of the Ducati kicked out on a turn, and Emmett managed to catch us, but not without both of us taking a dip to the right. At the same moment, a muzzle flashed off to our right, and the trunk of a massive ponderosa pine exploded with splinters of bark and yellow-white pulp.

"Shit," Emmett muttered, and then he grunted. The next shot pinged off one of his barriers; I watched sparks light up the spot where the round had struck. "Help me get the bike up."

Emmett eased the bike onto the service road's muddy shoulder.

"What are you doing?"

The Impala creaked past us; Sharrika was driving, and Jim leaned over the dash.

"Jim told you we had a plan," Emmett said.

As though that had been a cue, the entire mountain seemed to catch fire. It wasn't a white-hot blaze, not the hottest fire Jim had ever produced, but it was enormous. It stretched as far as I could see, flames dripping from branches, smoldering in the wet brush, crawling up the next slope. I thought I heard screaming off in the distance, and my stomach flipped.

The Impala rolled forward, and we trailed after it. The fire pushed out ahead of us like a vanguard, swallowing miles of forest, chewing along wet tree limbs as though they were soaked in kerosene. The whole effect was terrifying and, in an uncomfortable way, pleasant: the blaze warmed the air and smelled like a campfire. I doubted the men who had been roasted alive felt the same way, and that made my stomach flip again.

"How long can he keep this up?" I asked as we drove another mile.

Emmett didn't answer.

The fire spun out ahead of us, snaking through the darkness, lighting our way. Another mile. And then another. And then another, all of them achingly slow on the bad roads. But no more shots sparked against Emmett's barrier.

And then I heard water. The crackle of the fire was almost too loud, but the water was making a lot of noise—and around the next bend, I saw it jumping out in a short, broad waterfall and then racing down a rocky vee of the mountainside.

We came over the next slope, and I saw it: the valley, the bent heads of buffalo grass, the crooked cottonwoods along the water, the lake, and there, on a shelf overlooking the valley, the massive cabin. Chapee.

That was when the earthquake hit us. The ground slewed to the left, toward the water, collapsing into a slide of dirt and gravel. The Ducati pitched under us, and we fell, tumbling toward the river and the precipice of the waterfall. Ahead of us, the Impala dipped, its rear tires spinning empty air, and then more ground crumbled away, and the car tilted back onto its bumper, balancing for a moment like a seal on its nose, and then—

And then the ground kept shaking, and gravel and earth and a small juniper bush slid below me, but Emmett and I weren't falling. The Ducati wasn't falling. The Impala actually bumped up a few inches, floating in the air, and then slowly tipped forward, righting itself.

"Temple Mae?" Emmett asked, his voice bubbly with what sounded like relief.

"Kaden," I breathed. "That motherfucker might actually be worth something."

The bike drifted uphill until it reached a rocky shelf that marked the edge of the new precipice. The Impala glided after us. It had to be Kaden doing this. I could tell by how hard the Ducati landed, by how the Impala groaned when it hit solid ground, bouncing on its suspension. Temple Mae had finesse; Kaden was like a toddler kicking his way through Tiny Town.

I glanced back over my shoulder and saw the Charger skidding into a patch of wild onions, the tires snapping the delicate stalks and releasing their scent into the mixture of dust and fresh-turned earth and hot metal. Behind Austin, Jake's truck settled onto a soft patch of sod—like a baby rocking in its cradle. That was Temple Mae's work.

Another tremor shook the valley, and the Ducati's wheel skipped along the rock shelf, the rubber squealing.

"He's going to bring down the whole fucking mountain," Emmett said.

Before that could happen, the Impala's doors popped open, and Jim and Sharrika got out. Jim looked like shit: the only color left in his face was his eyes and the flurry of cinders inside them. His hair was the color of copper glinting in the sunlight, and all the rest of him looked like newsprint kept in a damp basement. Sharrika scrambled around to the Impala's trunk, shouting Kaden's name as she did so.

Overhead the clouds slowed, and then they sped up. A static charge raised the hairs on my arms, and my next breath carried ozone. I clutched Emmett's waist as another tremor rolled through the valley, and the Ducati bounced with a horrible metallic jangle.

"What the fuck are they doing?" Emmett muttered.

"Whatever they're doing, they'd better hurry."

As though in answer to my words, Kaden sprinted past the Ducati, his face whitewashed, his shoulders curled forward. Sharrika motioned for him to help, and together they rolled a bundle of rebar out of the trunk. Speaking into Kaden's ear—too low for me to hear over the ripples moving through the earth—Sharrika pointed. I followed her gesture, and lightning arced through the clouds overhead, and then I saw him. Kyle Stark-Taylor stood on a boulder wedged against the valley wall. Then the lightning died, and Kyle disappeared into the darkness.

Whatever Sharrika said, Kaden must have understood because he untied the bundled lengths of rebar, and they floated into the air, drifting into a line in front of him, like a row of spears ready to launch in Kyle's direction. Another tremor ripped through the valley. And another. Harsh, distressed cracks came from the stone shelf underneath us; a few more like that, and we'd be back falling toward the river.

Sharrika said something again. Jim and Kaden both nodded.

The ground heaved and bucked. A cottonwood below us shrieked as its trunk snapped, the heavy crown of branches tumbling into the water before being whipped sideways.

Then there was fire. A huge, imperfect globe of it that swallowed the spot where Kyle had stood—and swallowed the boulder as well, and a good twenty yards in every direction. It was like a miniature sun, filling the valley with ruddy light so that I could see every blade of grass, pick out every wavering shadow. Even from several hundred yards the heat made me flinch and squint, and snowflakes hissed on the ground and boiled away, and Emmett dropped the visor on his helmet like he wanted a welding mask.

Lightning struck. I squeezed my eyes shut, but too late, and the concussive brilliance of the bolt lingered in a purple afterimage. The boom rocked Emmett and me on the Ducati, and then through my eyelids came another incandescent punch, and Sharrika was screaming something, but the thunder following those massive blasts of lightning kept me from making out the words.

Then a final clap hit me in the chest, vibrated along my bones, and darkness swept down.

I blinked an ultraviolet afterimage out of my eyes and squinted out into the night. Ozone prickled the hairs inside my nose, obliterating everything else, and for a moment, in that total darkness, it seemed like those blasts of lightning had wiped out the world.

Then a vein of blue-white bled across the sky. More lightning, I realized. Only instead of crashing down to earth, it kissed something high above the Bighorns and vanished.

No more tremors, I realized. Ahead, Jim wavered, clutching at the Impala's passenger door, and then he fell. Kaden watched him fall. Sharrika didn't even seem to notice; her eyes were on the clouds, where another vein of blue-white bled out, sparking against something overhead and vanishing. A cough of thunder followed, but nothing like the last wave of force that had rocked Emmett and me on the Ducati.

At the third, smaller flare of lightning, I glimpsed it: a black thread hanging from the sky. At the ground, the thread spooled around a human figure. Kyle. He wasn't moving. He wasn't trying to bring down the mountains.

Lightning bled from the clouds again, and this time, when it licked the top of that black thread, I understood.

"It's a goddamn lightning rod," Emmett breathed.

I clapped him on the shoulder, grinning as I remembered what had happened last year at Belshazzar's Feast. Electricity had disabled Makayla when she'd become seemingly indestructible; we had tried the same thing in the hospital, and it had worked. For a minute, until Kyle had torn himself free. But with Kaden keeping the metal conductor in place, and Sharrika generating a steady current—I fought a sudden smile.

"We'll keep him here," Sharrika said, wiping sweat onto her *Star Trek* t-shirt. "You need to hurry; they're not going to wait—"

Something whistled through the air. I barely had time to glimpse it—a whiffle ball—before it disappeared into the tangles of grass and weeds. I whopped Emmett on the shoulder again, and he hit the gas. The Ducati leaped forward and whipped right. We missed Kaden by about six inches, but he was so concentrated on keeping that tower of rebar in the air—and cocooned around Kyle—that he didn't even blink.

Then the whiffle ball exploded. The blast wave flattened the Junegrass, and a ring of fire and plastic shrapnel spun out. A piece of it nicked my shoulder, biting through my coat and shirt, and I had to swallow a shout. Another piece grazed my ear, spinning so close that I could hear its hum before it sliced through cartilage and was off, disappearing into the blackness of the valley.

"Go," I shouted.

But ten yards later, Emmett turned into a skid, halting our progress as quickly as he could.

"Fuck," he shouted. "Fuck, fuck, fuck, that's exactly what they want."

He hunkered down, his brow furrowing in concentration, and the air around us stilled. He had put up one of his barriers. Something moved out in the darkness, and I had the impression of speed, and then the sound of a small motor. So. Leo wasn't operating on foot.

Something—another whiffle ball, maybe—exploded inches from the barriers. Shards of melted plastic clung to the invisible wall, and the fire left tongues of soot hanging in the air.

Then Jake's truck shot past us, rocking over the uneven valley floor, fishtailing as it cut hard around a rocky outcropping. The tail lights burned back at me like eyes as the truck herky-jerked across the dips and hummocks hidden by the tall grass.

Two hundred yards ahead, where the valley floor dropped toward the lake, I caught a glimpse of muzzle flare. Jake must have seen it too—or Temple Mae, maybe—because the truck swerved. I couldn't see the projectile. I couldn't tell if it had hit or not. I guessed it was a standard rifle round, but in Leo's hands, nothing was standard.

The explosion was so sudden and so bright that it ruined my night vision, and I blinked again, helpless. As my eyes adjusted, I saw the truck. On its side. Burning.

Digging my fingers into Emmett's shoulder, I said, "Go, Em. Go."

He gave the Ducati gas, and we lurched forward. But not toward the burning truck.

"Em." I grabbed a handful of leather. "Turn this fucking thing over there. Jake and Temple Mae—"

"Knew what they were signing up for." He bent lower over the Ducati's handlebars, and tension tightened his shoulders.

"Damn it, Emmett."

But he wasn't listening to me. He was trying to keep the Ducati upright on the rough valley floor, and he was also trying to keep a barrier in place—it flowed ahead of us, trampling the grass, leaving glossy, broken stalks behind it, their seed pods burst and peppering everything.

I glanced back at the Charger, which roared behind us. I couldn't see Austin's face, not with the headlights in my eyes, but he didn't swerve toward his brother's truck. He was still following me. They were all still following me into this mess.

The squeal of tearing metal brought my head whipping to the side, and I watched as the entire truck—an F-150, maybe the only thing Jake loved as much as Temple Mae—ripped down the middle. It was like watching a can opener tear off the top of a can of tuna. And then the two halves skidded across the grass, flames spitting and catching in tiny fingerlings on the vegetation.

Two figures limped away from the truck's shell. I wanted to shout. I wanted to warn them. Another flare from the muzzle came near the water's edge, and—

And then something like a firefly caromed off toward the valley wall. When it exploded, the sound ran through the whole valley, and an entire slope of scree kicked and tumbled its way through the firelight toward the water. It fell with the sound of rain on a tin roof, an enormous pattering that swallowed everything else. And as it poured across the valley floor, it parted around those two limping figures.

"Jesus Christ," I whispered.

"I knew they'd be fine," Emmett said with what he probably thought sounded like confidence.

I leaned into him, ready to tell him exactly what I thought about that statement.

A sudden weight dragged me off balance—dragging the Ducati off balance too, as Emmett swore and tried to correct—and a line of heat opened along my shoulder. The knife that should have taken me across the throat skipped off bone instead.

The pain lit up my brain brighter than the fires in the valley. It took me only a few seconds to process what I was seeing: the Crow boy had come out of nowhere, and somehow he was clutching onto me, his weight all on the right side of the bike, and in his free hand he carried a knife.

As I turned my head, the Crow boy braced his feet, leaned out, and slashed again. I moved to block him, catching his arm with my own. He passed through my grasp like air as the weight vanished and the bike overcorrected in the opposite direction.

Some part of my brain remembered his trick in the hospital, and my body twisted more out of instinct than anything else. A fresh weight pulled directly behind me, and a second blade skipped along my ribs. I couldn't look back—I didn't have time, and I couldn't take my eyes off the little fucker in front of me—so I threw an elbow back hard and felt the Crow boy's nose crumple.

"Em," I called as the boy on the side of me—his nose now busted and bloodied, even though my elbow had only caught the one behind me—readied another slash. The one behind me was choking on blood.

Emmett reached back and grabbed my coat, shouting, "I'm laying it down. Stay on top of it and follow it down."

Then he laid the bike down on its right side, and I moved left with him, losing sight of the Crow boy. I heard a high-pitched scream as a sudden weight pulled me to the right and then was gone.

We hadn't been going very fast, thank God, and the valley floor was carpeted with last year's dead grasses and the tender crop from this spring, all packed down by Emmett's barrier. I clung on to Emmett and rolled left with him, mostly keeping the bike under me. We skidded and slid over the uneven terrain. We slowed; then we came to an abrupt halt as we collided with a deadfall mostly hidden in the grass. I spilled off the bike onto the ground.

My head was spinning from the adrenaline rush, and white dots floated in my vision. Not stars. Not even those forking bolts of lightning. Just white like snow.

And then, I realized, it was snow. And it was coming down even harder. Snow in fucking April. That felt like the ultimate outrage, and the fact that it made me so upset left part of me wondering if I'd gotten a concussion.

I pushed myself up and looked around, even with the cuts on my shoulder and my ribs screaming at me. Smoke drifted across the valley now; multiple fires burned along the north slope, including the burning wreckage of Jake's truck. More fires were good, I thought, coughing as each breath brought the smell of burnt grass and cooking rubber. More fires meant Temple Mae was still alive, still fighting, throwing back Leo's explosive.

I turned back and could just make out the outline of the Crow boy against the light snow pack. He limped toward me, a knife in each hand. It looked like it hurt him to move, and that made me smile. I flicked a glance left, then right. Two more coming from either side, and they were limping too.

"That's a good trick," I said.

They kept coming.

Someone was jogging toward me, just a silhouette against the fires burning on the north side of the valley. Emmett? Austin? I guessed Austin because he was carrying a rifle, and Emmett hadn't had a gun.

"You make these little copies of yourself," I said. "But only one of them is real. Is that it?"

They closed another yard. I had maybe thirty feet left.

"Nobody ever sees you coming. They think they've got you, and then you're right behind them." I glanced over my shoulder, and there he was. Four of them.

Another yard. And then another.

"One of you is real. The rest of you are just smoke and mirrors."

For the first time in all our encounters, the Crow boy smiled. It was vicious—too mature and too horrible for a boy his age. His canine teeth looked like they'd been sharpened.

No, I thought. That wasn't right. Not smoke and mirrors. Because the boy on my right side had stabbed me as I was unbalanced by his weight. But so had the second boy, as he dragged me backward with his weight.

They were both real. And heavy.

But I couldn't touch the boy hanging on my right. And I couldn't feel his weight anymore either. I couldn't touch the copies of the Crow boy in the hospital. It had been like running my hands through smoke, every time except when I'd elbowed—

When I'd elbowed the one behind me without looking at him. Just like tonight, when I elbowed the one behind me without looking at him. When the weight had slammed down on me, he had been real. When I wasn't looking at him.

Fifteen feet.

"No," I said, pushing myself to my feet. "Not smoke and mirrors. Not exactly, right? You're real. All of you. But you're only in one place at a time. And you're always in the place I'm not looking."

Ten feet.

The silhouette coming toward me had slowed. The head cocked. Was he listening? Or was he lost? Was he trying to figure out which one was the real one?

Eight feet.

"Austin," I shouted. "Austin, get a bead on one of these motherfuckers, close your eyes, and shoot."

Five feet.

I dropped, the wet grass brushing under my chin, the sudden thickness of the green smell of crushed stalks making my stomach turn, and I waited for the sound of a thrust as the closest Crow boy stabbed. When I heard him, I'd kick out as hard as I could and hope to catch him right in his pubescent balls.

The shot sounded right overhead, a clap of thunder so loud that it ran down my back like a hand. I waited for something. Anything.

"Vie?" And then a warm, callused hand on my neck.

Austin's eyes. Blue-green even in the twilight. And the smell of gunpowder and his sweat as he grabbed a handful of my coat and yanked me upright.

"Are you ok?"

"Jesus."

"Vie?"

"Jesus Christ, did you shoot him?"

"He's gone. He disappeared."

"Fuck." I scrambled to my feet, wobbled. Someone jogged at us with a flashlight, the brilliant white cone slashing back and forth over the valley floor, picking out a patch of Queen Anne's lace that had somehow so far survived tonight's battle. And then the light dipped, splashed over a pair of Chucks, and I could see Becca's eyes.

"Emmett?" I asked.

The disappointment came down in Austin's eyes like a hard black veil. He shook his head. "I haven't seen him."

Becca shook her head too.

"We've got to—"

"You've got to get to that cabin, Vie." Austin's hand swallowed my shoulder, spinning me toward the lake and, beyond it, the shelf of stone on which the ancient building stood. "Right now, while the way is clear."

"That Crow boy—"

"I heard you. I know how he works now. We'll get him."

I hesitated. Austin and Becca were at my back; before me, the slate mirror of the lake, and the cracks of yellow light where the cabin broke the darkness.

"I'll find him," Austin said. Then he shoved me. "I'll make sure he's ok."

I wanted to—I don't know. Say sorry, I guess. Or explain.

But I glanced back, and he shrugged and turned away, the rifle coming down, and said, "You'd better go."

"Becca."

"Vie, you'd better go."

Austin looked once at me. His eyes could have been the far side of the moon, all the blue and green washed out, just a lunar gray like death.

I turned and ran.

I'd been running for a long time. For years. And this was the only time it had ever really mattered, so I ran, and I ran as fast and as hard as I could. Buffalo grass and cheatgrass and heavy-head purple thistles scratched at my jeans. Smoke and the lingering ozone filled my lungs, but as I got farther around the lake, the haze thinned, and the stars came out. I gulped down air that was clear and tasted of mud and steelhead trout and the bruised leaves of cow parsley.

I'd gone thirty yards when a gunshot rang out behind me, and I glanced over my shoulder, swerved to keep my footing, saw nothing but a gauze of smoke thickening, heard nothing but my own breathing—no shouts, no screams, no cries for help. No Austin. No Emmett. Then another gunshot, but off to my left, where I'd last seen Jake and Temple Mae. No explosion followed the crack of this bullet, and that meant Leo hadn't been the one who fired it—and that meant Jake was still going. Or Temple Mae. Or both, God, let them both be all right.

At the edge of the lake, my sneakers caught a rock smoothed by the lap of lake water, and it spun out, skipped once like it had cracked against ice, and then disappeared under the surface. The ripples from its passage shattered the slate mirror, turning it into a thousand distorted reflections, a thousand different sunken cabins with a thousand different swimming lights. It reminded me of throwing stones at Lake Thunderbird. I jagged hard to the right, following the lake's muddy shoulder, and cold mud slopped up over my sneaker; it squelched every other step.

Lightning webbed the sky, snapped out against the darkness like a bullwhip and clipped that tiny iron needle that was holding Kyle in place. How long? The thought hammered inside my head in time with my steps. How long could Sharrika keep the lightning going, even with a lightning rod to make it easier? How long could Kaden keep the iron armature suspended and tight? How long could Emmett and Austin and Becca hold out against a kid who could only be hurt when you weren't looking at him? How long could Temple Mae lob grenades back at a psycho teenager with an unlimited supply?

Not long. They were all tough and strong and brave, but we were outmatched. Eventually, they would tire. And Leo only had to land one of his homemade explosives to turn out the lights on Jake and Temple Mae. The Crow boy only had to get close enough to slide a knife into Austin or Emmett or Becca. Sharrika just had to miss one lightning bolt, and Kyle would pull the mountains down on our heads.

So I ran. And the slate mirror smoothed out beside me, and my shadow ran along the water, and then I reached the cabin.

My shadow veered left.

And I realized it wasn't my shadow.

# Chapter | 37

With all that power running through me, with all the energy that my friends had channeled into me, opening my second sight was like breathing, and on my next inhale, the other side spiderwebbed to life in front of me. And then I saw that it wasn't my shadow lounging against the door. It was my half-brother. It was River.

Or it was his ghost, or whatever haunted the other side after a person had died from supernatural trauma. He leaned against the cabin, hands buried in his pockets, and shook out his long, curly hair. In the hypersaturated colors of the other side, he almost looked alive again; his smile, directed at me in full force, was very much alive.

"You made it."

"I made it."

I reached out with my mind, brushing against River, testing. Urho's presence on the other side enhanced whatever abilities he must have had while he was alive, and one of those powers included controlling the dead. That's why the dead, even when I could find them on the other side, were never able to tell me who killed them. Urho had silenced them. That's why they had only been able to give me indirect guidance, clues, hints. And even then, Urho had made them pay for every crumb they dropped in my path.

But unlike all the other times I had encountered River on the other side, there was no shadow of the cord reaching off from him into a nowhere place. That, in the past, had been Urho's power binding River. And now it was gone.

"He's too focused on crossing over," River said. "He can't spare the energy to keep me under control. And he's vulnerable, Vie. Right now, if he makes a mistake, you could get him."

Letting out a relieved breath, I grabbed the doorknob. The swirl of colors coming off River brightened, and he dropped an arm in my path—an insubstantial arm, true, but I still stopped and glanced at him.

"I've got to get Tyler and Hannah. I don't have time to talk, and I don't want to hear whatever last warning Urho told you to give me."

River shook his head. "No messages. No warnings. No threats. At least, nothing from Urho." He paused, and his hair drifted in some unseen current of energy flowing through the other side as though he were floating in water. "I do have something to tell you, though. You knew that."

"I guessed that."

"Then you're really, really going to be pissed when I tell you what it is."

"I'm going in there, River. Whatever you think you need to tell me, spit it out and get out of my way. It's not going to stop me. It's not going to make me turn back. I'm not scared of them."

"Then you're pretty fucking stupid." The arm blocking my passage bent, and he placed a hand on my shoulder. I couldn't feel it, and at the same time, I could: not his touch, but a cool tingle that blew into heat. "He's vulnerable. But she's not. She's hungry, Vie. She's so goddamn hungry she . . . she'll eat you. She's been careful for a long time, just bites here and there, leaving most of them alive so she can remain undetected. She slips every now and then. Like someone popping open a bag of chips and pigging out instead of just one or two like they tell themselves. But when Urho comes back, she won't have to be careful. She'll devour you, and she'll leave your shell, your body, for Urho."

"Is that all? Just a vague threat about how dangerous she is? Move, River."

"I'm going to tell you something you aren't going to like."

"Did you and Emmett go to some kind of fucking remedial class? How to break bad news or something?"

River's lips twitched, and those long, loose blond curls spun out in that invisible current. I was starting to realize what that current was: Tyler's ability, dragging things on this plane of existence toward him. As I got closer to Tyler, the effect would grow stronger, and I remembered my dream, and a chill ran through me again. What did kids do with the things they caught? What did kids with all the kindness burned out of them, what did they do when they caught a stray? And I thought of Francis Valentino and the M80 and the dog's bloody stump of a tail.

"You aren't going to like it," River's voice stayed even, "but it's the only way you can walk in there and walk back out with those kids."

Behind us, another explosion chased the length of the valley, and it rapped between my shoulder blades like a dead man's hand.

"Faster. A lot fucking faster because people I love are out there fighting. Maybe dying."

River nodded. "Somebody you love betrayed you. And you're going to have to kill him to get those kids back."

"Austin." I pictured him disappearing into the night, the rifle over his shoulder, his lie about finding Emmett still on the air. I had trusted him. No, fuck that, I had loved him. And he had—

River was laughing. "Jesus, you little fucktard. You are so fucking stupid sometimes. 'Austin.'" He mimicked my voice, fluttered his eyes, pressed the back of his hand to his forehead. "You're just so fucking inside-assward when it comes to him it's kind of unbelievable."

"Emmett?"

"Jesus Christ."

"Well, just tell me then. You don't have to play this sick game, or whatever you think you're doing."

Something ironed the laugh lines out of River's face, and his hand tightened around my shoulder, and that prickle of heat dug into the muscle so that I could almost imagine his grip. "I didn't get to do big brother things for you. I wish I could do this. Big brothers are supposed to turn on the lights and show you there's no monster in the closet. And if there is a monster, well, big bros are supposed to lie and make those lies stretch as long as they can." He tried to smile; it fizzed off like a factory-second bottle rocket. "But you and me, we got to a place where lies don't work anymore. The monster is about to walk himself out of the closet and flip the lights on his own goddamn self. You know who I'm talking about."

"Dad."

The monster walks himself out of the closet. Walks himself right out. Flips the lights on his own goddamn self. The doorknob rattled in my hand.

I forced the fear to one side. "Big bro? You sound like a shitty afternoon special." I shrugged, trying to throw off his touch, and the gesture was purely symbolic because my shoulder passed through his hand. Then I twisted and threw open the door. "If there are any monsters in there, I'll flip on the lights myself and drag them out of the closet by their balls."

"Vie, a true psychic can touch both sides. And remember: we're blood. I'm here if you need me."

"Take care of yourself, River."

I stepped into the cabin's front room, which was about the size of Sara's whole house, and paused. I recognized this room with its fireplace and its spatter of drying wax on the floor and the elk-antler chandelier with real candles. The sofas were still in the same configuration; on one side, Hannah's physical body lay still—like a corpse, the voice at the back of my head commented—and on the other sat Tyler, his little face fixed in a mask of such hatred and contempt that I barely recognized him. It was like they had ripped out the essence of the boy I had known and sutured in a twisted, ancient horror. For a moment, I thought I was too late.

"Vie?" It was Hannah's voice, and her technicolor spirit slunk out from behind the sofa, her eyes darting from side to side. "Vie, you shouldn't be here. Vie, you need to go. Now. They're going to hurt you, Vie. They're going to—"

Urho's power clamped down on her so hard that I felt the shockwaves, and Hannah's tiny features twisted into an expression of agony. He was here. Urho. Not manifested in that ferocious, rabid beast that stalked the other side. But he was here, his power was here, and he was waiting.

The thought gave me pause. The thought made my heel scuff the threshold. The thought made my breath hitch.

Waiting for what?

Before I could consider the question, the crack of hard steps brought my attention to an arched doorway on the far side of the room, and then my dad stepped through.

"Come here," he said.

Tyler hopped off the couch and ran, pressing his head against my dad's legs, his features still fixed on me with so much hatred and fury that I knew that if the boy had a weapon of any kind, I'd be dead.

My dad stroked Tyler's hair and made a noise I remembered from childhood: a gravelly, shushing sound from deep in his throat. When his fingers curled at the base of Tyler's neck, he set the muzzle of a pistol against the crown of the boy's head. And then he looked up at me and smiled.

# Chapter | 38

Dad held the gun steady against Tyler's head, and if Tyler felt any fear or pain, they didn't shadow his face.

"Hello, son."

Dad looked like he'd been beat to shit not too long ago, with the bruises still purple and the scabs still fresh. But the hand holding the gun was rock solid. And he didn't have any trouble meeting my eyes.

*You're going to have to kill someone you love.* That's what River had told me. I wanted to laugh because River had been so totally, completely wrong. Kill my dad? For the love of God, I'd dreamed of about a hundred ways to kill him. I'd dreamed of so many ways to hurt him that, if anybody had found out about them, they would have shut me in a padded room and bricked over the door. This motherfucker had hurt me more ways than I could count. He had humiliated me. He had left me with her, he had fucking left me, and that was worse than all the rest of it combined.

But my dad, I could deal with in a moment. If I had to kill him, I'd kill him. If I could get out of here otherwise—well, fuck. Maybe I'd kill him anyway.

I focused on Tyler, reaching out, my mind brushing his. It was like running my fingers over barbed wire. I hissed a breath between my teeth and yanked back my mind. Whatever they'd done to him, they'd shattered his mind and planted all the broken pieces in cement, sharp edges pointed out to catch whoever came for him. The splintered-glass feel of touching him, even for that brief moment, ached in me, and if I hadn't been channeling a much larger power than my own, it might have put a stop to everything right there.

As I panted in pained breaths, Tyler's eyes came up, and he smiled like he'd ripped the wings off a fly.

That smile. That decided it. No matter what happened, no matter what it meant for me, I was going to kill Urho and the Lady. I was going to destroy them so that no ability or power or psychic could ever find a trace of them, not even a shred, not even a mote. For doing this to Tyler, they would be erased.

"Vie," Hannah whispered, her voice unsteady as it came across the ether of the other side. "Vie, something's wrong with me. Something's wrong with me like it's wrong with Tyler. Vie, they want me to do something and I—I think I'm going to do it."

I reached out again, more tentatively, and brushed against my dad's mind. Nothing. Silence. Like running my hands over cold concrete. That was Urho's power, blocking me from reaching my dad, making sure this all played out the way they wanted.

"It's ok," I said to Hannah. "Everything's going to be ok."

Dad nodded slowly. His eyes never left me; the gun never left the crown of Tyler's head. "I like that. I like the way you say that." Dad's lips curled, and the smile looked like River's. It looked like mine. "You've got a lot of practice gobbling that particular mouthful of shit. But saying it doesn't make it true." He cocked his head. "It never did, did it?"

My attack came without my even realizing it. It unfolded from me. It was like watching a thrower uncoil taut muscles and launch a javelin. It came from me with seventeen years of tension finally released. Psychic energy lanced into Bob Eliot's brain, driving through the barriers Urho had put in place as though they were straw or paper or smoke. And I followed that spear of psychic force, the weight of my power and all the power I channeled coming down on his mind like I was pinching a burning wick.

Darkness.

I floated inside his mind. With this much power running through me, I could do what I'd done to Krystal: I could rip every stitch out of his soul and drag his spirit to the other side, where a psychic wind would tear him into fluttering, burning tatters. I could do worse. I could shut down his access to the outside world, leave him trapped in here. I could turn on the lights, shine kliegs on the dark corners so that no matter where he turned, he saw every worry, every hurt, every fear. The rest of his life would be an eternity trapped in the nightmare of his own mind.

River's words throbbed in time with the pulse of my anger. The monster walks out. The monster walks himself out of the closet, flips the lights on his own goddamn self.

I shut out that thought. Death was too good for Bob Eliot. After what he'd done to Tyler—but really, the voice in my head was saying, to me, after what he'd done to me—death was just too good for him. Even that kind of final psychic destruction, his soul flaking away like paper borne aloft on fire, even that was too good for him. My dad deserved his own private hell.

After all, that's where he'd put me.

I gathered myself, gathered all that power, and it was like making a fist. A fist that held nothing. The conduit from my friends had narrowed. The raging river of power had thinned to a trickle. I thought of Ginny's words: *The minute you try to attack, the minute you let anger and hate and fear sharpen your mind, become your weapons, that precious lacework is going to burn away, and it'll be you facing Urho alone. No friends. No love. No power.*

It would be enough. That dark, vicious part of myself lunged against the last restraints I had in place. I needed to hurt him. I needed to do it now, here, when he had the muzzle of a gun biting into Tyler's scalp. Whatever I did to my dad now, it would be justice. It would be more than justice. It would be me trying to save a kid, and nothing was going to stand between me and saving a kid. A trickle of power was still flowing through the bond, and that trickle would be enough for me to do what I had to. It would be enough to drop the bar on every door and window inside his mind, turn up the lights, and let the monster walk himself out of the closet. Even if that monster was me. For Tyler's sake.

I almost believed it. Almost. Gripping that cord of power was like gripping sand, now—it sifted out of my hold no matter how tightly I clutched at it, weaker and thinner and shallower by the heartbeat. If I was going to do it, I needed to do it now.

*What do we do when we're the ones with the power? What are we willing to do to other people? And what aren't we willing to do? The rest of it, those are just excuses.*

They were my own words, and they rushed back at me through the smoke and the hate and fear. I had been here before. I had done this to my dad once before. Not to the same degree. Not even intentionally—not completely, anyway. And every day since, I had been happy that I'd done it. And every day since, I had hated myself for doing it. It swam up at me out of dreams. It slunk behind me in mirrors. I had been here before, and with a clarity that extinguished everything inside me, I realized I wouldn't do it again. I couldn't. I had my own monsters in the closet, to borrow River's metaphor, but unlike my dad, I could put a chain on the door. I could keep those nasty fuckers locked up. For today, at least. For this moment. And maybe for the next. And maybe the one after that, too.

I snapped back to my body. Sensation filtered in: the heat from the fireplace, the unsteadiness in my legs—exhaustion, part of my brain noted—even an old-lady smell like lavender and mothballs. My dad still stood with the pistol buried in Tyler's downy hair. Dad was cocking his head, as though waiting for something. Then a smile greased his face.

"You look like me. You talk like me, sometimes. But shit if you've got my balls, kid." Then the barrel of the gun swung up and toward me, and I stared into a black hole.

Yes, I thought. This is right. Things implode, and then all they can do is collapse, falling in on themselves. So it made sense that it would end this way, with the whole world disappearing down a gun barrel.

"No, Mr. Eliot." Babria, Lady Buckhardt, stepped through the archway, hands prim at her waist, her long hair pinned into a mound on top of her head. She looked grotesquely Victorian; with my second sight, I could see clearly the ravenous, shriveled soul inside that shell. It gnawed on old bones. It clawed and scrabbled, mad, desperate to get out. "Not like that. You remember our agreement."

I reached for the golden channel of power that had flowed into me, but I caught only cold wind and the taste of char. *That precious lacework is going to burn away,* Ginny had said. And she'd been right. Maybe Urho and the Lady had known what seeing my dad would do to me. Maybe they had simply hoped it would throw me off, and this was an unexpected bonus. Maybe, maybe, maybe. *It'll be you facing Urho alone,* Ginny had said. *No friends. No love. No power.*

Maybe. Maybe, maybe, maybe.

"Let Tyler go," I said. "Hannah too. Help them be normal again. As normal as they can be, after everything you've done to them. And then I'll help Urho cross over. I'll bring him to this side."

Lady Buckhart's pursed lips tightened. She wasn't wearing makeup, but red stained the thousands of fine lines webbing her mouth. Not lipstick, my brain said. That's not lipstick. She stepped around my dad, her bony fingers feathering Tyler's hair. The boy's huge, hateful eyes didn't register the touch. When she spoke, her voice was thoughtful.

"There are many paths, and the young must learn which one to follow. When a hound hunts, he must scent the quarry's trail. Drag a smoked cod across the fox's path, and the hound will go astray. Tie a silk scarf around a boy's eyes, and he will lose his way."

"You can make him better. Ginny helped you before. If you need her help again, she'll do it. She'll make sure you can fix him."

"Fix him?" The Lady's chin came up; those brick-orange eyes hardened. "Why should I fix him? He is perfect. His sister, on the other hand, has been difficult. She has been willful. She has been obstinate, ungrateful, proud. A lying, deceitful, mischievous child.

She will do what she must—she can't help herself—but afterward, she must be punished."

If I hadn't been watching Tyler's face so closely, if I hadn't been studying the hard, dark mirrors of his eyes for anything resembling the boy I had known, I would have missed it: a ripple like a minnow about to break still waters. And then gone.

Hope sparked inside me, and I meticulously ground out the glimmer. I kept my breathing even. Careful, I thought. Careful. Not yet, not quite yet, but soon.

"You," the Lady said, her skirt whispering against the ground as she crossed the room toward me. Her fingers stung my cheek with cold; I waited for skin to blister and crack with frostbite. "You will be delicious. I will begin the dust feast with you." Then, whirling, she pointed at Tyler. "Let us begin."

Somewhere out in the valley, under the thick snowfall and the clouds and the hidden stars, somewhere out in that whirlwind of fire and ice and darkness, someone screamed, and the scream went on and on.

The Lady smiled.

I took a step forward. She was frail and old. I was young and strong. I didn't need to be psychic to break her. I just needed to get a good grip.

As I grabbed at her hair, she spun and clutched my throat, shook me, shook me again. My head rattled so hard on my neck that, for a moment, I thought my spine had snapped. My arms and legs waved like a rag doll's. My feet slapped the floor in a horrible dance. She was so strong. Just like mom. Too strong, and I hadn't even considered it.

The Lady tossed me.

When I hit the ground, I hit so hard that I skipped, and I flew another two feet before I crashed into a roll. The roll brought me up hard against the hearth, where my head cracked against river stones and my blood mixed something like iron into the scent of burning pine and smoke and lavender.

I tried to roll onto my knees. My body, however, didn't respond. I was too tired. I hurt too much. I had tried and I had failed, and every horrible thought drifted over me, burying me in black snow, each icy granule sucking the heat and life from me. I had never been strong enough. I had never been smart enough. I couldn't save the people I loved. I couldn't save the people who deserved to be saved. I couldn't even save myself, and I was shit, and I was worse than shit, and I deserved everything that had happened to me. All of it. I had deserved it because if you laid the iron and the vacuum cleaner cord and the cigarettes and all the rest of it, if you laid all of that on one side of the cosmic scale, I still came up short. For a lot of reasons. But mostly because of this night. Another scream, a longer scream, came from the valley and blew through the cabin like a frozen wind. This epic failure.

Get up, I told myself.

Get up.

You can either die like the broken fuck you are, or you can get up.

Tyler had called me Thor.

Hannah had held my hand.

Austin had loved me against every good reason.

Emmett had dragged a razor up the inside of his arm.

Somehow, I flopped onto my stomach.

Somehow, I got my knees under me.

The scene playing out in front of me froze me for a moment. Tyler stood on one side of the room. On the opposite, Hannah's spirit perched above her body. A psychic gale ripped through the other side: the hypersaturated colors bled and swirled and streamed toward Tyler. I could feel the tremendous energy he was exerting, dragging the other side toward himself. From her place on the other side, Hannah was pushing. Between them, the glass-edged outline of the War Chief slipped and bled toward Tyler.

In a matter of moments, he would pass through the boy and to this side of reality, and then he would need a host, and—

The pistol touched the gash that the river stone hearth had opened in my head, and I hissed with pain and tried to jerk away. The gun followed.

"Stay nice and still," my dad said. His voice was flat. Flat like river stones. Flat like the small gray disc that once he had cupped my hand around. Flat like that perfect oval when he had gripped my wrist and guided me into the throw, and it had snicked through the air and then splish-splish-splish dimpled the water. "It'll be over soon, and they told me you won't feel anything."

That day skipping stones had been one day. One summer day, just a blip, nothing special, really, except I had felt loved. And I had loved him. That was what hurt so much, just as it had with Mom, just as it had with Gage. Love dug its roots deep, and you couldn't rip it out or burn it out or cut it out. All you could do was stop feeding it and hope it died, and it almost never did. That was the worst part: that I had loved Dad, that I had loved Mom, that I had loved Gage long after they had hurt me. That I still loved them, in fact. That I might always love them in some weird, twisted, aching way that made me feel foolish and weak and desperate and so very, very stupid.

"I love you."

Dad ripped down with the pistol, the muzzle gouging my scalp and forcing my head down. My jaw clicked shut. Blood slicked my teeth.

"Shut up."

"I do." Twisting, trying to find a way around the unrelenting pressure of the gun, I said it again, "I love you."

"Shut up."

This time, I managed to slide until the muzzle skipped past my ear, and I turned, the iron sight biting into my neck deep enough that warmth trickled down my collarbone, formed a hot bead in the hollow of my throat.

"It's fucked up," I said. "I wish I didn't. But it doesn't work that way." I swallowed, closed my eyes. I thought of River. I thought of the monster letting himself out of the closet. In my mind—in my heart—I reached out for that closet door and threw it open. Nothing. No monster. And then I breathed out and looked up. "You're my dad."

Something unfurled inside my mind: the curling edges of a scroll, the wings of a great bird, the roots of an aspen running under loam.

The gun cracked against my face low, the sight slicing along my cheekbone, and then struck again. The blows exploded in white, powdery bursts. Like snow, I thought, clutching at the hearth to keep from falling. Like somebody kicking the best powder after a fresh fall. And then the pain avalanched, and I bent and tightened my throat to keep from puking.

"You can say whatever you want, kid." His eyes crystallized above me, the hard blue crust of a mountaintop in summer. "This is the way it's got to be."

"I know." Those roots shimmied under loose soil, spreading, reaching out into the darkness.

"You try anything funny, and I'll shoot you. You know me. You know I wouldn't fuck around about something like that, even if you are mine."

"I know." The roots spread and tangled and spread again. They glowed like aspen leaves in October sunlight. They were part of me shooting off into the black spaces of my mind. Maybe they were my brain, I thought, feeling my whole face snap into a grin. Maybe they were my brain leaking out my ears.

"Jesus. Jesus Christ, will you turn the fuck around? I'm just doing what I've got to do. That's all. It's not personal."

And it wasn't personal. Not at all. I felt a crazy smile skid across my lips and then burn rubber out into space. "I know. But I do love you."

The roots in my mind twisted and spread again, and this time, they touched water. Water rich with minerals, cold and clear and deep. Water like moonlight and silver and glass. Only it wasn't water. It was power. It was love. It was my friends. The people who cared about me, even if this man didn't. The people who made me more than I would have been otherwise. Austin, a blast furnace of red-hot steel. Emmett, the ultraviolet stitching between the stars. They balanced inside my head. They turned me into fire.

Then, "You do what you've got to do. So will I."

And then I slipped out of my body. Completely. Totally. The way I had left my body at Emmett's and reached the other side. With the sudden rush of power, it was easy, and it came over me the same way as before: the sudden numbness, an anesthetized relief at the absence of everything: pain and hate and tears and hope and love. My physical body crumpled, my head sliding down my dad's leg until I sprawled on the floor. I turned my back on him and on my body. I heard the gunshot behind me, and I steadied myself with a breath. Well, there it was. He had shot me. I couldn't feel it, thank God, not this deep into the other side. But I knew what he'd done. I'd known he would do it before I made my decision. If I survived the nightmare in front of me, I would get back into my body just in time to bleed out.

It didn't matter now. I focused on the scene ahead of me. This deep into the other side, I could see Urho—not just the shadow, not just the glass-edged monster that had ripped open my neck. The man. He was short, his paunch spilling over rawhide chaps, and his hair fell in long braids down his back. He looked old. His eyes, when he saw me, were like two chips of asphalt that a dump truck had kicked up—a dirty, greasy black that had looked cheap from the first minute.

"You're too late."

He was sliding across the floor, the hypersaturated colors of the other side streaming past him as Hannah used her ability to push him out of the other side and Tyler dragged him onto the physical plane. Urho wasn't a visitor here; he wasn't like me, his psychic self projected from a physical body. This was all that was left of Urho, and he was rooted here even more deeply than Hannah. Hannah's spirit they had pinned here by damaging her chakras; Urho was here because he was dead. And what they needed to bring him back, to carry him through the veil between worlds, was a psychic. A true psychic. I could have helped him across because I could touch both sides. Lacking my ability, they had improvised two psychic engines to pump him across: two kids. Two innocents who had never hurt anyone.

"You're going to hell," I said to Urho.

He laughed, and his paunch jiggled, and his braids danced a tarantula dance across his back.

"And I'm going to send you there."

"You had your chance. And now that time is gone. We will keep you. You will be the first in the dust feast. These children will follow you in the feast. And the feast will never end."

He slid another few inches. Around him, reality shredded and tore, the tatters snapping like pennants in a strong wind as the combined force from Tyler and Hannah drilled between planes of existence.

She is hungry. River's words echoed in my mind. A true psychic. She is hungry.

"The dust feast," I said.

"You will know pain like you've never imagined." Urho laughed again. His belly bounced, creasing the rawhide chaps. "Each scrap of your mind, each quivering slice of flesh, each drop of blood will become flesh of her flesh."

She is hungry.

A true psychic.

I took another step toward the punctured veil between worlds. Urho's eyes followed me with open amusement; he bared his teeth in what might have been a smile. He was missing an eye tooth. He looked like he'd never owned a toothbrush.

She is hungry.

A true psychic.

I looked past the ragged edges of existence. I saw the Lady, her hands still primly at her waist, the shrunken creature inside her howling and scratching and clawing. Urho slid another inch. From between that torn partition, a howling noise rose—the shriek of the walls between worlds going under the psychic equivalent of an augur.

She is hungry.

A true psychic.

Like me.

I grabbed Urho's braids before he knew what was happening and lunged. He shouted, stumbling, as I swaddled him in my power. He slipped free of the psychic magnetism that Hannah and Tyler were driving, lurching after me, his hands going to his head, his eyes wide with shock. I dragged him with me. I was here, fully here, in a way that I had only been once before, and I was in the fullness of my strength, channeling a river of molten power.

Ginny was right. I couldn't attack with this power. I couldn't tear Urho to shreds the way I had pulled Luke into ribbons or sent Krystal drifting away in motes of cinder and ash.

Love was about navigating the black spaces of the universe. Love was a lighthouse at the edge of the world. Love—a smile crossed my face as I remembered months before, how simple it had been, how hard, trying to understand my power.

Love was a bridge.

And so I built a bridge across two planes of reality, and I tossed Urho across it. For a moment, the shock on his face waxed into indignation; I don't know if anyone had ever pitched Urho like a sack of dirty socks before. And then awareness swept over him, and victory sparked in his face. I watched as his spirit raced across the span of power I had extended through the veil between worlds. I watched the glow of triumph go stellar in Urho's face. I watched, and I saw the moment of horror when he realized what I'd done.

Urho did need a vessel. He needed a body for his spirit. But he sure as hell didn't want the one I gave him.

As realization burned out Urho's expression from the inside, he turned, trying to scramble back along the span of power I had extended, trying to drag himself back into the other side. But the bridge was long and steep and it was mine, and so I shunted him along its length, letting it crumble behind him, leaving no way back.

And his spirit lanced straight into the husk of the Lady's body. For a moment, his spirit swelled, smoked up, filling the nooks and crannies of the Lady's physical form, seeking an escape. The shriveled, nightmare abomination that lived inside the Lady twisted. It writhed. Its sallow, hollow cheeks quivered.

And then, shrieking with rage and helplessness, it launched itself at Urho's spirit and began to eat.

It began to feast.

The screams reverberated across the other side.

I watched as Urho first tried to resist, tried to restrain the Lady's spirit. But River was right: she was hungry. Hungry and rabid, and Urho's spirit might have been like old, tough jerky, but it was still food, and she ripped into him like he was a turkey dinner. I felt a certain vicious satisfaction as I listened to their shared screams because I knew that the Lady didn't want this any more than Urho did, but she couldn't help herself. She'd been saving up for her fucking dust feast. She should have paced herself. Maybe had a snack.

The current of power rushing through me was still strong, but I could tell that I was starting to flag. I turned my attention to Hannah. The psychic floodgates that she and Tyler had opened were now closed; Tyler sat on the floor, his face fixed in a kind of impersonal hatred that looked like it was locked into muscle memory. Hannah was crying, her head on her knees. Sobbing.

"Come on," I said, taking her hand and squeezing it.

"I didn't want to. I didn't, Vie. I didn't want to, but they did something to me, and then they did something else, and part of me isn't working. Part of my head, I mean. I can't—" She started crying again.

"Come on. Let's get you home."

I helped her to her feet and led her to the sofa where her body lay stretched out on the cushions. The vortex of power in me was slowing. The well of moonlight where I dipped my hand was shallow; soon, my fingers would scrape gravel at the bottom. I tried to stretch another bridge between worlds, and I couldn't.

"River."

He was there, hands in the pockets of his denim jacket, before I'd finished saying his name. "That was pretty good work."

"We're blood."

He nodded. "We're brothers."

Steering Hannah's spirit by the shoulder, I set her between us. "You push. I'll pull. And River?"

He raised an eyebrow.

"Gently."

I didn't want to go back to my body. I didn't want to die. But the numbness of this place worked on my heart like ketamine. It hadn't bothered me to rip every stitch out of Krystal's soul as I dragged her to the other side. It hadn't bothered me to imprison Urho inside the Lady's body and watch as the two souls savaged each other to pieces. It had amused me. Even now, I couldn't feel any horror at it, only a detached interest and a lingering sense of satisfaction.

And that was the danger. I might be able to stay. My body would die, and I might be able to keep a version of myself alive here. I would have River for company. And Samantha, if she was still around. And I could find Emmett in his dreams. And I could watch the world spin by without me.

But a part of me knew that Urho had made the same decision. He had stayed on the other side, and he had become more of a monster in death than he had been in life. I had already faced all the monsters I needed to. I didn't care for the idea of becoming another one. River's words came back again: *The monster walks himself out of the closet, flips the lights on his own goddamn self.*

I'd wanted to die for a long time. That black hole in my head had eaten up so much of my life. It had ruined every good thing in my life. Even Austin. Especially Austin. And now, with death riding toward my front door, I finally wanted to live.

What we want, though—that's never what we get.

So I closed my eyes and slipped back into my dying body, pulling Hannah with me across the barrier between worlds. There was tension, resistance. Then I felt my big brother give a very gentle push. And then we were across.

# Chapter | 39

First was the pain. All the cuts and aches that had followed me up the mountain, plus some new ones. In my face. On the right side of my face. And a ringing in my ears that washed out all other sound. But it didn't hurt as bad as I'd thought. Maybe he'd shot me in my head. That's why my face hurt. That's why the pain wasn't as bad as I expected it to be; he'd blown out some crucial center of my brain, and I was in shock, and in a few minutes, I'd be gone.

Except no wave of blackness crashed over me. And the pain didn't get any better. If anything, it got worse, and I groaned as the ringing in my ears seemed to double, and the side of my face throbbed in a dozen different places. I'd only been out of my body for a few minutes—had he cut me? Was my face in ribbons?

The part of my brain that was still working disassembled that idea rather quickly. I could feel my face, and although it hurt, it was more like a series of sharp pinpricks than long, sustained cuts. I blinked, forced my eyes to stay open, and a migraine rushed down my optic nerve. It was so goddamn bright. Not the steady yellow of electric bulbs; flickering, and I remembered the candles, and the spatter of dried wax. But this light was much brighter than candles. And there was heat, too—pressing against me, walling one side of my body.

"Vie?" That was Hannah's voice, and it pierced my head like a steam whistle. I groaned and tried not to throw up. "Vie? Are you—oh."

Then the steel-capped toe of a boot dug into my back, low, just above the kidney. "Up, boy-o." Then harder, and this time, I had to flop onto my stomach, gagging against the pain. "Up, right fucking now."

Something pricked my nose. I forced myself to concentrate, to pay attention. With my forehead resting on the boards, I was nuzzled up to a bullet hole in the floor. Splinters poked and prodded my nose.

I ran fingers over the side of my face and found more slivers. I jerked one loose, and it felt like my head was a balloon and I'd just popped it. The world went white.

I didn't even realize my dad was dragging me upright until my soles scuffed the floor. He had a good grip on my collar, twisting it until it choked me—not enough to make me black out, but enough that it was about all I could do to stay on my feet and suck air. Black pinwheeled across my vision, and I tried to pick out details.

Fire. Fire licked up the wall opposite me. The cedar log siding spat and popped, and the smoke whirled on thermals toward the high ceiling. From the hearth, a trail of still burning logs and embers ran to the base of the wall. Someone had spread the fire. Someone had intended for it to catch.

The Lady stood still as the blaze crept along her hem. The ancient black skirt burned easily, the flames twisting around her like crepe paper. From this distance, I was close enough to see the wrinkled flesh of her hands blister in the heat. I could see the first black fissure open where the heat ate at the fat in her arm, and the skin split and yawned open.

But she didn't move. Her hands were still in that posy knot at her waist. Only her face showed any flicker of life, and it was horrible. Her jaw sagged. Drool glistened and dripped off her chin. Firelight spun yellow yarn in that drool. Her cheeks quivered, spasmed, clenched. Her eyes spun. Black drifted over the orange like ink in clear water, and then the orange would burn off the black again. The battle was still going on.

Hauling me up another inch, Dad walked me backward until I was pressed against his chest, and he leaned over my shoulder, eyes intent on the nightmare struggle in the Lady's eyes.

"You did that, did you? You're one lucky son of a bitch. Guess I was right not to put all my chips on that old bitch." He watched another moment. "Aw, fuck, that fire isn't fast enough."

The pistol glided up. He aimed for the length of one slow, steady breath, and then his index finger crooked hard, and the pistol kicked. The sound of the gunshot that close to my head left my ears ringing again, but I didn't care about my ears.

Dad's shot had taken the Lady in the throat, and what spilled out of her didn't look like blood. It was black and thick and textured. At first, it reminded me of the oldest, wettest leaves at the end of autumn, the ones at the bottom of the mulch pile that have gone dark with rot. But this was blood, I realized. Old, yes. And thick, yes. Clotted, ancient blood.

Would the same thing come out of my mom's throat?

My knees went out at the thought, and the twisted collar of my shirt bit into my throat, and blackness snowed across my vision.

Dad shook me. "Walk, boy. Right fucking now."

Hannah peered over the sofa. My Hannah. In her body, all of her. She stared at each of us. The pistol dug into my back, in the same spot where the boot had kicked me. She didn't say anything, but her eyes flicked to the right.

Then I saw Tyler. He was kneeling on the floor, his face vacant, his little hands hanging at his side like he'd just fumbled his first pass or biffed it at t-ball or caught nothing but air when he ran up for a kick in soccer: a boyish disbelief mixed with total disappointment.

"Tyler?" I struggled against Dad's grip, never mind the gun jabbing me in the kidney. "Tyler, wake up!"

Fire snaked along the chandelier's rope, gobbled the wood, blackened the tips of elk antlers. As the fire grew, wax rained down in huge fat drops. One struck Tyler's cheek and hung there like bird shit. Even though it must have hurt—the wax was hot, and when a gobbet smacked my hand, right between my fingers, I yelped and tried to shake it off—Tyler didn't move.

"Leave him. He's fucking retarded anyway." Twisting tighter on my shirt, Dad dragged me, and my heels slipped and skipped along the polished boards as I tried to get purchase and pull myself free. I spun, slapping at the gun at my back, raking my nails along Dad's hand, grabbing his belt and yanking on it as though I could somehow reverse his momentum.

We made it about five yards like that, two cats scratching in a burlap sack, when Dad gave me another shake and shoved me away from him. I hit the floor on my knees. Air rushed into my lungs; everything brightened and pressed closer as oxygen rushed to my brain. I closed my eyes to keep from falling over. I breathed cedar smoke and tasted blood and the raw, lingering bile in my throat.

"You can fucking burn with them, then," Dad said, and I glanced back and saw him at the doorway. "You ever come looking for me, or you tell your bitch mother about any of this, and I'll personally cut off your balls and—"

His jaw sagged. His eyes went wide. For a moment, he looked like a man in an ecstasy, like a saint or martyr about to be hauled up on some sort of divine fly-line. Then he dropped, his knees folding, his face planting hard on the boards.

Behind him, Austin drew back the butt of his rifle and aimed the weapon into the cabin.

Our eyes met.

"Are you—" He shouted hoarsely over the crackle of the flames. "Are you you?"

Slowly, I got to my feet. The rifle followed me. Flames danced in the green-blue mirrors of Austin's eyes.

"What the hell do you think I'd say even if it weren't really me?"

"Vie?" Hannah shouted. "Vie, the fire's getting really hot. Vie!"

Austin's mouth hardened and thinned. The friction burn on his neck from Krystal's vine was ugly in the firelight, and his voice rasped as he said, "Tell me something so I know it's you."

I didn't even think. The words just came out. "I know we broke up. I know I don't have any right to say this. But you deserve better than Kaden. You deserve someone who loves you totally, completely, for the amazing person you are, not somebody who will sleep with you because he wants to save you. I don't care if you fuck every other guy in town, I don't care if we're broken up and it's none of my business, I'm telling you that he's going to be the biggest fucking mistake of your life if you let him."

Austin's head lowered infinitesimally as he sighted down the barrel. His finger was tight around the trigger. Then he fired.

It took me a moment to realize I hadn't been hit, and I shot a look over my shoulder. Lawayne Karkkanew took a stumbling step back, his hand over his chest where a rose blossomed wetly across a canvas shirt. Then Lawayne sat down hard. Blood bubbled pinkly at his mouth; he was breathing like he'd climbed a mountain, which I guess he had. And then he sagged against the corner of the fireplace and died. A pistol clattered onto the floor.

Lowering the rifle, Austin cast another cold look across the cabin before his gaze settled on me. "You are possibly the most jealous person I've ever met."

"I'm not jealous. I'm telling you he's bad for you."

With a shake of his head, Austin stepped over my dad's body and limped toward the sofa. He encircled Hannah with one arm and lifted her onto his hip; he was breathing funny.

I followed his example, jogging back to where Tyler knelt and raising him in my arms. His skin was hot; blisters welled on his neck, and he flinched when I pressed him to me. But he didn't speak, and after that initial reaction, he didn't shift or struggle. I brushed his mind with mine and found those same lines of broken glass and barbed wire, and I hissed and swallowed a swear.

When I rejoined Austin, he was pressing Hannah's head into his shoulder, whispering into her ear, "Don't look. I'll tell you when you can look, ok?"

She nodded once, her small frame molding itself around Austin, her back trembling as she sucked in air and cried. Austin dragged the rifle's strap over his shoulder and then stroked her back once with his free hand. Then again. And he whispered something else in her ear, and her whole body jerked once, and then, after a few more moments, once more, and then she lay quietly against him. He wiped her cheeks and patted her back one more time.

"How'd you do that?" I asked as I followed him to the door.

Under the starlight, everything was pale about him except the abraded skin of his neck, which looked black and rough in comparison. He led us out into the snow, which sloughed off my fevered cheeks, melted, dripped off my jaw.

Austin fumbled something out of his back pocket and spoke into it: a walkie-talkie. Jake's voice crackled back, and off in the distance, headlights bored holes into the night. They rocked and bounced toward us. A way out of here. A way home.

We stood there together, waiting.

As the headlights came closer, Austin broke the silence between us. "You don't care if I fuck every other guy in town, huh?"

My hand trembled on Tyler's back, trying to massage the tension out of the child's body, and in spite of my best effort my voice came out with a million little shakes in it. "Just not Kaden."

"Every other guy?"

"Everybody's allowed one slutty phase."

His wheeze of laughter sounded grotesque but honest, and Hannah jolted upright in his arms. He had to soothe her against him, still laughing, pausing as he stroked her back to wipe his eyes and keep laughing. And the headlights bounced through the snowscape.

When he'd stopped laughing, he looked at me, and his eyes shone with firelight and with the refracted gleam off the snow and with something else, with something that came from deep inside him and burned like the last star before morning.

"There's really only one guy." He shifted Hannah to his other shoulder, and he could have looked away then, but he didn't. He'd always been the brave one. He'd always been much braver than I. "For me, you know. Just one. And I know I messed up, but—"

The Charger roared out of the darkness, a cobalt streak like electricity in a blackout, and as it spun hard on the soft prairie soil, the passenger door flew open, and Emmett stumbled out. He hit me at a full run, clutching me to him, his hands turning my head, pulling out my arms, spinning me, checking every inch of me like he wanted to make sure every piece was still in place, and then he clutched me again, his mouth on my mouth, his mouth on my cheek, his mouth on my jaw, his mouth on my ear, his mouth whispering. "I love you, Jesus Christ, you're ok, oh my God, I fucking love you, oh Christ, oh Christ, you're ok, Jesus Christ, you're here, you're ok, right, you're ok? Right, Vie, right? Tell me you're ok."

When he pulled back to study my eyes, I looked past him. Just for a second. For one single instant. And I saw Austin, soot blackening the bridge of his nose, blood staining his coat where a knife had parted fabric and flesh. In spite of the wound, he was still standing, and his hand moved slowly down Hannah's back, and he whispered softly in her ear, and she raised her head slightly and looked around, and then she laughed, just a soft little laugh, but it was the first pure sound that pocket of hell had ever heard, and then she shivered and snuggled back against Austin, and his eyes never left mine, never flicked away, never wavered, because he'd always been the bravest one.

"I'm fine," I said, my eyes going back to Emmett, and then Em kissed me, dragging me against him, trying to squeeze me even with Tyler's body between us.

One last, treacherous, traitorous glance. Just one. And I saw Austin smile, and maybe it was just a trick of the snow and the shadows, maybe it was just my imagination, but he nodded his head, and I thought I saw the starlight wink out in his eyes.

# Chapter | 40

We drove out of the mountains: Em and I on the Ducati, Jake and Temple Mae and Austin and Kaden and Becca in the Charger with the kids, and Sharrika driving the Impala with Jim passed out in the seat next to her. When we got off the last service road and turned onto the state highway, Sheriff Hatcher had his cruiser parked across both lanes, and he got out and leaned hard on the hood, like he'd almost fallen over, and stared into the glare of the headlights.

His breath steamed and spun snowflakes in reverse. "What the hell happened?"

I shook my head.

"Damn near felt like the mountains were coming down on us."

"It's over."

He breathed out again slowly, his faced washed white and two-dimensional by the halogen bulbs. "Is that a fact?"

I thought of Kyle Stark-Taylor, whom we had left with a line of electricity running into his body. What would he do when that last charge ran out? Would he come after us? Would he pull down the Bighorns and bury Vehpese? Temple Mae had told me with one single word what had happened to Leo: *Dead.* And her feline eyes had filled with tears, and she'd slapped me. So Leo wasn't a problem. But Kyle.

I shrugged.

"You need a hospital."

"Some of us."

"Let's go, then."

And our shitty little parade streamed after the blues and reds until we reached the Western Bighorn Hospital, west of Vehpese—the closest medical facility after Kyle had torn down the hospital in town. As we got out of the cars, the sight of my friends hit me like a sucker punch. None of us looked good. I knew that I looked like shit, and a long bloody rash ran down Temple Mae's forehead, and Sharrika kept looking around and letting off these shrill bursts of laughter. Becca, somehow, had survived with nothing but a palmprint of dirt smeared across one cheek. Jake had a bloody lip—no, scratch that. When I got closer, I saw that a part of his lip had actually been severed and was dangling by a scrap of flesh. And the kid hadn't complained, hadn't even made a noise. Emmett looked like he'd been kicked down a few different hills—his leather jacket was scuffed and torn in a dozen places, and the cut on his neck had reopened and soaked his shirt.

But they were the walking wounded. They were the ones who had come out more or less in one piece.

Kaden and Jim and Austin hadn't. Kaden could barely stand, and Jake and Emmett had to lift him out of the car by the elbows, and the granola boy with a hand-stitched peace sign on his Vineyard Vines polo went into some kind of seizure the minute he touched the ground. His back arched, and his head shot from side to side, and for one terrible moment I thought he was trying to bite Emmett and Jake. Then he lurched forward, bending in the opposite direction, and spewed frothy white vomit all over the curb. Jake's face was grim, but he kept a strong grip. Emmett danced backward. He was trying to save his retro Jordans. A crew of nurses and techs got Kaden onto a stretcher while the rest of us watched.

Jim, in contrast, was unresponsive, and no amount of calling his name could rouse him. They took him on a stretcher too.

Austin, though.

I knew I'd have nightmares about him, about this night, the rest of my life.

That cut in his coat, the one that had left a bloody oval on the fabric? It was bad. Really bad. A lot worse than Austin had let anyone know. When he tried to stand, still clutching Hannah against him, he wheezed, and pink spume ran around his mouth like coral. I shifted Tyler's weight and went for Austin, trying to get an arm around him, and Austin slapped my chest with the back of his hand and shook his head and grinned, just this huge motherfucking shit-eating grin, and that pink spume popped around his mouth and surged back with his next breath.

"Uh uh," he said, and the words sucked and gasped in his chest, but he was still smiling. "I get to do this. Me."

"Austin, you need—Christ, I don't know what you need, like ten hours of surgery or something, but you can't—"

"Vie." He gave me another soft whap with the back of his hand.

Pressing Tyler's head against my shoulder, I stumbled out of Austin's path. He took a step, and his knee folded, and Becca lunged for him. But Austin didn't fall. And he shook his head at Becca, and she fell back. He took another step. More nurses and techs were pouring out of the building now, some with stretchers, some with first-aid kits, some just staring. Austin headed to the closest one, a dark-haired woman with pinched eyes, still stroking Hannah's back. He coughed, and his knee went out again like a trap door, but he caught himself, coughed, and some of that pink coral spattered across the back of his hand. I would dream about this. That was the only thought in my head as I clutched at Tyler. I would dream about this forever.

"Hannah," Austin said with those horrible, gasping sucks of air from the wound in his chest. "This is Nurse McDonald. She's going to take you inside, ok? And I'll be there in a few minutes. And your mom."

Hannah raised her head for an instant, scanned her surroundings, and dropped back against Austin's chest. She must have said something because he ran his hand up and down her back one last time. "Sorry, Hannah, but you have to. You've got to go—what?" He cocked an ear toward her. "Yeah, Vie'll be there too. Ok. Ok. Here you go."

And he passed her to Nurse McDonald, whose pinched eyes looked like they'd been forced open with sticks of dynamite. But to the woman's credit, she took Hannah gently and helped her onto the stretcher, and then she turned, and the crowd parted and jogged the stretcher toward the building. A few others went with her.

Everyone else was frozen.

Austin looked like a breeze was lifting him. Or like a current. And then he gargled something, and blood shot out of his mouth, and he fell. A big, bald guy in scrubs caught him before he could crack his head on the pavement, and it was like some invisible clock had suddenly resumed ticking.

Everyone flew into motion. Some of them whisked Austin into the hospital; others swarmed my group, separating us out, a kind of triage-blitz that resulted in all of us being dragged in separate directions, even Tyler being pulled from my arms. He didn't protest. He didn't even blink. I met his eyes once, and I brushed against his mind, and I found the same broken-bottle pieces turned out against the world, ready to cut anyone who tried to come and help.

I found myself alone in an exam room. The curtain was the color of old paper, and the room smelled like drugstore liniment. A built-in cabinet was papered over with a flyer for a blood drive (October 19, 1999), a detailed explanation of the Bird Flu, an irregularly-sized, hand-lettered piece announcing chlamydia statistics for the fall of 2017 in Mather, Sheridan, Big Horn, Washakie, and Johnson counties. I decided I needed to have a talk with Emmett. And, maybe, with Austin.

The Crow woman was wearing a different pearl snap shirt, but the same jeans and the same boots, and tonight her white coat had a name tag that said *Dr. Bird*. She eyed me up and down, whistled, and jotted something on my chart. Something about the little flourish at the end annoyed me, and I said, "What did you write?"

"Stray got in a dog fight."

"Fuck you."

She laughed, and the lines around her eyes deepened. It was a surprisingly deep laugh, and it was so pleasant and good-natured that I felt a small smile on my mouth. And then my eyes stung, and I had to tuck my face into my elbow and snort a few times and really scrub with my sleeve to keep from falling apart.

When I looked up again, she was sitting on a stool facing me, a tray with sterilized instruments and gauze and a hypodermic needle on a syringe. "As far as I know," she said, filling the syringe from a small bottle, "they're all in good hands. Most of them are already in recovery."

"Most of them?"

"This is a lidocaine solution. Otherwise it's going to hurt like a mother when I work on those splinters and the other cuts you've got."

"What do you mean most?"

"One boy is still in surgery. And two of them—it's hard to know what's wrong with them. Shock. Exhaustion. Traumatic stress." She shrugged and held up the hypo. "You can't do anything except wait, so we might as well get this part done."

"Are you supposed to be telling me this? Isn't it confidential?"

One of her dark, bushy brows went up. "Keep asking stupid questions, and I'll put enough lidocaine in your face to keep you from talking for a week."

"Is Austin going to be ok?"

Her eyes were kind but frank, and she took my chin and turned my face before the needle stung me. "That's a stupid question. I don't know. He's still in surgery."

My cheek seemed to balloon, and I probed the puffiness with my tongue. The words that came out sounded mushy on the edges. "I think I'm still in love with him. You don't even know me, but I've got to tell somebody, or my head is going to explode, and what the fuck am I supposed to say to Emmett? What he did for me, what the fuck am I supposed to say about that?"

She eyed the hypo as though trying to decide whether or not to give me more—to get me to shut up, I guessed. Then she laid it back on the tray. She clasped her hands between her knees. Her boots had fresh mud on them. She looked like the kind of woman who could shoe a horse and till a field and fill a hypo with lidocaine all in the same day.

"You're in love."

I shrugged.

She waited.

I nodded.

She nodded. "That explains all the stupid questions, then." She picked up a pair of what looked like tweezers and turned my face toward the light. "Every boy who's ever been in love is an absolute moron."

I was about to object when she yanked out the first splinter, and she did it so forcefully I half expected, even with the anesthetic, for half my cheek to come off with it. After that, I decided Dr. Bird didn't need to hear about my love life.

The problem, of course, was the way Austin looked at me when I said Kaden was bad for him. The problem was the way he had looked at me when he cradled Hannah and stroked her back. The problem was the way his voice had gone soft when he said, *There's really only one guy*. And then the little crack that had followed, the little crack in his voice when he said, *For me, you know. Just one*. That crack was the sound of his armor falling off him, hitting the ground in pieces. That crack was the sound of him being the brave one. Again. And that was the problem. The problem was that Austin had always been the brave one, and I'd always been the coward.

"Houston, hello, Houston." Dr. Bird waved a hand in front of me. "You got a problem?"

I blinked and touched the side of my face. My fingers found gauze taped over the wounds. Her laugh lines crinkled as she studied me. I forced myself to meet her eyes. "Yeah. A big one."

"You guys have a fight?"

"I was an asshole. A jealous asshole."

"I dated a jealous asshole once. It was fun until it wasn't."

Behind her, the curtain twitched. Chucks poked under the bottom of the curtain. And then a pair of retro Jordans.

"You need to talk to someone? The hospital has a shrink. I could find her for you."

I shook my head.

The stool's castor creaked as she wheeled away from me. Patting her white coat into place, Dr. Bird stood, snapped back the curtain, and said, "You take a few minutes, just stay here. If we need the room, though, I'm kicking you out."

I nodded.

"Bye, stray."

I gave her the middle finger, and she laughed again and was gone.

Becca was standing there when Dr. Bird left. The owner of the retro Jordans, however, was gone.

For a moment, Becca and I just watched each other. I wanted to ask about those retro Jordans. Instead, I said, "Are you ok?"

She nodded.

Somewhere out in the waiting room, a baby was crying. Shrieking, really, just this intense, high-pitched note that seemed like it went on forever.

"Kaden? And Jim?"

"They won't let us in to see them. They won't say anything. Ms. Meehan left. She took Mr. Spencer's car, and she's gone, Vie. Jake and Temple Mae want to leave. They're only still here because Austin's in surgery and his parents are on their way, but I think if it were up to Temple Mae, they'd walk out that door and go to Mexico or Aruba or somewhere and just disappear. She won't talk to me. She won't even look at me. And it's not like we were friends or anything, but she won't look at me, Vie, like she can't even stand the fact that I exist, and I can't—I can't—" She clapped both hands over her face and sat down, and her foot tipped up so that only the toes of her Chucks scuffed the vinyl tiles, and her heels bounced against the empty air.

"I need to see Austin."

"Well, they're not going to let you see him." She brought her hands down, and her face was dry and flushed, and her palms cracked against her knees. "He's in surgery. And his family is here. And—" She bit off the word so savagely that she tore her head to one side

"And he broke up with me."

"Can we just go home, Vie? I just want to go home tonight."

I thought of Sara, here, in the Western Bighorn Hospital, just a few floors above me, still recovering from a heart attack and a gunshot wound. Austin's dad had driven here last night—Christ, was it only last night?—to make sure his sister was still alive. He was doing that drive again tonight, only this time it was his son, and his son might not make it through the night.

"We're going to have to hitch."

The toes of her Chucks squeaked on the vinyl. "I've hitched before."

"No, you haven't."

"We did something good, today, right? That's what I keep telling myself. We did something good. I should be proud of that. I helped with something that's going to save a lot of lives. Save a lot of children.

But then I think about Jim and Kaden and Austin. Then I try to talk to Temple Mae. I look at your face, and I don't know anymore. None of it makes any sense."

"What's wrong with my face?"

She ran the ridge of her hand under her nose.

"It's a pretty fucking ugly face, I guess."

She sniffled. "You're so stupid sometimes."

"Sometimes I breathe through my mouth and look like I need to be on life support."

She sniffled into her knuckles. Her eyes zipped up to mine and then back down.

"When it's summer, I get these ugly patches of freckles, and Pete Bernier told me in third grade that it looked like God took a dump on my cheeks."

She laughed, and the volume of it shocked even her because she steepled her hands over her mouth. "You are probably the dumbest boy I've ever met. And I've seen you in the summer. And you don't really have freckles anymore."

"Tell that to Pete." I stood, held out a hand. "I want to do one thing before we find a long-haul trucker who won't slit our throats and drop us at a rest stop."

The soles of her Chucks smacked down. "I bet you say that to all the girls."

But she took my hand. And we wound a way through the hallways until we stood outside a third-floor room, where the door spilled open and light arced across the vinyl. From inside came the soft, struggling breaths, and the click of a woman's heel, and then the rustle of paper.

"But they're going to be all right? I just want you to tell me they're going to be all right."

That was Shay.

And then, her mother's voice: "They've been over this. They can't—"

"I want him to tell me they're going to be all right. And then he can go do whatever he needs to do."

"It's not that simple, Ms. Cribbs."

"It's Harwood. I'm changing it back. Back to Harwood, I mean."

"Ms. Harwood, your daughter is fine—physically, anyway. Aside from a few scrapes and bruises, she's in very good health. It's hard to know, though, the extent of the psychological trauma that she's undergone, and at her age, without some of the resilience that comes with age—"

"You mean she's not tough. But she is. We're all tough; we had to be. Hannah will be fine. It's Tyler I want you to tell me about."

"We just don't know. I'm sorry, but that's all I can say. We just don't know. He reacts to physical stimuli—his pupils respond to light and movement; his hearing is undamaged; his reflexes—"

"He just sits there. He just sits there and stares. I don't want to hear about reflexes, and I don't care if you shine something at him and he blinks. I want to know where my baby is."

"And he can't tell you." That was Lucy Harwood's brittle snap. "He's not going to lie—"

"Ms. Harwood, he's exhibiting behavior typical of post-traumatic stress disorder, a kind of catatonia, and that means he's not able to move and react the way he should. We've got a lot of options for treatment, and we're going to . . ."

I tugged on Becca's sleeve; she wiped her face and followed me. We left those voices behind us, and when I stopped in an alcove where a vending machine had a 3 Musketeers bar hanging halfway off a silver spring, I met Becca's eyes and said, "Did we do a good thing?"

She nodded.

"Let me run to the bathroom, and we'll go. Meet me downstairs?"

She nodded again. I took a step away, and then Becca said, not looking at me, "I'm glad we saved those kids. And I'm glad . . . I'm glad nobody else will have to go through that again. But why do I feel so awful?"

I shook my head. "Just shock. Stress. And you're exhausted. It'll be better in the morning. Gotta pee, Becca. I'll see you downstairs."

I trotted away from her and didn't look back, but instead of ducking into the restroom, I found the closest flight of stairs and climbed to the fourth floor. The fluorescent lights were louder here; the buzz went all the way to my bones, and I had a million almost-invisible shadows petaling around me on the vinyl. It was quieter here. I paced the length of one hallway. Then I paced the next one. And then I saw Don and Debra Miller in a waiting room, and I stopped.

They looked like the Road Runner after he'd gone under a bulldozer. Flattened. Lifeless. Don kept grabbing at a pink paisley tie; he was still in his suit, his hair still in its perfect part, and he'd grab that tie and weave it between his fingers and every once in a while yank on it like it was choking him. Debra wore yoga pants and a Lululemon quarter-zip and was on her phone. Her fingers scrolled up and down, tapped, swiped, and then scrolled again. Her eyes held thin rectangles of blue light and nothing else. If she blinked once during the whole ten minutes I watched her, I didn't see it.

Becca's question kept coming back at me. It was like those hundred different shadows I was throwing on the floor, all of them so faint they were barely ripples in the vinyl tile. Her question spread open around me, circled me, a hundred different versions of it. We did something good, so why did I feel so awful?

The answer I'd given Becca—you're in shock, you're exhausted, you'll feel better in the morning—had the taste of horseshit. But maybe it was true for her.

It wasn't true for me. I knew why I felt awful.

I left Don and Debra Miller in the waiting room, and I found Becca smoking in the parking lot. When she saw me, the cigarette tip flared, and she tilted her head back, and her throat flexed as smoke made a silver screen between us.

"Do you want to talk about it?"

I shook my head. I scanned the lot. The Charger was still there, painfully out of place among the minivans and family sedans. The Impala was gone, though. And so was the Ducati.

"Emmett's ok." Becca jabbed with the cigarette, the red star pointing east. "He got stitched up, and they said the cut really wasn't even that bad. He . . ."

"He heard."

Becca drew heavily on the cigarette. She clamped her lips tight and jogged the pack inside her coat pocket. Then she flicked the cigarette from her mouth with her tongue, and it tumbled through the air like a spark falling toward a pool of gasoline. But there wasn't any gasoline. Just slush and asphalt, and the coal-bright tip went out, and Becca ground it into the frozen ground just to be sure.

I nodded; it was all the confirmation I needed. "Ok." Then, a little stronger. "Ok."

"Just give him a night to cool down. He knows things are complicated; he's not stupid."

"Let's go home."

# Chapter | 41

I slept alone in Sara's house. I couldn't figure out the thermostat, and the place felt almost as cold as outside, so I slept bundled in my quilt, fully dressed, while the wind shrieked and slapped the windows and pried fingers under the edge of the roof. When I woke, the clock said it was eleven thirty-seven in the morning, and the clouds were gone. The sun barged through the window like the cheeriest asshole I'd ever wanted to kick in the teeth.

I showered. Alone. I dressed. Alone. I changed the dressing on my face. Alone. And I thought of what cheap motel soap smelled like. And then I felt guilty for that thought, so I thought about what Austin's breathing sounded like, the way he was always trying to curl an arm around me, the calluses on his palm that came from rope and leather and hard work.

In the fogged mirror, I wrote the question that I wasn't brave enough to ask myself. Two words stenciled with my fingers, the oil on my skin keeping the humid air from swallowing up the writing. *Which one?*

Austin was a rock. Austin was the ground under my feet. Austin made me better. Austin loved me.

Emmett was fire. Emmett was heroin. Emmett made me feel alive. Emmett loved me.

Austin was there day and night. Austin put up with my shit. Austin had taken a knife for me.

Emmett understood me in a way Austin never would. Emmett was there with me in the darkness—he had walked all the way into the black with me. Emmett had given half of himself for me, surrendering perfection to a crazy bitch with a knife.

I swiped the question out of the fog, stared at the blurry bastard, and scrubbed at the glass until all I could see were streaks. Streaks were a kind of nothing. Like the wind.

I walked four miles before somebody picked me up, and all four miles were bright, happy, Disney-wildlife-singing fucking nonsense. On a day like that day, the Wyoming sky was blue streaked with white, like a goddamn Dodgers jersey. And that pissed me off because I hated baseball and I really hated the Dodgers, and the only reason I even thought about those jerseys was because Austin had made me watch hours of spring-training games. On days like today, the air on the high plains was so thin and so clear that it felt like I could throw a fastball twenty miles and still see the rawhide splash down in the buffalo grass and the rangegrass and the Junegrass and watch the ripples spread through the sea of tall, waving stalks.

The woman who picked me up looked like her pink polyester suit and pillbox hat weighed more than she did, and she even had on lacy white gloves like she was on her way to church or a funeral or a royal wedding. She drove a red station wagon that had to be at least fifty years old, and this woman looked like she'd already lived a lifetime before the car even rolled off the line. On its side, the car wore a mixture of chrome letters and the darker outlines of the ones that had fallen off; they spelled out Lakewood. She rolled up next to me, eyed me through the window, and then stopped. When I opened the door, she must have gotten a better look because she squeezed her sequined purse against her lap and didn't let go of it until she dropped me in the hospital parking lot.

I knew my way, more or less, and I found Tyler's room, and then I stopped. A man in a Mather County deputy's uniform stood outside the door. I didn't recognize him; he might have been the hire who replaced the late Fred Fort. But it wasn't the fact that he was a deputy that froze me. It was the fact that he was staring into space, the muscles of his jaw relaxed, his hands tucked limply into his Sam Browne belt. I took another step. And then another. He didn't blink. I wasn't even sure he was breathing until I saw the slight swell of his chest.

I opened my second sight. Sleeping half a day had done a lot to bring me back to fighting shape, but at some point over the night, that conduit of incandescent power connecting my friends and me had shut off. I wasn't sure why. But I remembered hearing the sucking, gasping noises in Austin's chest. I remembered seeing those retro Jordans under the exam room's curtain. And I thought I knew why I wasn't connected to my friends anymore. Nothing lasts forever.

In the hypersaturated, textured reality of the other side, a slick of golden energy shone on the deputy's mind. I recognized that energy, and I recognized its effects, and I thought, briefly, about taking the deputy's gun. The last time this woman had been free, she had tried to put a bullet in me.

When I stepped into the room, Ginny stood next to Tyler's bed, her frisbee-disc hands folded around Tyler's small, pale ones. Ginny's eyes were closed, her head was down, and the same sheen of an aura surrounded her and Tyler. In tubular chairs next to the bed, Shay sat with her expressionless gaze fixed on the wall, while Hannah stared sightlessly into her mother's shoulder; both of them had the same goldfoil slick that I had seen on the guard.

"Step away from him."

Ginny drew a deep breath, a ripple running down her like she was waking from a dream, but she didn't lift her head or turn to face me. She rotated her hands, turning Tyler's palm up, and I saw the raw abrasions where the duct tape had ripped the flesh on Ginny's wrists.

"I can't undo what they did to him." With another of those deep breaths, another of those full-body shudders like she was trying to swim up out of sleep, Ginny lowered Tyler's hands and patted them against the mattress. Then she teased aside the papery collar of Tyler's hospital gown, exposing a bandage that ran the length of his chest. "The damage was intentional, severing key chakras."

"She didn't just sever them. She turned them against him. She made a fortress out of his own broken mind."

Ginny sighed and tugged the collar back into place, hiding the bandage.

"She made him into a weapon."

"She did."

"She did things to those kids that nobody should have done to them. Nobody. Let alone a kid."

Ginny nodded. Her back was still to me, and again I was struck by how solid she was, built like a cement smokestack, and how she somehow managed to look fragile even with all that mass. Fragile, and broken.

"You taught her how to do those things."

Once, Ginny's chin jerked to the side, as though she might shake her head and try to deny the whole thing. But then she caught herself. Her voice was so low you could have swept it under the bed. "I didn't teach her. But yes, I . . . helped her. I put her on the path."

"I stopped them when they wanted to torture you. That was a big, fucking mistake. If I'd had any idea—" I bit my tongue and tasted copper sparks. "You were wrong, by the way. The Lady is dead. Urho is dead. They're gone. Erased. Obliterated. And it's no thanks to you." One of my hands was clutching the door jamb now, the other was balled at my side. "You know what I think? I think you knew my dad was going to be up there. I think you knew they were keeping him. Weapon of last resort, isn't that what they call it? I think you knew, and I think that's why you were so sure that I'd lose. How am I doing?"

Raising both hands, she wiped at her cheeks.

"Don't cry. You don't have any right to cry. Am I right?"

She wiped her cheeks again. Fluorescent light glanced off her fingers.

"Am. I. Right. Because if I'm right, if you let me walk up there knowing that my dad was waiting, knowing that he was ready to put a bullet in me, knowing that if I tried to stop him, I'd lose the power I needed to stop Urho, if you knew all of that and still let me go without warning, I'm going to kill you."

"I warned you about your power. I tried to warn you, anyway. I tried to tell you what would happen if you . . . if you let your anger take control."

She bent. Her frisbee hands smoothed Tyler's small ones against the white linens, and the golden aura around both of them shrank and slid and retreated from Tyler until it only wrapped around Ginny. And then it winked out, and she turned to me and raised her head, and the pebbled rash of scabs around her mouth where duct tape had been ripped away gave her face a diseased look, as though she suffered from a plague that would spread with her next breath.

"But, yes. I knew."

My balled-up fist twitched. I thought of the deputy's gun. But I didn't need to sock her in the chin, and I didn't need to put a bullet between her eyes. I could use my ability. I'd already lost my connection to that river of power from my friends; I didn't have to worry about my hate and fury burning away the connection. I could bar the doors and lock the windows and leave her trapped inside her own mind, haunted by what she had done to these children. To my friends. To me.

"Vie?" It was Tyler's voice, and the word had so much dust and creak to it that I barely recognized my name. Tyler was running his hands up and down the hospital gown, as though verifying by touch what his eyes were seeing. Then he swallowed, the movement sending pain flashing across his face, and his little fists gathered handfuls of the cotton. "Vie, I'm thirsty."

I stared at him. In the hall, somebody shouted, "Bangarang," and then laughter boomed out, and a wheel squeaked on a service cart, and a machine shrilled out a long beep, and those were all signs that the world was still moving, the clock was still ticking, time hadn't stopped. But I stared at Tyler and didn't move, didn't speak, didn't blink.

His head swiveled; he wet his lips. He still looked like a lost kid, the kind on the back of a milk carton, when he said, "Mom?" And then, "Vie, is my mom ok?"

"You said you couldn't undo it." My voice sounded like it was six feet deep under talus. "You said—"

"There are many paths in the mind." Ginny shrugged, and it was like watching an anvil shrug or a bulldozer shrug. "He won't be the same, but he can find a way back. You can help him find a way back."

"Vie, I'm really, really thirsty."

"Yeah, Tyler. Yeah, buddy. I'll—just a minute."

Ginny met my gaze for the first time since I had entered the room.

"This doesn't make it right," I said.

"I know."

"If I ever see you again, ever . . ."

"I know."

She shambled toward the door, and I stepped out of her way. Thank God she didn't tell me she was sorry or she wished she'd done it differently because I don't know what I would have done. But she didn't. And when she was gone, the deputy in the hall cleared his throat, and Shay blinked, shifting Hannah's weight, and Hannah made a little cry when Shay bumped one of the girl's bruises. Tyler coughed and said, "Can I have some water, please?" And the please dragged out about a mile long.

"Oh my God," Shay said, getting up so fast, that she almost dropped Hannah. "Oh my God."

I snagged the pitcher of water and poured out a cup, and Tyler drank it down in two gulps. When he handed it back, he ran his arm over his mouth and licked his lips and said, "Vie, do you think that TV has cartoons?"

# Chapter | 42

I ate a vending machine sandwich. I drank two Cokes. I spent an hour with Sara, trying to make conversation with her while she played with the volume on the TV, until finally she brushed her cloud of blond frizz back from her forehead and looked me in the eye and said, "Vie Eliot, you are currently the light of my life, but I'm trying to watch my shows, and if you keep talking I might put tape over your mouth."

"Oh.

"Some of that Gorilla Tape."

"Maybe I'll just take a walk."

"That's a nice idea, sweetheart."

I might have gotten up a little fast because Sara's thumb was dimpling the rubber buttons on the remote control and I was starting to think she might pitch it at me. My heel clanged against the tubular chair. Sara's knuckles popped as she jabbed at the volume so she could hear *Days* over the racket.

"Love you," she said as I scurried toward the door.

"Oh. Yeah. Um." I yanked open the door and darted into the hall. "Loveyoutoo." It wasn't so much a word as it was a high-speed train shooting out of my mouth.

"Maybe you should keep walking until about four," she called after me.

In fairy tales, in dreams, there are times when every path takes you to the same place, when every turn turns in the same direction, when a choice isn't really a choice because everything is running on twin rails toward the same point. So I went left. And then I went right. And I went down the stairs until I hit bottom. I went outside, and I tramped up onto the overgrown shoulder where the wet grass dripped into my sneakers and soaked my socks, and the gravel crunched underfoot. A buttercup on the end of a long, weedy stalk bobbed in the air of passing cars and smacked against the inside of my hand. Before I knew what I was doing I'd plucked it and cupped it and turned my hand toward my leg so no one could see what I was carrying. And for all I knew, I went on like that, walking ten miles, twenty, toward Vehpese.

And somehow, I ended up back in Western Bighorn Hospital, standing outside Austin's room. Just like in a fairy tale. Just like in a dream. Just like in a nightmare. He was alone, which seemed like a miracle, and he was asleep. He'd gotten so big over the last year, packing on muscle, but with only the thin hospital linens on him, he looked thirteen again, or maybe twelve, the stripped-down slenderness of his face making him look like just a kid.

I took the chair next to him, followed the IV line to where it entered a vein on the back of his hand, and touched the tips of my fingers to his. The roughness of the calluses shocked me; I had to bite my lip to keep from making a noise. His fingers flexed once, and I shot a look at his face, but his eyes were still closed, and his breathing didn't change, and the white flag of a bandage still showed under the hospital gown. When I brushed the pads of his fingers again, they stayed still. I slipped my hand around his. I tucked the buttercup in the crook of his elbow and wondered if he'd find it when he woke.

How many nights? How many nights had we slept like this, hands linked? How many movies like this, how many study sessions like this, how many dinners when he hooked a pinky around mine just because he could? How many afternoons kicked out on the sofa, how many sleepless midnights when I couldn't breathe, when that black hole at the back of my head stole away every good thing except this, except the fingers crooked around mine? How much of my life could be calculated by my skin against his?

And then I had to get up because something was trying to claw its way out of my chest, and I let his hand slide across the white cotton sheet, and I stumbled into the hallway and caught the bathroom door with my shoulder and bounced off the counter with my hip and slammed the faucet handle so cold water sprayed out. I scooped up double handfuls and splashed them on my face. I was surprised they didn't boil off. Those claws were still digging their way out, cracking my ribs, punching through muscle and flesh. My breath had a knot in it every few inches. I scooped more water. I thought maybe I could drown in it.

But eventually the pain in my chest was a little better, and I hammered off the faucet with one fist, and then I was just standing there: the front of my flannel shirt soaked, my sneakers soaked, a puddle around me on the tile. I mopped myself up—and the floor—with handfuls of paper towels. And then I looked in the mirror. And I told myself I had to choose, even if it hurt this bad, even if it hurt this bad for the rest of my life, because if I didn't choose I'd lose both of them. Then I went back.

In the doorway, I stopped. Kaden sat in the chair I had vacated. His hand curled around Austin's hand. His hand. Kaden's hand cradling the hand that I had just been holding. His thumb pressed against the ridge of Austin's knuckles. His blunt-tipped fingers hid in the concavity of Austin's palm. The buttercup was gone.

"Get out."

Kaden shook his head. He tried to smile, and I realized, for the first time, that he really looked like shit. He was in a hospital gown too, and with his other hand he clutched a rolling stand with an IV bag. He'd lost any color in his face except a bruised, greenish tinge under his eyes and around his mouth. He met my eyes. He made sure I was watching. And then he traced the bumps of Austin's knuckles with his thumb.

"Get the fuck out. I don't care if you're still not well. I'll throw you out the fucking window if you don't get out."

"Sit down."

They sounded like the first honest words, the first really honest words, I'd ever heard from Kaden. None of his granola, buddy shit that he usually injected into every sentence. No posturing. No threats. Just two flat words while his thumb scaled the strong, hard lines of Austin's hand.

I took a seat by the door.

"You're not gay."

"Maybe I'm bi."

"You're not. You're not gay. You're not bi."

"I kissed you."

He had kissed me in the basement dungeon at Belshazzar's Feast. And, for a straight boy—hell, for any boy—it had been a real whopper of a kiss.

"One kiss doesn't make you gay."

He shrugged. That was somehow worse than everything else—even worse than the slow rise and fall of his thumb. That shrug. That total dismissal of me. Like he'd already erased me.

"Why do you hate me so much?

His thumb froze. Then a hint of the old Kaden came back, a megawatt smile that blinded me. "Jesus, Vie. I don't hate you. I . . . I meant what I said. At the motel. I'm your friend. I care about you. There's this part of me that does love you; that's the truth, whether you believe me or not. What we went through at Belshazzar's Feast, that's everything. That's my whole life, and you saved me. You got me out of there, you gave me a second chance. Even after the shit I did, you gave me a second chance. You're a good guy. If half the stuff Austin told me about your life is true, you're a pretty fantastic guy. If you want me to walk into hell behind you, I'll do it." That megawatt smile flashed out, and then he winced and touched his head, and the smile died. "I think."

"Hell." Those knots in my breathing were tighter now. Closer together. "You'd follow me to hell. Ok. And you're not gay. Don't even fucking try to tell me you're gay. But you're going to play this game out with Austin—why?"

"It's not a game."

"It's bullshit."

"It's not bullshit." The words came out in a shout, and Kaden clamped his mouth shut after them. Then, in a voice so low I had to lean forward, he said, "I care about you, Vie. I do. But you're . . . I don't know, you're messed up, ok? You're dangerous. And you're toxic. Austin's not himself when he's with you, ok? He worries. A lot. And he gets OCD about stuff with you. And I get it: he came out, you were part of that, he's got a lot of emotions tied up in the whole thing. He's not thinking clearly. But I am." Kaden's eyes pinned me. "I see the whole thing clearly, and I know how it's going to go."

"How's it—"

"I know it's going to get worse and worse. I know you're going to hurt him. Maybe get him killed. I know it. You want to talk about lying? You want to talk about playing a game? Fine. Truth. I'm not gay. That's the truth. But you need to admit that you're not good for Austin. You need to admit that you're too much of a risk. That he's better off without you."

Shaking my head, I said, "You've got no idea what you're talking about."

"Yes. I do. I've known him my whole life. He's my best friend. And you know what?" Kaden paused, chewing something over, his whole body tensed. "I do love him. I mean, I love him. And if I can save him—honest to God save him, Vie, save his life, save his sanity, save his future—then you know what? I'll take it up the ass for a few months, and then I'll break it off, and yeah, his heart will be in fucking pieces, maybe, and yeah, he'll hate me for the rest of his life, maybe, but at least he'll be alive. At least he'll be able to move on. With you, he's never going to get that chance."

"You'll take it up the ass? No straight guy takes it up the ass just because his buddy needs it."

"Whatever, man. Tell yourself whatever you need to. You can run off with Emmett, right? Fuck around with him for a while. Or are you bored with him now that he's not pretty anymore?"

The air was doing funny things. The lights were doing funny things. Everything was contracting to the size of a penny, and a corona of light glared off it. That ring of light was the color of snow. It was the color of the bandage on Austin's chest, where a knife had gone in and cut through his lung like it was a ribeye. All I could hear in my ears was the sucking, gasping sound of a straw at the bottom of a rapidly emptying cup, and that was the sound Austin had made when he tried to talk with a hole hacked into his lung.

"Do the right thing by Austin. If you care about him, you'll do that much for him."

I didn't see the hallways. The air was still funny. The lights were still funny. I just followed the penny-bright spot that I could focus on. It was like those old singalongs. Follow the bouncing ball. I did follow it. I followed it until I was out in the April day, and the light wasn't quite as funny, and the sun seemed to levitate everything around me: the asphalt, my sneakers, my wrists and elbows and shoulder blades, the blocky outline of the HVAC units on top of Western Bighorn Hospital, the mountains, the sky. It was like falling up. Gravity had gotten fixed on something bigger than Planet Earth. It was fixed somewhere out in that darkness. It was fixed somewhere in the back of my head.

I walked ten miles before the red Lakewood showed up again, stopped, and the ancient lady behind the wheel in her polyester jacket and skirt the color of Pepto eyed me like I was holding a gun on her, but she settled her purse and clamped it against her leg and reached across the seat to open the door. When she dropped me at the far edge of Vehpese, where another state highway cut up toward Sara's, she adjusted the pearls around her neck and said, "Young man, I think I'd like to take you to my church."

"Is it a Christian church?"

"Of course."

"Forgiveness? That kind of thing?"

"I should say so. Our Lord and Savior—"

"Even for guys that really fu—" Sara's angry face snapped across my mind. "That really mess up? Mess up everybody's life, all the people around them?"

Her face softened. The pearls shone as she counted them between her fingers. "Young man, those are exactly the people who need forgiveness the most."

"And you believe they get it?"

"I've got my Bible here." She squirmed in her seat like she'd dropped a winning lottery ticket, her hands running into the footwell, searching. "Let me just read you something, and then you'll know that anything can be forgiven, and the darker the sin, the brighter the dawn—"

"Not interested," I said, and I slammed the door and stomped the rest of the way to Sara's house.

My head was hurting. My throat was dust. Even inside, where daylight only entered as an oblique film across the furniture, my eyes throbbed like the worst hangover I'd ever had. In the pantry I found another envelope of raspberry lemonade, and I mixed up a gallon and drank it down, and the sugar rush buzzed through me like honeybees under my skin. I made a sandwich—swiss and ham and a limp leaf of romaine, mustard, rye—and I ate it even though my stomach had shrunk to the size of a grape seed.

As I rinsed the plate, I stared out onto the high plains, where the wind cuffed the rangegrass, flattened it, spread it out until I felt like I could see farther than anybody had ever seen before. But I wasn't really seeing anything. I was inside my head. The darkness was eating me up, and I was looking into it.

For some silly reason, I had thought that the problem was that I couldn't choose. I had somehow convinced myself that I had a chance at happiness with both of them and I had to choose. I had thought—*There's really only one guy. For me, you know. Just one*—that I needed to decide: safety or danger, steady or wild, love or a drug that scorched along every neural pathway.

But maybe that wasn't the right choice. Maybe the right choice was about me. Who would I hurt less? Kaden was right: Austin had a chance. He could go to college, find a great guy, live a decent, happy life. Not with me in the picture. That might have sounded arrogant, but it didn't come out of the conviction that I was the best thing to happen to Austin Miller. It came out of the knowledge that I was the first thing to happen to Austin Miller, and knowledge that Austin was loyal, that he made sacrifices, and that he'd keep being loyal and making sacrifices until I'd wrung out every last chance he had at happiness and left him a wreck.

Emmett, on the other hand. Emmett had a mountain of his own baggage. Emmett was broken, like me. Emmett had some kind of night vision that let him see into the black spots inside me and give me what I needed: drag a razor up his own arm, for example. I'd fuck up Emmett's life, too. But he knew that. He knew how to handle it. When it got to be too much, he could kick me to the curb. The plate spun out of my hands, clanged against the stainless steel sink, and rolled to a stop. I turned it over in both hands, looking for cracks and finding none. I was smiling. It would be better with Emmett. He knew how to kick me to the curb. He'd done it before, hadn't he?

And didn't I owe it to him? Half his body had a new landscape of scars and mutilations, and he'd done that for me. Didn't I owe him the best of whatever I could give him until he'd had enough of me, until he was done with me? Couldn't I give him that much?

Everything felt so clear. Everything settled in my head, and I shoved the plate into the drying rack. Everything made sense. But it was like dusk: the light just kept dropping away. Right now, for this minute, I could still see to the horizon. But that was an illusion because it was getting darker and darker inside my head, and I wondered why making a decision, making this decision, hadn't swamped everything like a klieg light.

Perched on the edge of the sofa, with the smell of Sara's potpourri in my nose, I settled the weight of the heavy phone on my leg and dialed twice: first, just tracing the numbers. Then a deep breath. Then I punched them.

He answered, but he didn't say anything. He was just breathing. His normal breath. I'd heard it a hundred times. A thousand times.

"Your parents ever come back?"

"They're not coming back. Lawayne made that really clear to my dad."

"He's dead, Em."

"They're not coming back."

"Are you going to—to wherever they are?"

His breathing changed. There was a hitch in it. Maybe pain. Maybe hope. "That's not what you want to ask me, tweaker."

"Are you going to leave Vehpese? Are you going to move back in with them, or are you going to go somewhere else? Start a new life?"

Another of those hitches. Like maybe he was crying. But his voice didn't sound like he was crying. "Just ask what you want to ask me."

"Will you run away with me?" It sounded so juvenile once it was out of my mouth. It sounded like clubhouses and a backpack stuffed with Kraft Mac & Cheese.

Another hitch. And then a rasping noise like he was wiping his sleeve across the phone. "Yeah."

# Chapter | 43

Emmett picked me up on the Ducati. He didn't come to the door. He didn't call to let me know he was there. The roar of the motor announced him, and because in spite of everything that had changed, Emmett Bradley was still one big fucking showboat, he expected me to trot out as soon as he pulled up. And I did. No more games. No more jerking him around to try to show him who was boss. When the Ducati crunched gravel outside, I shouldered my backpack and trotted.

Dusk. I could still see the horizon. Or maybe I just thought I could. That was the thing about light going out: you thought you could see right up until you couldn't. The wind smelled like wet grass and the Ducati's exhaust and hot engine grease. My skin prickled. Some of that was the cold. Some of that was Emmett's leather jacket hanging open, the thin tee underneath not hiding the taut lines of scar and muscles on his chest.

"Where's your bag?" I asked as I climbed up behind him, my backpack heavy on my shoulders.

He grinned at me from behind his visor. The scars twisted the corner of his mouth. "I've got credit cards, tweaker."

"Don't call me that."

He opened his mouth, paused, and the savaged corner of his mouth pulled into a frown. "I'm sorry."

Wrapping my arms around his waist, I settled my chin on his shoulder and let that be my answer.

I didn't ask where we were going. I didn't care. Anywhere but here. We drove. We drove fast. So fast, in fact, that when we hit those long stretches of snakeback highway curving along the high plains, the Ducati felt like it was coming off the ground, like the air was picking us up the way it grips the underside of a plane's wing, like nothing could keep us here, not even the traction of tires on asphalt.

Night closed down, hung over us in a black cup full of stars. We kept driving west. And then there were lights ahead of us too. Most the dirty yellow of sodium vapor streetlights. Some brighter, whiter. A few red winks.

The Ducati slowed.

My fingers tightened, coiling the zipper of his jacket, gathering inches of his cotton tee.

Buildings massed on the right side of the road. I recognized those buildings. I'd been here earlier today, and Western Bighorn Hospital hadn't changed in the last six hours. Heavy heads of ragweed smacked against my jeans and left mustard-powder prints as the Ducati bumped onto the shoulder.

"I don't want to say goodbye to Sara. It's better if I don't, Em. I'll call her. I'll tell her not to worry."

He rolled his shoulders. He twisted at the waist. It was like his clothes were too small, or—no. No. Like I was holding him too tight. Letting the bike lean, he dropped the kickstand and swung off. Swung free of my grip. His eyes were those funhouse, fallaway dark again. He held out a hand. "Take a walk with me."

"This isn't a very romantic spot."

"Take a walk with me."

"I just want to go, Em. Can we just go? Let's go as far as we can tonight. I don't care if we sleep in a ditch, but let's just go."

"Vie Eliot," he said, and I was in those eyes again: no up, no down, no falling, no flying. "Please take a walk with me."

The Ducati's headlight sprayed a rainbow across the film of motor oil and gravel. The halogen incandescence hit us at mid-thigh, and it slipped lower as we walked down the stretch of shoulder. We were walking into the blackness. Together. And Emmett's hand found my wrist, and then my palm, and then my fingers. The bandage on the inside of his arm rasped and rustled. When we got to the turn-off for Western Bighorn and the gravel ended at a strip of freshly-patched blacktop, Emmett stopped.

He didn't say anything. Maybe he couldn't say anything. His eyes were darker than the darkness, and I reached out and brushed against his mind and found the invisible wall still there, just as high and hard as it had ever been, but I didn't need to read his thoughts because I already knew.

"I told you I was going to do two things that would piss you off." He must have taken a breath because his chest rose and fell, but he barely had the air to say, "This is the second."

"No." I shook my head. "No. Absolutely not. I choose you."

His voice came out dark and thick like molasses. "You still love him."

"I love you."

"I'm not stupid, twea—" He bit the scarred corner of his mouth. "I'm not stupid. I know how you feel about me. And I know how I feel about you. But you love Austin. And he loves you."

"I love you. And you love me."

"I'm not any good to you like this—" His hand traced a half-moon over the scarred side of his face.

"No." The leather jacket's zipper bit into my palms as I shook him. "No. No fucking way. You don't get to do that. You don't get to say that you're no good for me. You don't get to pretend like things will be better this way. You don't get to make that decision." And I knew I was a hypocrite. And I didn't care.

For a moment, genuine amusement glowed in Emmett's face. "You still don't understand. I get to do whatever I want. Whenever I want. And you'll let me."

"I won't."

"Yes. You will. You're going to walk down to the hospital. You're going to take the elevator to the fourth floor. And you're going to tell Austin you're sorry for all your fucked-up behavior and tell him how you feel."

My eyes were burning; they felt hot enough to turn the whole night to fire. I shook my head.

"Vie—"

When he touched me, it was the breaking point, and I jerked away, shaking my head, shaking everywhere like a flu had settled into my bones. "I can't. I can't, Em. He doesn't understand how . . . how fucking broken I am. He looks at me and he thinks everything's ok, or that everything can be ok. He doesn't get it. I'm a wreck. A total shitpile. Nothing's ever going to get better. There's something wrong with me, something that goes all the way down, like this—like this black hole in the back of my head, and it's eating me up, and Austin will never understand that. But you do. You know it. You can see it. And you—you can still love me, even though I'm fucked up beyond repair. Please don't do this, Em. Please don't. Please don't do this."

He laughed. It was soft. It was a surprise. It raised the hair on the back of my neck, and it would have made me furious except it was so kind. And I'd never heard that gentle, kind laughter from Emmett Bradley before. His whole face had a firefly-light with that laughter.

"Tweaker, you are just so damn stupid sometimes."

I stared at him, realization flooding in. Of course Emmett wouldn't want me to go with him. He might be broken, but I was shattered, and Emmett didn't deserve to be the one who got cut on all the sharp edges. The rest of it—the fantasy that Emmett could see through the pitch-black shadows—that was just in my head. This, right here, this was reality.

"Fine." I tugged on my coat, trying to settle it on me in some way that would smother the frantic beating in my chest. "You'd better go, then. Before the sheriff starts thinking clearly and decides he wants to know more about what happened up at Chapee."

"I'm sorry I laughed. It's just—sometimes you're so dramatic. You know that? You don't mean to be. You're all tough and grim and make those faces like you could chew through an airplane hangar, but that's the drama right there. That's all part of the show."

"I get it Emmett: you don't want to be me with me. You don't have to be a fucking prick about it."

"Vie, I love you. Like, a crazy person kind of love. When you touch me, when you talk to me, when you look at me like you're going to chew through another airplane hangar or two just to get to me, just so you can rip my clothes off—I'm not sane anymore when you look at me like that. I'm not rational. You think I'm addicted to heroin because I shoot up at night, because I can't sleep? I'm addicted to you. The last few months, not being near you, heroin was my fucking methadone. That was what kept me from kicking in your window in the middle of the night and who cares what Austin would have said."

A beat-up little Ford Focus drifted by us. Ragweed bowed in the rush of air following the car. The heavy yellow heads tickled the inside of my hand.

"That's got to be the most messed up way of saying I love you. Ever."

"Maybe." A smile ran across his lips, a zig-zag lightning crooked smile. "But what you're talking about, all that stuff about a hole in your head, how you're broken, how there's something wrong with you, that's bullshit. Kind of heinously stupid bullshit, actually, considering it's the twenty-first century."

"Will you flip your asshole switch to off for one second and—"

"Vie, you're not screwed up. You're not broken. You don't have a black hole in the back of your head." Another of those jagged lightning smiles pulled his lips crooked. "You're depressed. You need help. You've been through shit most kids, most adults, most people never have to handle in their lives. And you know what the good news is?"

I pushed past him, checking him with my shoulder, my heels striking hard on the asphalt. He caught my arm. Wrestled me toward him. I was stronger, and I got free, but my back smacked against one of his invisible barriers, and I was stuck facing him.

"This time. This one fucking time you have to listen to me."

"Don't give me that depression bullshit. I'm not depressed, I'm—"

"What? Because you're psychic, you can't be depressed? Everybody else in the world, everybody else who feels the way you do, they're depressed, but for some magic reason, you're different? Bullshit. Heinous bullshit."

"You don't have any idea what you're talking about."

"Sure I do. I love you. All I do is watch you and think about you. Every fucking hand on the clock points at you—at least, that's the clock in my head. You're depressed—"

"Stop saying that."

"You're depressed—"

"Shut up, Emmett."

"You're depressed. Or you've got depression. Or whatever the right way is to say that. But you know what the good news is?"

I met his eyes. I was thinking about how fast I'd have to throw a punch to flatten his nose, and I decided I probably couldn't throw faster than he could put up a barrier.

"The good news, sweetheart, is that they've got ways to treat depression. They've got meds. They've got therapy, and baby, you need like a lifetime of therapy." One of those lightning smiles sizzled at the ruined corner of his mouth. "And it's going to take a lot of hard work. But the good news is there's nothing magic about depression, ok? The good news is you can get better."

My whole body was on fire, and I dashed at my eyes with my wrists, and my throat and nose and head were full of snot.

"Come on," Emmett said, hugging me against him, the smell of leather and bergamot and his skin running through me like a horse tranquilizer.

I snuffled into the jacket. Getting him snotty was poor payback for what he'd done to me, but he'd have to live with it. "It doesn't feel like that," I mumbled into his chest. "It doesn't feel like it's ever going to get better."

"Yeah, but it will. It will. Come on. It's going to be ok. You're going to be ok. You're not broken or any of that stuff. You're going to get better. And you're going to have a great life. Maybe it's with Austin."

"Em—"

He shushed me. "Maybe not. You can figure it out later. But for now, anyway, you're going to walk in there and tell him how you feel. And then you take it from there. Day by day."

"Em, it could be with you. My life could be with you, and we could get on the bike right now, and I promise I'll find a doctor, I promise, and—and I'll get better. Just like you said. Only you've got to let me get on the bike with you. And we've got to go tonight, now."

"No."

"Why not?"

He released me and stepped back, and when I put out a hand to touch him, my fingers glanced across an invisible wall. The night had darkened. His lips peeled back; he probably meant it to be a smile, but it just looked like a dissection with the skin folded over. "You know why, tweaker. You were never what I really wanted. Fun to fuck around with, good for a lay. But I've got big things ahead. I've got a life, and what am I supposed to do? Take you home, introduce you to my parents—" His voice wobbled, and the struggle of controlling it showed on his face. "Tell them your mom likes to burn you and your dad smokes crystal meth and you're a delinquent but you're also the crazy kind of fuck that makes me keep coming back? Nah. No thanks."

The words should have hurt. They should have lanced right through me. But his eyes were wrong, and his voice was wrong, and his smile was wrong, and his hands were shaking until he noticed and clamped them around his thighs.

"You don't mean that. You don't mean any of it. You just told me you loved me, and I love you, and I'll do whatever you want. I'll see a shrink. I'll take meds. I'll—"

"Tweaker." He broke the syllables hard and stretched them out. "You don't get it: I always get what I want. And I don't want you."

"You're still lying. You're still fucking lying. You don't even know why you're doing this, you don't even know why, so you're just saying shit to hurt me." Something crazy flashed through my mind. Something totally batshit insane, but my mouth was moving before I could stop myself. "Em, if you think you don't deserve me, or if you think you don't deserve anybody, or if it's anything stupid like that, you've got to get your head out of your ass and start thinking clearly. I love you—"

Pain crystallized in his face and then shattered and then everything was smooth and wiped clear. He was crying, just a little.

"I don't deserve you? After all the times I've had to put up with you, all the times I've had to drag your ass out of trouble, all the nights I got jabbed by your raggedy toenails? Fuck that. I'm leaving because this, between us, this is a match and gasoline. It's not good, Vie. I mean, it's great. But it's not good. Not for either of us."

"It is good. You know it's good. You know how it feels, how this feels between us. I know you do."

"Yeah. I know how it feels. And that's why I'm going now."

I had one last weapon. One last chance. "What did you ask my mom for?"

Emmett froze. It took him a moment too long to answer. "I told you: I didn't want to sit on the sidelines anymore. I wanted to be able to take care of myself."

"That's a lie. You're lying to me again. What did you ask her for?"

"Goodbye, tweaker."

"You asked her for a way to keep me safe."

The only noise between us was the wind in a great emptiness.

Then he nodded.

"This isn't keeping me safe, Em. You can't keep me safe if you walk away. You can't protect me if you leave."

"Don't you get it? Don't you fucking understand? This is it. This is me protecting you. Protecting both of us, tweaker. This is the only way to keep you safe. And I'm going to do it even if it kills me."

For a moment, as he walked backward, the only thing left of him was his face, half marked with whorls of scars, the other half the perfect beauty that had hit me like a telephone pole when I saw him the first time.

"Em, don't go. Please don't go. I need you."

He looked like he might say something else, and his eyes weren't dark anymore. They weren't that fallaway blackness that left my stomach in the air. They were bright and liquid like the moon on the Bighorn River. All of the sudden I thought of the first night I had been in his bedroom, when he had played the guitar for me and I had watched the wind ruffle the rangegrass, and I could almost hear it again, the song he had played, and it sounded like every heartbreak in the universe played in the same chord.

Then the moment passed, and Emmett shook his head, and he trotted to the Ducati, and the engine roared to life, and when Emmett sped past me, the visor was down, and he was nothing but black leather and muscle crouched on the bike. And then he was red stars winking in the tunnel of my vision. And then he was gone.

# Chapter | 44

The sky was a cupped hand of oil and sand. The April breeze picked up. Long stalks of rangegrass licked the insides of my legs as I climbed the berm, away from the road, my back to the road, my back to that puncture hole at the end of my vision where two red lights had extinguished. The grass had dried during the bright, sunny day, and the blades hissed between my fingers. I gathered handfuls of it at my waist. The granules of seed in the compact heads crumbled inside my palm, and I counted the upper windows on the Western Bighorn building until I thought I had found the right one. Then I folded my legs and sat, the seed pods bumping against my neck, the only sound the rush of tires on the road behind me.

Nightmares.

The window—if I had counted correctly, I reminded myself—didn't look any different from the others. The hue and warmth of the glow were the same. The shape of the window was the same. The moth-colored shadows from the parking lot lights were the same.

Behind that window, Austin Miller was in bed. Awake? Asleep?

Awake.

Behind that window, Austin Miller was in bed. Awake. His short, preppy-boy hair sticking up, those big arms visible beneath the sleeves of the hospital gown, the bandage on his chest as bright as winter light, his knees knobbing the blanket across his legs.

I ripped a stalk of grass and then took it by the end and shredded it into thinner strips, following the grain lengthwise. Yes, Austin was right there. I could see him. I could reach out and touch him. The window was the same as every other damn window, but for a moment, it was like there was something else shining through. A warmth. A glimmer. Like turning black soil and finding gold flecked throughout.

The grass stained my fingers; the pungent greenness of it hung on my next breath. Austin was inside that room with the gold-flecked glow. He was there. I knew it like I knew I was breathing chlorophyll and dust and spores from crushed seed pods. Austin was in there, and what was he doing? It was like I had x-ray vision. It was like I could see through steel and plaster: Kaden stretched out in one of those shitty tubular chairs, his fingers threaded through Austin's, that million-watt smile so close to Austin's face that it was probably going to give him a damn sunburn. They were talking. They were flirting. They were kissing. They were fucking.

Everything was getting going again at the back of my head. That black wheel was spinning again. My heart was thumping again. My thoughts galloped again. Was that what I wanted to walk in on? Was that how I wanted this to go? I jiggle the chrome handle on the door, the latch doesn't catch—just an accident, they didn't shut it all the way—and I get to see Kaden's bony ass bob up and down while he rides Austin. Was that the last memory I'd have of my boyfriend—of my ex-boyfriend, a chilly little voice reminded me?

I let the tattered strips of grass fall, and they lay like pick-up sticks across my legs. I scrubbed my green-stained fingers on my jeans. I planted my hands on the cold, wet ground, and I found a hard wad of old chewing gum and four cigarette butts and an empty can of hornet spray. Then I pushed myself up. I'd walk back to Vehpese. I'd crawl back if I had to.

But I couldn't stop staring at that window. The exact same color, the exact same light, the exact same shape as every other window on the whole fucking building. And why was I so sure that it was even his window? Why did I think that counting floors and rooms would put me at the right spot? What kind of messed up, idiotic thinking was that? What kind of—

It was still there, though: the flecks of gold, the summer warmth, the smell of leather and hard work and cedar and tobacco flakes dusting my fingers. There was still that feeling that I could see through stucco and steel and plaster.

And then I was touching his mind, not even meaning to, just brushing it, and I saw a rerun of *Magnum, P.I.* on the hospital TV and the crackle of a thought—that Tom Selleck had been hot, and the mustache was a big part of it—and then unfiltered shock as he recognized me.

Vie?

I slammed the connection shut.

I walked to the highway.

I held out my thumb.

Headlights fogged together in the distance, separating as they came toward me, slowed, stopped.

The station wagon was still red. The chrome letters, even with some missing, still spelled Lakewood. She was wearing the exact same suit as the day before only this one was in a shade of turquoise that probably hadn't been manufactured since the 1950s, but she clutched the exact same purse in her lap as she stared out at me.

The engine rumbled softly. The exhaust was poison sweet.

"Do you want to get in?"

"I don't know."

"I won't make you go to church."

"I know."

"If you're coming out here every day to visit someone, maybe I should just plan on picking you up." Her wrinkled face puckered into a smile. "I think God might be getting tired of scheduling these meetings."

I didn't think God had anything to do with it. Luck. Chance. The coincidences of a state that was mostly empty, and the added coincidences of being in a pocket of the state that was emptier than the rest.

A second set of headlights in the distance turned the dark to gray.

"We'd better get going."

"Thanks."

She coiled the strap of her purse around her wrist. She glanced at the oncoming headlights in the rearview mirror. She looked back at me. "We'd really better get going."

"Yeah," I said. "I know." And then I turned and walked back toward the hospital. Over my shoulder, I called, "Thanks, though."

Headlights washed between my legs, turning the asphalt white, and then they were gone.

I was right about the door to Austin's room: it was closed. I wrapped fingers around the handle, burying the chrome under my sweaty grip, and then breathed in the lemon-crisp air and stale coffee and when a nurse with huge curls of brown hair pinned up passed me, a whiff of bleach off her scrubs.

We'd really better get going.

I turned the handle. And I knocked.

"Come in."

No bony ass. No Kaden at all, in fact. Austin's face was white, his hair lank and dull, one hand curled into a fist over his chest, while the other hand clutched something at his side. He was working his thumb on it. A ballpoint pen, maybe. A nervous tic.

"Oh. Hey."

"Hey."

He swiped at his face, and his hand went right back into a fist at his chest. "I'm not really feeling good."

"Ok. I'll just—"

"No. I mean. I'd like you to stay. But I just—I might not be very good company."

We watched each other. His thumb was still clicking.

"Will you sit down or something? You're giving me a crick in the neck."

So I sat.

Tom Selleck was still on TV. He was doing something with a filing cabinet. He had a hat pulled low on his forehead. His mustache did look pretty damn good.

"How are you feeling?" And then I blushed because it was such a dumb question.

Austin smiled, and the smile evaporated. "Not great."

"It hurts?"

"They give me this thing." He turned his hand, exposing a small plastic device with a button. "I press this, and it's supposed to release more painkillers."

"Supposed to?"

"I don't know. It's been ok most of the day, but the last few hours." Sweat made his face glisten; it made the rings under his eyes uglier.

"Are you going to be ok?"

He smiled again, and it lasted a few more seconds this time before drying up. "I'm here, aren't I?"

"Why the fuck didn't you tell me you'd been stabbed in the fucking chest?" The words exploded out of me. "Jesus Christ, Austin. Jesus fucking Christ. You could have died. Did you think about that? We took our goddamn time driving over here. We were practically strolling. And you didn't say one word. What the fuck was that about?"

"Yeah, well, I didn't die, did I?"

"That doesn't matter."

"The doctors said the knife barely punctured the lung. Barely. In fact, it didn't even cut completely through at first, which was why I could—"

"What? Walk up a mountain, carry a child, and damn near get yourself killed by being stubborn?"

He shook his head. The purple under his eyes looked like the fucking rings of Saturn. "Why are you even here? I thought you'd be gone by now. Or is this your last stop? Did you just want to check in, make sure everybody was still breathing before you jumped on the back of Emmett's bike and got out of town? Don't look at me like that. You think you're so mysterious, but you're an open book, Vie. Kaden told me what you said when you came here. He told me you wanted him to tell me that it was better this way, better if you went somewhere else, better if I never talked to you again. That's how you decided to send that message? By having Kaden tell me? Why didn't you just put a knife in his hand and tell him to dig a little deeper while he was at it? You're such a fucking coward sometimes. And now you're here, and you're yelling at me and—" He cut off with a sharp cry; the fist he held at the level of his chest flexed open and then spasmed shut, as though he were trying to chain something in place. The pain, I guessed. The pain that was running roughshod through him.

"You're the one yelling," I said, my voice harsh and low. "And you're the one with a fucking hole in his lung, so you shouldn't be yelling. You shouldn't be getting excited. I never told Kaden to say that stuff to you, and I came here because I am still fucking in love with you. I was hoping maybe you were still in love with me. Now give me that fucking pain pump and let me see if I can get it to work."

I pried his fingers off the plastic, studied it, jammed the button a few times, and glared at him.

The pasty color to his skin was worse. Sweat poured off him like a river. He stared straight ahead, like I wasn't even there, and said, "They limit how much I can get out of it. So I can't OD. It's not broken, and you can't fix it."

"Aus—"

He shook his head; his fist spasmed again, and he grunted.

The next words I chose carefully. I was building a bridge. Or a ladder. Something rickety. Something that had a long fall under it. "You asked me what was wrong. With us. With me." I had to take a long, slow breath; I was shaking so hard I was about to rattle to pieces. "It wasn't us. It was me."

"No. It was us. There was something fundamentally wrong with us."

"Oh." I ran both hands through my hair. I smoothed my jeans. My fingers left sweat prints on the chrome arms of the chair and I pushed myself to my feet.

"Did you listen to the rest of it?" He wasn't looking at me. He was staring at Tom Selleck's fucking mustache.

"What?"

He just gave a sharp shake of his chin.

"No," I said. "I shouldn't have listened to any of it. I know that. I knew that. And I'm sorry."

"Do you still have it?"

My face was burning. "Yeah."

"Well."

It took me a minute to realize what he was saying. Then I dug through my backpack and found the cassette player. I rolled my thumb across the triangle on the play button. And then I pressed down.

"It's just, sometimes I think it'd be so much easier if he weren't here." His voice sounded tinny over the cheap speaker, and Austin squeezed his eyes shut. The recording continued: "I know I'm dodging the question. You asked me about me. And the answer is, I'm . . . I'm having a hard time. Not just with coming out. And not just with . . . with the violence. With the bad things that have happened. I'm having a hard time figuring out who I am. It's like, when I was dating Samantha, or, I mean, any girl, it made sense. I knew who I was. I was supposed to be tough, I was supposed to protect her, I was supposed to be the shoulder to cry on, I was supposed to fix the sink, I was supposed to play football and rope steer and—" A noise of frustration made the player rumble in my hand. "And with him, I know it's different. I know it doesn't have to be that way. But there's this part of my brain that just keeps pushing me to take care of him, to be the guy, if that makes any sense. I know it's stupid because he's tough and he's a guy and he could probably fix a sink better than I can. He's so brave that sometimes I don't think he even realizes anymore when he's doing things nobody else would do. And that scares me."

The therapist's soft voice came on next. "Gender roles in a same-sex relationship can be difficult, but they're also an opportunity to negotiate—"

"No." On the recording, Austin blew out a wet breath. "That's not what I'm trying to say. I just . . . I don't know how to be me with him, not yet, so I'm just being this one part of me, and it's . . . it's claustrophobic. Like I'm back in the closet all over again."

"There's something I'd like you to try—" the therapist said.

"That's enough," Austin said. His eyes were still shut.

Neither of us said anything. A machine beeped, and then it beeped again, and Tom Selleck made a wacky shot behind his back and caught a bad guy right in the chest, and outside, the wind brushed the buffalo grass and stirred the sage into silver glimmers. "You're supposed to rope steer."

He laughed. It was a wet laugh, almost a cry, and didn't open his eyes. "You're such an asshole."

"I'm terrible at plumbing."

"Ok, Vie."

"I don't know how to fix a sink."

"I get it."

"Unless I can solve it with Draino, I am totally, absolutely lost."

Austin was crying now, his eyes still shut, and he wiped his cheeks with the back of his hand.

"I . . . need you. I love you. And I need you to take care of me. Not because I'm an overgrown kid who can't cook anything besides Top Ramen—although, to be totally honest, I can't. And not because I can't live without you, although it would be pretty fucking hard. I need you to take care of me—a little, just sometimes, anyway—because that's part of who you are. You're this amazing guy who makes sure other people are ok. And I love you. I love that part of you. I love how you make me feel. I love that you care that I'm ok." I drew a breath and ran my hand across my chin, felt my lips against the back of my hand, tried to pull words from the thunderstorm in my heart. "But I don't want that to be the only part of you I get to see. And I don't want you to feel claustrophobic. I want to get to know all of you. And I want you to yell at me when I'm messing up. And I want you to tell me when you're not happy. And I want you to grow and be the best person you can be. And if it's not always going to be with me—"

He sobbed and then wiped his mouth with both hands and said, "Just shut up, please."

"I'm serious."

"I know, and now I'm telling you I don't want you to talk like that. I don't ever want you to talk like that." One hand clenched over his chest again; he was trembling, and pain drew tight lines in his face. "Vie, can we . . . can we do this another day? I'm sorry I started this. I'm sorry I made you say things that you probably weren't ready to—"

"One more thing. Maybe we weren't doing so well because I didn't know how you felt. I didn't know you were . . . trapped, I guess. Into always being supportive, always being protective, always taking care of me. I should have known. But there's something else. Those times you asked me, those times you knew something was wrong and you wanted to talk about it? I should have told you."

My eyes were hot. The chrome railing blurred into a long bar of white light, and I had to blink and breathe through my mouth and chafe my palms on my knees. "I've been really, really unhappy. I think . . . I think I'm depressed. Or I've got depression. I kept telling myself it was just about my powers and Urho and the Lady and about my dad and about my mom, but it's more than that I think. It's something in my head. Something's wrong, and I've felt so shitty for so long, but I didn't want you to know. I didn't want you to think it was because of you, so I just kept telling myself everything was ok. I kept telling myself everyone felt like this, and I never want you to think I wasn't happy with you because—"

Austin's eyes were open: bloodshot, swimming in tears, blue-green like perfect water. "Come here."

I got up, the motions jerky like all my joints were steel. "I'm going to get help. I promise. I'm going to see a doctor and I'll take something and I'll even go see a shrink if you—"

"Vie, please come here."

I took another of those tin-man steps. My knees cracked against the bed. "I'll get better, Aus. I promise I'll get better."

Austin blinked his eyes clear and patted the bed beside him.

I sat down.

He kissed me.

And then I was crying so hard I couldn't hold myself up. I tried to. I knew this boy had just gotten stabbed in the chest, and I knew I should stay upright and not collapse onto his shoulder like a fucking maiden in a medieval fairytale, but I just couldn't do it. I cried for a long time, and he ran one hand across the back of my neck, and he whispered in my ear, telling me it was going to be ok, and after a long time, after a really long time, I stopped and sniffled and managed to scoot back a few inches.

"Are we in a fight?" he whispered.

I shook my head.

He looked like he might say something, but the pain made him gasp, and his fist spasmed above his chest. He wasn't going to get any more pain meds for a while, and I couldn't stand seeing him like this. I slipped my hand around his. I opened my second sight, and I flowed across the connection between us until I floated in the darkness of his mind. Sleep. He needed to sleep and rest and heal. And I thought of the last night I had slept beside Austin: the smell of his hair, his breath on my neck, the sticky heat where our legs tangled, the coil of bedding that I had shoved to my waist. I remembered the way I had counted my heartbeats that night like I was counting the cars on a train, a train slipping off into darkness, and then I had slept. I felt the memory echo inside him, and when I returned to my body, he was asleep, his face turned to the pillow, his breathing even, the rigid lines of pain melting.

I dragged the chairs into a makeshift cot, and I slept too.

It was the same dream that had followed me for the last few months: snow lying heavy on the ground, fog lying heavy above the snow, the trees laying heavy limbs above me, their broad trunks marching in every direction. Urho came behind me—that vicious, insane wolf that was the manifestation he took in dreams. He was hunting me. And if he caught me, he would tear me apart.

Part of me was awake enough to know that this was only a dream, that Urho was dead, that terror and trauma and months of nightmares were the reasons for this dream. But even knowing that, I was still afraid. I ran, my breath a bonfire in my chest, my legs slowing until they froze, as heavy as snow and wood. And the wolf came behind me. The wolf was as fast as ever. And the wolf darted between the trees, crouching, coiling, launching toward me, jaw open, fangs tearing at flesh—

"Hey, hey, hey, stop. Vie, stop. Vie! It's ok."

The words dragged me out of the dream, and I flopped on my makeshift cot, mopping my face with my sleeve. Austin leaned on the chair, the plastic bending along a white crease as he supported all his weight on it, but Austin's attention was on me. He pushed sweaty hair back from my face. A cool, callused hand lay against my cheek.

"That was one hell of a nightmare."

I dropped onto my back, falling away from his touch, and covered my face. He didn't move. His breathing was labored, though, and I could hear the barbs of pain in it.

When I trusted myself, I wiped my eyes and said, "It's stupid for you to get out of bed like that." Then I got up. "Come on. You need to lie down."

I helped him back into the hospital bed. The strain of moving, of standing, showed in his face. As I tucked the blanket around him, I talked. Just stupid stuff. Stuff I couldn't keep from coming out of my mouth.

"It's just a dream. Sorry I woke you. It's just—I thought they'd be over. Gone. Now that—well, after what happened. Anyway, you shouldn't have gotten up."

Austin caught my hand when I pulled back.

I took a breath, and then I kept going. "And I'm sorry I said it was a stupid thing for you to get up because I know you were trying to help. But sometimes I think you're so worried about me that you don't take care of yourself, and that really starts to fuck with my head. I don't know how to think about it, much less talk about it. So I say stupid stuff. Like I tell you you're stupid for helping me. Or I—or I show up in your hospital room and yell at you. And I guess I'm just trying to say I know why you came up to the cabin at Chapee. I know why you didn't talk about how bad the cut was, because you were worried about me. I guess I'm just trying to say, I'm sorry."

"I do worry about you."

"You don't need to."

"I love you."

"You don't need to do that either."

That surprised a laugh out of him, the first genuine one I'd heard in this room, and he squeezed my hand. He squeezed hard. Some of it was for me; some of it was for the pain. "I'm sorry about what I said."

"You don't need to apologize. You didn't do anything wrong. Kaden's right: I should get out of your life."

"Vie," he said, and tears hooked along the purple shadows under his eyes. "You are my life."

I bent and kissed him, and he tasted like medicine and sweat and, underneath that, the familiarity of his mouth. When I broke the kiss, his fingers tightened around mine, and he gave me a smile. "I thought I wasn't supposed to get excited."

"I was just checking."

"Checking?"

I ran a hand up his thigh. "Making sure everything still works."

"Playing doctor?"

I slid my hand higher. "Something like that."

I kissed him again.

When I pulled back, pain shone in his face like the edge of a sword. I disentangled our hands. "I'm going to go. You're going to get some sleep. I'll come back tomorrow, and we'll . . ."

"We'll take tomorrow when it comes."

I nodded. "Day by day." And I wished it didn't sound like an echo.

When I stepped away from the bed, Austin said, "The nightmares. You've been having them for a while?"

"A few months."

"Every night?"

I started to shake my head; then I made myself tell the truth. "Almost."

With obvious effort, he scooted to one side of the bed and turned down the sheet.

"Aus, you need to—"

He patted the bed.

"You're hurt, and you're in pain, and the last thing—"

"No orgies."

I blinked. "What?"

"No reverse cowgirl. No peek-a-boo."

"What the hell are you talking about? Reverse cowgirl?"

"We're going to sleep. That's all. Sleep." He smiled, and it was fragile and shy and laced with fear. "Please? Tonight? I don't want to be alone tonight."

"Tonight," I said, already kicking off my sneakers.

As I settled in next to him, smelling his skin, the plastic rustle of the hospital gown, the sponge-bath soap, all of it, he dragged up the sheet up over me. And then he pulled my head to his shoulder. His arm went around me.

"Your chest," I said.

"Tonight." His hand ran up and down my back, and I remembered the way he had stroked Hannah. His nails scratched lightly, pleasantly through my shirt. My next breath came out easier. And the next even easier. He had some magic in his hands: animals and little kids and even feral things like me.

"I love you," I said.

"I love you. Now get some sleep."

I slept. And I only had one dream that night: a high meadow, and the sun breaking on my face, and Austin.

# Epilogue

The letter came three months later with E. Bradley and no address in the envelope's corner, and my name and address printed in jagged, nervous scratches in the center.

*Dear* (A smudge of gray graphite where Emmett had scribbled out a word.) *Vie,*

Somebody in group said I was an asshole for calling you tweaker all those times. I told her I knew I was an asshole. She said that wasn't the only reason, and I said I knew that too. It's a hard habit to break.

I'm ok.

How are you?

(A long, scribbled out section.)

I hate this. I want to talk to you. I want to—

(More scribbles.)

Do you know what a twelve-step program is? I guess you do. The one here, at this place, has amends as step eight. So I guess I'm on step eight. Only really, in my head, I think I got stuck somewhere around step three because I don't think I believe in God. I guess I believe in something because something brought you to Vehpese. Something good. Something amazing. So I guess I believe in that. But I'm not sure I believe in God.

I put you on my list of amends. Then I took you off. I put you on again. I took you off again. Jerry says I should leave you on, and he's pretty cool, and Dana, that girl in group, says I should get my balls cut off because of how I treated you, and Jerry told her you can't say things like that in group.

(Another scratched-out paragraph.)

Can I start over?

This place is pretty nice, and before you ask, I'm not going to tell you where it is. I just don't think I could—

(Scratches.)

It's kind of like a spa, I guess. I wear slippers all day. And the clothes are basically pajamas. And there are a lot of waterfalls and they play New Age music and they have jasmine in the gardens. I like to sit out there at night. I can see the stars, and they make me think about home. I think about you a lot when I'm out there.

I didn't scratch that part out. Are you proud of me?

They tell me I'm supposed to make amends for people I hurt because of my addiction. They don't tell me what I'm supposed to say to the person that is my addiction. I guess most people can't write letters to coke or meth. I mean, they could, but it probably wouldn't help very much.

You know the first thing they told me when I got here? You never stop being an addict. And you know what I learned writing this letter?

They're right.

(A long paragraph followed, scribbled out so vigorously that the paper had torn in places.)

Here's what I want to apologize for:

I'm sorry I lied to you.

I'm sorry I hurt you.

I'm sorry for the way I left you. The way I left us. But I still think it was the right thing to do.

I'm sorry for all the other stuff I did. If you want to send me a list, I'll apologize for all of it. Kind of joking. Kind of not joking.

I hope you and Austin are happy. If you guys broke up, then I hope he has a blowout case of herpes, and I think you should revenge-fuck Kaden. I know you think he's straight, but that kid is definitely bi.

I almost scratched out that stuff above, but I'm going to leave it. I want you to know what I really hope, the thing I really want, is that you'll happy. And well. I hope you kept your promise. I hope you're doing what you need to be doing so you can get better. Because I am.

(A scribbled-out line.)

(A scribbled-out line.)

(A line scratched out so hard it creased the paper.)

Well, fuck, I keep writing it and keep scratching it out and I guess I'm going to write it again and just send this stupid thing. I love you.

Emmett

PS—Are you going to college? My parents want to put me in a final year of prep school, but I think I'm just going to do my GED and start at the community college.

PPS—I know, I know. I asked you questions and I didn't give you a way to write back. I guess I'm still an asshole; group can only do so much.

PPPS—Want to hear something weird? Guess who I saw. Jim Spencer. He's—

(Long, deep scratches.)

He's having a really hard time, I guess. He said he left Vehpese without telling anyone. He said he can't be there anymore. He said he heard I was here, and one day he just needed someone to talk to, and he showed up, and I basically had a heart attack. He's been coming a lot since then. We've been—

(Scratches.)

I know I said I didn't want to tell you where I am. I still don't. Knowing you, you'd probably try to hitch a ride, and you'd end up with a serial killer, and I'd be responsible for you getting your skin made into a dress or something like that. But I miss you so much it's crazy. And I want to know you're ok. Jim said if you email him, he'll print it off and bring it to me, and then I can write you back. He might be a cool guy except he's twenty-five or something so he's basically an old man. He promised not to read whatever you wrote, and I actually kind of believe him. I'll put his email address at the end. It's up to you, but I hope you'll write.

Write me. Pleasepleasepleasepleasepleasepleaseplease. Ok. I'm going to say it again before I go all chickenshit. I love you.

# Acknowledgments

My deepest thanks go out to the following people (in alphabetical order):

Justene Adamec, for her extensive reading (and re-reading) of the final manuscript, for her insight into Vie and Emmett's evolving relationship, for pointing out the parts that didn't make sense, and for being the first to catch the broken nose that was really a punch to the stomach!

Austin Gwin, for the incredible amount of support and encouragement he provides over email. Austin identified sections of the book that dragged, helped me see why, and—as usual—put his finger on a problem that I could feel in my gut without being able to name. And I'm sorry (again) for accidentally bringing back a hated nickname!

Alyssa Ma, for all her excellent corrections to the text.

Cheryl Oakley, for pointing out the fundamental weakness in the book's ending—and for managing to do so with kindness and a wealth of generous ideas to resolve the issue. If you enjoy the epilogue (or if you hate it, but you needed to know a little of what happened with Emmett), thank Cheryl!

Tray Stephenson, for catching so many of my typographical (and other) blunders, for emails full of good humor and encouragement, and for many kind words along the way!

And Jo Wegstein, who disassembled and reassembled so many parts of this novel: for providing expansive feedback on topics ranging from asphyxiation to the physics of boys who vanish from motorcycles. Jo's insights into the characters, the plot, and the array of technical problems that this story posed have made the book what it is today, and I am deeply indebted to her—and I probably owe my life to the fact that she's a patient person, especially after the hundredth run-on sentence she caught!

# About the Author

For advanced access, exclusive content, limited-time promotions, and insider information, please sign up for my mailing list at **www.gregoryashe.com**.

Made in the USA
Las Vegas, NV
10 February 2023

67204841R00267